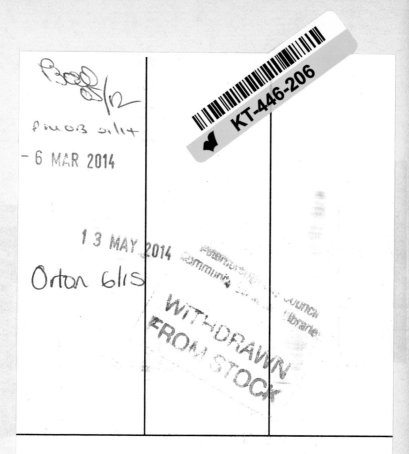

PETERBOROUGH LIBRARIES

24 Hour renewal line 0458 505606

This book is to be returned on or before the latest date shown
above, but may be renewed up to three times if the book is not
in demand. Ask at your local library for details.

Please note that charges are made on overdue books

Bryce Courtenay

The Story of
DANNY DUNN

PENGUIN BOOKS

PENGUIN BOOKS

Published by the Penguin Group
Penguin Group (Australia)
250 Camberwell Road, Camberwell, Victoria 3124, Australia
(a division of Pearson Australia Group Pty Ltd)
Penguin Group (USA) Inc.
375 Hudson Street, New York, New York 10014, USA
Penguin Group (Canada)

Penguin Books Ltd

Penguin Ireland

Penguin Books India Pvt Ltd

Penguin Group (NZ)

11 Community Centre, Panchsheel Park, New Delhi – 110 017, India

67 Apollo Drive, Rosedale

(a division of Pearson New Zealand Ltd)
Penguin Books (South Africa) (Pty) Ltd
24 Sturdee Avenue, Rosebank, Johannesburg 2196, South Africa

Penguin Books Ltd, Registered Offices: 80 Strand, London WC2R 0RL, England

First published by Penguin Group (Australia), 2009
This edition published 2011

3 5 7 9 10 8 6 4 2

Copyright © Bryce Courtenay 2009

The moral right of the author has been asserted

Cover design by Cathy Larsen © Penguin Group (Australia)
Text design by Tony Palmer © Penguin Group (Australia)
Cover photographs by Ian Waldie/Getty Images (Hat) and Steven Rothfield/Getty Images (Beer)
Typeset in Goudy Oldstyle by Post Pre-press Group, Brisbane, Queensland
Printed and bound in Australia by McPherson's Printing Group, Maryborough, Victoria

National Library of Australia
Cataloguing-in-Publication data:

Courtenay, Bryce, 1933–
The story of Danny Dunn / Bryce Courtenay.
9780143203513 (pbk.)
Bars (Drinking establishments) – Australia – Fiction.
World War, 1939-1945 – Veterans – Australia – Fiction.

A823.3

penguin.com.au

FSC
www.fsc.org
MIX
Paper from
responsible sources
FSC® C001695

For my beloved Christine

CHAPTER ONE

———

DANNY DUNN RETURNED TO Balmain from the war understanding that he was no longer indestructible. When he'd joined up to fight at twenty, he'd been bulletproof. But coming home five years later, his childhood nickname – Dunny – seemed wholly appropriate. His life, almost since leaving the peninsula, had been shithouse, and it frightened him to think how he would cope as a civilian.

Back then, it hadn't taken long for some smart-arse kid in primary school to realise that by adding a 'y' to Danny's surname, in time-honoured Australian fashion, he could change it to the name for the toilet at the end of every backyard path. But a scattering of broken teeth, a few bloody noses and black eyes soon persuaded them that it was a cheap crack made at great personal risk to the joker.

By the age of fifteen, Danny was already a big bloke, a pound or two off fourteen stone. With feet as big as flippers, he swam like a fish and played in the Balmain first-grade water-polo team. On Saturday mornings he laced up his size-twelve football boots and played rugby union as a second-row forward for Fort Street Boys High, then in the afternoon he fronted in junior league for the mighty Balmain Tigers at Birchgrove Oval.

The old-timers at Balmain Leagues Club had been keeping an eye on him ever since he'd been in the nippers, and forecast big things for his football career. That he also played water polo as his summer sport was a matter of great concern to them. Everyone knew that water-polo players were a bunch of yobbos who played dirty and that severe or permanent injury in the pool was not unusual. In fact there was some truth in this. A game of water polo generally consisted of punches, kicks and scratches, resulting in bloody noses, bruises and torn ligaments that sometimes led to permanent injury. In an average game a player swam more than two miles and had three times as much hard body contact as a rugby-league player.

Furthermore, the Balmain polo boys and their followers richly deserved their dubious reputation for dirty tricks beneath the surface. As a venue, the Balmain Baths possessed an unenviable reputation. There was decking on only one side of the pool, which limited the referees' range, and the green murky water washing in from the harbour limited their vision, therefore a great deal of illegitimate underwater activity went undetected. Balmain polo players seldom lost a home game. They were renowned for their dirty tactics and considered to be the roughest players in the grade, a reputation in which their fans took considerable pride.

On several occasions Danny had been approached by a Tiger football coach who suggested that he take up a less dangerous summer sport than water polo; competition swimming was the one most often suggested. They pointed out that a truly special athlete comes along once in a generation and a Danny Dunn playing for a future Tiger's first-grade team was the kind of talent that could win premierships.

In football-mad Balmain it was advice a young bloke would be expected to follow, but Danny proved surprisingly stubborn and it was clear he had a mind of his own. He'd pointed out that he greatly enjoyed playing water polo, which kept him fit all summer for the winter football season, and that, unlike swimming, for which he had to be up early four mornings a week for two hours of intensive training, polo practice was in the evening and so met with his mother's approval. He could do his homework in the afternoon, practise in the evening, then get a good night's sleep and be ready for school in the morning. While he agreed he'd copped the odd bruise and bloody nose playing polo, even on one occasion a pair of black eyes, this was no different from playing football. Finally, he pointed out, if he were to maintain race fitness for swimming it would need to be his preferred sport summer *and* winter, and rugby league would of necessity become his second choice. This ended the discussion.

However, it had all come to a head when the *Daily Telegraph* did a feature in its sports pages on water polo and noted that it was one of the oldest team sports, along with rowing, in the Olympics and that water-polo was first played in Australia at Balmain. The article went on to say that, despite Australia's long history in the game and the genuine and enthusiastic support for it, we had never played at Olympic standard. The upcoming Berlin Games were an ideal opportunity for Australia to test its mettle in the water.

As further proof that we were ready for international competition, the newspaper cited as its authority György Nagy, the Hungarian Olympic coach at present visiting the country. Nagy had announced that he was greatly impressed with the standard of the local game and that, in his opinion, an Australian team could hold its own against any European team. He strongly recommended that Australia attempt to qualify for the Berlin Olympics.

The *Daily Telegraph* then picked a tentative Australian team from the various polo clubs, justifying their choice. For Danny Dunn, the singular selection from Balmain, they'd added a note of caution:

While his brilliance as a centre back is unquestioned, it is to be hoped that such a young player will not be injured or permanently incapacitated in the rough and tumble of international competition. Young Dunn will be sixteen when the games are being held, and therefore eligible, but his progress at any future Olympic trial should be carefully monitored.

All this was pure speculation on the part of the newspaper, and what followed was at best a storm in a teacup, but, in Balmain, a small, close-knit and mainly working-class community, any contention involving sport and one of their own had the potential to roar out of the teacup and develop into a gale-force storm. Like a quarrel between a father and son that starts as a conniption and erupts to involve the entire family, the future of Danny Dunn, included in the speculative water-polo team going nowhere, soon involved the entire peninsula.

There wasn't much joy during those dark post-depression years, so pride in the sporting achievements of Balmain's sons and daughters often sustained the entire community. Danny, barely sixteen when he would supposedly represent his country, was big news regardless of the sport involved. So the argument was infinitely more complex than simply football versus water polo. For a poor Balmain kid, top-level sporting prowess of any kind was a way out. It meant a future, ensured a job and, providing you didn't hit the grog or go off the rails in some other way, earned you respect for life. It also brought high regard and honour to your family. So while most folk were Tiger fans, regardless of their loyalty to the rugby-league team, they found themselves ambivalent, thus effectively removing themselves from the front line of battle.

This left only the diehard football fanatics opposing the water-polo fans, the latter seeing Danny's selection as the ultimate vindication of their sport. The numbers were roughly equal, which always makes for a good stoush, and that afternoon in the pubs it was on for one and all. Moreover, everyone involved had long since forgotten that the selected team was no more than the informed musings of a bored sports writer searching for a different topic to write about.

The football mob finally had all the ammunition they needed: the danger to Danny wasn't only *their* considered and long-held opinion but also that of the *Daily Telegraph* – the authority on racing at Randwick, the dogs at Harold Park and the trots at Wentworth Park, and therefore expert in all things. Danny Dunn's carefully nurtured rugby-league career was about to be placed in jeopardy by a bunch of thugs in swimming trunks.

The new thrust of the footballers' argument was that, if local games were clearly dangerous, any mug could see what it would be like when your country's honour was at stake. If Danny was to play against those dirty, filthy, no-holds-barred wog and dago teams it would almost certainly greatly endanger his career as a footballer. In their minds they had him returning from the games a permanent cripple in a wheelchair.

The vernacular, liberally punctuated with invective, flowed like wine at an Italian wedding.

'Mark my words, that kid belongs on the football field. He's a Tiger to his bootstraps. And one day he'll be a Kangaroo – nothing more certain – he'll play for Australia!'

The reply from the polo mob was just as insistent. 'Mate, he's a fucking porpoise! Six foot two and built like a brick shithouse. He's the best centre forward in the country and he's not even sixteen!'

'Yeah, and that's the flamin' problem, ain't it? Why do you think we're keeping him in mothballs, in the juniors away from the big blokes? The lad's still growin', that's why!'

'Growin'? Ferchrissake, he's fourteen stone! He *is* a big bloke! Mate, yiz don't play centre forward if you're not as strong as a bloody Mallee bull!'

'You water-polo bastards don't give a fuck, do yiz? Use him up, spit him out . . . plenty more where he come from! Well, there ain't, see! Danny Dunn's a fucking one-off, a sporting fucking genius! Youse could bugger him forever!'

'How's that?'

'Mate, in rugby league it's all out in the open. You biff someone. He biffs you back. A bit of claret, fair enough. The ref blows his pea and blame is duly apportioned, a warnin' or even an occasional penalty gets handed out. Open, fair, decent – handbags at five paces – all out in the open. Nobody gets hurt. Not like your mob. The ref can't see underwater, and soon as blink you'll knee a bloke in the balls or worse, tear his bloody arm off!'

'Bullshit! Danny can take good care of himself. Just you watch, mate, the kid takes no prisoners. Them wog players will jump into the pool baritones and come out fucking sopranos!'

By six o'clock closing on the night of the announcement of the hypothetical Olympic water-polo squad, several fights had broken out on the pavement outside various Balmain pubs, and a fair amount of claret was spilt. However, all blood was spilt in vain. The following morning, just after ten o'clock opening time, the argument was settled by Brenda, Danny's mother, in the front bar. 'I'm not taking sides. Danny's still at school and won't be playing in any Olympic team. That's all I've got to say!'

The water-polo supporters on the peninsula had gone from ecstasy to agony in twenty-four hours. At the soap and chemical factories, the ferry workshops, the foundry, coal loader, power station and wharves, there was little else discussed all day. In fact, the water-polo supporters grabbed anyone who was prepared to listen. 'The first water-polo game played in Australia was right bloody here! Here in the Balmain Baths! We was the first swimming club in Australia. Started in eighteen fucking eighty-three! Jesus! Yer don't go abusin' stuff like that! Lissen, mate, we was playing water polo before fucking rugby league was invented. We're the bastards with the tradition. Compared to us, them in league are still wet behind the bloody ears!'

By three-thirty knock-off time, it had been decided by the polo mob that a delegation would be led by Tommy O'Hearn, the union shop steward at the Olive, as the Palmolive soap factory was known to the locals. An ex-player and now assistant coach for first grade, he was ideally equipped to persuade Brenda Dunn to change her mind. The O'Hearn family had been polo boys for three generations; the game was in their blood.

Changing Brenda's mind was a task nobody took lightly; every attempt to persuade her to let an SP bookmaker to take bets in the pub had failed – her pub was the only one in Balmain that wouldn't allow gambling on the premises. 'Silly bitch . . . who does she think brings in the drinkers? They come in to have a beer and a bet; ya don't have one without t'other.' They didn't add that the SP bookmaker bought a lot of grog for his clients and also paid rent for the privilege of operating illegally on the premises. Nor did they reflect that the Hero never had any trouble with the police. And it wasn't because of bribery. Like every other publican, Brenda'd buy a cop a beer or two or serve him a free counter lunch, but that was it. The truth is there were no SP bookmakers, no stolen goods sold on pub premises and no other scams.

But Tommy O'Hearn was a smooth talker, a clever, persistent and patient bloke who had a fair idea what he was up against when it came to Danny's mum. He knew she was stubborn, and that approaching her directly would be pointless. The key was her husband, Half Dunn. 'Useless prick – all piss and wind. But maybe he has some influence, yer know, behind the scenes?' O'Hearn suggested.

Mick Dunn, six foot one inch and twenty stone, could drink twelve schooners of Reschs Draught and still appear reasonably sober as he sat propped on a reinforced bar stool at the main bar in the Hero from ten o'clock opening to six o'clock closing. He always wore exactly the same clobber, a white shirt and a humungous pair of grey tailor-made pants, the waistband of which reached almost to his armpits. From each knife-edged trouser leg protruded a pair of pointy-toed black and white, pattern-punched, patent-leather shoes, the instep and ankle of which were covered by carefully blancoed spats. Above them were grey silk socks held taut by suspenders. His open-neck shirt was collarless to accommodate the several chins that scalloped downwards to his chest, and he wore a solid-gold collar stud in the top left-hand buttonhole, to show that the omission of a starched detachable collar was deliberate, a matter of style. Finally, Half Dunn added a pair of crimson American barbershop braces with four square chrome clips. He was, he believed, a natty dresser, in the Runyonesque style he imagined Nicely-Nicely Johnson sported in *Guys and Dolls*, a book he tucked under his pillow each night before falling asleep.

It was often said of Half Dunn that he possessed an opinion on everything. There was no subject too obscure or trivial that he couldn't mature into a conversation. To give an example, on one occasion a punter came into the pub carrying a bag of corn on the cob he'd no doubt nicked from a produce boat he'd been unloading on the wharves. He ordered a seven, which indicated he was skint, and walked over for a chat with Half Dunn.

'What you got there, mate?' Half Dunn asked, pointing to the hessian bag.

'Yeah, mate, corn; fresh, straight off the boat. Let you have half a dozen for sixpence.'

'Nah, don't eat corn. No good fer ya,' Half Dunn replied.

'How's that, mate? Corn's good tucker,' the bloke said, taking the knockback in his stride.

'It don't digest,' Half Dunn volunteered.

'Digest? What d'yer mean by that?'

'You know, it gets into yer stomach, all them acids and stuff, fermentation, taking out the nourishment . . . it don't happen with corn.'

'Fermentation? Yer mean like grog . . . beer?'

'Yeah, gettin' the good out've the corn.'

The man looked quizzically at Half Dunn. 'How d'ya know all this shit?'

Half Dunn never missed a chance. He could pick up a double entendre in a flash.

'That's it precisely! Shit!'

'What's that suppose'ta mean?'

'You eat corn. Next mornin' you go for a shit. What do you see?'

'Eh?'

'Nothin's happened to the corn, mate. Them kernels are still in their little polished yellow jackets, same as when you swallowed them, digestion juices can't penetrate, see. No fermentation.'

The corn man took a sip from his seven and shook his head. 'Crikey! Ya learn somethin' every day, don't ya?'

'Stick around, son,' Half Dunn said, pleased with his erudition.

While Half Dunn could be described as a useless bastard, with no authority to do anything whatsoever except talk crap, like many seemingly unthinking people he possessed the capacity to talk to anyone on any subject, mining clues from their inanities and developing these to advance the conversation. Pubs by their very nature attract misfits and lonely men, and Half Dunn could talk to them all, adding to the pub's air of congeniality and increasing its appeal.

While Half Dunn drank more than his fair share of the profits and dispensed bonhomie and mindless opinions on everything from the perfidy of politicians to the training of ferrets, his wife, Brenda, put in a fifteen-hour day ending at 8 p.m. when she'd finally balanced the day's receipts, checked the cellars, cleaned the beer pipes and personally polished the bar surfaces. Tommy O'Hearn was right to treat her with respect. Nothing escaped her. Before the cleaners arrived, she always removed the Scott industrial toilet rolls, then replenished them after the cleaners had left, to prevent their being replaced by near empty ones brought from home in a cleaner's shopping bag. The Great Depression had left a residue of bad habits among basically honest people, and Brenda was onto every cleaning shortcut and sly trick in the trade.

Even the bartenders knew better than to pocket the cash from the odd middy. Brenda had been known to stand on a bar stool and punch the daylights out of a six-foot barman she'd caught short-changing a drunk patron. She ran a tight ship and a spotlessly clean pub. While she left the bragging to Half Dunn, she would occasionally claim, with justifiable pride, that her last beer at night tasted as fresh as her third one (the first two were always discarded), and no one ever disputed this.

But generally Brenda came as close as a woman may to being taciturn. She was different in almost every way to Half Dunn. Just five foot and half an inch, at seven stone she was as petite as Mick was grossly fat. Even though Michael Dunn's name appeared above the main entrance to the pub as the licensee, she was most definitely the boss. While she was as conscientious as any wife in the 'Yes, dear' department and never put her husband down in public, it was apparent to the regulars that his opinions counted for bugger-all. She opened the pub doors precisely at ten each morning and she'd show the last drunk the pavement at precisely five minutes past six each evening; in between opening and closing, the decisions she made ensured that the Hero was one of the most successful and best-run pubs on the peninsula.

Brenda Dunn fuelled all this effort with half-consumed cups of sweet black tea and Arnott's Sao biscuits, ten of which she'd place in her apron pocket of a morning. When the pub closed she would repair to the backyard where three magpies waited expectantly for the brittle Sao crumbs. She also smoked three packets of Turf Filters a day. More precisely, she'd light sixty fags, take an initial puff to get each one going, then carefully rest the cigarette on one of the heavy glass ashtrays advertising a brewer or whisky distiller, which she placed, she always imagined, at points she frequently passed. More often than not, as she reached for the cigarette to take a second drag, it would have collapsed into a fat grey ash worm. Some clever patron once worked out that if she got an average of one and a half drags from every fag and there were twenty potential puffs in each, she'd only smoked four and a half cigarettes a day.

What Tommy O'Hearn didn't know, was that Brenda's character had been forged out west in a poor farming family, where hard, thankless work began at dawn and ended after dark. There was never time for idle chatter, even about rain, that rare and precious, almost legendary occurence. She'd lost her two elder brothers in the Great War, one at the Somme and the other, who'd come through the horrors of trench warfare relatively unscathed, in the Spanish Flu epidemic that raged through Europe in late 1918 and in the next two years spread around the world killing more than twenty million people. The eldest of the three remaining daughters, Brenda was sent at sixteen to work as an upstairs chambermaid in Mick's parents' pub, the Commercial Hotel in Wagga Wagga. Lonely and entirely ignorant about sex, within six months she was up the duff to eighteen-year-old Mick Dunn, their only son.

He would come into her tiny upstairs bedroom at the crack of dawn before anyone was up, gently shake her awake, then sit on the end of her narrow iron bed and invent outrageous and amusing stories about the town's notables, soon sending her into stifled giggles. An initial bold wake-up kiss on the forehead had developed over time into a cuddle on a freezing winter's morning when she'd let him creep under the bedcovers. Mick was already a huge lad, six foot one inch and starting to go to fat. The bed was very narrow, and the tiny housemaid failed to understand that the fumbling, kissing and rearranging of their bodies was bound to lead to penetration and, for Mick, almost instant ejaculation.

Soon after Brenda arrived, the regular barmaid fell ill and Brenda was called from her duties upstairs to clean the tables, wash glasses and keep the bar area clean while Dulcie, Mick's mother, took over the bar. By the end of the week Dulcie Dunn was so impressed with Brenda that she kept her downstairs and Fred raised her salary by two and sixpence a week. 'If Bob Barrett asks, you're to say you're eighteen,' she'd instructed Brenda. A rise in pay to pass on to her family was all the incentive their young housemaid needed to conceal her age from the local police sergeant. Besides, the downstairs main bar was far more interesting than making beds, sweeping and scrubbing floors, and cleaning out toilets and bathrooms. Never again would she have to scrub the upstairs passage on her hands and knees, enduring the leers and sly winks from commercial travellers bound for the bathroom with only towels that bulged with their early-morning erections wrapped around their waists.

Brenda proved to be a hard worker, quick to learn, good with the till, and demonstrating remarkable initiative for one so young. She was generally liked by the patrons, had a pleasant but firm way of persuading inebriated drinkers to go home, possessed very nice table manners, was modest, disarmingly shy and scrupulously honest, and was a Roman Catholic to boot. But soon the sharp-eyed gossips and stickybeaks in town started to whisper and point as the diminutive Brenda began to show. Dulcie and Fred were secretly delighted once they learned of the clandestine early-morning coupling. A generous donation to the church building fund allowed Father Crosby to waive the reading of the banns and the wedding proceeded as quickly as possible. Mick, their phlegmatic, indolent and generally useless son, had at least succeeded in sowing the seed for what they hoped would be their first grandson.

Fred and Dulcie Dunn had also married at eighteen and sixteen respectively, though, in their case, from choice rather than necessity. They'd been inseparable since their last year in primary school. Five years after their wedding, they'd taken over the Commercial Hotel from Fred's parents, and their son, Michael Donovon, was born in January 1900, the year before Federation, ten years after the marriage, when they'd just about given up hope of having a child.

Fred was a big man by most standards and as strong as an ox. Dulcie was long limbed and taller than most of her generation, so it was no surprise when she gave birth to a large child. Michael was the apple of his mother's eye and spoilt rotten from the very beginning. She would hear no ill spoken of him or his ballooning weight, until at eighteen, she had to face the truth. The army refused to recruit him to fight on account of his *obesity*. They'd never heard the term before and consulted Dr Light, the family physician, who told them the word basically meant grossly overweight. Dulcie was finally forced to agree with her husband that her precious son was a bone-idle slob and dangerously close to becoming an alcoholic. Fortunately, armistice was declared before the real reason for their son's rejection was revealed. Mick's only assets – dubious in a country boy and in particular a publican's son – were that he was mild mannered (in fact a coward) and could talk the hind leg off a donkey.

Mick and Brenda were married at the newly consecrated St Michael's Catholic Cathedral on a scorching January Saturday. Brenda's twin sisters, Bridgit and Erin, were the bridesmaids and Brenda's father, Patrick O'Shane, gave her away, despite the 104 degree heat, in the same heavy Irish tweed suit, good woollen shirt with starched detachable collar and side-buttoned boots he'd worn when he married her mother Rose in 1895 in the town of Galway on the shores of the River Corrib in County Galway.

However, all the hasty 'bun in the oven' wedding arrangements turned out to be unnecessary; at four months Brenda miscarried a baby girl. Young Dr Light, after performing a curettage, advised Brenda to try to delay a year before the next pregnancy. 'You're very small and all the Dunns are big men,' he warned. 'You'll need to be in excellent health.'

Danny Corrib Dunn, nine pounds four ounces at birth, was born on the 4th of July 1920. The long and painful labour was no surprise to Dr Light, nor was the damage to Brenda's plumbing; he warned her never to attempt to have another child.

Dulcie and Fred were delighted with Danny, apart from the initial shock when the nursing sister unwrapped the swaddling blanket and they observed their grandson's dark hair, tiny brown fists and olive complexion.

Although Mick's incompetence couldn't have had anything to do with the miscarriage, they had nevertheless been secretly worried and then vastly relieved when the second pregnancy turned out well. The marriage had proved fruitful in two ways: a grandson, but also a highly competent daughter-in-law.

By the time he was christened, the baby weighed eleven pounds two ounces and his abnormally large feet protruded from the end of his christening gown. It was impossible to ignore his jet-black hair and olive skin, surprising when both parents were so fair skinned and freckled. Brenda's hair was commonly referred to as titian and Mick's was the colour of a red house brick. At the christening party held at the pub afterwards, when the baby had been produced for inspection, Fred had heard one of the inebriated guests snigger, then ask in a loud whisper, 'Any Abos seen hanging around outside the pub this time last year?' The publican had grabbed him by the scruff of the neck and sent him out the back door nose first into the dirt.

Brenda, flat as a pancake in front, had no means of satisfying Danny's voracious appetite, so he was bottle-fed from an early age. Nor was she allowed much time to enjoy her baby. Fred and Dulcie realised that they now had a daughter-in-law who had the basic nous to run the pub, with a bit of training. Fred had always wanted to go on the land up north to breed racehorses, possibly the Hunter Valley, but somewhere close enough to Sydney, and Randwick Racecourse. Dr Light had diagnosed a dicky heart and advised him to remove himself from the daily stress of running a busy pub. Both parents had realised that Mick wasn't capable of taking over and it had seemed for a time that they would have to sell. But the arrival in their lives of the little Irish lass, now their daughter-in-law, changed everything, and they could begin to plan for a retirement in which Fred could fulfil his long-held ambitions.

Danny was handed over to a young nursemaid and Brenda's training as a publican began in earnest. Meanwhile Mick was earning the sobriquet Half Dunn, never quite able to complete a given task and spending more and more time on the customer side of the bar, where his elbow and his mouth were the only parts of his rapidly expanding person put to serious work.

Three years into the marriage, when Brenda had assumed almost the entire responsibility for running the pub, and Fred was on the eve of his early-retirement dream, Dulcie was diagnosed with breast cancer.

They had to move instead to Sydney so she could have a mastectomy and undergo the latest radiotherapy treatment. The pair bought a rather grand Federation house in Randwick with the twin advantages of being close to a major hospital and the famous racecourse, where Fred hoped over a few years to establish himself as both a racing identity and a breeder of quality bloodstock if all went well.

They returned to Wagga to say their goodbyes to family and friends and to finally leave the pub in Brenda's care, although not before the little vixen had handed them a lawyer's document requiring them to put the pub into their son's name. In Brenda's mind this was a necessary precaution. As a child she'd often enough heard the axiom from her mother, Rose, that gambling defeats the rewards of a woman's hard work, and that horses in particular send families to the poor house, especially the families of Irishmen. Fred's declared ambition to breed racehorses and his love of the turf concerned her greatly, and she didn't want a destitute father-in-law and his cancer-riddled wife descending on them and resuming ownership of the Commercial Hotel. One rotten Dunn was enough in Brenda's life. Mick's parents still demanded half the monthly income from the Commercial Hotel, even though they were wealthy by the standards of the time, and had been saving for Fred's dream stud farm all their lives.

Fred agreed to Brenda's demands, with the proviso that, if the pub were sold before both he and Dulcie died, they would be entitled to half the proceeds. With the change of ownership, there was now a pub in the Dunn name for the third generation, and Fred was justifiably proud.

More hard years followed the drought in the south-west, and while the Commercial Hotel continued to do well, dividing the profits was burdensome. Brenda was still supporting her family on the farm and paying for her twin sisters to attend the Presentation Convent boarding school at Mount Erin. Making ends meet was a constant struggle. Her one consolation was that young Danny was growing into a lively boy – quick, lean, long-limbed, active and intelligent.

No matter how rushed she was at the end of each day, Brenda made sure she read to him in bed every night. Danny, she'd decided, was going to go to university, even if it killed her. She was aware that this was a lofty ambition, well beyond her station in life, and that she could never divulge it to anyone without appearing presumptuous and uppity. She was still regarded by the town's respectable Protestant families and wealthier Catholics as bog Irish, and definitely from almost the bottom of the working class, despite her new status as a publican. At that time, women like her were not expected to achieve anything through their individual efforts, and to even entertain the possibility was considered immodest, unseemly and suspicious; such women simply married their own kind, bred, cooked, scrubbed, skimped and struggled until they died of overwork and lack of attention.

Brenda had been dux of her small country school when she finished in form three, the level at which most students, having reached the permitted school-leaving age, discontinued their education. Her parents had not attended the end-of-year prize-giving, where she'd received two books by Ethel Turner, *Seven Little Australians* and *Miss Bobbie* – the first tangible evidence that she was a bright and clever student.

Shortly afterwards, her parents had received a visit from the district school inspector, Mr Thomas, prompted by the young teacher, Linley Horrocks, on whom Brenda, along with every other girl in her class, had a secret crush.

Horrocks had not himself gone out to see Mr and Mrs O'Shane because he was a Protestant and a Baptist and felt that the much older and more senior Mr Thomas, a Catholic and known to be a prominent lay member of St Michael's, Father Crosby's parish in Wagga Wagga, would have much more influence with them.

By his later account to Horrocks, the interview with Brenda's parents had not gone well. As it transpired, they'd just received the news of their son's death at the Battle of the Somme.

Brenda had not been permitted to be present at the interview, which had taken place in the tiny front room of the farmhouse, referred to by her mother, with the little pride she had left in her, as 'the front parlour'. It was only used for the very occasional socially superior guest who visited the lonely homestead.

The curtains were drawn against the fierce sun and the window kept closed to protect the precious brocade curtains, brought from her mother's home in Kilcolgan, Ireland, so the room was at damn-near cooking temperature. Mr Thomas was clad in weskit and tie, having removed his jacket as a concession to the unrelenting heat, but was decidedly uncomfortable; the inside of his starched collar was soaked, the rim cutting into his neck. His white shirt under the woollen weskit stuck uncomfortably to his stomach as he addressed Brenda's parents.

'Mr and Mrs O'Shane, it is not customary for me to travel to a pupil's farm to talk to her parents,' he began somewhat pompously. 'However, in this particular instance I consider it a pleasure rather than a duty.' He paused for the expected effect, didn't get a reaction, put it down to nerves, then continued, 'I have, some might say, the onerous task of being the school inspector to all the schools in the south-west of this great state of ours. I say this only to emphasise that I am in a position to witness the progress of several thousand children, some tolerably competent, others, I regret to say, less so.' He uncrossed his legs and leaned forward for emphasis, his soft hands with their clean nails resting on his knees. 'But, every once in a while, a rose appears among the thorns. That is to say, an exceptional student.' He paused for further effect before continuing. 'I am happy to tell you that your daughter has a very good head on her shoulders. She is, I believe, one of the brightest we have in this part of the state.' Thomas leaned back, folded his hands over his stomach and beamed expectantly at the two still entirely motionless and expressionless adults.

The school inspector was sitting in one of the two overstuffed armchairs, upholstered in the same brocade as the curtains, while both parents, their backs pressed into straight-backed wooden dining chairs, continued to stare into their laps. It was as if they were yet again facing the bank manager.

Rose O'Shane had perhaps once been pretty, but now her face was work-worn and her pale-blue eyes no longer curious; her hair, pulled back into a hasty and untidy bun, was almost entirely grey, with just the faintest suggestion of her daughter's lovely titian colour. Patrick, her husband, was bald on top, with a few copper-coloured strands of hair mixed in among the grey. Surprisingly, considering the rest of his raw and sun-beaten face, his pate was smooth and unblemished. The rim of the battered bush hat he'd removed when he entered the parlour had created a clear line across his brow an inch or so below what must once have been his hairline. Above it the skin was undamaged; below it his face was pocked with skin cancers, its peeling, scaly surface bright puce.

The silence continued well after Thomas's deliberately prolonged smile had faded. He was not accustomed to being ignored and it was becoming clear that the O'Shanes were not receiving the good news in a manner he might have expected, nor showing him the respect he merited as a man of some standing in the south-west, a fellow papist and their obvious social superior.

'If your daughter is allowed to complete her high-school education in Wagga, who knows, after that she may well qualify for a scholarship to the university,' he ventured. Still getting no reaction he added quickly, with what was intended to be a disarming chuckle, 'When the time comes I dare say I can use what little influence I have with the Education Department in Sydney.' His tone clearly implied that a nod from him to the scholarship board was all it would take. 'We don't make a request very often, so when we do . . .' he left the sentence uncompleted, covering his arse just in case, not quite committing to the full promise.

Patrick O'Shane quite suddenly came to life, leaning forward, looking up from his hands sharply at Thomas. 'And for sure, who would it be paying for this fancy education now, Mr Thomas? I'll be tellin' you straight, it'll not be us.' As suddenly as if he'd spent his allotment of words, he fell silent, his eyes returned to his lap and his work-roughened hands, skinned knuckles and dirty fingernails; the thumbnail on his left hand was a solid purple, not yet turned entirely black, the result of what must have been a fairly recent and painful blow.

'Well . . . er . . . urrph,' Thomas said, clearing his throat, 'I'm sure we could come to some arrangement, some accommodation . . . with the school hostel, and the various textbooks she'll need . . . If you could possibly add . . .'

Patrick O'Shane looked up sharply, this time jabbing his forefinger at the school inspector, his expression now angry. 'Arrangement! Accommodation! Hostel! Books!' he repeated as if each word were intended as an expletive. 'And what would you be meaning by "add"? We've done all the adding we can, Mr Thomas. We've added two sons fighting for this country in a war no self-respectin' Irishman could justify, fighting on behalf of that unholy Protestant whore, Mother England! One of them will never come home. We've added the sweat from our brows and the strength of our backs to work the unforgiving and endless dust plain. The saltbush and pasture are all but gone and the few starvin' ewes still left to us can't feed their lambs; the dams are empty and so are our pockets. There's nothing left for man nor beast and we haven't had any decent rain for three years. And you ask . . . you have the *temerity* to ask, "If you could add"!' He slapped his right hand down hard onto his knee. 'Mary, Mother of God! Have we not done all the adding and has it not all come to nought, to bugger-all?'

Thomas, taken aback by the sudden tirade, could nevertheless see where Brenda's intelligence originated. He had the nous to know that offering his sympathy would only exacerbate the situation. 'Perhaps the convent?' he stuttered. 'I . . . er, could talk to Father Crosby . . . I'm sure —'

'That old fool and his building fund!' Patrick O'Shane exclaimed in disgust. 'You don't get my drift, do you now, Mr Thomas?' He paused momentarily. 'Never you mind the good head on her shoulders, our daughter *also* has two good hands and a strong back. She can scrub and clean and do domestic work for people of your kind in town. Her mother and I can no longer go it alone. We have two other daughters, twins, to feed as well. She's the eldest now. Don't blame us, sir. This godforsaken country stole my boys! Drowning them in mud, murderous shrapnel and sickness and robbing us of their strong hands and broad backs for years, one of them gone forever. She'll not be going back to school! You may be certain of that now, Mr School Inspector!'

Brenda accepted her father's decision calmly. After all, they were poor and she was a girl, with no reason to expect anything more than her mother had been granted in a thankless life of childbearing and hard work.

However, Danny's education had been her overriding ambition from the moment he was born, and she waited eagerly for the day when it could begin. A tall, sturdy, curious and confident little boy, Danny was more than ready for school at the age of five and a half. But in January 1926, disaster struck, at least in Brenda's terms of reference. Danny was due to start school in February, but a few days after Christmas he had asked if he could have ice-cream for dinner. As ice-cream was a special treat, Brenda asked him why. Danny had a voracious appetite and rarely refused to eat what was placed in front of him.

'Because my throat is very sore, Mummy,' he'd replied.

The following morning his face was deeply flushed, he had a

temperature and could barely talk. She'd taken him off to see Dr Light who, after an examination, announced that Danny had diphtheria.

Brenda, not usually given to panic, burst into tears, whereupon Dr Light attempted to reassure her. 'Mrs Dunn, Danny's a strong, healthy little boy – there's no reason he shouldn't recover.'

But Brenda wasn't new to diphtheria. She'd seen it in her own childhood when all three children on a neighbouring farm had died from the disease. She knew it as a scourge that killed hundreds of children every year. She was also aware that, even if a child lived, there was a danger of a weakened heart or damage to the kidneys or nervous system, in some instances even incurable brain damage.

Danny spent the following week in hospital drifting in and out of delirium. Brenda stayed at his bedside and watched in despair as his fever worsened and the disease spread its toxins through his small body. She would sponge him for hours in an attempt to reduce the fever and try by sheer willpower to draw the disease out of him.

She'd left the running of the pub to Half Dunn with no instructions – a recipe for certain disaster but of no possible consequence now. She frequently sank to her knees beside the bed and prayed, saying her Hail Marys promptly every hour, then begging God, if necessary at the cost of her own life, to save her son. If she slept it was for no more than an hour or two and she'd wake exhausted and guilt-ridden.

Half Dunn visited every evening and brought her a change of clothes and two cold bacon-and-egg sandwiches, the only thing he knew how to cook. Brenda would thank him, 'I'll have them later, dear,' and put them aside. She would feed them to an ageing golden Labrador named Happy, who was permanently ensconced on the front verandah of the children's ward when she went outside early for the first of four cigarettes she smoked each day. The old mutt thought all his Christmases had come at once. Happy had accompanied his master, who'd been admitted three months previously and had subsequently died. Afterwards the dog had refused to leave. On two occasions someone had agreed to adopt him, but he'd made his way back to the hospital at the first opportunity. On one such occasion he'd been taken bush to an outlying homestead and came limping back to the hospital a week later with his paws bleeding and one of his ears badly tattered and almost torn off. How he'd survived the trip through the bush at his age was close to a miracle. His wounds were dressed and he was allowed to stay.

Over the second week Danny's fever lessened and he began the slow road to recovery. Throughout this period Brenda lived with the fear that her son might suffer permanent damage to his heart or brain. Despite Dr Light's assurance that he was coming along nicely and that there appeared to be no abnormal signs in his recovery, the die was cast, and for the remainder of his childhood she would fuss over his health. The slightest sniffle brought her running with the cod-liver oil; a cut or abrasion, and the iodine bottle appeared at the trot. But Danny recovered completely and seemed no worse for the experience. Despite his mother's over-enthusiastic ministrations he was to become a rough-and-tumble kid, eager to play any kind of game and quite happy to take the school playground knocks and bumps without complaint.

Incidentally, Happy decided he couldn't live without Half Dunn's bacon sandwiches, and agreed to be adopted by Brenda as the pub verandah dog. She'd hoped the old dog would be a mate for Danny, but, as they say, you can't teach an old dog new tricks and Happy only had eyes for her. Half Dunn would make Happy's favourite tucker every morning, but the dog would only accept the offering from his mistress. On one occasion she'd been away at her parents' farm for the weekend and had returned to find an unhappy Happy with his nose beside four uneaten bacon-and-egg sandwiches, which he proceeded to wolf down the moment she granted him permission to do so.

Brenda, grateful for her son's full recovery, had only one abiding regret: the diphtheria and Danny's lengthy recuperation meant he had missed a precious year of school. In fact, when he started school she discovered half the class was aged either six or seven, but she ever afterwards felt that she'd let a precious year of her son's education slip by.

In April that year, after a long battle with cancer, Dulcie died at the comparatively young age of fifty-three, followed three months later by Fred, after a sudden and massive heart attack on his way to the corner newsagent to get the morning paper. His friends, travelling up together on the train from Wagga Wagga for the second time in three months to attend the funeral, agreed that he'd almost certainly died of a broken heart over his beloved Dulcie.

The mourning contingent were well prepared for the journey up to Sydney for Fred's funeral with two crates of beer for the men and four bottles of sweet sherry for the ladies. After drinking their way through Cootamundra, Harden and Yass, they were pretty well oiled by the time the train rolled into Goulburn.

The conversation had progressed beyond the virtues of the dearly departed to discussion of his origins. His father, Enoch Dunn, was claimed to have won the pub in a game of poker on the Bathurst goldfields in the 1860s. The general consensus was that, all in all, the Dunn name had stood for something in the town and there was speculation about the present and the future.

Sergeant Bob Barrett, clad in a brown worsted suit that must once have buttoned over his front and looking decidedly uncomfortable out of his blue serge police uniform, seemed to express all their thoughts – well, those of the males present, anyway – when he ventured darkly, 'Ah, a truly blessed union, Fred and Dulcie, a tribute to the town.' He paused and raised his beer in memory. 'But, I'll give it to you straight. The boy has turned out to be a bloody no-hoper. If it weren't for that splendid young lass he married there'd be no pub and he'd be in the gutter, mark my words, a regular in my overnight lock-up. She keeps him out of harm's way, though gawd knows why, the useless bastard!'

But this tribute to Brenda didn't go unchallenged. The chemist's wife, Nancy Tittmoth, sailed in for her tuppence worth, her fourth glass of sweet sherry turning to pure acid as it touched her lips. 'Don't believe everything you see, Bob. Bog Irish, that one! Still eat with their fingers. The only way her kind can get out of the gutter is to land with their bum in the butter! That girlie has lots to answer for. Little hussy housemaid gets herself pregnant to the publican's son, both Roman Catholics, so they have to marry. Then her keeping the boy in a state of permanent intoxication so she can rule the roost. The hotel is in his name, of course, but as long as she hangs on to him, well . . .' she smiled primly, '. . . the little tart and her son with the girly hair can enjoy all the benefits of a fortunate marriage.'

Bob Barrett held his tongue. Everyone in town knew that Nancy had earmarked Mike Dunn for her eldest daughter, Enid, a sweet enough girl, though very tall, exceedingly plain and rather dull.

With the death of his parents, Mick and Brenda now had the total income from the pub and expectations of a further inheritance that might mean they could afford not only Mick's enduring thirst but Danny's education as well. To Mick's consternation and lasting bitterness, when the will was read, the Randwick property, Fred's half-share in two racehorses stabled at the racecourse and a not inconsiderable sum of money in the Bank of New South Wales had been left to Dulcie's two older sisters, both nuns approaching retirement.

It never occurred to Brenda that she could now afford to be a lady of leisure; she had always worked and she would continue to do so. But now she was no longer beholden to her parents-in-law, Brenda decided she'd had a gutful of running a country pub. Mick was all piss and wind and contributed little, either as a husband or a worker, besides his gift of the gab. She'd had her fill of commercial travellers stealing towels or jacking off in bed and leaving sperm stains on the sheets; she was sick of locals defaulting on their monthly beer tab, of drunks fighting or throwing up on the pavement outside. And Sergeant Bob Barrett, older than her father, the dirty old sod, propping up the bar most nights for an hour after closing when she was exhausted, ogling her as he downed a couple of complimentary schooners and a plate of ham sandwiches. She was sick of it all. The final straw came when one morning she'd gone out to feed Happy and found him dead. The ageing verandah dog hadn't shown any signs of being poorly. He'd simply passed away in his sleep. Brenda shed a quiet tear, sorry that she hadn't been present to say goodbye and to whisper into his tattered ear that she loved him. She decided she wanted a bigger world, and it was time her bright young son was educated in the city.

Brenda felt she'd fulfilled her duty to her own family. She'd put the twins through convent and paid for courses in shorthand and typing. While she still helped financially with the farm, good rains had fallen and the saltbush was coming back. She'd even noticed a gleam of hope occasionally in her mother's pale-blue eyes. Confident she would survive in the big smoke, they sold the pub to Toohey's Brewery in August 1929 and moved to Sydney, where they rented a small house in Paddington while Brenda looked for a suitable pub to buy. She thought she'd received a good price for the Commercial, but she was astonished at the pub prices in Sydney. After a few months she was beginning to wonder if she'd been wrong to sell up and leave Wagga. Then the New York Stock Exchange crashed, the effect resonating around the world to panic investors and set in train the Great Depression. Suddenly, cash was king and she found two run-down pubs, the Hero of Mafeking, in the working-class suburb of Balmain, and the King's Men, in Parramatta. While the Parramatta pub was a slightly better buy, she'd discovered that each year the brightest two kids in their final year at Balmain Primary School would be chosen to attend Fort Street Boys High, a selective school with an enviable academic reputation. For a working-class boy it was the first step to a university education and Brenda fancied her chances with Danny, who was proving to be very bright. It was for this reason that she ignored the advice of the hotel broker and chose the more run-down of the two pubs.

The gathering hard times had bankrupted the licensee, but Brenda reasoned that men still needed a drink, no matter how hard things became. She soon discovered that the pub had been cheap for several very good reasons. The previous publican had a reputation as a surly bastard who drove away more patrons than he ever attracted. With thirty pubs to choose from on the peninsula, this was not a very intelligent way to conduct business. Furthermore, the Resch's brewery rep had cut off his supply when he couldn't come up with the cash for his deliveries. The place was so run-down, shabby and dirty that the brewery had decided not to follow their usual practice of buying the freehold and installing a lessee, thus tying the pub to their beer forever. The premises were infested with cockroaches and rats, although the former were a product of Sydney's humid summers and the latter – not exclusive to the pub – emanated from the wharves and ships anchored at the docks. In fact rats on the peninsula were in plague proportions, adding to the general sense of misery since the Wall Street crash. Everything and everyone went hungry, from the packs of emaciated dogs that roamed the streets, to the families who had once owned and loved them. Only the cats had full bellies.

Danny, now nine, was enrolled in the local primary school in time for the first term of 1930. Brenda wasn't happy that he was growing up in a pub, but she'd managed to keep him out of the pub in Wagga and she'd do so again in Balmain.

The Balmain peninsula jutting out into Port Jackson was distinguished by the beauty of the harbour and the polluting industry that festered at the water's edge. It was an inner-harbour suburb of Sydney, with Iron Cove on the west, White Bay to the south-east, Mort Bay on the north-east and Rozelle to the south-west. But Balmain did not regard itself as a part of anything or anyone. To the people who lived in its just over half a square mile, it was a different place, a separate village, a different state of being and of mind.

How this overweening civic pride had come about nobody quite knew. Clearly Balmain was superior to Rozelle, which was lumbered with Callan Park, a lunatic asylum. 'Yer gunna be thrown in the loony bin if yer don't behave!' was the customary threat to children growing up on the peninsula. Balmain boasted an impressive Italianate town hall of brick and stucco, and several handsome winding streets leading down to the two wharves or terminating in broad stone steps that led to jetties projecting into the sparkling harbour. Along Darling Street, rickety, swaying, clattering trams bore passengers down the steep slope to the

Darling Street Wharf where they could take the ten-minute ferry ride to the city terminus.

Yet, despite its beautiful setting and impressive civic centre, Balmain exhibited all the signs of working-class poverty. Spidering out along the peninsula on either side of Darling Street were humble back streets of run-down wooden and sandstone terraces of one and two storeys fronting directly onto cracked and weed-infested pavements. The tiny backyards contained only an outdoor toilet and a washing line, a rope or wire strung from the top of the kitchen door to the dunny roof. The *Daily Worker* once described these workers' hovels as not fit for dogs to live in.

A coal loader left a residue of fine coal dust on Monday's washing, blackened the rind of dried mucus round the nostrils of the snotty-nosed kids, and added a sharp, acrid smell to the atmosphere. The air was filled with coal smoke from a power station and sulphur from a chemical factory near the Rozelle end, causing throats to burn and eyes to water. Two soap factories contributed the fetid stink of sheep tallow, and a host of small engineering factories added to the din and stink, squatting in niches and coves around the harbour.

Others may have described Balmain as poverty-stricken during the Great Depression and the ongoing misery of the thirties, but locals were largely unaware of their particular misfortune. While many of its working-class residents struggled more than most to survive – unemployment in Balmain was double the state average – they nevertheless possessed a peculiar and unreasoning pride: they came from Balmain and were therefore fiercely, even foolishly, tough and independent. 'Balmain boys don't cry' epitomised the breed.

They needed every bit of determination as the 1930s progressed. Moonlight flits were common – a huddle of cold and hungry urchins together with their desperate parents escaping down a dark street at midnight carrying between them everything they owned, unable to pay the rent or persuade the landlord to extend them any more credit. In winter people were reduced to rowing out at night to ships waiting to unload, dodging the water police, then stealing aboard like rats to pinch coal or vegetables from the holds. War veterans sold matches or busked outside pubs on harmonicas, playing the popular songs of the Great War and the roaring twenties. Men turned up at dawn to get a place in the labour queue, their stomachs rumbling or cramping with hunger after a dingo's breakfast – a piss and a good look around.

Balmain became a place of hungry, bronchial, barefoot children, many suffering from scabies. Paradoxically, the children attending school were well scrubbed, unlike those from other poverty-stricken neighbourhoods. Similarly Balmain men standing in the labour queues were, as a general rule, neatly shaved. This came about, not from fastidiousness, but because soap and shaving cream were stolen from the production line of the local Colgate Palmolive and Lever Brothers soap factories and handed out to friends and neighbours. There was always soap beside the tub, even if there was no food in the cupboard.

But Brenda had been correct. Although poverty gripped the peninsula and per capita beer sales had dropped, pub patronage increased. Tired and defeated men could go to the pub and know that they were not alone; it was neutral territory, where they could share a middy or a seven, have a whinge and a joke and talk football or the race results at Wentworth Park and Harold Park or at Randwick. They could linger over a beer beside another bloke and forget the labour queue they would both be joining the following morning, competing for a dwindling supply of jobs.

The Hero of Mafeking needed a lot of work if it was to become a decent pub, and although it had been cheap, repairs and renovations soon depleted the money in the bank, except for a small emergency reserve. In fact they went close to bankruptcy on several occasions. However, the resourceful Brenda, by skimping and saving, short-staffing, and working until she dropped as barmaid, cleaner, cellarwoman and publican, kept them afloat. She'd often enough wake with a start in the small hours of the morning, having collapsed from sheer exhaustion in the beer cellar, slumped against an eighteen-gallon kilderkin of beer. But somehow she contrived to build the pub's popularity as well as enable her parents to save their farm.

By the time the Depression had started to wane slightly towards the end of 1934, the Hero of Mafeking was considered one of the best of the thirty pubs on the peninsula. Brenda had introduced several innovations. In the main bar she got rid of the sawdust on the floor and, to the amusement of the competition, laid bright red and white checked linoleum and a couple of dozen three-legged bar stools along the length of the polished teak bar.

'Stupid bitch. Wait until some drunk slips on his own vomit or beer slops and breaks his fucking neck.'

She strategically placed three brightly painted firemen's pails each filled with an inch or two of sawdust so that anyone feeling the urge to throw up could reach them quickly.

Brenda made sure there were always fresh flowers in the parlour – the ladies bar – and laid a pretty rose-patterned carpet; she placed a couple of nice still-life prints on the wall together with a large glossy picture in an ornate gold stucco frame of the two royal princesses, Elizabeth and Margaret.

The first counter lunches were offered at the Hero of Mafeking: threepence for a middy of beer, two thick slices of bread (twelve slices to the loaf), cheese, boiled mutton or German sausage. Other pubs followed suit, but their mostly male publicans did little else to raise the spirits of their patrons.

Photographs of the great Balmain rugby-league players as well as other sportsmen of the past appeared on the walls of the main bar decently framed behind glass and not screwed permanently to the wall.

'Mark my words, they won't last ten minutes. Bludgers will soon have those under their jumpers and into the pawnbroker!'

But, with some rare exceptions, the patrons did no such thing. They responded well to being treated decently. Having a beer at the Hero became a pleasant experience, and to be banned for bad behaviour was considered a genuine disgrace.

Far and away Brenda's greatest innovation was her ladies' soiree. She invited the neighbourhood housewives to congregate in the shade of the pub's back verandah each weekday afternoon to enjoy one another's company while darning, mending, shelling peas or peeling potatoes for the family's evening meal. The single schooner of shandy that lasted each of them through the afternoon was free twice a week and half the usual fourpence on the other three weekdays.

'Silly drongo! Soon go broke handing out them free drinks to the sheilas!'

At this very popular afternoon gathering, involving at any time two or three dozen women, Brenda would be rewarded for her generosity with all the gossip, hard news and rumour from around the peninsula. No one in Balmain could scratch his bum without her knowing, and anything the opposition tried she'd know about, often before it happened.

To his credit Half Dunn had never objected to the financial help she gave her family, even when they'd been pretty skint themselves. Brenda never forgot that, accepting him for the lazy, bullshitting, useless lump of pomaded and nattily dressed lard he in fact was. In the end drinkers regarded him as a fixture, someone never short of a word, a cheeky remark, a clever quip or the latest joke.

By 1936, the year of the Berlin Olympics, the Hero was solidly in the black and Brenda's reputation as a publican was at an all-time high. But the day she declared that, come what may, Danny wasn't going to the Olympic trials, many of the chairs on the back verandah of the pub remained empty, despite it being a free shandy day. Brenda was shocked. She had come to regard the women as friends and confidantes, but the empty seats symbolised a general disapproval. The women were appalled by her decision; they could never have afforded and would never have dared to make it themselves, and some thought she was giving herself airs.

Opportunities for working-class boys in Balmain were few and far between: they could excel as sportsmen or be selected to go to Fort Street Boys High School. It ultimately meant the opportunity for a decent job in the city, a clean job where you wore a white shirt, collar and tie, shone your shoes every morning and came home with clean fingernails, or with an honourable ink stain on your second and third fingers where you held your Croxley fountain pen. On a rare occasion it meant a scholarship to Sydney University. Even by proxy, Fort Street and sport made a big difference to how folk felt about themselves.

The alternative for a young bloke who wasn't super bright or couldn't kick a football, swim like a flaming porpoise, race a bike at the velodrome or go ten rounds in the ring at Rushcutters Bay Stadium was to follow his old man into the Colgate-Palmolive or Lever Brothers soap factories, the iron foundry, the ferry repair workshops or as a trainee crane driver at Walsh Bay. That is, if he was lucky enough to get an apprenticeship and didn't end up as a common labourer shovelling shit and guts at the Flemington abattoir, working at the chemical factory or as a labourer on the wharves, repairing the roads or, worst of all, working on the coal loader.

Danny was already at Fort Street and clearly a superior athlete; to most folk such good fortune would not only guarantee their son's future but their own as well. Publicly the men denounced Brenda for denying the community the reflected glory of a favourite Balmain son's fame, and the women protested by staying away from the soiree. But Brenda maintained a stubborn silence on the subject.

The water-polo delegation assembled on a vacant block behind the backyard of the Hero of Mafeking around four-thirty one Tuesday afternoon. A Hero regular among them was sent to coax Half Dunn out of the pub, so as not to alert Brenda, who would probably give them the benefit of her acerbic tongue. Half Dunn, who only left his reinforced stool to take a piss, would be urged to slip out the back of the pub to the meeting spot in the vacant lot.

The plan wasn't quite as simple as it seemed. Half Dunn weighed over twenty stone, and by four o'clock already had eight schooners sloshing around in his enormous belly. A thirty-yard waddle in the late-afternoon sun was asking a fair bit. Then there were his two-tone patent-leather shoes to consider; they were for display purposes only, not for walking on rough, stony ground.

However, Half Dunn knew he couldn't refuse the invitation, for if he did, he'd look weak as piss. Furthermore, while everyone knew and accepted that Brenda ran the pub and made the business decisions, it went without saying that a man was still the boss in his own home. Brenda never put him down in public and so the delegation would have no reason to suspect any different. This was, after all, a family decision, not pub business, and they had every right to assume that, as her husband, he could come down on her like a ton of bricks; certainly demand she change her mind.

Half Dunn made it to the vacant block, panting heavily, his shirt wringing wet, pale-blue eyes blinking away the stinging sweat under his brilliantine-darkened ginger brush-over.

'Yeah, good on ya, Mick. Thanks for coming,' Tommy O'Hearn greeted him.

'I've scuffed me fuckin' shoe,' Half Dunn replied, looking forlornly down at his left foot.

'Yeah, righto. Spot o' polish'll fix that,' O'Hearn replied, glancing at Half Dunn's shoes. 'Mate, we'd like to talk to you about your unfortunate decision.'

'My decision? What decision?' Half Dunn panted, mopping his face with a large white sweat-soaked handkerchief.

'C'mon, mate,' O'Hearn said impatiently. 'Yer boy Danny . . . not goin' to the Olympics.'

'Brenda!' Half Dunn replied by way of a one-word explanation. His wife's name seemed to give off a firm, hard sound, like a heavy brass padlock snapping shut.

'Yeah, mate, we know.' O'Hearn waited for a further explanation.

Half Dunn stuffed the hanky absently into his trouser pocket and stared at his buggered shoe, thinking, *you can't polish patent leather.*

'So?' someone asked, breaking the silence.

'I dunno, mate,' Half Dunn said. Danny, the cause of this kerfuffle, wouldn't have dreamed of bringing his disappointment over his mother's decision to his old man, to use him as an ally in an attempt to make her change her mind, two against one. He had long since sussed his father out as a major crap artist. Although never openly disrespectful, he seldom if ever asked his opinion on anything.

Last night Half Dunn'd heard the boy crying in his room upstairs, but knocking at the door and going in to offer him comfort was pointless. Brenda's word was law. He knew he was piss-weak as a father, as a husband even worse. He'd willingly handed over any authority he might have once possessed a long time ago, although he couldn't quite remember how that had happened. Take the Commercial. One moment he'd been happily propping up the bar in his childhood home, the next she was buying a pub in Balmain. 'Sign here, dear,' forefinger on a line appearing in the same place on several sheets of typed paper he hadn't the energy to read or the nerve to question. 'Sign here,' was practically her maxim.

It hurt. It hurt like hell having no particular purpose, sitting on his reinforced stool getting slowly pissed and crapping on to the customers from opening to closing time. He was, in his own eyes, a useless prick, but he no longer had any idea how he might assert himself. He wouldn't have understood the term 'emasculated', but he knew how it felt.

It wasn't as if they ever quarrelled or even raised their voices. She'd simply say, 'Yes, dear' or 'Never mind, dear' or 'Trust me, dear', then go ahead and do as she'd originally intended. The worst part, in terms of the eventual outcome, was that she was seldom wrong.

'I'll talk to her,' he promised the men standing with their arms folded in front of him.

'What, you haven't already?' someone asked, shaking his head in disbelief.

'Jesus, mate,' yet another exclaimed, his disdain obvious.

O'Hearn, as the union shop steward, was accustomed to doing the talking and there was a grumble of disquiet beginning to come from the delegates. Any moment now, he knew, they were all going to be having a go at Half Dunn. He took a step closer to deliberately separate himself from the mob. It was basic union training – you own the mob, they don't own you. 'Glad to hear it. So tell me, watcha gunna say to the little missus?'

Half Dunn looked at him alarmed; he hadn't thought that far ahead. He was being pushed into a corner and didn't like it, but he wasn't game to object. 'Er . . . I'll . . .'

'Can I make a suggestion,' the shop steward cut in firmly – it wasn't a question. 'You're going to point out to your good wife that half . . . no, more than half the blokes who drink at the Hero, at *your* pub, support the water-polo team. That's half the flamin' profits if I'm not greatly mistaken! I mean, if they should decide to drink at any of the other twenty-nine pubs we've got on the peninsula . . .' He paused to let his meaning sink in, then stabbed his forefinger at Half Dunn and added, 'We're disappointed see, *very* bloody disappointed, and disappointed people who have been let down badly can get very cranky, know what I'm hintin' at, mate? They've been known to change their mind about where they drink. Get my drift?'

'Yeah, righto,' Half Dunn growled in an attempt at bravado. Despite his misgivings, he was annoyed that the union man felt it necessary to labour the point. 'I got the fucking message the first time.'

'Good on ya, matey. Just wanted to make sure. We'll send someone over in the morning to get the good news,' O'Hearn said, smiling. Reaching out he squeezed Half Dunn reassuringly on the shoulder, his thumb sinking to the base knuckle and still not meeting any muscle. Pulling it out of the layer of blubber under the wet shirt made a small sucking sound. He rubbed his glistening thumb absently down the leg of his blue King Gee overalls and Half Dunn saw the pink blotches on the back of his hand where he'd been burnt by the raw caustic soda used for making soap. He also picked up the rank smell of sheep tallow that permeated the skin of workers at the Olive and the Lever Brothers soap factory, especially when they perspired. The union man grinned, then winked. 'Might even buy you a beer, hey?' His expression changed suddenly to a quizzical frown. 'You're not gunna let the side down now, are ya, mate? Balmain's depending on you to come through for the water-polo team.'

'I don't need your fucking free grog, I own a fucking pub!' Half Dunn blustered.

'You'll need somethin' a damn sight stronger to drink if you don't have some good news termorra, big boy,' one of the blokes laughed.

'Nah, she'll be right,' O'Hearn said confidently, ushering them with a sweep of both hands towards the entrance to the vacant lot.

They began to shuffle away, two of them touching him lightly on the cuff of his sleeve, the only part of his sweat-soaked shirt not clinging opaquely to his enormous ginger-haired pink-skinned chest above his trouser line. Half Dunn wasn't sure whether this gesture was meant to be an additional threat or an encouragement. Both smelled of sheep fat.

Half Dunn stood alone for a while, trying to think. The afternoon sun was beginning to sting his scalp, burning through the wisps of pasted-down ginger hair. Partially formed thoughts misted and dissolved like passing clouds. *Where do I start?* A wave of panic swept over him. *How? When? Jesus! Fuck! How do I put it to her? Make her see the consequences. She won't like losing customers one little bit. Fucking O'Hearn's right. Customers, that's the key. Do it at tea, with the boy at the kitchen table? Nah, if Danny blubs she'll blame me. They'll both agree I'm shickered. Tell her tonight in bed? No good. It's her private time to read the new* Women's Weekly. *She's up at sparrow fart . . . tackle her then. Good idea. She won't expect me to be up. Make her a cuppa. Catch her unawares.*

He glanced up to see the three magpies gliding in to land on the backyard fence on their late afternoon Sao-biscuit run. *Shit, she'll be out the back any moment emptying her pinafore pocket. Shoe's fucking ruined!*

Even at fifteen, Danny Dunn was becoming a 'somebody', moreover a very fortunate somebody. Not only was he a brilliant young sportsman, he was also one of the select few who'd made it to Fort Street from primary school. His exam marks were good and there wasn't any doubt that he'd pass. But, of course Brenda wanted to make sure he obtained university entrance level once he matriculated. Going to the Olympic trials and then maybe the Olympics would undoubtedly distract him from his studies, and Half Dunn knew Brenda wouldn't have a bar of that. Over my dead body, mate! She was fanatical about her precious son going to university. It was the major reason they'd left Wagga. Just about the major reason for everything she did. Unlike the rest of Balmain, the football crowd included, even if the water-polo team won gold in Germany and gave Danny a hero's welcome and a street parade, he knew she couldn't have given a fuck, if, in the process, he hadn't made it into Sydney University. And that was the basic problem. Her way of thinking wasn't the way the peninsula saw things. Her values were not the same as theirs. He could clearly understand their resentment.

As it transpired, Danny had gone down to the pool to face his mates that night, take the flak, cop it sweet, accept their agro. Half Dunn and Brenda had tea alone in the pub kitchen, where he seized the opportunity to tackle her on the subject. He told her about the visit of the water-polo delegation and the very real threat they'd made. As usual she listened politely. That was the thing. She was a feisty woman with the staff or anyone else who gave her strife, but never with him. It was as though she thought him so far beneath her contempt that he wasn't worth getting all hot under the collar about.

But, then again, she was unfailingly polite, often even sympathetic. It was just that, in the end, she never took any notice of his opinions.

When he brought up the prospect of half the patrons deserting the pub, her expression barely changed. When he'd finished talking and she'd brought him his pudding – IXL canned peaches and custard – he asked, 'Well, what do you think we should do?'

'Nothing, dear,' she replied evenly, starting to clear the dishes.

'Nothing? Jesus! You mean, you ain't gunna change your mind?'

'That's right, dear. No need to take God's name in vain,' she chided gently.

Sometimes he got this terrible urge to punch her, smash in her bog-Irish teeth. Blood everywhere. Serve her fucking right.

But then, smiling, she placed her hand on his shoulder and said, 'Never mind about the shoe, dear. We'll get you a brand-new pair.'

Fuck me dead! He hadn't even mentioned his scuffed two-tone brogue.

Now here's the funny thing. Three days later, the Australian Water Polo Association decided in their annual committee meeting that eighteen was the minimum age for a player to represent his country at water polo and, at the same time, issued a statement saying they lacked the funds to bring the top players from the various states for team trials, let alone to meet the cost of sending a team to Germany, but they were considering the following Olympics as an opportunity to qualify.

The storm in the teacup abated and there was no noticeable fall in patronage at the Hero. It was business as usual, both inside the pub and at the peas-and-spuds soirees. In fact, purely by coincidence, a day after the announcement that there would be no Olympic water-polo team, Doc Evatt, once the Labor, then independent member for Balmain, turned up at the Hero of Mafeking and stayed an hour, which did no harm whatsoever to Brenda's reputation as a publican. There were thirty pubs on the peninsula and he'd chosen hers three times in a row. Evatt, though not born and bred in Balmain, was nevertheless a favourite son, so much so that when he'd split from the main faction of the Labor Party after a quarrel over policy, the almost totally reliable Labor vote on the peninsula switched and he was voted in as an independent. He'd left politics to be appointed the youngest justice ever to the High Court. Occasionally, if he was passing, he'd drop by to keep in touch with his ex-constituents – once a politician, always a politician; you never know where life could take you. The stickybeaks were quick to point out that this was his third consecutive visit to the Hero and the scuttlebutt was that the Doc was sweet on Brenda. If he was, then it was a very public affair; his driver would park directly outside the pub for all to see in a big black Buick and he and Brenda were never seen together on the same side of the bar. Hardly the stuff scandals are made of.

As Danny grew towards manhood, it became clear that he really did seem to have just about everything going for him. He was genuinely popular, had an easygoing nature, was modest, self-effacing and loyal to his mates, and when it came to the birds, he had a smile that could turn a nun into a harlot. In fact, he was astoundingly good-looking. In the terminology of the day, Danny Dunn was sex on a pogo stick.

His looks were commonly referred to as black Irish. Popular history, while wildly inaccurate, goes like this. Way back in 1588 when Sir Francis Drake fought the Spanish Armada, a whole heap of Spanish galleons were wrecked in a storm and washed up on the Irish coast. Legend has it that, as fellow Catholics, the shipwrecked sailors were immediately welcomed ashore by the Irish, who even then regarded the English as the enemy. The Spaniards took an instant liking to the fair-skinned local sheilas and the feeling, it seems, was reciprocated. One thing led inevitably to another and the dark Latin blood proved to mix well with that of the titian-haired Celtic colleens to make a generally interesting combination. However, as a passing note, the Irish, regardless of their shared faith, brutally slaughtered the shipwrecked sailors almost to a man.

Occasionally an almost pure 'Catalan' throwback occurred, known as black Irish, a look and colouring in a male or female that usually turned out to be spectacular. Danny was one such 'throwback'. His skin was polished amber in winter, a shade darker in summer. A mop of jet-black hair extended in soft curls down his neck in defiance of the traditional short back and sides inflicted at the time by the barber's brutally efficient clippers on every kid and his dad. Despite her son's constant, often tearful, pleading as a small boy, Brenda had never allowed this fierce instrument anywhere near his dark curls. Instead, to his absolute mortification, she would cut his hair with a comb and scissors on the back verandah of the pub during the afternoon peas-and-spuds soiree, a terrible humiliation perpetrated before the entire neighbourhood, or so it had seemed to Danny, who endured countless taunts and bloody battles in the school playground as a result. But, in the process, it toughened him up and earned him the respect of his mates, until eventually his almost flowing locks became his trademark and were no longer ridiculed. Danny's dark curls marked him out on the football field and it would have seemed odd and entirely inappropriate to fans and spectators had he ever decided to shear them off in conformity with the rest of the Tigers.

At almost six foot four inches, Danny Dunn at sixteen could easily have passed for a man of twenty-one, with his lazy assurance and apparent confidence. However, the truly spectacular element in his dark good looks was a brilliant dash of pure Irish: the addition of a pair of dark-lashed, deep-blue eyes that set the breasts of young girls heaving and their tongues flickering lasciviously and entirely unconsciously over their lips. Young, strong and innocent, he was the exact opposite of what most married women had to endure.

A typical husband, usually after a skinful at the pub or the football of a Saturday arvo, would proceed to get motherless on the half a dozen bottles of pilsener he'd brought home. Later, stumbling to the front bedroom, often on her arm, he undertook and she underwent the obligatory once-a-week leg-over, performing the dreaded deed from thrill to spill in one minute flat. Sweating like a pig and smugly assured that his manhood was intact and that he'd serviced the little woman for another week, he'd roll off her unrequited thighs onto his back, where, in a moment, his heavy panting would change into thundering snores, the occasional beery belch and the sudden ripping sound of a happily escaping fart. His wife, shutting her mind to this combined bronchial, gastric and anal chorus, would put pliant fingers to work as she fantasised over young Danny Dunn, a usually successful way to conclude the disappointing events of the evening and take her mind off the noxious fug that passed for air in the tiny bedroom.

CHAPTER TWO

DANNY SAT FOR HIS final Leaving Certificate examinations in November 1937, and in January the following year his name appeared in the *Herald* with excellent marks. Matriculating, he was then eligible to enter Sydney University. Shortly afterwards he received a letter advising him of his admission to the Arts faculty.

Brenda was over the moon and quite unable to contain herself. It was the fulfilment of her dream, and after all those years of struggle, she wanted to celebrate. She decided to give Danny a surprise party. Half Dunn cautioned against it but, as usual, Brenda took this as confirmation that it was a grand idea. To put Danny off the scent she suggested a small party for his closest friends from Fort Street to celebrate the end of school, and Danny agreed. Instead she threw the biggest private bash Balmain had ever seen, secretly inviting all his childhood mates and seemingly half the peninsula, including all the pub regulars and their wives, the mayor and town councillors and a host of others including his friends from Fort Street, who felt decidedly uncomfortable and left as soon as it was polite to do so.

Danny was mortified. He accepted the handshakes and slaps on the back from most of the two hundred people with characteristic good humour, but in reality he felt humiliated and ashamed: he was by no means the first person from Balmain to go to university. After it was all over and the last of the drunks had left the beer garden, Danny confronted his mother in the upstairs kitchen.

'Mum, how could you do such a thing?' he cried, his emotions barely under control. 'How could you humiliate me like that? We agreed, just a few of my closest friends from school, not the whole of Balmain! What are people going to think?'

'But you're going to university, my darling boy!' Brenda protested. Still on a high from the party, she was unable to see what the fuss was about, and underestimated his distress.

'We agreed, no fuss! Just a few mates!'

'Oh, that! That was only to put you off the scent. So you wouldn't become suspicious,' Brenda countered.

It was too much. 'Mum, you lied to me!' he screamed. 'You fucking lied to me!'

Danny had never used the 'f' word in front of his mother. Brenda's euphoria popped like a party balloon. She'd taken enough. Her son had accused her of lying to him when all she'd done was to honour him and show her love for him. The memory of Half Dunn warning her not to do it rose like bile.

'You ungrateful bugger!' she snapped, jabbing Danny in the chest with every word. 'Do you have any idea what it's taken to get us to this day . . . to this moment?' She glared up at him. 'Do you think it's been easy? This is the first party we've ever had for us, for you and me and your father! The first time we've patted ourselves on the back just a little bit! And you say you're humiliated!'

'I tried to warn you,' Half Dunn said quietly from where he sat at the kitchen table, knowing not to interfere between mother and son but unable to avoid being involved in the fracas.

Brenda turned on him. 'Oh shut up, you fat fart! What would you know?' she shouted, then turning back to Danny she hissed, 'You are mortified! Well, now I'm the one mortified, see! Because yer such a bloody coward! Afraid of what people will think. I don't care what people think – I don't give a shit!'

Danny had never before heard Brenda swear, but he was damned if he was going to cave in.

'Mum, can't you see – it's showing off! It's bragging!'

Brenda burst into tears. 'Can't I show off . . . even once?' she asked.

Danny, shocked to see his mum cry, tried to make her understand. 'It's making them eat crow! Mum, most of my best mates haven't even got permanent jobs and neither have their fathers. They're still lining up at Pyrmont every morning hoping for the privilege of a day's work. Their brothers and sisters go hungry as often as they eat, and here am I boasting because I was lucky enough to go to Fort Street then get into uni! Throwing a party for a bunch of freeloaders . . . Jesus, Mum, it's just not on!' Danny yelled, now close to tears himself, but unable to stop. 'Your speech today about me going to uni to get a BA, how proud you were I'd be a somebody, it's rubbing their noses in it! Don't think it doesn't all add up! Stopping me going to the Olympics, when they'd have killed to have one of their sons selected, this bloody stupid piss-up, and then going on and on about me having diphtheria when I was six and missing out on a year of schooling and now, hooray, I'm off to uni. Ferchrissake! It's only a fucking BA!'

Brenda burst into fresh tears. Danny's university career was her emotional blind spot. Scrubbing the pub floor at midnight in the bad old days, wiping up the vomit in the toilets, or the piss on the tiles, or the crappy toilet lid where somebody had been too drunk to know it was down, all of this and more she'd happily endured in the knowledge that Danny Corrib Dunn, her precious son, who'd very nearly killed her in childbirth, who'd come close to dying as a small boy, would one day go to university.

The vision of her father in his Irish tweed marriage suit, woollen shirt and polished side-buttoned boots in the scorching heat of her wedding day in Wagga had never left her. She could still see the great beads of sweat trickling down his scrawny cheeks and neck as he led her to the altar at St Michael's, blinking the perspiration out of his eyes. She recalled his blistered, sun-scabbed face, his hopeless, pale-blue eyes reflecting all that he'd silently endured, the bitter lines etched around his mouth by a pitiless and unforgiving land; a man who had left the sweet grass and green fields of Ireland, never again to feel the evening breeze blow in from Galway Bay, who'd lived his young life in a crofter's stone cottage looking out onto the sparkling waters of Lough Corrib as he woke each dew-glittering morning. He'd left to make his fortune in a new land that had rewarded him with nothing more than a baking corrugated-iron roof over his head, a handful of dust and a weekly charity handout from his daughter. It was never going to happen again.

Her son would be a 'somebody', an educated man who could hold his head up in any company, a man who didn't have to remove his hat and hold it by the brim in both hands and look down at his feet when he was addressed by a smug, patronising bank manager leaning back in his captain's chair behind his big desk with his thumbs hooked into his braces.

Brenda didn't see the beautiful boy who caused a young woman's knees to tremble when his deep-blue eyes picked her out in a crowd or the lopsided grin that every girl knew she would be unable to resist. She didn't care about the brilliant young sportsman who was being spoken of as almost certainly a Kangaroo rugby league international player and who could have played centre back in the water-polo team had they gone to the Olympics. She didn't see the six foot four, strong-limbed, seventeen-stone lad who, just by being who he was, made Balmain folk feel better about themselves. Half Dunn understood this lionisation of the young sportsman. He overheard more than he let on as he sat in the pub each day.

'Yeah, Danny's our boy! Mark my words, mate, that lad's gunna be a league international – shit it in. Got a bloody good head on his shoulders too. And the sheilas flock around him like bees round a honey pot. I reckon he could shag any sheila he wanted on the peninsula.'

'Yeah? How about your daughter?' some smart aleck quipped to roars of laughter.

'Yeah, well, providin' I knew about it, I'd wait a month or two then go round to Brenda and tell her me daughter's up the duff and —' he grinned and cupped his right ear, 'I can hear *weddin'* bells ringing!'

More laughter, then someone asked, 'You reckon she'd buy it? Castin' no *nasturtiums* at yer daughter, mind, but you know what she's like . . . stubborn Irish. Remember the water polo and the Olympics? She wouldn't have a bar of it. Even if your daughter had a bun in the oven I reckon she'd hand you the money for an abortion and tell ya to piss off.'

'Abortion? Bullshit! Brenda's a tyke! If she paid for an abortion it would screw up her immortal soul forever. The bloody tykes take that sort of stuff real serious. They've got this thing called . . . something or other, I forget, you cross a river and the other side is a sort of halfway house to heaven where you hang around until all the sins you committed in yer past are forgiven and all your relatives have paid the priest heaps fer yer ticket to heaven. But if you done an abortion, yer history! No more questions asked, over and fucking out, down you go, straight to fucking hell!'

'Yeah? Well, I hope fer yer daughter's sake it don't happen. But I reckon she's got a right to be proud of Danny. I reckon we all have.'

Half Dunn knew how the locals regarded Danny, but he kept his counsel. All Brenda saw was her boy standing in cap and gown in the Great Hall of Sydney University holding a parchment scroll, proving her mum and dad hadn't left Ireland for nothing and that she and her twin sisters could hold their heads up high. Danny would reach down and pull them all up out of the gutter. She knew she shouldn't have made the speech, but she couldn't help herself. Danny had started the last climb to the Everest of her aspirations.

Danny copped it on the chin, never complaining about the party again, but he believed he would never live down the shame. As a small indication of his remorse, he refused to join the University Rugby Union Club, the oldest in the nation, and stuck with rugby league; in the summer he played water polo for his old team. In the 1938 league season he appeared as a front-row forward in the firsts for the mighty Tigers. He also passed his first year at university the same year.

By the end of the following season, when the club won the league premiership, if there had been any lingering resentment about the party, the good folk of Balmain had well and truly forgiven him. Danny had fulfilled all their hopes and met their every expectation.

Then, having almost completed his second year, Danny turned on the wireless in early spring to hear that Neville Chamberlain, the British prime minister, had declared that Great Britain was at war with Germany; then Bob Menzies went on air and said that if Britain was at war, so was Australia. Two weeks later at breakfast, Danny announced that he wanted to join up.

Brenda went very still. 'I don't think that's wise, do you?' she said coolly.

'All my mates, the whole team at the Tigers and the polo boys, they're all joining up this week. Mum, I can't just sit on my arse and let them go and fight for England while I get a lousy degree! I'll be qualified to teach high school. What's more, I don't want to be a bloody teacher! Mum, I'm going! I'm not sixteen and this isn't water polo and the make-believe Olympic squad. If you try to stop me I'll quit uni anyway! And I'll leave home.'

'We'll soon see about that! You're not twenty-one yet, my boy!' Brenda warned, an ugly flush staining her neck. 'England! That Protestant whore has taken my two brothers and now she wants my son!' She turned her back on Danny and busied herself at the sink, banging pots and splashing noisily.

Danny still remembered how she'd lost her temper after the party, and how challenging her had achieved nothing. She must have sensed the general disdain that had been the lasting result of the party, but she'd never apologised or indicated that she'd been even slightly in the wrong. Now, in this thing, he knew he had to confront her. He couldn't simply stand by and let his friends fight for him. He'd been awake half the night trying to prepare for the row he knew must come. He'd hoped she wouldn't refuse her permission because he wasn't twenty-one, that it wouldn't come to the ultimatum he'd now been forced to give.

Half Dunn gave Danny the wink, levered himself out of his chair and approached Brenda, placing a conciliatory hand on her shoulder, but when she felt his touch, something in her snapped and she spun around fiercely to fend him off, still holding the heavy porridge pot half full of dishwater. It caught him on the point of the jaw and he staggered backwards, slipped on the water that had spilled from the pot and went crashing down like some great behemoth, the back of his head smashing against the oven door. His eyes rolled in their sockets and he lay senseless on the kitchen linoleum.

'Jesus, Mum!' Danny shouted, and wrenched the pot away from her.

'You ungrateful bastard! After all I've done for you!' Brenda hissed, then stormed out of the kitchen.

Danny dropped to his knees beside his father. For all he knew, Half Dunn could be dead. But then he saw his huge gut rising and falling with each breath. 'Dad, you okay?'

Half Dunn opened his eyes and let out a loud groan as Danny extended a hand, and winced as he was pulled into a sitting position with his back against the oven door. 'Okay, mate?' Danny asked again.

Half Dunn nodded gingerly and touched the back of his head with care, drawing his hand back in alarm, first sensing then observing that the tips of his fingers were covered in blood. He gave a small moan and collapsed into a dead faint. It look Danny another five minutes to bring him round, get him to his feet and back into a chair. He examined the back of his father's head and saw that the wound wasn't too serious – with luck, all Half Dunn would need was a dab of iodine to prevent an infection.

'Hmm, you've taken a big hit,' Danny said, shaking his head in mock consternation, then turning to the kitchen cupboard to retrieve the bottle of antiseptic and a wad of cotton wool from the first-aid kit Brenda always had at hand.

'Bad, is it?' Half Dunn ventured bravely.

Danny saw a way for Half Dunn to regain some ground, and added a large crepe bandage to the pile. He'd been shaken by his mother's outburst against Half Dunn, rarely having witnessed the scorn she felt for him. He knew it was largely a result of her anger with Danny himself, but the poor bastard seemed to cop all the shit. The least he could do was show some sympathy for his old man who had, after all, only been trying to help him.

Danny was frustrated and angry at his mother's reaction but he tried to stay calm by telling himself it was pretty well what he expected. Brenda had never liked the Brits. She'd blamed them for the loss of her brothers in the First World War, and he now saw that she wasn't going to let him join up without a fight and certainly not before he'd completed his degree. Besides, she'd withdrawn from the argument, and throwing a shitty in front of his pathetic father wasn't going to help.

'It'll need a dressing. You're probably going to have a pretty sore noggin for a few days; the bump on the back of your head is the size of a golf ball,' Danny exaggerated.

'Yeah? Jesus, what do you think? Concussion?' Half Dunn asked somewhat hopefully.

Danny held three fingers up in front of Half Dunn's face, one of the tests if you got a bad knock on the football field. 'How many fingers?'

'Three . . . I think,' Half Dunn replied, clearly disappointed. Danny reduced the finger count to one. 'One,' his father called.

'Three and one are both correct. No concussion. Now hold still while I fix this dressing.' Danny attended to the superficial wound with several unnecessary dabs of iodine, each one accompanied by a sharp indrawn breath or an *ouch* from his father. He then covered it in a wad of cotton wool the size of the back of his hand, and secured this with wide strips of Elastoplast to the bald patch at the back of Half Dunn's head and to his neck. It was time for some revenge. Danny wound the bandage several times over the top of Half Dunn's head and under his father's several chins until he looked as if he'd been the victim of a major accident. Brenda would be truly alarmed when she saw it. 'If I were you I'd play this one for all it's worth, Dad,' he advised, grinning, knowing that his father didn't need to be told twice.

Danny helped him down the stairs, Half Dunn sure he was too dizzy to navigate them alone. Looking suitably pathetic, Half Dunn, practising a few quiet but manly groans, levered his great carcass onto the reinforced stool at the main bar.

Danny then attended to all the jobs Brenda would normally be doing to get the pub ready to receive the first customers of the day. At a quarter to ten he realised he ought to be gone. Half Dunn's moment in the sun was about to arrive as Brenda appeared to open the pub, and much as he would have liked to be present, if he was, Brenda might just play it straight and not react. She was tough enough. Half Dunn must have shared his thoughts, because he said, 'She'll be down soon, son – never misses opening. I'll tell yer mother you've gone to uni, eh?'

Danny, perhaps out of childish pique, didn't attend university that day, but instead spent the morning walking around the peninsula, then went down to the pool and trained for two hours. Hungry after the swim, he bought a sandwich and spent the rest of the afternoon playing touch football and then a game of pool at the club with some of his unemployed mates. The talk was all about the war and joining up with the Sixth Division. He arrived back at the Hero of Mafeking just after six o'clock closing, knowing he must confront his mother once more.

Brenda was in the beer garden feeding six magpies, now several generations removed from the original Sao triplets. 'Mum, can I talk to you, please?' Danny said.

Brenda turned from feeding the birds. 'Oh, hello; there you are, dear,' she called back calmly, as if nothing had happened.

'Mum, about this morning . . .' Danny began.

Brenda threw a final handful of Sao cracker crumbs for the greedy birds, then, turning back to Danny, she brushed the remaining crumbs from her hands and the front of her apron. 'It all came as a bit of a shock this morning. Will you give me two or three days to think about it?' She paused, smiling, her head to one side. 'Please?'

What could he say? He could hardly refuse. 'Yeah, sure,' Danny mumbled. 'Promise you'll think about it?'

Brenda laughed suddenly. 'Your father's head, you well and truly got me there.'

'Oh?'

'I nearly died when I saw the bandage.'

Despite himself, Danny grinned. 'I hope you apologised?'

'Worse, I called a taxi and took him straight to Dr Keeble.'

'He didn't object?'

'Object? He milked it for all it was worth. We got to the surgery and there were half a dozen people in the waiting room. An old lady came out just as we arrived. "Sorry, everyone, this is an emergency!" I called out and barged straight in to Doc Keeble's surgery, dragging your father by the hand. Well, you know what a curmudgeon old Keeble is. He unwound the bandage, removed the enormous wad of cotton wool, then sniffed. "Mrs Dunn, is this a joke? If it is, I'd be obliged if in future you didn't waste my time!" He was as cranky as all get out.'

'And Dad?'

'"What about the golf ball? Could be concussion!" he said.' Brenda chuckled, '"Or more brain damage," Doc Keeble replied.'

Danny laughed. 'Yeah, I told him about the golf ball; a bit of an exaggeration, I guess. The concussion was his own idea.' Danny caught his breath, suddenly serious. 'Mum, please don't think this is all over, me enlisting.'

Brenda turned to go back into the pub. 'You agreed to give me two or three days, Danny,' she said crisply, her mood changing as suddenly as her son's.

The following morning Brenda called Doc Evatt's court clerk, asking that the judge phone her as soon as possible, but to her surprise he put her through, cautioning her to be quick – the judge was very busy. Brenda was flustered, and said abruptly, 'I'm sorry, Doc, but I need your advice . . . urgently.'

'Happy to oblige,' Evatt replied. He'd always had a soft spot for her.

Brenda was profuse in her apologies, but he cut her short. 'Tell me what I can do for you,' he said.

So she did, concluding with an invitation for him and Alice to join her for dinner at Primo's on Wednesday.

There was a pause while Evatt consulted his diary, then he said, 'You're in luck with me, but not with Alice. She has a prior engagement, I'm afraid, and we'll have to be quick because I have a complex matter in court the following morning and have to brush up on my notes. Make it six o'clock at Primo's, out by eight-thirty?'

Brenda, breathing a sigh of relief, thanked him.

Brenda wore a spiffy new ensemble purchased from David Jones and chosen with advice from the fashion department manageress. Normally she would have found something at Freda's Frocks in Darling Street, relying on Freda Morgan or Gwendy, her sister, to advise her. But both were notorious stickybeaks and understood that nobody bought a complete outfit, including hat and gloves and matching shoes, unless there was something going on that the two of them felt they, and therefore the rest of Balmain, should immediately know about.

Brenda wasn't the browsing type and felt completely lost in the big city department store. She'd picked a green dress, a colour Freda and Gwendy always said was 'quintessentially her', and was in the process of looking at a blue felt hat when the manageress approached. Smiling, she proffered her business card. 'Madam, blue and green should never be seen,' she said in a light but assured voice. Normally Brenda would have told her to go to buggery and gone ahead and chosen the blue hat with gloves and shoes to match, but the authority represented by the personal card had undone her, and besides, she couldn't recall having ever seen blue and green together in an ensemble in the *Women's Weekly*. The manageress reached out and removed a smart-looking, deep maroon hat from the display rack. 'Ah, lovely. Shall we try this, madam? Green and wine are simply divine.' Brenda tried on the hat and was forced to admit that it suited her. Besides, she was going to a posh restaurant with a High Court judge, where there would be smart, fashionable people; she felt out of her depth. The manageress was confident and sophisticated and so she ended up with the deep wine-coloured hat, gloves and shoes, assured that, 'The gorgeous green sets off your lovely little figure and titian hair, madam,' and that the accessories were 'understated and simply splendid'.

Brenda was never what you might call beautiful, but at thirty-seven she still had her petite figure, and despite the years of hard toil, was pretty enough in her new glad rags to turn a few heads at the cocktail bar as she entered the restaurant at precisely six o'clock. When the maître d' indicated the bar and suggested a pre-dinner cocktail she refused and asked to be escorted directly to her table.

'Of course, madam.' He seated her, unfolded the large cone-shaped damask napkin and with a flourish placed it on her lap, then proffered the wine list in a heavy leather folder embossed with a gold coat of arms and the name of the restaurant. 'I am expecting Dr Evatt,' Brenda said, pausing before adding, 'the High Court judge.'

'Ah, always a welcome guest, madam.'

'He's in a bit of a hurry,' Brenda added a little breathlessly, for a moment forgetting her poise.

'Always,' the maître d' said smugly, scoring a second time. 'I shall advise the chef to prepare a rump steak and *pommes mousseline*.'

Brenda had felt both of the previous putdowns and she'd had enough. 'Whatever you wish to call them they're still mashed potatoes,' she said dismissively.

While she'd been to some of the nicer restaurants in town at the invitation of various breweries, Primo's was regarded as a cut above the others and this was confirmed when Brenda examined the wine list. While she didn't have much call to sell wine at the Hero of Mafeking – none, in fact – except for the fortified varieties, sweet sherry, port and madeira, she was familiar with the wholesaler's liquor price list and was quick to note that the restaurant mark-up on a bottle of chablis was three hundred per cent, sufficient validation in Brenda's mind of the establishment's stratospheric reputation. Fortunately Doc Evatt drank scotch (one hundred per cent mark-up) and she sarsaparilla, or very occasionally a dry sherry, having read in the *Women's Weekly* that it was a ladylike thing to do in polite company.

The Doc didn't waste time on the usual pleasantries. He greeted Brenda with a nod and a grunt, sat down, ordered a scotch from the now obsequiously smiling maître d', then a steak, any way the house liked to cook it as long as it came with mashed potatoes. With that out of the way he squinted through his thick glasses across the damask-covered table and came directly to the point. 'So, Brenda, tell me, what's the problem?' he demanded.

Brenda laughed. 'But I haven't ordered, Doc,' she protested, turning to see the maître d' had been replaced by a waiter wearing a white apron down to his ankles.

'Steak's good,' Evatt offered with an impatient flick of his wrist. 'So, what can I do for you?'

Brenda glanced up and said, 'I'll have the same as Judge Evatt, only half the portion.'

'Madam, I'm afraid all the steaks are the same size, aged beef, hand cut an inch and a half thick by four and a half inches across,' the waiter replied pompously.

Evatt gave him a sharp look. 'Hand cut, eh? Then cut the bloody thing in half!' he demanded, turning back to Brenda, who proceeded to outline the situation as succinctly as possible.

'If you can delay him from joining up, he'd have his BA in another year,' she concluded.

Evatt looked up. 'What's he want to do, teach?'

'No, definitely not.'

'Pretty worthless degree, unless of course he goes on and takes law,' Evatt observed, confirming Danny's own assertion.

'Well, useless or not, he's not going to finish if he joins up. All he wants to do is follow his mates into the Sixth Division.'

'Hmm, not surprising; mates are everything at that age.' He thought for a moment. 'Not the Sixth, definitely not right for him,' Evatt pronounced firmly. 'When he's graduated he'll go to officers' school. We need educated men as leaders. I'll talk to him. When is the lad home?'

'Oh, thank you, thank you, Doc!' Brenda said, unable to hide her relief. 'He's usually home around five o'clock. He helps at the main bar during rush hour at the pub.'

The following day at almost precisely five o'clock, Doc Evatt's driver drew up directly outside the pub in a big black Buick.

It was an unseasonably warm spring day and the pub windows were open, so there was a sudden lull among the patrons as the judge opened the back door and stepped out onto the pavement. Brenda hurried to meet him, calling Danny over as he entered the pub, then ushered them both upstairs.

Brenda, aware that the judge hated any sort of fuss, had placed a pot of tea, two mugs, a milk jug, a sugar pot and a plate of assorted biscuits on the upstairs kitchen table.

Doc Evatt sat down and indicated to Danny to take the chair opposite. Brenda poured them each a mug of tea, adding the milk and sugar first. Accepting the mug absentmindedly Doc Evatt glanced up at her and said, 'I'll see you downstairs to say goodbye.' Danny was impressed as he watched his mum leave without a word.

'So you want to join up, son?' Doc Evatt asked.

'Yes, sir.'

'Because your friends are all doing so?'

'Yes, sir.'

'Do you always do as they do?'

'No, sir.'

'So, you must have a special reason this time.'

'Well, yes, sir. It's the war. I want to do my bit.'

Doc Evatt thought for a moment. 'This *bit* you want to do – is it for these friends you talked about?'

'No, of course not, sir! For my country.'

'Ah, I see; your country! So, even if your friends stayed at home, you'd join up?'

'Yes, I think so, sir.'

'Think so?'

'Yes, I would.'

'So, you believe your country comes first, ahead of your education?'

'Yes, of course, sir.'

'Hmm . . . very commendable.'

'No, sir . . . it's my duty,' Danny said, beginning to feel decidedly awkward. Evatt's simple questions, which he sensed were far from cursory, were slowly backing him into a corner.

'And if your country asked you to jump headlong into a hail of machine-gun fire to meet almost certain death, would you do so unquestioningly?'

Danny hesitated. 'Well, yes. I don't suppose I'd have a choice.'

'Ah, Gallipoli, eh? Leave a letter for your sweetheart with your mate then scramble out of the trench when your officer blows his whistle and into a hail of Turkish fire.' He looked up, one eyebrow raised quizzically. 'Were you not taught at school that we lost that stoush?'

'Yes, sir.'

'Could it be that while we acted with incredible, dare I say, foolish bravery, we failed to ask ourselves what we hoped to achieve by our actions? Brave men may win posthumous medals, but the real objective is to keep them alive so we can win battles.' Doc Evatt was silent, hands resting on the kitchen table, fingers curled inwards so he could examine his nails.

Danny groaned inwardly; he knew, or thought he knew, what was coming next. Doc Evatt was going to point out that his country *was* giving him a choice. He did have permission to complete his degree before joining up. But he'd guessed wrong. Without glancing up Evatt asked, 'What if your country had a different agenda this time?'

'How do you mean, sir?'

'Well, you're aware of the economic situation. In this constituency alone the rate of unemployment is still appallingly high. The centre for the Unemployed Workers Movement is right here in Balmain.' He paused momentarily. 'I assume it's the Sixth Division you want to join. Is that right?'

'Yes, sir.'

'Well, I hope you'll believe me when I say that for most of the men who join up, it will be the first job with steady pay they've had in quite a while. Some of the younger ones have never known a regular job. Some are permanently unemployed. Too many men are still doing it tough, so it stands to reason the ranks will be swelled by the unemployed, unskilled and hard doers. That's just a fact of contemporary Australian life.'

'Sir, I don't think I'm anything special; I'm not any different to them . . .'

'Ah, but you are, son; your education is what separates you.'

Danny frowned. 'Sir, all my mates, the blokes I grew up with, fit your description. I'd like to be in it with them.'

'That's quite understandable, even commendable. But in terms of your country's needs, it's not sensible. It's a fact of modern warfare that rank and file – ordinary soldiers – are wasted as a fighting force unless there are sufficient men qualified to lead them.'

Danny felt that, judge or not, he couldn't let Doc Evatt get away with a statement like that. 'Sir, in the *Herald* yesterday the editorial pointed out that the rush to join the Sixth Division from the professional classes is such that there is sufficient officer material to lead an army.'

Evatt hardly missed a beat. 'I hope the *Herald* is correct – I cannot comment – but I am led to believe that you are a highly regarded sportsman and I guess not altogether stupid either. You captained your school in rugby and I've heard you described in Balmain as a born leader, someone young blokes choose to follow. During the First World War, the officers were almost entirely "educated",' he gave the word an ironic inflexion, 'but nevertheless there were few men who could lead, and

I include the generals in this list of ineffectual leaders. Australia also had its fair share of nincompoops – private schoolboys from our better families, professional men, officers who, when it came to leading in the battlefield, didn't possess an ounce of commonsense. But we also had men such as Monash and Pompey Elliott, who, I'm sure you will agree, support my point; men who had completed their education, honed their intellect and so could understand the complexities of modern war.'

'But . . . but, it's only an Arts degree,' Danny protested. 'It has nothing to do with the complexities of modern warfare!'

'True enough. But a degree, any degree, cultivates your mind, teaching you how to think, organise, analyse and research. Besides, you'll receive the appropriate officer training when the time comes and if, as has been suggested, you have the instinct to lead, the rest will follow naturally.' Doc Evatt leaned back and folded his hands across his pot belly. 'Take my advice, son. You owe it to your country to complete your education, the education your country has granted you, to be used, one would hope, in its service. War is to be avoided at almost any cost – I myself lost two brothers in the last one – but now we're in another we all have to contribute what we can. If I might put it differently, your country needs all your capabilities rather more than it needs another trigger finger.'

Evatt rose to his feet. He looked steadily at Danny until the younger man was forced to drop his gaze. 'Complete your degree, son. You'll enjoy officer training. Take my word for it, this war isn't going to be over in a year or even two or three. There will be plenty of opportunity to do your duty by your country when the time comes. Generally speaking, an athlete who is a natural leader makes a damn good officer. If men are prepared to follow you willingly, you must be competent to lead them intelligently.'

Danny was suddenly conscious that he was being addressed by a justice of the High Court, living proof of what a boy from an ordinary background can achieve in Australia. 'Thank you, sir. I'll try to do as you say.'

Evatt smiled. 'Good. Now I must go.' He extended his hand. 'Good lad. Don't disappoint me, or your country. Give us all you've got to give. That way we'll win this war.'

Danny watched from upstairs as Doc Evatt's big black Buick pulled away from the front of the pub. The drinkers had spilled onto the pavement to see the great man leave, his mother at the forefront, giving the judge a farewell peck on the cheek. Brenda had won, Danny thought sourly. She always won.

Doc Evatt's logic couldn't be faulted. Danny would go back to uni and eat crow while locals watched their sons marching off to war, thinking to themselves that he was the gutless wonder who would remain behind. Any explanation – that he planned to complete his degree and then go on to officer training – would only increase their silent scorn. Balmain boys were born with a healthy suspicion of authority and stuck with their mates come what may. A famous example, taught to every kid when he was knee-high to a grasshopper, was the story of the six Balmain boys, waiting in a narrow trench at Gallipoli to go over the top when the officer blew his whistle. The first boy handed his mate the letter he'd written to his sweetheart. The whistle blew five times and the first five were, each in turn, mown down by Turkish machine-gun fire. The sixth eventually returned home with five letters for five sweethearts. In fact the legend was so well known among Balmain folk that it was simply known as 'Five Letters to Five Sweethearts'. When unity of opinion or effort against an outside opponent was called for, it was shortened further: 'Okay, fellas, Five Letters!'

Danny went downstairs to help with last drinks, then cleaned the bar and afterwards went for a long walk, crossing over to neighbouring Birchgrove where he sat on a bench in a small park.

Half Dunn had watched his grim-faced boy silently leave the pub without calling goodbye or indicating, as he usually did, when he might be back. He had no need to ask how the meeting had gone upstairs. Danny's silence as he cleared the glasses and cleaned the bar was answer enough. She'd won.

He felt for his son, recognising his own impotence in the face of Brenda's determination. He still hadn't recovered from the recent scene in the kitchen. Passing out at the sight of a drop of his own blood in Danny's presence had been pathetic. After returning to the pub from Dr Keeble's with a silent and humiliated Brenda, he'd waited while she went upstairs and shortly after returned with a hand mirror and led him into the ladies toilet. Making him stand in front of the mirror she'd held the second mirror up to the back of his head to show him the extent of the wound on his bald patch. It was truly nothing and he'd felt ashamed and worthless. Despite the satisfaction he'd obtained from the huge scare he'd given her, by silently demonstrating her contempt with the mirror, she'd ultimately made it seem like the cheap and unworthy trick it was. The large and tender bruise that came out around his coccyx caused him considerable pain when he sat down, but it could not be seen and, of course, he daren't mention it now. He knew it would heal in time, but his humiliation would remain.

Now, here was more of the same with Doc Evatt: the cursory way the great man had acknowledged him on arrival, a mere nod of the head as he and Brenda had sailed past and she'd called out to Danny to follow; then ignoring him completely on the way out. It hadn't even occurred to her to include him, the father, in a discussion involving the boy's future.

She'd left the pub two nights previously dressed to the nines, new dress, hat, gloves, silk stockings and high-heeled shoes, hopped into a waiting taxi she must have ordered earlier, and when he'd called out to her from the front door, she'd waved and called back, 'Primo's, Doc Evatt!' She'd made no mention of her assignation the next day.

Now she returned from farewelling the judge wearing a decidedly smug smile, but, as usual, didn't bother to tell him a thing. She'd gone directly into her office, closing the door behind her. To hug herself gleefully? To gloat?

Half Dunn felt a tightening in his chest, a feeling of frustrated rage that had been occurring more and more lately, in fact, since the declaration of hostilities a couple of weeks earlier. He had always felt a private shame that his obesity had prevented him from enlisting in the AIF towards the end of the last war. He traced his subsequent lethargy and sense of worthlessness to this rejection, which had been further exacerbated when the diggers returned home to bands and parades. He was fully aware of the deference shown to the men who had served their country, and of the way people in Wagga regarded him – girls in particular – with their slender arms around the waists of returned diggers, the corners of their pretty-coloured lips curled in contempt when they thought he wasn't looking, or of how they'd coolly survey him under their lashes as they exhaled the smoke from their cigarettes, then disdainfully turn away. He'd sought solace in grog and covered his hurt with bombast, bonhomie and bullshit.

This self-serving explanation for his early decline wasn't strictly true. Lethargy, gluttony and a somewhat cowardly demeanour had marked him from childhood, but his large and abiding thirst had appeared promptly with the arrival of his legal drinking age and wasn't necessarily due to his rejection by the army. We all seek comfort in excuses of our own invention and Half Dunn had come to believe in these largely fallacious reasons for his failure to live up to his own and others' expectations.

But this new conflict was Danny's war, his rite of passage. His son was everything he would have liked to have been and wasn't. Danny's misfortune was that he'd come up against a formidable mother, a veritable force of nature, if not a virago, then certainly the single most determined person Half Dunn had ever known.

Pathetically he realised that any effort he might make to support his son wasn't worth a pinch of shit. Brenda was capable of cutting him down to size any time she liked, that is, when she didn't simply ignore him. Even her former token 'Yes, dears' had now been replaced by an impatient tongue cluck and a flick of her hair.

Half Dunn didn't regard the Doc Evatt episode as an act of desperation on his wife's part but perhaps uncharitably as an act of sheer determination. Now he watched helplessly from the sidelines as she schemed to get her way and in the process whipped the kid back into line.

However, Brenda, after farewelling the judge, had barely made it to the safety of her office before she began to weep. Danny's threat to leave home and university had been real. She could no longer bulldoze her son. The boy who had torn the porridge pot from her hand with such a look in his eyes was now a man who, unlike Half Dunn, was prepared to defy her. Had it not been for Doc Evatt's silky logic, she realised, she might have lost both her son and her long-held ambition for him. The possibility that all she'd done might come to nought filled her with terror.

She could see her mother's pale-blue eyes with their look of resigned despair, her stoic father sweating in his wedding suit. With her help her twin sisters had progressed to shorthand and typing and held down nice clean billets, then regressed by marrying no-hopers, drinkers and gamblers, who condemned both women to lives of drudgery, with too many kids tugging at their aprons and too little money to nourish them properly. She'd tried so hard to lift them out of the mire and it had all amounted to nothing.

She sometimes wondered if the smug, self-righteous middle class were correct about the hopeless lower classes being unable to rise above their misery, content to be pigs wallowing in their own filth. She had to prove them wrong, show them, and she would do this through her son. Danny carried the responsibility of the past and the future, redemption and fulfilment. If he failed her, then it had all been pointless, and she felt sure she lacked the strength of purpose to continue. She rose from her desk and, sinking to the small carpet beside it, began to pray. *Mother Mary, Mother of God, Blessed Virgin, grant me two more years. In the name of God and all the saints, will you allow me to see my Danny holding that precious piece of paper?* she begged on bended knees.

Doc Evatt had been right. The raising of the Second AIF was a godsend to a lot of the young blokes on the peninsula. They were jack of bosses keeping them on casual rates or short-term employment. The Depression, in Balmain anyway, seemed to be grinding on endlessly. What work was available was exploited by the bosses, who constantly demanded more than they were entitled to from their workers. Furthermore, when a safety issue or legitimate complaint arose, they'd be quick to point out that there were another couple of hundred hungry men wanting a job; that if you didn't toe the line, you'd be back on the pavement on your arse wondering what had hit you.

Young blokes fed up with the insecurity saw the war as a chance to get off the poverty treadmill; not having to stand in the long line at Pyrmont docks at dawn trying to catch the foreman's eye, hoping for a day's mindless and backbreaking work; not forgetting at the end of the shift to seek out the bastard who'd hired you to thank him personally for the privilege, the sycophantic smile: 'Remember me, mate. I'm good and I don't make no trouble.'

Seven bob a day was a bloody sight better than they were averaging in civilian life. In addition they'd have the status and respect given to the mighty Anzacs – Gallipoli and all that. But best of all, it was a chance to tell the boss to shove his fucking job up his fat arse!

In January 1940, after initial training, the Sixth Division was sent somewhere in the Middle East for further training, no one quite knew where (Loose lips sink ships). It was becoming apparent that the war wasn't progressing in the way everyone expected, and was far from coming to a successful end. By March, the beginning of the third and final year of Danny's course, things had settled into what was being called the 'Phoney War'.

Danny reluctantly resolved to complete his third-year studies. A month into the new university term he met Helen Brown, a tall, leggy blonde, feisty, steady eyed and pretty, a student taking her MA in ancient history who didn't go weak at the knees when he approached. She wouldn't even let him kiss her until their fourth date and then only after she'd taken him home to get the approval of her dad, a chemist in Birchgrove, and her mum. When they gave him the nod, she gave him his first demure kiss, light and on the cheek, with no encore and strictly no pashing or groping to follow.

Danny metaphorically pulled up his daks, buttoned his fly and said goodbye to those several generous girlfriends on the peninsula who'd indulged him more or less on request. He did it as nicely as he could, explaining how he was going to join up the moment he graduated and it just wasn't fair. His deep-blue eyes, looking gravely into theirs, did the trick. Each in turn, sobbing, begged him to change his mind, but when they saw that his duty to his country must come first, they ended up demanding one for the road. Danny felt it his duty to oblige them before delivering himself body and soul to Miss Helen Brown, even though she and he had only reached the stage of a chaste kiss, lip to lip, with tongues safely confined behind teeth. He wasn't within a bull's roar of taking her to bed.

Then, in early June, the Phoney War was over and the empire was suddenly in deadly peril. The unimaginable had happened – the Maginot Line had collapsed and France had fallen. There was the chaotic scramble to withdraw Allied troops from Dunkirk, and now Britain stood alone facing a victorious and triumphant enemy across the narrow expanse of the English Channel. Defeat looked a real possibility. What, people asked, would happen to Australia if Britain fell? Australian troop divisions were in the Middle East. With the British Navy out of the picture, the German U-boats would control the seas. Our available fighting men would be stranded. A resurgent Japan was beating an aggressive drum. There was every possibility they would join the war on the German side. What then? Australia would be alone, undefended, with the Japs coming at us through South-East Asia. White Australia's oldest fear would be realised: the yellow hordes of Asia would be upon us. The excrement, as they say in the classics, had well and truly hit the rotating blades.

Danny agonised about what to do, working hard at his studies, but resenting every minute of it. Then, when he had only months to go at university, a deciding factor in the form of Billy Scraper walked into the pub on a Saturday afternoon, resplendent in an RAAF uniform so new you could smell the pine resin from its wooden packing case. He was with his old man, Sky Scraper, so named because he drove the big crane at Mort Dock Engineering, who was beaming fit to burst at the congratulations the patrons were shouting out to his son as he lapped up the reflected glory. Billy's old man peeled off to join a rowdy group he obviously knew, but Billy, pausing only to receive the odd back slap, walked directly up to Danny behind the bar.

Observing his approach, Danny grinned, holding up his hand. 'Don't even think of buying a beer, mate. Today you drink on the house.' It was winter, and because he hadn't seen Billy for a couple of months, he'd assumed he'd joined up. Often the period between joining up and being sent to training camp was no more than a couple of days and you couldn't get around to saying all your goodbyes. Besides, Billy was essentially a water-polo friend; they'd never been close mates.

Scraper was a reasonable defender who played in the second-grade comp, though occasionally he'd sit on the reserves bench for the firsts and get a few minutes of pool time when a player was subbed or dragged off by the coach for performing badly and made to sit on the bench in disgrace. In the hierarchical world of young sportsmen, Danny was an aristocrat while Billy, at best, was a serf. Danny didn't observe these unspoken distinctions and treated everyone the same, but nevertheless they seldom mixed much beyond the confines of the pool.

'Make it a seven, mate, same for me dad. We got a fair few pubs to go yet and we been at it all afternoon.' He laughed. 'The old bloke can't believe his luck; we haven't paid for a single beer yet.'

'Fair enough, it's your big day,' Danny grinned, pouring two seven-ounce beers and placing them on the counter. Billy turned to where his old man was talking to the group of older blokes. 'Dad!' he yelled. 'Beer, mate.'

Billy's dad occasionally came into the Hero but usually did his drinking at the Dry Dock Hotel down at the wharves. He walked over and picked up the seven of beer and turned to go back to his mates.

'Hey, mate, it's on the house,' Billy called. 'Say thanks, will ya?'

Sky Scraper propped, then turned slowly to face Danny, lifting his hand slightly to indicate the beer he held, then pointing at it with his free hand. 'I'll return the favour when I see yiz in uniform, son,' he replied, then turned his back and went over to rejoin the group.

Danny flushed deeply but managed somehow to keep his composure.

'Take no notice – he's shickered. We've been on the piss all morning,' Billy Scraper said. 'Mostly I've been drinkin' shandies but the silly bugger prides himself he can hold his grog.'

'Yeah, fair enough,' Danny replied, attempting a smile, but he was gutted, his heart thumping. 'So where to next, mate?' he forced himself to ask.

'Canada. Training to be air crew.'

'Hey, good one! Bloody cold in the winter, though.'

'Yeah, mate, have to find meself a local bird,' Billy grinned. 'They say them Canadian sheilas know their way around the cot. Must be all that cold weather!'

'Could be. We had one lecture us in my first year at uni. She was supposed to be half Red Indian, come here on some sort of teaching exchange with Canada.'

'Yeah? Good sort?'

'Not bad.'

'You bang her?' Billy asked bluntly.

Danny laughed. 'Christ, no! You know the rules, mate. Never piss on your own doorstep.'

'Shit. Never *shit* on yer own doorstep,' Billy corrected.

Danny attempted to hide his surprise. These things were subtle, but he wouldn't normally have expected Billy Scraper to have the courage to correct him like that. He was obviously using the newfound authority he imagined his RAAF uniform granted him. In his mind he probably thought the tables had been turned; new rules – war was greater than sport. 'Yeah, right,' Danny said.

'How long you got to go?' Billy asked.

'What, uni?'

'Yeah.'

'Few months.'

'Jesus! In a few months I'll be on night bombing raids over Germany! Jerry searchlights tryin' ta locate us. Them little puffs a' smoke hanging in the air from ack-ack shells exploding every fuckin' which way in the sky. Us in our Wellington shittin' ourselves!' Billy said excitedly.

Normally Danny would have grinned, allowing his mate to bullshit, amused by the well-rehearsed fantasy. Plainly Billy Scraper had seen too many war movies and was revelling in his new blue uniform. But Danny wasn't his normal self. Sky Scraper's insult had kicked him in the emotional crutch and, anyway, he felt guilty and was already hurting.

Billy had almost finished the seven. 'One for the road?' Danny offered.

'Shit no! Gotta go, mate.' He drained his glass and slapped it down on the counter, smacking his lips ostentatiously. He wiped his mouth on the back of his wrist and stretched over to shake Danny's hand. Head slightly to one side he gave Danny a sardonic grin. At least, that's how Danny interpreted it. 'So long, mate. Don't hang around too long . . . you'll miss all the fucking fun.'

In his mind Danny translated this to mean: *Bludger! Dodging the war while your mates are doing their bit.*

Danny watched as father (somewhat unsteadily) and son departed to a chorus of good wishes from the patrons, then somewhat grim-faced he moved down towards Half Dunn's end of the bar, collecting the empty glasses.

'You okay, son?' Half Dunn asked as he drew near.

'Yeah,' Danny responded, not looking at his father.

'Never mind, not long to go at uni and then it's officers' school. Pass before you know it,' Half Dunn comforted him.

Danny looked up angrily. 'Jesus, Dad! It's months! Then there's another four months doing the friggin' course . . . that's the best part of a year! Then I'll probably have to hang around for a posting to a unit overseas. Could be a year or more before I see any action!' He jerked his head towards the door. 'And in the meantime Billy's dropping bombs on night raids over Germany!'

At that moment Brenda entered the bar. 'Talk about it tonight, eh?' Half Dunn said *sotto voce*.

He and Danny had grown a lot closer in the months since the declaration of war and the porridge pot incident. Half Dunn had announced that he was going to cut down on his drinking as his personal contribution to the war effort.

'Be able to buy a couple of Churchill tanks with the money you save,' some wag had noted.

'Does that mean he halves his bullshit quotient as well?' another joked.

To everyone's surprise he stuck to his guns and in three months he'd lost four stone. While fifty-six pounds missing from a three-hundred-pound bulk isn't all that noticeable, he felt a lot better. It also meant he was sufficiently sober to listen nightly to the ABC news with Danny at nine o'clock, both of them seated at the kitchen table upstairs. It had become a ritual; they all missed the seven o'clock broadcast because they were required to help clean up after six o'clock closing. Brenda, on the other hand, evinced no interest whatsoever in the war, both as a matter of Irish principle and as a consequence of her stand on Danny joining up. She usually retired to bed to read the *Women's Weekly* or to listen to a play on her bedside radio.

Danny found that he enjoyed the company of his father and was constantly surprised at Half Dunn's grasp of the war and the significance of news from the front. He persuaded his old man to take some exercise, and while this amounted to no more than a morning walk to the newsagent a third of a mile up Darling Street to fetch the *Sydney Morning Herald*, it represented a major effort on his part. Moreover, the swap from the *Daily Mirror* to the more serious broadsheet was yet another manifestation of Half Dunn's more earnest demeanour. Danny, who'd always taken his cue from his mother, was discovering that there was more to his father than he'd previously imagined. Perhaps, he concluded, his father's ability to construct constant, amusing and inventive bullshit had had the effect of actually sharpening his mind.

The late news on the evening following Billy's visit was particularly woeful, the ABC newsreader impassively reciting a litany of disasters in France and elsewhere. Danny, who had grown increasingly sombre as the day progressed, finally said, 'Dad, how can I possibly sit on my arse with this going on? I feel like I'm cheating.'

'Yeah, mate, that's perfectly understandable, but you're not cheating. Like I said this afternoon, it's not so long to go.'

'That's bullshit, Dad. It could be almost a year! It's a Five Letters call and I'm not there for my mates. I'm going to join up now . . . tomorrow!'

'It's Sunday,' Half Dunn reminded him.

'Yeah, right, Monday then. I've had a gutful.'

'Danny, I heard what Sky Scraper said to you downstairs. He was pissed – don't take no notice.'

Danny suddenly turned on his father and shouted, 'Pissed or not, he was fucking right!'

'Danny! Danny, calm down, mate. You'll bring your mother running,' Half Dunn said in an urgent undertone.

'Well, why not? Sort it out right here and now.'

'Yeah? Like the last time?'

Danny sighed. 'I'm sick of the way people look at me in the street. Last Wednesday I bought a pie and a cup of tea in a cafe on Parramatta Road opposite the uni and this old woman brings it and there's a white chook feather sticking out the top of the pie. "Ma'am, I ordered a meat pie, not a chicken," I joke.

'"That's a meat pie, son," she says.

'"What's the feather for then?" I ask.

'"Ask your father," she says, mouth like a duck's bum. I should have laughed, but I didn't. I lost it . . . I completely lost it! I picked up the pie and hurled it against the wall and then I poured the cup of tea on the floor and walked out. "Don't ever come back, yer bloody coward!" she shouted after me.'

Half Dunn looked down at his hands, then sighed deeply and looked up at Danny. 'Mate, what can I say? I've always felt like a weak bastard because I didn't join up in the last stoush against the Jerries. They said I was too fat to fight.'

'Dad, that's a medical reason. I'm not too fat.' He nodded in the direction of Brenda's bedroom down the hallway. 'She's the only reason I'm not in uniform.'

Half Dunn sighed again. 'Son, your mother's never going to give her permission. You'll just have to wait until your birthday next year, then you can do what you bloody well want!'

'No, Dad. I don't want to join up because I hate Mum! Because I don't – I love her. I want to join up now *right now*, because it's the right thing to do. Last time, when I agreed to finish university, everyone said the war would be over in a matter of months and that we were bound to win. But that hasn't happened, and Britain, we, the allies, we're taking a hiding. There's talk of the Japs joining the war. If they do, we're in deep shit. You know that, you said so yourself. This time it's different. This time Doc Evatt could talk until he was blue in the face and it wouldn't make any difference.'

Half Dunn didn't speak for some time, but when he did it was prefaced by a growl, or perhaps it was a groan. 'Go down to the post office Monday morning – not the one in Darling Street, or Balmain East, they might tell your mum – go over to Birchgrove, get the parents' permission form and I'll sign it.'

'Jesus, Dad, she'll kill you!'

'Yeah, well, maybe. I'm still your father. I might not have been much of a one, but it's time your mother realised it too.'

On Monday morning Danny woke early, though not early enough to beat his mother, who he could hear talking to the early cleaning lady from her office downstairs where she did the accounts first thing, wrote the orders for the day and completed her other office duties. He dressed quickly then walked quietly along the polished wooden corridor towards her bedroom. It was next to Half Dunn's, and he paused to look in through his father's half-open door. Half Dunn lay on his side like a great beached whale in grey striped winter pyjamas. As Danny watched, a small bubble formed at the left corner of his mouth then immediately popped with his next breath. Danny noted that the pillow directly below his cheek was wet with spittle that shone against the side of his cherubic chin.

Danny smiled; his fat slob of a father, now fifty-odd pounds lighter, had come good in the end. He didn't envy him the day that lay ahead, in fact it was going to be pretty trying for them both, but he'd soon be gone and Half Dunn would have to continue to live with Brenda.

Danny moved to his mother's bedroom next door. The bedhead was positioned against the wall between two standard windows, so when she lay in bed Brenda looked directly out of the bedroom door into the hallway, giving her a sense of supervising the affairs of the pub, of being in charge, even while she slept. Set into the wall above the pink silk-shantung padded headboard was a small wall safe. It was where she kept the previous day's takings, and she was probably downstairs stuffing them into a canvas bank bag at that very moment. Brenda trusted no one but herself with the banking.

The safe contained a long thin black box that held his parents' marriage certificate, the contracts for the sale of the pub in Wagga and also for the purchase of the Hero of Mafeking. He picked up a single folded sheet of paper, browning with age, and casually unfolded it to see it was Brenda's final school report card. It showed she'd received a distinction in every subject. At the bottom of the page in fading copperplate script was a handwritten notation: *The best student I've ever had the privilege to teach. It would be a great shame if Brenda were not allowed to continue her schooling. Linley Horrocks, Teacher.* The final document in the tin proved to be what he was looking for – his birth certificate.

Danny pocketed the certificate and returned the box to the safe, closing it and thumbing the combination to a random set of numbers. As he passed Half Dunn's door his father sighed in his sleep, then with a great creaking of bedsprings, turned onto his back, gave a snort and began to snore.

Shortly afterwards Danny emerged via the back stairs and the beer garden into Darling Street just in time to see the rattler approaching, coming back up from the ferry terminal. He sprinted to the tram stop and hopped aboard, leaving it again at the closest stop to the post office. He walked the remainder of the way, arriving moments after it opened.

He was back at the pub just before opening time and was fortunate enough to catch Half Dunn alone, polishing the wooden surface of the main bar. Brenda was out the back supervising the unloading of a beer delivery.

'You'll need your birth certificate,' he said to Danny.

'Yeah, thanks, Dad. I've got it.'

'Haven't changed your mind?'

'No, of course not!' Danny put his hand on his father's shoulder. 'Thanks, Dad. This isn't going to be easy for you, mate.'

Half Dunn smiled sadly. 'Never has been, never will be. Your mother isn't an easy woman, son.' He sighed. 'But there you go, it's done now.'

Danny arrived at the army recruiting centre at one o'clock, a wooden hut in Martin Place directly over the underground toilets, hence the immortal expression, 'Mate, I'm in Shit Street.' Inside the hut, around a dozen young blokes were waiting.

At last it was Danny's turn to stand in front of the recruiting sergeant's desk. The heavy-set military man looked up as he handed Danny a form. 'Well, well, first gollywog all day. When'd you last have a haircut, son?'

Danny grinned. 'Never known a barber's clippers, sir.'

'Not sir! Sergeant! Well, take my word for it, son, you won't be fighting in this army with that haircut.'

'Cutting it is fine by me, sergeant,' Danny replied, grinning. 'But I'm afraid you'll have to ask my mum's permission.'

The recruiting sergeant didn't react, though the slight smile indicated he bought the joke. 'Army's about the only place where your mum's permission isn't needed, except if you're not yet twenty-one, of course.'

'I'm not, but I have my dad's permission, sergeant.' He handed over the permission form along with his birth certificate.

The recruiting sergeant glanced at both, noting that Danny was about a year shy of his majority. He looked up in some surprise. 'Couldn't wait any longer, eh? Well, your timing's perfect. We're raising a new division – the Eighth. You can get in on the ground floor.' He pointed to a row of desks. 'Fill in the form and bring it back here.'

Danny, having completed the form, once again stood in front of the recruiting sergeant. 'At university, eh?' He looked up. 'Two further choices. You can defer or apply for officer training.'

'Neither, sergeant, I just want to get on with it.'

'Good on ya, son – it's your call. Come back at two o'clock for your medical. Shouldn't be a problem – you look pretty fit.'

By late afternoon Danny had completed the paperwork and had been to Victoria Barracks for his medical examination. He was instructed to return to the Barracks the following day to be sworn in before being transported to the military training camp at Wallgrove, an hour's journey to the west of Sydney.

On his way home to Balmain he detoured to Birchgrove, to Helen's house. She was at home alone when he arrived and they went into the garden. She sat on the swing hanging from the branch of a gum tree that stretched high over the back fence. The birds had begun their evensong and the winter afternoon was drawing to a close.

Danny broke the news to Helen, not quite knowing what to expect. They'd only been together a couple of months and there was a whole heap of stuff he still didn't know about this tall pretty blonde wasting a first-rate brain on Egyptian hieroglyphs. For instance, to his utter bemusement, she was excited about doing her doctorate on mummy bandages.

Helen kicked the swing into motion but said nothing. 'Well?' Danny asked after a few moments. The swing made a creaking sound as it moved back and forth, the rope having burnt a polished groove into the branch from years of friction. Helen placed her feet on the ground, skidding to a dusty halt. She squinted up at him. 'Just as well I know now, or I could have ended up marrying a bloody fool.' She released a hand from the swing rope and waved it dismissively at Danny. 'Go on, piss off, Danny Dunn!'

'Hey, wait on!' Danny protested. He'd never heard Helen swear or use such a common expression. No bird had ever treated him like this. She didn't even seem unduly upset at losing him. 'It's my duty to my country,' he added self-righteously, unaware of how pompous this must sound to her.

Helen sighed and rose from the swing. 'For God's sake, spare me the scene from a bad melodrama, Danny. You're the little boy marching down the garden path with his popgun over his shoulder. There's the postie. Bang! Bang! Bang! The postman's dead! Don't expect me to play that silly game, to think of you as a hero, doing your bit for king and country! The ever-faithful sweetheart, waiting at her candlelit bedroom window for her soldier boy to return. Because I won't be! What you're doing is woefully stubborn and stupid!' She walked up to him and took him by the hand. 'Come!' she demanded.

'What now?' Danny asked, confused, holding back. 'You just told me to piss off.'

'You might as well know what you're going to miss before you go,' she said archly, pulling at his arm.

'But . . . but . . . ah, aren't you . . . you know, a . . . ?'

'Virgin? Don't be such an arrogant prick!'

CHAPTER THREE

___

TWO HUNDRED AND FIFTY men – mostly but not exclusively Australian prisoners of war – had gathered at the camp gate, not knowing what to expect, or for that manner what to do if it were suddenly flung open and they were free to leave. Did they march to Bangkok, leaving behind those mates too sick or fearful to fend for themselves? Or did they sit tight and wait? Freedom, coming so unexpectedly, had completely flummoxed them.

That morning, when they'd received double rations for breakfast, they immediately thought that the Japs wanted something they couldn't beat out of them, but what that might be was pure speculation. The prisoners had become accustomed to the irrational behaviour of the enemy and had long since given up trying to guess their motives for doing just about anything. They had simply reached the conclusion that the oriental and occidental minds work very differently. But the double rations had heralded the appearance of the Japanese commandant, Colonel Mori, at *tenko* or rollcall, a highly unusual occurrence. Without any fanfare or fuss and with not the least show of emotion he'd simply announced, 'War over! Japan *suwenda*! All men now *flends*! All men go home!' Then he snapped a salute and returned to his office. It was as if everything was perfectly normal, and it was this sense of the ordinary that confused the prisoners – nothing and everything had suddenly changed.

Soon after the announcement, Lieutenant Hiro, who had been in charge of the airport work gangs, walked up to Danny. As his right hand automatically rose to his forehead, Danny realised that he need no longer salute the Japanese soldier. At the same moment, he understood that the announcement of peace must have had a similarly profound effect on the Japs, who, with the exception of two guards who remained at the gate, had abandoned their normal duties and passively returned to their barracks to wait their turn to be incarcerated. They were no longer members of a master race with the power to inflict random and cruel punishments on those they regarded as their inferiors. The sudden loss of authority must have caused them to feel as strangely dispossessed and ambivalent as the Australian prisoners of war now felt with their newfound liberty and power.

Lieutenant Hiro unsmilingly addressed Danny in Japanese. One of the main reasons Danny had been a successful negotiator was because he'd taken the trouble to learn the enemy's language, down to the argot the guards used. As far as it was possible for an Occidental, he understood their peculiar way of thinking, which had often saved the men under his command from needless punishment and bloodshed. '*Watashitachi wa kore kara tomodachi ni nareru yo* [We can be friends now],' Lieutenant Hiro said, and offered his hand to Danny.

'*Sore wa zettai ni muri da yo* [That will never be possible], *Hiro-san*,' Danny replied, ignoring his hand.

The officer, showing not the slightest reaction, announced in Japanese, 'No more work. All Japanese go to barracks.' He proffered a small bunch of keys. 'Rice store house . . . also *Led Closs*.'

'Red Cross?' In the time they'd been in captivity they'd received just one Red Cross handout, each box to be shared between four men. Danny knew that as prisoners of war they were entitled to receive one Red Cross parcel per man per month. Initially there had been six hundred prisoners in the camp . . . He did a rough calculation, using forty months of captivity instead of forty-two, that was 24 000 Red Cross food parcels, less the 150 they'd distributed. The bastards had stolen well over 23 000 parcels.

'Led Closs box,' Lieutenant Hiro explained.

'How many?'

'Many. Maybe four hundred, maybe more.'

'Jesus!'

Danny knew it was pointless asking him what had happened to the remainder. Hiro snapped to attention and bowed, then turned and marched briskly towards headquarters. Danny pocketed the keys, deciding that rather than distribute the Red Cross parcels, he'd tell the head cook, Corporal Alan Phillips, about them and instruct him to include the food content in the men's daily rations. The other items, such as writing paper and pencils, sewing kits and cigarettes, would be issued to the men as they left the mess hut, each with a dixie can containing something more than just boiled rice, edible weeds and a tiny scrap (if they were lucky) of gristly meat.

Alan had been a chef in a Brisbane private school for boys, and ran the prison kitchen staff and the cooks under him with crisp efficiency. He was trusted to dole out precise rice rations to each man, regardless of rank – there could be no exceptions; equal quantities of food were not only a matter of fairness, but also a matter of life and death. Perhaps the most rigid rule of them all was that there could never be any favouritism, and in this, Danny trusted Phillips completely. He also supervised the roster system which ensured that every man in the camp got his turn for an occasional extra helping from the meagre dollops of rice left in the pots after everyone had received his ration.

Danny moved towards the area of the camp gates where the new masters of the universe, the survivors of three and a half years of imprisonment, were milling around entirely unprepared for the mantle of authority. Most of them were wordless, sunk into themselves, almost uncomprehending; too bewildered to cheer. They were as powerless as ever, unable to decide what to do next.

Starving men who are constantly beaten and mistreated find a space in their heads to which they retreat to lick their wounds. There they repair to summon the mental energy to survive. All of them had learnt to treat every unanticipated event with passive, incurious resignation: a severe beating inflicted on a mate working beside you, a sudden incomprehensible outburst of spit-flecked rage directed at you by a camp guard, or a day's ration withdrawn for some unexplained misdemeanour – all were accepted without comment and with a stoic mindset. All the individual quirks of character had long since been beaten out of them – compassion or any sense of injustice had been buried very deep – and they were, for the most part, hollow men who simply obeyed instructions.

But there are always a few men who manage somehow to keep their heads and not succumb entirely to despair; men who, when called upon, will still reach out to a severely beaten friend and help him to his feet in front of his smirking tormentor, knowing that it could well cost them their own lives. In such circumstances their actions are downright foolish, but for some unknown reason many earn the grudging respect of the enemy and manage to stay alive against all odds.

Among the mob during that first hour of liberation was a prisoner named Paul Jones, known to most of the onlookers as a competent medic in the camp hospital. He now walked towards the flagpole at the entrance to the camp carrying a small rice bag. Jones – nicknamed 'Spike' after the American bandleader Spike Jones, famous for his demented percussion and crazy satires – was a tiny man further diminished by four years of starvation. Some wag had given him the nickname instead of the ubiquitous 'Taffy' because in civilian life he'd been a kettle drummer in his colliery brass band. Spike Jones wasn't in any sense made of the stuff of heroes; a quiet, reserved type, you'd have thought he wouldn't have said boo to a mouse. Reaching the flagpole, he placed the bag at his feet, then brazenly began to haul down the Japanese flag, the despised fried-egg symbol that had fluttered so menacingly above their heads during their captivity. When the Japanese flag was finally within his grasp he untied it and dropped it in a heap at his feet.

As the senior NCO and therefore the highest ranking Allied prisoner in the camp, Danny hadn't thought to lower the flag, and felt obscurely ashamed. 'Well done, Spike!' he called, loping towards the flagpole with several others who had suddenly become aware of what was going on. 'You've shamed me, mate. Should have been the first thing I did.' Stooping, he picked up the Japanese flag and handed it to the little Welshman. 'Make a great keepsake. Pity we don't have one of our own to replace it.'

'Oh, but that we do, Sergeant Major,' Jones replied, removing a Union Jack from the bag. 'It's not the Welsh dragon, mind —'

'Jesus, Spike, where'd you get that? It could've cost you your life!'

'Two years ago Micky Sopworth, a Geordie lad – miner like meself – gave it to me in the hospital. He was dying of dengue fever. "Fly it when we beat the boogers," he begged me. I made a false bottom on the bandage bin; with the flag folded flat you couldn't hardly tell the difference.'

'Go ahead then.' Danny pointed to the Union Jack. 'Let's get the true colours flying.'

Spike Jones started to tie the flag to the halyard, but he'd been so anxious to unknot the Japanese flag that he hadn't noticed how it was attached. Danny, watching, said, 'Here, let me. At home we always flew the flag above the pub. I've done it a million times.' Danny swiftly tied the flag that signalled their liberation to the halyard. 'Okay, haul her up, Spike – No, wait! What the hell am I thinking?' He turned to the men who had gathered around. 'Sergeant Catterns and Corporal Osmonde, get the men on parade for a flag-raising ceremony, here in front of the flagpole, at the double!'

'Yes, Sergeant Major!'

Some five minutes later, galvanised into action by the two NCOs, fifty men stood at ease in five rows. Danny barked, 'Attention!' The men responded as a well-trained group, but most of them were barefoot or wearing sandals made from old rubber tyres, so the coming to attention lacked the percussive effect of hobnailed boots crashing into the dirt. However, it was notable for the earnest expressions on the men's faces. The hated flag had been toppled and now one of their own was about to be raised. This was something tangible they could grasp.

'I have called you to attention. Next I will call you to the salute. Then Private Jones will raise the Union Jack and we will all sing the national anthem at the salute!' he commanded. 'Company! Salute!'

Danny snapped a salute and, standing at rigid attention, started to sing.

> God save our gracious King,
> Long live our noble King,
> God save the King.

The men followed, the anthem growing louder as they watched the flag moving up the flagpole, their discordant voices rising to the familiar words so long absent from their lips. It was as if a dark spell had been broken and they began to understand for the first time that they could, on this day and from this hour, once again act as free men.

> Send him victorious,
> Happy and glorious,
> Long to reign over us:
> God save the King!

'Parade! At ease!' Danny addressed the men. 'The Jack may not be exactly the right flag for most of us, but it sits in the left-hand corner of my own flag and that's good enough for me. I don't know about you blokes, but who'd have thought that after breakfast on what seemed like just another day of moving rocks and sand, we'd be free men? But we are, and now I want us to observe one minute's silence for those of our mates who didn't make it.'

Danny waited until a minute's silence had passed. 'Right then,

I don't know quite what happens next in terms of our liberation but I'm still responsible for you until then, so I guess it's time for a new set of standing orders. The Japs may have surrendered, but our mob here in the camp are still armed, so do not attempt any retribution. They could as easily kill us all before nightfall if we give them any aggro.' He paused. 'There will be no trouble. We're going home, so let's not fuck it up now!' Danny waited a moment to let the message sink in. 'Dismiss!' he called, whereupon some of the men let go a ragged cheer as they broke away, while others simply stood and wept, and some few dropped to their knees and silently prayed.

Danny turned away, smiling and offering his hand to Spike Jones. 'Thank you, Private Jones,' he said formally. 'I salute your courage. You're a bloody brave man. I shall see to it this doesn't go unmentioned.'

Jones shrugged. 'It was a promise to me mate, wasn't it then, Sergeant Major.'

The little medic had broken the evil shackles that had so thoroughly controlled their minds, and Danny now realised that no one, including himself, had yet summoned the courage to walk through the camp gate – a gesture that would symbolise their freedom more powerfully than anything else. The camp gate was an unprepossessing and primitive structure of barbed wire and bamboo, lacking any of the normal fortifications an entrance to a prison compound might have been expected to exhibit. As the senior NCO it was Danny's duty to be the first man out, if only to stroll a few yards down the road and back. He clapped Spike on the shoulder and pointed at the gate, beyond which the two Jap guards stood. 'Come on, mate, you and me are going to walk through that bloody gate,' he said.

As the two of them walked towards the entrance to the camp, they suddenly became aware of the sound of a motorbike approaching. Danny stopped and turned to the little medic. 'Wait on; could be the first of the cavalry arriving!' He glanced around and realised that most of the men had spontaneously fallen into formation behind them. They all watched as a military motorcycle with sidecar roared towards the gate and skidded to a halt only a yard or so from where the two Japanese sentries, having laid their rifles hastily at their feet, now stood rigidly to attention saluting.

The men behind Danny spread out along the perimeter of the fence on either side of the gate so that they could more easily witness what was about to take place. As they watched, a huge Yank in jungle-green uniform and high boots dismounted almost casually and reached into the sidecar to lift a Tommy gun from its interior. Several grenades were clipped to his waist, a colt .45 automatic was strapped to his thigh, and ammunition belts crossed his chest. His sleeve chevrons indicated that this one-man walking armoury held the rank of master sergeant. The Yank turned to face the gate and stood, feet apart, towering above the two Japanese guards who stared straight ahead, their eyes focused at a point somewhere close to infinity.

'Open the fucking gate!' he commanded with a flick of his crew-cut head.

The guards, not understanding, made no move, whereupon the Yank, switching the Tommy gun to his left hand, approached the sentry nearest to him and brought his right hand down hard against the side of the Jap's head, knocking him off his feet. The watching men gasped. Had anyone raised a hand to a camp guard just a few hours earlier it would have meant certain death. The guard, expecting more, curled up into the foetal position, his arms covering his head, preparing for the boot that must follow. 'Open!' the Yank barked at the second terrified Jap, switching the Tommy gun back into his right hand and prodding it in the direction of the gate. Finally understanding, the second guard ran the three steps towards the gate and began to unlatch it.

Along with the flag-raising ceremony, this gratuitous slap was the thing that, many of the watching men would later claim, seemed to switch on something in their heads, and they began to understand that they were no longer prisoners of the Japanese but free men all. Danny himself remarked later when he described the scene that had the big American simply mowed down the two guards with a burst from his machine-gun, like a scene in a John Wayne movie, it may well not have had the same effect on them as the loud and powerful slap.

Having dealt with the guards, the American scanned the men behind the barbed wire. Pathetic, emaciated, bearded, sun-blackened, barefoot, ragged, near-naked prisoners stared back at him. 'Jesus Christ! What you motherfuckers done to my brothers?' he exclaimed. Then, in a burst of pure rage, he gripped the second guard by the back of his neck and slammed him face-first into the heavy wooden gatepost, releasing him so that he fell unconscious into the dirt. Without further ado the American swung the gate open, mounted his motorbike, dumped the machine gun in the sidecar, kick-started the engine, and roared past the two guards, the first of whom had risen to his feet and stood once again at rigid attention in a haze of exhaust smoke. The second was either unconscious or playing dead beside the gatepost. The motorcycle came to a halt in a cloud of dust in front of Danny and Spike Jones, the American sergeant revving the engine once (perhaps to punctuate his arrival) before killing it.

There was nothing to indicate that Danny was the senior NCO in charge – like everyone else he wore a ragged pair of khaki shorts and a pair of crude motor-tyre sandals – so the huge Yank simply included him and Spike Jones in his greeting. 'Howdy, folks. How y'all doing?'

'Gidday!' A dozen or so of the men standing closest responded, while others, murmuring excitedly, approached their lone liberator and his clumsy-looking motorbike, which Danny had now identified as a Harley-Davidson.

The American cast a concerned eye over the skeletal prisoners. 'Hey, you guys,' he called out. 'I'm real sorry, but I got no rations! Thai kids ate all the candy bars.' Then he indicated the sidecar with a grin. 'But I got a shit-load o' Camels and Chesterfields. Help yourselves. You guys mostly from Australia, right? Who's the head honcho?'

Spike Jones pointed to Danny. 'Company Sergeant Major Dunn, Sergeant.'

With the news of the cigarettes a couple of dozen prisoners began to move uncertainly towards the motorcycle. They were unaccustomed to acting on their own initiative, even when invited, but when they saw the sidecar heaped with cartons of cigarettes they began to mill, then push and shove, each anxious to lay hold of such unimaginable treasure in case it should disappear in front of their very eyes.

'That's enough!' Danny shouted. 'Nobody touches the fags! Get into line! No shoving! Corporal Thomas, take charge. Count the packs. There's 410 men in camp, another 63 in sick bay!' He turned and extended his hand to the American sergeant. 'Danny Dunn. Bloody good to see you!' Before the big American could reply, he asked, 'How many packs have you got in there, Sergeant?'

'Hell, man, I don't rightly know,' the Yank said, squinting up at him. 'I reckon maybe twenty cartons.'

Danny did a quick calculation: twenty cigarettes to a pack, a dozen packs to a carton, twenty cartons, that was half a pack per man – ten cigarettes. 'Corporal, five smokes a man. Anyone gets out of line he gets bugger-all! Five more after breakfast tomorrow! Forsyth, you help him,' Danny instructed.

He turned back to the sergeant, realising he hadn't allowed the American to introduce himself. 'Jeez, sorry, Sergeant. I didn't even give you the chance to introduce yourself. Had to stop the stampede. It's been a fair while since any of the men enjoyed a smoke. Very bloody good of you, mate.'

'You're welcome, Danny. It's Billy du Bois, OSS, New Orleans, Louisiana,' the Yank said, looking directly at Danny and once again extending his hand. 'They do that to your face?'

'Yeah – Singapore. I took a beating from a *kempeitai* officer.'

'*Kempeitai*?'

'Yeah, the Japanese military police . . . cruel bastards. I tried to interfere when I thought they were about to kill one of my work detail for stealing food.'

'Jesus, man! They gone hurt you bad!' the American exclaimed wide-eyed, looking directly at him, man enough not to avert his gaze.

Danny gave him a lopsided grin. 'Yeah, I'm an ugly bugger, I know. Fortunately we're not big on mirrors in camp. But I'm alive and now it seems we're going to make it. Never thought we would.' He paused. 'Not too sure how I feel about that yet.'

'Hey, maybe we can send you stateside. Have you one o' them plastic-surgery operations,' Sergeant Billy du Bois said. 'They doing great work, I hear. That's one good thing about war; surgeons they get themselves a whole lotta practice.'

Despite himself Danny was forced to smile at the obvious concern the big ingenuous American was showing for him. 'Yeah, maybe, Sergeant,' he replied without conviction. Then, anxious to change the subject, he indicated the road beyond the gate with a nod of his head. 'When's the rest of the cavalry arriving?'

Sergeant Billy du Bois dismounted and stood beside Danny, who was genuinely surprised to see that they were about the same height. In fact the GI probably wasn't any bulkier than Danny had been when he'd left Australia for Malaya, but to him, and no doubt the other starving Australian prisoners, the Yank appeared to be a giant, a creature filled to the brim with life, with personal power and natural authority, confirmed by the way he'd so casually dispatched the two Jap guards. Billy du Bois chuckled. 'No, like I said, it's just me, Sergeant. Parachuted into Thailand four weeks ago to help train the Thai resistance.'

'What? Just one bloke?'

'Sure. The Brits did it in France. We're doing it here.'

'And you decided to come here on your own? I mean, liberate us solo, with fifty Jap soldiers armed to the teeth waiting for you?' Danny asked.

The American laughed, patting the crossed ammunition belts. 'Hey, man! I'm armed to the teeth too.' He paused, glancing down at his torso. 'All this shit, it ain't for patrols. Too fuckin' heavy, man. I wear it on the rig 'cause it impresses the holy Jesus out o' the Thais. They neutrals, but when their young guys see this get-up together wid the rig it makes recruiting them as resistance fighters a damn sight easier.' He grinned. 'Young guys the same everywhere. Long as they get one o' these ammo belts and a Tommy gun they gonna join.' He laughed. 'But the Japs they surrendered, ain't no cause to be afraid of them now. They ain't like us. They gonna cut their own throats . . . commit hara-kiri, because they ashamed, see. Now they their own worst enemies, no way they gonna be no danger to us no more.'

'Hope you're right, mate,' Danny said, unconvinced, 'but if I was you I wouldn't hang around and ask Colonel Mori to hand over his sword.' He pointed to the rig. 'That come by parachute too?'

'The pig? Yeah, it goes where I go. Harley's got real good shocks – it don't have no trouble landing.'

'The Japs didn't see it coming down?'

'Not at night. Paddy field makes a soft landing.'

'So you knew all along we were here?'

'Sure. Ain't you bin gettin' fresh food from the locals?'

'That was you? It's been a godsend. Most of it has gone to the hospital – made all the difference. Half a dozen blokes might not have made it otherwise.'

'You're welcome. Glad to be able to help, buddy. Thais don't like the Japs any more than we do.'

The men who'd already received cigarettes were talking excitedly, though none of them had lit up. Observing this, Billy du Bois reached back and undid the buckles on a canvas bag strapped to the rear of the seat. 'Hey, wait on! Should be a dozen Zippos in here.' He handed the lighters out to the men nearest him. 'Share 'em around, buddy.' He turned back to Danny. 'I was half a mile away from my base camp when I remembered the fucking Zippos,' he laughed.

'They'll be worth their weight in gold,' Danny replied. Then, growing serious he said, 'Okay, so what now, Sergeant? Do we stick around or attempt to march to Bangkok?'

The American scratched his head. 'Cain't say, buddy. They ain't wrote the script yet. This goddamn war, it's not suppose to finish till

1946. But now the president, he dropped the atomic bomb, suddenly it's all over, the whole goddamn shebang!'

'The *what* bomb?' Danny asked, not understanding.

'Atomic. We got us atomic bombs now. One bomb can take out a whole goddamn Japanese city. They dropped two, first Hiroshima, then Nagasaki – that like Memphis and New Orleans – totalled in jes two motherfucker bombs. After that the Japs decide they had enough; they don't want no war no more.' Billy shrugged then smiled broadly. 'That happened yesterday, so now we got us peace before we's had time to make arrangements.' He spread his hands. 'I ain't got no instructions about peace. So I thought maybe I'd jes take the pig, load up the sidecar wid cigarettes and mosey up to liberate you folk in the name of Uncle Sam. After that,' he shrugged, 'I'm afraid I ain't done a whole lotta thinking. But I guess you right, buddy – cain't see no point in a fancy surrender ceremony.'

'It's all come as a bit of a shock to us, too,' Danny replied. 'We had no idea until after breakfast this morning. I guess we'll just have to lie low, wait and see,' he added, not knowing what else to suggest.

'Yeah, I don't think you should have yourself a prison revolt,' Billy replied. 'Soon as I get back I'll radio HQ, arrange for an airdrop.' He grinned. 'I'll tell them to throw in a crate of Hershey bars, eh?'

'Hershey bars?'

'Chocolate candy; you gonna love 'em, buddy.'

'No! No, please don't! Too rich, mate. We'll get bad stomach cramps. Bully beef, canned veggies, canned fruit, sugar, tea, condensed milk . . .' Danny turned to Spike Jones. 'What are your most urgent medical needs, Spike?'

'We don't have urgent needs, Sarge. Everything's urgent. We need the lot – bandages, swabs, antiseptics, quinine, anything they've got for malaria, dysentery, tropical ulcers, but we can use whatever they can spare. We've got bugger-all, not even Aspro,' Jones replied.

Danny turned back to Billy du Bois. 'That would be great, mate . . . Oh, yeah, and maybe more cigarettes if that's possible?'

'Beer?'

'Jesus, you mean it?'

Billy laughed. 'You'll have to drink it warm – an ice-machine drop takes a little longer to arrange.'

Danny laughed in turn. 'Don't worry, mate. I've just realised we've got one. Colonel Mori's got a petrol generator and his own fridge; I guess I just took it over.'

Billy du Bois grinned. 'Yep, that's the idea. You're a free man now, buddy.' He swung his leg over the Harley. 'Hey, gotta kick the dust if I'm gonna get Uncle Sam's air force to do a drop today, even tomorrow morning. I'll keep in touch. So long, Danny.' With this he kick-started the Harley, then manoeuvred the clumsy rig around with staccato bursts of power from the accelerator and the help of his booted right leg. The men were cheering as he waved a salute and roared back out the camp gate, hitting a patch of loose gravel and careening sideways, narrowly missing the now conscious Jap guard. He straightened with a burst of accelerator and a wave, and then the Yankee liberator shot off down the bumpy dirt road.

Spike Jones turned to Danny, pointing to the two Japanese soldiers at the gate. 'If you don't mind, Sarg'n Major, I'll just take a look. One of them may need a wee bit of attention.'

Danny grinned. 'Yeah, okay, mate, but I daresay it won't be a popular move,' he advised. He knew that it wasn't the generous and brave Sergeant Billy du Bois who'd liberated them, but the diminutive Welshman who'd risked his life to keep a promise to a dying mate to raise the flag. He watched now as Spike bent over the guard who was sitting with his back against the gatepost; Danny could see he was bleeding from the nose and mouth. The little Welshman's hand rested sympathetically on the Jap's shoulder as if he were one of his own men. Jones was one of those rare men who, in his heart, carried no hate for his fellow humans.

Ten days after the announcement of the Japanese surrender, the prisoners of war had been trucked to a Japanese-built airport near Bangkok and flown in twin-engine Dakota transport planes to Rangoon, the capital of Burma, where Danny spent the first month out of prison camp in a British army hospital.

In spite of gaining nearly ten pounds, Danny still looked as if the next breeze would blow him off his feet. He'd also lost an inch in height and now walked with a slight stoop, in fact, an inch worth of stoop, brought about by being struck repeatedly in the small of the back with a rifle butt by Japanese or Korean guards. He'd been shown the X-rays of his spine and told bluntly that he was one of countless prisoners of war who would probably (read certainly) suffer from a bad back for the remainder of their lives.

Major Craig Woon, the Australian army doctor in Rangoon, had given him an extensive examination lasting almost three hours. Danny had entered his surgery, come to attention and saluted him, but the young officer had simply waved him to a chair. 'Forget all the formal crap, Sergeant Major. Take a seat. You've been through enough.' Danny immediately warmed to him as he went on, 'I've read your army record and I'd like to ask you one or two questions if I may. Cigarette?' He extended a slim silver monogrammed cigarette case.

'Thanks, sir, I don't smoke. Please, go ahead, ask away.'

Craig Woon grinned at the habitual 'sir'. 'Army habits die hard, but you'll soon be back in civilian life. Better get used to no longer having to respect someone who is technically your superior but very unlikely to be your better.' He snapped the cigarette case shut with a flick and returned it absently to the top pocket of his uniform jacket. 'It would help me if you would allow me to make notes,' he said, and when Danny nodded, went on, 'Perhaps you'd like to tell me how your face got into such a mess. The damage obviously didn't come about from an explosive device.'

There was a pause, then Woon added, 'If you'd rather not, that's fine, it's just that sometimes it helps to talk about these things. Buried too deep they can cause problems later on.'

'You mean psychological problems?' Danny asked.

'Yes. I confess we don't really know a lot about the condition we used to refer to in the First World War as shell shock. But it's an area I believe we ought to be looking at more carefully. Some of us are beginning to think that there is a lot more to understand about the long-term effects. In this hospital we have over a thousand beds and we know through anecdotal evidence from men like yourself who survived the prison camps that many prisoners of war just gave up, refused to eat, and died – in a manner of speaking – from despair.'

Danny nodded. 'Yeah, in the first eighteen months we saw it all the time. Nothing you could do about it. Blokes would sink into a state of despair and when they stopped eating their rice ration you knew it was only a matter of time. You could try talking them out of it and occasionally someone would respond, but mostly they got a certain look in their eyes, as if they were no longer listening to you, but to some inner voice. After that it was usually only days or a week or two at most. There was no telling who it would hit – other blokes, seemingly physically worse off, made it through to the end.'

'Yes, it's a story we're hearing all the time and there are patients who, now that it's all over, are falling apart mentally right here in this hospital. We're more concerned with treating tropical diseases here than mental problems; we're a general hospital, with only two psychiatrists on staff, and they can't begin to cope with the load.' Dr Woon shrugged. 'As I said, I'm not yet qualified to have an opinion but I have a feeling it's going to be important to understand the effects of war when we get around to running the peace. So, thanks for agreeing to talk to me, Danny.'

'Go for your life, doc. But there's not a lot to talk about. I simply got bashed up by a Jap officer and a bunch of Jap soldiers under him.'

'Perhaps a little more detail? The how, why, when and where . . .'

'It's a while ago now, doc. I'll have to think . . . never talked about it before.'

'Perhaps the day of our surrender in Singapore might be a good place to start?'

'Oh, okay then. It's not something I'm likely to forget in a hurry.' Danny sighed, and his eyes lost focus as he began to recall. 'We'd fought all night, held our position until dawn, thought we were doing pretty well holding the Japs off in our sector. That is, until a radio signal came through that Percival had surrendered.' Danny's voice rose. 'Shit . . . like I said, we were doing okay. We reckoned everyone was; after all, we outnumbered the enemy two to one on the island. They, the Nips, had no more reinforcements, no backup. Jesus! We had sufficient ordnance and supplies to damn near mount a counter invasion on Japan and it was us who hoisted the white flag, who surrendered!' Danny was warming to his story.

'It had a lot to do with water as I remember?' Dr Woon volunteered.

'Well, yeah, as it turned out. Talk about biting yourself on the bum. Percival made no arrangements to build defences against a Japanese invasion, in particular for the holding reservoirs on the island, all of which were close to where the Japs landed in the north-west sector. The pipeline that fed them brought the island's water from Johore on the mainland, and in the process of blowing up the causeway from Malaya the Brits also blew up their own pipeline, their main source of water, ferchrissake! The Japanese took possession of the holding reservoirs – the island's only remaining supply of drinking water – so they could turn off the taps to Singapore city at any time they wished. No water, no war. Sit down and wait for everyone to die of thirst. Nice one.'

'I daresay there were other issues,' Woon said, in an attempt to be fair.

'Yeah, sure. The Japs had a brilliant general in Yamashita and we had a bloody nincompoop in Percival. Not that our Australian bloke was much better. Bloody General Bennett hopped onto a boat and fucked off back to Australia as soon as the surrender was announced. That was after he ordered us not to attempt to get off the island. Cowardly bastard!'

Measured analysis was beyond Danny, after three and a half years of being a prisoner of war as the result of the biggest military defeat in British history, almost entirely due, in the view of most of the fighting men, to a monumental cock-up. It was obvious that Danny had built up a deep resentment against his leaders. Woon was later to discover this same resentment and humiliation in a great many other prisoners of war, who felt they had lost something unnamed but akin to their manhood, and had undergone a kind of mental emasculation that would continue to haunt them for the remainder of their lives. They were young warriors who were sent up against the enemy with their hands metaphorically tied behind their backs.

The young doctor generally agreed with Danny's viewpoint, but he was more anxious to hear his personal story, to have Danny revisit past experiences he may have buried deep in his subconscious. 'Your facial injuries, did they happen on the day of the surrender? Tell me about that incident,' he said.

'Nah, later. The first day we walked – marched, I suppose – but we were that buggered and disillusioned, we walked or dragged ourselves through the streets. I remember the crowds gathered by the Japanese to watch our humiliation were as silent as we were. Everyone, it seemed, was in a state of shock. Before the invasion Singapore was full of Chinese. Now there wasn't a Chinese face to be seen in the crowd. We soon enough understood why. In the weeks that followed, when we worked in the warehouses on the waterfront, we witnessed the killing of dozens of Chinese and saw the results of hundreds more.

'All along the waterfront the Japanese erected several hundred poles sharpened to a point at one end and about five and a half feet high. On each pole, they stuck the severed head of a slaughtered Chinaman or woman. Each morning as we marched to work from the old colonial barracks of Selarang there would be fresh Chinese heads on public display, staring at us at eye level, a black cloud of flies buzzing around them.' Danny glanced at Craig Woon. 'I don't know whether the Japs had worked out the height of the average Allied soldier, but there is something very bizarre about a severed head every three feet staring you straight in the eye as you pass. If the Nips hated us, it was nothing compared to how they felt about the poor bloody Chinks.'

'These warehouses . . .'

'They call them godowns, and there were literally hundreds of 'em.'

'Aha, godowns. And you were . . . ?'

'Loading the contents into Japanese merchant ships, virtually the wealth of Malaya, Britain's second-richest colony after India. You name it, tens of thousands of tons of tinned food and other goods, hundreds of shiploads of rubber and tin, both of which the Japs needed badly. Then of course there was the captured military equipment. My work gang of forty blokes only did the godowns. But some of the other blokes who did the dumps said they were huge and placed all around the island: tens of thousands of guns and millions of rounds of ammo, thousands of brand-new trucks and cars, hundreds of heavy guns and thousands of shells.

'There was, I remember, a warehouse we entered that had all the equipment and medicines needed for a major military hospital and several field hospitals. In effect, there was enough captured field equipment, armaments, food and medical supplies for the Japanese army to continue their invasion of the Pacific without requiring very much more to be sent from Japan. The Brits had advanced the Japanese invasion of the remainder of the Western Pacific, and equipped them better than in their wildest dreams. And they supplied them with an intelligent labour force they didn't have to pay to do the hard yakka.'

'Your face, Danny . . . the bashing?' Craig Woon reminded him, noting that his patient seemed to prefer to stick to generalities.

'Oh, yeah, right, but first I have to explain about our sudden change of diet because it's relevant to the story. After the first few days, five days to be exact, we'd pretty well eaten all the rations we carried. Then we realised that the Japs were going to give us only rice to eat, and not very much of it at that. The immediate result was bloody catastrophic. We were constantly hungry, but even worse, the change of diet seized up our bowels: constipation on a massive scale; we were shitless in Gaza, or, if you insist, Singapore. Corporal Catterns held the record – thirty-eight days without a shit. We ate almost nothing and grew extremely weak, something the Nips, accustomed to a diet based on rice, couldn't understand, and they thought we must be on a hunger strike. Savage bashings with rifle butts, pick handles or boots were so common they were almost the norm. They'd discovered a warehouse that contained thousands of pick handles and it became the weapon of choice among Nip NCOs, even over the much-loved heavy bamboo stave. We were severely beaten for the smallest things: if you didn't spring to attention quickly when a Jap approached, or if your feet weren't properly aligned, or your bow wasn't considered respectful enough to satisfy the ego of the gibbering peasant in front of you. But worse, far worse, was if you were a big tall bloke: the smaller the Jap and his cohorts, the greater the pleasure they took in beating you to a pulp until you lay unconscious at their feet. It was clear that the Nips thought of us, particularly the big guys, as less than human; after all, we had surrendered and so we were, in their culture, beneath contempt. Starving, constipated, and having the shit beaten out of us every day, we —'

'Perhaps not the appropriate expression?'

'Huh? What isn't?'

'Having *the shit beaten out of you* would have brought some relief, I'd have thought.' Craig Woon grinned.

Catching on, Danny chuckled. 'Oh, okay, you're right,' then added quickly, 'Well, to put it differently, we were forced to endure a great deal of crap!'

'And then some, it appears. I think we'll stick with the original metaphor,' Dr Woon added, regretting his levity.

Danny continued. 'And then some luck – one morning at the height of the constipation crisis, we were given a godown to clear that was chocka with food and general supplies. We gorged ourselves all day and within hours some of the blokes were creeping into dark corners to take their first crap in two weeks and coming back with smiles on their gobs as if they'd just won the lottery.

'I'd warned the men not to take anything back with them to the barracks because the godown was going to take a week to clear. I told them we'd load the waiting freighter so that the edible stuff went into the hold last; that way we'd have a week at least on a decent diet.

'We'd also found a store of medicine – quinine, emetine for dysentery, although that wasn't our problem at the time, other valuable stuff we realised the Japs were never going to supply to prisoners. So we loaded up on those, concealing them on our bodies. The risk wasn't that big. Our underpants hadn't yet worn out so we could hide most of the medicine in them – it wasn't hard when you were wearing the overlarge khaki shorts the Brits called Bombay bloomers. Besides, by the end of the day the camp guards barely bothered to search us – a cursory pat over the shirt pockets, slap on the thighs to locate anything in our trouser pockets and that was about it. Bob's your uncle, nothing easier.

'But that night proved to be different. We marched back into camp and instead of the usual pat 'n' slap before we went on our way, there were shouts of "Ki o tske!" (Stand to attention!) Then a truck roared up and came to a halt directly behind us. A platoon of Jap soldiers jumped out and lined up on either side of the road, flanking us. *What now?* I thought. We were learning that you could never tell what was likely to happen next with the Japanese, and these blokes looked different.

'Well, what did happen next was that a Japanese officer stepped out of the front passenger seat of the truck, a British Bedford by the way. He was short and fat, his uniform obviously specially tailored, which was unusual in their officers, who didn't much go in for anything fancy in their everyday uniforms. The point about this bloke was that he also wore a monocle, just like those propaganda cartoon posters sending up the Japanese you used to see at the post office and town hall. Of course we all bowed deeply and that's when everything came unstuck in a helluva hurry.

'Snowy Pitt had disobeyed orders and concealed a can of Nestlé's condensed milk under his slouch hat. It was standard practice to strap your hat on so it couldn't be snatched off your head in a quick search, but he can't have fastened it under his chin because, as he bowed, out it tumbled, landing with a thud on the road in front of him and rolling directly toward a Japanese corporal standing almost beside him. I stood maybe three steps from him and couldn't believe my eyes. The Nip let out a bellow of rage, and lifting his heavy bamboo stick in both hands, he smashed it into Snowy's face. Snowy went over backwards, landing hard on his arse. A second soldier rushed forward, his bayonet aimed at Snowy's guts. I don't remember how, but the next thing I knew I was holding the Arisaka rifle with that wickedly long bayonet, and the Jap soldier was on his back with a blood nose beside Snowy. Thank Christ I didn't react instinctively and stick him. Suddenly there were guards with fixed bayonets coming at me from everywhere.' Danny grinned. 'I was about to have more holes in me than a kitchen colander. Then the Jap officer barked out a command and everyone froze. He was behind me so that I couldn't see him, but the next moment there was an explosion of pain in my lower back and I sank to my knees. The next blow was to the kidneys, the pain so intense I was unable to even scream. My legs folded under me so that I was seated on the back of my thighs. Everything was a red blur that cleared just sufficiently for me to see the officer in front of me holding a soldier's rifle by the barrel and stock. Then the steel-capped butt came down hard into my face. I recall a brilliant flash of pain and then nothing more.' Danny paused and glanced at Dr Woon, who held his head in his hands, staring down at his desk. 'That was the last time I saw through my left eye. It seems he had a couple more goes with the rifle butt.' Danny shrugged. 'It turned out the Japs in the truck and the officer in charge were *kempeitai*, Japanese military police, renowned for their cruelty and greatly feared even by the Japanese rank and file soldiers.' He glanced up, Woon now acutely aware of his ruined eye. 'Well, that's about it, doc. The recovery took about a year and it wasn't a lot of fun.' He grinned. 'But here I am, ugly as sin.'

Dr Woon thought again about the prisoners of war, those who had died of despair. How had Danny, with very little medical help, painkillers or drugs to stop infection, made it through to the end? Not just made it, but, as the highest-ranked NCO, taken on the additional responsibility of running the camp and maintaining discipline and morale among the prisoners.

In reading Danny's war record, Dr Woon realised that he wasn't your average recruit. He'd noted that Danny had passed his first two years at university with distinction and had jacked it in with only months to go to complete his degree. This alone seemed to offer a clue to his personality. He was also a sporting hero, accustomed to the approbation of others. Moreover, he was obvious officer material, someone young men would happily follow into combat. Yet he had elected to join as a private. Again, his rapid promotion to sergeant major proved that he was not so egalitarian that he was opposed to climbing the ladder of command, and he had clearly demonstrated his willingness to exercise authority. According to the men who had survived the concentration camp, his leadership had been exceptional. Some claimed that he had saved many a prisoner's life by fearlessly confronting the Japanese guards in their own language, and complaining directly to the commandant, Colonel Mori, over the harsh and cruel treatment of his men. He'd often stoically taken a private beating afterwards from the Japanese guards or the even more vengeful Koreans who, while under Japanese jurisdiction, were allowed to mete out punishment and took great delight in outdoing their masters in every form of cruelty.

This was a young man grown prematurely old, who seemed to contain a whole bundle of contradictions. One wrong decision to abandon his studies had led to his undoing; his dreadful disfigurement and the scars resulting from four and a half years of medical neglect pointed to trouble ahead, including the possibility of revulsion from the opposite sex. And his spinal injury was yet another burden, ruling out any chance of rebuilding his self-esteem through his sporting prowess. As a civilian he would lack the responsibilities and rank that had sustained him in the prisoner of war camp and this, added to everything else he had suffered, could easily lead to acute depression.

Dr Woon understood only too well that people might find it difficult to hire Danny and he might find it equally difficult to hold down a job.

Danny Dunn was a good man, perhaps even an exceptional one, but it would be easy for him to become bitter and aggrieved. He should have faced a bright future, but it was now in jeopardy. As a doctor, Woon wanted to know more, and was sufficiently concerned to realise that the next few weeks were critical to the ultimate rehabilitation of Danny Dunn.

'Danny, when you get back to Sydney will you keep in touch? You're going to need quite a lot of work on that face. We've got an ear, nose and throat specialist coming from Melbourne in a week or so, a Dr Adams. He'll take a look at your nose and advise. Besides, if you agree, I'd like to get to know you better.'

'Sure, I'd like that, doctor . . . er, Craig,' Danny said.

'Just one more question. What happened to Snowy Pitt?'

'They turned on him after they'd beaten me up. Unfortunately he lost both eyes to the *kempeitai* lieutenant's work with a rifle butt,' Danny said quietly.

Dr Woon cleared his throat. 'I see,' he said quietly. 'Did he make it?'

Danny laughed quietly. 'Sure did. We made him the camp barber.'

'You didn't!' Woon exclaimed, laughing.

'It helped his self-esteem, knowing he was needed. At first he was pretty rough, but I guess it didn't matter: we weren't going anywhere. But in the end he became a bit of a tonsorial artist.'

'And he got through?'

'Yeah, he made it. I'll look him up when I get home, see how he's going.'

Woon hesitated a moment then asked, 'You're not bitter?'

'What . . . over the can of condensed milk? Shit, no. He was taking it back to camp for his best mate. Snowy was always going to cop shit. He was six feet tall, hair the colour of Bondi Beach, blue eyes . . . everything the Japs hated. Besides, he'd probably have gotten off with a severe beating if I hadn't grabbed the Jap's rifle.'

Dr Woon didn't reply. He felt he was learning a new culture, a mixture of the singular determination to survive and the unspoken duty of care for your mates, the two things almost amounting to a contradiction in terms. He made a mental note to follow up on such unexpected behavioural phenomena to see if they appeared elsewhere in the various prisoner-of-war camps.

Then, reaching for Danny's war records, he said quietly, 'I read these last night, made a few notes. Would you mind if we carried on a bit longer?'

'No, go for your life. I guess the worst is over. Don't know if talking about it has helped any but thanks for listening.'

'University. Two, no two and a half years,' Woon looked up. 'You didn't complete your degree?'

'No, sir . . . er, Craig.'

'May I ask why?'

'Didn't seem much point at the time.'

'With only months to go?' Woon asked, obviously a little surprised.

'In hindsight it was stupid, I guess. As it happened I could have completed my exams and still made it overseas in plenty of time. We hung around Malaya doing bugger-all, waiting for the Japanese army to arrive.'

'You don't think it may have been worth completing your degree?'

'Now? Yes, of course. But at the time all my mates had signed up and had left Balmain. My parents own one of the pubs and I was getting looks from the patrons. Where I come from, university isn't big on the agenda but fighting for what you believe in is. And fighting for your country is top of the list. On the other hand my mum was determined I'd finish – it was sort of the whole purpose of her life. Sometimes it seemed like she lived for nothing else, and it was putting me under a lot of pressure – Mum or country. Then there were a couple of incidents, one in the pub and another when an old woman working in a cafe gave me a white feather, that kind of thing. Dunkirk came, people were talking about the Japs joining the war and Australia being in danger of invasion. I guess I cracked or something, just wanted to get away from it all. Besides, I couldn't really see what good an Arts degree would do me.'

Danny shrugged. 'As it turned out, it wasn't the smartest move I could have made.'

'You didn't think of becoming an officer? After all, you had the qualifications.'

'Another no. Not where I come from. They'd have called me a bludger.'

'Peer pressure, social conformity, then the added pressure of your mother's expectations?'

'Yeah, dumb as it sounds, that's just about it, doctor.'

'Not at all. Those are among the commonest reasons why people do things.' Woon put down his fountain pen. 'Well, Danny, may I suggest you think about completing your degree? It's as good a way of handling your rehabilitation as any and it's going to be a while before you fully recover.' He paused and looked straight at Danny. 'The bastards have made a fine mess of you, old son,' he said leaning back in his chair.

Danny attempted to grin, knowing that his expression was closer to a grimace than the wry grin he'd intended. 'Yeah, there were one or two moments, doc.'

'Well, we'll see what we can do here. I feel reasonably certain we can cure any tropical diseases, ulcers and whatever else we find, and we can build up your weight and strength a little before you go home. But any plastic surgery to your face will need to take place in Sydney. Not a great deal we can do about your back except to strengthen it and teach you how to use it differently. I've looked at your papers, it seems you were quite an athlete – rugby and water polo, eh?' He paused. 'I'm afraid you won't be playing either again, unless you want to end up in a wheelchair. But if you can swim regularly it will help your back immeasurably.' Danny watched as he wrote out a prescription for the hospital pharmacy. 'Better get used to taking these. They won't cure you but they'll help a little with the pain.'

Danny grinned. 'Thanks, doc. I confess, even a little will help.'

'There is one more thing.' Woon glanced down at his notes for a moment, then looked Danny in the eye. 'You may be sterile. We suspect that severe starvation may cause permanent sterility. I'm sorry —'

'Doubt it'll be a problem, doc. I can't imagine women are going to be queueing up.'

'Well, let's wait and see,' Woon said, then went on briskly, 'We're going to put you into traction, see if we can release the pressure on your vertebrae; it sometimes helps. I've also made an appointment for you with Dr Adams for early next week, see if he can do something to open those sinuses and advise on your nose reconstruction.'

But traction didn't do much to relieve Danny's chronic back pain. Dr Donald Adams, the nose bloke from Melbourne, didn't help much either. He was a civilian who cultivated a carefully clipped RAF moustache to go with the gratuitously acquired rank of captain. He was grossly overweight in a hospital where the patients were all walking skeletons, which added somewhat to the incongruity of his presence. The brand-new tropical officer's uniform he wore, complete with enormous Bombay bloomers and khaki hose pulled up to his very pink, sun-starved and chubby knees, explained why his patients dubbed him 'Colonel Blimp'. He wore army boots and not the usual officers brogues, no doubt to support his ankles, and waddled like a penguin, his new boots squeaking with each step, so that they announced him well before he appeared. In size he compared favourably to Half Dunn but lacked his *joie de vivre* or sense of humour. His clipped, often monosyllabic speech, coupled with an abrupt and condescending professional manner, made it very difficult for the patients to warm to him.

Dr Adams sat opposite Danny for his examination, sausage-like fingers digging and jabbing into his sunken cheek and ruined eye, pulling the scar tissue around the eye as if testing it for elasticity. The examination of Danny's nasal area was left until last. He proceeded to prod and pinch the immediate area around the nose as if it was composed of putty and he was committed to the process of moulding a new one. The examination was extremely painful and it took all of Danny's courage not to cry out. Finally Adams rose and without comment walked over to a small washbasin and began to wash his hands, rinsing and then repeating the process twice over, as if, Danny thought, he'd been contaminated.

While Danny knew Adams had a job to do, he really didn't much like the way this bloke from Melbourne had gone about examining him. Apart from regular grunts, he hadn't said a word. Danny, sore from being prodded and poked as if he were a piece of meat, was not just annoyed, but felt Colonel Blimp's complete lack of regard for him as a person differed little from that of the Japanese.

Dr Adams returned to sit at his desk, hands clasped and resting on his extensive belly. 'Ha! If I'd rammed you into a brick wall face first at sixty miles an hour I couldn't have done a better job, Mr Dunn,' he announced happily. 'As for that smashed cheekbone,' he frowned, 'I just don't know. Maybe they can reconstruct it, put in a plate . . . can't say, not my area, what? The left eye, of course, is gone forever, but I should think they'll fit you with a marble, eh? Never convincing, in my opinion, no natural movement, you're looking to the right and it's looking left, ha, ha. The nose? Not much a plastic surgeon can do, I shouldn't think; a little cosmetic reconstruction perhaps. We'll have to remove most of the broken bone, then attempt to open up the sinus passages. It's a big job – skin grafts, rearranging the tissue mass, never going to look much good.' He paused at last. 'Well, that's all, Mr Dunn. You are free to go.'

Danny rose and, attempting to conceal his anger and humiliation, said in a steely voice, 'You're in luck, doctor. I'm still in the army. Had it been Mr Dunn, by now your nose would have been in a very similar condition to mine. Let me assure you, you fat arrogant bastard, it won't be you who gets to work on my nose!'

On the morning of the 6th of November 1945 Danny disembarked from the Circassia, a troopship that had begun life as a passenger ship, one of the many requisitioned by the Australian army to bring our prisoners of war home. A huge crowd stood on the dock at Circular Quay to welcome the boat – whole families, sweethearts, wives, children – an aggregation of joy, laughter and tears as beloved sons, husbands, fathers and brothers were reunited with their families that came close to bringing Danny to tears of self-pity. There would be no one to meet him because he'd deliberately asked the army authorities not to inform his family of his arrival. He'd written to Brenda from the hospital in Rangoon. *I have a crook back and my mug's been rearranged a bit, so don't expect the old Danny boy. I'm not sure when I'll be home.*

Brenda had replied to say how overjoyed they'd been to hear he was still alive, and that no matter what, he was still her son and she'd love him in any shape in which he came back to her. She also said that Helen Brown had asked if she could write to him. Half Dunn, adding to the letter, wrote to say that since the army had notified them that he was alive the pub had been completely repainted and renovated in anticipation of his return and that Brenda had ordered enough flags and bunting for the welcome-home party to match the launch of the *Queen Mary*.

The Cinesound newsreels played every Saturday night along with a movie at the hospital had shown the ecstatic crowds at the dockside welcoming the returned soldiers back home. They'd been warned to expect an even bigger welcome for their own return as prisoners of war from South-East Asia. Danny simply couldn't bear the idea of his mother waiting excitedly on the dock with Half Dunn and possibly Helen, then seeing him, a walking fucking nightmare, emerge out of the crowd of joyous, laughing and happy people.

He'd known Helen less than a year before leaving for Malaya and much of that time he'd been at training camp or away from Balmain or Birchgrove. The contained Helen he'd first seen at university with the cool, confident, even appraising look that had attracted him in the first place had proved to be a woman of a great many surprises and not a few contradictions. She'd made him work for every demure kiss, and then only after she'd taken him home, seemingly to seek the approval of her parents. Like a leggy nine-year-old she'd sent him packing when he'd gone over to tell her he'd enlisted, and then minutes later had jumped from the swing, taken him by the hand and led him upstairs to her bedroom. The education of Danny Dunn had been about to begin.

They hadn't made love in the 1940s version Danny expected – he dominant and active, she supine and compliant. Instead she'd taken over, undressing him carefully, and without haste. Then, sinking to her knees, she'd begun to use her pretty mouth to excite him.

'Do you like that?' she'd asked, after a moment or two.

He'd been unable to do much more than groan, so she went to work again, experimenting with pressure and speed, until she had brought him almost to the point of no return. Still on her knees she'd reached over and opened the drawer of her bedside cabinet and withdrawn a contraceptive. 'That's the advantage of having a dad who owns a chemist shop,' she'd giggled, then, undoing the packet, she'd tried to slip it on.

'Here, let me.' Danny looked at her, bemused. 'Helen, you planned this all along, didn't you?'

'No, I just knew that sooner or later I'd need one. I don't suppose you carry one in your wallet, do you?'

'Not usually.'

'I thought not. Silly thoughtless boy.' She'd proceeded to undress slowly, her eyes never leaving him, a mischievous grin on her lovely face as she watched his reaction. Then she'd moved into his arms and kissed him deeply, more so than ever before, finally extricating herself and moving to the bed, where she lay on her back.

'You're beautiful,' Danny heard himself saying. He'd never said that before; he'd said different things, paid casual compliments to the women in the past who had been generous with their bodies, but never that plain and simple 'You're beautiful'. Now he knew he meant it.

As he approached the bed and pressed one knee between Helen's long slender legs, she stopped him. 'Whoa, Danny boy,' she said, grinning. 'My turn now.'

Danny looked confused. 'Yeah, well, that's just what I'm —'

'No!'

'What?' he asked, perplexed, drawing back, his leg in mid-air.

She pointed to his erection. 'I'm sure we'll need that later. But right now I want your tongue, your whole mouth in fact.'

'Huh? Whaffor?' Danny grunted, too surprised to stop the words. 'You mean . . . ?' He pointed at Helen's thighs. Then, in an attempt to recover he asked, confused, 'French? French love?'

Helen smiled. 'Danny darling, I want you to caress me with your tongue! You may use any language you're fluent in.'

They both started to giggle. Finally Danny managed to say, 'I'm not sure I know how. I mean, I haven't . . . ever . . .' he admitted, grinning stupidly.

Helen, attempting to contain her mirth, looked up at Danny. 'Well, darling, are you ready for your first language lesson?'

They proceeded to experiment, with her guidance, she reaching what seemed like several orgasms until Danny was forced to come up for air. 'Jesus, that's hard work. Did you enjoy it?' he asked, wanting some reward for his efforts.

'Your grasp of oral French is very promising, young man. You seem to have a natural gift for speaking in tongues. One or two more lessons and you'll have the whole thing licked,' Helen said, grinning wickedly, pleased with her naughty wit. 'Now, perhaps some swordplay?'

Helen proved as obliging as she'd previously been demanding, and for at least an hour they'd made love variously and deliciously, mostly following her suggestions.

Afterwards, lying in each other's arms, Danny started to worry. He'd obviously got it all wrong; all Helen's romantic reluctance, her ban on anything touchy-feely, her insistence on his meeting her parents, her initial cool demeanour. Now this. He imagined he'd fallen in love with a highly intelligent but thoroughly chaste girl, someone who kept her legs tightly crossed, and all the time he'd had a nympho on his hands. All the things they'd done in the last hour, none of the women he'd been with knew any of that stuff, and neither did he! With other women it was just straight up and down, ordinary sex, what you'd expect. Maybe Helen was the town bike and everyone at uni knew except him. Still, it had been pretty awesome, well, the first bit . . . and the last bit. He told himself he could do without the middle bit, but then that was the big surprise – it seemed to arouse her the most. He wondered if maybe there was something wrong with her. Was she a lesbian? Blokes didn't talk about stuff like that. He'd never heard anyone admit to doing it, whereas the converse – a blowjob – was a badge of honour the older guys boasted about in the showers after a match. He didn't talk about it, but today wasn't his first blowjob; he'd had several, even one or two in his final year at school. Her saying, what's good for him is also good for her . . . I mean, how could you argue? She'd have you trapped in a moment. But it wasn't the same thing, definitely not. No way!

Assuming what he hoped was a casual tone, Danny said, 'Remember that time when I suggested you were a virgin and you told me I was an arrogant prick?'

'Which you were,' Helen interrupted.

'Well, I didn't believe you. I thought you were just putting me in my place, that you actually *were* a virgin.' Danny laughed. 'Little did I know, eh?'

'Oh, but I am . . . or rather, *was*, until one delicious hour or so ago,' Helen said.

'Ah c'mon, Helen, that's bullshit! All that stuff, the things we just did! You know heaps more than me about making love.'

'Ancient history.'

'That's what I'm getting at.'

'No, dope. I mean really ancient history.'

'Huh?'

'I learned all of it studying tomb and temple paintings, hieroglyphs, the Egyptians, then the Greeks – the cults of Dionysus and Aphrodite, the *hetaera*, the poems of Sappho, the poet of Lesbos . . . And the Romans – Ovid, Catullus, Sextus Propertius, the erotic art unearthed at Pompei, Apuleius,' Helen reeled off the names. 'The tale of the Golden Ass, that's got just about everything in it you could imagine and then some.'

'Fair dinkum? You mean, that was the . . . I was the . . .'

'You were the first? Yes. I'm a very good student, and a great theoretician. Now you've helped me with my prac.' She smiled sleepily.

Danny was astonished. 'So, they did those things way back in ancient times? Why didn't I choose classical studies?'

She laughed. 'Danny, the missionary position was about the only thing they didn't seem to practise, though the ancient Egyptians included it among others. They don't seem to have used it a lot – it was probably too boring!'

'Yeah? And all this stuff we did today, they did that?'

'Of course! And a great deal more. I even thought about shaving.' She giggled.

'Shaving? You mean, down there?' Danny said, shocked.

'Uh-huh. The Egyptians recommended removing all body hair.' Helen couldn't resist the urge to shock him still further. 'You're lucky you weren't met with a bald pudenda!'

'Christ! So that's where you discovered French love?'

'Well, they didn't call it that. The Gauls didn't exist as a tribe at that time.'

'Galls? As in galling?'

Helen laughed. 'No, but you might be onto something, judging by your response. You should have seen your face!'

'Well, I mean . . .'

'Yes, what do you mean?' Helen demanded.

'Well, God gave men dicks, didn't he. So obviously you're not supposed to do it with your tongue. I mean, anyone could do that!'

'You mean it doesn't require a man?'

'Yeah.'

'You're right there. Just ask Sappho. But what are you saying? Sex is all about the biblical injunction to go forth and multiply? Impregnate the nearest female and go thy way rejoicing in the Lord? What fun for you!'

'Didn't you enjoy what we did?' Danny asked, adding, 'You sure as hell seemed to.'

'Which part?'

'You know, me and you together . . .'

'Yes, very much.'

'What part was best?'

'You mean what part of the missionary position?'

'It wasn't *only* that. Coming inside you from the back, then you on top . . .'

'Sweetheart, of course I enjoyed it all, your lovely, strong body, your breath, the life in you, you in me, it was wonderful, the way of a man with a maid . . . that's also biblical by the way.'

Danny seemed pleased. 'Me too. Your body, the closeness, the smell, the movement, I thought it was wonderful. When I came inside you I wanted to . . . it . . . it was a bit like dying, but a wonderful sort of dying.'

'That's beautiful, Danny.'

'You didn't feel the same?'

'When I climaxed?'

'Yes.'

Helen sighed. 'Bloody men! Danny, when you caressed me with your mouth I came four times. When we made love I came once.'

'Yes, but . . .'

'Danny, don't say it!'

'Don't say what?'

'That it's quality not quantity.'

'Well, isn't it?'

'No, that's rubbish. Why does a man judge everything on the performance of his penis, as if it's the gold standard for sex?'

'Well, it's natural isn't it? The penis is made to fit into the vagina, that's its primary purpose,' Danny declared pompously.

'What are you saying? The penis is king, it's the warrior, his sword and the conquest all in one, while the vagina, and therefore the woman, is the quiescent vessel?'

'C'mon, Helen, I didn't say that.'

'Danny darling, you didn't have to. Think about us tonight. I take you into my mouth and that's entirely appropriate. I ask you to do the same to me and you're shocked. That's a different matter, that's kinky, that's dirty, perverted, yuk!'

'But it's not as good as the real thing, me and you —'

'You know, Danny Dunn, you *are* an arrogant prick.'

'But —'

'Heaven forbid you men might do something that pleases a girl. We can't have that, goodness no. It's not decent, not respectable, not at all *nice*, and it doesn't make babies. Worst of all, there's nothing in it for the bloke.' Helen was warming to her subject now. 'And if I'm wrong, then why is the "c" word the worst expletive you can call a man?'

Danny was deeply shocked. He'd never heard a woman refer to the word before. 'Jesus, Helen! That wasn't necessary!' he said, blushing to the roots of his hair.

'Oh, but, darling, it was. It illustrates how men instinctively think about the female, about the opposite sex. You might boast to your mates about what I did to you, but you'd rather die than admit you did the same to me.'

Danny was suddenly angry. 'I'm not in the habit of discussing my private life with my mates.'

'What? Not in theory? C'mon, be honest now.'

'Well, yes, it's true,' Danny admitted. 'Blokes talk like that, but it's just stuff in the showers. Most of them are still virgins. Most have never even seen a woman's vagina.' Danny hesitated, a half-grin on his face, 'In fact, to be strictly honest, I hadn't until tonight. You don't look down there, even if you're not in the dark. It's a feeling thing.'

'Prod and then hope to be guided home. That's how my married girlfriends describe their husbands' approaches. They know it's down there somewhere . . .' Helen chuckled.

'Yeah, something like that,' Danny admitted, grinning. 'I didn't know girls talked about things like that.'

'Of course we do, or some of us, anyway. Up until now, most of my talk has been theoretical. Part of my masters degree takes in some anthropology, which has been very helpful, an excellent primer,' she said, in her best schoolmarm's voice. 'For instance, did you know that throughout the ages and across cultures, not very many women achieve an orgasm through penile penetration alone?'

Danny looked bemused. 'But you just said you did.'

'Yes, and it was a very nice surprise; the whole experience has been a very nice surprise.'

'You mean you didn't know if you would? Hey, wait on, what say you hadn't . . . would you have told me?'

Helen gave a little laugh. 'I don't know. My married friends don't usually tell their husbands.'

'You mean they fake it? No one's ever done that with me.'

'Oh? How would you know?'

'I reckon I'd know . . .'

Helen smiled. 'Darling, you've got a lot to learn about women.'

Danny hesitated. He was getting in too deep. But he couldn't stop now. 'You mean women go through their whole married lives, have kids and all that, but never achieve an —'

'Orgasm?'

'Yeah.' Danny frowned, concerned. 'All their lives . . .' It was clearly a new thought.

'Only the very silly ones do,' Helen said crisply. 'Sex is a hands-on business, as I'm sure you know.' She raised one eyebrow.

'Oh? Oh, I see what you mean,' Danny said quickly. Wanking was something he'd taken for granted since puberty, but it never occurred to him that girls, women, had the same basic urges or got up to the same tricks.

Helen laughed. 'Well, that's enough theory for now. I'm not finding this conversation in the least erotic, so don't think you can skip French language lessons in future. I want the lot: everything that's natural between a man and a woman. And I don't want that decided by the Pope or the convocation of the Church of England. What do they know about what pleases a girl? They rabbit on about what's decent, and respectable, and *nice*, about making babies, but it's all for blokes. And women put up with it. But not this one. I won't be short-changed, Danny Dunn.'

Danny laughed, 'Sure thing, Miss Brown. May I enrol for ancient history lessons as well, please?'

Danny wasn't inexperienced with women, but it counted for very little in his new relationship. It wasn't only that Helen didn't go along with the prevailing social and sexual mores – the Friday or Saturday night special, the drunken grope in the dunes or the back seat of a car, the obligatory marital bout of panting, probing, mumbling and fumbling; she also constantly challenged the order of things.

Helen simply didn't know her place as a woman. She didn't fit into any particular class for the simple reason that she didn't go along with most of what passed for conventional wisdom. She certainly didn't think a woman's place was in the home, though she was nevertheless an inspired cook. After the war she was planning to take her doctorate and thereafter pursue an academic career. In the working-class ethos of Balmain she would be seen as an absolute disaster by the men, a bitch who didn't know her place, while the women would refer to her as a stuck-up snob – 'Too many brains for her own good, that one!' Most young blokes would run a mile from a sheila like Helen.

Danny had initially been afraid to introduce her to Brenda. Both were strong women, both held strong views, though not necessarily the same ones. His mother was a Catholic, and while not a regular churchgoer, she attended mass at Easter, Christmas and New Year's Eve and said her rosary every day. She was a dormant but far from lapsed Catholic. Danny couldn't imagine anything even vaguely sexual going on between her and Half Dunn. Like most children, he felt reasonably certain that apart from conceiving him, his parents had never had it off together. He tried to imagine them in the missionary position, Half Dunn on top, and although it brought a grin, inwardly he felt ashamed; you didn't think in those terms about your mum, and poor old Half Dunn lacked the energy to raise himself off the mattress.

Helen wasn't in the least religious, even though she was a biblical scholar. She blamed the church for most of the crimes against humanity committed over the past millennium or so, describing the Crusades, perpetrated in the name of a just and supposedly loving God, as the greatest mass murder in history.

By the time he'd returned for his first home leave, Danny knew he couldn't delay the two women meeting. At Helen's insistence he'd taken her to meet Brenda. They'd liked each other immediately. 'Don't you lose that girl now!' Brenda admonished him on his next weekend leave, 'What you've got there, son, is a "somebody".' She'd never become reconciled to his leaving university and still never mentioned the war, even though Danny was now permanently in uniform. But Helen's appearance in her life had made a notable difference to Brenda's general demeanour. The two women seemed to have become friends, truly good friends, spending time together when he was in camp, Helen even occasionally helping out in the pub.

Danny had written to Helen every week from Malaya and then Singapore, right up to the day before they'd been captured, that is, if the last mail to Australia got out safely, possibly on the same boat as that cowardly bastard Bennett. Danny knew that he loved her and she him – she'd admitted as much. But Helen wasn't keen on the 'until death do us part' bit, and they'd finally agreed to see what happened after the war.

She'd completed her masters degree towards the end of his battalion's stay in Malaya, majoring in Egyptian history, and had written to say she'd joined up as a cryptologist, her study of hieroglyphs at university an ideal preparation for code-breaking . . . *and other things!* She'd also started to study Japanese as part of her course. *I hope to discover a few new oriental secrets that the Egyptians, Greeks and Romans didn't know about!* she wrote in the same letter. They'd given her the rank of second lieutenant and she'd ended the last letter he'd received with, *'Next time we meet you'll have to salute me, Danny Dunn, and high time too!'* He'd received it two days before they'd surrendered to the Japanese, and his final letter, the one that may or may not have reached her, was addressed to *Lieutenant Helen Brown*. On the back of the envelope he'd drawn a crude version of his face wearing a slouch hat with a hand on the right brim at the salute.

That had been three and a half years ago and Danny had convinced himself that she'd have long since forgotten him and met someone else. He'd told himself that it was logical that a woman as good-looking and intelligent as Helen, not knowing whether he was alive or dead, wouldn't hang around if the right guy came into her life. Nor would he expect her to, knowing that she wouldn't accept him the way he was now, anyway, that no woman would. He'd been lucky, he'd had his fair share, women had always been generous to him, but now he'd better get used to flying solo. She'd been the best and at least he'd had that.

He'd taken on the task of burying her in his mind and had all but succeeded in erasing her from his memory when Brenda's letter had arrived. He'd written back to say he didn't think a reunion was possible and he didn't want her to renew their correspondence.

Danny had never been concerned about his looks, simply accepting that women found him attractive, a fortunate circumstance he wasn't going to analyse. He was grateful that he was lucky with women, and accepted, with an enigmatic smile, the joshing he received from envious mates. Now he realised how thoughtless, even arrogant, he had been. Why, when Helen Brown hadn't fallen into his arms, he'd discovered that there was more, so much more to love than casual conquest.

Most of his mates had gone off to war as virgins and had lost their virginity in a brothel in Lavender Street in Singapore or with a clumsy knee-trembler hastily taken in a dark, stinking, rat-infested alley in a Cairo slum or some equally seedy whorehouse – a raucous and drunken evening with their barrack-room mates, culminating in a loss of innocence they couldn't remember much about the following morning. Now they'd be the conquering heroes returning, to get all the nooky they wanted, while he would have to endure the phoney smile on the lips of a King's Cross whore as she counted his money.

They arrived home on a morning with clear skies and brilliant summer sunshine to a welcome that started a fair way out to sea when the pilot boat and the first yachts appeared to accompany them through the Heads. As they drew closer, Danny could see that North Head was crowded with thousands of people while South Head, a naval base, was empty, but as they drew even closer and he could see Vaucluse lighthouse on the point of South Head, there, standing on a rock ledge on the cliff face, was a lone piper. Moments later, as the swirl of the pipes reached him, Danny began to weep.

> Oh, Danny boy, the pipes, the pipes are calling,
> From glen to glen and down the mountain side;
> The summer's gone and all the leaves are falling;
> 'Tis ye, 'tis ye, must go and I must bide.
>
> But come ye back when summer's in the meadow,
> Or when the valley's hushed and white with snow;
> 'Tis I'll be here in sunshine or in shadow;
> Oh, Danny boy, oh, Danny boy, I love you so.
>
> And if ye come when all the flowers are dying,
> If I am dead, as dead I well may be,
> Ye'll come and find the place where I am lying,
> And kneel and say an 'Ave' there for me.
>
> And I shall hear, though soft ye tread above me,
> And o'er my grave, shall warmer, sweeter be,
> Then if ye bend and tell me that ye love me,
> Then I shall sleep in peace until ye come to me.

The Circular Quay welcome had been even bigger than the newsreels had promised. Every military and civilian brass band in the city seemed to be playing 'Waltzing Matilda', and the dockside cranes were spraying large arcs of white water into the harbour as the *Circassia* came in to berth. As they'd sailed up the harbour, thousands of small boats and yachts flying flags and bunting had come out to welcome them, some displaying hand-lettered signs that read, *Welcome home, Tom . . . or Kevin . . . or Jack*. The familiar green-and-cream ferries, brought to a standstill, blew their horns, and Danny could see people gathered on the foreshore by the tens of thousands. The noise from the cheering crowds on the wharf throwing streamers was almost deafening. Sydney had come out in force to welcome home its physically and emotionally broken sons, returning to their loved ones, who were about to discover how very different they were now from the happy, excited, strong and robust young men who had departed with a final kiss for Mum and a manly handshake for Dad maybe five years previously.

Danny had been given a warrant for a taxi, but despite his bad back, he'd shouldered his duffle bag and begun to walk the twenty minutes or so from Circular Quay over to the Erskine Street Wharf where the ferry to Balmain berthed. Six years previously, had a young bloke arrived in the peninsula in a taxi, they'd have thought him a wanker. Danny couldn't think of a convincing reason why things might have changed. Even if he was no longer bulletproof, he knew Balmain would be just the same as ever. It would take more than a global conflict to alter the beliefs of the people with whom he'd grown up.

He still thought of himself as a young bloke, although his physique belied that description and his face told a different story. He'd left Australia standing six feet and four inches in his socks and weighing seventeen stone, but you don't strip six stone off a big bloke who isn't carrying any excess weight and expect him to look like Charles Atlas. Now, lugging his kit over from Circular Quay to Erskine, he could feel the two painkillers he'd taken coming through the heads into Sydney Harbour starting to wear off.

Ten minutes or so from the Erskine Street Wharf with perhaps a thousand yards to go, a young bloke of about eighteen approached. He seemed to Danny to be bursting out of his skin with good health and wore a wide grin. 'Lemme help you with yer kit, mate. Yer look tuckered out,' he offered.

Danny turned to face him and noticed the look of shock when the young cove saw his face. 'Bugger off!' he snapped, suddenly furious. He dumped his kitbag onto the pavement and began to kick it. 'Bugger off! Bugger off!' he yelled, and kept kicking until the pain in his back became too much and he was forced to stop. Panting furiously, bent double, his hands on his knees, Danny attempted to catch his breath.

The young bloke was still there. 'I thought I told you to bugger off?' Danny gasped.

'Yeah, you did, but I ain't,' the young bloke said mulishly. He bent and hoisted Danny's duffle bag onto his shoulder. 'Ready when you are, soldier. Where to?'

Danny attempted to laugh. He was, to misquote a popular song, bent, buggered and bewildered, but he was home and the first bloke he'd met ashore had shown him kindness. 'Just until I catch my breath then. Erskine Street Wharf,' he said, extending his hand. 'What's your name, mate?'

'Lachlan Brannan. I missed out, turned eighteen the day they dropped the atom bomb on Japan.'

'Count yourself fortunate, son,' Danny gasped, shaking his hand but forgetting to introduce himself. They had resumed walking towards the ferry terminal and Danny had gained his breath sufficiently to ask, 'Brannan? I played water polo with an Adrian Brannan, three or four years older than me. Good bloke. As I remember he had four younger brothers and a sister, Doreen, who was older than him.' Danny grinned. 'Damned good sort. Any relation?'

'Yeah, Adrian's me oldest brother. I'm the youngest! Doreen's married now,' Lachlan said, taken aback. 'You from Balmain then?'

'Yeah, my folks own a pub there, the Hero of Mafeking.'

'The Hero? Me old man drinks there! Jesus! You ain't . . . ?'

'Sorry, mate, bloody rude,' Danny extended his hand. 'Name's Danny . . . Danny Dunn.'

'You're kidding! *The* Danny Dunn? Balmain Tigers, first-grade front row? You won the grand final for us just before the war. I was just a kid, but I was your number-one fan! We used to fight about which of us was gunna be you when we played touch footy in the park.' Lachlan shook his head in amazement. 'Shit, eh? Danny Dunn, who'd a thought?'

'Look I'm sorry about giving you a mouthful back there, mate. It's just . . . nah, forget it, just one of those days. You work around here, Lachlan?'

Lachlan laughed. 'I wish. Mum gimme sixpence for the tram, told me to go into the city and find a job. I missed out yesterday and the day before and she's getting really cranky. I heard they was hiring casual labour down at the passenger wharves so I come down.'

'No luck?'

'Nah, there weren't no casual; bloke at the gate asked to see me union card.' Lachlan grinned. 'I told him if they gimme a job I'll join for sure, nothing more certain. The fat fart told me to piss off. He reckoned I didn't have the right fucking attitude.'

'Oh? And what might that be?'

'Dunno, mate. But I should'a known. Wharfies union, closed shop, Joe Stalin's mob, lotsa commos.'

They walked on silently for a while, until Lachlan asked, 'You gunna play again, Danny? F' the Tigers?'

'Why? They looking for an ugly one-eyed ten-stone prop with a crook back?' Danny laughed.

'You could bulk up – looks don't matter none. You're a front-row forward,' Lachlan offered naively.

Danny grinned and pointed to the duffle bag Lachlan was carrying. 'Back, mate – it's buggered. Can't even carry that bastard. Lawn bowls, if I'm lucky.'

They'd reached the ferry terminal and Lachlan dumped Danny's duffle bag on the jetty where the ferry pulled in. 'I'd come home with you, Danny, carry your clobber, but if I get home before five I'll cop a tongue-lashing and a clip behind the ear from me mum.'

THE STORY OF DANNY DUNN   115

Danny had a sudden idea. 'What if I paid you? You know, treat it like a legit job?'

Lachlan shook his head. 'No way! You come from Balmain. Yiz coming back from the war, yer got a crook back. I take your money, me dad would take his belt to me. Anyway, I wouldn't do it, I mean, take your money. Maybe I'll still find a job. Sometimes there's late-afternoon loading at a packing house I know about in Darling Harbour.'

Danny felt fairly certain Lachlan was fibbing. 'Nah, she's right, mate. My back's rested now. It's that tough, eh? I mean, finding a job?'

'Yeah, all the blokes comin' home from the war, they get first go. Me dad reckons it's only fair, but me mum don't take no notice. If you're willing to work there's always something, she says.'

Danny put his hand into his trouser pocket and felt for a two-shilling piece. 'Well, thanks, Lachlan. Come and see me at the Hero – I'll buy you a beer.' He extended his hand as if to shake the kid's and in the process slipped the coin into his palm.

Lachlan Brannan drew back, pulling his hand free. He looked down at the silver coin, not quite believing what he held. Then he shook his head. 'No way!' he cried, genuinely upset. 'No way . . . no effing way! Like I said, I ain't taking your money, Danny.'

'It'll be lunchtime soon enough. Buy yourself a pie,' Danny offered.

Lachlan took a step forward and held the coin out for Danny to take. 'A pie costs sixpence.' He patted his back trouser pocket. 'But I already got a sanwitch.'

'A milkshake then,' Danny said, conscious that he'd upset the kid.

'No way!' Lachlan insisted, then reached out and dropped the coin into the shirt pocket of Danny's army fatigues.

'Sorry, kid. I didn't mean to insult you. I guess it's been a while. I'm not accustomed to spontaneous kindness. Where I've been there wasn't much of it going around. It's just, well, when you came up and offered to help me carry my kit I reacted badly, but I appreciate it. I really do. I'll never forget that I'd been back in Australia half an hour and a young bloke, a stranger, offered to help me. You didn't have to do that.'

Lachlan grinned and shrugged. 'I wasn't doing nothing else.'

'Okay, no hard feelings then. Come and see me at the pub. Be a pleasure to buy you a beer, mate.'

'Yeah, okay, Danny, after I've found meself a job.'

'No, come anytime, tomorrow if you like.'

'Nah, I ain't no bludger. I'll wait till I can buy a shout.'

Danny could see the little ferry approaching, a wash of white water as the prow turned coming under the bridge. Nothing had changed. He was right about not taking a taxi. He was back in the Balmain mindset. 'See you soon, Lachlan.' Danny set off, then suddenly turned back. 'Here's an idea, mate. When I was at uni during the holidays, just so I didn't have to work at the pub, I'd work as a messenger, usually for a law firm, but once I applied to an advertising agency. I didn't get the job because they wanted someone permanent to start as a dispatch boy; it's a sort of messenger boy, but you eventually move up into the other departments, and if you're bright it can lead to a whole career. That's not the sort of job they're going to give to a returned soldier.' Danny paused, thinking. 'Wait on, let me remember the name, they were in Commonwealth Street . . . George something? Yeah that's right . . . George Patterson Advertising.' Danny looked at Lachlan, who was wearing a pair of khaki shorts and shirt with the sleeves cut out and a pair of well-worn worker's steel-tipped boots, with an inch or so of odd-coloured socks showing above the top of each. 'Got any good clobber at home?'

'You mean Sunday best?'

'Yeah, you know, jacket, daks, white shirt, tie, shoes?'

'Nah, but I can borrow me brother Charlie's. He's at sea – he's first mate on a coastal freighter, he won't mind. Mum can take up the trousers a bit.'

'Okay, come round to the pub tomorrow and we'll buy the *Sydney Morning Herald*, and we'll also get stuck into the telephone book, see if we can find something between us, eh?'

'Yeah?' Lachlan said, surprised. 'Fair dinkum?'

Danny grinned, spreading his hands. 'We can only try, mate.'

'Shit, eh,' Lachlan said, pleased. 'Wait till I tell Mum.'

'You'll have to learn a bit of telephone patter. You know – what to say, how to answer their questions, but I'll teach you all that interview stuff. I guess I can still remember it. It's all about showing lots of enthusiasm and energy, then when they give you a month's trial, you run everywhere, smile a lot . . . volunteer, kiss arse.'

'Gee, thanks, Danny.' Lachlan stepped forward and once again shook Danny's hand. 'Do yer think it'll work? I didn't do too good in me leaving certificate.'

'Like I said, we can only try. Did you pass?'

Lachlan grinned sheepishly. 'Yeah, but only by the skin o' me teeth. I can't go to uni or nothin' like that. Not that I could, even if I could, if you know what I mean. We ain't never gunna have that kind of money, anyway.'

'Well, you got through and you passed, that's all people – prospective employers – will want to know,' Danny said, remembering how he'd simply walked out of university in his third year. What might have happened had he not been so bloody pigheaded didn't bear thinking about.

'I should probably have left at the intermediate certificate,' Lachlan admitted, 'done an apprenticeship like me brothers, but Mum said some of us had to have a proper education, get through high school, not like her and me dad during the Depression. If you got an education, you can get a job.'

Danny couldn't help liking this kid who didn't mind a chat. Most working-class eighteen-year-olds, as he remembered, were all acne, shuffling feet, mumble and grunt. 'I seem to remember your sister Doreen went to Fort Street Girls? She was pretty bright, as I recall. Didn't she get offered a scholarship to teachers' college?'

'Yeah, but me dad was in the queues, two days casual a week if he got real lucky, Adrian was a boilermaker's apprentice and earning bugger all and Mike the same for fitter and turner. Charlie and me were still at school, so Mum said Doreen had to learn shorthand typing and go out and work – too many mouths to feed. Now she works as a senior clerk at Trades Hall in Goulburn Street, but her and Tommy, they're going to have a baby soon.'

Danny thought for a moment. 'You don't strike me as stupid, kid.' He pointed in the direction of the city. 'You can bet your sweet arse, somewhere in that heap of bricks there's a job for Lachlan Brannan. They didn't drop that bomb on your eighteenth birthday for no reason. Japan surrendered, the world is at peace again and soon there'll be jobs for everyone.'

To Danny's surprise Lachlan disagreed. 'Nah, that's the whole problem. There were lots of jobs when the war was on; now with everyone coming back it's different.'

The boy can think and has an opinion, Danny acknowledged, then said, 'Yeah, you may be right, but we're going to find a position for an eighteen-year-old that they don't want a returned soldier like me to fill.'

The passengers had disembarked from the ferry and it was time to board. Danny hoisted the duffle bag onto his shoulder. 'See you tomorrow, Lachlan. Come around about ten-thirty, after we've opened. Unless things have changed, it's not a busy time of the day.'

Danny made his way to the front of the ferry so that the six other passengers could only see the back of his head. He was suddenly aware that he'd made his first peacetime commitment, and on the quarter of an hour ferry ride to Balmain he wondered whether he should have offered to help the kid. It was a small gesture, yet now he wasn't sure if he was ready to take on even this much responsibility for someone else's life. He told himself he could barely scratch his own arse and hadn't any idea how he was going to cope in the real world. He no longer had three stripes on his sleeve and a mob of tattered and broken blokes who accepted his authority without question. In fact, he had no authority and what's more didn't want any. He just wanted to be left alone so that he could work things out, learn how to conduct life with a face like a truck smash and a back that needed a handful of painkillers every day. He knew he was becoming depressed and understood that this was a luxury he couldn't afford.

In the camp he'd had a singular obsession: to stay alive. There were no other considerations, except to keep an eye out for your men. Depression would simply have killed him as it did countless others. Besides, he had the additional problem of trying to mend a fractured cheekbone, heal an eye socket and repair a nose broken, as it turned out, in several places. Then there was his back, which kept him in constant pain. Added to all this were the ubiquitous tropical ulcers, bouts of dengue fever and malaria, worms, skin infections and a multiplicity of tropical pestilences visited upon them all at one stage or another. All this on a starvation diet based on rice, a few scraps of meat and the edible weeds they could scrounge or the few veggies they were allowed to grow. For many of his mates it hadn't been enough. But Danny had adopted Dr Albert Coates's motto and made it virtually a mantra for his men: 'Your ticket home is in the bottom of your dixie.'

Now all that had changed and his world had suddenly become complicated. Meeting Lachlan Brannan had forced him to dig deep into the past, to use social skills in a way that to anyone else might have seemed simple, even natural. When Danny had offered to help the boy, he'd squandered energy that was intended to keep him alive. He didn't know if he could go through with it; take responsibility for helping the kid. It was a moment of recklessness that could cost him dearly, an emotional boilover he knew he couldn't afford.

Danny was scared – very, very scared – as he saw the stretch of sun-brightened water between the harbour and the shore diminishing and the Balmain ferry terminal approaching. He knew with some certainty that when he stepped ashore onto the peninsula it would be the beginning of a new life that would have little or nothing to do with the old. Danny Dunn, boy hero and lover, was effectively as dead as if he'd actually been killed.

The next step was to call Brenda from the public telephone on the jetty. He was shitting himself at the prospect. He wouldn't take the tram, he'd decided – too many stickybeaks, too many curious eyes. Instead he'd walk up Darling Street, up the hill, a fair climb carrying a duffle bag on a hot spring day, then he'd walk around the back, down the covered alleyway to the side of the back garden that led up to the private back door to the pub. He'd envisioned it all, sneaking in the back way where Brenda and Half Dunn would be waiting. Brenda tiny and tearful, Half Dunn filling all the available space in the small hallway. Jesus, what then?

Maybe he should turn back, not make the phone call, just disappear. They weren't expecting him. There'd be no hue and cry. He'd write to them, explain. He'd go somewhere way up north where there were lots of other misfits and where nobody had previously known him and would only see him as the freak he now was. He had three and a half years' pay coming to him. He'd be okay for a good bit while he tried to sort himself out, find out who the hell he was. Doc Woon had said he thought they could do something about reconstructing his nose. Maybe have that done first, check into Concord, the repatriation hospital. Then if he was swathed in bandages, Brenda and Half Dunn could visit and slowly grow accustomed to the idea of his new freak face.

Shit! What to do?

CHAPTER FOUR

DANNY WAITED UNTIL ALL six passengers had left the ferry, allowing them to walk some way down the wharf before he disembarked. He selected a bench outside the terminal that allowed him to look directly up Darling Street yet concealed him from the view of anyone getting on or off the tram. Now he watched as the tram came rattling down the hill, slowed in its headlong rush by the counterweight under the road. He well remembered the urgent clatter of the trams, bells ringing, sparks spluttering from the nexus of the cable arm and the overhead wires, the downhill ride still an event to delight a child and shake the bones of an ageing adult. Now, as he watched the return journey, the enthusiasm of its downhill romp was missing, the slope so steep that without the counterweight the tram would not have had the power to make it up the grade. The great contraption had slowed down with a mechanical groan and it seemed fortunate that only six passengers had climbed aboard. The frisky young girl coming down was transformed into the rheumatic old crone going back up.

Danny grinned to himself, remembering the times when the tram was packed to capacity and making hard work of the climb. The conductor would yell out, 'Righto! Males under eighteen off!' If this still wasn't sufficient to lighten the load, he would yell, 'Males twenty-five and under off!' They'd walk up the hill beside the slow-moving tram and then jump aboard again as it breasted the rise, each of them loudly demanding a penny discount and taking delight in the conductor's rebuff: 'Bugger off, the lot of youse!' At least this hadn't changed. Behind him the ferry's idling engine lifted then settled into an insistent hollow-sounding throb before it eventually pulled away, leaving the smell of diesel fumes in the air as it headed back to the city centre.

Danny remained on the bench for nearly an hour before finally summoning up the courage to call Brenda from the red telephone box outside the terminal. His hands trembled as he pushed the three pennies into the slot and dialled the six-digit number. Moments later he heard the ringing start at the other end.

'Hello, the Hero.' It was Brenda who answered, so there was no turning back. Despite having been born in Australia she affected an accent with a soft edge to it. Whether natural or practised, it had been there since his childhood – she was a tough little woman with a deceptively soft comforting lilt to her voice that had tricked many a presumptuous liquor salesman into thinking she was a pushover. Danny thumbed the silver button on the black pay-box and heard the sound of the coins dropping to trigger the connection. 'Mum?'

A moment's silence, then a hesitant voice. 'Danny? Danny, is that you?'

'Yes, Mum.' Danny swallowed. 'Home from the war.' He could picture Brenda standing with her back to the main bar counter, the black Bakelite desk phone placed on the mixer counter, the four mirror-backed shelves lined with spirits rising above her head with the seldom requested liqueurs at the top. He remembered that the Drambuie bottle, the most popular of the rarely requested liqueurs, was on the second-top shelf with all the other blue, green, yellow and orange bottles, altogether a dance of reflected light. Brenda always had to stand on a bar stool to reach it, evoking an occasional wolf-whistle from a customer seated at the bar who had caught a glimpse of the back of her knees as her skirt lifted. The top shelf contained a jeroboam of Moët champagne Brenda had been given by a liquor wholesaler when she'd won a sales competition. It was not for sale. Sometimes a customer, usually much the worse for drink, would demand it, emptying his week's pay in crumpled notes on the bar counter. 'Sorry, love. It's an empty, for display only,' she'd say so that he wouldn't persist. With a sudden pang Danny remembered her excited promise when she'd won the giant bottle. 'It's French, the real thing! We'll pop it to toast you at your graduation, my boy.'

'Danny! Where . . . where are you?' she said, her voice at once tremulous. 'Oh, Danny . . .' she continued, then followed wrenching sobs as the full impact of his phone call struck home.

'Mum! Mum, take it easy. Don't cry. I'm on my way home!' Danny shouted. But Brenda was unable to contain her sobbing, repeating his name over and over, as if she was grieving beside his grave. 'Mum, Mum! Listen, will ya?' Brenda's outburst had, unexpectedly, calmed him, putting him in charge. 'Mum, can you talk?'

But all he could hear were her sobs, then, 'Sorry . . . sorry, my darling. I'm just so happy!' This was followed by a fresh outburst of tears.

'Mum, is Dad there? Can you put him on the phone, please?' Danny knew Brenda wasn't normally the weepy type. But none of this was normal.

'Yes . . . sob . . . my boy . . . oh, oooh,' Brenda howled. By now Danny imagined Half Dunn would have seen her reaction to the phone call from where he always sat and would have squeezed through the counter flap, an anxious Puffing Billy.

Brenda's sobbing was soon replaced by Half Dunn's tentative voice. 'Danny?'

'Yes, it's me, Dad.'

'Danny, where are you?' his father shouted. Then, not waiting for an answer, 'Can you catch a taxi? Tell him we'll pay at this end.'

'No, Dad, listen! I should be home in twenty minutes. Can you and Mum be at the back door, just the two of you, nobody else?' He paused. 'Please, Dad, definitely nobody else!'

'Sure, son, we'll be waiting, just your mother and me. Gosh!'

'Dad . . . just one more thing.'

'Yeah, what is it, son?'

'I'm a bit of a mess . . . my face. Be prepared for a shock.'

'Son, your mother's okay . . . she wants to talk to you,' Half Dunn replied. Had he heard?

'Danny darling, please come now! Hurry, dear!' Brenda called.

'Mum, it's . . . it's not the same . . . me.'

'I know, dear, we've heard on the news – you've all been starved. As long as you're alive, nothing else matters. Please hurry, darling boy!'

'No, Mum. There's something else.'

'Danny, nothing matters, just having you here . . . Come home quickly!' she pleaded.

There seemed no point in explaining further. 'Righto. Be there in twenty minutes. Back door. Remember, just you and Dad!' Danny replaced the receiver. That was it then. There was no turning back now.

It was lunchtime when at last Danny reached the pub. The beer garden around the back seemed filled with people drinking in the sunshine. He was perspiring profusely, the light cotton shirt of his tropical uniform clinging to his back. In fact, he'd been forced to rest on two occasions. On the second a truck smelling strongly of sheep's tallow had stopped beside him, the driver offering him a lift. Danny had waved him on. His back hurt like hell, but it was important for him to walk up the hill to the pub. He needed to feel the peninsula under his feet, the hot sun on his back, the evocative and distinctive smells peculiar to Balmain in his nostrils.

There had been too many sudden changes since the morning Colonel Mori had announced at breakfast, 'War over! Japan *suwenda*! All men now *flends*! All men go home!' The trucks arriving at the camp with a convoy of ambulances, the long bumpy ride to Bangkok, hospital in Rangoon then by military plane to Singapore to get the ship home.

All of it by command and under orders. Now he wanted to give himself sufficient time to arrive on his own terms. To smell, touch, feel the peninsula, like an animal checking out its territory.

He realised he was hungry. His stomach, so long shrunken from lack of food, was beginning to adjust after the two-month stint in hospital, demanding some little sustenance, since he'd skipped breakfast parade on the boat. He thought longingly of his mother's breakfasts, which brought the Hero vividly before him. In his mind's eye he could see the old pub with its familiar cream paint, mid-green windowsills and frames. 'Early Depression cream and green' was the usual name for these two colours, though no one seemed to know quite why, except that most of the public buildings and vehicles at the time – the pubs, buses, even the harbour ferries and railway stations – were painted inside and out with these two nondescript colours, neither of which promised any joy. Helen had once pointed this out to him, adding, 'Perhaps it's called Depression cream because it's so depressing. The green's not much better.'

In Rangoon he'd received mail at last, a letter from Brenda with a postscript from Half Dunn telling him that the pub had been repainted and noting that Brenda had bought flags and bunting for his return. At the time he'd cringed inwardly at the news, and now, seeing the pub painted a gleaming white with dark laurel-green trim, it seemed quite wrong – brash and garish. He pictured the Hero he loved as a generous middle-aged Balmain housewife first thing in the morning, her hair in curlers, wearing a chenille dressing-gown and worn felt slippers, with the day's first cigarette sticking out of the corner of her mouth. Brenda may have transformed the inside to make it the friendliest and most comfortable of all the pubs on the peninsula, but she'd kept the outside as it had always been, repainting sections when necessary in the same two colours, the idea being that a pub should blend into its neighbourhood. But now he thought it stuck out like a sore thumb. Danny wasn't expecting the change and found he resented it. Thank goodness he'd surprised Brenda and she wouldn't have time to add the bunting, the final visual insult. He was soon to discover that his image of the pub, like the faces and places he'd carried with him to war, was redundant.

Careful not to be seen by the lunchtime crowd, heart thumping, mouth dry, he walked up the covered passageway to the back door. Danny climbed the four back steps to the outside landing, dumped his duffle bag beside the door, pulled the brim of his slouch hat as far down over his eyes as he could, took a deep breath and turned the doorhandle. Brenda stood directly in front of him, six or so feet down the passageway, Half Dunn behind her, now half the size Danny remembered him – his giving up fat for the war had evidently been successful. The sharp midday light streaming in behind him lit her face, revealing every detail. She'd aged noticeably, her pale-blue eyes puffy from crying and now creased at the corners, a suggestion of grey showing through her titian hair. His own face was in shadow, so that it wasn't until he'd stepped further into the interior, turned and reached for his duffle bag, that she was able to see him properly. The shock on her face was palpable. Her mouth opened in horror and both hands shot up to cover it as she sank slowly to her knees. 'No! No! No! What have they done to my boy! To my beautiful, beautiful boy!' she howled.

Danny dropped to his haunches and drew Brenda in to his chest. 'Mum . . . Mum! I'm so sorry. I should have spared you this. I shouldn't have come!'

Brenda pulled away and forced herself to look directly at Danny, then reached out and lightly touched his face, first his eye socket, then his sunken cheekbone, and finally the tips of her fingers ran down the bumpy tissue that passed for his nose. Then, placing her hand behind his neck, she pulled his face down towards her and kissed him on the mouth. 'Welcome home, my darling,' she said quietly in her soft, lilting voice. The strong Brenda was back.

She released him and Danny sat for a moment, too emotionally overcome to move, hot tears running down his cheeks. He became aware for the first time that the tear duct in the ruined eye still worked. 'Sorry, Mum, Dad,' he sniffed. 'I'm afraid I've come back a bit of a freak!'

Half Dunn reached down to put a comforting hand on Brenda's shoulder, taking his son's hand and raising him to his feet. Looking directly at Danny he said, 'Welcome home, son. I'm afraid the freak rights in this pub have long since been claimed by me.' He smiled. 'And I'm not giving them up.'

Danny reached down and lifted Brenda to her feet. His back hurt like hell but he ignored the pain and hugged her briefly, the warmth and softness of her body threatening to bring him undone again. 'I'm starving,' he said hurriedly. 'What does a man have to do for a cuppa tea and a corned-beef sandwich with hot English mustard?' he asked, then in case she'd forgotten, 'No milk, no sugar.'

Brenda arranged for one of her off-duty barmen to come in to work so that she and Half Dunn could spend the afternoon in the upstairs kitchen with their son. While Danny had been able to construct an almost impersonal narrative for Dr Woon in Rangoon, he found it near impossible to tell his parents the story of his three and a half years in captivity under the Japanese. He had already begun the lifelong task of finding a compartment in his mind where he could begin packing away those memories he didn't want to revisit, memories that had no purpose other than to haunt him. Now he heard himself recounting a series of the less horrifying incidents, but even these seemed a bit too much for them to absorb. He saw silent tears running down Brenda's cheeks as he described how they had treated tropical ulcers by scraping out the pus and rotting flesh with a sharpened spoon.

When Half Dunn asked about the Japanese, Danny found himself telling his father about the punishment they meted out for any assumed disobedience to a Japanese officer. 'They put you into The Cage,' he began, 'a box made of wood and chicken wire only big enough to sit in with your knees pulled up to your chest, then they left you in the hot sun for three days. The rest of us were forbidden to bring the poor sod any water on pain of being placed in The Cage ourselves. The bloke would often be dead or raving mad when the time came to take him out.' The three of them sat for a time in silence.

Danny knew he would have to tell them the details of his beating by the *kempeitai* officer, and when he did, his mother actually covered her eyes, then her entire body, racked with grief, started to shake uncontrollably and she whimpered, unable to restrain herself. Danny forced himself to complete the story, knowing that the telling would stop there, that he would not need to continue. It was apparent that they were incapable of understanding what he and his mates had been through. How could they possibly grasp the world he had until recently inhabited? Toes that rotted on your feet; tropical ulcers that suppurated and ate down to the bone; malaria; cholera that could kill in twenty-four hours, or, if you survived, leave you a shrunken husk; recurring dysentery that sapped what little strength you retained; beri-beri that bloated your body and ruined your heart. Your body, and those of all around you, mere skeletons with a thin layer of skin stretched over them. The only robust aspects of a man were his beard, hair and nails – ironically the parts of the body already 'dead'.

They couldn't possibly understand and he realised that he belonged to a fraternity of men who, in their minds, played host to the ghosts of the past, the unclean, beaten, forsaken, disgusting – the detritus of human life – images and emotions they couldn't share with anyone, which they must carry with them to the grave.

Above all, Danny didn't want his parents, or anyone else, to pity him. Already the look that had come into the eyes of the few civilians who had seen him since he'd left the ship had made him realise that people would never again accept him for his own sake. That his face would always trigger questions and underpin the way he was regarded in the future. That the public anonymity he had enjoyed, the sense of living in one's own private world, was gone forever. He had a face that led to bizarre speculation. He was public property, a walking story that triggered every stranger's curiosity. Long before Danny had completed what he hoped would be the first and last telling of his story he had ached to end it. It made him feel worthless, whereas he knew that Brenda and Half Dunn were trying to reconstruct him as the conquering hero returned, someone in whom they could take justifiable pride and accommodate within their own uncomplicated world.

Danny, finally exhausted, asked to retire to his room after supper (Brenda had somehow managed to prepare a roast dinner – the works, roast lamb, roast potatoes, roast pumpkin, fresh green peas, all smothered in thick brown gravy), where he spent until near midnight lying on his back staring at the ceiling desperately trying to reacquaint himself with the simple ways of his former life. But the high bed and the yielding mattress made him feel as if he was suspended and slowly being smothered by a soft sponge. Three and a half years of sleeping on a bare bamboo shelf had conditioned him to a hard surface. Even in the hospital, after the nine o'clock inspection and distribution of pills and medicine, many of them had abandoned their beds and slept on the floor beneath them. Now, stretched out on the hard wooden surface of his bedroom floor, he fell into a fitful sleep.

He awoke at 4 a.m., a habit he'd acquired in the camp where he was up half an hour before the other prisoners, needing to organise the day ahead, sort things out, go through the work roster, so that the men who were sick could be rested and those who'd been given time off to recover could take their place in the work gangs. He dressed slowly, deciding on his army trousers because the ones in his bedroom were too big for him around the waist, and an old shirt, also too large for his emaciated frame, but less noticeably so with the sleeves rolled up. At least an old pair of sandshoes fitted, his feet the only part of him that hadn't shrunk.

He left his room, being careful to tread softly down the hallway. It was unlikely that Brenda would be up quite this early, but she was a notoriously light sleeper. To his surprise, her door, which was usually left ajar, was closed, and just as he was passing, he heard her start to sing, her voice carrying to him quite clearly. He recalled how she would sing to him as a child – those lovely old Irish tunes – although at the time he hadn't realised that she carried a tune very well, with a light agreeable voice that was better than most. He was about to tiptoe towards the stairs when he heard his name and at the same time realised the tune was familiar – an old tune he remembered from his childhood, when Brenda would sometimes sing him to sleep. Guiltily aware that he was intruding, he nevertheless felt compelled to listen.

> Here I sit on Buttermilk Hill,
> With salty eyes I cry my fill,
> And ev'ry tear would turn a mill,
>   Danny's gone for a soldier.

> Shule shule shule aroo,
> Shule shule shule aroo.
> And every tear would turn a mill,
>   Danny's gone for a soldier.

> With pipes and drums he marched away,
> He would not heed the words I'd say,
> He'll not come back for many a day,
>   Danny's gone for a soldier.

> Shule shule shule aroo,
> Shule shule shule aroo.
> He'll not come back for many a day,
>   Danny's gone for a soldier.

> Me, oh my, I loved him so,
> It broke my heart to see him go,
> And time will never heal my woe,
>   Danny's gone for a soldier.

> Shule shule shule aroo,
> Shule shule shule aroo.
> And time will never heal my woe,
>   Danny's gone for a soldier.

I'll take my needle, take my reel,
And try my broken heart to heal,
I'll sew my quilt and wish him weal,
Danny's gone for a soldier.

Shule shule shule aroo,
Shule shule shule aroo.
I'll sew my quilt and wish him weal,
Danny's gone for a soldier.

I'll dye my dress, I'll dye it red,
The colour of the blood he's shed,
For the lad I knew has from me fled,
Danny's gone for a soldier.

Shule shule shule aroo,
Shule shule shule aroo.
For the lad I knew has from me fled,
Danny's gone for a soldier.

The song had barely come to an end when he heard Brenda sobbing. Danny's heart was thumping and he knew he was on the edge of panic, paralysed and unable to think what to do next. Brenda began to wail, deep despairing cries muffled by the bedroom door. The song was unmistakeably about him – she'd substituted his name for Johnny in the lyrics – and she was lamenting her boy who had returned a freak. Should he tap lightly on the door and attempt to comfort her? But how could he? It was just after four in the morning, a time she'd chosen to grieve so that nobody would catch her at it. Brenda was a proud woman; if she knew she'd been discovered it would be mortifying. It was his fault, all of it; if he'd heeded her desire for him to complete his degree, none of this would have happened. He would summon all his courage and go in and apologise. But how could that possibly help? Wouldn't that make things worse? She'd forever after feel compelled to make a show of her love for him to assuage her guilt, all because he had overheard her grieving for the way he'd returned to her.

Dr Woon had advised him to complete his degree, but he hadn't yet decided whether he would take the doctor's advice. Now he knew it was the very least he could do for his mother. Too little too late, but at least something could be salvaged from this tragic mess. Danny continued towards the stairs, placing each foot cautiously, grateful that he was wearing sandshoes and not army boots. With luck the loud snoring coming from Half Dunn's bedroom would drown out the odd creaking floorboard.

As he stepped into Darling Street, a three-quarter moon hung over the harbour, turning the water to soft pewter in the pre-dawn light. For the next two hours he wandered through the streets of Balmain trying to marshal his thoughts and to plan for the day to come. He was conscious that, for all he'd gained by being liberated from slavery, he'd lost the ability to simply be himself. While it hadn't been much of a self when he was a prisoner of war, it was the truth; what you saw was what you got. Wounded, sick and starving, there had been nothing to hide, no artifice, no special agenda. But now he was forced to do everything in his power to conceal who he was, and camouflage his sense of inadequacy and shame, his frustration and amorphous anger, the detritus of his particular war. He was an alien who was learning to emulate the habits of being in a society to which he could never again truly belong.

As dawn broadened into daylight Danny walked down a set of stone steps that led onto a landing stage constructed of Sydney sandstone. Waves slapped against the wall, an incoming tide lifting the water to less than a foot from the top of the platform. Danny removed his sandshoes, rolled up his trousers to above his knees, and sat on the edge of the wall, submerging his legs almost to the knees in the salt water. The skin over his ankles and shins, stretched tight over bone, was pitted with ulcer scars, some barely healed, still tender to the touch. At one of the camps along the railway there had been a small river where the prisoners had learned to immerse their legs to allow the tiny tropical fish to feed on the decaying flesh of their leg ulcers. It had worked a treat; the ulcers had healed in almost half the time, allowing the men to avoid a trip to the medical hut and the painful procedure with the sharpened spoon. If only, he thought, he could find a similar cure for his mental wounds. Then, on a sudden impulse, he dipped his hands into the water and scooped it over his head, dousing himself over and over again, bawling like a baby, as if he could purge the horrors from his mind with the sting of salt water. Finally, when he could no longer raise his arms, his sobbing ceased and he sat quietly, drenched to the skin. Curiously, he felt as though something had indeed been purged during this baptism in the harbour, and he found he could think just a tad more clearly.

Danny sensed it would not be easy to fit into a post-war society that was anxious to forget the war and get on with the peace. How simple it is to forget the past when there isn't a great deal to remember, when the load you carry doesn't force you to your knees each morning. He accepted that he had to develop a way of coping that would allow him to appear to live a normal life, or at least one acceptable to the people around him. He knew he must make a desperate effort to fight the depression and hopelessness he was already feeling, the sudden irrational rages he tried so hard, though not always successfully, to repress, like the incident with the bloke at Circular Quay, his unreasonable fury when the kid had first offered to carry his duffle bag. People must think that what they saw on the surface was the real McCoy. They must never discover that, beneath the conventional exterior, he was an emotional mess.

His mother's words came back to him and he realised that they might contain a clue to a place where he could hide. He would become 'a somebody', keeping people at arm's length, so they saw only the outside and never what lay within. One thing was certain: he must remain single – a loner. Nobody must be harmed by his neuroses, his seemingly baseless anger or his depression, his anxieties or obsessions. Nobody must see the damage.

Danny now brought to mind his first emotional hurdle: Helen. Just thinking of her when he was in the camp had often given him the strength to go on. By pure force of will he hadn't allowed himself to think of the consequences for their relationship of the brutality he'd experienced, the damage he'd sustained to body, spirit and mind. Once he'd been liberated and was safe in the hospital in Rangoon, he was forced to face reality. He'd needed her as his anchor and he'd hung on for dear life, but now he was adrift, convinced that the storm he'd experienced had broken his mooring and that he'd been washed onto the rocks.

Danny had never stopped loving Helen, not for one moment, but in the unlikely event that some high-ranking officer hadn't already swept her up and married her, he knew she'd take one look at his face and run for her life. She was ambitious, and the last thing she needed was a one-eyed, broken-nosed freak at her side.

He'd expected her to be long gone, expected to find the 'Dear John' letter waiting for him. So when Brenda told him Helen wasn't hitched and was, on the contrary, anxious to see him, he'd panicked. He wasn't ready. It was as if she'd been resurrected from the graveyard in his mind, where he'd already grieved for the loss of her. It wasn't fair, he thought childishly, that he should be put through the agony of seeing her, knowing the inevitable outcome. For her sake, as well as his own, he'd have to avoid a meeting between them – perhaps write a letter telling her he no longer loved her nor wished to see her again. That would spare her embarrassment and be the kindest thing he could possibly do. Best to do it right away, this morning; get it over with.

The kid! Danny suddenly remembered that he'd promised to help – what was his name? – Lachlan, Lachlan Brannan, find a job. Jesus! He'd be at the pub just after opening. Why had he opened his big mouth? He wasn't ready to help anyone find a job. He could barely help himself.

Danny waited for the sudden panic to subside, the old familiar feeling he'd so often experienced in the camp – let it subside so the Japs don't see it. After all, it was only some snotty-nosed kid. He'd send him to the newsagent to buy the *Sydney Morning Herald*, show him how to work the classifieds, let him use the phone. Maybe that was enough. If the kid lucked in, fine; if he failed, well, Danny would have kept his promise. He'd be rid of him by lunchtime, then he could get on with the more important task of ensuring Helen Brown understood that, for them, there could be no possible future.

Even so, he longed to see her just once. Helen was a seeker after truth, and with her incisive mind and strong character, she would be the kind of friend he needed to stiffen his battered spine, to give him the fortitude to start again in this new and alien environment. On the other hand, how could he bear having her only as a friend, knowing she pitied him, was perhaps repulsed by him, but was tough enough to understand and stubborn enough to endure? The trouble was, Danny wasn't at all sure that *he* could endure. He felt like an old jalopy stalled on a railway crossing, with Helen an express train coming full pelt down the track towards him. Helen was strong-minded, even obdurate, never a quitter and not one to run away from a problem. She never had, never would, take any shit from him. Theirs, he finally decided, was a collision he must at all costs avoid.

He climbed the hill from the harbour, turning his head away as the eight o'clock tram carrying city office workers to the ferry passed him by. The passengers didn't need to see his scars first thing in the morning. That was another thing he'd have to learn: to look directly at someone without wondering, or assuming, what they were thinking.

Brenda was in her office when he returned, and he tapped on the half-open door. 'Morning, Mum,' he called.

'Come in, dear, come in,' Brenda replied. He entered, forgetting the state of his clothes. 'Danny, you're soaked! Where on earth have you been?' she cried, rising from her chair, her face showing her consternation.

Danny grinned ruefully. 'Trying to wash away the last three years, Mum,' he replied, attempting to keep it light-hearted but not fooling her for a moment. Brenda took the half-dozen steps to reach him, then put her arms around his waist and, standing on tiptoe, kissed him on his damaged cheek, then let her head rest against his chest. 'Oh, Danny, Danny,' she cried.

'Mum! I'm wet!' Danny protested, not wanting to create a scene in her office and suddenly very glad he hadn't entered her bedroom to comfort her earlier.

'You're home, that's all that matters, my dearest,' she said, drawing away slightly and looking lovingly into his face as if the old Danny with two blue eyes, a straight nose and a smooth-skinned left cheek were still there. Danny realised how much courage it had taken just to do this, but he was embarrassed by the expression on his mother's face. He knew that Brenda had done her crying, probably for most of the night, then finally sung the lament he'd heard in the early hours, her grieving over. Now, he knew, she would bury her grief and hide her distress at his broken face forever. It was she who was truly bulletproof.

Brenda drew away from her sodden son and said with sudden mock severity, 'Go on, upstairs at once!' It was as if he were still a small child caught in a sudden rainstorm while playing outside. 'Take a hot bath or you'll catch your death!'

Danny looked down at his wet clobber. 'I guess I'll have to get some new duds; nothing fits,' he said, not knowing how to react and quite incapable of clasping his mother to his chest and thus returning her love with a simple gesture.

Upstairs Danny lowered himself into the hot bath, and sighed. This was the first opportunity he'd had to really study the damage to his body. He hadn't examined the whole of himself when he'd been a prisoner of war – there were no mirrors and no reason to see the stages a body goes through in the process of starving to death. Later, in Rangoon, he'd simply been aware of the dressings that covered the still suppurating ulcers. On the boat home he'd been billeted in a small cabin with six other men and his daily ablutions took place in a communal shower room with only just enough time allotted every morning for each man to shave, shower and shit. Seeing the scarred and pocked condition of one or another of the ex-prisoners of war, he supposed he looked the same. Now he saw that his shins were a mass of purple craters, the legacy of tropical ulcers; his back and shoulders were ropey with layered scars from the beatings handed out by the Japanese and Korean guards; his neck was pitted with the remains of boils, the result of long-term vitamin deficiency. Then, to cap it all, there was his smashed-in face, sallow from recurrent bouts of malaria. His only remaining physical assets were his one deep and exceptionally blue eye and his hair, which was still black as a crow's feather and thick as it had always been. With a grunt, Danny picked up a scrubbing brush and worked it hard over every inch of his body, scrubbing fiercely and painfully at the tropical ulcers, some freshly healed, and the scars left by the cuts, beatings and accidents sustained and then forgotten from his time as a slave of the Japanese.

Filled with shame and loathing for what his once powerful body had become, Danny towelled himself and changed into an old cotton tracksuit from his water-polo days. It was miles too big but he used a belt to gather and fasten the excess material at the waistline and then dropped the top over the belt to neaten things up. He put his army uniform in the copper, which, he was surprised to notice, no longer required a fire to heat the water but was now connected to the electricity with heating elements beneath it. Then he headed for the kitchen and breakfast.

Some weeks later Danny was to learn from Half Dunn that the day after he'd left Australia for Malaya, his mother had packed her bags, closed the pub and warned him not to attempt to open it again until she returned. She was off to visit her mother, Rose, she'd announced.

'When will you be back?' Half Dunn had asked, surprised.

'I don't know. I can't explain. It's a family thing, with my mother. It's time for me to learn the song and bring back the grieving quilt.' She paused. 'A week, I'll be back in a week,' she'd said.

'What quilt? What song?' Half Dunn had asked, confused.

'It's how my mother's people have grieved for generations in Ireland and here, when my brothers . . .' Brenda didn't complete the sentence.

'But I can run the pub while you're away,' he had protested.

'Yes, you could, but I want it closed. That way I can do what I have to do without worrying about you or it.'

'But what about our regulars?'

Brenda had suddenly lost patience. 'For God's sake, Michael Dunn, I ask you! There are thirty pubs in Balmain. They're not going to go thirsty now, are they?' Whereupon, Half Dunn explained, she'd phoned for a taxi to take her to the train leaving from Central that evening, which would stop at Wagga Wagga around three o'clock the following morning.

She'd returned a week later very pale, looking as if she'd aged five years. He waited patiently for her to settle then explain her absence, but she failed to say anything, although she'd come back with a large, badly scuffed, brown leather trunk. Pointing to it, Half Dunn asked, 'That the . . . er . . . grieving quilt?'

'Yes,' Brenda replied.

'May I see it?'

'No!' she said quickly, adding, 'It's bad luck until I know what the addition will be, and that won't be until Danny returns.'

'Did you . . . did you learn the song?'

'Yes, but that's also for when Danny returns, *if* he returns,' she replied darkly. Then, seeing Half Dunn's dismay at being fobbed off so brusquely, she softened. 'Michael, I can't tell you any more. Please, will you trust me?'

'But nothing's happened! Danny's on board ship, they're going to Malaya, there isn't even any fighting yet!' Half Dunn had protested one last time. Then, to his enormous surprise, Brenda had burst into tears.

'That's not what Rose sees,' she'd wailed.

Half Dunn had known better than to question Brenda further. Trying to comfort his distraught wife, he had felt his usual clumsy, useless self.

'Well, I've returned now. Have you heard the song at least?' Danny asked, hoping like hell Half Dunn hadn't. He recalled the morning he'd heard it, unsure if he'd ever quite recover from the sadness of the lament, and realising in that moment that all his headstrong stupidity had culminated in his mother's grief, grief for the boy who'd left her, only to return broken and beaten. It could all have been so different had he not been so insanely anxious to throw his life away.

Half Dunn shook his head. 'Nah, it's driving me nuts, not a tweet.'

'What about, you know, what's she call it . . . the grieving quilt?'

Half Dunn shook his head again. 'She keeps that big ol' trunk locked in her bedroom. Maybe she's doing, yer know, something, with the bits of yer clothes she's kept since you were a baby. She said they were to remind her of how you were – school clothes, yer favourite blue shirt when you were at university, football jumpers, cozzie – they're all there. I went into her bedroom the other day looking for Aspro and there were scraps on the floor where she'd been cutting them up. I reckon she's back in her bedroom sewing something to do with that bloody quilt. Once when Helen visited I overheard them. I wasn't stickybeaking or anything, it was at the main bar and your mother mustn't have realised I was in my usual spot. She was asking if Helen had anything, a dress or blouse that you liked when you were going out with her. She wanted to buy it. Helen said she had this blue crepe dress that was cut quite low at the front, teal blue, that you always said you liked, and that she could have it with pleasure. I remember her saying, "It carries too many memories now, all too painful to recall. I can't bring myself to wear it."

'"Maybe the hem is deep enough," your mother replied. "I only need a small piece."'

Danny had a sudden lump in his throat. 'I remember that dress, she looked terrific in it,' he said quietly, recalling that it buttoned right down the front and that Helen would let him unbutton it. When he reached the last button she'd throw the front open and yell, 'Surprise!' because she'd be in the nuddy, whereupon he'd toss her onto the bed and they'd make love laughing. It was bloody stupid. He could feel the tears welling in his good eye and in the socket of the other and turned away from Half Dunn so they couldn't be seen. 'Sounds like she's doing something all right,' he observed, attempting to sound matter-of-fact.

Danny knew Half Dunn would be loyal to Brenda to his last breath, but he was also aware that his father was a teller of tales, famous for his ability to retell a story that was a vast improvement on the original. Now here was something on which he could really build – the song and the quilt and, best of all, a prophesy by Brenda's mother, Rose. 'There's got to be a grand story to be told here,' Half Dunn muttered. 'It's bloody frustrating, I can tell yer!'

Then there was that other story, the one that might never be told. Right from the moment he'd clapped eyes on Danny's broken face, Half Dunn had realised it was a story in hiding, and when it came to sniffing out a good yarn – snooping and sleuthing for details – there was no room for scruples. Danny wasn't sure whether Half Dunn's reaction to his battered face was an illustration of his father's sensitivity or just the opposite. His father seemed to have accepted the change in Danny, and they'd resumed their friendship as if nothing particularly untoward had happened. But Danny suspected his broken face might yet figure in a story brewing in Half Dunn's mind, as a detail to add poignancy and drama to the overall narrative he was concocting. Even if Half Dunn never actually told the story to anyone, nothing could stop him from formulating it in his mind, and the lack of those missing pieces was obviously driving him crazy. Even so, Danny would never admit to either of his parents that he'd heard his mother's lament.

Danny was surprised to find Brenda in the kitchen cooking him breakfast. 'Your father's downstairs,' she said, 'and he's organised your clothes,' she added. 'Pineapple Joe is coming around at nine to measure you up for a suit.'

Danny fought back a surge of sudden and unreasonable rage. He hated surprises. He needed time to prepare himself, to plan how to react. Didn't she realise? He wanted to scream at her, 'What do you think you're doing? You didn't bloody ask me!'

Brenda, unaware of her son's seething anger, laughed, and went on, 'He told your father, "For zat boy only za best. For him I am making special suit from *Esquire* magazine, American atom bomb double-breast six button, no less, hunnert per cent pure merino vool, best English *schmutter* I still got already from before za var! No expense spared wit my compliments for vinning za var for our side!"'

'Pineapple Joe is going to shout me a suit? But the government gives me a free suit when I'm officially demobbed, you know.' Danny had his temper under control again. 'Do you think he'd delay it until I've put on a bit of weight?'

'I doubt it, dear. He's told half the peninsula about the American atom bomb suit he's making for you.' Brenda dropped back into his accent – she was a good mimic, but nothing compared to Half Dunn. '"Special cut, very snazzy, trust me." I expect he wants to make it his new line and you're the model. You'll break his heart if you refuse. Besides,' she smiled, 'don't look a gift clotheshorse in the mouth – we've earned it. He's made a fortune tailoring your father's clothes over the years and now that he's losing weight, Pineapple Joe is busy making a second one.'

'By the way, what the hell is an American atom bomb suit?' Danny asked.

Brenda laughed. 'When your letter arrived from the Rangoon hospital, your father was having a fitting for a new pair of trousers. He told Pineapple Joe the good news about your liberation, and then he said something about how the Americans dropping the atom bomb had forced the Japanese to surrender, which, like you said in your letter, probably saved your life. That's when Pineapple Joe said, "For him I am makink zat Danny boy American atom bomb suit for comink home alive!"'

Half Dunn, sensing a story, had once asked Pineapple Joe how he'd come by his nickname, as his real name was Maurice Ruberwitz. The little tailor had replied, 'I am comink off zat boat from imma-gra-tion nineteen turty-one and dat imma-gra-tion man, he's stamp my peppers, then is saying, "Righto, off you go, Joe." Now I have mine first new names for mine new contree. Next is by za dock's fruit barrow. I am liking already very much dis place – za sun is shinink and dat man, he is shouting, "Apples, gripes, fresh fruit, juicy pineapple!" Apple, gripes, dis I know already, but what is dis pineapple? I am looking at dat pineapple. "Pliss, what I must do wid dis fruits?" I am asking, very polite. I don't tink dat man, he like foreigner comink to Australia, because he says to me, "As long as ya buys one, ya can stick it up yer dago arse fer all I care, it's a bloody pineapple, mate!" Pineapple Joe chuckled, shrugging his shoulders and spreading his hands. 'So now I am gettink already mine second new names.'

Pineapple Joe had become as much a part of Balmain as anyone born on the peninsula. He became a Tigers fanatic early on, never missing a game. At the beginning of every season he outfitted each member of the entire first-grade team with a free grey worsted suit and two shirts, making them the best-dressed team in the premiership. 'Goot for advertisemint; mit de goot bodies, already dey makink mein suits look vunderful.' Moreover, he made his business terms very plain and very simple, as many Balmain kids soon learned. Any of them fortunate enough to get a city office job went to Pineapple Joe for their first suit, dubbed a Pineapple Special. So did every worker getting married. Each new gainfully employed lad was required to pay it off himself at sixpence or a shilling a week, depending on his starting wage, regardless of whether his parents could afford to pay cash for it, which was highly unlikely, anyway. 'Zat boy, he must be learnink money is not growink on za trees like za lifs and flowers,' Pineapple Joe would insist. While a Pineapple Special, run up in a single afternoon on his pre-war industrial Singer sewing machine ('Mine American sew-machine'), was far from a sartorial triumph and paid absolutely no heed to current fashion, it was well made and the recipient usually outgrew it or did well enough in his job to be able to afford something more stylish. Young blokes paying off their Pineapple Specials wouldn't have dreamed of welshing on the deal, and sufficient shillings and sixpences continued to roll into the tailor's shop to keep the wolf from the door and allow him to put a little aside.

In the mid-fifties, Maurice Ruberwitz opened a Pineapple Joe tailors shop in the city, producing cheap but well-made suits. A sign outside his shop read, *American Cut, Double or Single Breast – Only the Best! Cash Only.* Eventually he became, by Balmain standards, a wealthy man. He drove a chocolate-brown Dodge sedan on which he replaced the chrome charging-ram emblem on the top of the radiator with a small silver pineapple, made for him by young Ian Buchanan who was doing his apprenticeship as a silversmith, and welded into place by Harry Bezett, who worked in the maintenance section for buoys and beacons at the Maritime Services Board. While it was said to be solid silver and very valuable (it was in fact nickel-plated brass), nobody in Balmain would have dreamed of nicking it, even if it had been solid gold. Pineapple Joe was inordinately proud of what he referred to as 'Mine American Dodge car', and he would spend Saturday and Sunday afternoons in the summer driving slowly up and down Darling Street. As he knew everyone in Balmain, he would stop if he saw a housewife carrying her shopping and call gallantly, 'You are hoppink aboard, Mrs Selkirks, and ve are takink you verever you wish, compliments Pineapple Joe. Put za begs in za beck seat and now you come sit in za front mine American Dodge car.' With a hearty chortle he'd add, 'Maybe already you are seeink somebody and are makink vaves.' When he was duly thanked for the lift he'd say, 'Acht! I am sharink already mine goot fortune for comink to Balmain. Cheerio. Up za Tigers!'

Brenda's fussing was so remote from Danny's experience in captivity that he found himself growing nervous, almost afraid. While he knew she was demonstrating her love for him, her fussing made him feel vulnerable. It was as if he were somehow not entitled to or worthy of her caring or attention. Now she came and stood behind his chair as he ate, brushing her fingers lightly through his hair. 'I think I'd better go downstairs and see what your father's up to. When those two get together they talk both hind legs off a donkey,' she said.

After she'd gone he remembered that her great love had been to cut and shape his hair with comb and scissors and Danny decided to ask her to do so again. He'd allow it to grow long – nothing like the army's short back and sides, or the shaved heads of the camp inmates. Despite the prevailing fashion, it had been his unique style since he'd been a child, and it would be the one thing he'd retain from the old Danny; from now on people might say what they liked – it would be his single defiance. Seen from the front he would always be a dreadful fright; seen from the back – provided he wasn't in the nuddy, and with his mother's help – he would look like his old self, with his hair eventually resting just above his shoulders.

He had just buttered a couple of slices of toast, poured himself another cuppa and was reaching for the marmalade jar when he heard Brenda calling from the foot of the stairs, 'Someone here to see you, Danny!'

Danny froze. It must be Helen, a conspiracy, she and Brenda had worked out a sneaky arrangement to trap him. He wasn't ready. He hadn't worked out in his head precisely what he wanted . . . what he was going to say to her. He felt the anger rising in his chest. Bloody hell, fair go, it was almost five years ago! 'Who is it, Mum?' he called back, struggling to control his voice.

'Young lad, says he met you yesterday near Circular Quay. You asked him to come and see you this morning.'

'Oh, yes,' he cried. The boy! He'd completely forgotten that he'd arranged to meet him. Danny's sense of relief was palpable. Now he walked to the head of the stairs from where he could see Brenda and called down to her. 'He's Lachlan Brannan. He tells me his old man is a regular here.'

'Brannan?' Brenda called back. 'His sister must be Doreen. She's married to Tommy O'Hearn, who wasn't very nice to your father over the water-polo thing. He's been climbing the union ranks while everyone else has been away fighting. He's supposed to have flat feet . . . the only flat he's got is *flat out* taking advantage! Doreen's much too good for him.'

'Lachlan's a good kid, Mum. Can you send him up please?'

Danny, back at the kitchen table munching toast, heard Lachlan coming up the stairs and called out, 'Turn right, first door on the right. Come in, mate.'

Moments later young Lachlan appeared smiling at the kitchen door in a suit that suggested its owner, or perhaps several owners, had taken a fair old belting from life. Danny couldn't believe his eyes. The lapels were frayed and stained and the baggy trousers were cut in some fashion from the distant past. It was a suit that had never seen the interior of a dry-cleaning shop but had been the recipient of a thousand soapy sponges and countless hot flat irons applied through a sheet of brown paper, which was intended to prevent the fabric singeing or developing a shine. Or perhaps not, because Lachlan's borrowed finery was a perfect example of the damage a hot iron can do if applied directly to ageing grey serge. The jacket was too big by half and fell almost to his knees, and the sleeves were rolled back a good six inches to reveal a mattress-ticking lining brown with age. The lapels, jacket front and two sagging pockets were stained with all manner of indelible substances that testified to the desperate though futile efforts of somebody's wife to remove them. The trousers, equally frayed and stained, billowed in a distinctly Chaplinesque manner then pooled over his shoes, their length, Danny estimated, at least eight to ten inches longer than the wearer's legs. Lachlan wore a white school shirt and an ancient, brown, moth-eaten knitted tie. In his hand he carried a battered brown felt hat, the crown resting against his knees so that Danny could see that it had been stuffed with newspaper to fit Lachlan's head.

'Come on in,' Danny called. 'Piece of toast?'

'No, thanks, I already et,' Lachlan replied, stepping towards the kitchen table.

'Couple'a slices of toast can't hurt, eh?' Danny said, feeding two slices of white bread into the toaster. 'Peanut butter? Vegemite?'

'Can I have peanut butter please?' Lachlan asked, obviously glad that Danny had insisted, then grinning he said, 'Whaddaya reckon, Danny? Good, eh?' He was obviously referring to his suit.

'Oh . . . yeah . . . Your brother's?'

'Nah, Mum took his to the pawnshop. We'll get it back when he comes home with his wages from the ship.'

'So?'

'We got real lucky. Old Mr Foster three doors down died last week and they was going to bury him in it . . .'

'What? In the suit?'

'Yeah, but luckily old Mrs Foster said, "Waste not want not, maybe it could do some good to the living. And Herb would be more comfortable in his red nightshirt that Shirley, his daughter, give him last Christmas."' Lachlan shrugged, causing almost no observable movement in the overlarge jacket. 'So that's what happened. She give it to me mum last night.'

Danny, unable to contain himself, started to chuckle and Lachlan joined him, both of them soon convulsed with laughter. He couldn't remember when he'd last laughed – simply, deliciously laughed, unable to restrain his giggling. They didn't hear the toaster popping or Brenda coming up the stairs and into the kitchen. 'What's so funny?' she asked.

'Nothing, Mum,' Danny chortled, 'it's just that (giggle) Lachlan's suit was rescued from a dead man!' Both boys burst into fresh laughter.

'What? Taken off a corpse?' Brenda asked, aghast.

This caused fresh guffaws. 'No, Mrs Dunn, luckily for me he liked his red nightshirt best,' Lachlan said, milking another laugh.

'Well, I'm glad to hear that,' Brenda answered, mystified. From her expression, it was clear to Danny that she thought the suit belonged in the same wooden box occupied by its last owner. 'Pineapple Joe's arrived for your fitting, Danny. The saloon bar is empty – why not do it there?' she suggested.

'Your toast!' Danny exclaimed, remembering.

'That's okay,' Lachlan said. 'I already et, like I said.'

'Toast? Honestly, you men!' Brenda said in feigned disgust. 'When Danny was your age he ate like a horse. I expect you're the same. How about a couple of fried eggs and bacon *with* the toast, eh?' It was an offer simply too good for the boy to refuse. Not knowing quite what to say he grinned and nodded. 'In the meantime, a cup of tea? Sugar?' Brenda asked, fetching a cup and the sugar bowl and nodding to Danny with a jerk of her chin. 'Go on downstairs, I'll take care of Lachlan.'

'Velcome! Velcome!' Pineapple Joe spread his arms as Danny entered the saloon bar. 'Za atom bomb kid, already! Mein Gott, you looks terrible, terrible, Danny,' he said, patting Danny all over, squeezing his thin arms and shoulders.

Danny laughed. It was obvious that Pineapple Joe wasn't referring to his face but to his general condition. 'Yeah, lost a fair bit of weight since you last saw me.'

'Nineteen turty-nine Tigers, ve are vinning za premiership zat day! Mein Gott, I vas so proud of you Danny, za youngest and also lock forward, strong like za bull! Zat night I am dronk, first time mein life. Stonkered! Mudderliss! Up za Tigers!'

'As I remember we were all motherless by the end of the night.'

Pineapple Joe removed the tape measure from around his neck and whipped it expertly around Danny's waist, reading the measurement then tut-tutting. 'Skins and bones, skins and bones,' he repeated, shaking his head in dismay. 'Pliss, so tell me, Danny, how I am making American atom bomb double-breast hunnert per cent merino vool from before za war on zis body? Zat bastard Japanese, zey are makink you like za bean sticks!'

'Beanpole?' Danny suggested.

'Ja, zat also,' Pineapple Joe said.

'What say we wait six months, eh? I've already put on twenty pounds. In six months I should be right as rain.'

Pineapple Joe paused to consider, then shook his head. 'I am making already shoulder pads for za jacket and zen I am leaving plenty material for za hems. Later I take out za pads and za hems and zen we havink perfek number vun atom bomb result, no?'

Pineapple Joe only answered to three forms of address: Pineapple Joe as a business name, Pineapple as a personal name, and Mr Joe for formal occasions. Danny opted for formality. 'Mr Joe, I wonder if you could do me a favour?'

'Mein pleasure, Danny, for vinning za var.'

Danny chuckled. 'Thank you, but I'm afraid my contribution to the final victory was fairly insignificant.'

'So modest already,' Pineapple Joe noted to himself.

While Pineapple Joe took his measurements, writing them down in a small spiral-bound notepad, Danny explained that he wanted him to make Lachlan a suit that he personally would pay for, but that it wasn't a simple matter, because the boy and his mother were very proud; in fact, the whole family was proud, and he was fairly positive they wouldn't accept it from him, considering it to be charity. He described the dead man's suit and explained that he had hoped to get Lachlan several interviews in the city, but that the oversized, aged, ragged and stained suit made the boy look like a tramp. 'You know better than most how people are judged by their appearance,' he concluded.

'So let me see zis boy, pliss,' Pineapple Joe said immediately. 'Maybe only sixpence a veek ven he get za job.'

'Yeah, righto, but he won't accept it until he does . . . get a job, I mean. In the meantime he needs the suit to get the job.' Danny shrugged. 'Problem?'

'No problem! Vere is zat boyz?'

'Upstairs.'

'Bring, bring . . . From boyz I know already.'

'Sure, I'll go fetch him. You will be, you know, careful?'

Pineapple Joe rocked his open hand in the air in front of him, 'Gentle like za fezzer fallink,' he said with a benign smile.

Several minutes later Danny and Lachlan entered the saloon bar. Danny had explained to him that Joe was making a suit for him and was happy to take up the sleeves and the trousers of old Mr Foster's suit without charge. 'No problems. Just a couple of minutes on his sewing machine,' Danny said, to reassure the boy. 'My dad gives him heaps of business,' he explained, adding, 'He's an old friend of the family.'

'Hello! Zis is zat boyz you is tellink me about? Come, come, let me see zat suit you are wearink.'

'Lachlan, this is Mr Joe, the best bespoke tailor in Sydney.'

'How do you do, sir?' Lachlan asked, extending his hand.

'Goot! Excellent and even better zen zat,' Pineapple Joe said, smiling and shaking Lachlan's hand. Then he reached out and felt the lapel of the dead Herb Foster's suit, rubbing it between his forefinger and thumb. 'Mein Gott!' he said, almost under his breath. 'Zat material only for officer zey are getting special after za Boer War! English officer only getting zat material. Zat vool belong sheeps from Scotlandz.' Pineapple Joe clasped his hands to his chest, his head to one side. 'Pliss, for my collection I am wanting zat suit. So now we are makink a plan. Zis suit it is make a deposit, zen ven you are gettink a job, you are paying me sixpence every veek for four years, zat five pounds. For zis I am makink bran-new suit, yes?'

'You mean you'll make Lachlan a brand-new suit in exchange for that one plus sixpence a week for four years?' Danny asked, smiling broadly.

'Absoloot!'

'You hear that, Lachlan? What do you say, mate?'

To Danny's surprise, Lachlan didn't answer, instead looking down at the ill-fitting, ragged old suit he was wearing. 'You mean it's valuable then?' he asked, somewhat surprised.

'For me, yes, for uzzer pipple, no.'

'I'll have to ask my mum, sir. She got it from old Mrs Foster. Maybe she'll think we ain't grateful or somethin'.'

Danny liked this; the kid wasn't a fool. Asking if the suit was valuable showed he was thinking, then worrying about old Mrs Foster's feelings. That was nice, but, on the other hand, he wasn't thinking for himself.

'No, mate. Time you made your own decisions. What's it to be then?'

Lachlan looked up at Danny, 'It's not charity, is it? Me mum says when you lose your pride and start taking charity it's like being a beggar; eventually you lose yer self-respect.'

'No, mate, it's not charity, you'll be paying for it. The old suit is only a deposit.'

'What if I can't get a job?' Lachlan asked.

'In that old bag of fruit we've got a problem; in a new suit we've got every chance. Old Mr Foster's dead-man's suit just isn't right, it's like putting a fine horse into the Melbourne Cup with nothing but a tatty saddle blanket.'

'Me mum says "neither a lender nor a borrower be". She says debts make you somebody's slave.'

Danny was rapidly growing weary of Lachlan's mum's ubiquitous influence, and her sayings. He sighed impatiently. 'First a beggar and now a slave. You're not easy to help, are you, kid? Let me put it to you this way. Think of the city as a concrete jungle. The enemy is anyone who is competing with you to get a job. If they get it and you don't, then they've taken you out, in a sense eliminated you. If they got the job offer and you didn't there has to be a good reason. Right?'

'Yeah, right,' Lachlan agreed, enjoying the military terminology.

'Could be lots of reasons they got it – better preparation, better weapons, better knowledge of the battlefield, whatever. Do you agree so far?'

'Yeah. I never thought of it like that,' the boy admitted.

'Well, remember how you told me the story about the bloke at the gate at the docks who asked you if you were a member of the wharfies union, and when you told him no, he told you to piss off?'

'Yeah, well, I told you, they're a bunch of commos!'

'But you knew that all along and you still wanted the job.'

'Yeah,' Lachlan agreed reluctantly.

'So you had the wrong weapons to win, didn't you? Don't answer. I think you get the general idea. Now say you'd gone to the union offices first and told them you wanted to join the union but didn't have a job. There was one going at the docks, so could they give you a note or something, and if you got the job you'd pay your union fees pronto. Think about it for a moment. You even had the inside running, your sister works at Trades Hall and your brother-in-law, Tommy O'Hearn, is a union official. That's what's called being armed with the right weapons. The new suit is the same – you're presenting yourself to a new employer as a recruit ready and properly armed for combat in the concrete jungle.'

'I've made up me mind,' Lachlan announced. 'I'll take it. Even if I only do odd jobs I could find sixpence a week, I reckon.'

Pineapple Joe was called down to measure Lachlan and obligingly left with old Mr Foster's suit, which he promptly deposited in the nearest rubbish bin. Later he would tell Danny, 'Oi vey! Ven pipple zey seeink me mit zat terrible schmutter I'm goink broken already!'

'Going broke,' Danny corrected without thinking.

'Broke? No, no, dat only one piz. I am broken, many, many pizzes ven pipple seeink me wid dat Grice Brudder suit. Like zat dumpty humpty ven he is fallink off zat wall and all zoze soldiers and zoze horses belonginck ze king zey cannot fixink him . . . no vey, José!'

Danny knew it was time to give up. Pineapple Joe had managed splendidly with his own peculiar syntax for almost fifteen years; who was he to argue? Half the peninsula tried unsuccessfully to imitate him, but Half Dunn was one of the few who'd managed to do so, it being an essential part of spinning any yarn that included the little tailor.

Lachlan was sent out to buy the *Herald* and they spent the morning going through the situations vacant columns. By lunchtime they'd made over twenty phone calls and secured three appointments for two days hence, sufficient time for Pineapple Joe to make the suit and a couple of white business shirts. Lachlan knew of an afternoon shift job going at a dockside packing shed and left after having first managed a pub lunch consisting of a lemonade and six sausage rolls pressed on him by an insistent Brenda, who seemed to have taken a liking to him.

Danny had decided to go in to Sydney University to see about completing his Arts degree. It would be, he hoped, a little good news to give Brenda. The Grace Brothers Emporium was almost opposite the university and he planned to go in and buy a pair of grey flannels and a couple of shirts so he'd look half decent for his interview, and he'd select a tie as a gift for Lachlan. He'd thought about getting a brown trilby and trying to persuade Lachlan he'd bought it for himself and later decided he didn't like it. He'd think of a reason why it just happened to be two sizes too small for him, if the kid noticed.

He was about to leave when the kitchen phone rang. Half Dunn was having his afternoon nap and Danny, thinking it must be for him, answered. 'Danny, it's Helen. Please don't hang up,' she said quickly.

'Oh!' was all Danny, shocked beyond words, could say.

'Danny, *please* can we meet?' Helen asked. 'I've waited nearly five years!'

'Did my mother put you up to this?' he demanded, recovering from his initial shock and instinctively going on the attack.

'Yes . . . yes, as a matter of fact she did.'

Danny had expected her to deny that the two women had colluded, but he'd forgotten that Helen didn't play those games. 'She told me that you didn't want to see me. Didn't want me to welcome you home.'

'Yeah, well . . .'

'Danny, please. I've thought of very little else these past four years, wondering whether you were still alive, whether I'd ever see you again. Surely you can give me five minutes.'

'Oh? What was it you said? Ah yes, I recall: "Don't expect me to play that silly game, to think of you as a hero, doing your bit for king and country! The ever-faithful sweetheart, waiting at her candlelit bedroom window for her soldier boy to return. Because I won't be!"' Danny quoted her verbatim, then added, 'What? So you're telling me you *have* been the ever-faithful sweetheart waiting for your soldier boy to come home?' Danny hated himself, he knew he was being a dickhead, but told himself he had to find a way to reject her.

To his surprise he heard Helen giggle on the end of the line. 'Well, whatever they've done to you it doesn't seem to have affected your memory, and you're still an arrogant prick, Danny Dunn.'

'Hmmph,' Danny said, amused despite himself. 'Same old charming Helen. And what does that mean, in particular?'

'It means that I am now in a position to make a comparison and you're still the best fuck I've ever had, but apart from that purely incidental detail, I've never stopped loving you, Danny.'

Danny's heart started to pound. 'Helen, I'm not the same . . . it's not the same. I've changed . . . I'm not me any more.' He hesitated. 'You won't like . . . what I've become.' It was a pathetic thing to say and the moment the words were out he felt ashamed and braced himself for her reply.

Helen's voice at the other end was calm when she spoke. 'You're very probably right, but I think I deserve a cup of tea or, if you like, a drink, at some neutral place, so I – we – can decide what we want to do.'

'Helen, you don't understand – my face . . . I'm a freak.'

'Danny, I've seen your face.'

'What?'

'I watched you walk down the gangplank yesterday. You seem to have forgotten I was in an intelligence unit, a lieutenant colonel by the end of the war. I've even read your medical report from Rangoon and Dr Woon's excellent notes.' Helen paused to allow Danny to absorb what she'd just told him, then added, 'Now, can we please stop all this nonsense?'

CHAPTER FIVE

———

DANNY ARRANGED TO MEET Helen at a cafe across from the university off Parramatta Road late that afternoon after his meeting with the dean of admissions. He'd phoned for an appointment, expecting to see a clerk in the registrar's office, but when he explained that he was a veteran wanting to complete his degree, he was asked to wait, then shortly afterwards granted an appointment with the dean.

Danny wasn't at all sure about his future, about his capacity to rise to the challenges that civilian life would surely present. Now he recalled that final session with Dr Woon before leaving Rangoon, when he had asked, 'So, what plans have you got for the future, Danny?'

While it seemed like a normal enough question, Danny had successfully avoided it. Thinking about what might lie ahead was too daunting for his frail ego, and all he could think of was finding somewhere to hide and lying low. He'd answered in the vernacular so that he sounded more assured than he really felt and didn't seem to be stalling for time. 'Buggered if I know, mate . . . I'll stumble across something.'

Craig Woon was silent, lips pursed, tapping the end of his unopened fountain pen on the desk. It was obvious to Danny that he wasn't going to accept such an answer. 'What about completing your degree?'

'That would please my mother, but otherwise it's pretty meaningless.' Danny shrugged, thinking that once Brenda saw his face she might realise that it was now out of the question for him to be a 'somebody'.

'Danny, you'll be arriving in Australia in November. It will probably be March or April before there's a chance of any surgery on your face – Concord Military Hospital is already overwhelmed with urgent cases – and it will take at least six months for you to heal properly, possibly longer, before you're really fit to face the outside world. Why not complete your degree and think of further study? Law, for instance; you'd make an excellent lawyer . . .'

'As a matter of fact you're not the first to suggest that. Dr Evatt, the judge, is a mate of my mum's and he suggested it once, although it was before this, of course.' Danny pointed to his face, then smiled as an amusing thought occurred to him. 'What happens when the defending lawyer looks more of a villain than his client?'

Craig grinned. 'I imagine it would make the prosecutor extremely happy.'

'But I don't know about law, mate. I'll probably help out at the pub. I pull a bloody good beer, and where I come from that's a very significant achievement. If you know how to give a good head,' he grinned, 'half an inch, no more, with the amber fluid beneath it clear as a toddler's eyes, then nobody will care what the barman looks like.' Craig chuckled as Danny concluded, 'If you forced a choice between the two sorts of head, most of our patrons would choose a beer with a perfect head over the female variety any day.'

Craig laughed. 'You'd be good in a courtroom, but I'm not so sure about the rough and tumble of a pub. You're going to find that some days are difficult for you no matter where you are: dealing with the public won't be easy, dealing with a drunk looking for trouble might be impossible. You may find you're on a very short fuse at times. Perhaps you should think about that.'

After he'd attempted to wash some of the uglies out of his head that morning in the harbour, Danny had promised himself that he would complete his degree, if only for Brenda's sake. But the thought of taking law increasingly preoccupied him. It was a profession constrained by rules and traditions, and it just might prove to be an excellent place to hide. So he'd phoned for an appointment to discuss it with someone at the university who knew nothing about his history.

He was rather nervous as he crossed the quad. This once-familiar hunting ground was now completely alien. Then, he'd seen himself as a young bloke taking a degree he thought he'd never need, bursting to get on with his life and to fight for his country. Now, he felt like an old man who had already had the shit kicked out of him by life.

Arriving on time he was made to wait almost forty minutes. His nervousness was soon replaced by impatience, and he grew decidedly irritable. His back hurt and he was on the verge of leaving when he was finally admitted to the dean's office.

The dean looked up as he entered and gave Danny a thin smile. 'Ah, Mr Dunn. Welcome back. It's always nice to see old faces, particularly when they belong to men who've served their country with distinction.' He spoke somewhat pompously in the home-counties accent affected by many well-educated or simply pretentious Australians. Half Dunn described this particular accent as 'Bob M.' – 'He spoke in a Bob M. accent' – meaning in the somewhat patronising tones of Bob Menzies, known in academic circles as standard or received pronunciation. Despite the November weather, he wore a tweed suit with leather elbow patches, and a white business shirt with detachable starched collar, the gold collar stud peeking out above the knot of what looked like a club or old school tie. His cuffs were fastened with small monogrammed gold cufflinks of the sort that an advertising copywriter might describe as being worn by a gentleman of distinction.

Danny, despite his annoyance at the long wait, smiled at the inappropriate welcome. 'I doubt if three and a half years of slave labour under the Japs can be described as serving one's country with distinction, building a railway to Burma plus two airfields intended to be used to more effectively bomb the Allies,' he said, not adding the mandatory 'sir' to his reply. Somewhere out to sea on the voyage home from Singapore Danny had decided that he would take Dr Woon's advice and never again refer to anyone as if they were superior in position or rank. He'd used up a lifetime supply of kowtow, of being obsequious; from now on, as far as he was concerned, Jack was as good as his master. But having decided to abandon the appellation 'sir', Danny now wondered how to address the man. Was it Dean? Or was it Mr McCarthy? Dean McCarthy? Wayne? The man had a distinctly pernickety air about him and didn't seem like the sort of bloke you'd call Wayne – Charles perhaps, or Samuel, even Cuthbert, but not Wayne, certainly not if you were a student.

The dean half rose and reached across to take Danny's hand, his grip decidedly limp. The glass-topped desk, the only modern furniture in the room apart from the dean's swivel chair, was ostentatiously big and completely free of clutter, apart from a large and spotless blotter, a telephone, a pipe stand containing two pipes, and a nameplate in dark wood bearing the name Wayne McCarthy, carved and picked out in gold paint. It looked like something from an Asian street market. Each of these objects was placed sufficiently far from the others to give them the appearance of isolated islands on a sea of glass.

McCarthy was a man in his mid-fifties, tall and fairly slim, with greying sandy hair, a neatly clipped moustache and eyes so pale that if the sum of their blue had been doubled it wouldn't have matched the intensity of Danny's single almost violet eye. The dean's cherubic complexion clearly seldom saw the sun, despite its rubicund flush, which suggested a better than nodding acquaintance with a scotch bottle.

'Kindly take a seat,' the dean invited, adding, 'The armchair is mine.' He pointed to a traditional brown leather armchair, appropriately scuffed and aged, opposite a matching two-seater couch, either side of a small and well-worn Persian carpet. The wall behind the desk consisted of a floor-to-ceiling glass breakfront bookcase containing green, maroon and black leather tomes, the titles in gold on the spines. Most of them seemed to deal with university by-laws, and though they were indeed books, they would never be read unless a question of protocol or precedent needed to be answered.

Danny seated himself, conscious of the sharply creased newness of his elegant grey flannels and the slightly starchy feel of the smart, mid-blue, open-necked shirt he'd purchased less than an hour before his appointment. He'd left a large Grace Brothers paper bag containing his old clobber, as well as the tie and trilby he'd bought for Lachlan, with an obliging receptionist, a bespectacled lady he judged to be in her fifties, wearing sensible brown shoes, lisle stockings, a tartan skirt and a starched white blouse, whose presence perfectly matched the general ambience of the office of the dean. Danny hungered for these small details of normalcy. The three and a half years in which he and his men had worn only ragged khaki shorts or loincloths and broken army boots had made him an avid observer of the different ways people dressed, no two quite the same, and usually with some small detail that told you more than they realised about themselves. For instance, the receptionist wore a heavy silver skull-and-crossbones ring on the third finger of her left hand. How did one explain that?

His own manner of dress for the interview was not a rebellion against the ubiquitous white business shirt, tie and sports jacket a gentleman student would be expected to wear to a formal appointment, but rather pragmatism: it was pointless buying a sports jacket that in a matter of months would be too small for him. Besides which, when he chose his next suit or sports jacket, he wanted to do so with great care. His army gear, acceptable on almost any occasion, was in the wash, probably boiling away in the newfangled electric copper. Anyway, he didn't want to wear a uniform to his assignation with Helen and, of course, Pineapple Joe's suit probably hadn't yet reached the cutting table.

The dean rose and reached for one of the two briars on the desk, then came to sit in the armchair, his legs crossed at the ankles to reveal sensible grey woollen socks rising from a pair of brown brogues. He produced a tobacco pouch and proceeded to prepare his pipe in silence, finally striking a match and squinting as he drew the flame down through the tobacco, puffing until his head practically disappeared in a cloud of aromatic blue smoke. Danny observed this ritual with a wry smile, reminding himself that he was back in a world where leisurely affectation had its place, where he would have to learn almost from scratch how to live.

'Now let me see, your file shows you left us a little precipitously, one might even say impetuously, when you were mere months from taking your degree.' The dean paused. 'A trifle injudicious, wouldn't you say?'

Danny was no longer a young student wet behind the ears. 'Well, at the time, in my opinion, no. France had collapsed, the Japs looked like linking up with the Germans, our troops were stuck in the Middle East and it looked as if we might very well lose the war.' Danny paused. 'It seemed the right thing to do, wouldn't you say?' he asked pointedly, his look challenging the dean.

The older man's head jerked back in surprise as if he wasn't accustomed to being questioned. Sucking at his pipe to give himself time, he finally withdrew it, cleared his throat and said, 'Quite so,' leaving Danny with the clear impression that he disagreed.

Irritated, Danny said, 'If you want to know if I regret it in retrospect, then take a look at my face. The answer is, obviously, yes, I do. I was young, foolish, impetuous and regarded myself as bulletproof. That's why I've returned, hopefully to take up where I left off.'

Before the war Danny had seldom needed to be assertive; things came easily to him. A big, good-looking bloke, a noted sportsman and local hero, he'd always found that folk wanted to be helpful, to be associated with him. As a prisoner of war, assertiveness was a characteristic you soon learned could get you badly hurt or even killed. Now being assertive felt good.

'Yes, I applaud your decision, Mr Dunn,' puff, squint, puff, exhale, smoky silence. 'With your war experience you'll make an excellent teacher.'

Teacher? Danny was tempted to ask him why. Was it because he'd learned how to be an absolute bastard? 'Oh, but I don't want to teach,' he said instead.

This produced another series of thoughtful puffs, then finally, 'Ah, I see. What then did you have in mind?'

'I hoped to go on and do law.'

'Hmm.' The briar went back into his mouth to buy some more time but, alas, it had gone out. With his prop now missing the dean was forced to reveal prematurely the ace he'd been holding up his sleeve. 'Well, I can't say I entirely approve. One would have liked to have seen you complete your first degree, but if you've successfully completed seven units of your Arts degree you may apply to the law faculty in Phillip Street. Your results were excellent, and I feel sure you would have been invited to do honours or perhaps undertake a masters. A generous Canberra government has decided that ex-servicemen should be given every encouragement. I shall have my secretary prepare a letter informing the law faculty of your eligibility and no doubt you will receive confirmation in the mail of an interview.' As he spoke he patted his pockets busily, and eventually found the one containing the matchbox. Then, as Danny was about to ask him if this meant he had been awarded his Arts degree, he shoved his pipe into his mouth, struck a match and began the lengthy process of lighting his tobacco all over again.

It seemed to Danny deeply ironic that, should he receive his degree in return for going to war, Brenda's grand moment would have come and gone in a puff of pipe smoke. She had always imagined herself seated in the great hall, dressed to the nines, her eyes moist with gratified tears, while he, in cap and gown, received the precious scroll from the hands of no lesser person than the vice chancellor, resplendent in tasselled velvet cap, black gown and gold braid. Now her moment of moments had been reduced to a sharp blast of the postie's whistle and a soft thump in the letterbox. He knew Brenda would insist on hauling down the jeroboam of French champagne from the top shelf of the main bar and, after chilling it in the ice tank under the counter, proceed to conduct a brave, poignant ceremony of her own. In his mind's eye he could see the cork exploding from the champagne bottle and smashing into the ceiling to leave a dent or other mark, a lasting reminder of that day of days when Danny Corrib Dunn became a 'somebody'. Half Dunn, offering a toast, would make a characteristically exaggerated speech and Danny, knowing that his mother needed some kind of ceremony, would do his best not to show his acute embarrassment. The jeroboam contained more champagne than the three of them could drink in a week and, after they'd consumed a glass or two, was destined to go flat or be offered to the men drinking in the pub at the time who, never having tasted French champagne, would no doubt privately declare that it tasted like Frog piss with bubbles.

The pipe was finally alight again, and the air above the dean's head was clouded with smoke rising lazily to the ceiling when Danny finally asked, 'Does that mean I've been granted my bachelor's degree?'

'Oh, no, no, dear boy. You have two choices: you can simply change to law, in which case that will be your degree, or you can complete the missing three units of your bachelor's degree while you are studying law and be granted both degrees when you graduate in four years' time. And did I mention that the government has agreed to pay for your studies? Again, I'm not at all sure that a free education for ex-servicemen is a good idea. I should warn you that the law faculty will be crowded with over eleven hundred first-year students, mostly back from the war. I fear that few of them would have qualified for the privilege under peacetime conditions.'

'Surely you mean few of them could have afforded the fees?' Danny shot back, appalled. 'But they were qualified to sacrifice their lives . . .' He drew back just short of saying *so old pipe-smoking farts like you could sit on your socially superior bums*, but instead concluded, ' . . . for their country.'

The dean took two further pulls at his pipe, withdrew it, exhaled, then looked directly at Danny. 'Well, then, we must agree to disagree,' he said, giving him one of his thin smiles before dismissing him with the words, 'That will be all for today, Mr Dunn.'

Leaving the campus to meet Helen, Danny reflected that he simply couldn't take a trick. He grinned wryly. His mother would have to learn that her moment of glory, when Danny Corrib Dunn became a 'somebody', had been postponed for another four years. Oh, well, at least the champagne would benefit from the delay and she'd have two degrees, two 'somebody' scrolls to frame.

Danny entered the cafe Helen had suggested in a quiet lane just off Parramatta Road expecting he'd have to wait. He was early, but as he entered he saw her seated at a table towards the back, her head down, writing on a small yellow pad. A teapot, sugar bowl and two white cups stood on the pale grey Formica table. He was halfway across to her when he realised that this was the same cafe in which he'd been given a pie with a white feather stuck in it. He'd thrown the pie against the wall and emptied his teacup on the floor before walking out in high dudgeon without paying. He hesitated momentarily, wondering if the evil old bitch was still here.

Then Helen looked up and smiled, a soft easy smile such as he might have expected had they been together a couple of hours previously and not apart for the last four or so years. Danny was forced to respond in kind or appear churlish, and so without opening her mouth she'd settled any tension there might have been between them, although Danny wasn't quite sure whether he should kiss her on the cheek or on the lips. But again Helen had anticipated him. As he reached the table she said, 'Danny Dunn, I shall close my eyes and you will decide where you prefer to kiss me.'

'Good Lord, not here!' Danny quipped. 'We'd be arrested! Besides, my French is pretty rusty.' Both of them were laughing when he kissed her lightly on the lips.

'I'm sure I can arrange for a refresher course,' Helen grinned, then not missing a beat she abandoned the double entendre. 'How'd you go with the dean?'

Danny seated himself across from her. 'Well, it seems I can go straight into Law without completing Arts.'

'Law? Oh, Danny, that's wonderful!' Then as suddenly she did a back flip. 'But poor Brenda. Oh dear, I feel so sorry for her!' Helen exclaimed.

'She called me, absolutely tickled pink that you were going to complete your degree, and now she'll have to wait another four years.' That was the thing about Helen, she cut to the chase. The irony hadn't been lost on her.

'Cuppa tea would go down well,' Danny said, pointing to the teapot. He wondered to himself how many phone calls there had been. 'Is that a fresh pot or shall I get another?'

'No, I've only just ordered it. I took the liberty of ordering you scones. I seem to remember they're very good here.'

'Yeah, beaut. I've hit ten and a half stone; only four stone to go. After living on the smell of an oily rag for three and a half years I seem to be ravenous all the time.'

A young waitress arrived moments later with four scones, a small pot of cream and a dish of strawberry jam. Danny noticed how she avoided looking at him. 'Excuse me, Miss, do you have an old lady, uglier than me, working here? You know, from before the war?'

The waitress forced herself to look at Danny. 'No, sir, nobody like that. Maybe before . . . my parents only bought the business a year ago.'

When the waitress had departed, Helen asked, 'Danny, "uglier than me"? What was that all about?'

Danny grinned. 'I was hoping to settle an old score.' Then he told Helen about the white feather. 'A good thing she's not still here. I probably would have cocked it up.'

Helen reached out and put her hand over his. It was such a simple gesture but it was suddenly more than he could bear and Danny began to tremble. 'Oh, Jesus, I don't think I can do this,' he whispered, looking down into his lap.

Helen lifted her hand from his and grabbed him by the wrist, then pulling his arm towards her she held his hand against her cheek. 'Darling, please give me a chance . . . please,' she begged.

Danny looked up, directly into her blue eyes. She'd once remarked that whomever their children resembled they'd be sure to be blue eyed; now hers were glazed with the tears she was attempting to hold back.

'It's just . . . I mean, it's not just my face, Helen. I've changed. You have to understand, I'm not the same Danny.'

'What, not the same arrogant prick?' Helen choked, and the tears welled and began to run down her face.

'Ferchrissake, look at me, Helen. What you see comes with a crook back as well and a filthy temper I can't seem to control anymore. I bloody near clocked that pompous bastard at the uni.'

'Who – the dean? McCarthy?' Helen asked with a sniff.

'Yeah, the one with the starched collar and cuffs . . . monogrammed gold cufflinks.'

'Danny, Danny, oh no!' Helen cried, shaking her head.

'Why? What's wrong?'

'All four of his sons were killed in the war.'

'Oh shit!'

'His wife was my ancient-history tutor before the war. She had a nervous breakdown, and now I believe she's in Callan Park. The dean, poor old codger, is in denial. He should be on an indefinite sabbatical, but he's refusing, showing the world a stiff upper lip. Esme, his secretary and receptionist, says sometimes he closes his office door and she can hear him crying.'

'Jesus, how do you know all this?'

'Esme is a good friend of my aunt – Mum's older sister. But a month after I was demobbed I enrolled to take my masters and the whole university was in mourning. His oldest son, Martin, was a senior lecturer in chemistry at thirty-one, said to be brilliant and very popular. Like you, a very good sportsman, captain of the university cricket team. He was offered an associate professorship and could have opted to stay out of the war, but he insisted on joining up, together with his three younger brothers. He joined the RAAF, and he and his crewman went missing when their Beaufighter went down over Rabaul early in August. Our forces found their bodies in the wreckage soon after the surrender.'

'Christ, that close to the finish. And the other three?'

'The twins, the middle two, went down with the *Perth* in the Sunda

Strait on the 1st of March 1942, and the youngest was with Maroubra
Force and also died in New Guinea somewhere along the Kokoda
Track – I don't remember the exact date – some time in July or August
1942. The McCarthys lost three sons in the same year. It was too much
for Thelma and, according to Esme, she's not expected to recover. I've
been to see her, but she hasn't the foggiest who I am.'

'And all the time I thought he was a pompous prick. Well . . . so
much for whingeing over a crook back and an ugly mug,' Danny said
ruefully. 'Jesus!'

Helen, fully recovered, said, 'Danny, I think we ought to discuss your
face. It's obviously causing you some distress.'

'What are you saying – that I'm feeling sorry for myself?'

'We haven't been together long enough yet for me to decide,' Helen
replied with a grin. 'But I'll let you know if I think you are. I don't suppose
much can be done in the short term about the trauma, shell shock, or
whatever other names they have for it. I've read everything I can get
my hands on about that sort of thing and I must say it's a controversial
subject and precious little makes sense. Your Dr Woon seems to think
there's a lot more to it than just handing out free prescriptions for
sedatives. He believes that it may be a long-term medical problem. Let's
hope he's wrong.'

'Yeah, bloody doctors! Woony excluded, of course. Give you a pill
and think you're a bludger when you tell them it isn't helping.'

'So that leaves what you've just referred to as your ugly mug and, of
course, your back. What advice have you had about both?'

'Not a great deal. Not much hope, according to an ear, nose and
throat specialist, a fat civilian from Melbourne sent to Rangoon for a
fortnight to play soldiers in his tailor-made uniform . . . He made a crack
about a marble for my eye, and said my nose was permanently buggered
and he didn't think plastic surgery would help. He said I should have the
chipped bone removed when I got back and that he wasn't in the business
of mending cheeks but expected some sort of plate would be needed.'

'Oh, charming. Nothing since? I mean medical advice?'

'Ah, Woony, er, Doc Woon, said as far as my back was concerned my footy days were over and that it had to be "managed".'

'And?'

'Next week I have to have a complete medical at Concord Military Hospital. I guess they'll be a little more specific.'

'Possibly, but don't expect too much.' Helen was silent, then asked, 'Danny, would you mind if I got involved?'

'Hey, wait on! You want to be my nurse? Christ, Helen, you're not backward in coming forward. We haven't even decided whether we're getting back together again and you're already at my bedside feeding me soup.'

'No, darling, *you* haven't decided. I don't have to decide. I've never stopped loving you and I don't give a shit about your face – you were too pretty for your own good anyway – and I feel a lot safer now that it's been squashed a bit.' She giggled wickedly. 'Too bad about your back . . .' Then, with a look of mock horror, she added, 'Tell me, quick, they didn't damage your tongue, did they?'

Danny, despite himself, was forced to laugh. 'Helen Brown, besides being a conniving bitch you also have a very dirty mind. So, tell me, do you think an MA in mouldy old mummy bandages equips you to be a nurse?'

'Don't be such a deadshit, Danny Dunn. I'm sorry if I offended your sensibilities, Sergeant Major.'

'No, go on, tell me, ma'am.' Danny broke a scone open and began to add dollops of cream and strawberry jam to one half.

Helen was suddenly serious. 'Well, one of the advantages of having some rank and also being in intelligence is that you can get hold of anyone, high-ranking Australian officers as well as Americans, with lots of influence. Lieutenant colonel is just about the right rank, or was. Being a woman with rank also helps.'

'And a very pretty woman to boot,' Danny interjected.

Helen ignored the compliment. 'Yes, well, I've talked with Dr Woon – he now sits on the Victorian branch of the Assessment Board for the

Repatriation Commission – and he's already checked out Concord. As he suspected, there's a long waiting list for surgery, as much as a year for plastic surgery. The burn victims are getting priority. He also mentioned that the best facial reconstruction people are in the States. This confirmed what I'd heard in Brisbane.'

'You were stationed in Brisbane? I didn't know that.'

'It was after your last letter, the one where you addressed the front of the envelope "Lieutenant Brown" and on the back you drew – very badly, I might add – your face wearing a slouch hat with your hand at the salute.'

'Ah, good, you got that. I often wondered. It must have gone out on the last boat from Singapore with that excrement, General Bennett, making his escape, sneaking off and leaving his men behind to face the Japs.'

'We worked with the Americans in Brisbane for nearly three years,' Helen explained. 'That's where MacArthur's headquarters were, where we all went to genuflect.' She laughed. 'Or, to use the correct term, to closely cooperate with the Yanks.'

'And doing whatever it was you did in intelligence you met these, what . . . general staff officers?'

'No, that happened mostly at receptions with the Americans, MacArthur's people. My area cooperated closely with their Western Pacific operation. Our navy even had an Intelligence operator in the field with the US marines.' Helen shrugged. 'Staying close to the Americans was important to Canberra, and I guess I had both the looks and the rank.'

'Not too close, I trust?'

'Danny, we've already been there,' Helen reproved him. 'What I'm trying to say is that it wouldn't be too difficult to arrange for you to go to the States for the surgery you need.'

Danny laughed. 'Funny you should say that. Yours is the second offer I've had.'

'Oh?'

Danny proceeded to tell her about Master Sergeant Billy du Bois, lone liberator on a Harley-Davidson, concluding, 'It was a spontaneous and generous offer but I don't suppose he could have pulled it off, although, come to think of it, he managed to get the US air force to do a food and beer drop in less than twelve hours. As an NCO I wouldn't have liked my chances of achieving the same with our air force.'

Danny knew Helen wasn't easily distracted once she'd got her teeth into something. Now, the senior rank she'd so recently held was evident as she brought him briskly back to the subject of his face. 'Does that mean you'd consider going?' she asked.

Danny helped himself to the other half of the scone, busying himself with cream and jam while he thought. 'I don't know. I'll be starting in law next year. Only hope I can knuckle down and do it. My mind's like mashed potatoes.'

Helen laughed. 'It's not your mind you need to worry about. It's being a student again when, like me, you've been accustomed to having all the authority. Kowtowing isn't easy.'

Danny was about to ask how she knew he'd been accustomed to giving the orders to his own men in the camp when he remembered she'd read his records. 'I guess I've had my fair share of knuckling under. At least I won't be beaten or shot for defying these authorities.'

'Oh, Danny, I'm sorry. How insensitive of me,' Helen cried.

'No, not at all. I really have to try and forget all that shit and get on with it.'

'Danny, it's only been three months; give yourself a chance,' Helen said, trying to keep it light. Then, changing the subject she reverted to Danny's surgery. 'I guess you could defer your studies and get your face done . . .' She hesitated, then added, 'We'll need to be away at least six months. I could probably defer as well.'

It was Danny's turn to ignore her last remark. 'It wouldn't be right, jumping the queue like that when there are blokes worse off than me needing surgery. I'd feel bloody guilty, and besides, I want —'

'For God's sake, Daniel Dunn!' Helen exploded. 'Here we go, the

Balmain Boy strikes again! *I don't want to be an officer, my mates will think I'm a wanker . . .'*

Sometimes, Danny thought later, time seems trapped in a vacuum where nothing happens, the seconds tick by unused towards our ultimate demise; then, on other occasions a passing moment is so crammed with stimuli that it sputters and spits, sending out emotional sparks like a shorting electric plug. Danny experienced a host of emotions, crowded together in sounds and pictures, a kaleidoscope of events that tumbled and danced and seemed to go on endlessly from the moment he'd left university to join up, fragments of the past, jumbled together: a flash of Helen's long legs on the swing in her backyard; the sound of the condensed-milk can dropping from Snowy Pitt's slouch hat and hitting the ground at his feet; the *kempeitai* officer's grunt as he drove the butt of the rifle into his face; a brilliant scarlet flash of pain as he did the same to the base of his spine; the sound of the slap as Sergeant Billy du Bois hit the Japanese guard at the prison-camp gate; a snatch of discordant *God Save the King* as they raised Spike Jones's flag; the barking tone of Colonel Mori's words, '*All men now flends!*'; a decapitated Chinese head stuck on a pole at eye level; the dazzling snowy-white sheets in the hospital at Rangoon; a staring, unmoving glass eye; the poignant call of the pipes carried on the wind from the lone piper standing on a rock at South Head. While, through it all, he could hear Helen verbally lambasting him.

'What is it with you?' Helen's voice was rising. 'You're right! Your head *is* full of mashed potato! You'd better make up your mind and stop this puerile bullshit! It's the same stubborn mindset that got you hurt in the first place. If you'd been an officer this probably wouldn't have happened. Mind you, you'd still be an arrogant prick, but not the pathetic creature you seem determined to become!' Helen paused to catch her breath, then, close to tears, added plaintively, 'What's more you've got strawberry jam on your chin.'

Danny felt the urge to rise from his chair and run for his life, then as quickly to explode into incandescent anger, but the ridiculous thought of running away or raging at her with strawberry jam on his chin became too much and, like a little boy, he wiped it away using the back of his hand. Staring down at the smudge of sticky jam he started to laugh and said, 'Game, set and match to Miss Brown.'

'*Phew!* That was close,' Helen said, grinning in an attempt to hide her relief as Danny reached for a paper napkin.

'Okay, smartypants, if you're so good at winning friends and influencing people —'

'It wasn't like that,' Helen interrupted. Still emotionally charged, she went on, 'It was standing in a pair of black court shoes, the high heels an agonising civilian addition to my army uniform, which the CO of our intelligence unit insisted on for these soirees, though I might add didn't pay for. It was endless hours spent listening to colonels and generals in every branch of the army, navy and air force trying to flirt with me or yakking on endlessly and self-importantly about their careers. It was watching them get steadily plastered until their braggadocio hopefully reached a point where they'd reveal a piece of useful information I could put in my report. Listening to their whingeing about the foolishness of Canberra or Washington or one of their senior contemporaries, usually MacArthur or one of his aides. Or on our side that fat buffoon Blamey and his toadies. I was required to bat my baby blues, stick out my chest, swing my derrière and appear to be fascinated while proving capable of the odd intelligent or pertinent question, all in the name of gathering intelligence for and from my own side, sustained only by a glass of soda water with a slice of lemon masquerading as a gin and tonic. My reward at the end of what seemed like an eternity was a handbagful of phone numbers and a dozen or more sloppy kisses on the cheek or a sly pinch on the bum . . . oh, and, of course, the right to request a favour at some later stage.'

'Speaking of favours, I need one. But first, tell me how you found the time for cipher work or whatever you did? You must have been pretty good at it, for them to make you a lieutenant colonel . . .'

'One day I'll tell you exactly what I was doing, but, yes, I'd like to think so. Marg Hamilton, one of my counterparts in naval intelligence in Melbourne, once summed it up perfectly. We'd occasionally be summoned to Sydney or Melbourne for one of those combined forces soirees, usually in Government House and most often with MacArthur in attendance. I remember on one occasion we were both in the powder room. She was a gorgeous-looking girl, and always immaculately groomed. I made some crack about how it was a hard way to earn promotion. Too bloody hard. She'd taken off her high heels and was massaging her toes, but she laughed and quipped, "Behind many a successful man you'll find an exhausted woman. And behind many a successful woman you'll find a successful behind!"' Helen smiled. 'That just about sums up the way the female component of the Australian Intelligence Unit in Brisbane was regarded at the time. During the day they worked you like a navvy, and at night you were required to flaunt your tits and bum without, I should add, ever getting involved in an assignation, unless of course it promised to yield more information. Not exactly romantic. Most of the time I'd get back to my quarters after one of these combined army, navy or air-force shindigs almost too exhausted to wash my undies and hang up my uniform.'

'Well, I guess I asked for all that. Now, back to my original question . . .'

But he'd hit another sensitive spot. 'What – a woman's place is in the cipher room?'

'Christ, Helen, you haven't changed, have you? I said I need a favour, but it's not for me. I need your help to get one of the blokes in the camp, a Welshman named Paul Jones, a citation.' Danny then proceeded to tell Helen the story of Spike Jones and the raising of the Union Jack.

The story Danny told of the little Welsh medic seemed to finally calm Helen down. 'That's a lovely story. I'd love to try and help, although I didn't have a lot to do with the British – not a lot of them about – but I met the British high commissioner at Government House on one or two occasions and he seemed a very approachable chap. I'll see what I can do, but I'm sure he'd like to hear the story directly from you.' Helen grinned. 'Of course, it would be simple to get to General Bennett. Give you the opportunity to tell him what you think of him.'

'Jesus, you watch it, Brown. You're skating on very thin ice,' Danny laughingly threatened. He suddenly realised that he was back with this impossible, witty, intelligent and forthright woman and loving every moment of it. He couldn't wait to make love to her. The miracle was that she seemed to want him back in her life. 'The dean said there would be eleven hundred first-year students enrolled in the law faculty at Sydney University next year. I guess they'd happily allow me to defer for the operation.'

Helen's eyes widened. 'So you'll go to the States?'

'Yup. Your tantrum convinced me.'

'May I come?'

'Sure. But that means you'll have to defer as well.'

'*Tut-tut*, with a masters degree, and eventually a doctorate, I'll probably be around universities for years to come, so six months or more away would be lovely. We'll try for the Mayo Clinic.'

'Why? That the best place?'

'I keep forgetting you've been incommunicado for a few years. You've got a bit of catching up to do. The American Army had a huge General Hospital in Brisbane, over two thousand beds, where they treated their serious medical and surgical casualties from the islands – New Guinea, the Solomons and New Britain. I met a lot of high-ranking surgeons and doctors. They'd have regular hospital dances and throw great parties. They were the only ones I really enjoyed – there are no dark secrets to wheedle out of a doctor, so we could have a glass or two of champagne, forget the war for one night and have some fun. I've already . . . I mean, I *could* easily contact two surgeons I knew, was particularly close to. Both are known to be among the best in their field at reconstructive surgery.'

'How close exactly?' Danny asked, somewhat tongue-in-cheek.

'Oh God, you're a suspicious idiot, Danny Dunn. One of them married one of my lieutenants and the other married a gorgeous Australian nurse, also a friend. I'll write tonight.'

'You mean you haven't already?'

'Yes, but I'll have to confirm possible surgery dates.'

Danny shook his head. 'Jesus, Helen! What if I'd said no?'

'Ah, but you didn't.'

Danny discovered to his surprise that he'd eaten all four scones and that the cream pot and jam dish were empty. He licked his forefinger, then, dabbing at the scone crumbs on his plate, placed them on his tongue.

'Hmm. Is that confirmation that your tongue is in perfect working order?' Helen teased gently.

Danny ignored the dig about his table manners. 'By the way, you haven't by any chance spoken to Brenda about all this, have you?'

'Danny, what kind of a question is that?' Helen cried, taken by surprise.

'A straight one, which deserves a straight answer.'

She gave Danny the full benefit of her baby blues. 'Well, yes . . . now that you mention it, we spoke briefly on the phone this morning. How very perspicacious of you, Danny.'

'Perspicacity be buggered! How bloody *stupid* of me to even bother asking.'

Helen leaned down to pick up her handbag and briefcase, then, rising from her chair, she bent over and kissed him lightly on the forehead. 'Come on, Danny, darling,' she said softly. 'I now have a bedsitter in Glebe Point Road, five minutes' walk from here. Time you resumed your French lessons.' She reached to take his arm.

'Hang on, I haven't paid.' Danny hesitated and gave her a questioning look. 'Unless . . . ?'

Helen grinned. 'No, I haven't. Some things ought to remain sacred.'

Danny spent two full days in the company of Lachlan and the *Sydney Morning Herald* classifieds. They'd put in several hours on the telephone on both days, almost becoming accustomed to rejection, the usual reasons being lack of experience or age. There wasn't any doubt that a bias existed in favour of returned servicemen. They'd finally secured five interviews that seemed promising, all for the following week. Two had requested that a parent or family member accompany the job applicant to the interview, but Lachlan had returned the following day to declare that his mother didn't have the right clothes to wear and his father, now a garbo with the council, had practically passed out at the prospect of having to front up with him, hurriedly claiming that he couldn't leave his job. Furthermore, Doreen, his sister, was expecting her baby any day and the doctor had confined her to the house. 'We'll have to give them two appointments a miss,' Lachlan had concluded.

'Not on your life, mate. One of them is George Patterson, the advertising agency I told you about that needs a despatch boy. I'll call them, tell them your parents can't make it and your sister is expecting any hour, but that I'm a very close friend of the family. I'll ask them if I may deputise. Remember, this is a war zone.'

George Patterson agreed to Danny accompanying Lachlan, but the second company, a prominent city law firm, refused, the very officious man at the other end of the phone demanding to know if the non-attendance of either parent indicated a criminal record. Danny had retaliated by saying, 'Yeah, they're related to Ned Kelly on the mother's side,' upon which the phone had promptly gone dead in his ear.

The following day Danny presented himself at Concord Military Hospital for his compulsory check-up and assessment, an all-day affair he wasn't much looking forward to. But he couldn't be demobbed without undergoing a final medical to determine his 'future prospects', or so he'd been informed.

'What does that mean?' he'd asked at the time. 'All I want to do is get out of the bloody army.'

'We need to check your medical condition and assess what we can do for you,' the clerk at the other end replied smoothly, adding, 'You may need help for years to come, Sergeant Major. Ten hundred hours; be on time.' Danny heard the phone click at the other end and grinned; poor bugger probably had smart-alec remarks like his coming at him all day.

Danny took a taxi to the hospital, arriving just after nine-thirty in the morning for his ten o'clock appointment. The ride in the taxi had made his back ache and he decided a walk might ease it. He could have a decko at the hospital grounds at the same time.

The hospital was laid out along the Parramatta River and buildings had obviously proliferated around the multi-storeyed red-brick main building. Dozens of single-storey buff-painted timber huts were connected by a spider web of covered walkways spreading over acres of lawn that was just starting to brown in the heat. The whole complex was an army builder's dream: infinitely expandable, utterly dull, a dead-set clone of every military base he'd ever seen. Halfway into his wander it occurred to him that finding the correct hut might take up the remainder of his time, and as it happened he came across it with only five minutes to spare.

He made himself known to the desk corporal, who ticked him off on a clipboard. Danny noted that his name was first on the medical assessment list for the day. The corporal pointed to a second room. 'We're an hour behind, Sergeant Major. There's a tea urn in the waiting room.'

'How come, Corporal? I'm first on your list; ten hundred hours is commencement,' Danny said, using the correct army jargon.

The corporal sighed and shrugged. 'Don't blame me. Only following orders.'

Nothing had changed. It was the same old junior-rank disclaimer. Danny poured himself a paper cup of black sugarless tea and prepared for an even longer day.

An hour and a half later he was still waiting and had been joined by three other men, all wearing their army uniforms. The last of the three to enter the room had lost both hands and the bottom half of his chin. Danny noticed as he walked to the centre of the room that he had no gaiter on his right trouser leg, which hung loose over his army boot. He looked around, cackled with laughter, then declared, 'No limbs missing, hey? Tough luck, fellas!'

The two other men in the waiting room remained silent. 'What's the lucky part, mate?' Danny called, thinking that with his own broken mug he could get away with the question.

'Sheilas, mate. Yer don't have to do the work. Lie on yer back and the jig-a-jig is free!' He started to giggle. 'See what I mean? No arm, no puff needed, get me?' Then, jumping in front of Danny, he pushed his chinless mug right up into his face. Danny smelt the soldier's stale breath as he asked again, 'Get me?' Then, not waiting for an answer, he danced over to the next bloke. 'Get me?' he asked again, this time waiting for a nod before repeating the same performance with the last soldier. Holding his handless arms to his stomach he laughed uproariously, then, as suddenly as he'd started, he fell silent, looking around like a frightened animal.

It was all too familiar to Danny. 'You on the Burma Railway?' he asked.

The soldier snapped to attention. 'Speedo!' he yelled in the Japanese manner, answering Danny's question. He then performed a smart about-turn before marching across the room, stumps swinging in the approved manner. At the far corner of the waiting room he barked, 'About-turn!', faced the three of them again and cried, 'Stand at ease!'

'Explosives?' Danny asked, indicating his own hand but keeping his voice and manner casual.

'Boom! All fall down!' the soldier shouted, jumping backwards into the corner where he sank slowly to the floor, then pulled his knees up to his chest with his arms clasped around them and his eyes closed. When he next looked up at the three of them he immediately began to shriek:

> *Blow up his hands,*
> *cut off his chin.*
> *Then throw what's left*
> *in the loony bin!*

Whereupon his head sank onto his chest and he began to sob piteously like a small child.

'Jesus! Poor bastard,' Danny whispered. The two men waiting beside him, eyes downcast, nodded. Danny rose and left the room, walking over to the corporal at reception. He explained the situation briefly and requested a doctor.

'No can do,' the corporal replied airily, not in the least sympathetic. 'He hasn't been assessed yet.' Glancing at his clipboard he declared blandly, 'He's fourth on the list.'

'Look, the poor bastard needs to be sedated. He's going through a bad patch. I've seen it before,' Danny said, angry but holding himself in check.

'They try it on all the time – bludgers. They're after a permanent disability classification,' the corporal said smugly.

'Corporal, the poor bugger has no hands – he already qualifies!' Danny had witnessed two similar accidents with his own men, both due to faulty fuses going off prematurely. Neither man had survived the shock of the operation to remove what was left of his hands. It was all the more reason to help this poor bastard, who'd somehow miraculously survived.

'Oh, is that so? You one of them trick-cyclists or something, then?' the corporal smirked.

'No, mate, a prisoner of war under the Japs, and let me tell you something else, sonny boy. You wouldn't have lasted a month where that poor bugger's been!'

'He'll still have to wait his turn . . . mate,' the corporal said mulishly.

It was the 'mate' that finally did it for Danny. He very nearly grabbed the smug little twerp by the shirtfront and hauled him over the desk. But then, without being conscious of the change, he grew very calm, his will, cold and resolute, replacing his sudden anger. He was back in the camp, back in the combat zone. It was his ability to control himself without cowering or raising his voice that the Japs had learned to respect. His opponent was once again a soldier of inferior rank who nonetheless seemed to have the power to destroy him or one of his men. The fact that the ingrate seated at the desk in front of him wasn't a Japanese or Korean corporal but a recalcitrant Australian one meant nothing to him; he was no less the enemy.

Danny spoke quietly in a measured tone. 'I may be in civvies,

Corporal, but I'm still your superior. You call me mate again, not only will you be on report for insubordination but I won't stop until they tear those two pathetic and ill-considered stripes from your shirt sleeve. You're a disgrace to the uniform I fought in to save your miserable arse.' Keeping his eye on the corporal, Danny pointed at the waiting-room door. 'There's a man in that waiting room not much older than you who has no hands and is dealing with demons not of his own making. He deserves our help – your help.' Danny's voice grew very quiet. 'Now, be a good boy and get on the phone and request a hospital orderly, or a nurse or doctor to attend to him at the double.'

The kid obviously had more balls than commonsense. 'No!' he said, just the single word, his eyes downcast, his jaw set.

'Where's your internal phone list?' Danny barked. The corporal jumped at the sudden change of tone.

'What's going on, Corporal?'

Danny turned to see an officer – a major in the army medical corps, he noticed – almost certainly a doctor.

The corporal leapt to his feet and stood to attention, saluting. 'This man wants to abuse the system, sir,' he shouted.

'At ease, Corporal.' The major flicked his right hand, barely raising it to his shoulder. Turning to Danny he asked, 'Are you a civilian, sir?'

'No, Major,' Danny answered, 'not yet.'

'Then why are you not in uniform?'

'I am trying to adjust to civilian life, Major. Wearing a uniform doesn't help.'

The major nodded. 'Well, you seem to have grasped the fundamentals quite well. No more "sir" or saluting, I see?'

Danny, assessing his man, grinned. 'That was one of the easier bits, Major.'

A small smile played on the officer's lips. 'Now, what seems to be the problem? You need an earlier assessment time, is that it?'

'No, no, I'm first on the list. I was attempting to get a hospital orderly to attend to one of the men in the waiting room, an amputee who probably needs sedation, and your corporal is refusing to cooperate, in fact is being a thorough-going bastard.'

'And you'd be competent to make such an assessment?'

'Yes, in both instances,' Danny replied. 'I was a Japanese prisoner of war for three and a half years. I can tell when a man is undergoing a mental collapse.' He glanced meaningfully at the corporal. 'I can also tell when an NCO isn't up to the task he's been given.'

The major turned his attention to the corporal. 'What's your name, Corporal?'

'Hoskins, sir.'

'Corporal Hoskins, call Emergency and have them send over two orderlies and a gurney, or an ambulance if there's one available, then get the duty nurse to bring in my medical bag from the surgery.' He turned to Danny. 'Come, let me have a look at this man of yours.'

An hour later and two and a half hours after Danny should have begun his assessment it finally got underway, although Danny was happy enough at the delay. The poor bugger with no hands or chin had been helped. And when Danny had to return to the waiting room to await the result of an X-ray, he noted that Corporal Hoskins had been replaced by a pleasant-looking medical corps sergeant. He grinned to himself. The incident in the waiting room would almost certainly be the final influence he would exert as a military man, but it was a fitting and satisfying conclusion. That it should involve someone he would have regarded as one of his own pleased him mightily. When the ambulance orderlies lifted the sedated soldier onto the gurney, his right trouser leg with the missing gaiter rucked up to reveal the unmistakeable purple scars of the tropical ulcers that had once clustered above his ankles.

Late that afternoon when his assessment was all but completed, Danny was ushered by the cheerful and pleasant-looking sergeant receptionist into the surgery of the major who had ordered the ambulance. To Danny's surprise the officer rose from his desk and came from behind it to shake his hand. 'I apologise for this morning, Sergeant Major Dunn,' he said smiling. 'I neglected to introduce myself: Rigby . . . Roger Rigby. How do you do?'

'It's Danny, Major. Thank you for trusting my judgment this morning.'

'Ah, poor devil. I shall see to it that he gets the right care. As to your judgment, I've since read your records and, I must say, you're better qualified than most of us. Remarkable that you and so many of your men survived,' Dr Rigby paused, looking directly at Danny, 'though at some real personal cost, I observe.'

'I guess it's all a matter of opinion, doctor. An ugly mug and bad back come a poor second to no hands and a mangled head.'

'Hmm. You're adjusting well to civilian life, then?'

Danny laughed ruefully. 'I can't say I don't have my moments, occasions when my head is pure mashed potato and I'm a tad less than rational.'

'We're hearing that all the time,' Roger Rigby observed. 'I've read Dr Woon's Rangoon Hospital notes in your medical record and I'm inclined to agree with him. This shell shock, war neurosis, whatever you want to call it, needs a lot more psychiatric investigation. We have half a dozen names for it, yet it remains a stranger to my profession, a medical enigma,' Rigby said. Then, indicating the chair across from his desk, he added, 'Please take a seat and we can go through your assessment.'

Danny seated himself while Major Rigby returned to his desk, reached for several single-page reports and busied himself collating them. Finally he looked up. 'You don't smoke, do you? It must have been a small blessing among a great many disasters. Most of the POWs under the Japanese claim that giving up cigarettes was harder than adapting to a starvation diet of rice.'

'I was a reasonable footballer and played water polo before I enlisted, so happily I never got around to cigarettes,' Danny grinned, recalling, 'although getting used to nothing but rice was bloody awful. One of my men went three weeks without a shit.'

'Glad I wasn't with you for several reasons, one in particular relating to the absence of rubber gloves,' Rigby laughed, then asked, 'Well, shall we begin?' Not waiting for an answer he picked up the first medical report. 'Your Rangoon medical records are pretty comprehensive and we found very little to contradict them. There are two matters we believe we can constructively address: the damage to your back and to your nose. We would concentrate mainly on your sinuses, but we may be able to improve your cheek as well, to relieve the pressure on your teeth on the top left side. We can fit a prosthetic eye, of course, although they never seem to look quite right and most men find them a damned nuisance and end up with an eye patch instead. I'm not surprised you suffer from headaches. How often do they occur, would you say?'

Danny laughed. 'It would be easier to tell you how often they cease, doctor. I guess they're pretty constant, but the intensity varies.'

'Right, that's where we'll start. My guess is that they're caused by your sinuses, which, like your nose, have taken a terrible hiding.' He started to write on a pad. 'Are you taking anything for the pain? Codeine?'

'No, I ran out so I've just been taking aspirin.'

'How many a day?'

Danny thought for a moment. 'Ten . . . no twelve or so – I forgot the two when I go to bed – sometimes a couple more when I wake up at night.'

Doctor Rigby looked up, startled. 'You'll have to stop that. You'll end up drilling a hole in your stomach. We don't want an ulcer to develop. We'll slot you in for an operation to your sinuses as a major priority with the cheekbone next; both are probably contributing to your headaches.'

'My nose, doctor . . . I mean, can they rebuild it?'

'Ah, no easy answer there, I'm afraid. As you can imagine, we have a great deal of facial reconstruction to deal with, so when I say we'll give your sinuses and cheekbone priority, I'm talking three months, perhaps a little more. If we're successful, that should give you a working nose, but that's about it.' He hesitated just a moment longer than might have been necessary. 'There's a limit to how far current practice can take us.'

'What? We don't know how to rebuild noses, or we don't know how to do them here?' Danny asked.

'It's not hard to see why you were good at running a prisoner-of-war camp, Danny. You read between the lines very well. The truth is that we haven't got the time. Our job is to get you into decent working order; the cosmetic side is pretty much irrelevant.'

'You don't consider that such brutal disfigurement could have a psychological effect on a man?'

'The task of second-guessing personality outcomes is not on the agenda of the army medical corps at this stage; it's a luxury we can't allow ourselves. Besides, our brief is to get a patient back into productive civilian life as soon as possible. As I've said, we have a large number of patients with facial injuries still hospitalised, and the backlog of outpatients such as you is enormous. Frankly, there are too few experienced surgeons available to do the work.'

'You mean they're all in private practice?'

'No, most of the good ones work with us already. It's a question of training. Reconstructive surgery isn't a big area of medicine during peacetime, so when a war comes along there are simply insufficient trained surgeons available.'

'So, tell me, doctor, is good plastic surgery even possible? Does someone, somewhere, know how to do it?' Even though Danny had agreed to go to America, he couldn't shake the feeling of guilt about jumping the queue. Paradoxically, he still wanted some sort of permission from this man. It was the old problem of not acting in a superior manner to your neighbours or your mates. You simply didn't take advantage of your more fortunate circumstances or flaunt your own good fortune, even though Brenda and Half Dunn were well off by the standards of the day, and by Balmain standards they were rich.

Billy Scraper, who'd joined the RAAF to fly as crew in a Wellington bomber, had been returning from a bombing raid over Dresden when his plane had been shot down over the English Channel by a German fighter. It had caught fire, and Billy had sustained third-degree burns to his face before ditching. According to Half Dunn, compared to Billy's facial injuries, Danny's practically qualified him for movie-star status. Billy simply lacked a face at all. 'Two little holes blowing snot bubbles, a bigger hole where his lips used to be, and in between just mushy-looking scarred flesh . . . no eyelids, so his eyes are always open, just staring.' Half Dunn had described Billy's face in his usual graphic style.

Danny could still hear Billy's comment as he left the Hero to do his air-crew training in Canada. 'Don't hang around too long . . . you'll miss all the fucking fun.' Hopefully Billy had found that pretty Canadian bird who loved to go to bed in the cold weather but not to sleep alone.

The Balmain code of behaviour, whether you were rich or poor, didn't allow you to buck the egalitarian system. If you had to wait to have your nose fixed, no matter how long it took at Concord, well, that's what you did because that's what your mates would have to do; what Billy Scraper would have to do. His time as a prisoner of war had reinforced these values, because survival had depended on everyone having the same chance, the same number of rice grains. Danny had needed to understand what the situation was at Concord. Now that he knew there wasn't a queue to jump he felt a whole lot better, but he still needed to confirm, despite Helen's optimism, that going to America was worthwhile.

'What about the Americans?' Danny added, trying to sound casual.

'Yes, of course, the Americans are way ahead of us in cosmetic surgery, but the Brits are doing the truly cutting-edge work with burn victims, under a New Zealand plastic surgeon, Archibald McIndoe, though almost exclusively with RAF pilots and crew, I believe.' Rigby paused. 'Now, he is someone who interests himself, controversially, in the psychological aspects as well as the physical aspects of his art. Not my field, I'm afraid.' Rigby seemed disinclined to discuss the subject further and Danny got the feeling that he was a man who told you only what he knew and didn't like to trespass into areas of conjecture. 'Now, the injury to your back is quite another matter. A spinal fusion may be one way to go and we can certainly do a creditable job on it here at Concord.'

'What does that involve, doctor? Fusing sounds pretty drastic!'

'Well, it's simple enough. We take bone from elsewhere, usually your hip, and use it to fuse the vertebrae to protect the spinal cord from further damage. It's basically a hammer and chisel job, the operation takes about nine hours and while the recovery is tedious the results are usually reasonable.'

'Tedious?'

'Well, yes, you'll be completely immobilised in bed with a plaster cast from neck to knee for three months, then it'll be roughly a year before you're fully recovered. Not much you can do in that time and, of course, strenuous exercise or even touching your toes after that isn't going to be possible.'

'You said the results are reasonable. You don't sound over-enthusiastic, doctor. If it's *one* option, then . . .'

'It depends on the degree of pain you're experiencing. If you think you can live with your back, then regular physiotherapy, massage, certain exercises, that sort of thing, might be sufficient. Spinal fusion is a simple but brutal operation and doesn't always achieve the intended results. If it were me I think I'd wait and see, opt for non-surgical intervention until circumstances forced me to consider the alternative.'

Danny was silent for a moment. 'So, basically it's sinuses and cheekbone?'

Roger Rigby placed his pen on the desk and leaned back in his chair. 'I'm afraid so, Danny. In years to come we may have another look at that nose – you never know. In the meantime I'm pretty sure I can get you in for surgery some time in the next three months.'

'How would that affect my discharge from the army, doctor? I really am rather anxious to see the end of it.'

Rigby smiled. 'Yes, that was the distinct impression you gave me a minute or so after we met. I am recommending your immediate discharge. Your injuries were sustained due to your war service. I shall recommend to the Assessment Board a disability pension of fifty per cent. This means that you qualify under the Repatriation Commission's Medical Scheme, which entitles you to free medical and pharmaceutical benefits for the remainder of your life. Of course, nothing is set in concrete; you may appeal any decision the board makes.'

Danny laughed. 'Free benefits and now you've forbidden me to take aspirin!'

At dinner that night Half Dunn wanted all the details of Danny's assessment and was almost pop-eyed with excitement when he repeated the sad little rhyme the soldier with the amputated hands had recited. Danny knew that it was details such as this that formed the true grist for his father's storytelling mill; he also knew that cautioning his father to keep any information to himself was pointless. Details of his own operation would also come out soon enough, and it wasn't a bad way to prepare people for what they'd see when they first met him again.

The following week, returning from the city with young Lachlan, whom he'd accompanied on his initial interview with George Patterson Advertising, Danny arrived home after five o'clock, the busiest time in the pub and known as the six o'clock swill. He slipped around the back, avoiding the drinkers in the beer garden, and went up the stairs to the kitchen to make a cup of tea. Brenda called up, 'I thought I heard you coming in. Someone to see you, dear.' She was amazing. The pub was crammed with late-afternoon drinkers and the noise they made practically raised the roof, yet she'd heard him come in while no doubt serving at the main bar. Danny knew he ought to go down and help but told himself he wasn't quite ready to face the Balmain drinking crowd. Many were regulars who'd known him for years and he felt sure they'd show an almost proprietary interest in him.

Danny told himself he'd done enough for one day – he felt exhausted. He was surprised how much Lachlan's interview had taken out of him. For once he'd been happy to show his mutilated features in public, aware that his presence as a veteran who had copped a fair wallop but who wanted to help a friend's son get started in life would add to the sum of the interview. And so it appeared to have turned out. At the conclusion of the interview the personnel manager had taken them in to see the managing director, a man called John Farnsworth, who had been more than cordial. Afterwards, when the personnel manager saw them to the front door, he'd shaken Lachlan's hand and then drawn Danny aside. 'We'll get back to you in a few days, but it's going to be fine. He's a nice lad, well groomed, and just the kind of young man we like here.'

Now, Danny walked to the head of the stairs. 'Mum, it's been a long day. Who is it?'

'From the Tigers, love. Bullnose Daintree and Sammy Laidlaw.' Bullnose was the reserve-grade coach who used to boast he'd discovered Danny way back in the nippers. More importantly he wouldn't let him play first grade until he was certain his body was mature enough to sustain the impact of crash tackling. Sammy Laidlaw was the club's chief masseur, and never lost an opportunity to remind everyone that he'd done one year's study as a physiotherapist before the Depression came. His healing hands were legendary. Brenda, hearing the reluctance in Danny's voice, added, 'They've been waiting two hours and haven't touched a drop. They'll be pretty disappointed if you don't see them. Bullnose says they want to make you an offer.'

'What, to be a ball boy? Tell 'em I can't bend down far enough to pick up a football.'

'Please, dear. Bullnose has had five glasses of soda water. He's on the verge of collapsing from the shock to his system. Sammy's not far behind.'

Danny sighed. 'Yeah, okay, send them up. Pour them each a schooner on the house – draught for Bullnose and a bottle of Flag Ale for Sammy, if I remember correctly.'

If the two old boys were shocked by Danny's face they didn't show it. 'Jeez, mate, welcome back. Half Dunn reckoned ye'd taken a fair old belting. No point beating about the bush now I seen you, and no disrespect to yer father, but I reckon for once he ain't bullshittin'.'

Sammy took a long and grateful drag at his schooner of Flag Ale then smacked his lips. 'That's real subtle, Bullnose. Give the lad a break, will ya?' He looked at Danny. 'Take no notice, Danny, yiz good as gold compared to Sky Scraper's boy. If he come round a corner on a dark night I'd shit meself.'

Danny started to laugh. 'You two out on a recruiting drive, are you, looking for a one-eyed, broken-nosed forward with a crook back?' he asked.

Both men cackled then Bullnose said, 'Yeah, pity about yer back, Danny. Yer face? Yer a lock, son, nobody's gunna notice the difference. Most of the time yer got yer head up a prop's arse!'

Danny was once again brought to laughter, which continued when Sammy added, 'Bloody hell, talk about one-eyed, that bastard ref last week against the Parramatta Eels – what was his name?'

'Alan . . . Alan Philips,' Bullnose supplied.

'Yeah, him. We was playin' against an extra man and a one-way whistle. Bastard musta been on weekend leave from Long Bay!'

Danny realised that, while his entire world had changed – in fact, *the* entire world had changed – very little had changed for these two. 'So, what brings you here? I'm afraid my football days are over, fellas.'

Bullnose had almost finished his schooner and now did so, upending it and throwing his craggy head back, draining the remainder in one long swallow. 'Ah, bloody marvellous,' he declared, then looked directly at Danny. 'Yeah, well, Half Dunn told us you'd copped a heap of shit from them Jap bastards and wasn't no good for football and all that. So one thing led to another and Sammy and I got to talkin' and, well, yer know how it is – once a Tiger always a Tiger.' He held up a meaty hand. 'Understand, it ain't because we feel sorry for yiz – it's bloody tough luck what happened – and, mate, naturally we can't do nothin' about yer face, but Sammy here, you know from before, he's got fuckin' magic hands. Half Dunn says the quack at the hospital said maybe a spinal fusion but —'

'That's ratshit advice, Danny!' Sammy, realising Bullnose was making a meal of it, cut in. 'You don't want to listen to them doctors. Three of our past players got it done. They been rooted ever since. Mate, I should know, I bin workin' on the poor buggers. They reckon it was the worst thing they ever done and I agree. Lemme try massage and exercise, hey?'

'Yeah, mate,' Bullnose added. 'Don't let them butchers near you, son. Best thing you can do is build them muscles so they support yer spine. Sammy's gunna do the deed best he can and they don't get no better, but he reckons we gotta get yer in the swimmin' pool.'

'Can't be too hard. Yer practically lived down there with the fuckin' water-polo mob,' Sammy said, then added, 'Half Dunn says you ain't been near the baths since you come back.'

Danny grinned. Obviously there had been no improvement in the relationship between the football old-timers and the water-polo mob. He made a mental note to tell Half Dunn to keep his over-energetic mouth shut. 'Another beer?' he asked, stalling for time. He pointed to the kitchen fridge then looked at Bullnose. 'Plenty of bottles in there, but if you want a draught, I'll have to go fetch it downstairs.' Then, realising what he'd said, added quickly, 'Not a good idea. You know what a shit fight it is in the bar at this time of the day.'

'Nah, bottle's fine,' Bullnose said, noting that Sammy had also finished his schooner but was pouring another half a glass from the Flag Ale bottle. 'Long as it isn't that piss Sammy drinks.'

Danny removed the cap from a Toohey's Pilsener bottle and placed it on the kitchen table beside Bullnose, suddenly aware of an uneaten ham sandwich and cold cup of tea at his elbow. 'There you go, mate.'

Bullnose immediately busied himself nursing his beer into the used glass to avoid too large a head. 'So, whatcha think, mate?' he asked, eyes fixed on the rising level of beer.

Danny had to concede to himself that their tremendously generous offer made a lot of sense. But he didn't want anyone to see the scarred and broken body that went with the freak face. The very thought of all those furtive eyes stealing a secret look or the pitying expressions on their faces as they caught sight of his own mangled face filled him with apprehension. He wasn't naturally vain, but he'd once had a beautiful body and he couldn't help being aware of the looks women had given him when he climbed from the pool. Helen, watching him get out of the Balmain Baths on one occasion, had observed, 'If eyes could turn thoughts into pictures, Danny Dunn, then the ones you trigger in women would be banned as pornographic.'

'Maybe when I've put on a bit more weight, hey?' Danny replied.

Bullnose, having achieved the perfect head on his schooner, now looked directly at him. 'Son, your trouble is that you're feeling sorry for yerself. Yeah, you were the best. Forwards or backs, I mean it, it was a lay-down misère you'd'a played for Australia, maybe one day even captained the Tigers. But you fought for Australia instead, son. You kept us safe. In my book that's the greater achievement. You honoured us all. You got injured on the field and so it's now our job, Sammy and me, to get yer back on yer feet. The real reason yer haven't got back in the pool is yer afraid of what the sheilas'll think, feeling sorry for you and all that shit. Me daughter once told me yiz was sex on a stick, and now yer a broken fuckin' stick. Well, Sammy and me, we reckon we can mend you. Not all, but some.'

Danny looked up at Bullnose and said nothing.

CHAPTER SIX

SAMMY'S YEARS MASSAGING INJURED footballers meant that there wasn't much he didn't know about damaged backs and the muscles and tendons that can, with careful work, be built up to support the spine. But he was accustomed to strong, firm young bodies at the peak of health and fitness and not the wasted wreck he now found under his hands. 'Jeez, Danny, we've got a fair bit of work to do. Bloody wonder yer can still walk. Them bastards really give you a proper workin' over, matey.'

Bullnose Daintree, always present if only for the chat, growled. 'Bloody mongrels. I see one o' them chinks in the street, I'm gunna headbutt the bastard all the way back'ta fuckin' where he come from!'

'Japanese, mate, they're not Chinese; different race,' Danny observed with a grin.

'Yeah? Yer could'a fooled me. They got slant eyes, ain't they? Bandy legs? Bastards can't see in the fuckin' dark.'

'You've seen too many propaganda posters, Bullnose,' Danny chuckled. 'Although, come to think of it, the Japanese officer who did this to me was short, with bandy legs and thick glasses.'

'Yeah, chinks, Japs, they all look the same,' Sammy said, in defence of his mate. 'Swimmin', Danny, like I said before. It'll help fix ya. Me hands can only do so much.'

'I know, Sammy, and I'm grateful. Thank you.'

'Nah, ain't nothin'. You done your bit. It's the least a man can do.'

'Oath,' Bullnose added. 'Sammy's got magic in them hands. Yer gunna be bran' new, Danny.'

The long road to recovery had begun and it wasn't all pain. Helen worked her own magic in the little bedsitter in Glebe Point Road. Danny, despite the dark moods that sometimes overtook him when he knew he had to be on his own, was happier than he had thought possible, but the unrecognised heroism of the little medic, Spike Jones, weighed on his conscience. It was unfinished business, and so he called on Helen, the lieutenant colonel with the contacts, for help.

Helen, in turn, called on one of her fellow wartime colonels, now in the permanent army but then on the general staff, who in turn referred her to Colonel Napier, the senior staff officer in the Australian army in charge of protocol in Canberra, who advised that he wanted a written submission before deciding whether he would grant Mr Dunn an interview.

Danny's detailed submission had concluded with the story of the hoisting of the Union Jack that Spike Jones had kept, at the risk of his life, for three years, and both Danny and Helen had every confidence they would be granted an interview. But no such thing happened.

'Listen to this,' Danny fumed, waving the letter he'd received that morning. '"*Military procedure requires that an officer must have personally witnessed the behaviour in question. Without such confirmation, no matter how commendable the action, the application for recognition at any level must, unfortunately, be rejected.*" Jesus Christ!'

'Oh, Danny, how unfair!' Helen cried.

'The bastards *know* the prison camps were commanded by the senior NCO, that the Japanese separated the men from the officers.' Danny's dismay, not to say disgust, was palpable.

Helen embraced him. 'Oh, Danny, I'm so sorry.'

Danny felt a black rage rising inside him. '"Commendable!" No matter how fucking *commendable*!' he roared. Pulling away from her embrace he tore the letter into pieces and stamped on them like a small child. 'They send us into the jaws of hell, and yet the word of an ordinary serviceman can't be trusted, and their deeds, no matter how —' he practically gagged on the word, '*commendable*, are of no worth unless they are pronounced upon by some toff wearing a Sam Browne! One rule for officers and another for their men!' He flung himself into a chair and winced as his spine jarred against the back.

Helen watched as he struggled to regain his composure. She knew better than to try to comfort him when he was in a rage, but it tore at her heart to see him so distressed about one of his men. Danny, she realised, was a good man, loyal to a fault when it came to his friends, but he was developing, or had already developed, a chip on his shoulder when it came to conventional authority figures. She wondered what their future together might bring. The one thing that was quite clear in her mind was that she loved him and, whatever happened, she wasn't going to give up on him. But she wasn't at all sure that Danny felt the same way. She was sure he loved her, but she was beginning to realise that it wasn't just his mutilated face that troubled him. He feared that the demons within might prove beyond his control, which therefore made him very wary of a permanent attachment. She knew it wasn't her; he liked being with her, even felt safe with her, and their love-life was nothing short of wonderful, although sometimes he simply couldn't respond. They both knew it was himself he was going to have to contend with in the future and he feared he might not manage with a partner in tow.

Helen, as usual, had her own practical take on the matter, but Danny was reluctant to discuss anything permanent. 'Darling, we were warned that there's a strong likelihood I could be permanently sterile. Those three years of starvation in the camps may have destroyed any chance I had of fathering children. Please think about it. You may never be a mother if you marry me.'

Helen would have none of it. 'Darling Danny, I love you and hope that I always will, but if our love isn't strong enough for me to remain happily childless or for us to adopt a couple of kids, then I shall simply divorce you. In the meantime, let's get on with having you fixed up. Besides, I've already done my homework and I've heard of two returned prisoners of war with a similar background to your own whose wives are pregnant.'

Helen had insisted that Danny couldn't possibly go to America for plastic surgery without her to care for him, and, like it or not, they would have to marry; it would be almost unthinkable for an unmarried couple to travel successfully as partners in America. And that was that.

If Helen was determined to marry Danny, she was less concerned about the type of wedding she would have, to the distress and fury of her mother. Barbara Brown was determined to have a big slap-up wedding at St Andrew's Cathedral in Town Hall Square, where she and Reg had dutifully worshipped all their married lives as insurance for just such an event. The reception afterwards would be at the Australian Golf Club in Rose Bay, where Reg had recently been admitted as a member after the mandatory ten years of reapplying annually while waiting for a vacancy. But Helen was proving maddeningly stubborn. 'Mum, two days after the wedding Danny and I are leaving for America, where he will be undergoing months of plastic surgery. Save the wedding money and give it to us as a wedding present – we can use it for a deposit on a flat when we return.' She'd looked pleadingly at her mother. 'When we get back, Danny will be a law student and I'll be applying for a tutorship; we'll be broke and we'll need all the help we can get. We're not sure how long we'll be living in America but all we've got to live on is three and a half years of army back pay, which Danny is entitled to as a prisoner of war. It's not much, Mum.'

'Can't you think of someone other than yourself for a change?' Barbara replied angrily. 'Your father was looking forward to inviting all our friends to the golf club for the reception – people from Rotary and the Pharmacy Guild, some of his major suppliers, your school friends from PLC, of course. You know we don't entertain a great deal and this is our chance to say thank you. There are several important people he's met at his new club, too. It's simply not fair. The least you could do is consider the family. I know my sister, your Aunty Agatha, would love to come up from Adelaide. With your Uncle Jim recently passed away, it would give her something to really look forward to and make her feel part of our family. I don't know how I can possibly face Bishop Johns now; he has already agreed to officiate at your wedding.'

'Mum, I haven't been inside St Andrew's since my confirmation!' Helen protested.

'Oh, that doesn't matter. We're Anglican, for heaven's sake. Your father and I have more than made up for you. Can't you, for once in your life, consider *our* feelings? These things are important, and the people of Birchgrove expect nothing less from someone with our standing in the community.'

'Mum, the people of Birchgrove couldn't give a hoot about where I'm married. Dad's their local chemist – he gives them stuff to take when they've got a cold, that's all.'

'Well! That puts us firmly in our place, doesn't it!' Barbara snorted. 'Your father works very hard for this community, I'll have you know. He's been invited to put his name up for possible nomination for the National Council of the Pharmacy Guild. It's a chance he can't afford to miss. The wedding, and then the reception at the golf club, would be a major social event. It would be in the Sunday newspapers. It's a single stroke of luck in this whole unfortunate business and it could make all the difference to his nomination. Can't you see, Helen. It's a once-in-a-lifetime opportunity, even if it does cost an arm and a leg.'

Helen let her mother's obvious disapproval of her choice of partner pass unremarked, knowing that any comment would only lead to a row. She seldom thought about her looks, but in truth she was a stunner, and knew it. In her mind's eye she saw herself, the radiant bride in flowing white wedding gown, with Danny at her side, his poor broken face grimacing in a valiant smile. The story had all the essential ingredients – beautiful, intelligent bride with her master's degree, and war hero with the ruined face. It would mean that not only the social editors but also the regular journalists would have a field day. Helen winced as she imagined the distress it would cause her friend and future mother-in-law when Brenda opened her beloved *Women's Weekly*.

'Mum, if you want us to make it into the social pages, then we can go to something at Dad's club when we get back from America,' Helen suggested, 'that is, if Danny is allowed in . . .'

'And what's that supposed to mean?' Barbara asked tartly.

'I once made enquiries to the Australian Golf Club for an American colonel on MacArthur's staff who wanted to play golf and who was to be stationed in Sydney for a period of duty. I was told that he could be made a visiting member, providing that he wasn't a Jew or a Catholic.'

'Well, of course that doesn't apply to wedding guests at a reception,' Barbara snorted.

'Mum! I'm marrying into a Catholic family! Would you feel comfortable at a club that banned Protestants?'

'I wish this unfortunate business with that boy had *never* occurred! It's . . . it's *impossible!*' Barbara cried out. 'Why don't you *listen* . . . can't you see what's going to happen? That *face*! That *terrible* face! Yes, they're Catholics and, if you ask me, bog Irish! The mother runs a public house, for goodness sake! Why couldn't you find a decent, clean-living boy we could be proud of?' Barbara Brown, frustrated, was beyond watching her words and was close to tears.

This was the second time her mother had referred to the 'unfortunate business' of her choice of life partner and it wasn't in Helen's nature to let it pass twice. But she didn't raise her voice when she spoke; rather, she said, as if to herself, 'Danny's "terrible" face was once handsome, Mum. When I first saw him walking towards me on the campus of Sydney University I thought he was the most beautiful creature, male or female, I had ever seen. Before he'd opened his mouth I was head over heels in love with him.'

Barbara tossed her head and gave a disgusted cluck, but Helen went on. 'Then, standing concealed among the cheering hysterical crowd on the dock at Circular Quay, I watched silently as a tall, stooped, emaciated young man with a missing eye and a mutilated face walked slowly down the gangplank and I knew that I loved him even more.' Helen looked at her mother. 'As for decent and clean living, it's young men like him who were prepared to sacrifice their lives for complacent old women like you, Mother. Never forget that and please don't ever attempt to separate us! When I look at Danny, all I ever see is the boy who walked towards me that first day on campus.' Helen paused and looked coldly at her mother. 'With your prevailing sentiments I would rather die than put Danny through the kind of pretentious and ostentatious wedding you have in mind. Understand quite clearly, the answer is no, Mother. *No!*'

Helen had always hoped that her mother would have understood that the kind of social wedding she so desired was out of the question. There was simply no possibility of it happening with Danny in his present situation. But, ever since she could remember, whenever Helen had had a firm or committed opinion on any subject, it had clashed with that of her mother.

Besides, there simply wouldn't have been time to organise a big reception before they left for the States. They were booked to sail two days after the wedding and Helen was going to need all that time, a matter of six weeks, to make the arrangements, even with her formidable organisational skills. She had begun with a letter to her former assistant in intelligence, Jennifer Coombs, now married and living in St Louis with her surgeon husband, Dr John Glicks.

Jennifer had been an enormous help and instrumental in their choice of St Louis and the Barnes Hospital. John Glicks had initially been transferred from Brisbane to Valley Forge General Military Hospital in Pennsylvania because of his success with bad facial wounds sustained by American and Australian troops in the Pacific War. During his medical training, plastic surgery, as it became known, wasn't recognised as a part of the American Board of Medical Specialities, and was considered simply a part of normal surgery. In 1941, when John was already a military surgeon, it had finally received recognition. Not an area in which most military surgeons felt comfortable, it was nevertheless one to which he felt intensely drawn, and as a result, he'd been given most of the cases coming into Brisbane from the islands. His reputation had reached the States, where there was an enormous need for competent plastic surgeons to treat troops returning from Europe and the Pacific, and he'd been drafted to Valley Forge.

Jennifer had written to say that, despite her husband's considerable military reputation and senior surgeon status in the army, he'd wanted to learn more and that, in civilian life, this meant working under John Barratt and Vilray P. Blair, known to be among the best plastic surgeons in America. He had accepted a post as a surgeon at the Barnes Hospital, where they both practised as senior plastic surgeons. She had, after consulting with her husband, suggested that Danny come to St Louis, where John Glicks could be his personal surgeon under the supervision of the great Vilray P. Blair, adding that all Danny and Helen would be required to pay would be the hospital costs – her husband would waive his surgeon's fee. Helen winced when she heard what these additional costs might be. They were considerably more than Danny's army back pay, which they had hoped would stretch to cover their living expenses over the six months they'd be away. Her plans were almost in tatters before she'd begun.

But Helen wasn't easily daunted, and when it came to someone or something she cared about, pulling strings she might not strictly speaking be entitled to pull was the least of it. Helen with a cause was a formidable opponent. She called the American embassy, using her obsolete army rank, and asked them to help locate Doctor John P. Mulhall Jnr, another senior army surgeon she'd known in Brisbane. They replied that he was still in the army and based at the Walter Reed Army Medical Centre in Washington, DC. She had written to him, including copies of Danny's medical history, to see if she could get him admitted to a military hospital as a gesture to the Australians who had fought alongside the Americans in the Pacific. The Americans were known to be generous, but even so it was drawing a long bow. Danny wasn't happy when he heard the lengths to which Helen was prepared to go for help.

'Helen, don't do it. Using your former rank could get you into a lot of trouble. Besides, we don't have to beg. I'll go to uni instead and one day we'll be able to afford it.'

A couple of weeks later Dr Mulhall wrote to say it could be arranged but that the waiting list for surgery of the type Danny would need to undergo was two and a half years at the very least. For now at least, that seemed to put the kibosh on the whole idea.

Next, Danny, at Helen's urging, had turned to Dr Craig Woon and Colonel Rigby, the doctor at Concord Repat. They'd hastily arranged for Danny to go in front of the Disability Allowance Board, which had allocated a disability allowance that covered some of the costs, although it was obvious they were still miles short. But Helen had remained cheerful. 'At least we've got enough to live in the States now. It's comparatively cheap apparently,' she volunteered.

'Yeah, great, but how do we get there in the first place?' Danny asked. 'Helen, you always wanted to do your doctorate after your masters. That's something tangible we can do with this money, and if you get a tutorship in combination it will just about pay for our living expenses while I'm at university. My face may not be very pretty but I don't think my brain has been damaged.'

'That remains to be seen,' Helen said with a smile. 'But, Danny, that's way, way into the future. Firstly, I have to apply for the right to prepare a dissertation for my doctorate. Then, I'll have to go on at least one dig with a British archaeology team to Egypt or Mesopotamia, and then, as you know, I can't do a doctorate in ancient history in Australia, so I'll have to apply to the University College, London, to do my dissertation. Then, of course, it has to be marked and accepted. It could take years. Thanks for thinking of me, darling, but for the moment I'm concentrating on getting us to America.'

Danny could see why Helen had risen to such a senior rank in army intelligence. She was like a dog with a bone and simply never gave up. He'd tried unsuccessfully to dissuade her from the American idea but now he had to level with her; this time he feared she'd met an insurmountable obstacle. 'Well, get that brilliant brain of yours around this: Ben Chifley is restricting overseas payments to prop up British sterling; we're only allowed to take two hundred pounds' worth of foreign currency with us. Even if we had all the money we needed, that's not enough to live on *and* get my mug done.'

'Half Dunn's working on that.'

'Half Dunn?'

'And Brenda.'

'What, through Doc Evatt?'

'No, of course not! We're going over to the Hero for dinner tonight.'

'Helen, what's going on? Have you been talking to Brenda about money?'

Helen looked at Danny, her big blue eyes innocent. 'No, Danny Dunn, *she* has been talking to me.'

'Jesus, I'm embarrassed —'

'Well, don't be. As you say, it can't be more than two hundred pounds anyway, and she's going to insist and I'm going to accept. If you're going to be stubborn about it and we're going to have all that Balmain boy bullshit, then we'll sign an IOU.'

'How's it going to help if we're still miles short?'

'Don't be so bloody negative, Danny. If this operation were for me you'd be asking Brenda to mortgage the pub.'

'Yeah, sure, but it's for *my* ugly mug and I'm learning to live with it quite nicely, thank you.'

'Bullshit. Then why do you cry in your sleep?' Helen asked, deliberately cruel. 'It's affecting your entire life. Besides, if there is something that can be done, then it ought to be done,' she said firmly, refusing to back down.

'Okay, I apologise. Christ knows what the boat tickets will cost, and then we'll need another – what was your estimate of the hospital costs in St Louis?'

'About six hundred pounds.'

'Jesus, that's two and a half grand in American dollars!'

'Two thousand four hundred to be precise, and that's only an estimate,' Helen answered. 'But the fact that John Glicks is doing you pro bono has saved us around three hundred pounds. Isn't that nice, darling,' she added in a soothing voice.

'That's fucking ridiculous! Let's say three grand American all up. That is, if we could take it out of the country in the first place. We could buy a new motorcar for far less than that and it would buy us a house, *if* we had it in the first place! Let's get real for a change, sweetheart!'

Helen laughed. 'We don't need a motorcar and when we get back we can rent a flat a short tram ride from uni. And, as you say, there's still the boat tickets, that is, if we can even find a boat that isn't fully booked and has a cheap cabin in steerage.'

'Which is very bloody unlikely,' Danny cried.

Helen had heard enough. 'Danny, in a few weeks we're going to be married. In my mind I'm marrying a man who never gave up, who ran a concentration camp and kept his men alive against all the odds. Your papers show that a near-record number of your men survived, despite enduring the most terrible conditions of any camp on the Burma Railway. That takes a lot of character, hope, tenacity and guts . . . but it also takes imagination and leadership of a very high order.' Helen slapped him hard on the arm. 'Now *wake up* to yourself! If you can save your own life and the lives of your men, you can do this! If you think we can't and you're going to give up and creep into a corner and hide your face and spend your life feeling sorry for yourself, then tell me now so I can walk away! I'm far too good a woman to want to marry a coward or anyone who's sorry for the cards life has dealt him!'

'But . . . but it's only for my face . . . it's always going to be ugly,' Danny protested.

'Oh, shut up! You make me sick! Now get this straight. You're about to marry a beautiful woman and, it's true, right now you're an ugly bastard. But I think we may be able to do something about that. At least make you a slightly less ugly bastard. If I'm going to have to wake up to you in the same bed for the next thirty or more years, I want you to be the best-looking ugly bastard it is possible for you to be!' Helen suddenly burst into tears. 'Now get your jacket. We're going to your parents' for dinner,' she sobbed.

Danny may have had very little time for most officers, but he was going to have to change his mind about at least one of them. He drew Helen towards him and kissed her on the forehead. '*Shhh!* Lieutenant colonels are not supposed to cry,' he chided softly.

'Go to hell, you bastard!' Helen sniffed, pulling away from him.

Brenda had made a nice dinner and they'd talked mostly about the wedding, with no mention of the American trip, but afterwards, over a cup of tea, she'd turned to Half Dunn and said, 'Well, go on then, Mick.' She was obviously pleased about something.

Half Dunn, a sly grin on his face, rose with what for him was alacrity. He was no longer enormous – portly but mobile would be a more accurate description of him now – and sometimes showed surprising energy. He left the kitchen and went down the hall into Brenda's bedroom. Danny would later realise he'd gone to the safe set into the wall above her bed. When he returned he was carrying what looked like a red morocco leather folder somewhat resembling a large wallet. He slapped it down on the table in front of Danny and said, 'Go on, son, open it.'

'What's this?' Danny looked in turn at each of his parents.

'Go on, Danny, open it!' Brenda said excitedly. 'It's sort of a wedding present, for when you go to America.'

'Shit!' Danny gasped as he opened the wallet, not quite believing his own eyes. The large wallet contained a wad of banknotes three inches thick – not pound notes but American dollars. He fanned them out, noting they were mostly tens and twenties but that there were also hundreds – a lot of everything.

'Mum! Dad! What's going on?' He looked at Helen. 'Did you know about this?'

Helen looked at him wide-eyed. 'What, darling?'

'This . . . money.'

He pushed the wallet over to Helen, who opened it. 'Goodness, no!' She looked at Brenda, obviously completely surprised. 'I thought it was the two hundred pounds we talked about and the money Daddy gave me converted to dollars. This is more, much more!'

'Oh well, Mick and I got to talking. We were going to give you a new motorcar for a wedding present. But then when you and I were having a cup of tea last week and you mentioned, you know, how Mr Chifley says you are only allowed to take out two hundred pounds in foreign currency, blah, blah, blah . . .' Brenda explained. She looked up at Half Dunn for him to continue.

'Well, you don't sit on your arse on the same stool in the main bar for eighteen years without knowing a thing or two about . . . well, a thing or two,' Half Dunn began.

'Now don't you go into one of your long stories, Mick, or we'll be here all night,' Brenda scolded, but with a smile that meant he had permission to wax on a bit.

'Well, two things,' Half Dunn continued. 'Jim Black, who works for the customs at Circular Quay, and Tater Murphy.'

'Tater? You mean Sean Murphy, the sly-grog merchant's son?' Danny asked.

'The same,' Half Dunn agreed.

Brenda jumped in again. 'It just goes to show that in the end thieves never prosper!'

Half Dunn laughed. 'Stupid ones, anyway.'

'Didn't Tater Murphy join the Sixth Division, and get sent to Cairo?' Danny asked.

'That's him. He got shot in the leg in Bardia – there's some say it was probably self-inflicted – but either way they sent him home with a crook knee, a bit of a limp and a fair old thirst he must have picked up in the desert. They discharged him early and he went into the old man's business up at Kings Cross and in the brothels in Crown Street, selling grog to the nightclubs, strip joints, whorehouses – excuse the term – as well as to the Yanks during the war. His old man, Sean, once tried to put the hard word on us to supply him but we told him to go to buggery, even though there was a fair quid in it. It didn't stop him dropping in for a drink and a bit of a whinge every once in a while. Still occasionally does.'

Brenda poured Half Dunn a fresh cup of tea. 'Get on with it, love,' she said, though not unkindly. She and Half Dunn seemed to have long since sorted out their differences. Danny had returned from the war to find them seemingly content in each other's company, with Half Dunn now very much more than a bloated barfly, though Brenda still made most of the decisions.

'Anyway, father and son expanded their grog business and started taking Yank dollars direct in payment, then by various ways and means using them to buy stuff at the Yank PX stores – you know, nylons, Scotch, chocolates; if you had the money, you could order what you wanted and they'd have it for you the next day. I mean, even prime American steaks, big as your two hands and yay thick,' he said, indicating a good two inches with his thumb and forefinger.

'Well, when the Japs surrendered in a hurry after Nagasaki they were caught, pardon my French, with a shit-load of American dollars. So, Sean figures the war's over, everything's okay again, and he trots off to the bank to see the manager. Lucky for him it's Harry Farmer and he and Harry went to the local school together. Harry tells him he's in all sorts of strife, that Sean'll be up for profiteering and working the black market and he advises him to forget that he ever came into the bank in the first place, and to get the hell out of his office and take what's in his so-called legitimate bank account with him.'

Brenda grinned. 'They've been stuck ever since with this funny green money they can't change at the bank and the local black market doesn't want it except for practically nothing. Then, Helen had an idea for the boat and then we had one as well to turn the motorcar into dollars.'

Danny looked mystified. 'What idea for the boat . . . what boat? I don't know anything about a boat.'

Helen grinned. 'In the end it was simply supply and demand. Three of my American wartime contacts are still in Australia. One of them, a senior colonel who must remain nameless for reasons that will soon be obvious, is responsible for getting Australian war brides to their American husbands. The army has contracted a pre-war Matson Line luxury cruise liner, the SS *Lurline*, and converted it to war trim – that is, basic steerage – to transport over seven hundred war brides to the States. But several first-class cabins have been permanently reserved for returning officers who, for various reasons, remained in Australia after the Japanese surrender.' Helen paused. 'Well, Brenda told me about the cheap dollars available when I first mentioned the American trip and the hospital money we were going to need. So, I called my American contact and suggested that perhaps some of the officers returning to the States had surplus Australian pounds, and that instead of an official conversion rate of four US dollars to the pound, I could offer six in exchange for one of the first-class cabins on the *Lurline*. The offer was pretty good – they'd been paid in American dollars, converted them officially in any bank for Australian pounds, then sold me the pounds for a fifty per cent profit in returned American dollars, and a first-class cabin.'

'And he, this officer, bought the deal?' Danny asked, somewhat surprised.

Helen shrugged, suddenly giggling. 'He wanted to know if we'd like the stateroom.'

'But, isn't all this a bit shady? I mean, on our part?'

'You mean mine, don't you?' Helen didn't wait for a reply. 'I daresay it could be seen as money laundering by some overzealous bureaucrat, but sometimes you have to bend the rules a little. I learned that in intelligence . . .' She laughed. 'Nice girls come last.'

Danny was beginning to understand that one man was no match for two good women but he felt compelled to show some resistance. He shook his head slowly, a wry grin on his twisted face. 'A man should say no . . . Just another example of *who* you know, officer bloody privilege, let the rank and file sweat down in steerage while the officers swan around in first class.' Danny paused and with just the semblance of a grin said, 'I want you to know that I've given it thirty seconds of serious thought and decided on this occasion to forego my principles and not object.'

This brought a cheer, and Helen, not to be outdone, cocked her head and said with a wide smile, 'Well, I am so glad you've managed to overcome your proletarian prejudices on this occasion, Danny Dunn, after such lengthy deliberation. Being always mindful of your sensibilities – otherwise known as the bloody great chip on your shoulder – I have had you listed on the manifest as my batman. The cabin has been allotted to Lieutenant Colonel H. Brown. As a former intelligence liaison officer, I made sure the Americans had no record of my decommissioning; I was therefore still on their official Allied Forces Liaison Officer list. Hopefully you will not object to eating in the first-class dining room, my good man, formerly known as the officers' mess.'

Both Brenda and Half Dunn applauded spontaneously and Brenda returned to the story. 'Helen had moved a lot of American money for Sean Murphy, and when he phoned to say how grateful he was I asked if he could drop round for a chat. He told me that he'd decided to retire and was handing the business over to his son, Tater, who would be around pronto.' She glanced over at Helen. 'Please don't be upset, but business between Balmain people is different. When I explained that you were going to the States for plastic surgery, Tater offered me seven dollars to the pound – very generous. So, when I'd got him to agree to eight American dollars to the pound I called Helen, who asked us to add the hundred pounds her father had promised as a wedding gift.' Brenda looking very pleased with herself, then concluded, 'With the car money, there's your money for America. Just over four and a half thousand in green bills.'

Helen wasn't going to take any chances with Danny's ridiculous pride interfering, and before he could respond she said, 'Thank you, both, very much. It's a wonderful thing to do for Danny.' She smiled. 'And I get a handsome husband into the bargain!'

Danny was overcome with gratitude. 'Mum, I'm afraid I'm marrying way out of my class and much, much more woman than I know how to handle.' He threw a glance at Half Dunn. 'But then you weren't much good at the love, honour and obey bit with Dad either.'

'Bloody good thing too,' Half Dunn grinned. 'Gawd knows where we'd'a ended up without yer mum.' He paused and cleared his throat. 'One more small detail: when you're going through customs, Jim Black's the head man at Circular Quay – you remember he used to do the halftime water and oranges with Bullnose Daintree and Sammy Laidlaw for the Tiger Nippers?'

'Yeah, I remember him well,' Danny laughed. 'He once told me if we won the Junior Grade Premiership, there'd be a job for me in His Majesty's Customs after I left school.'

'Yeah, well, he'll be looking out for you, see you through customs without any embarrassing questions or rummaging through your suitcases. He looks just the same – beer gut's got a bit bigger, that's all.'

Danny and Helen married on the 12th of March 1946, at the Sydney Registry Office in a quiet ceremony attended by both sets of parents, with Helen's girlfriend Sylvia Holmes as her witness and Dr Craig Woon, who was up from Melbourne to attend a three-month course at the Military Repatriation Hospital, acting as Danny's best man. The reception, equally quiet, was held in a small private dining area at the Australia Club, as a sop to Barbara. No confetti, but plenty of roast lamb, peach melba and champagne, followed by a long, lugubrious speech from the father of the bride, intended to be humorous but only occasionally succeeding (though everyone laughed politely). Reg Brown explained that while Helen had been a wonderful and in many respects exemplary daughter, even as a child, she'd never resembled in either looks, habit or character any member of the Browns or the Mortlocks, Barbara's family. He bought a cheap laugh when he suggested she could well have been switched in the hospital maternity ward. Then, hypothesising further, he claimed that perhaps she was a throwback to a great-great aunt in England, Jasmine Maude Brown, who was known to be wilful and headstrong and even 'contrary'. Jasmine had run away from home at the age of sixteen and returned at the age of fifty-two in possession of a great deal of valuable jewellery and a sizeable fortune in large uncut emeralds, the source of which she never divulged, other than to say that she had spent her life 'having fun in other parts', and that 'one is forced to do unto others as they do unto you', whatever this was supposed to mean. Rich Aunt Jasmine could also occasionally be heard shouting in Spanish in her sleep. Reg concluded by remarking, 'It has occurred to us from time to time that our darling daughter may well have a fair allotment of rich Aunt Jasmine's genes!' This got another polite laugh. Helen cast a quick glance at her mother, whom she noted had not joined in the laughter.

When it was Half Dunn's turn to speak, cautioned by one of Brenda's 'Don't try to compete with that story about your grandfather winning the pub in a card game' looks, he kept his speech surprisingly short and sweet. However, the sour expression on Barbara Brown's face when Half Dunn acknowledged their family's good fortune in acquiring Helen as both daughter and wife would have curdled milk.

Two days after they were married Danny and Helen boarded the SS *Lurline* at Circular Quay, having been escorted through customs like VIPs by Jim Black. They'd been allocated a very large first-class cabin with its own bathroom and a double bed, referred to as a double bunk simply because the legs were fixed to the floor. Helen, having inspected the cabin thoroughly and declared it to be satisfactory, made Danny come over to stand directly in front of her. She cleared her throat dramatically. 'You may recall, Sergeant Major Dunn, that you are listed on the ship's manifest as my batman. Now, there are over seven hundred war brides on board this ship who haven't had a man for several months. You will be confined to this cabin for the duration of the voyage and be required to make constant love to only one of them!' Helen suddenly flung her arms around Danny, smothering him with kisses. 'And, hooray! That one is me!' she cried happily.

They'd begun to make love soon after they'd passed through the Heads and into the open sea. Danny, after undressing hastily, scrounged through his suitcase to find Reg Brown's parting gift. Helen's father had drawn Danny aside at the wedding reception and slipped a packet of three contraceptives into his hand. 'For tonight, old son,' he'd said out of the corner of his mouth. 'Advantage of being a chemist, what.' Then he'd asked Danny to visit the Birchgrove pharmacy the next day. 'Little surprise waiting; not for Barbara's eyes,' he'd winked.

The following afternoon Danny had called Brown's Pharmacy, its name recently changed from Brown's Chemist Shop, and arranged a time to come over. Upon arrival, he was ushered into the inner sanctum where Reg made up prescriptions and was handed a carefully wrapped brown-paper package roughly the size of a shoebox. 'Samples, every imaginable configuration,' Reg had winked, adding, 'Have fun, son,' and patted Danny on the back.

Now, as the liner breached the first waves in the open sea and the rocking became more pronounced, Danny lifted the lid on Reg Brown's gift, offering it to his bride as if it were a box of chocolates. 'For your pleasure and delectation, madam,' he said.

Helen, seated on the edge of the double bunk, squealed with delight. 'Oh, what fun! Danny, where on earth . . . ?'

Danny grinned. 'A parting gift from your father. Samples he's been ordering, mostly from France, Germany and America, and collecting for God knows how long. I must say, your dad looked very pleased with himself. "None of these are available in Australia, son. I've searched the international market, got most of them, except for three Japanese brands, and they'd probably be too small," he explained to me proudly.'

Helen snorted. 'Good Lord! My bold father! There must be fifty here and all different. Whoever would have thought, with Daddy a vestryman at St Andrew's! Goodness, I had no idea there were so many different shapes!' She selected half a dozen small packets and dropped them into her naked lap, then, picking one at random, read out its name. 'Oh, look! It's called The Virgin Tickler! I'm not sure that what I need most at the moment is tickling, and, alas, I'm no longer a virgin.' She discarded the tickler and selected another, translating from the French: 'Leap in the Dark! What do you suppose? Intended for a couple who've only just met?' She reeled off the other names: 'Pretty Fingers! Maiden's Bliss! Sweet Joy! Ecstasy! *Amore!*' Then she suddenly cried out, 'Oh, how appropriate! This one's called Sweet Caution!' She glanced up at Danny to see that he was standing, stark naked, holding the box lightly between thumb and forefinger as it balanced on his erection. 'Oh dear, is that my batman I see standing at the salute?' Helen cried, eyes dancing.

'Lieutenant Colonel, madam, if you would kindly make your selection, I am at your immediate service and ready to once again fulfil my marriage vow to love, honour and cherish you!' Danny gasped in one rapid sentence.

'Oh, my poor darling!' Helen exclaimed, dropping to her knees on the carpeted floor and scattering small packets everywhere. She removed the box from its precarious resting position and murmured, 'I've made my selection, darling. We're going *au naturel*,' whereupon she allowed her mouth to accept his impressive salute.

To the faint throb of the turbine engines, Helen worked Danny to the point where he was beginning to whimper softly, then withdrew her lips, rose to her feet, kissed him deeply, and took him by the hand. 'Come, lover boy,' she said softly, climbing into the double bunk. 'It's time we practised making a baby!'

The voyage to San Francisco was uneventful, that is, if you discount seven hundred excited, not to say randy, war brides being on the same ship. Helen had told one of the ship's senior officers their reason for going to the States, more as a way of preventing speculation and to explain Danny's battered face than anything else. She'd simply told him Danny had been a prisoner of war and his facial scars were due to an atrocity committed by a Japanese officer. Unfortunately, the bare bones of any story need to be fleshed out, and this one, which travelled like wildfire through the ship, became more and more exaggerated with each telling. With the young war brides outnumbering the men on board approximately five to one, Danny was soon regarded as their own Errol Flynn, a war hero who had brought the Japanese whimpering to the surrender table practically single-handedly. Despite his looks, or perhaps because of them, he became an object of romantic and almost maternal interest. He couldn't leave his cabin without being swamped by excited or sentimental females, with the result that he spent a lot of time reading on his bed. To his intense chagrin, the ship's captain ordered one of the smaller decks out of bounds to his fellow passengers so that he could catch a breath of fresh air and get some exercise.

Helen and Danny were standing on this little private deck at six in the morning as the liner sailed into San Francisco Harbour and they watched as the soaring red pillars of the Golden Gate Bridge loomed out of the morning mist. By the time they'd passed under the bridge the mist had all but cleared and the City on the Bay seemingly rose out of the sparkling harbour. 'The city of grand promise and dire warning,' Helen observed. 'Look to your left, darling – the rock of Alcatraz, one of the truly grim American prisons.'

'Yeah, I've read about it. The only escape is via the harbour and that simply delivers the prisoner à la carte to the sharks, or so they say. I think I'd take my chances. I've been swimming in Sydney Harbour since I was a kid and only once saw a live shark. Mind you, with the shit that pours into the harbour from Balmain – the soap factories, chemical factory and the other effluent producers around the rim – there isn't anything for a self-respecting shark to eat on the harbour side of the Heads. It's probably the same here, if the prisoners only knew.'

The decks below them were filled with excited brides who began screaming as the liner started to dock and they caught their first glimpse of the mass of waiting husbands crowded on the passenger terminal wharf. 'I think we might stay on board until the happy reunions are over,' Helen laughed, then turned to Danny and kissed him. 'Well, my beautiful ugly man, we've made it this far.' Then she grew serious. 'Oh, Danny, it's going to hurt all over again, isn't it?'

Danny laughed. 'Yeah, probably, but there are two immediate advantages I can think of this time that were absent on the first occasion: anaesthetics and painkillers. I shall either be out like a light or drugged to the eyeballs.'

It took a good two hours before the wharf below and the customs hall beyond were reasonably clear and Helen and Danny were able to make their way onto dry land and through US customs with a minimum of fuss. The taxi took them away from the harbour, up a steep hill and past a tram, then down the other side again to Union Square, where they booked into the St Francis Hotel. The taxi driver, crew-cut and built like a pro footballer going to fat, didn't say a word throughout the entire journey, which somewhat dampened their spirits. Danny paid the fare when they arrived and added two quarters of the unfamiliar money. 'What's this, buddy?' the driver asked.

'A tip,' Danny answered, bemused.

The driver shook his head. 'No, man, this ain't no tip. This is a fuckin' insult!' He tipped the two quarters onto the pavement, gunned the engine and moved off shouting something that sounded like, 'Muthafucker!'

'Screw you too, mate!' Danny called after him angrily.

'Welcome to America,' Helen said quietly, then looked up to see a bellhop pushing a birdcage trolley towards them. He left it and ran to retrieve the coins from the gutter, popping up beside Helen and holding out the two silver quarters, a small dark-skinned boy with big brown eyes and a cherub's face who didn't look much older than twelve. He was dressed in the traditional maroon figure-hugging jacket with gold buttons down the front and epaulettes on the shoulders, his pillbox hat set at a jaunty angle, the strap secure about his chin.

'Ma'am, sir, we 'pologise in da name of da St Francis Hotel,' he said earnestly. 'Dat ain't no way foh dat taxi driver to behave, cussin' jes beecause yoh tip him so bad.'

Helen laughed, and Danny, despite his anger of moments before, was forced to grin. 'What's your name?' Helen asked, accepting the two quarters and immediately falling in love with the little fellow.

'Samuel Pentecost Tucker, ma'am,' he replied, then added seriously, 'but dey jes call me Sam, ma'am.'

'Well, Samuel Pentecost Tucker, we're from Australia where we don't really understand tipping, so you're going to have to help us. How much should we have tipped that rude taxi driver?'

'Well, he got hisself a grow'd up job, so he gonna get one dollar min-a-min, dat da rule. But if'n he ain't polite and he don't help wid yoh suitcases, den he don't get nuttin'. He gonna curse and holler some, dat only natural, but he gonna know why he don't get nuttin'. Yessir, ma'am, one dollar, dat da min-a-min, all things considered.'

'And you, sir, do you get a dollar?'

'Dee-pends, ma'am,' Samuel Pentecost Tucker said, his expression serious. 'Yoh all got three portmanteaus, I see. Now, I ain't grow'd up so I gets a quarter foh evey one – dat seventy-five cents, ma'am.' He moved over and picked up the first suitcase using both hands. He managed to lift it and with some effort place it on the luggage trolley.

Danny lifted the other two suitcases and placed them next to the first, to the apparent consternation of Samuel Pentecost Tucker. 'Now I ain't done yoh no full service, sir,' he protested.

'She's right, mate. I reckon you've earned yourself the full entitlement plus a bonus.' He handed the boy a dollar. 'Lead on, Sam, my man,' he instructed.

'Thank you, sir, much obliged,' Samuel Pentecost Tucker said, beginning to push the luggage trolley towards reception, but then he stopped. 'It ain't necessary yoh give ree-ception no tip, sir.'

The hotel, built just before the great San Francisco earthquake and fire of 1906, miraculously survived relatively unscathed, and was typical of turn-of-the-century architecture, twelve storeys of sandstone and brick facing onto Union Square. At reception they were told, with profuse apologies, that they would need to wait an hour because the previous occupant of their room hadn't yet checked out. They stowed their suitcases in the baggage room, checked their passports and money into the hotel safe, then, aching to use their legs on dry land, stepped outside.

First, they took the tram – or cable car, as the locals called it – down to Fisherman's Wharf. Then they spent the remainder of the day walking, doing all the touristy things, stopping for lunch in Chinatown at the Hang Ah Tea Room, famous for its dim sims, which Danny deemed no better than the ones from the chinks in Darling Street, Balmain. By the time they reached the Golden Gate Bridge, they were exhausted.

Helen, as usual, had done all her homework, and they made a late afternoon visit to Macy's in Union Square, where a sign pronounced it the largest department store outside of New York. She bought a pair of sensible walking shoes, chosen from a great variety that were cheaper than anything she could have found in Sydney, and a pair of sexy high heels with peekaboo toes, again selected from an astonishing range of styles. It was obvious that America was revelling in its success: it had won the war, it had the atom bomb and it was prosperous. Americans were excited about the future, they accounted for over half of the world's industrial wealth, and they were upbeat and generously prepared to rebuild the broken and tattered world beyond their shores. The only shortage they seemed to be experiencing were hours of the day in which to enjoy their secure and happy lives.

Australia, still on rationing, was as yet unable even to imagine post-war recovery. It was more like a small nation dusting itself off and counting itself lucky to have survived a disastrous war and escaped a Japanese invasion than one girding its loins for boom times to come. The war had left Europe in ruins, and Great Britain no longer great, exhausted and on its industrial knees, but America was different. San Francisco wasn't a big city, but the bay was wider than Sydney Harbour and the bridge was longer than the Sydney Harbour Bridge, and yet it was so redolent of Sydney that Danny and Helen felt comfortable and almost at home. It was a good place to disembark when visiting such a new country.

The hotel was pleasant without being grand, and unlike that first taxi driver, everyone was extremely friendly and polite. They spent the evening visiting two jazz joints on the Barbary Coast, back down in the wharf area. At one they ordered hamburgers for supper that had so many fillings they stood nearly six inches high, including pickled gherkins, which neither Danny nor Helen had ever tasted. By such silly and often trivial things do we remember places and events.

They left the hotel early the following morning to catch the eight o'clock Santa Fe train from Oakland Station to Union Terminal in Los Angeles. Helen had demanded that Samuel Pentecost Tucker handle their luggage and order a taxi, which he did with a twin-fingered whistle, in a manner that was surprisingly loud and sophisticated for one so young. Helen handed him a two-dollar tip and thanked him for his very grown-up service. He received it with a gracious, 'Much obliged, ma'am, sir. Now, yoh folk come see us again soon, yoh hear? One day I'm gonna come see me some them kangaroos.' Samuel Pentecost Tucker held the back door open for Helen to enter the taxi and in a loud whisper advised Danny, 'Oakland, dat a long ride, dat two dollars tip, sir.'

The Santa Fe Streamliner to Los Angeles was a day train, and they were shown to comfortable seats in one of the first-class carriages, or railroad cars, as the Yanks called them. Helen, having decided that this trip to America was probably going to be the only holiday they'd have for several years, insisted they do things properly wherever they could. It was their honeymoon, after all, and with the luxury of Brenda's dollars they didn't have to skimp; in fact, they seemed to be extremely well off. America was surprisingly cheap and Helen was going to make the most of it before Danny's surgery. They reached Los Angeles only just in time to join the Super Chief for the two-night journey to Kansas City.

The Super Chief, known as the train of the stars – the Hollywood variety, of course – stretched the entire length of the Union Terminal platform, and the gleaming silver and black train with its huge throbbing diesel engine seemed like something out of a Jules Verne science-fiction novel. Helen and Danny had never seen anything remotely like it except in the movies. They were glimpsing an America where everything was bigger and better, but even here this train was considered topnotch – the most modern train in the world.

The head porter who escorted them to their compartment was stout, with a wide gleaming smile that matched his immaculate white jacket and gold epaulettes. He wore a black bow tie, black trousers and shoes burnished to near perfection. Danny felt a sudden pang for Glossy Denmeade, then turned his attention to the porter who announced grandly, 'Ma'am, sir, this is drawing room number four and it is entirely for your pleasure with the compliments of the Super Chief and staff.'

It was impressive, to say the least, and contained a gleaming modern bathroom with shower, washbasin and toilet, large fluffy monogrammed towels and perfumed soap. The compartment itself had two large comfortable seats and a central table beneath double-glazed windows fitted with venetian blinds. Two roomy bunks folded down from the walls at night. A porter named Maurice, dressed in a similar uniform to the head porter but without the epaulettes, presented himself at the touch of a buzzer. They only just had time to shower and change for dinner, served with gleaming silver and bone china on white damask at a table for two. The menu, once they'd got over the curious fact that in America the main course was referred to as the entrée, was worthy of Primo's in Sydney.

Danny, finally replete with a double helping of apple pie and ice-cream, wiped his lips and placed his napkin on the table. 'Beats the hell out of the last dinner I had on a train, which, if I recall correctly, was a handful of cold rice that I ate standing up cheek by jowl in an open truck on the Thai–Burma Railway.'

The Super Chief pulled into Kansas City late in the morning, just over forty hours after leaving Los Angeles, having travelled across the immensity of the Great Plains. Helen was reminded that enormous herds of buffalo once roamed across these vast grasslands, the herds stretching from the southernmost tip of North America to the Canadian border, millions of these large, handsome bearded beasts with hardly a single one left to graze the sweet native pasture as humans opened up the plains for Indian corn and habitation.

Less than an hour after reaching Kansas City they were on the train to St Louis, 240 miles away, passing through several medium-sized towns, the first of which was Independence, Missouri, the home town of President Truman, the current occupant of the White House. The journey took them just short of the Illinois border, with the track following the mighty Mississippi River. To Helen and Danny, accustomed to Australian rivers that were often dry for months on end, rarely a torrent and never a vast stretch of water, the Mississippi was a seemingly never-ending expanse, beyond their wildest imaginings.

St Louis was a small city in the middle of nowhere. Formerly a gracious sleepy old French river town, it had become an American city after it was bought from France in Thomas Jefferson's Louisiana Purchase in 1803. Most of the old money had been made on beer – it was the home of American Budweiser – and in the old days the city accumulated much of its wealth by funnelling the agricultural bounty of the endless plains through the city's river port down to New Orleans for shipment to the world at large. The new money and the jobs it brought with it were in manufacturing, which was given a huge boost by the war economy. Workers from the impoverished south came in tens of thousands, attracted by work in the booming factories supplying the war effort and jobs in the giant Curtiss-Wright aircraft factory.

Barnes Hospital, where Danny's operations would take place, seemed to be innovative, and not only in plastic surgery. It was linked to the Washington University School of Medicine, and was partly staffed by Washington University faculty members, serving as a centre for research as well as education.

Helen had phoned Jennifer Glicks from Los Angeles, telling her the time of their arrival, and she met them at the station and drove them to the Roberts Mayfair Hotel in the centre of downtown St Louis. Helen had arranged a special rate for the three weeks they would need to stay for the operation. Jennifer had, of course, offered the hospitality of her home, but Helen insisted that it would be best if they stayed in a hotel.

That night they had dinner with John and Jennifer Glicks. The two women talked almost non-stop about Australia and the old friends they had shared during the war. Mid-morning the following day, Danny attended Dr Glicks' consulting rooms at Barnes Hospital.

John Glicks was a quietly spoken, serious man who tended to give answers to questions rather than to volunteer information. It was the unconscious attitude of many doctors, Australian as well as American, based mostly on the belief that laypeople wouldn't understand the mysteries of the medical profession. Sometimes they had come to believe in their own privileged status, and that it put them above the need to explain their decisions. Danny believed that no man was innately superior and that explanations were necessary in all areas of life.

John Glicks had received by mail a copy of Danny's complete medical history and Helen had brought all the X-rays of his face with her. Danny now handed these over.

'We may need to take some of our own, but I'll look at these later and decide,' Dr Glicks said, accepting and laying them aside.

'I think you'll find they're in focus; there's certainly plenty of them,' Danny said, with just the slightest suggestion that he didn't want to be patronised.

John Glicks didn't miss a beat. 'Perhaps you forget I worked in your country and was frequently impressed with the high standards of your medical system. It's unlikely, but there may have been some slight changes since these were taken.'

Danny realised he'd been put in his place and that he'd been out of order; his paranoia was showing. 'Doctor, before we start, I am very grateful for your offer to do this operation pro bono, but Helen and I believe that this is too generous. We have enough saved to pay your fee and I'd like to make that offer now before you begin.' Danny, while including her in the decision, hadn't discussed this option with Helen, but he'd thought about it a lot – they had a little more money than they needed, and he didn't want any more freebies. Helen had worked a miracle to get them here and that was enough.

To his surprise John Glicks didn't brush him off and tut-tut over the idea of being paid. 'We all like to be rewarded, paid for what we do, but in your case that would be extremely awkward, Danny. Let me explain. Dr Vilray Blair has agreed to work with me simply because you are . . . er, well, not an American citizen, and the hospital can be seen to be making a contribution outside normal practice. Both he and I have had to obtain permission from the hospital board to perform your surgery. In fact, while Jennifer originally informed Helen that you would need to pay the hospital costs, I was about to tell you that the board has decided that these, too, will be available to you free of charge as part of our ongoing research budget. It would be very awkward, and certainly delay proceedings, if you now insist that you become a paying patient.'

Danny could do no more than gracefully accept. 'Thank you, John. When will I meet Dr Vilray Blair?' he asked.

'I shall be in close consultation with him after I've examined you, but he will only attend during surgery, when you will undoubtedly be under anaesthesia. Now, if you'll get onto the examination table, I'd like to have a closer look at you, Danny.'

After nearly fifteen minutes of gentle prodding and tweaking, very different from the rough handling Danny had received from the fat buffoon in Rangoon, the American surgeon clipped several of the X-rays Danny had given him to a large light box. After examining them for some time he remarked, 'These are excellent, but they show that the damage to your nose has been extensive.'

'You don't need to tell me, doctor. I'm aware of that every morning when I shave,' Danny said ruefully. 'I live in fear of the slightest sniffle.'

Dr Glicks, busy examining the remainder of the X-rays, didn't appear to hear. 'Hmm, difficult,' he remarked at last. 'The bones and cartilage that give the nose its shape have been smashed in and pushed to the left.' He looked up. 'That's not good news but it could have been a lot worse.' He grinned. 'If the blow from the butt of the Jap's rifle had been directly front on – that is, square – you would almost certainly have been killed.'

'I didn't wake up for three days as it was, and when I did I can remember wishing I was dead. Do I need to go through all that again? And can you do anything to fix it?' Danny asked.

'Oh yes, almost certainly. As far as plastic surgery goes, we should be able to get your nose looking almost as good as new. But, in answer to the first part of your question, the procedure is complicated by the fact that the bones, and in fact the entire structure beneath the skin, has long healed and knitted together in the new traumatised shape we now have.'

'And what will you do to fix it?'

The surgeon hesitated. 'I'm not sure you'll want to know.'

'Please, doctor. I have discovered that knowing is far less worrying than leaving it to my febrile imagination. I guess the advantage is that this time I won't be awake while it happens.'

'No, of course not. We'll perform what is known as rhinoplasty, which is a relatively simple process had you come directly off the battlefield. Then we would simply manipulate the tissue from inside the nose and bring it back into shape, cleaning up the broken bone, but that method is no longer available to us. Now, we will need to make a series of incisions to open the nose up from underneath and inside to expose the structures, and then we will cut the bone where it has knitted incorrectly and reconstruct the damaged bridge and septum, reattach dislocated cartilage and realign the bone structures as far back as your frontal sinuses.' He paused, took a breath and smiled. 'I don't believe I've gone into that much detail since my med exams. When that's all done, of course, we close everything up again. With a bit of luck you'll heal well and make a quick recovery and be almost as good as new, with little or no scarring apart from a few small lines around the base of your nose.'

'What about my cheekbone – any luck there?'

'Ah, a much simpler procedure. We'll do that at the same time as your nose and you can expect a full recovery and no noticeable scars.'

'And how long – I mean, in weeks or months – until we'll be able to go home?'

'Well, that depends; not everyone heals at the same rate. There will be some discomfort, of course, and you'll be on strong pain medication, but you'll be able to leave the hospital after ten days. You'll have to wear a facial plaster cast to keep everything in alignment until the bones knit. There may be some swelling, though not necessarily after the first two weeks. I'll want to see you again, with Dr Blair, in two months, then we'll decide if you can go home.'

If Danny had previously experienced any doubts about John Glicks, he'd long since dismissed them. They had expected to be away a year, so two or three months was great news. What's more, his questions had been answered in a forthright and direct manner and he began to wonder why the surgeon needed the help of Vilray P. Blair. 'I must say, you've given me a great deal of confidence, John. Thank you,' Danny said.

Dr Glicks laughed. 'I hope so, Danny. While war is hell, it's heaven for plastic surgeons. A year in the Pacific and then Valley Forge Military Hospital, where I've done more than two hundred facial reconstructions – most much worse than yours – is the kind of experience one can never gain in peacetime. Believe me, the damage a bullet, shrapnel and explosives can do to a face is horrific, not to mention the burns sustained by a pilot or rear gunner in an aircraft accident.'

Danny thought of Billy Scraper's face, so much worse than his own. John Glicks continued. 'The work on your face is by comparison fairly straightforward and I have every confidence that with time and care we'll get a better than good result. I'm sure Dr Blair is going to agree with my diagnosis and prognosis. I'd like you to check in the day after tomorrow, which will give me time to consult with Dr Blair and arrange a theatre time that suits us both.'

'This is very good of you, John. I only hope when you and Jennifer visit Australia we can repay you somehow.'

'You already have, Danny. I get to work with Vilray P. Blair and, medically speaking, that's a special treat.'

Fifteen days later, Danny, looking a fright with the middle section of his face in plaster of Paris, was released from Barnes into Helen's care. She, of course, had made detailed plans for his recovery.

Billy du Bois, in response to a letter from Danny, had said that the moment he was released from hospital he was to come down to Louisiana to recover. He would not hear of them holing up in a hotel, and pointed out that there was a refuge for Danny at the du Bois plantation, where he and his family would show the newlyweds a little southern hospitality. He asked Helen to call him in New Orleans, where the family had a house, to discuss their plans. Danny, with both the missing eye and the good one edged in deep purple – usually referred to as a pair of black eyes – looked so bizarre that Helen realised he either had to stay cooped up in their hotel room or accept Billy's invitation.

Billy du Bois immediately offered to cancel several appointments and drive up and fetch them back to 'N'awlins'.

'Thank you, Billy,' Helen said, 'but it's simply no trouble to take the train. Danny is well enough to travel.'

'Uh, y'all sure now? Give me the time you get into N'awlins and I'll meet your train,' he insisted, then added, 'But how will I recognise y'all now Danny has had his operation?'

Helen laughed. 'Easy,' she said. 'He's the one with a plaster cast covering part of his face.'

Helen had a clear impression of Billy du Bois as a swashbuckling, larger-than-life character, for while Danny seldom spoke of the prisoner-of-war camp, he was fond of recalling the day they were liberated by the giant Yank, festooned in ammunition-belts on the Harley-Davidson with its sidecar filled with cigarette cartons. She pictured him in cowboy boots and jeans with a large Stetson hat and an open-neck shirt, hairy chest protruding, and said as much to Danny. He laughed, unsure himself how Billy might look in civilian clobber, but guessing it would be casual, or perhaps one of those light-blue American seersucker suits. It came as something of a surprise when the unmistakeably huge young man waiting for them was dressed in an immaculate and obviously tailor-made grey pinstriped suit, black business shoes, white shirt and conservative blue and red striped tie. He, of course, immediately recognised the face in the plaster cast and realised the beautiful blonde woman beside its owner must be Helen.

'Well now, welcome to N'awlins,' he said, his arms held wide as if to embrace them. His obvious pleasure and open-hearted declaration seemed to be welcoming them on behalf of the whole of the state of Louisiana. Looking directly at Helen and extending a bearlike paw he declared, 'Uh, welcome, Mrs Dunn. We are most honoured and privileged to have y'all visit us. This is a truly grand occasion.' He spoke with what they would come to recognise as a Louisiana drawl – slow, carefully enunciated, and seeming to convey that the speaker had all the time in the world.

'Helen, it's Helen. I don't answer to anything else,' she said with a smile. 'We are equally delighted to be here. I've heard so much about you from Danny.'

'G'day, mate,' Danny said, trying to sound cheerful. The painkillers he'd taken before they'd left were beginning to wear off, and although his speech was greatly improved it was still a bit wobbly after the operation on his cheek. He attempted to shake Billy's hand, but Billy grabbed him, and the two big men – the American and the Australian who'd met under such unique circumstances – hugged each other. 'It's a long way from the rice paddies of Thailand,' Danny managed to say, his throat constricting with sudden emotion.

Billy drove a very large, new black Buick with whitewall tyres. 'Uh, y'all say if it ain't convenient, but I thought maybe you'd like to stay in the town house tonight and tomorrow, then on the weekend we'll go visit La Fonteine. What say y'all?'

'That sounds lovely,' Helen said from the back seat. 'But where and what is La Fonteine? Danny has to take things pretty quietly for a while.'

'Ain't nowhere quieter in the State of Louisiana, Helen. It's further south. Been in the du Bois family now two hundred years.'

'Two hundred years!' Helen exclaimed. 'That includes the time of slavery?'

'Sure does, ma'am. We've been right lucky with our coloured folk; many of the original families have stayed to this day. There was no good part of slavery but I guess my forebears were a might more tolerant than most. La Fonteine is a lucky place for us; the original old house was requisitioned for officers' quarters during the war, which saved it from being burned to the ground.'

'Oh, I hadn't realised that you were directly affected by the war. What was it, fifth column sabotage? American Nazi movement?' Helen asked, curious.

Billy du Bois threw back his head and roared. 'Only one war round these parts, ma'am, and it ain't the one you and I and Danny just fought in. The war I was referring to was the Civil War. It's a habit I acquired from my daddy – everything in this part of the south is dated either before or after the Civil War.'

They had entered what appeared to be an older part of New Orleans and so it turned out to be. 'Uh, this is Vieux Carré, the old French Quarter. I guess we've had a home here almost as long as we've had the plantation.' The big Buick drew up in a quiet street and Billy sounded the horn. The street was not unlike one of a row of large terrace houses in Sydney, with wrought-iron balconies fronting directly onto the street, and which, apart from elegant front doors and a carriageway on the side, would have looked at home on a leafy street in Woollahra. It was only when the whole of the house was seen that the difference became obvious. It was built entirely around a magnificent courtyard garden, with a continuous balcony upstairs and a verandah downstairs that ran all the way around it. It was a perfectly preserved example of a wealthy antebellum home in New Orleans and was at least three times the size of a large terrace in Sydney. The house was called La Trianon and there was little doubt that it represented serious money.

Their luggage was taken inside by a manservant named Jackson, whom Billy informed them also acted as chauffeur and would be taking them around when Billy wasn't available to do so himself. Inside they met Aunt Mary-Louise, the coloured housekeeper and cook, who looked after Billy but came from La Fonteine, as had Jackson. Both lived in the servant's wing of the large house.

Aunt Mary-Louise had set out afternoon tea in an elegant drawing room that Helen would later describe to Brenda as positively reeking of old money. The tea service was antique Limoges, and the cutlery antique silver. Several varieties of home-baked French pastries were displayed on an elegant platter.

For Helen, who had developed an eye for the authentic and well preserved, the house was like a page from history, though on second glance she realised that the antebellum ambience and sense of grandeur disguised the latest in kitchen and bathroom appliances, and that the house, although sporting a grand fireplace in the main drawing room and smaller versions in every other room, was centrally heated.

Billy du Bois may have been a knockabout master sergeant in the Special Forces of the United States army, but he was every inch an old-fashioned aristocrat in his native Louisiana. He explained that he was the youngest of the three sons of Marcel and Heloise du Bois. His father, now retired, was still fussing and taking unnecessary trips to the plantation to make a nuisance of himself with Billy's brothers, Frank and Andre, who ran the plantation and the mill respectively.

'What, cotton?' Danny asked.

Billy laughed. 'No, sir! That's the standard notion of the old south. Mark Twain probably didn't think sugarcane was as romantic as tote'n' cotton along the Mississippi; "The old sugarcane fields of home" doesn't have quite the same ring to it. But, in fact, my family have been growin' sugarcane at La Fonteine nigh on one hundred and eighty years. The spring sowing is just over so there's a bit of time to welcome y'all to the plantation.'

Billy went on to explain that his parents now spent most of their time at La Trianon but that his father made a point of being on the plantation for sowing and harvesting, where he drove everyone mad, and his mother went along in a mostly vain attempt to stop him doing so.

'And you, where do you fit in?' Helen asked.

'Uh, I run a distribution company that my uncle, William "Billy" du Bois, left to me after I graduated from Louisiana State University. He was a youngest son, and had no heirs. Youngest son to youngest son, both with the same name – I guess it was meant to be. The business was left in the care of a manager when I enlisted and now I'm in the process of building it up again.'

'Distribution?'

Billy grinned. 'You're right, it could mean anything. In fact we're in entertainment machinery and equipment as well as cash registers. Before the war, William "Billy" du Bois Entertainment was the biggest distributor in the south of pinball and slot machines, gaming machinery, roulette wheels and the like, as well as cash registers. I guess you couldn't go into a Bourbon Street jazz or illicit gaming joint, cathouse or speakeasy during prohibition without seeing at least one machine supplied by William "Billy" du Bois. That's where it all started. Now the boys in Chicago and New York are beginning to talk about Las Vegas in Nevada. Gambling's always been legal in Nevada and William "Billy" du Bois has always been there, but it's been penny-anti, wayside casinos and clip joints. If the mafia – the New York and Chicago mobs – get interested, I guess I'll need to go speak to them. We can bring in all the I-talian machines they want, of course, but we'd prefer to source them here. Nobody has better knowhow, or rather, used to have better knowhow, than William "Billy" du Bois. It's a business that goes beyond supply and demand – after-care protection is an important element.'

It was a long explanation and Helen hadn't wanted to interrupt, but now she asked, 'William "Billy" du Bois – is that the actual name of your distribution company?'

Billy grinned. 'Sure is, ma'am. My uncle was very well known around these parts, and for a period he was even mayor of N'awlins, but with his name on so much "entertainment" machinery found in places that never should've been there in the first place, he was eventually obliged to step down from his civic responsibilities. There's lots of folk said it was a pity – William "Billy" du Bois had a good vision for this city and he was a great friend of Huey Long, the governor of Louisiana, and between the two of them they got a lot done for poor folk.'

Billy paused. 'Enough about me. We'll visit all the N'awlins sites in the next day or two, if y'all are up to it, but then I have to go to the East Coast on business. You're welcome to stay here at La Trianon, but, I warn you, my daddy will want to show you everything, and if you need a rest to recover from your operation the plantation would be ideal. Either way y'all stay as long as you like, you hear?'

And so Helen and Danny stayed at La Fonteine for nearly two months, coming up to New Orleans from time to time, where Helen and Heloise du Bois got on like a house on fire. The plantation was run much as it always had been, the workers regarded almost as family, most of them having adopted the du Bois surname as their own. Many of the coloured folks' forebears had been on the plantation well before the Louisiana Purchase.

Marcel was inordinately proud of the fact that the plantation had its own school and clinic, and ten coloured families had children who attended the all-coloured college in St Louis, paid for by the du Bois family. 'Many folk round these parts don't hold with the notion that people of colour have the brains to be educated to book learning, but I intend, most assuredly, to prove them wrong,' he chuckled. 'They say to me, "Marcel, they'll take your good name and drag it through the mud," but I tell them, "I think y'all misconceived what happened, sir. It was people of colour who dragged a horse and plough through the spring mud in the name of du Bois, and planted and harvested the sugarcane that gave my family its good standing in the great state of Louisiana. It is these folk who earned the good life for us white folk, and I am most grateful and rightly proud that they would want to use du Bois as their family name.' He sucked on his pipe, discovered it had gone out, struck a match and reignited it, then, blowing blue smoke towards the ceiling, said quietly, 'White folk, they don't like that much, but I cain't see how we got much reason for pride. The du Bois family is one of the very few old southern families round these parts that can truthfully say there never was a Negro lynched that they had the personal responsibility for.'

'Lynched?' Helen said, shocked. 'You mean the Ku Klux Klan?'

'Hell no, ma'am. The Klan is white trash and reason enough today for all southerners to be rightfully shamed. But in the old days before the war, a troublesome slave was a possession a plantation owner could dispose of any way he damn well liked.'

'It wasn't any better with our Aborigines and the white squatters in the early days in Australia. They referred to murdering blacks as "duck hunting" and notched the butts of their rifles after a kill,' Danny said.

When Danny started to feel better, he and Helen borrowed Billy's 1939 Chevy two-seater with the dicky seat. It had been on blocks in one of the garages at La Fonteine, and with the help of Jimmy Sugar, the mechanic on the plantation, they got it going sweetly again. It was the car Billy had used while at university and with it they toured the south, calling this their proper honeymoon.

The three months' recuperation soon passed and they returned to St Louis and Barnes Hospital, where the great Vilray Blair and a delighted John Glicks removed Danny's plaster cast and pronounced his nose job excellent, beyond expectations. While Danny was still somewhat discoloured and blotchy, Helen was delighted with the result. 'Darling, it's a face that looks well used and not, as before, abused. You were far too handsome as a young lad. Now most men would like to have your face; it has a life that, like a well-told tale, is full of interest. I simply can't wait for Brenda to see you.'

Danny, looking at himself in the bathroom mirror at the hotel, could see that if you compared his new face to the old, there was a definite improvement: this one could have belonged to a prize fighter who'd fought half a dozen fights against heavier opponents he should never have taken on. If it wasn't pretty, at least it could pass in public with perhaps only a second glance.

It was time to go home.

Danny began his Law degree, and Helen went looking for a flat that was small enough and cheap enough for them to afford, finding one at the top end of Darling Street almost next door to the Callan Park Mental Hospital. It wasn't at all bad and the real estate agent confided in her that the rent was low because 'people don't want to live close to a loony bin'.

Helen laughed. 'I think we're going to be right at home here. We'll take it. Is there any key money?' She had landed a job at the university tutoring in ancient history, and was able to supplement her small salary by taking private students, while Danny worked two afternoons and Saturdays at the pub, where she also occasionally helped out. To Danny's surprise Helen enjoyed working on the bar at the Hero. 'It's social anthropology,' she'd once explained.

'What? Watching men getting pissed?' Danny snorted.

'Well, yes, in a way that's true, but there hasn't been a period in the evolution of mankind where humans haven't performed rituals using a mind-altering substance of some sort. For us, going to the pub is a social ritual and alcohol is the substance. I'm sure it wasn't very different in ancient Egypt,' she replied.

Danny's time at Law School seemed to pass very quickly – he struck up a friendship with another Law student who, though considerably younger and fresh out of Scots College, one of Sydney's elite private schools, was in his own way also something of a loner. Franz was Jewish, and had left Austria with his parents in 1932 when he was two years old. Once they had arrived in Australia, they almost immediately started one of Sydney's first genuine delicatessens in Bondi Road – Landsman's Delicatessen and Continental Smallgoods. They were smart enough not to make it kosher and almost from the day it opened it had prospered, being frequented by the wealthy, sophisticated and more widely travelled customers from nearby Bellevue Hill, Double Bay, Rose Bay and Vaucluse.

With the advent of the Second World War, they were no longer able to import smallgoods from Europe. This was followed by the blow of Josef, an Austrian Jew, being sent to Hay Internment Camp. Hester, his wife, a capable and enterprising woman, had immediately set to work establishing a smallgoods factory, initially in a rented double garage, as well as sourcing private outlets. Using the knowhow and skills of other migrants from the Continent, she developed the techniques to make or source from these various families the sausages, cheeses and smallgoods she'd formerly imported.

After a year in the local primary school Franz had been recommended for Woollahra Opportunity School, a primary school for bright kids, and at the age of thirteen had been given a scholarship to Sydney Boys High, the state school in the Eastern Suburbs that catered for gifted boys.

However, each year the various private schools in the Eastern Suburbs kept an eye out for a truly bright student whose parents couldn't afford the fees for a private school. It was their social-conscience scholarship. Scots College in Bellevue Hill offered Franz their scholarship in 1941. His mother had been in a quandary. The selective high school had the better academic reputation and normally this was all that would have counted with Franz's parents, but with her husband away she'd listened to the advice of one of their wealthy Vaucluse customers, Bryan Penman, himself a fifth-generation Australian Jew, who came from a well-connected family who had several vineyards in the Hunter Valley and a distillery that produced fortified wines. 'He's a clever boy,' he'd advised Mrs Landsman, 'so it doesn't much matter where he goes, he'll do well. But there's one thing you ought to consider.' He paused, so as to add weight to his next words. 'Connections. In this country it's called "the old-boy network". You say your boy wants to go into the law? Believe me, Mrs Landsman. I'm a trained lawyer, though I don't practise. It will come in more than a little useful in his career if he goes to Scots. In fact, I'd venture to say it would be foolish not to avail yourself of this opportunity for your lad to have a private-school education. In this city, and particularly in the law, it is less about what you know and more about who you know.'

Hester had written to her husband in the Hay camp and he'd replied, *It's good advice, in Austria it was the same.* So Franz's parents had taken Bryan Penman's advice and enrolled their son at Scots College. While Franz was indistinguishable from any native Australian, with his father in an internment camp he was immediately regarded as a 'bloody Kraut', not a good thing to be in the midst of the war, so he copped a fair amount of schoolboy shit from the sons of the privileged minority in the exclusive Eastern-Suburbs private school. He soon became known as a swot and, while he wasn't exactly a sissy, he was the next best thing – good at chess and debating, and hopeless at sport – and so was rewarded with the double status of being referred to as 'unco' (uncoordinated) and nicknamed 'Snake Mouth', quickly shortened to Snake because of his so-called poisonous tongue. He could more than match his persecutors in sharp, sometimes cruel quips. Thus, he effortlessly gained the reputation for having a dangerous tongue and for being essentially a loner.

Franz Landsman completed his final-year exams in 1946 and achieved the third highest pass in the state, by far the best Scots College had ever achieved in the state-wide exam. As his ultimate revenge, his name was transcribed in perpetuity in gold letters on the honours board in the school assembly hall. Franz Landsman had improbably joined the list of the school's immortals.

In the tradition of Scots, and to the delight of the headmaster, Franz Landsman elected to study law, although he didn't meet Danny until partway into his first year, shortly after Danny had instigated what was to become a famous incident among his fellow students.

Danny had avidly followed news of the War Crimes Tribunal, set up to try the officers and guards who had murdered and tortured his fellow prisoners of war. During one lecture, his Law professor, discussing the universal rule of law, had claimed that the War Crimes Tribunal was an excellent example of international justice finally administered fairly and impartially. Danny could feel himself becoming agitated and tried in vain to control the fury building inside him. Jumping to his feet, he signalled to the lecturer that he wished to speak, then, barely waiting for permission, he called, 'With the greatest respect, Professor Dodds, that's simply not true. It seems you can starve prisoners, punish them with indiscriminate beatings, lock them into a small wire cage so that they cannot move in the blazing tropical sun without water for three days, force them to eat salted rice until eventually they die of thirst or sunstroke, deny them fundamental medical treatment so that they die of preventable tropical diseases, and finally, with impunity, work them to death. Provided you don't actually line them up and shoot them in cold blood, you've acted according to the rules of warfare and so go unpunished. My Japanese commandant, Colonel Mori, spent six months in a military prison in Singapore before his case was summarily dismissed. His incarceration in Changi was very different from my own; the food was good and plentiful – in excess of 2000 calories a day, contrasting with ours, a starvation diet of 1000 calories of mouldy rice – he wasn't required to work and every medical treatment and care was available to him. The War Crimes Tribunal then deemed the six months he'd spent awaiting trial as sufficient punishment for my three and a half years of beatings, brutality and starvation and paid for his ticket back to Japan. I believe in such cases, and they are too numerous to be exceptions, that the law has failed in its moral and legal duty. As usual, the law has been applied in a typically discriminatory manner! There is one rule for officers, and another rule for the rank and file.'

Until this outburst Danny had kept a low profile on campus – one look at his face was enough to earn him the respect of the younger students – but this single short, eloquent speech brought him instant notoriety. When he sat down, his chest heaving, there was a spattering of applause from the braver students.

'See me afterwards,' Professor Dodds said tersely, and Danny's heart sank. He knew what was coming.

But he was wrong. The professor commended him on his performance. 'You seem to have all the prerequisites for becoming an excellent barrister, Mr Dunn,' he said with a wry smile. 'You should consider the bar.'

A week after what students called 'The Great Jap Spat', Franz Landsman had approached him in the university canteen. 'Mind if I join you?' he'd asked.

'No, go ahead.' Danny pointed to a vacant chair, then stuck out his hand. 'Danny Dunn.'

'Yeah, I know. Franz Landsman.' He shook Danny's hand, adding, 'Congratulations on the other day with Dodds.'

'Oh that,' Danny laughed. 'You'd think at my age I would have learned to keep my big mouth shut.'

'My problem precisely,' Franz replied, 'though I reckon we could make a bit of a splash as partners in the debating society. What say we give it a go – two Law students with big mouths and a brain or two to spare.'

Danny liked the young guy immediately; he wasn't sycophantic like so many of the other students who'd approached him since the confrontation with Dodds. Franz's approach had been straightforward – he'd come with a mission and put the idea of joining the debating society without any preliminary fawning. Like a kid from Balmain – like Lachlan Brannan, Danny suddenly thought – Franz Landsman appeared to be a cheeky young bugger. But, unlike Lachlan, who, like so many Balmain kids, hadn't been led to expect much out of life, Franz Landsman had a confident demeanour and assured grin and seemed to have a fair idea of his self-worth. As someone who'd once possessed the same easy confidence in great abundance, it was a quality Danny immediately recognised. And so began a friendship that, unbeknown to either of them at the time, would eventuate in a law partnership that was going to last into their dotage.

'Debating, eh? Never thought of joining,' Danny said.

'Be good, the WASP and the Yid – formidable!'

'WASP?' It wasn't an expression he'd heard in Balmain, probably because most people who lived there answered to that description. And the only Jew he knew was Pineapple Joe, who didn't count because he was, well, just himself.

'Yeah, White Anglo-Saxon Protestant,' Franz explained.

Danny grinned. 'Oh, then we're off to a bad start, mate, because my background's Irish Catholic.'

'Shit, eh? That's better still. A German Jew and a Tyke, two blokes with hefty chips on their shoulders who are angry at society and can think on their feet – that's a pretty impressive combination.'

Danny pointed to his face, which, after the plastic surgery looked almost normal, though, as he sometimes said, it was good panel beating but easy enough to tell where the prang had occurred. 'If I'd thought on my feet, my physog wouldn't look like this,' Danny replied.

'Okay, I'll do the fancy footwork – the tap dancing – and you supply the emotion – the anger, the vehemence. You were bloody excellent the other day with Dodds and neither of us lacks for brains. I reckon we could debate the arse off the rest of this university.'

'Careful – you haven't met my wife, Helen.'

'She in the debating society?'

'No, but if I join she might, and she'll insist on always being on the opposing team.'

'She good, then?'

'Yeah, and then some. She takes no prisoners.'

'She a law student?'

'No, archaeologist. She's got her masters in ancient history.'

'In other words, a good brain wasted,' Franz said dismissively.

'Hey, whoa . . . hold on, mate! Life's not all about making a quid,' Danny protested.

'It isn't? Shit, now you tell me!' Franz quipped.

Danny grinned. 'What was it Henry Adams said? Oh yes. "Those who ignore the past are condemned to relive it."'

'See, you need me, Danny. Henry Adams didn't say that and the quote is wrong. It was George Santayana who said, "Those who cannot remember the past are condemned to repeat it."'

'So what have we got here . . . a smart-arse?' Danny said, slightly defensive.

'No, no, the point you make is still valid,' Franz Landsman insisted. 'My family, Mum and Dad and I, we escaped the Nazi death camps by leaving Germany in 1932. Six million Jews didn't escape. Persecution of the Jews is a fact of history – it's happened several times before and we simply forgot to remember, and now it's happened again.' Franz Landsman paused, then said quietly, 'I apologise for being a smart-arse and belittling your wife's vocation.'

'Don't worry, mate. If you ever meet Helen and try to belittle her, you'll have your hands full.'

'Good mind, eh?'

'You better believe it, son,' Danny said, liking Franz Landsman for his own good mind, forthright manner and honesty. It was like having a younger quick-witted brother who kept you on your toes. 'Well, okay, let's start by being friends,' Danny said, extending his hand again. 'But you need to understand I'm not one of your mob.'

'What, a Jew?'

'Christ, no! I mean from the soft underbelly of the Eastern Suburbs and the North Shore, a private bloody schoolboy. My folks own a pub in Balmain.'

'And mine own a delicatessen in Bondi Road.'

'Righto, that's about equal; the chips on our shoulders are roughly the same size. But you have to do the legwork for the debating society, okay?'

'Shit, already the Yid is being persecuted by the Gentile.' Franz laughed. 'Then you pay for another Coke. Two good minds working together is thirsty work.'

'Stuff'll rot your gut. In the army we'd leave our dirty brasses in it overnight, and next morning they'd come out shining like a new pin.'

'Won't bother me, mate, I was brought up on Jewish cooking.' The boy from Bondi was quick.

Danny came third in his first year, with Franz Landsman ahead of him in second place, first place going to an ex-serviceman called Ron Ridge, who had missed the last three months of his first year due to an operation on his lung and elected to repeat. Danny had completed his Arts degree during his first year of Law and Helen believed that was why he hadn't topped the year, although Danny was chuffed with his result, if secretly a little annoyed that Franz had beaten him. But he pulled away quite significantly in second year to take the top spot, with Franz Landsman second and Ridge still in the top ten. After two years full-time at university, Law students began work in a law firm and continued their studies part-time.

The city law firms would line up to select those students they wanted to invite to serve their articles with them for the next two years. This was when well-connected parents flexed their social and business muscles, using any means available to influence the big important firms. It was a no-holds-barred contest that roped in uncles, cousins and friends, and employed dinner parties, nominations to exclusive clubs, the calling in of old favours, sometimes even threats or occasional blackmail, to help work the legal profession and the old-boy network. It was the time when who you knew in town really mattered.

So, there were quite a few powerful noses out of joint when Danny and Franz, two nobodies, a Tyke and a Yid, not only filled the first two places for second year but, despite their total lack of legal connections, were selected by the venerable Sydney law firm Stephen James &

Stapleton, who until then hadn't employed a single Jew or Catholic on its staff of twenty-four lawyers. As Franz put it to Danny, 'Mate, I've done my research and you can hear the buzz from that particular WASP nest from three blocks away.'

They completed their articles during their third and fourth years and sat their final Law exams, with Danny again topping both years and Franz Landsman coming in second and fourth respectively (he'd met a girl in his final year).

While Stephen James & Stapleton dealt more with commercial law than criminal, one or two of their solicitors worked the criminal courts and Danny quickly sought them out. Not surprisingly, it was the injustice he saw that prompted him to choose criminal law. As Helen put it when he told her of his decision, 'Darling, what else? With your anti-establishment ethos, it was a done deal.'

'You mean the chip on my shoulder?' Danny said defensively.

'No, I didn't mean that. I'm proud of your decision,' Helen replied. 'Somebody has to do it.'

In fact, the casual disregard for due process of those who worked within the law – the police force and magistrates, in particular – had been a constant topic of conversation between them on evenings when Danny had been in court. The police seemed to decide for themselves whether a defendant was guilty or not, and backed up their prejudices with verbals that suited the prosecution case. He noted that this scant regard for true justice all too often involved working-class defendants, who were easily dismissed as the criminal element in society and automatically assumed to be guilty. Magistrates saw rape victims as cock-teasers or sluts, almost by definition, and it was rare for a rapist to be convicted. Wife-beating and violence against children was seen as a domestic matter, and was yet another area in which the law wore blinkers.

Danny wasn't allowed to practise on his own, and the senior lawyers were either too busy for or too uninterested in the pro bono cases that began to pop up in Balmain now Danny was, in the eyes of the locals, a proper lawyer. Danny would, at Brenda's instigation, attend one of her afternoon soirees at the pub and advise the women preparing their veggies on their legal rights, in particular in the area of wife-bashing and even sometimes rape. This didn't help his popularity with some of their husbands, amongst whom this category of crime went largely unreported. He would even visit errant husbands and threaten them with an injunction, which would often scare the daylights out of them and change – for a while, anyway – their aberrant behaviour. In one or two cases when a husband continued to bash his wife, Danny persuaded one of the solicitors at work to allow him to prepare a brief and to let him function as his associate in court. They'd won the cases and the solicitor, Gary Murphy, was so impressed that he took, under Danny's instruction, three further cases: another battered wife, a rape victim and children assaulted by their father. They'd lost only the rape case.

Danny had earned a reputation in Balmain: amongst drunken husbands, who saw it as their right to beat their wives, it was as a meddler and a do-gooder; amongst wives, it was as a hero and a white knight. These were poor people but proud, and Helen would often arrive home from university to find a pot of stew, a batch of scones, a meatloaf or a cake on the doorstep with a note that said something like, *Thanks, Danny, return pot to Brenda.*

Helen was to learn that Danny never forgot or forgave an injustice, no matter how small. 'All that is necessary for the triumph of evil is that good men do nothing' had become one of his favourite sayings. Helen would often wake at night to find him missing from their bed. She had learned not to go after him, because often it was his demons that kept him awake, but sometimes he'd confess at breakfast, 'Couldn't sleep last night for thinking about . . .' and name some incident that was worrying him. Two that were most frequently on his mind were those concerning Captain Riley and Glossy Denmeade's boots, and Colonel Mori, his Japanese camp commandant.

Danny assiduously followed the fate of officers who had served under Mori, often asking Helen to call in favours, and scanning the newspapers for news of the trials. Several of the NCOs and soldiers from the camp were executed or jailed for crimes they'd committed while following Mori's direct orders. Danny continued his research in an attempt to build a new case against Mori, and discovered through a contact supplied by Helen that the American occupying powers in Japan had requested his unconditional release and his immediate and urgent repatriation to help with post-war reconstruction. Danny was learning that affluence and influence went hand in hand; Colonel Mori's aristocratic family were the owners of one of Japan's largest engineering firms and the Americans claimed he was needed to bring it back into effective production. If being a prisoner of war had taught Danny anything, it was never to give up, and he became obsessed with this injustice.

Helen, as forthright as ever, replied, 'Danny, you've got to forget Mori! You have to stop this battle against injustice and make peace with yourself, or the war is going to kill you as surely as if you'd taken a bullet in the heart from Mori himself. The world is a cruel and hateful place. For God's sake, Danny, you should know that better than anyone! Are you to take all this accumulated hate with you to the grave?'

But Helen knew that her husband had inherited his stubbornness from Brenda and that her pleas were useless; it was Danny's obsessive nature that kept him going – it was what made him formidable in whatever he tackled. Danny hated to lose, either at tiddlywinks or in a court case. As a young man before the war he could put his aggression and determination into water polo and rugby league, but now his bad back restricted him to swimming endless early-morning laps of Balmain pool. All his energy went into social justice, or, for that matter, justice itself. His experience as a prisoner of war had clearly and irrevocably demonstrated to him what it was like to be at the bottom of the pecking order. He wasn't a goody-goody – he was a Balmain boy, after all – but he hated anyone who took advantage of the innocent or underprivileged. It was his tenacity that was going to earn him a reputation as a formidable opponent in a court of law. He never knew when to quit, even when it might have been to his advantage.

For instance, not long after he graduated as a lawyer, in what the
military authorities and the government decried as 'grandstanding' he
had petitioned the government to reconvene the War Crimes Tribunal
and to reinstate the prosecution trial of Colonel Mori. But once again
it proved a case of might being greater than right. The government
denied the request, dismissing the charge that the authorities had been
influenced by any request from the Americans. In their letter of rejection
they also failed to mention that they were currently being pressured by
the Americans to sign a formal peace treaty with the defeated Japanese.
Pragmatism *über alles*, with truth and justice always easy victims.

CHAPTER SEVEN

———

IT HAD TAKEN THIRTY years for Brenda's moment of glory to finally arrive, when Danny was to receive not one but two mighty scrolls on the same day: his Arts degree as well as his Law degree. Brenda had put off writing to her parents until Danny had received the results of his final-year exams and notification that the graduation ceremony would take place at 10.30 a.m. on Tuesday the 30th of January 1951 in the Sydney University Great Hall.

She'd spent several days writing and rewriting the letter in an attempt to persuade them to make the trip. Over the years, especially when she made her annual visit to the farm near Wagga, she'd tried to get them to visit, but without success. They'd always agree when she asked, but then Patrick, her father, would find some excuse not to go at the last minute – the drought or the rains, lambing, fencing, fixing the tractor she'd bought him, digging a dam – always something to prevent them coming, and always to the bitter disappointment of her darling mother, who would usually confess in a letter that she'd 'been to the chickens'.

Rose O'Shane had never allowed her children to see her cry, although they all knew as kids that when she appeared with red puffy eyes it meant she'd been to the chickens. The chicken run was a place

Patrick never visited. The hens were his wife's responsibility. So when life became too unbearable she'd visit the hens for a good old Irish keen. Letting a hen roost on her hands was very comforting.

In the end, Brenda wrote a very formal letter, spending the entire Christmas break composing it and taking care with every word. In the years since she'd left school she'd forgotten about the importance of paragraphs and the letter seemed somehow all the better for this, because, while formal, it also had the virtue of appearing to come, as indeed it did, from the heart.

Brenda decided to take the bit between her teeth and talk about Danny's injuries and war record as well as his two degrees. While she desperately wanted her parents to be present at his graduation, it had to be on her terms. Her father had bullied her for long enough with his refusal to visit. This time she wasn't going to take it on the chin. She had, after twenty-nine hard years, achieved her ambition for a member of her family to be a 'somebody'. Now there could be no more compromises.

> Dear Father,
>
> Your grandson is to receive not one, but two university degrees. While I know your stance on the first war and this recent one, nevertheless, Danny served with great distinction. I often receive letters from the men he was responsible for in the Japanese concentration camp. They all say the same thing – that he should have received a DSO for bravery. Many claim he saved their lives and some describe how he did this. Many of their stories make me weep, but I also take great pride in my son, your grandson, who is soon to become a lawyer. They also speak of the terrible injuries to his face and back, which he sustained at the hands of the Japanese while defending one of his own men. I feel sure my brothers were heroes in the last war and Danny has followed in their footsteps, in your, our family's footsteps. I know life has been hard for you and Mother Rose, but since leaving Ireland you have shown a steady courage, which has been passed on to your grandson. As the first member of our

family to receive not one but two university degrees, we have cause to celebrate in the knowledge that it has not all been in vain, that at last we are somebodies. Without you and Mother Rose at Danny's graduation it will not be a true family celebration. In the name of my two dead brothers I beg you from the bottom of my heart to be with us on this grand day, the triumph of the O'Shane family.

   Your loving and obedient daughter,
   Brenda

She then attached two first-class return tickets for the train from Wagga to Sydney and a money order for five pounds for travel expenses. She was ecstatic when Rose wrote to say Patrick had agreed they would definitely be coming as he wanted to see his grandson get the first degree ever earned by a family member.

Brenda's own preparation for graduation day had lasted nearly a month, so that on the big day she was dressed to the nines with everything brand-new and of the very best quality. Helen, whenever she was free from the university, became her constant companion and consultant, as Brenda wouldn't trust herself in such matters. Her accessories were chosen with the help of Madam St Clair, dressmaker to the Eastern Suburbs' rich and famous, who'd created Brenda's outfit and then insisted on accompanying them, for an appropriate fee, to Mark Foys (underwear and stockings), David Jones (shoes and handbag) and Anthony Hordern (hat and gloves). Finally, to set off the whole outfit, Helen had lent her a genuine pearl necklace and drop earrings left to her by her grandmother – much to the chagrin of Helen's mother, who'd always had her eye on them but had received instead her mother's wedding band and (very small diamond) engagement ring.

While Brenda and Half Dunn were considered well off, even rich, by most standards, it had never occurred to Brenda to spend very much on herself. Like everyone else she depended on Freda's Frocks to tell her the latest fashion and length of hem required for the year to come. Every Wednesday she'd have her hair and nails done at Nina's Beauty Salon, and once a year on the 31st of December she had a permanent booking to have 'the works' – a facial, which included a mudpack; and hair and nails – in preparation for midnight mass at St Augustine's to see the new year in.

In fact, the last time she'd splurged on clothes was when she'd gone to dinner at Primo's with Doc Evatt, then a judge in the New South Wales High Court, but later President of the General Assembly of the United Nations, and now being spoken of as the next leader of the Labor Party should the ailing Ben Chifley retire from parliament.

For the big occasion, Brenda's make-up, usually a hastily applied lick of Rita Hayworth-style red lipstick to show off her pretty mouth and sometimes a smudge of eye shadow and a dab of rouge, was now personally supervised by Nina from the beauty salon. She'd brought all her paraphernalia in a large suitcase over from the salon in Darling Street to the pub, arriving just after eight in the morning.

Danny and Half Dunn privately agreed the result was somewhat over the top, but they were nevertheless quick to compliment Brenda, who had become increasingly nervous after breakfast, lighting twenty single-puff cigarettes that were later discovered burnt out in various ashtrays around the premises. By the time the taxi taking them to the university for the mid-morning graduation ceremony arrived, she was very close to tears from a mixture of anxiety and overwhelming excitement.

Brenda sat in the Sydney University Great Hall between Rose and Helen, whose parents, Barbara and Reg, sat next to their daughter, with Patrick next to Rose, and then Half Dunn next to his father-in-law. While the dolled-up version of Brenda didn't look any prettier for all the expense, at forty-eight, despite the years of hard work – or perhaps because of them – she was still a trim and good-looking woman. She was blessed, as some people would have said, with good bone structure and a nice figure.

Rose had been to Freda's Frocks, too, where Brenda had insisted she have a new outfit: a pink mid-season rose-patterned dress, white shoes, hat and gloves, the loveliest undies she'd ever owned and real nylon stockings. Half Dunn was in a new Pineapple Joe suit and Patrick, at his insistence, once again in his Irish tweed wedding suit, starched detachable collar, black tie and button boots, though this time the weather was a little kinder.

But the day, as so often happens when we eagerly anticipate an event, didn't quite turn out as Brenda had always imagined it would. Later, when Half Dunn told the story of Danny's graduation, he would begin by saying, 'When, as Brenda has done, you wait almost thirty years for something, you tend to build up a fair head of steam.' He'd pause, then say meaningfully, 'That can be dangerous . . . very dangerous.'

They'd arrived an hour before the ceremony was due to begin, to ensure good seats. With the first rows in the centre block being reserved for the faculty, they'd settled into seats three rows back, the first row available to the public. By the time the vice-chancellor, resplendent in floppy gold-tasselled velvet cap and black gown festooned with gold braid, had led the long, colourful procession of professors onto the stage and they'd taken their seats, Brenda was already crying softly. Helen reached down and held one of her hands while Rose held the other.

The vice-chancellor welcomed the guests, then launched into the usual dry and dusty stuff about the importance of hard work and carving a worthy career while maintaining a strong sense of duty to and respect for society, but then he went on to say, 'At last year's graduation ceremony, and again at this one, we take a special pride in those graduates who returned from serving their country to complete or undertake degrees. While this great institution acknowledges its debt to all these exceptional men and women, one man in particular stands out. I speak of the recipient of this year's University Medal for outstanding scholastic achievement. He is a man who endured captivity and torture under the Japanese. While working on the Thai–Burma Railway and later in Thailand, he was solely responsible as the senior NCO for the men in two prisoner-of-war camps, enduring the onerous conditions of starvation, sickness, lack of medical facilities and harsh cruelty with which we are all too familiar. In performing his duty, this man managed to save many lives, in fact a greater proportion than in most other prisoner-of-war camps in Burma and Thailand. It is an indictment of our military system that such a man has received no formal recognition for his extraordinary achievements.' The vice-chancellor paused before continuing. 'I hasten to add that the University Medal is given solely for scholarship, without regard for past endeavours beyond the walls of the Academe, no matter how worthy those endeavours may have been, and, in the case of this man, undoubtedly were. This medal will be presented later in today's ceremony when we are only permitted to highlight the academic achievements of this fine young man, but it would have been remiss of me not to make mention here of this remarkable student, as well as those others who served their country and do us all proud. I am speaking of Daniel Corrib Dunn.'

Brenda's quiet weeping had turned to audible sobbing and then to an uncontrollable soft wail so that Helen was finally obliged to lead her out of the Great Hall. Rose had moved to follow but Patrick placed a rough, sun-damaged hand on her arm to restrain her.

Helen guided Brenda to a bench in the quad and held her to her breast while she continued to weep, finally crying, 'That medal, it was won by Doc Evatt, too!'

Helen was more than a little surprised by her mother-in-law's emotional outburst. While Danny had told her about the incident that had occurred just before dawn on the morning after he'd returned home, he'd made a point of Brenda's stoicism, saying that he had rarely heard or seen her cry. She was a woman firm in resolve, deeply proud, who kept her sadness to herself, or, as Half Dunn suspected she'd done when Danny had left to go to war, took it home to share only with Rose. It was not that she was phlegmatic or emotionally circumspect – she had a quick temper and a sharp tongue, as many a drunk could testify, although these were balanced by her ability to laugh at herself. For Brenda to break down in public was entirely out of character and it testified to the extraordinary depth of her feelings. The sole purpose of her life was about to be fulfilled, and although she had steeled herself for what was, after all, a long-anticipated event, it had been the vice-chancellor's unexpected tribute to her war-ravaged son that had crashed through the carefully constructed barrier behind which she'd always contained her emotions.

It was almost half an hour before Brenda recovered and allowed Helen to wipe away the mascara, and most of the vestiges of Nina's cosmetics, to restore the naturally pretty Brenda, albeit with eyes puffy and red from crying. She had missed the very moment she had waited so long for, the conferring of Danny's double degree, making him a double 'somebody'. One of the university ushers arrived to say that the vice-chancellor had deferred the medal presentation until last and hoped she might return to the Great Hall to be present when her son was honoured by his professors, the academic staff and fellow students. She straightened her shoulders, and patted her hair. She would be present when he won the trifecta and became a triple 'somebody'.

As Brenda and Helen re-entered the Great Hall, the audience spontaneously rose to their feet and clapped until she'd resumed her seat. And although fresh tears coursed down her cheeks she wore a smile a stonemason couldn't have chiselled from her face.

Danny, wearing the cap and gown of a Law graduate over a brand-new suit ('For knowink already a genius, no charge and compliments of Pineapple Joe'), received the University Medal to a standing ovation, a rare or perhaps singular occurrence for a student with a bachelor degree.

The eight of them – Brenda and Half Dunn, Rose and Patrick, Reg and Barbara and, of course, Danny and Helen – had gone back to the Hero for lunch, a low-key family affair at Danny's insistence. While Barbara smiled quickly when spoken to, Helen couldn't help noticing that in moments of repose, when she was unaware of anyone looking at her, she'd largely remain po-faced, though when Danny received his medal there had been a flicker of gratification. Perhaps she was surprised to discover that Catholics could also be brilliant, Helen thought to herself.

Helen had made a *boeuf bourguignon*, to be followed by fresh strawberries and ice-cream topped with a chocolate cognac sauce. She had taken a course in French cooking when they'd visited Billy du Bois in Louisiana. The French cooking was to complement the jeroboam of champagne that had been waiting patiently on the top shelf of the main bar for a decade or so. By anyone's reckoning it now qualified as vintage. Danny had brought it down from the shelf that morning and Half Dunn had immersed it in a tub of ice cubes.

While the celebration lunch was low key, Brenda insisted that it take place in the dining room. The only other time anyone could remember using the dining room for an actual meal was when Doc Evatt had visited just after the war. But even then they'd ended up eating pudding and sharing the best part of a good bottle of brandy in the kitchen. The dining-room table was really only used for an occasional game of cards or Monopoly and Danny had studied on it in the evenings before the war.

However, Brenda didn't care how much it cost or what Danny wanted – she was going to celebrate his graduation in style. She'd shopped with Helen at Anthony Hordern's, where they'd bought a complete set of Wedgwood crockery, a posh silver-plated canteen of cutlery, and an Irish linen tablecloth and napkins with a 'D' hand-embroidered in a corner of each. Brenda wanted the 'D' to be in scarlet, as she'd once seen the 'T' embroidered at a special Tooheys banquet for their most valued customers, but Helen had persuaded her to have it in white. Finally, champagne glasses had been a must – Waterford crystal from Ireland. Brenda justified all this extravagance to Helen by saying, 'When you married in such a hurry before going off to America for Danny's operations we never set you up properly. Now that Danny's a lawyer you'll be entertaining a fair bit, I suppose, so after Sunday it will all be yours, my darling.'

Now, on the big day, the table was perfectly set following instructions Brenda had cut out from the *Women's Weekly* and saved on an impulse years ago. 'If the Queen was coming to lunch I wouldn't be ashamed of this table,' she said to Helen, happily surveying it, head on one side.

With everyone seated, the moment to open the famous jeroboam had finally arrived. Crystal glasses were lined up in front of Half Dunn, who had rightly assumed the role of master of ceremonies. He began the opening ceremony with the story of the champagne. 'This jeroboam has stood on the top shelf of the main bar through much of Danny's school days, through a war, a first degree at the university and then a second. During that time it has had to resist the efforts of countless drunks who've thrown their week's wages on the bar and demanded we open it. But Brenda has dealt with them, as only my darling wife knows how. Now, at last, its time has finally come.'

In truth, Half Dunn hadn't opened many bottles of champagne in his career as a publican. The Hero and its patrons didn't call for a lot of champagne, in fact, almost none. But he knew the general principle, or had seen it in the movies. It was simple enough: you removed the foil, untwisted the wire loop and then worked the bulbous crown of the cork with the pad of your thumb up and away from the neck, pointing it at the ceiling, while everyone waited excitedly for the pop. The cork then exploded from the neck at a thousand miles an hour to hit the ceiling with a resounding bang, leaving a mark to be happily recalled ever after.

But, alas, no such thing happened; the cork wouldn't budge. Half Dunn then tried to twist the cork out of the bottle. It still didn't move, even after several attempts, so that he had grown somewhat red in the face and was breathing heavily from the effort by the time Danny volunteered to take over. But the result was the same. The cork may as well have been welded to the neck. Danny then gripped the large bottle between his knees and twisted with all his might, unwittingly agitating the champagne, but again to no avail. The cork remained firmly in place. Finally, in desperation, Danny retrieved a shifting spanner from the toolbox downstairs, fitted it to the cork and began to twist. The cork creaked and moved a fraction.

'Got the bugger!' Danny cried, just as the cork shot from the bottle and hit the ceiling with a report that must have been heard at the ferry terminal. Almost simultaneously an angry geyser of champagne gushed out in an umbrella-shaped shower, thoroughly drenching Brenda's beautiful table setting and all who sat around it.

Helen, the first to recover, let out a delighted yell. 'Hooray! I always wanted to bathe in vintage French champagne!' Then she calmly reached for her sodden monogrammed napkin to wipe her face.

This set off a gale of laughter as everyone dabbed furiously at their clothes, all except Brenda, who sat at the end of the table looking utterly stricken. The champagne had flattened her carefully coiffed hair so that it fell over her eyes in a tangle of dark-red strands. 'I don't think I'm ever going to get the knack of being a "somebody",' she said in a forlorn little voice. Then she sniffed and shrugged, surveying the ruined table setting. 'Oh, well, back to the kitchen, everyone.' A corner of her mouth quirked and she was soon laughing too.

Suddenly Patrick got to his feet. Throughout the day, he'd been more taciturn than usual, and even the congratulatory handshake he'd given Danny after the ceremony had been accompanied by only a gruff, 'Well done, son.' Now he peered at the bottle Danny was still holding and said, 'If me old eyes don't deceive me, there's a wee drop left in that Frenchy bottle. If it's only a mouthful, then it's still enough for a toast to me darlin' daughter.'

Brenda was deeply shocked, not only by his suggestion but by the endearment. She couldn't remember, even as a small child, the slightest sign of sentiment from her father, although Rose had once told her that he was 'quite the loving lad' in Ireland. Australia, that godforsaken country, had taken his two sons in England's brutal war and had instead granted him the burden of daughters. He was left a bitter and silent man.

Brenda had always been aware of the shame he felt at having to accept her help over the years, and she felt no rancour that a mixture of pride and resentment had prevented him from showing her the slightest gratitude. She was certain that this was the reason why he had constantly refused her entreaties to visit Sydney with her mother. While the notion that she might expect some repayment, if only emotionally, had never entered her head, Brenda knew it to be Irish logic that the giver must be punished for giving in order to preserve the pride of the beneficiary.

Brenda had also discovered that poor relatives were an emotional as well as a financial burden. The twins, with their fifteen children, both expected and resented her help, sending begging letters about their parlous situation so that Brenda was always compelled to help, but never a thank-you letter or even the smallest gesture of love. She'd arranged with a local grocer to deliver the basics to both families each week so the children didn't go without when the fathers were out of work or had spent their wages on drink. Similarly, a local department store supplied their school uniforms and other necessities. The accounts would be sent to Brenda each month, but whatever she did for them would never be enough and she understood that they saw no reason to be grateful. As with her tears, Brenda kept her disappointment and grief to herself.

Danny held the bottle up to the light, and discovered that about three inches of champagne were left, enough to fill each glass with a decent mouthful. He poured the now precious liquid as Half Dunn handed the glasses around.

'It would please me if we all stood while Brenda remained seated,' Patrick O'Shane said in a stern voice to hide his anxiety. Chairs scraped backwards and everyone stood silent, holding their glasses. That is, all except Barbara Brown, who, lips pursed, still dabbed at the champagne-spattered oyster satin blouse that concealed her ample breasts. Their rapid pumping, together with her sour expression, signified her extreme annoyance at the ruin of her best blouse. While Helen's father was a nice chap in a regular Rotarian sort of way, her mother was a snob who quite obviously thought that her woefully wilful daughter had married well beneath herself. Danny's winning of the University Medal was all very well, but you can't make a silk purse out of a sow's ear and the fact that the boy had a modicum of brains didn't make up for his Irish Catholic background and barely passable face, and the lamentable behaviour in the Great Hall of the particular Irish sow in question. Later, when she unburdened herself to her friends about Brenda's weeping, the debacle with the champagne and much else besides, she would use words such as *atrocious*, *cheap*, *gauche*, *vulgar*, *common*, *unconscionable* and *shameful*, but at this moment the epithet that sprang into her mind was *bog Irish*. Really, what had Helen been thinking!

Patrick waited patiently until Helen's mother had ceased her angry dabbing and finally rose from her chair to join them. 'I'm a plain-speaking man without the words to express my feelings, but I will try to say what I feel in my heart.' He paused and looked directly at Brenda. 'When Rose and I lost our sons in that terrible, terrible war, we lost our hope. The land they could have worked when the drought finally broke was barren, the stock dead, and we had three girls to feed.'

Brenda listened, stunned, as he told the story of the school inspector's visit and his mortified refusal. 'It wasn't her brains we needed but her strong back and a good pair of arms that could scrub floors and be useful to others more fortunate than us. So we sent our clever daughter into town to work as a room maid in the hotel. And thanks to her efforts since that time we have all survived. Time out of mind when we had nowhere else to turn, our daughter has been our only support.' He paused and looked around. 'It was me who robbed her of an education, but I couldn't rob her of her character, determination and love. It was me again who was too proud to thank her, to tell her how much we loved her. She has been the embodiment of my two sons as well as a remarkable daughter. She is the sum total of all the good in us. If ever there was a "somebody" in our family, then it is our darlin' daughter. I would now like to propose a toast to the most remarkable woman Rose and I have ever known.' He held his glass aloft. 'To Brenda, our beloved daughter.'

'To Brenda!' they all cried and drained their glasses.

Danny took one look at his mother, hurried to her and held her in his arms.

'Oh, dear, Danny, this is supposed to be your day,' she said tearfully. 'I've had much too much attention.'

'No, Mum, it's yours. I've kept you waiting long enough.' Danny helped his mother to her feet and led her to the kitchen. 'I guess I've never told you, but I could not have wanted for a better mother,' he said quietly. It was the closest he'd ever come to telling her he loved her.

'To the kitchen, everyone, for beer and Irish stew!' Helen laughed, instantly converting her *boeuf bourguignon* to a dish more suitable in the circumstances.

By late afternoon Helen had cleared away the plates from the strawberries and ice-cream doused in chocolate cognac sauce, which she'd renamed Irish Mudslide to much applause. Half Dunn then produced Scotch glasses and brandy balloons, together with a bottle of French cognac and another of aged Irish whiskey and poured each of them their preferred after-dinner tipple. With everyone's glasses charged, Danny stood up to say, as Half Dunn would later put it, his two bobs' worth. Patrick, the happiest Rose had seen him since they'd left Ireland, tapped the rim of his glass with his dessert spoon and demanded silence for his grandson.

Danny thanked both his parents for their love, patience, understanding and loyalty, then finished by saying, 'If I can show my darling Helen the same loyalty and understanding as my father has shown my mother while allowing her the freedom to be herself, then I feel sure that I will have served her well. While my mother has received the attention she so justly deserves, my father has always been a loyal husband, unquestioning, patient and cheerful. Please, everyone, I would like to propose another toast to Mum and Dad. How fortunate I am to have them as my parents. To Mum and Dad!'

'To Mum and Dad!'

'To Brenda and Michael!'

And so the day had ended, on a suitably sentimental note, with Patrick and Half Dunn falling asleep at the kitchen table, Helen's parents having taken their leave as soon as it was polite for them to do so. Rose and Brenda, happily aproned, were clearing up and doing the dishes, adamant that Helen should not help ('You're the cook and we're the bottle-washers, darling!'), so she and Danny were able to finally take their leave and return to their little bedsitter in Glebe Point Road.

'God, I'm totally whacked,' Danny sighed, emerging from the bedroom barefoot, having changed from his good clothes into a pair of rugby shorts and an old Tigers' football jumper. He heard a loud pop and cried, 'Christ! What's that?'

Helen, smiling, head to one side, stood at the doorway of the tiny kitchenette holding two champagne glasses and a bottle of French bubbly. 'I didn't spill a drop!' she declared triumphantly.

'Jesus, darling, haven't we had enough?' In fact Danny, with the exception of the mouthful from the jeroboam, hadn't touched a drop. He was aware that booze was no place to hide, and that it was capable of exposing him and bringing all his demons to the surface.

'Like you, darling, I barely touched a drop. A glass now to celebrate is entirely appropriate.'

'I think I'm celebrated out. I'm sure your mum and dad didn't make this kind of fuss when you got your masters degree.'

Helen laughed, placing the glasses on the small coffee table in the room that served as both lounge, dining room and office. 'They took me to dinner at the Australia Club. We had oysters and duck à l'orange and a drop from what Reg referred to as "a good bottle of wine", explaining that it had been recommended by a friend who really knew his onions.' Helen started to fill the glasses.

'By the way, your mum was hardly a bundle of joy today,' Danny said, accepting the champagne from Helen.

'Oh, you should know by now she's an awful snob and the champagne shower would have been the last straw.' Helen grinned. 'Look at it from her point of view. Her only daughter, always a stubborn and wayward child, ends up marrying a tyke with an ugly mug, well beneath her notion of my station in life who hasn't given her any grandchildren, and who now has the effrontery to somehow win the University Medal. It's all pretty harrowing stuff.'

'Well, the last person I want to drink to is the barren bloke with the ugly mug.' Danny smiled. 'Darling, you've had to manage the whole shebang from start to finish – Mum's outfit, shopping for the posh table setting, Mum's weeping fit at the uni, cooking lunch, humouring everyone after the champagne shower, regrouping in the kitchen and turning a French banquet into an Irish dinner and, last but by no means least, finally winning over my grandfather with your "Irish stew". Since I was a child, I've regarded the old bastard with fear and loathing as a taciturn old bugger who treated my mother like dirt.' He stepped forward and kissed his wife lightly on the lips, careful not to spill his champagne. 'To my darling Helen, who indeed is much, much more than I deserve and way, way above my station in life.'

Helen shot out a hand, covering his glass and saying, 'Whoa! Not so fast, lover boy! This isn't a toast to you or me but to a someone neither of us has actually met.'

Danny looked at her quizzically. 'What's that supposed to mean?'

In a portentous tone she announced, 'Danny Corrib Dunn, I am pleased to announce that, after a period of four years and nine months, I am pregnant!'

Danny's mouth fell open and he began to shake. He placed his glass on the coffee table rather unsteadily and said, 'A baby?' as if tasting the word, then looked at Helen and added, 'But you said . . . no, surely not . . .'

'Yes, yes, yes! We're having a baby!' Helen squealed, unable to contain herself.

'You mean an actual *baby*? Why didn't you tell me, Helen?' he yelled, grabbing at her.

'I wanted to be sure, darling,' she giggled, drawing away. 'Look out, I'll spill my champagne!' Helen hastily placed her glass beside his.

'Come here, woman!' Danny demanded, suddenly aware that he couldn't see her clearly. 'Jesus, I'm going to cry . . . it's been four years!' He grabbed her, holding her to him and smothering her in kisses.

'And nine months – remember we started practising on the ship going to America, just after we'd sailed through the Heads.' Helen began to weep, and they held each other for what seemed ages until finally she pulled away. 'The toast . . . we haven't —'

'And you kept it all to yourself all this time?' Danny interrupted.

'It wasn't easy,' Helen sniffed, knuckling away her tears. 'Every time I looked at you I wanted to tell you, and when you were awarded the medal I wanted to yell out, "Darling, you're going to be a father!" Keeping it to myself has been the hardest thing I've ever done. I missed a period two weeks ago, and you know I'm regular as clockwork. Imagine what Brenda would have been like if this had been added to her day?'

'You're sure . . . I mean, *positive*, aren't you?' Danny found he was trembling as he reached down and lifted the two glasses from the coffee table, handing her one of them. 'A baby! Jesus!' Then, lifting his glass, he said solemnly, 'To the baby! May he have his mother's brains and character!'

They raised their glasses and Helen looked into Danny's eyes. 'And her father's looks and courage,' she said quietly. Then, taking him by the hand, she turned towards the bedroom door. 'We won't be able to make love for a month to six weeks after the baby's born, so that's approximately twenty orgasms you're going to owe me and there isn't a moment to lose. I've never slept with a University Medal winner. Oh, darling, I am so proud of you!'

Danny was still having difficulty comprehending the news; he'd long since believed that he was sterile, that the years of starvation in the camps had cost him his children as well as so much besides, and while they enjoyed a full and satisfying sex life – Helen demanded she received as much as she gave – in the four years and a bit they'd been married they'd taken no precautions and she had not become pregnant. Sometimes after they'd made love and she'd fallen asleep in his arms he'd been overcome by panic, convinced that she was going to leave him.

For Danny's graduation, Helen had worn a straight chemise dress nipped in at the waist and falling to just below her knees, à la Norman Norell, finished off with a flared jacket. Under her outer garments she was equally fashionable, as Danny discovered. He loved the ritual of undressing Helen, working slowly, first removing her dress to reveal her nylon strapless bra – the latest fashion – then, with a deft flick, unclipping the back, then kissing and gently sucking her breasts. He would take each nipple in his mouth until it stiffened and bounced against his tongue, pointing, as he would laughingly put it, to the moon.

Now he eased her slip over her head so that she stood in her brown satin French knickers trimmed with cream lace, her garter belt, nylons and high heels. It was a sophisticated version of the New Look, rather than the hooped skirts, petticoats and nylon corsets the jitterbug era had made all the rage. It was Helen's only good outfit and had taken her months to accumulate.

Undressing his wife had never been this complicated before, or perhaps Helen's news had destroyed his powers of concentration, but on several occasions Danny needed instructions. Finally, he removed her gorgeous knickers and went down on his knees, his hands clasped around her nice firm buttocks so he could demonstrate his immaculate French and bring her to her first climax of the night. Then he hurriedly removed his own clothes and they slid into bed, where Helen opened her legs wide to receive him and said with a low chuckle, 'Two medal-winning performances in the same day! First the University Medal and now the *Légion d'honneur!*'

An hour later they lay back in bed, happy and exhausted, though less from the joy of making love than from the long day. Danny went to the kitchen and returned to their bed with fresh champagne, unable to wipe the grin off his face. 'Imagine . . . who would have thought . . . a baby.' He made it sound as if procreation were a unique process known only to them. 'Just you wait – I'm going to be a terrific father, the best. He'll play for Australia!'

'What if it's a girl, smarty pants?' Helen replied.

Danny hesitated, then sniffed back fresh tears. 'Swim,' he said. 'She'll swim for Australia.' His voice shook with emotion. 'Let's see, born 1951 . . . She'll be twenty-one in 1972, an Olympic year! Yes, yes, swim – or row – for Australia!'

Helen frowned. 'What about *think* for Australia?'

'Hah? Oh yeah, that too!' Danny said happily.

From the moment Helen announced she was pregnant Danny sensed that he'd been given another chance; that his life was not effectively over; that with children he could be himself, come out of hiding and be completely honest. From that day on, Danny would always celebrate the anniversary of the day on which Helen broke the news of her pregnancy with a bottle of French champagne. It wasn't a difficult anniversary to remember – the news of Helen's pregnancy had come on the same day as his graduation in what would ever after be known in the family as 'Weepy Day'.

If Helen had waited almost five years to become a mother, she might have expected that she could now relax, but she would discover that nothing was as she had expected. As her pregnancy progressed she grew more and more enormous, so that at six months she was waddling around like a Jersey cow and was forced to give up work. Danny's salary as a solicitor was barely enough for food once they'd paid the rent. One evening Franz paid them an unexpected visit and found them eating baked beans on toast for supper. He said nothing, but twice a week thereafter, a hamper from Landsman's Delicatessen and Continental Smallgoods, now with four shops and a state-of-the-art processing plant, appeared on Danny's desk. When Danny questioned Franz he simply shrugged and said, 'Hester!' as if that explained everything. Then, when the hampers began to arrive three times a week and Danny was becoming a little embarrassed, he'd added, 'Jewish mothers.'

Of course Brenda would have seen that they didn't go without. They actually had a plain but very good diet despite their lack of money, and the food from Bondi Road was actually a bit rich. While Danny enjoyed it, Helen was very careful that she ate the right foods and stuck to the 'Triple "B" Plan – How to build a better baby', in the Dr Spock book she'd adopted as her baby bible.

Helen's contractions had become very close and her waters finally broke just before six o'clock on an early spring evening, the 24th September 1951, when Danny had not long arrived home from work. Panic-stricken, he'd driven Helen in Half Dunn's Holden FX, borrowed for the occasion, in to the Crown Street Women's Hospital.

They arrived at reception – a window set halfway down an interior wall and fitted with a broad wooden writing ledge for people filling in registration forms. A male clerk asked for a surname, then checked a list and pushed a form through the window. 'Your details, please, Mr Dunn. You must come down and see the cashier before you leave, sir.'

Danny hurriedly filled in the form and pushed it back to the clerk, who then attached the form to a clipboard and made a phone call. Covering the mouthpiece he said, 'Please wait, sir. The admission sister will be down shortly to collect you.'

Danny looked around to see that the foyer contained no furniture other than a small table with a large, tired floral arrangement on it. 'Is there a waiting room? Somewhere my wife can sit?' he inquired.

'The ward admission sister will be down soon, sir,' the clerk replied.

'Yes, but —'

'Shouldn't be long,' the clerk interjected, turning away from the window and disappearing around a corner of the office.

Danny, already anxious, felt his anger rising. 'This is ridiculous!' he shouted at the window in frustration. Helen's contractions had been coming more quickly in the car on the way to the hospital, but she was steadier than Danny.

'It's all right, darling,' she gasped, attempting a smile. 'It's probably ages yet. I'm sure someone will be coming soon.'

Just then the lift door opened and a large veiled starched figure in her fifties, clad from head to toe in spotless white, emerged – the ward admission sister. She ignored them, crossing to the admissions window where the clerk, who must have heard the lift doors opening, appeared again to hand her the clipboard. She glanced down at it. 'Mrs Helen Dunn?' she asked, even though Danny and Helen were the only ones in the foyer. Then without waiting for a reply, she said, 'Follow me, please,' and stalked off towards the lift.

Danny held a panting Helen by the arm, carrying her overnight bag in his other hand. The bag contained several changes of undies, two nightgowns, a chenille dressing-gown, bed socks, new slippers, six freshly ironed hankies, a new toothbrush, a new tube of toothpaste, fancy face cream (Brenda's gift from Nina's Beauty Salon), lipstick and a small manicure set. He'd personally packed it weeks before, fussing over every small detail. Now he was doing his best to appear in control when he knew he was very close to panicking. They entered the lift and rose three floors, emerged, walked down a long passage, passing open doors that led into various wards, until they reached a room with five beds, four of them occupied by expectant mothers. The empty bed was nearest the door, and Helen, exhausted from the long walk, sat on the edge of it panting as she waited for another contraction to pass. 'Please get into your nightgown and climb into bed. A nurse will be around presently,' the sister instructed.

Danny lifted the overnight bag onto the bed, opened it and removed a nightgown, dressing-gown and slippers. 'Don't move, darling. I'll get you ready for bed,' he offered.

'No, that won't be necessary, Mr Dunn. A nurse will be along shortly,' the sister said firmly, starting to draw the curtains around the bed.

Danny ignored her and dropped to his haunches to remove Helen's shoes. 'Come along now!' the sister said briskly, her impatience clear.

'Better be off, darling,' Helen whispered.

Danny rose and began to unbutton the front of Helen's maternity dress. 'Won't be a moment, sister,' he said, trying to sound cheerful.

'No, no, this simply won't do. Your wife is in our care now!' The sister had drawn the bed curtains so that only the triangle formed by her veil and her head protruded into the space around the bed. Danny noticed that the bright-red lipstick she wore had started to leak into the heavy face powder, giving her mouth a distinctly bloody appearance. In his mind he dubbed her Sister Dracula. 'You'll have to leave at once, Mr Dunn,' she insisted. Then she pulled her head back and gave the curtain a sharp tug to indicate her annoyance.

'My wife . . . I can't leave her . . . what if . . . ?' Danny called in a panicked voice. 'It won't take long. I know where everything is – I packed it myself,' he added lamely.

'Better get along, darling,' Helen said, attempting a reassuring smile that was suddenly cut short by a fresh contraction.

Sister Dracula's voice called from beyond the curtain. 'At once please, Mr Dunn! This is a maternity ward and no place for a husband! Your wife is going into labour!'

Danny, not wanting to upset Helen, knew he was beaten. 'See you soon, darling,' he said, kissing her tenderly on the lips. 'Just going downstairs. Be back in a moment,' he whispered.

Helen grabbed him by the wrist. 'Danny, please! Don't do anything foolish,' she hissed.

Danny grinned and gave her a thumbs-up sign, showing an assurance he didn't feel. Then, turning, he parted the curtains to see the sister with her bloodied lips drawn tight in obvious disapproval, holding the clipboard and waiting impatiently at the entrance to the ward. She began to walk down the corridor immediately he appeared, her back rigid with censure. Danny followed her, his footsteps making a soft squeak on the linoleum floor, never quite catching up to her until they'd reached the lift, where they waited in silence. On the way down Danny asked, 'Will you direct me to the waiting room, please, sister?' adding hopefully, 'Perhaps someone will call me when the baby arrives?'

'No, no, Mr Dunn. Please understand. You have to go home now. Your doctor will contact you by telephone after his rounds tomorrow.'

'No waiting room?' Danny asked, dismayed.

'It is not hospital policy to allow relatives to stay overnight, Mr Dunn.' She sighed, thoroughly fed up with him. 'Really! I should have thought you'd understand that much. I must remind you that this is a busy maternity hospital. We simply can't have people – men – hanging about!'

'I'm not "people" or "men", sister! I'm an expectant father. I'd like to stay,' Danny persisted, a hard edge to his voice.

The lift arrived and opened on the ground floor and Sister Dracula strode out, not answering or waiting for him to leave. 'Please go to the admissions window,' she called, then, all sharp, starched white angles from the back as she slipped through one of two doors leading from the foyer and closed it somewhat too firmly behind her.

Danny walked over to the reception window. He was becoming more agitated by the moment, expecting to see his nemesis appear before him, but there was no sign of Sister Dracula or, for that matter, the original clerk. Instead, a very thin, weary-looking woman looked up at him, sighed audibly, then rose slowly from her desk and approached him. Danny assumed she must be the cashier he had to see. She appeared to be in her forties or early fifties but it was clear that life hadn't been kind to her and she had come to expect nothing good. The only colour that showed on her sallow oily face was two rosy-red circles of rouge on her cheeks and a thin line of orange lipstick, the two colours incongruously bright on her pale, forlorn face. She was dressed in a navy-blue serge skirt with an uneven hem that shone from frequent ironing and, despite the spring weather, a cheap brown machine-knitted cardigan buttoned all the way up. Her ratty hennaed hair was drawn back in a scrappy bun with strands of hair sticking out at every angle. A pair of frameless glasses hung from a cheap anodised chain around her neck. She too held a clipboard and Danny noticed that her fingernails were broken or chewed but retained traces of crimson nail varnish.

'I have to check your details and you'll need to pay the hospital costs,' the clerk said automatically. 'I see you have Dr Leader. You will have to make separate arrangements to pay him.' She paused then asked, 'Will that be cheque or cash?' When Danny didn't answer immediately she added, 'Or do you wish to undertake an instalment plan where we make arrangements with your employer to garnishee your pay?' All this was said in a monotone, a litany she had obviously performed a thousand times before.

'Cheque,' Danny replied, grateful to be able to assume some sense of control.

'The name of your bank, Mr Dunn?'

'It won't bounce, madam,' Danny replied.

The clerk sighed. 'It's purely routine, sir.'

'Bank of New South Wales, Balmain. The manager's name is Harry Farmer.'

The clerk wrote this down on the clipboard, then slid a slip of paper across to Danny. 'Please make your cheque out for this amount. That will be your deposit on account and you will need to pay any extra costs over and above that amount before your wife and baby leave the hospital.'

Danny wondered momentarily what might happen if a family was unable to pay the bill. Did the hospital keep the baby? He wrote out the cheque, grateful that Brenda had insisted on topping up his bank account.

'I'll need your home and business phone numbers to contact you in case of emergencies. I take it your doctor has these as well?' She gave him a wan smile. 'To let you have the good news.'

'Sure, but in both instances that won't be necessary. I'll be waiting right here in the hospital.'

The clerk looked up in surprise. 'Oh, no, sir! That won't be possible. We'll . . . your doctor will inform you . . . telephone you at home some time tomorrow.'

'What if the birth occurs during the night, madam?'

'Some time tomorrow morning, after he's done his rounds.'

'No, no, you don't understand. It's essential I know the very moment my child is born. What if there are complications? I'll have to be here,' Danny insisted.

The clerk sighed. 'Dr Leader could be busy. This is not his only hospital.'

'All the more reason to stay,' Danny cried, knowing he was rapidly losing control.

'We don't have suitable . . . er, facilities. The waiting room is only open until six; it's already been locked for the night.'

'Have you got a public toilet?'

'Yes.'

'And a spare chair?' Danny turned and indicated the foyer behind him. 'I could put a chair somewhere here. There's plenty of room.'

'I don't have that authority, sir.'

'What? To lend me a chair?'

'No, to allow you to remain in the foyer. It must remain clear at all times, for emergencies.'

'Then who has?' Danny could hear his voice beginning to rise.

'That would be the superintendent, and he's gone home,' the woman replied.

'Who is in charge then?'

'Miss Kirk, Miss Alison Kirk, the night-duty matron.'

Danny pointed to the phone on a nearby desk. 'Will you call her, please?'

This last request proved too much for the weary clerk. 'I am permitted to call only in an emergency, Mr Dunn.'

'But this *is* an emergency!' Danny insisted.

'I don't think so, sir.'

Danny was suddenly back in the camp facing Colonel Mori. He knew shouting at her was pointless, though that was exactly what he itched to do: to wreck the joint, make someone listen, reach though the window and grab this poor scrawny bitch and shake some sense into her, even though he was aware that she was only doing her job. He knew he was being unreasonable, but he didn't care. He had to be near Helen in case something happened, something untoward. Everyone knew it happened all the time; you were always hearing about mothers dying in childbirth, and Helen was huge, almost twice normal size. People kept observing that she might be having twins. If so, this gave her twice the chance of dying in childbirth, didn't it? Oh, Jesus! He had to be near, near enough to get to her bedside if something happened during the night.

Danny composed himself, smiled, and said in his Colonel Mori voice, 'Your name, please, madam?'

'Mrs Gibson.'

'Mrs Gibson,' Danny began, 'I'm a lawyer, and a hospital is a public building, and this is one where the public come to have babies. Now a baby isn't simply one parent's responsibility but both, and although of course my wife has to do the lion's share, I am an expectant father and naturally I am very, very concerned and consider myself directly involved. There are especially good reasons for my request, though I won't go into them here, but I'm sure the legal implications of a public hospital denying a husband the right to remain in a designated waiting room, which has been deliberately locked, while his wife gives birth, or could possibly be dying,' he added darkly, 'will not serve this particular hospital well in a court of law or in the newspapers.'

Mrs Gibson looked thoroughly confused, as Danny had expected she might. He hoped to hell he'd guessed right about her and that she wouldn't call his ridiculous bluff. He'd laid it on pretty thick and he knew that Helen would have practically killed him if she'd witnessed this ridiculous melodrama. Anyone with half a brain would know his words were an idle threat.

'Mr Dunn, you'll have to speak to the matron; this has nothing to do with me,' the clerk said.

'Of course, Mrs Gibson. I understand your position and that you *would* help if you could,' Danny said soothingly, adding, 'I know you're only following instructions. As you say, I need to speak to the night matron.' Danny gave her a forlorn look. 'But without your help, I can't think how I can possibly gain her attention.' He grinned. 'Without picking up that vase of dead flowers and hurling it through a window.'

It was a ridiculous threat and Danny intended it to be funny – but then he thought that perhaps she was responsible for the foyer flowers – so he was pleased to observe that Mrs Gibson, despite herself, smiled, breaking the tension between them.

'I'd like to help you, Mr Dunn. I truly would. People – husbands anyway – should be allowed to wait at night. Some travel up from the country and can't afford a hotel, and often the Salvation Army hostel down the hill is full, so they have to sit on a bench at Central Railway Station until the morning – that is, if the railway police don't move them on – and then they have to walk the streets all night.'

'If matron will give me just five minutes of her time I won't ask for a second more,' Danny said quickly. 'I understand you are not permitted to call her directly. Perhaps you could simply leave the list of hospital extension telephone numbers here on this ledge for ten seconds? Then, if you are questioned later you can deny either telling me, writing down or giving me the number. You can swear on a stack of Bibles in a court of law you didn't give me her extension number. I should know – I'm a lawyer,' Danny said soothingly, adding, 'I promise I won't ever mention your name.'

To his surprise she smiled. 'I only wish my husband had cared this much about me, Mr Dunn.' She turned and unhooked a phone list and placed it on the ledge. 'First line, second page, Alison Kirk.' She smiled again, seeming to enjoy the conspiracy.

Danny flicked to the page and memorised the number. 'Thank you, Mrs Gibson,' he said quietly, pushing the list back through the window. 'Now, pink or red roses?' he asked.

'I beg yours?' Mrs Gibson asked, surprised.

'You've been very kind. Pink or red . . . or white, for that matter?'

'Oh, red, please. I've never been given roses before.'

'And I've never had a baby!' Danny said, laughing.

'There's a phone box on the pavement directly outside,' Mrs Gibson offered. 'The hospital one next to the lift is padlocked after six and the superintendent has the key.'

Danny had no idea what he was going to say to Miss Alison Kirk, the night matron. When Danny was a kid, Half Dunn had once advised him on what to do when he found himself in an awkward situation. 'Talking's always better than not talking, son, then just trust your Irish luck; the gift of the gab will usually get you through a crisis.' Danny dialled the hospital number and, when the switchboard answered, said in an authoritative voice, 'Dunn here. Matron, please, extension 151. Has she come on duty yet?'

'Yes, doctor,' came the cheery operator's reply. 'She came on half an hour ago. I'll put you through.'

'Thank you,' Danny said in the distracted professional manner he'd heard some of his older legal colleagues use when calling from the public phones at the courts. Even in the army, where as a Sergeant Major he could command instant obedience, he'd learned that authority works best not when obedience is demanded but when it is simply assumed.

He heard the extension ringing, then a rattle as the receiver was lifted. 'Hello. Matron Kirk.'

'Matron, my name is Dunn, Daniel Dunn; we haven't met.'

'Oh? Are you a doctor?'

'No, a lawyer, madam.'

There was a pause. 'Is it a matter concerning me or the hospital, Mr . . . what did you say your name was?'

Danny had to hand it to her – she was quick. Without thinking he replied, 'It is Daniel Corrib Dunn. I'm a solicitor and it concerns both.' Danny went on in a relaxed, easy voice, 'But let me quickly add, matron, that it is an informal matter – an important request but not one that should give you or the hospital the slightest problem. I'm calling from close by and could see you in the foyer or your office in a matter of minutes. I promise to take no more than three or four minutes of your time.'

Danny held his breath, conscious that the matron's reply would decide whether he won or lost. He couldn't think of a single reason why she'd agree to see him. If she asked, he'd have to stumble through some kind of explanation or pathetic admission; tell the truth, beg. To his surprise she caught him completely off-guard by saying, 'Corrib. Did you say Corrib? That's a county in Ireland, isn't it?'

Danny realised she was playing for time, deciding how to react to his request. What did he expect? She was a matron of the biggest maternity hospital in the city and he didn't doubt for one moment she was a formidable woman, not one to be easily conned. 'No, matron, rather more the district around the lake of the same name. It's where my grandparents came from. My grandfather was born and raised in a crofter's cottage on the lake shore.' *What now?* Danny thought, inwardly wincing, certain he'd blown it.

'Daniel *Corrib* Dunn, unusual,' the matron remarked, adding quickly, 'Strange coincidence. The only time I've heard that name before was at my niece's graduation ceremony at Sydney University earlier this year. A law graduate who won the University Medal.' There followed a slight pause, then, 'Was that you?'

There is a God in heaven, Danny thought. 'Yes, matron, I'm afraid my darling mother became a little distraught on the day.'

'Nonsense, it was lovely and quite understandable. I must say, the vice-chancellor's opening address and then the presentation left us all very close to tears.' Then, as if he weren't on the other end of the phone, she remarked, 'Not a day I'll easily forget. You seemed to epitomise all the brave, clever, decent young men who've fought and died for all of us. We felt very proud.'

Five minutes later Danny sat in the matron's office enjoying a cup of tea. Miss Kirk turned out to be a tall, slim, attractive woman, probably closer to sixty than fifty, with nice brown eyes and a set to her mouth that suggested she was not to be taken lightly. She spoke like Helen and obviously came from a good family.

'Well now, Mr Dunn, yours is not a face one is likely to forget, though they seem to have done a splendid job. Did you have it – the plastic surgery – done here in Australia?' she asked without a hint of embarrassment.

Danny laughed. 'Please call me Danny, matron. No, America. I spent many months in and out of the Barnes Hospital in St Louis. 'Not a time I'd like to have over again, although the Americans treated me extremely well.'

'Yes, lovely people. I spent some time as a young nurse in the Mayo Clinic in Minnesota before the war. Well now, Danny, what is this matter you wish to discuss with me?'

Danny took a deep breath, and when he spoke the words emerged in a rush. 'My wife came in an hour ago, matron. This is our first child – we've tried for almost five years. They told me that, because of the three and a half years of severe malnutrition as a prisoner of war under the Japanese, I was likely to be sterile and then . . .' Danny paused, suddenly realising the immediate implications. 'Helen told me she was pregnant directly after the graduation ceremony in January.' He paused again, overcome with emotion. 'The joy I experienced was a thousand times better than anything that's ever happened to me before,' he finished quietly.

'My dear boy,' Matron Kirk said quietly, 'what is it we can do for you?'

When the moment came to ask, Danny couldn't think of anything reasoned or persuasive to say. 'Matron, please let me stay here while Helen has our baby – anywhere, the toilet will be fine.' He inhaled sharply. 'Then let me see my wife and baby just as soon as it's over. Please, Matron, I won't be the slightest trouble,' he begged.

Matron Kirk was silent for some time, then she asked, 'Your wife, what floor is she on?'

'Three, ward 3M.'

The matron picked up the phone, dialled a number and asked for the duty sister on the third floor. 'Yes, sister, it's matron here. Can you tell me how Mrs Dunn's labour is progressing? [pause] Oh I see, how intense? [pause] Uh-huh. [pause] The doctor is on the floor . . . [pause] a previous delivery? How fortunate. Thank you, sister, I shall be up immediately.' She turned to Danny, smiling. 'It all seems to be going like clockwork. Dr Leader is here, your wife has gone into intense labour, he's scrubbing up and they're preparing her right now. I shall visit myself. In the meantime you must remain here, please.'

'Thank you, thank you, matron,' he cried, not quite able to believe his good fortune.

'It could be a long night, Danny.' Matron Kirk pointed to an easy chair in the corner of her small office. 'You had better make yourself comfortable. I have to do my rounds and won't be back for a while. Please do not leave this office unless you hear from me. I will instruct a nurse to call you when you may see your wife. If you need the toilet, it's four doors to the left down the hall.'

Almost an hour later Matron Kirk reappeared. She was carrying a cup of tea and a plate of ham sandwiches. Danny jumped to his feet.

'Thank you, matron,' he said, acknowledging the tea and sandwiches but sensing that he should otherwise remain silent.

'Sit, Danny, I have something to say to you,' Matron Kirk instructed.

He sat down, thinking she was going to send him home. If so, he decided he was going to go down on his knees and beg. Coming out of the prisoner-of-war camp he'd sworn that he'd never humble himself in front of a man again in his life, but this was a woman and it concerned Helen, who was and always would be the exception to the rule.

'I've made a decision and I want to explain why,' Matron Kirk began. 'What I am going to allow does not have a precedent. I want to be perfectly clear about that. With the exception of perhaps half a dozen young obstetricians who have been allowed to be present, but certainly not directly involved, while their wives gave birth, I don't believe this hospital has ever agreed to a husband being at the birth of his child.' Danny was beginning to shake. 'I want to tell you why I have agreed to make an exception in your case,' she paused, 'and why Dr Leader has agreed.' She paused and looked directly at Danny. 'We feel that this is an opportunity to thank you, and the thousands of young men such as you, who fought and died to ensure that the next generation of Australians are born into a free society.'

Danny was very close to tears, his throat was constricted and all he could manage to choke out was an almost soundless, 'Thank you.'

'No, no, it is I who must thank you, but I must ask you to keep this away from the newspapers. While I am not acting against the law or even the official rules of this hospital, I would be setting a dangerous precedent. You do understand, don't you?'

Danny looked up at Matron Kirk. 'Somehow, and I don't yet know how, I promise to repay your kindness, matron. Thank you.'

Matron Kirk laughed. 'You already have, Danny. Come along now, you have to scrub up and change into a smock, cap and mask. I imagine you're not the fainting type, after what you've been through.'

At 11:33 p.m. on 24th of September, Samantha Dunn was born. It all happened with Danny thinking that at any moment Helen was going to rip his arm from his shoulder as she hung on to his hand, gasping and moaning. As Sam's head emerged, Helen let out a piercing and agonised scream. Danny's insides twisted in panic, but then, in moments, a baby was in the room, and Dr Leader was saying, 'It's a girl!' She was briefly laid on Helen's tummy, and both her parents gazed at her in awe, and then at each other, speechless. The umbilical cord was cut and tied, and, still unwashed, Sam was placed in Danny's arms, her first squalls quietening at once.

The midwife was just taking her from his arms to 'make her respectable' when Danny realised that Helen was still labouring. He'd read something about the afterbirth, but to his astonishment, another baby girl was placed on Helen's tummy, only six minutes after her sister: Gabrielle. Twins.

To Danny they were already the most beautiful little creatures he had ever imagined. He was permitted to sit with an exhausted Helen who was almost too weary to smile but managed to whisper, 'Daniel Dunn, I don't know how you managed this but I love you more than I can say.' She closed her eyes and Danny wiped her brow, while telling her a hundred times over that he loved her.

'Go to sleep, my darling . . . and thank you . . . thank you . . . thank you so much.'

Matron Kirk arrived and congratulated him and then shooed him away. He was totally worn out but jubilant, the single happiest man alive, with the nightmare behind him.

Danny called Brenda from the red phone booth outside the hospital. It was 1.30 a.m. and she answered immediately. 'Twins!' he cried. 'Girls!' He laughed for sheer joy. 'Congratulations, Grandma Dunn!' he yelled ecstatically.

'Oh, Danny. How is Helen?' Brenda managed to say before she started to weep. His tough little Irish mother was softening with age.

'I'm coming over, Mum.'

Danny heard a sniff then a tearful, 'Yes . . . *please*,' followed by a choking sob.

One minute after visiting hours began the following morning, Danny, bearing a huge bunch of pink roses, burst into ward 3M. Helen sat up in bed, a swaddled pink bundle on each arm. He'd been vaguely aware that both twins had been born with some matted darkish hair but he was not prepared for what he now saw. He'd expected – well, he didn't really know what he expected; some babies have fuzz, some are bald as eggs – but was simply not prepared for the blazing thatch of red hair above the two tiny, squished-up sleeping faces of his twin daughters. 'Oh my gawd, redheads!' he exclaimed, laughing. 'Two more fiery women in the family!' But that was all the levity he could manage. At the sight of Helen as a mother, he was suddenly overcome by a love so fierce that he dropped the pink ribboned roses onto the bed and fell to his knees beside her. With his head on her lap, he wept like a small child. Danny now loved three women so deeply that he knew with absolute certainty he would not hesitate to give his life for them.

In the months of Helen's pregnancy and the early months of the twins' lives, Danny and Franz completed their probationary year, the fifth and final of their legal studies. Despite their Law degrees, they were not allowed to practise on their own account until the following year. A week prior to Christmas the two young lawyers were called into the office of the senior partner, John Sharp, a veritable legend in commercial-law circles, who had concluded his review of their three years with the firm. 'We are pleased with your progress so far, gentlemen, but, as they say in our profession, there's many a slip between mug and lip, especially when you're young. You have both shown the qualities that will lead, in the fullness of time, to the prospect of a partnership with our firm.' He paused impressively. 'So, it gives me great pleasure to invite you to fill the positions of associate solicitors, beginning in the new year – 1952 – after the Christmas and January recess. You are both invited to share a glass of sherry with the partners in the boardroom at 6.15 sharp this evening, when I will introduce you formally and in the traditional manner to the other partners, with whom you are already well acquainted.'

Both young solicitors, by now accustomed to the firm's clubby atmosphere and their lowly order in the scheme of things, assumed suitably grateful and humble expressions and thanked the senior partner for his faith and trust in them.

However, Danny, perhaps because of his age and military past, couldn't refrain from asking, 'Mr Sharp, I hope you don't find my question inappropriate or impertinent, but, in your opinion, what period of time would you expect to elapse before we could reasonably be expected to be elevated to partnerships in the firm?'

John Sharp, a little taken aback by so direct and perhaps, indeed, impertinent a question, thought for a moment, then replied, '*Hrrrmph* . . . well, I suppose a little ambition in a young lawyer is not such a bad thing, as long as we allow some humility to prevail. I was made a partner quite quickly, in a little over eighteen years.' He chortled to himself. 'I recall at the time many of the more senior partners thought it a rather precipitate appointment, ha ha.'

Franz shot a quick glance at Danny. 'Well, sir, that certainly sets us a very difficult challenge,' he said.

John Sharp missed the irony. 'You would both do well to just get on with it . . . know your place. Patience is the very essence of the law. You young lads are always in a tearing hurry, but in this profession it's the tortoise and not the hare that will always claim the prize.'

'Yes, thank you,' Danny said, trying to appear grateful for the advice.

They'd attended the sherry charade, as Franz termed it, where they were formally re-introduced to the partners they'd known and worked with for the past three years as virtual messenger boys and dogsbodies. In the hour or so that the soiree lasted, they were each advised on several occasions by different partners to choose the more commercial areas of the law, or as one grossly overweight partner, appropriately named John Bull, pontificated, 'Go for the fatter fees, my boy, and avoid the cesspits of criminal law. Criminal lawyers . . . disgraceful bunch, what!'

With the ordeal over Danny mentioned to Franz that Brenda was babysitting for the night and he and Helen were going to the jazz club up at the Cross to celebrate. 'Perhaps you'd care to join us?' he invited.

Franz hesitated. 'Mate, I know you two don't get out a lot now you have the twins. Why don't you just enjoy the occasion on your own?'

Danny hesitated then said, 'No, mate, it wouldn't be the same. We've been in this together since first year. I've already talked to Helen; she'd very much like you to come.'

'If you're sure, then I'd love to. Thanks. Jimmy White, Bob Gibson and Don Burrows are playing.'

Helen had insisted they have a bottle of champagne and they toasted each other several times over. The bottle was nearly empty by the time the band took a dinner break and they could talk in normal tones. Danny, who'd restricted himself to a single glass of champagne, began by saying, 'Franz, I've discussed with Helen what I'm about to say and she and I are in complete agreement. We were thinking —'

'That to spend the next twenty years working our arses off for that bunch of fucking WASPS is bloody stupid,' Franz interjected, plainly a little tipsy.

'Well, yes, as you put it so succinctly. As a *fucking* WASP, I wholeheartedly agree,' Helen laughed, adding, 'Danny wants to make you a proposition, Franz.'

'Funny that, I was going to do the same thing,' Franz replied quickly.

'Oh? And what was that?' Danny asked, a bit miffed that the limelight had been snatched away from him.

'A partnership, of course,' Franz answered.

'Bastard!' Danny cried.

'Isn't that the point?' Helen laughed. 'You each anticipate the other's thoughts.'

'I anticipated first!' Danny exclaimed. 'My name goes first!'

Franz sighed. 'Mate, you're going to do criminal law while I'll do commercial. That means I'll make the money and you'll get all the glory. Money always trumps glory – I'm a Jew and I know these things! Landsman & Dunn, money and glory – the second isn't much use without the first.'

'Bullshit! You know what your problem is, Landsman? You're a smooth-talking lawyer! Mouth like a slippery dip!'

'Children!' Helen remonstrated.

'What?' both men asked simultaneously.

Helen balanced a two-shilling piece on her forefinger and thumb ready to toss. 'Heads it's the Jew, tails it's the Tyke.' The coin sailed into the air and, catching it in her right hand, Helen slapped it down onto the top of the left, keeping it covered. 'You agree to accept the verdict?' she asked. Both men nodded. Helen lifted her right hand, uncovering the coin. 'Heads! Landsman & Dunn!'

'Best out of three,' Danny growled.

'Danny!' Helen warned.

Danny extended his hand to Franz. 'I was only thinking of offering you a junior partnership,' he joshed.

'That's funny. My proposition to you included the same clause.' Franz accepted Danny's hand and added, 'What say another bottle?'

'Well, I'm glad that's settled. It's okay for the two of you, but I have to deal with my mother. The whole of her bridge club is aware that her brilliant son-in-law did his articles and has now been offered an associate solicitor's position at Sydney's topmost law firm, Stephen James & Stapleton! She's never going to live this down.'

'Wait until I take on my first dirty big criminal case,' Danny laughed.

CHAPTER EIGHT

LANDSMAN, DUNN & PARTNERS was the name they eventually settled on; as Franz said, it sounded weighty and reliable. Their reputation as a young, smart, hungry and aggressive law firm grew rapidly, with Danny looking after the criminal law and Franz doing the commercial. At Franz's insistence they'd agreed to pool their profits and pay themselves the same salary. This was generous of Franz, who knew his partner well; Danny was likely to put as much work into a pro bono case as into one that paid a hefty fee, so someone had to make the real money.

Helen was not able to work in the first year of the twins' life, caring for them devotedly until a few months after their first birthday, when she stopped breastfeeding and found a nanny. Mrs O'Shea, a widow in her fifties, was a trained Karitane sister, and Helen felt confident leaving the twins in her care. She returned to her former position at the university, where she was promptly elevated to the position of lecturer in ancient history, specialising in ancient Egypt. It was now twelve years since she'd obtained her masters degree and she started preparing her dissertation for her doctorate, warning Danny that she would have to attend a dig in Egypt or Mesopotamia under the direction of a British team at some time in the future.

Danny, absorbed in his work, had agreed without paying much

attention at the time. He was rapidly earning a reputation as the lawyer of choice in certain criminal circles, but not without putting enormous effort into his briefs. In addition he'd taken on a great many pro bono cases, representing people too poor to afford a lawyer, and in several of these he had successfully exposed the police for verballing. Hard work became a haven for him; if he buried himself in it and never allowed time to reflect on the past, then the nightmares weren't anything like as bad. But the moment he relaxed, the past came storming back in his sleep, in particular the terrible beating he'd taken from the Japanese *kempeitai* officer who'd used a rifle butt to mutilate him. *Stay busy, get involved, work, work, work* became his credo. His efforts in the swimming pool were every bit as frenetic. He'd pound through the water, back and forth, as if the water itself would serve to wash the negative thoughts from his mind.

Danny was always immaculately dressed in a beautifully cut dark suit, which Pineapple Joe had copied directly from the pages of *Tailor & Cutter*, using only the finest English worsted wool. He now sported a dark eye patch, the story of which was in the press often enough for at least one member of any jury to have heard it and, naturally, to relate it to the rest of the people sitting in judgment. Thus, he started ahead of most of the stuffy, patronising barristers in their sombre black gowns and horsehair wigs.

While Danny was entitled, in New South Wales, to act as a barrister and a solicitor and to appear in both the District and the Supreme Court – the High Court being the only exception – his legal colleagues generally disapproved of anyone doing so. A practitioner was expected to choose to be either a barrister or a solicitor. But Danny's experience as a prisoner of war had taught him to trust no one but himself, and his success in some pretty tricky, high-profile cases, where he came up against barristers with considerable reputations, soon proved the wigged-and-gowned mob wrong. He was good – very good – and the general consensus was that the young lion was way too confident and cocky (if only they'd known). Moreover, many of the cases he took on were ones in which barristers with solid middle-class upbringings and private-school educations were socially out of their depth. Danny understood the underlying psychology, social background and environment of the people he defended, especially the crims, who trusted his judgment. This often antagonised judges or magistrates, who tended to share the privileged background of the barristers, but it worked a treat with the jury, whom he addressed in his easy courtroom manner, as if they were his neighbours.

Danny didn't win all his cases, and some were doomed before they reached the courts – none more so than the case of one of Sydney's most notorious safe crackers, a recidivist known in Balmain as 'Blaster' Henderson. The ageing crim had used too much gelignite on a job in a CBD high-rise and the explosion had knocked him out, as well as several windows on the third floor, so that the police knew where to find him.

Blaster Henderson's case was dead in the water before it even began and the jury had no option but to deliver a guilty verdict, whereupon the judge, himself an old-timer, wearily pronounced the comparatively soft sentence of four years in Long Bay.

Danny had gone down to the cells to commiserate with the old bugger as he awaited transport to 'the Bay', to find Blaster not only cheerful but appreciative. 'Don't you worry, Mr Dunn. If it hadn't been for your plea in mitigation the judge would'a give me twelve years, no risk!' He'd chuckled. 'Yeah, fer sure. After yer finished tellin' the court about me daughter's 'ospital bills and me little granddaughter being whatzit . . . yeah . . . autistic, I think His Honour hisself was feelin' a bit sorry for me an' all. I'll be out in three wid good behaviour. I got your fee, Mr Dunn,' he added. 'Me daughter Dulcie's got it under the mattress. She'll drop it in to Brenda . . . er, old Mrs Dunn, at the Hero termorra.'

'Forget it, mate. She'll need the money while you're away.'

While Blaster Henderson insisted on paying, many didn't. Danny was a pretty soft touch, and while the pro bono cases he took on and usually won might have enhanced his reputation, they did nothing for the firm's bank balance. As Franz once said after a disastrous financial month, 'Mate, your wins and acquittals are from the wrong side of the tracks. A favour should always be redeemable, quid pro quo, but these people don't pay and, what's more, are never going to be in a position to help you; they can never return the favour.'

'Franz, as far as my mob are concerned, you blokes from the middle class are from the wrong side of the tracks. Take my word for it – in the years to come, it will pay off handsomely.'

'All right, Mr Counsel for the Hopeless and Hapless. Just how is that likely to happen?'

'Christ, you know how. Criminal law is all about inside information – the grapevine. People hit paydirt when they have their ears to the ground, not their noses in the air!'

'I hope that is merely a philosophical and not a practical approach, mate. A little cash in the kitty would be handy.'

'Ouch!' Danny winced.

It was the closest the partners ever came to a row. Franz, who was beginning to bring in some quite profitable conveyancing business, had always made the bulk of the money they divided.

Every young lawyer hopes a big case will come his way, and while this seldom happens, Danny got lucky. The wife of Bryan Penman, who'd advised Franz's parents that their son should accept the scholarship to Scots College, was discovered shot dead in her home. After their initial investigation the police charged Penman with murder. While he'd never practised as a lawyer – hadn't needed to, as the heir to Moresby Vineyards and Brandy Distillers Pty Ltd – and didn't play the social game, he was certainly considered to be a member of one of the leading families in New South Wales, and the case was big news in all the papers. Some of the most senior barristers in town waited eagerly for their telephones to ring, but while Penman could afford any barrister in the city, he chose, to the consternation of the legal fraternity and the delight of the press, the young, aggressive and relatively inexperienced solicitor from 'Gawd help us, Bal-bloody-main!'

Not only was it a high-profile case, but the evidence against Danny's client seemed pretty compelling. But either way it would bring Danny well and truly out of the shadows and into the harsh spotlight of public attention. Or as one journo wrote, 'This young lawyer has crept from under the grapevine into the distillery crush but has yet to prove whether he can turn on a vintage performance.'

The story seemed to have all the trimmings and most of them pointed to a guilty verdict for Penman. Neighbours reported constant and violent arguments and, in particular, one instance where, incongruously, Penman had been chased by his wife down the garden path with a cricket bat and beaten over the head so severely that he had required hospitalisation. To everyone's surprise, Danny didn't use this incident to prove that Penman, a small man, was in fact beaten by his wife, a large woman. Instead, the prosecuting barrister used it to indicate that Penman had shot her precisely because she was beating him. Her motivation for attacking her husband, he contended, was that he was having a longstanding affair with an unnamed popular actress.

The case appeared to be fairly open and shut. But no murder weapon was found and Danny, using forensic and ballistics evidence, showed that she had been shot with a standard-issue army 303 rifle. The bullet that entered her head through her left brow had been shot from a considerable distance, probably through the open bedroom window some twenty feet away from the bed. Penman had never been in the army, did not possess a rifle, and had never been known to use one. Danny succeeded in convincing the jury that nobody could shoot so accurately without a great deal of experience and skill. He also fortuitously managed to have the information about the actress, who had been described in the press with such heavy hints that everyone immediately knew who she was, excluded from the evidence. There was also a rumour circulating among the criminal underground about Mrs Penman, using the name Thompson, having been seen in various Balmain pubs, dressed in slacks and a jacket, flashing a wad of large-denomination notes and looking for a hit man to do her husband in. To the obvious fury of the QC prosecuting the case, Danny had interviewed his source – a prisoner in Long Bay – and the judge had allowed the witness, a notorious safe cracker, to give evidence in front of the jury. In the judge's summing-up he had instructed the jury that the jailbird's evidence was unreliable and should be disregarded, but juries are only human.

Convinced by Danny that his client was a pillar of society as well as a regular but quiet supporter of charity – the Salvation Army and in particular the Parramatta Boys Home – the jury contended that the prosecuting QC and the police had not proved Bryan Penman's guilt beyond reasonable doubt and acquitted he, whom the legal profession privately believed, almost to a man, to be guilty of murdering his wife.

The murder trial had made the headlines for weeks, but for Danny the best moment came when a legal wag told journalists, off the record, that 'The best way to secure a divorce in Sydney is to murder your wife and hire "Nifty" Dunn to get you off.'

Two major newspapers, the Sydney Morning Herald and the afternoon Daily Mirror, ran the anonymous quote, to the consternation and anger of women everywhere, and Danny immediately recognised that his moment had arrived. He realised that the unnamed barrister's use of the sobriquet 'Nifty' would serve him well in the future. Secretly delighted with the new nickname, he threatened to sue the newspaper for attempting to sully his recently acquired reputation. Furthermore, he demanded, in the name of the nation's women, that the papers name the barrister who was supposed to have made the remark. Both papers refused to reveal their source, so Danny took out an injunction to force them to do so. Rival newspapers eagerly latched onto his nickname, giving Danny 'Nifty' Dunn the publicity he'd hoped for, and then some. The matter was eventually settled out of court for an undisclosed but considerable sum. Danny was not only extremely well paid for the acquittal by his grateful client, but the money from the newspapers allowed Landsman, Dunn & Partners to purchase a ten-year leasehold on chambers in the heart of Phillip Street, the most prestigious legal address in Sydney.

In later years, when he had achieved considerable power, he would look back with gratitude on that first experience with the Sydney Morning Herald and the Daily Mirror. It taught him that threatened litigation, if used judiciously, was a powerful weapon against one's enemies, as well as nosey investigative journalists, although Danny knew by heart the ancient Chinese military maxim: keep your friends close and your enemies closer still.

Nifty Dunn, by making himself conspicuous, had succeeded in the first principle of disguise: that is, to allow people to see you for what you do and not for who you are. 'Nifty' was a splendid nickname, encompassing his dress sense and his sharp, quick mind. It was a great word to hide behind, and it attracted paying customers. After all, who wouldn't want a nifty lawyer conducting their defence? If some of his clients were not among the more morally upstanding citizens, they were nevertheless entitled to vigorous representation by the one-eyed lawyer with the panel-beaten face who in every other way looked as if he had just stepped out of the pages of *Tailor & Cutter*.

While his face was never going to be his fortune, it was a huge improvement on the mangled wreck it had once been, and was sometimes likened to that of the RAAF fighter pilot and now senator John Gorton, who, like Danny, had both his cheekbones and his nose smashed when his Hurricane was shot down by the Japanese and crash landed. Danny's face, with its missing eye now covered by one of the eye patches Billy du Bois had given him as a parting gift when he left New Orleans, had a certain raffish air that made it ideal for a criminal lawyer.

If it's true you are known by the company you keep, then Danny was building a somewhat questionable reputation in respectable legal circles. He'd successfully represented the notorious and now ageing Tilly Devine, the madam and sly grogger, on a tax-evasion problem. Kate Leigh, the equally notorious madam, hadn't paid up to the bag man from the Premier's Department and so had been raided by the police. This case was hurriedly dismissed on technical grounds. Danny and Helen both thought brothels should be legalised. Politicians, from the premier down, were supplementing their salaries with bribes, and the working girls and women had no protection other than their pimps. The whole system was corrupt.

Perc Galea, an SP bookmaker among other things, had his case dismissed when a key witness to the mysterious disappearance of a colleague left unexpectedly for an overseas trip. (Danny had nothing to do with this and didn't take the credit, although it looked like another win for Nifty.) Lennie McPherson approached him without success, for Danny hated standover men above almost all things. They always reminded him of Captain Riley forcing Glossy Denmeade to surrender his boots; he turned down the job.

Abe Saffron, known as Mr Sin, asked Danny to represent him after he'd been raided by the police for illegal gambling. Danny won the case by proving it was a social game among friends and that no money had changed hands. He had no real objections to illegal gambling, having grown up in a community where gambling was part of the local culture, and he considered the draconian laws a conspiracy between the church, politicians and wowsers. Gambling, like grog, had been part of the Australian ethos since the First Fleet, and, to his mind, the sooner it became legal the better off everyone would be, especially those with an urge to have a flutter on the gee-gees or chance their luck at the gaming tables. The six o'clock swill – where men chug-a-lugged half a dozen middies in the last fifteen minutes before closing and went home, often to beat the living crap out of their wives and children – had to be abolished.

Danny lived by his own moral code, and his bigger cases paid for the battered wives and rape victims he took on at no cost. As a child growing up in Balmain he had constantly been aware of kids coming to school with black eyes, split lips and broken noses, claiming they'd run into a door or some such bullshit explanation that nobody believed for a moment. As Danny had been a natural leader in the playground, they'd fess up to him that the old man had come home pissed and beaten them up. He also learned that for every battered kid there was usually a battered mum and even sometimes a sister who had been sexually abused. The boys eventually grew up and could defend themselves, but the women remained vulnerable. Helen's indignation at this cruelty to her sex and

Brenda's frequent reports of incidents she'd heard at shandy soirees had helped to deepen Danny's sympathy for these women into something of an obsession. But from the very beginning his support of women had got him into strife with the magistrates and judges who presided over rape cases. Men themselves, they allowed victims to be harried by the defence until it seemed that the women's morality was on trial; often the victims were accused of complicity or, in Balmain language, of being 'cock teasers'. Not surprisingly, there was a disproportionally high rate of acquittals from juries reluctant to convict in the face of the judge's or magistrate's obvious bias when summing up. In many cases involving domestic violence, the husband would be let off with a warning, on the usually spurious grounds that the court did not want to 'deprive the family of its breadwinner'.

There was, however, one aspect of these cases of violence against women that concerned Danny deeply, because he found himself emotionally involved. Some of the wife-beaters and child abusers he was taking action against were ex-servicemen suffering from the same demons as Danny – the same depression and irrational anger. These men often mistakenly took to alcohol to ease their suffering, frequently with disastrous consequences for their families. At such times Danny was reminded of how tenuous was his own mental health, and he resolved to continue to try and control his mood swings by staying as far away from the grog as possible and burying himself in work.

Danny knew he'd had quite enough of swimming after the first five years of early-morning laps at Balmain pool, which he'd taken up at the behest of Bullnose Daintree and Sammy Laidlaw, his one-time junior-team trainers at the Tigers. His health had greatly improved, and he knew he needed the daily exercise to avoid his back seizing up on him, but still he declared himself bored witless from tapping the ends of the pool a hundred times each and every morning. While his old coaches had long since given up supervising his exercise, Sammy, with Bullnose always in tow, would drop round to the baths once a week to give Danny a massage. No one could remember when or if the payment for Sammy's massage service had been negotiated. Six schooners each at the Hero was just something that had been quickly understood, by some sort of osmosis, even though Bullnose did nothing but talk while Sammy worked on Danny's back. Bullnose, in particular, was a veritable mine of information, but both of them seemed to know all the gossip, business, politics and domestic scuttlebutt on the peninsula. In fact they were a source of information that would one day become important to Danny. Bullnose, whom most regarded as not very bright, had almost total recall of any conversation he'd ever heard. It was an uncanny ability, and with his minor gift for mimicry he was often able to reproduce what he had heard fairly exactly, complete with pauses and inflections. It was as if he were a human recording machine.

However, the drinking rules for the pair were clearly delineated by Brenda, who stipulated that they could partake of their grog in one sitting, as they often did, leaving the pub almost legless, arms about each other's shoulders in mutual support, or over the entire week, but they couldn't carry over their entitlement to the following week, a thought that had obviously never occurred to them. Six schooners each was known to be their limit in one drinking session, after which they would famously fall down and, worse still, soon be snoring, unable to be roused. Both were widowers, their families grown and departed, and they lived together in rented accommodation near the harbour's edge. Because it was downhill from the pub, they could usually get home under their own steam, even with six schooners sloshing around in each distended belly. While they talked about everyone and everything, they never referred to the place where they lived, which Danny suspected was a boarding house, and obviously a pretty grotty one.

It was not long after the Penman case that Danny finally declared himself heartily sick of swimming laps. As a young bloke he'd played polo for the action it involved; swimming laps was too dull. 'Sammy,

I'm going crazy, mate. Do you realise I've touched the ends of the pool thousands of times over the past few years. And in between those touches nothing happens; I don't see anyone or feel anything, except salt water up my nostrils. I reckon I've swum halfway round Australia!'

'Shit eh! Halfway round Australia. When d'ya reckon you'll get back?' Bullnose exclaimed, obviously impressed.

Sammy sighed. 'Ain't nothin' else I can recommend, mate. Nothin' better fer yer back, bodyweight-wise, than swimmin'. No weight-bearin', see?'

'There has to be something . . . something almost as good? Just for a change,' Danny said desperately. 'I'm going crackers, Sammy.'

'Mate, halfway round Australia, that's fuckin' impressive,' Bullnose persisted, 'especially seein' yiz got a crook back.'

Sammy stopped working and thought for a moment. 'Yiz could always try rowin', mate. Y'know, on the rowin' machine in the club gym.'

'Yeah, row the other half. Swim halfway, row halfway. I bet that ain't never been done before. Bloody good thought, Sammy,' Bullnose said, excited.

'I can't see that a rowing machine would be any better, except on a cold winter's morning. It's the same old thing, going nowhere, just a lot more repetition,' Danny said. 'On the other hand it would make a change. There would be people to talk to.'

'What about fair dinkum rowin', yer know, mornin's on the harbour,' Sammy replied. 'See things, take an interest, no two days the same . . . harbour traffic, I-talians goin' out in their fishin' boats, a bloody good workout to boot. Couldn't be better. Beat the shit outa swimmin' up 'n' down.'

'Yeah? But what about a boat?'

'Well, ya see Wee Georgie Robinson's got this skiff fer sale,' Bullnose said disingenuously.

'I see, and you guys get a commission if you sell it?' Danny laughed.

'Mate, two birds with one stone,' Sammy replied pragmatically, quickly adding, 'Wouldn't have a bar of it if I didn't think it'd work fer yer back, mate. That comes first. Bloke's got a professional rep to maintain.'

'What, for massage or honesty?' Danny laughed again.

'Jeez, Danny, we would'n' betray yer trust, mate,' Bullnose insisted, looking hurt. 'Others maybe, but we's bin mates a long time, since you was a nipper.'

'How much?'

They both spoke simultaneously:

'Twenty (Sammy) Twenty-five (Bullnose) Quid,' they finished in unison.

'Tell you what. I'll give you fifteen, sight unseen,' Danny said, knowing he'd have to ask Brenda for the cash as he and Helen were only just managing to get by.

'Done!'

Danny was taking a chance; the price of a skiff could go as low as five pounds if it was in poor shape, but Wee Georgie Robinson had a reputation on the peninsula for good, well-maintained sailing boats and skiffs. He worked wearing felt carpet slippers – 'Mate, yer don't wear hob-nailed boots when yiz working with good wood. Mark it wid a dirty big scuff or dent. Ya gotta treat it wid respect or it don't let yiz work it nice 'n' clean.' He'd also famously been a member of the Balmain premiership side of 1915, so, by definition, if he couldn't be trusted, then no one could, Danny decided.

From the first morning Danny pulled the skiff into the water off Wee Georgie Robinson's boatshed ramp, having negotiated a cheap weekly rent to berth it there, he knew things were on the up and up. He simply loved being on the harbour in the early mornings, even when the weather was foul. The only time he didn't go out was on those rare mornings in winter when you couldn't see three feet in front of you through the fog. Sammy had been right – after four months of rowing, his back was in even better shape and there was never a time when he didn't feel rewarded by having been out on the water at first light.

One bitterly cold and blustery Monday in July, when he'd come back from his row chilled to the bone, Brenda called him to say that Billy Scraper had committed suicide by hanging himself from a rope suspended from the arm of a dock crane nearly fifty feet above the ground. Danny knew that he must have been sober on that dark, blustery, moonless Sunday night to have climbed along the arm of the crane, secured the rope, slipped the noose around his neck and jumped. His body had been discovered as dawn broke, swinging like a pendulum high above the grey harbour water.

Brenda asked Danny to attend the funeral, which would take place after the coroner's inquest, and offered to hold a wake for Billy at the pub. 'Most of the people around here say it's good riddance to bad rubbish,' she said quietly. 'I doubt many will attend. He's upset everyone who ever tried to help him.' She sighed. 'Darling, please make the effort.'

'Of course I will, Mum.' There was no need for her to urge him, for while Billy wasn't an ex-prisoner of war, he'd suffered facial injuries similar to Danny's – worse, in fact – and there could be no thought of Danny not attending.

Billy Scraper was a prime example of a man who chose to use booze to try to kill the deep psychological pain he felt. Danny had Helen to talk to when things got bad, and that helped, even though she sometimes didn't fully understand what was going on in his head, but poor Billy had had no one to turn to.

Danny was once again made aware of how little people understood the effects of shell shock or war nerves, as the condition was still being called. While people like Dr Craig Woon, now a psychiatrist and practising in Sydney, were beginning to see it as causing extensive and lasting psychological damage, officially it was still being dismissed as a temporary condition, a state of shock brought on by battle fatigue. People, especially those from Balmain, expected you to get over it and get on with your life, to stop whingeing. Danny understood this and played the game, but his real self had gone into hiding, and by exposing only the public face of a high-profile criminal lawyer, he had managed to conceal from most people the damage he'd suffered, except for those like

Helen and Brenda who knew him for what he was – a damaged soul. But Billy had let the booze get to him and you can't do your hiding behind an empty booze bottle.

Billy's face was an altogether different matter. It was something with which the people of Balmain could sympathise. Billy Scraper had been saddled with a terribly mutilated and fiercely ugly face. Danny had suggested that Brenda start a fund to raise the money needed for Billy's boat fare to England. She'd done this by upping the cost of a middy of beer by a penny, and by tuppence for a schooner. In a year, with a bit of a shortfall made good by Brenda herself, they'd raised sufficient money to send Billy to the Queen Victoria Hospital in East Grinstead for treatment by the famous New Zealand plastic surgeon Professor McIndoe.

Billy had already spent a year at the Queen Victoria Hospital burns unit after he'd been dragged from the wreck of his burning bomber. But before the long and gruelling series of operations could be completed, he'd elected to return to Australia. Now, with his burns healed, the authorities would not consider plastic surgery for what they regarded as purely cosmetic purposes, nor were they prepared to send him back to England. He could breathe and mumble, which, as far as officialdom was concerned, made him fit to be released into society.

Billy returned from the pub-sponsored trip eighteen months later after multiple skin grafts, with eyelids that now effectively closed, a mouth capable of forming recognisable words and a new nose formed from his own tissue. Almost miraculously, or so it seemed to the Balmain locals, the doctors had grown skin for the nose while it was still attached to Billy's shoulder, then cut it away once the blood supply was established in the new site. Like Danny, Billy was never going to be pretty, but he could now appear in public among adults, although he still often frightened small children.

However, after returning to a second hero's welcome, instead of showing his gratitude to those who'd put their hard-earned pennies into paying for his fare, he'd become a hopeless, difficult and often violent drunk. His father, Sky's, dreams of seeing Billy settle down, get his crane-driver's ticket like his old man, then eventually marry one of the many spare sheilas left spinsters after the war and perhaps even start a family were dashed, and Sky became more silent and morose with each passing year.

People had taken to referring to Billy privately as an ungrateful bastard and a bludger, and after a while very little community sympathy was left for the miscreant. Over the years since his return from England the people of Balmain had written him off as a drunken derelict to be avoided or left on the footpath to shout gibberish. Danny knew they couldn't possibly be expected to understand that the destruction of Billy's face, which they'd willingly paid to repair, was nothing compared to the wreckage inside. Like many of the men who'd been permanently broken by the war, to Billy grog seemed the only reliable anaesthetic – a cheap way to temporarily block out the pain, alienation and isolation he felt.

Only a handful of people attended Billy's funeral: some of his old ex-servicemen pals; a few water-polo teammates; his father, now a widower; and Billy's two older sisters. Balmain had a long tradition of looking after its own, but if they felt they'd been let down they found it hard to forgive. Danny remembered the young lad who, almost twenty years earlier, had shouted back at him as he left the bar, 'So long, mate. Don't hang around too long . . . you'll miss all the fucking fun', then headed off to Canada for his training. He knew it was futile trying to explain to people that Billy had suffered from hidden demons which they would hopefully never have to confront themselves.

After the funeral Danny attended the wake Brenda held for Billy in the saloon bar of the Hero. Sky Scraper waited until Danny was alone before approaching him. 'Mate, I owe you a beer and an apology,' he said. 'What I said back then when Billy was off to Canada was fucking out of order.' He gave Danny a straight look, and Danny noticed that he was as dry-eyed as he'd been at the funeral service (as good Balmain boys were expected to be). He recognised all the signs of a man only just hanging on, and without a thought he pulled the unresisting old bloke to his chest. 'Mate, how could we possibly have known how . . . how it would be,' Danny said softly. He then held Sky while he sobbed and sobbed, at last, for his beloved, brutally damaged, lost son.

Each morning Danny would stand in stockinged feet in front of the bathroom mirror adjusting his tie knot carefully until it was perfect, with the required dimple centre top and just below the knot of one of the very fine Macclesfield silk ties he'd select to wear each day. His obsession with clothes had begun after he'd returned from the Japanese prison camp, and by the mid 1950s had settled into a fortifying routine. For three and a half years he'd had no choice but to wear a torn pair of khaki shorts, his battered slouch hat, and dilapidated boots without socks or sandals made from old truck tyres. That was about it, except for church parades and burials, when the prisoners wore their tattered shirts to respectfully acknowledge a far from merciful God. That was until His servant, the Reverend John Ayliffe, who'd refused to leave the men and go to a separate prison camp for officers, died of starvation and assorted tropical afflictions, whereupon God's special days lost their meaning. Danny held the Reverend John Ayliffe to be one of those rare people who, like Paul Jones, the little Welsh medic, felt only compassion for their fellow man.

Each weekday as soon as he was dressed Danny would wake the twins and get them dressed, give them breakfast and then drop them off at preschool. It was his way of spending time with the kids, although he longed for the day when they'd be old enough, and he had a skiff safe enough, for Helen to agree to their accompanying him on the harbour. Helen's job as a lecturer and the work for her dissertation often kept her up late, and Danny knew how much she enjoyed those extra hours of sleep each morning.

In 1956, the year of the Melbourne Olympic Games, several things of importance happened in Danny and Helen's life. They began to talk about joining the Labor Party; they finally had enough for the deposit on a modest house; and Landsman, Dunn & Partners showed their first decent profit. Danny was getting regular work from clients who were prepared to pay top fees for his services; the only problem was that he was also doing a lot of pro bono work for battered wives and kids. Franz would sometimes chide him for this, but he'd simply answer, 'Being a lawyer isn't only about money, mate.'

'It isn't?' Franz would counter in a voice of mock surprise. He, too, was doing well on the commercial side.

Danny had managed to persuade Helen that they should buy a television set to watch the games with the bonus he and Franz had paid themselves. The twins had turned five and were old enough for Danny to put his secret plan for them into action. His ambition was to turn them into competitive swimmers, which for Danny meant champion swimmers. He was aware that champions were built not just from talent, but also through habit and repetition; anything extra, such as natural talent of the kind he was once supposed to have possessed, was a bonus. The work nevertheless had to be done. He had already decided that he would pattern their training on that of the young Balmain swimmer Dawn Fraser, who was winning races in every national swimming carnival she entered and was being spoken of as a potential gold medallist at the Olympic Games. He'd already spoken to Harry Gallagher, her coach, who'd agreed to brief Danny on a training schedule once the girls turned eight.

Danny wanted the twins to think of early-morning wake-up calls as natural, almost instinctive. At five they were still too young to begin early-morning swimming training, so he decided he needed a bigger and safer skiff to take them with him onto the harbour every morning.

He'd gone to see Wee Georgie to ask him to make a skiff that could accommodate the twins, and possibly even Helen occasionally, but one that was still light enough for him to row on his own.

'Yeah, I could do that, son,' Wee Georgie agreed.

'How much would it cost then?' Danny asked.

'Mate, if I make it, it's gunna cost yer two hundred quid, maybe more. Can't do it no cheaper.'

'So, okay, what sort of skiff are you suggesting?'

Wee Georgie appeared to be thinking, but Danny knew he was extremely knowledgeable and wouldn't need to think for long. He also knew he was building a state-of-the-art eighteen-footer, which he was calling, rather grandly, *Britannica*. Wee Georgie was simply searching for the single most persuasive argument for the boat he had in mind. He was no bullshitter; he'd deliver a verbal coup de grâce that settled any possible argument, or he'd keep quiet. 'The provedores used to use them to row out to the sailing ships in the olden days,' he said finally.

Danny didn't quite get the connection. 'You'll need to explain, Wee Georgie.'

'Skiff, seventeen-footer, light, for one or two rowers; one sits on the front thwart, t'other in the middle; go out in any weather; real sturdy, and yer gotta be pretty bloody stupid to capsize her in a hurry; high stem back, narrow raked transom, lapstrake construction,' he paused, finishing with a smile, 'and beautiful.'

'But you just said in the olden days.'

'Whitehall skiff – nah, modern as termorra. Been around since Noah was a baby but yer can't improve on perfect.'

'So, can you build me one?' Danny asked again.

'Better'n that, Danny, mate . . . I got one out the back.'

'Yeah? In good nick?'

'Never been on the water. I built it for a bloke in the city who had this accident, fell off his roof and broke his shoulder – bloody lucky that was all he broke. Now he doesn't want it no more but he's asked for his deposit back – fifty bloody quid! I told him no way, I done the work, I'm entitled.'

'You said two hundred quid, but you've already got fifty,' Danny protested, as any self-respecting Balmain boy might.

Wee Georgie grinned, having anticipated the comeback. 'Split you the difference. It's yours for one seventy-five.'

'Let me see it first,' Danny said.

Wee Georgie padded in his slippers over to a dark corner of his boatshed and switched on a naked globe hanging from the ceiling.

It was love at first sight. The beautiful little Whitehall skiff was exactly what Danny wanted.

'Nice! Pretty,' he said.

'If a boat looks good it will probably go well. This one's got good directional stability – glide – between strokes.'

'They always come varnished like that?' Danny said, deliberately stalling.

'Nah, mate, that's a Wee Georgie special. I should charge ya extra. Most boat builders just paint 'em; varnish, that's class, that is. I guarantee ya won't see nothing like it on the harbour.'

Danny had to have the skiff but he knew the game; some restraint was needed. 'Hmm, tell you what. If you paint – not stencil, I mean hand paint like I know you can – the name on the back, you've got a deal, Wee Georgie.'

'Yeah, okay, Danny, special script, copperplate Gothic, like I'm gunna use on *Britannica*.' He tapped the side of the skiff. 'What's her name?'

'*Calabash*.'

'Eh?' Wee Georgie's eyes screwed up and his small button nose practically disappeared into the centre of his head. 'What's a calabash?'

Danny thought for a moment. 'It's sort of a pumpkin with a long snout, you know, a kind of marrow.'

Wee Georgie looked distinctly put out. 'Yer gunna name my beautiful skiff after a fuckin' pumpkin?' he snorted.

'It comes from a song my twin daughters sing,' Danny explained, while not explaining.

'*Calabash*?' Wee Georgie growled, tasting the word then spitting it out. 'Jesus! I put a lot of work into that there skiff.' He looked directly at Danny. 'Where you gunna berth her?'

'Well, I thought like before . . . ?'

'Ten bob!' Wee Georgie shot back. 'It's bigger'n the last one.'

'Seven and six?'

'Righto then.'

'When do you want the money?' Danny asked, not sure where he was going to get the one hundred and seventy-five pounds from. He'd expected the skiff would take several months to build, as Wee Georgie worked alone and was a master boat builder and didn't do things in a hurry; it would take possibly six months, even a year. That would have given him the time to find the money. According to Franz, the six hundred quid they'd each paid for an Admiral TV had pretty well cleaned them out for the month, and Helen wouldn't let him borrow from the deposit put aside for a house.

They'd moved to a two-bedroom flat soon after the twins were born, but it was rapidly proving too small. The girls needed a garden to play in, and Danny thought he might have found just the house, but they still had to find the last of the money to send Helen to Egypt for three months on a dig. She'd been invited to excavate at Saqqara with a British team under the direction of redoubtable archaeologist Walter B. Emery, a Liverpudlian, and Danny wasn't going to deny her such a once-in-a-lifetime opportunity. She was doing her dissertation for her doctorate through University College London, and an Emery dig would be a huge plus for her submission. She was due to leave in three weeks, and while Franz had said there should be no problem with funds, they had yet to find the final payment. It was a bad time to be buying a boat.

Danny knew Helen too well to mention the skiff; while she would argue that he already had a boat, once she knew he really wanted it, she'd offer to forego her trip so that he could have it. Helen had needed a lot of persuading to agree to the television set. She didn't see the Olympics as a big enough incentive to spend money that could supplement the meagre deposit they'd saved for a house. Danny, on the other hand, had seen the TV as an important part of his secret plans for the twins: they could watch the swimming at the Games and be inspired. She'd assumed that it was for his own pleasure (perhaps correctly, he admitted to himself), and so she'd finally given in. Now, as recompense for her generosity, there was no way on earth he was going to stop her going to Egypt.

Besides, he'd never broached with her the subject of taking the twins out on the harbour. His own skiff was much too small and dangerous. Helen knew that a cargo freighter had once capsized him when it came too close, and he was pretty sure she'd veto his plan, despite the safety features of the new Whitehall. To Helen, the idea of taking the twins out on the harbour at dawn when they were only five would, he knew, seem completely insane. Now he realised that her absence was his one opportunity. If he could institute it while she was away and make it a regular routine that the twins enjoyed, she wouldn't be in a position to object by the time she returned.

He thought about taking the money from the house deposit they'd saved, but rejected the idea. He'd seen a house while rowing on the harbour, and there was just the possibility that the deposit they had might be enough. He daren't cut into it for the skiff. Besides, he'd be going behind Helen's back if he did and that wasn't on; they'd saved the money together. It was little enough, whatever domicile they finally settled for. They weren't going to cause the local real-estate agents to lose any sleep with their meagre deposit. Danny increasingly regretted the impetuosity of their trip to America, when they had seemed to have plenty of money, some of which they could have saved for hard times. But there you go – they didn't and now they were skint.

He needed time to pay Wee Georgie, but not too much time, because it all had to happen while Helen was away.

'When will you take delivery?' Wee Georgie asked.

'Do I get to try her out first?' Danny asked, stalling.

'Yeah, I suppose, but yer insulting me intelligence.'

Danny ignored the protest. 'Next week's not convenient. I could do it early morning, Friday fortnight.' It would give him another two weeks to find the money.

'Righto, Friday fortnight mornin', half-past seven sharp.'

'When will the name be painted on?' Danny asked. If he stalled for a couple more weeks, the firm might just have the money and Helen would be off to Egypt. He had a coroner's inquiry coming and a compensation case against a shipping firm's insurance company, representing a dockworker who'd slipped a disc – bread-and-butter cases he was pretty certain he would win.

Wee Georgie, in his usual manner, thought for more than a moment. 'Gotta find a nice piece of cedar for the nameplate, varnish it, paint the name white wid a black drop shadow, clear varnish that when she's dry – varnish don't dry in a hurry – drill and countersink two holes, fit two-inch solid brass screws flush, varnish 'em . . . I reckon ten days in between working on the *Britannica*.'

'Price?'

'Two quid; it's lotsa work.'

'Make that two weeks,' Danny said nonchalantly, knowing Wee Georgie was a great craftsman but a poor timekeeper; he'd take another couple of weeks at least. Danny extended his hand. 'Thanks, Wee Georgie. Nice doing business with you.'

'Hey, wait on. How d'yer spell that pumpkin widda snout, Cala . . . Cal?'

'Calabash. Got a piece of paper?'

Danny wrote it down in block capitals and handed it to Wee Georgie.

'Bloody stupid name, if you ask me,' the shipbuilder growled, fixing the piece of paper to a six-inch nail hammered into a stud.

Danny left Wee Georgie's place, thinking hard. He now had two things on his mind apart from finding the money: taking the twins out in the new Whitehall skiff behind Helen's back while she was away; and the house he'd seen from the water which she would need to look at before she left.

He had decided even before the opportunity to buy the skiff came up that he had to have a house near the water. While this had seemed pretty near impossible to achieve at this stage in his career, the house he'd seen was within reach. It sat among the factories in a narrow street lined with what had once been the homes of managers and workers but was now virtually a slum. This particular old house stood at the very end of the street and had an overgrown driveway to the front door. It was what, in an earlier age, would have been referred to as a mansion, a rambling old two-storey sandstone, fronting the harbour, and it stood on a large half-acre block, a good fifty yards from the nearest houses. It had the added attraction of its own boatshed and slip, crumbling and broken and clearly unused for a very long time. The sandstone was pitted and stained, and the ramp and the base of the boatshed were covered with green harbour slime.

However, Danny judged that the house was well constructed and fundamentally sound, unlike all the others in the same industrial locale, which had fallen into disrepair. Judging from its appearance, with verandahs on both the top and bottom storeys, it was probably close to a century old. At one time it would have stood on its own and had the wide harbour view to itself.

Without saying anything to anyone, Danny had made enquiries and discovered that it was to be auctioned by the public trustee the week before Helen was to leave for Egypt. Its previous occupants had been elderly spinsters, the Simpson twins, born in the house, and the last of a direct line who had occupied it from when it was built. One of the Simpson twins had died and the lone twin had been moved into a nursing home, where she too passed away a matter of weeks later.

Danny knew the next step was to get Helen involved before she left, and every morning for the following two weeks he would row up to the house and rehearse his arguments to persuade her they should attempt to buy it. He would be trying to persuade her to move the twins into a broken-down old house on a hopelessly overgrown block in a slum area, where if there were any kids, and he hadn't seen any, they'd probably have rickets and chronic nasal drip. If, by some miracle, Helen agreed to buying the house, neither of them had the time or money to do the renovating. Yet, despite these irrefutable facts, he convinced himself they'd manage somehow.

He knew that showing the house to Brenda was pointless. She would simply dismiss the idea with a sniff. Besides, she wanted them to build on the vacant block beside the Hero, which she'd recently acquired. Brenda had been in the business of running a pub for thirty-six years, and she'd started to talk about retiring in five or six years but taking it a little easier in the meantime. She wanted more leisure to enjoy her two granddaughters, especially as she'd worked so hard throughout Danny's childhood. While she didn't expect Danny to become a publican or take over the day-to-day running of the pub, she wanted him to supervise the business, which she and Half Dunn intended leaving to the twins. In order to keep an eye on the manager and staff, Danny and Helen would need to be close by; next door would be ideal. So, without consulting them, she'd purchased the vacant lot.

Curiously, over the years Helen had shown an unexpected interest in how the place was run. She'd help behind the bar if there was a crisis and would laughingly explain that she saw it as an exercise in social anthropology. 'For the adult males, it's the tribal meeting hut where many of the discussions and decisions that involve the community take place, and where kava, or its equivalent, is consumed in a ritual essential to the men of the tribe.' Danny knew that Brenda hoped Helen's interest would overcome her reluctance for the twins to grow up close to an alehouse.

Danny knew that there was every possibility Helen would hate the broken-down old dump on the water and that his mother would win her over to the idea of building next door to the Hero. One thing was certain: Brenda wasn't going to lend him any money to buy his harbourside dream.

So Danny decided to show the house to Franz before he took Helen to see it, hoping he would be able to tell her that Franz thought it a good buy, a good investment. Franz, in theory, believed deeply in real estate investment, and in waterfront properties. His parents already owned two in Coogee, a supposedly up-and-coming suburb, and Franz claimed they were both good long-term investments. Helen trusted his judgment, and if he agreed the house was a good buy, Danny knew she'd consider it. Danny no longer saw it as the wreck it indeed was; in his mind it had become a beautifully restored harbour-side mansion where the twins would grow up happy and healthy. Now all he had to do was make Helen see the same vision. A little enthusiasm from Franz, the would-be property investor, might be very useful.

However, Franz was appalled at the sight of the crumbling sandstone edifice. 'Danny, you've got to be out of your cotton-picking mind!' he expostulated.

'It's absolute waterfront,' Danny protested. 'Mate, where are you going to get that without paying through the nose in Sydney?'

'There's waterfront – that's the Eastern Suburbs – and there's cesspit-front – that's here,' Franz shot back. 'I can see three fucking factories belching out smoke from here and a street with houses that look like Armageddon has already arrived. You'd have to look hard to find a place as bad as this in the Old Testament, even during the plagues of Egypt!'

'It's going to go for a song, and over the years the neighbourhood will improve,' Danny persisted.

'Take a look, Danny. I grant you, this was once a nice house, a very nice house . . . maybe a hundred years ago.' He paused. 'That was the last time this neighbourhood was a good location. It's cheap because nobody wants to live in an industrial slum. Take my advice: rule one in life is, if you make any dough, you move *out of* a shit hole like this one to the east or, at a pinch, to the north, across the Harbour Bridge!'

'Hey, steady on, mate. I grew up in Balmain. You're talking about the salt of the earth.'

'Yeah, well, what can I say if you want to toil in a salt mine? Danny, you can't be serious!'

'I can have a boatshed at my front door. Where can you have that in the Eastern Suburbs?' Danny persisted.

'Boat!' Franz looked genuinely shocked. 'You didn't say *boat*, did you? Please tell me you're not going to buy a boat.' His consternation was real. 'Fuck! Why don't you just tear up five-pound notes, throw them in the harbour and watch them float through the heads and out to sea?'

'No, mate, not a yacht. A new skiff – Whitehall, seventeen-footer. Get me around the harbour faster.'

'What's wrong with the ferry? Only a dumb Mick would row somewhere when he can catch the ferry for a couple of bob.'

'Don't start, or I'll tell you about people who won't use their car after sunset on Friday!' Danny threatened.

Despite himself Franz grinned. 'Yeah, I know – your back, exercise. But you've already got a perfectly good rowboat, haven't you?'

'It's too small. I want to take the twins out of a morning.'

Franz looked at him warily. 'Does Helen know about this?'

'What – the house or the twins coming out with me?'

'Both.'

'No. Not yet. Nor the new skiff. We don't have a hundred and seventy-five quid available in the kitty, by any chance, do we?' Danny asked hopefully.

Franz sighed. 'Mate, I can't help it if you've had a sudden massive aberration and your brain has turned to mush, but count me out on both items. If you've made up your mind to live in a shithouse,' he shrugged, throwing his arms wide, 'what can I say? About the money for the boat, skiff, whatever, no, we don't have that much in the kitty.'

'Okay, but promise me one thing.'

'What's that?'

'You won't tell Helen you've seen it.' Danny hesitated. 'Also, not a word about the new boat.'

Franz sighed. 'Mate, it's Friday and it's after five and I'm going to get into my car and drive home to my rented flat overlooking Bondi Beach, while I wait for a suitable house in my neighbourhood to come up for sale so that I can live in it while it matures into a decent investment. To tell Helen anything about this proposition of yours would be to revisit the humiliation I feel at having picked not only a goy but a schmuck to be my partner in chambers.'

'It's so good of you to give me your blessing . . . mate.'

Franz bowed mockingly and turned to go back to his Morris Minor.

'Why do you persist with that Pommy shitheap?' Danny called, unable to resist a final shot. 'Get rid of it. Buy a Holden – a fair dinkum Aussie car!'

'Excuse me?' Franz turned. 'What was that about General Motors Holden?' he called back.

With time running out before Helen left, Danny finally summoned up the courage to broach the subject, expounding the virtues of a harbour-side dwelling, while going fairly light on the disadvantages of the one he was proposing. She agreed, though somewhat reluctantly, to view it. 'Why don't we invite Franz along? He's always on about waterfront property, and he's in commercial law and knows a bit about real estate.'

Danny cleared this throat. '*Hrrrmph!* Later perhaps. I'll arrange a private inspection. What say we see what you think first up, eh?'

Danny's heart sank when they entered the cold, damp building. It smelt overpoweringly of cats' piss, with a distinct tincture of mould to emphasise the general atmosphere of despair and neglect. They discovered later that the Simpson women had kept fifteen cats, not counting the stray moggies that customarily dropped in for a feed, that turned the house into a cats' toilet. Everywhere they looked there were stacks of newspapers, all, it seemed, the *Sydney Morning Herald*. The Simpson twins were obviously well brought up.

The interior, in its own way, was much worse than the exterior. Everything they touched was dirty, damp, and stank of cat and decay. But, to his surprise, Helen simply adored it.

'The furniture is mid-Victorian and only the best of its kind. If we can restore it, it will come up wonderfully,' she exclaimed.

'You sure, darling?' Danny asked, unable to believe his ears.

Every cupboard, sideboard and breakfront revealed more treasures: ornate chamber pots, bedroom jug-and-basin sets, five complete bone-china dinner services, beautiful copper pots, pans and kitchen utensils green with verdigris, antimacassars, doilies, embroidered tea cloths all stained with mildew. They found a canteen of Victorian silver cutlery, the bone handles on the knives loose and shrunken with age. Once-beautiful embroidered linen sheets were dappled with mildew. Hand-tinted colour portraits of ancient whiskered ancestors hung from the wall.

'It's like a combination of walking into an old newspaper repository and a visit to the Victoria and Albert Museum in London,' Helen cried. 'Oh, how divine!'

'It's a shitheap! I mean the contents, not the house,' Danny added quickly.

'It's a mess, I grant you, a terrible one.' She glanced up at Danny, eyes shining. 'But not a hopeless one.'

'Yeah?' Danny exclaimed, still not believing what he was hearing. 'Really and truly?' he asked, using one of the twins' expressions.

Helen laughed. 'Poor old dump. It's a bit like your face, darling. Once it was probably much too handsome, now it's been brutally battered, but I do believe we'll be able to improve it so much that I'll grow very fond of it.'

The house came up for auction two days before Helen was due to depart. There were only two bidders – curiously enough the other was also a lawyer, though it turned out he was acting on behalf of a client. He seemed taken aback by the presence of Danny and Helen and it was obvious he'd expected to pick up the property for a song, because he withdrew when he saw they were determined to continue, and fortunately long before the bidding had reached a level that would have required more than the deposit they had saved.

The result was that the property was knocked down in their favour for what seemed to them a bargain price, though probably most people would have disagreed. They even had a small amount over for clearing, cleaning and the first urgent repairs and renovations. Brenda guaranteed the loan, and Harry Farmer agreed to a mortgage, unable to resist pointing out that his common sense would probably have prevailed had he and Danny not both been Balmain Primary and Fort Street High boys and had Brenda not been an old and valued client who'd never required an overdraft.

A week later, Franz handed Danny a cheque for one hundred and seventy-five pounds. 'Buy your boat. A nice piece of city property changed hands last week – money for jam,' he lied.

'Thanks, Franz. I owe you.'

'Oh, sure,' Franz replied. 'Just don't drown the twins.'

The ship took Helen to Port Suez, at the southern end of the Suez Canal, where she would travel overland to the dig. Danny showed the twins on a map the route she was taking, and every night he'd invent a bedtime story that was set in Egypt and involved Helen. On her return she was often totally mystified by a great many of their questions.

By the time she got back four months later, looking tanned and fit, though a little too thin, the twins, out with Danny in the boat four days a week, were already old hands on the harbour. Helen was not pleased, so Danny took her to see Wee Georgie, who explained the almost uncapsizable qualities of the Whitehall skiff, and this, together with the obvious excitement of the twins, made her finally agree to allow Danny to continue the early-morning ritual.

By the time the Melbourne Olympics arrived in late November, the twins were so accustomed to being out on the harbour at sparrow's fart – a term Danny often used that sent them into gales of laughter, bending over, cupping their mouths and dancing in a circle – that they often woke him up before the alarm went off. Danny spoke constantly to them about swimming, preparing them for what was to come.

During the Olympics, the twins were bathed and ready for bed by 6 p.m. each evening when the day's results appeared on TV. Danny encouraged them to watch the swimming heats, yet another of his ploys, in the ridiculous hope that even at the age of five they would somehow soak up the Olympic dream. For days he'd made a huge fuss about Dawn Fraser swimming in the upcoming heats, and when she won the gold medal in the 100-metres freestyle final he'd practically gone berserk: 'Look, look, kids!' he yelled. Then, 'Go, Dawnie! Go, girl! You've got it, it's yours. Go, go, go! You beauty!'

The twins, excited because he was, danced around crying, 'You beauty!'

'It's ours, the gold medal's ours! Dawnie belongs to us, to Balmain!'

'Hooray!' Sam cried.

'It will be your turn one day, sweethearts!' Danny said, hugging them to him.

Despite all this excitement, the twins soon became bored, yawning, quibbling or plaintively demanding their bedtime story and bedtime song instead, a ritual he observed every night without fail. That is, until one evening when the rowing was shown. The girls became very excited. 'Look, Daddy. Rowing, rowing!' they chorused. The race was the final of the double sculls. As Mervyn Wood and Murray Riley crossed the finish line to win bronze, Danny suddenly realised, *Jesus! The girls could just as easily represent Australia in the double sculls.* Building up their strength and mental toughness for rowing would be much the same as training them to swim. Perhaps he could begin by training them as swimmers, then switch them to the double scull if it seemed they were not suited to swimming. He couldn't lose! Danny had always imagined them powering home, Sam first, Gabby second, but now he saw them crossing the line as a team in the double skulls, a length ahead of the boat in second place.

In a split second Danny clearly saw the path to fame and glory for his daughters. He'd never felt more certain about anything. It was the birth of an obsession, although to Danny it felt like an epiphany.

Settlement for the house had occurred two weeks before Helen returned. It was the beginning of two years of weekends spent restoring it, seeking professional help only when they could afford it or were out of their depth. Bullnose was a retired bricklayer, and with Sammy as his barrow boy, the two old mates worked together, teaching Danny and Helen the tricks of the trowel, tuck-pointing and how to lay new damp courses, mix concrete and mortar, and do basic brickwork. They took a small weekly salary, topped up with a schooner every night of the week at the Hero, in addition to their customary six schooners each week in return for Danny's massage. Wee Georgie gave up some of his precious time to restoring the original Baltic pine floorboards to beeswaxed perfection and also showed them how to varnish the old stair panelling and stair railings. Then he French-polished the cedar tables and helped restore the furniture. If they needed expert advice on just about anything, they told Half Dunn, who soon flushed out an artisan or somebody else who could advise them. When they discovered that the ornate ceiling moulding was soft from damp and mildew, Half Dunn produced a plasterer and moulder who had recently been employed to work on the Sydney Town Hall. He worked a veritable miracle and returned the mouldings to almost pristine condition.

Half Dunn lost two stone gardening at weekends with Lachlan Brannan, who was going from strength to strength in the media department of George Patterson Advertising. They cleared the overgrown garden of lantana to discover another garden underneath that still possessed the bones of the original design and revealed several beds of glorious camellias, azaleas and, remarkably, an old-fashioned rose garden. Lachlan's dad, now off the garbage trucks and working as a council gardener, miscalculated the number of rolls of turf required for an extension to the council gardens – by his own admission he'd never been good at sums – and miraculously the council truck dumped the makings of a large front lawn at the back gate after dark one Friday evening.

On a hot summer's day in January 1958, Helen, Danny and the twins moved into the mid-Victorian home. They gazed out at the magnificent view across the harbour from the French windows upstairs, over the tessellated verandah, which had been reproduced downstairs. From the front door and large windows they could look over Lachlan's father's sloping lawn and the original stone pathway and steps that led to the water's edge and the glistening harbour beyond.

There were only two drawbacks. The factories were still pumping crap out into the harbour and pollution into the air, and the disturbances from the slum dwellings seemed to have increased. More of the broken-down housing seemed to be used to accommodate a floating population of single men and, more recently, women and children. Friday and Saturday nights were a living hell, with the drunken brawling in the street often continuing into the early hours. The worst was the so-called boarding house closest to them, a neglected factory manager's double-storey building that seemed to contain a great many more boarders than the size of it suggested was humanly possible.

Increasingly Danny realised that there was something very wrong, and on several occasions he complained to the council with little or no effect. He simply received a letter to say that they would look into the matter and nothing would change. After nearly a dozen or so complaints he realised that someone somewhere must have been on the take. He'd spoken to Half Dunn, who asked around and said, 'Mate, you're on a sticky wicket here. Local Labor – you know him, remember he was the shop steward who humiliated me over the water-polo fiasco when you were a lad, scuffed one of me two-tones that day – Tommy O'Hearn. He's in it up to his eyebrows. He's on the council. Refused a nomination to be mayor because he's being nominated by Sussex Street to represent Labor in Balmain–Birchgrove at the next state elections, in effect a gift for past deeds well done. He's working with someone from the outside, can't find out who. But it goes right back to Labor headquarters in Sussex Street. The council is up to their eyeballs in it as well. They – whoever is behind this – are buying all the old shit boxes in the street, banging up plywood partitions and renting them as cheap accommodation for the down and outers.'

Danny realised that Franz Landsman might yet prove to be right; they had a lovely harbour-front residence set on a beautiful half-acre block, but the location might prove to be a real-estate disaster.

Danny, like Tommy O'Hearn, was a Balmain boy and knew better than to interfere with local arrangements, other than by observing the formalities and complaining to the council, like every other member of the community. O'Hearn was popular, energetic, trusted and local; as long as nobody was hurt, that was pretty well all that was required in Balmain. Furthermore, he'd paid his dues and the party was going to reward him, knowing he already had the blessing of the larger part of the local population.

However, Tommy O'Hearn was married to Lachlan's sister, and so Danny called Lachlan, who had recently been appointed an account executive at George Patterson. Lachlan was a frequent visitor to Danny and Helen's house and was aware of the weekend mayhem, but when Danny spoke to him about the street and the 'rumour' that his brother-in-law was involved, there was a noticeable silence. Then Lachlan said, 'Danny, mate, I'm between a rock and a hard place. I honestly don't know a lot. Tommy knows you and I are mates, and says very little in front of me. I've asked Mum and Dad and they just shrug, and my sister told me it was none of my business.' He laughed. 'She accused me of becoming a bloody white-collar, middle-class snob, in my fancy suit and my polished shoes. Said I was spreading bullshit, and my job was "irresponsible". I think she's on the defensive, but she has to stay loyal to her husband. I reckon the bloke behind the buy-ups and partitioning is head of a real-estate syndicate that operates from Double Bay – posh money.'

'What's the name of the real-estate syndicate?' Danny asked.

Lachlan sighed. 'I don't know, mate. I'm just putting two and two together. I've overheard him referring to the Double Bay mob on the phone, and once he said, "Finance is no problem. I've got a silvertail syndicate that's awash with cash." Sorry I can't tell you more, Danny. That's honestly all I know.'

Danny didn't want to push him any further. This was just the kind of issue that could divide a Balmain family. While he'd always regarded himself as Labor, he hadn't given it a lot of thought. Everyone in Balmain was Labor, or if you weren't you only told the ballot box. He realised that he was, in party terms, at best a loyal vote; certainly not an insider, and not a comrade. His vote was taken for granted but his opinion wasn't needed or, for that matter, desired.

He discussed the matter with Helen, who, as usual, cut to the chase. 'Darling, we're not moving from here and this isn't going to go away. While the women may love you, your support of wives and children hasn't made you very popular among some of the male members of our illustrious community. This issue, while it stinks to high heaven, is going to take more than a few complaints to council to resolve. The first thing we should do is become paid-up members of the Labor Party. We've been talking about it for a couple of years now.' She paused. 'Then at least we're not looking over the fence like a couple of gawking kids. This is not an issue for a lawyer but one for a good citizen, and in the end for Balmain. Labor use this community for any purpose that suits them because they know we'll remain faithful and our votes can be counted on. Look at it.' She began ticking things off on the fingers of her left hand. 'Power station; coal depot; five chemical factories, three of which we can see from the front verandah, all of them belching out smoke and pouring pollutants into the harbour; countless dirty little foreshore factories; and two soap factories. And now this slum settlement on our doorstep!' She hesitated. 'But, darling, I'm not going to lose my beautiful home, so we'd better get on the inside where we can see the corruption more clearly and keep an eye on the O'Hearns of this world.'

Neither Danny nor Helen had ever seen their new home as an opportunity to make money or as a stepping stone to a more salubrious location. They loved the old house – Helen had a library and study of her own, and the twins, now aged seven, had a big garden to play in – and they were more than happy. Each Monday the girls needed very little encouragement to rise and trot down to the restored boathouse to launch the Whitehall skiff. While Danny treasured its varnished beauty, the twins saw it as essentially belonging to them. They'd winch it into the harbour in minutes, then each would take up an oar mid-ship and wait for Danny to arrive to man the oars at the front thwart.

The twins were virtually identical, and strangers found it almost impossible to tell them apart. Even Mrs O'Shea, now more housekeeper than nanny, would become confused, a fact that delighted the girls, especially when she'd accuse one of them of some misdemeanour only to be met with a denial, the blame placed firmly on the other in a ping-pong game of catch the right twin. But Helen and Danny had discovered fairly early that there were differences, especially in their personalities. Helen defined this by referring to Sam as 'Miss I' and Gabrielle as 'Miss We'. Sam seemed to be the more competitive. But it wasn't a time when anyone took much notice of children or their personalities; they had no rights or entitlements except to be loved and nurtured. They did as they were told and behaved as they were expected to, accepting the rules of behaviour set for them. That children should be seen and not heard was still a widely held view among parents. The twins were polite, compliant, innocent and friendly; Sam loved books, and Gabby music. But at such an early age they were, according to Helen, who would take on the task of training their minds, best left untrammelled to develop as they might. It wasn't a time when children were expected to be gifted, and few Australians would have even considered the possibility of their child becoming a prodigy, except perhaps in sport, or music, which was too rarefied a pursuit to be considered by most families. This was a phenomenon that would come later, perhaps from European migrants.

While people might marvel and exclaim about their appearance, and although they often grew weary of being asked who was who, the twins showed no impatience, accepting their identical appearance as simple fact. They didn't think being twins was special, or that dressing identically was any different from simply dressing. Their marks at school were usually within a point or two of each other, but they accepted this as being the natural outcome of doing everything together. They also accepted that adults, confused by how alike they were, rarely used their names but simply referred to them as the Dunn twins. This would last throughout their sporting careers, and, if anything, made them seem even less individual, even to themselves.

But the twins did all the things kids of their age did: played hopscotch, skipped, chanted rhymes and giggled a lot, and while they were cute and said funny things, this was no different from every other contented child of their age.

However, there were differences between the twins and most other Balmain children. For instance, they went to school regularly, had never been beaten in what was known in the schoolyard as 'taking a belting from me dad'. And their father paid them a great deal more attention than most fathers gave their children. Danny had taken on responsibility for their mental discipline, preparing them for the sporting achievements his own ambition suggested they deserved. The twins simply responded to his instructions; ambition was still an alien idea to them. It was not until their early teens that they felt, like many others, they had a right to differ from their father. And it was even later before they thought to differ from each other.

There was one notable incident, however, where the twins showed a marked contrast in the way they responded. They'd been walking down what they had come to call 'Brokendown Street' on their way home from school one Thursday when they were approached by a man from one of the houses.

'Hello, young ladies,' he said with a grin. 'You look like the type of girls who like lollies. Am I right?'

'Yes,' Sam said, smiling, but Gabby remained mute.

'What sort of lollies are your favourites?' the man said, dropping to his haunches in front of Sam.

'Smarties,' Sam said excitedly.

'And yours?'

'Raspberry suckers,' Gabby said, still serious, but trying to be polite.

'Well, this is your lucky day, my sweet little twinnies,' the man chuckled. 'Guess what? Last night I won a whole bucketful of lollies in a church raffle and I can't eat them 'cause I've got a bad tooth and it hurts if I eat chocolate and lollies.' He stuck his forefinger in the side of his mouth and pulled upwards. 'See . . . the big one at the back's rotten.'

Sam stepped forwards to take a closer look, then pulled back suddenly because the man smelled nasty. He reached out and gently took her hand. 'If you come to my house,' he pointed to a rundown house two doors down, 'and give me a kiss, I'll give you the whole bucket just for yourselves. Will you come?'

Sam nodded, smiling.

'Come then, both of you.' He rose to his feet. 'Boy oh boy, is this ever your lucky day!' he laughed, releasing Sam's hand.

'No!' Gabby cried. 'Run, Sam!' Grabbing her twin's hand she jerked her into a run. Sam reacted instinctively to Gabby and started to run. It was the first time they had ever differed in their response to a situation, and while nobody understood the significance of it at the time, it was a defining moment in their lives.

The twins, panting, told their neighbour Mrs O'Shea about the lolly man, and were asked to describe him.

'He smelled nasty,' Sam said.

'He had black hair and a bad tooth. Sam saw it,' Gabby answered.

It wasn't much to go on but she immediately called the police and then Danny and Helen. The police came down in a van half an hour later with the sirens blaring, did a search of the house the twins indicated, but made no arrests, claiming they had no identification to work from and that there wasn't anyone in the house at the time. Very few men were about because they were all still at work. The police suggested a line-up of every male in the street, but Danny was unwilling to expose the twins to such an experience, aware that it would be pointless. 'It's time you blokes did a regular patrol down here. You must know what this street's like. It's out of control every weekend,' he said.

'See what we can do, sir,' the sergeant said impassively. Which turned out to be nothing.

From that day on Mrs O'Shea would collect the twins from school.

———

Friday was the twins' morning off, and although they didn't go rowing on the harbour with Danny, they'd usually be up to have breakfast with him and to compete in the push-up competition, so Danny was a little surprised they hadn't appeared by the time he was ready to leave for the office the next day. Sam had seemed none the worse for their experience, but Gabby had lingered after their mandatory bedtime story, asking for another. They hadn't been tucked in until a quarter to nine, when they sang 'The Fish Tummy Song' and finally kissed Danny goodnight.

While Helen got away with reading to them while they were in the bath, he was required to tell them a story to which they could contribute. It always ended in the same way with the singing of 'The Fish Tummy Song'. It was a routine that had begun when they were too tiny to remember, and he often wondered if they could go to sleep without it. The song was pretty basic, but once a verse had been established and added to the song, the twins policed it with a diligence that brooked no possible alteration.

The Fish Tummy Song

Sam and Gabby, I heard someone say,
You haven't been terribly good today.
You've given the next-door neighbour's cat
A nasty whack with a ping-pong bat.
And can you possibly tell me why . . .
You pulled the wings off a butterfly?

Chorus
May you eat boiled cabbage and pumpkin mash
And row inside the tummy of a great big fish
In a hollowed-out calabash!

Now, my girls, it's not very nice
When you torture poor little baby mice,
And squash the bug on the Persian rug,

With the brand-new rubber bathroom plug.
And can you possibly tell me why . . .
You made the butcher's parrot cry?

Chorus

May you eat boiled cabbage and pumpkin mash
And row inside the tummy of a great big fish
In a hollowed-out calabash!

It's not very kind to creep up behind,
And frighten a lady who's almost blind,
And make a poor little slimy slug
Dance a waltz and a jitterbug.
And can you possibly tell me why . . .
You told a fat little pig she could fly?

Chorus

May you eat boiled cabbage and pumpkin mash
And row inside the tummy of a great big fish
In a hollowed-out calabash!

Now it's really not good that you watched the dog
Eat up the frog on the log in the bog,
Or captured some tadpoles to put in the water
You gave to your favourite teacher's daughter.
And can you possibly tell me why . . .
The canary was dipped in bright-blue dye?

Chorus

May you eat boiled cabbage and pumpkin mash
And row inside the tummy of a great big fish
In a hollowed-out calabash!

But now is the time to go to sleep,
Snuggle right down and don't make a peep.
Grab your teddy and close your eyes,
Off you go to sleepy-byes.
And can you possibly tell me why . . .
You dream of ice-cream and apple pie?

Chorus
May you eat boiled cabbage and pumpkin mash
And row inside the tummy of a great big fish
In a hollooooowed ooout caaaalaabassssh!

After the children were asleep, and he and Helen had retired to bed, he would kiss her twice last thing at night. The first kiss meant, 'Goodnight, darling. Sleep tight,' and the second, moments later, meant, 'Wake up, beautiful. I'm off to work.' This was so that he didn't have to wake her in the morning.

Still a little disappointed at not seeing the twins before he left for work, Danny sat down on the bathroom chair to perform the last step in his morning toilet. He reached for his boots, as he did every morning, and said aloud, 'Glossy Denmeade, I haven't forgotten; I'll get that bastard Riley yet.'

The boots, hand stitched and slim, were highly polished in the military manner. Pulling them on served as a daily reminder of his origins, and his place in the constant fight against injustice and the class system. The boots had become a symbol, as had so much else that served to mould his character when he was a prisoner of war.

Danny, with all the other prisoners, had spent the first thirteen months in Changi Prison, prior to being sent to the death camps to work on the Burma Railway. During the period they'd spent in Changi, the officers were allocated separate compounds from the men, outside the walls. By the standards of captivity under the Japanese, the officers were relatively comfortable, unlike their men, who were housed in the prison itself. The officers had gone to great lengths to maintain discipline, none more so than the martinet Colonel Callaghan, who'd built his entire career on spit and polish, even maintaining a batman while in captivity. Towards the end of the first year, as their uniforms began to wear out in the harsh tropical climate, British, as well as some Australian officers began confiscating from the men under their command, for their own use, items of apparel in good condition. Perhaps they were under the illusion that their appearance in full uniform was good for general morale, and a sign to the Japanese that, although they were captives, they couldn't be intimidated.

This appropriation was deeply unpopular with most of the Australians, although their British counterparts seemed to accept it as part of the natural order of things. British officers, with a few exceptions, were notorious for not looking after their men, whereas the Australians were usually much more closely allied to the rank and file, though, in truth, a small percentage of them behaved in much the same way as the British. The officers in Danny's Company, B Company, played no part in this uniform appropriation, but there had been some talk of two officers in C Company who had demanded items of clothing from some of their men.

The day had come when Danny's company was arbitrarily separated from the remainder of his battalion by the Japanese to make up the numbers in a contingent to be sent to 'somewhere in Thailand'. The men were already in pretty poor shape, having worked as slave labour on Japanese projects on the island, existing on food that delivered no more than 1000 calories; in effect, a starvation diet. While life can be sustained for a time on 1000 calories a day, eventually it will lead to death, and the process is markedly accelerated by the addition of hard labour. The weakened body begins to waste away and its natural defences are overwhelmed by disease and infections. While over 30 000 Allied soldiers died in captivity, mainly due to cruelty, starvation and sickness, only a handful of officers perished in this way. The reason was quite simple. Officers were not required to do any forced labour. Those who died, like the Reverend John Ayliffe, were among the few who elected to remain and work beside their men.

However, the call to go to Burma was welcomed by the men in Danny's company, because Japanese propaganda had led them to believe that the Burma internment camps were a reward for the work they'd done in Singapore. In fact, they sounded almost like holiday camps, with plenty of food and a little light agricultural work. Previous detachments had been sent to Burma to what later became known as the death camps in horribly crowded cargo ships, but this time they were to proceed to the other end of the railway – to the Thai border – by train. Danny had inspected his men, who were lined up along the railway tracks prior to boarding the waiting trucks. By most standards they were not too badly equipped. A group in from Java, destined for Burma, had mostly been reduced to going barefoot, wearing only loincloths, while most of Danny's men still retained a half-decent pair of shorts and a shirt and, most importantly, their boots. So it had come as some surprise when he saw that Private Owen Denmeade was the only one of his men who stood barefoot on the hot stones that formed the track ballast.

Denmeade's nickname was 'Glossy', because he was renowned throughout the battalion for the magnificent shine on his now missing boots. He'd explain to anyone prepared to listen that a mirror finish to the toecaps of your army boots allowed you, when standing close to a good-looking sort, to glance down at your toecaps and see up her skirt. The fact that there was no way of testing this theory because there were no women wearing skirts in Changi Prison seemed not to matter to him; it was this deliciously lascivious notion that kept him polishing his boots for hours on end. It was also true to say that the result wasn't far short of being a work of art, and while they'd been stationed in Malaya, Danny had given Glossy permission to have a local leatherworker emboss the initials OD on the inside ankle area of both boots.

'Private Denmeade, why are you not wearing your boots?' Danny asked, thinking he might have put them in his kitbag for safekeeping.

'Confiscated, Sergeant Major!' came the reply.

'Confiscated by whom?'

'Captain Riley, Sergeant Major!'

Danny had difficulty containing his surprise. 'From C Company?'

'Yes, Sergeant Major.'

'And he didn't swap them . . . give you his?'

'They was fucked . . . er, beyond repair, Sergeant Major.'

'He didn't offer to buy them?'

'No, Sergeant Major. I wouldn't sell them for all the tea in China!'

'Tell me exactly what happened.'

'He come up to me and I come to attention and salute and he touches his cap and says right off, "Private, what size are your boots?"'

'"Ten, sir," I tell him. "Good. Remove them. I'm appropriating them," he says.'

'And then?'

'"Please no, sir," I beg him. I'm pretty choked see.' Glossy looked up at Danny. 'Them boots took more'n two year to get perfect, Sergeant Major . . . they was begun when we was in Malaya.'

'Yes, I remember. Did you explain this to Captain Riley?'

'Yeah, but he weren't interested. "That's an order, private, unless you want to be put on a charge," he said t' me, sarg.'

'Why didn't you report this to me, Glossy?' Danny asked, dropping the formality, which gave the hapless Glossy permission to do the same.

'Yeah, Danny, I'm sorry, but we was going to this holiday camp. If I didn't give the bastard me boots, he'd put me on a charge like he said, maybe insubordination, then they'd keep me in Singapore and youse would go without me! I'd miss out . . . be left behind without me mates,' Glossy said, his voice quavering.

Danny was angry. Glossy was one of his men and Danny knew that if he'd reported the appropriation of his boots before they'd left Changi Prison for the docks, he could have made an issue of the matter and almost certainly got them back. A sergeant major is not without power in the Australian army, and on a moral issue involving his men, it is a brave officer indeed who ignores his opinion. In taking his boots the bastard had taken away Glossy's self-respect, and that simply wasn't on. But, as they were about to board the train, there wasn't much Danny could do.

They'd eventually arrived at the Hin Tok death camp, one of the most notorious places on the Thai–Burma Railway. It hadn't taken them long to realise that they'd been tricked and had descended into a veritable hell on earth. The workers they joined were starved, beaten and suffering from chronic malaria, dengue fever, dysentery, tropical ulcers and cholera. On top of this, they were forced to work beyond the limits of human endurance by the constantly apoplectic screaming of the Japanese engineers. Already weakened, Danny and his men soon became indistinguishable from the legion of walking ghosts building a railway through some of the worst terrain in the world, a task the pre-war colonial authorities had rejected as impossible.

Because he'd lost his boots, Glossy Denmeade died at Hin Tok – like Hell Fire Pass, one of the many nightmare locations on the railway. Constantly harangued with the cry of 'Speedo!', after nearly fifteen continuous hours of backbreaking work, too exhausted to watch where he stepped while clearing the jungle, the barefooted Glossy trod on a bamboo spike. His left foot became infected, and the camp surgeon, Lieutenant Colonel Albert Coates, lacking sulphur drugs or any other medicines, could do little to halt the infection, finally resorting to amputation without anaesthesia. Glossy's frail, work-beaten and poisoned body couldn't withstand the shock, and he died in agony.

The Reverend John Ayliffe, shaking from a bout of malaria, conducted the burial service over Glossy's wasted corpse, in the midst of a tropical downpour when work became impossible, so Danny and his men could attend. The roar of the rain drowned his words, but it didn't matter; each of the men carried the eulogy in his head. Glossy's body was thrown into a huge covered bonfire kept continuously alight to consume the endless supply of bodies. As it does in the tropics, the rain stopped as abruptly as it had started, and the cries of 'Speedo!' were heard from every corner. But not before Danny and his men stood at attention while the company bugler, Corporal Steve Reiber, blew the Last Post. Glossy would never get the opportunity to test his boot-cap mirror theory.

Glossy Denmeade was just one of the 106 000 victims of the Thai–Burma Railway; 16 000 of them were Allied prisoners, and a further 90 000 were Asian labourers. It has been claimed that a prisoner of war or an impressed Asian coolie died for every wooden sleeper laid along its length.

At the completion of the Thai–Burma Railway, the men who'd survived, along with some of the officers from their separate camps, travelled over the railways they had built to a large camp in Kanchanaburi province on the banks of the River Kwai in Thailand.

Word reached Danny that Captain Riley was among the contingent of officers housed in huts in a small nearby village and he set off to see him.

Helen would hear the rest of the story after the first Anzac Day parade in 1946 when Danny returned pissed and she'd asked him how the day had gone. 'Yeah, great. Most of the boys were there, but still no sign of that bastard Riley,' he'd remarked.

Danny seldom spoke of the prison camp, even to Helen, and while she'd been able to piece together a fair bit, including the story of Glossy's stolen boots and his subsequent death, Danny had always stopped short of telling her too much about building the Burma Railway. What she did know came through casual comments, which she'd be quick to question in the hope that Danny would follow them up with more information. She'd always assumed that the story of Glossy's boots had ended with his death from septicaemia. Now she sensed there was more to come. 'Riley? The captain who stole Glossy's boots?'

'Yeah, the same deadshit.'

'What? You hope to meet him and confront him on an Anzac Day march?'

'Not confront him – I've already done that.'

'Oh? When was that?'

Danny had proceeded to tell Helen the rest of the story, explaining that when they'd been taken to the camp on the banks of the River

Kwai, he'd heard of Riley's whereabouts in a separate officers' compound, nearby but sufficiently far away to avoid contamination from the human detritus that formed the sick and starving rank and file who had survived the horror of the railway.

'I got to the officers' compound and was directed to a central hut where I was told a card game was in progress. The hut turned out to be a platform on stilts with a post at each corner supporting a thatch-leaf attap roof, the open sides designed to catch any passing breeze. Six men, presumably officers, were seated on wooden stools around a roughly hewn table playing cards. I didn't recognise any of them except for Riley.

'Like all of us, I was skin and bone, brown as a berry and shirtless, wearing only a ragged pair of khaki shorts, my battered slouch hat and a pair of sandals made from a discarded truck tyre. Unfortunately we hadn't learnt how to make the sandals until after Glossy's death. When my shirt finally wore out I sewed my sleeve chevrons and crown to the side of my hat where the badge usually sat, so that the Jap guards and engineers were aware of my rank and would relay their instructions through me instead of screaming instructions in Japanese at the uncomprehending men,' Danny explained. 'I climbed the three wooden steps to the platform, saluted and announced, "Sergeant Major Dunn!"'

'Then one of them, a captain, pointed to my slouch hat without even acknowledging me and quipped, "It seems your rank has gone to your head, Sergeant Major. Bloody silly place to put it."

'This produced a bit of a titter. Still standing at attention I replied, "With respect, sah! If some officers present hadn't found it necessary to steal our uniforms I might have had a shirt sleeve to wear it on."'

'Oh, dear, what happened then?' Helen asked, grinning. Then as an afterthought she added, 'Be so kind as to remember I held the rank of lieutenant colonel, Sergeant Major Dunn.'

'Well, with my ugly, broken, one-eyed mug confronting them they were probably somewhat taken aback, but one of them managed to say, "Take it easy, Sergeant Major. What is it you want?"

'"I've come for Glossy Denmeade's boots, sir."

'They all gave me a bemused look, even Riley. I pointed to Riley's boots under the table. Though they'd lost their former glorious shine and were scuffed, I could clearly see the initials OD over the inside ankle of the right boot. "Those."

'Riley coloured and started blustering. "What the hell are you talking about?" he stammered. Then, gathering courage, he said, "Be careful, Sergeant Major, or you'll find yourself on a charge."

'"Glad to be able to oblige, sir," I replied.

'"What's going on here? Perhaps you can explain, Sergeant Major," a colonel asked.

'"Ah, glad you asked, sir." I then told the story of Glossy's boots and ended by pointing a finger at Riley's chest and saying, "You ordered Private Denmeade to give you his boots, and by doing so you killed him as surely as if you'd personally executed him, sir. Now please give me Glossy's boots. B Company requires them as memento mori."

'The colonel turned to Riley. "This true, Captain?"

'I'll say this for Riley – by this time he'd regained his composure. "This man's mad, colonel. No such thing ever happened. These are the boots I was issued with shortly before the battalion left for Singapore." He looked up at me and said in a sympathetic tone, "Sergeant Major Dunn, I can see you've been through a fair bit. Why don't you just go back to your camp before I am reluctantly forced to put you on a serious charge?"'

Danny smiled at Helen. 'Sometimes the gods smile down on you. The lace on the right boot was undone and I suddenly dropped to my haunches, grabbed and pulled hard. The boot came loose in my hands just as Riley grabbed frantically at the edge of the table to stop himself from following it. "What the fuck!" he shouted out in alarm.

'I rose and placed the boot side-on on the table with the embossed OD showing. While the boot was scuffed and dull there were still several patches towards the top that showed it had once been highly polished. "These are the initials of Private Owen Denmeade, known in our company as Glossy," I said, pushing the boot so it rested in front of the colonel. "I should know as I gave him permission in Malaya to have them embossed on the inside ankles so it wouldn't show on parade. They were stolen from him by this officer and it cost Glossy Denmeade his life!" I turned to Riley and demanded, "May I have the other one please, sir?"

'The colonel looked over at Riley. "Hand it over, Captain Riley," he ordered.

'Riley hesitated. "He can't talk to me like this. It's blatant insubordination, sir!"

'"Don't be a bloody fool, man!" the colonel snapped. "If there's a court martial, how do you think this is going to look?"'

'Smart colonel,' Helen remarked, then asked, 'Did Riley hand over the other boot?'

'Yeah. I took it and snapped to attention, then said to the bastard, "Don't ever try to march on Anzac Day. Those of us in B Company who get back home will be waiting for you, and if I'm fortunate enough to be one of them, when we find you, I will personally break every bone in your fucking body, sah!" I did an about-turn and left without saluting. Later we heard that the other officers more or less ostracised him from then on.'

'And Glossy's boots, what happened to them?' Helen asked.

'They've been fully restored and they rest in a glass case at the RSL in George Street.'

'Do you know if Riley made it through to the end? Got back home?' Helen asked.

'Of course, he was an officer, wasn't he?'

'I wonder what's happened to him. Maybe he's taken your threat seriously, or now lives in another state or overseas.' Helen rose from the couch and kissed him. 'Darling, you have to get the war out of your head. Glossy, like thousands of others, is long dead. He could have died in a hundred different ways.'

'But he didn't! Some things you don't forget. Captain Riley is one such,' Danny growled.

Danny pulled on his boots and decided he'd get a coffee from the café across the road from his office in Phillip Street on his way in. Coffee was a beverage for which he'd only lately acquired a taste. The café was run by Italian migrants and featured what they referred to as an espresso machine. He'd have a bacon-and-egg sandwich as well, he thought. The rowing kept him fit and he didn't have a weight problem – a bacon-and-egg sango would do nicely.

He tiptoed into the twins' bedroom. They slept together in a double bed and now lay 'spoony', Gabby snuggled into Sam, sucking her thumb. He kissed them lightly then went back into the master bedroom and, crossing the carpet, checked that the alarm clock was set in time for Helen to wake and dress the twins, give them breakfast and drop them off at school. He'd kissed her good morning the previous night and told her he loved her.

He remembered that today was the day she was coming in from university to the office and they were going together to Labor headquarters in Sussex Street to become paid-up members. It was to be their first step towards, as he put it, 'auditing the cooked books'.

It was to prove a poor decision and the beginning of a very bumpy ride for Danny Corrib Dunn, solicitor at law.

CHAPTER NINE

HELEN SUBMITTED HER DISSERTATION for her doctorate in January 1960, the culminating event in her education, which had begun well before war was declared. Her ambition, never openly expressed except once or twice to Danny, was ultimately to be appointed head of the Department of Archaeology at Sydney University. As always she'd planned her path meticulously: tutor, lecturer, then senior lecturer, which was her current position, and once she had her doctorate, professor. The current head of the department was due to retire in 1968 or '69, when the twins would be seventeen or eighteen, and Helen wanted his job. There were some in academia who, had they known of her plans, would have described them as breathtakingly audacious, or insanely ambitious.

Helen was a woman who calculated odds but was never afraid of them. She was a realist and knew the academic pathway she had chosen would be full of obstacles and barriers, many of them supplied by her male colleagues. A male-dominated university senate would make it very difficult for a woman to reach such dizzy heights, and she'd have to contend with the cultural cringe, when competing with applicants from around the world. Professorships in archaeology, and particularly in her area of specialisation, Ancient Egypt, were rare as hen's teeth, and they invariably went to men, usually Englishmen. She didn't regard this as unfair – the English, not to mention the French and Germans, led the world in Egyptology, and the Americans were catching up fast. In fact, if she got the job she would be the first woman to do so in Australia. In order to get her head even a few inches above the crowd she would have to achieve a research breakthrough in her special field. But Helen wasn't unduly daunted; life wasn't meant to be fair, and academic life in Australia was anything but where women were concerned.

She told herself there were signs that the cringe the nation suffered from when it came to academia and the arts was slowly fading. It was over a decade since the mass migration of a million European migrants to Australia, and the cultural climate was changing fast. In another eight or nine years things could be vastly different. Helen had already proved during the war that she could compete with men. The army was predictably sexist and, she felt certain, far tougher than any university.

Helen had been working hard on her dissertation through University College London since returning from the dig in Egypt, and, as far as Danny was concerned, January 1960 was a red-letter day; the bloody thing was finally finished and on its way to some blokes in the UK who would mark it. Helen had no idea who these men might be.

Ever since she'd returned from Egypt she'd been talking, writing, thinking and arguing about what she termed the 'Arm of Djer'. She'd get very excited and go on and on about this ancient arm, and her ideas about it being royal. 'Darling, if I'm right, it's going to create a storm of protest, not only in England with the London, Edinburgh and Oxbridge crowd, but in France – and Germany as well – although the Americans will probably be more open to conjecture. But just imagine . . .'

Helen was a clever mimic and her voice changed as she sketched her reception by the rubicund old codgers in the Athenaeum Club in Pall Mall. 'I say, who *is* this person? Orstralian, did I hear you say? Good God, not a woman! Worked with Emery? Well, I suppose that's to her credit. Doesn't agree with him? Oh, I say, cheeky devil! What? She's disputing the North Saqqara tombs? Says it's a royal necropolis! Quite wrong, of course. No way to make a reputation, but then she *is* from the Antipodes. Vulgar, pushy lot. Met one once. Voice like a carpenter's rasp on a tin roof! Emery – splendid chap. Liverpudlian. Not his fault, of course. Can't choose your parents, what? Ha, ha, ha. Made the ladies on his dig wear culottes. Never do to have the wogs glimpsing their pink cambric knickers, what?' Helen paused, giggling. 'Can you imagine the excitement here if an Australian archaeologist, and a woman to boot, blows the roof off a theory that up to now has not even been in contention?' she laughed happily. All she had to do was prove her theory to the disbelieving and, in her mind, reactionary world of Egyptologists.

Danny, of course, would never have dreamed of telling her that he couldn't imagine a stampede of Australian news photographers, flashbulbs popping, storming the front door, closely followed by a mob of reporters clamouring for an interview. But he nevertheless loved his wife's enthusiasm, and was grateful that Helen had always supported him. He was more than happy to pay the price of having to hear about a bandaged arm found in a crevice in the wall of a tomb at a place called Abydos by a bloke named Petrie, which she firmly believed was an early example of mummification and which, in addition, she now believed she could prove belonged to Egyptian royalty.

He could almost recite her argument, having heard it a dozen times over the years since her return from her first archaeological dig. 'Listen to this, darling. Emery contends that because Abydos is about 250 miles south of Memphis, the capital of Ancient Egypt, and because there was no mummification at the time of the First Dynasty, no royals could have been buried there – the bodies would have decayed long before they arrived by boat. On the other hand Saqqara is close to Memphis and so it's the logical place for royal burials! And quite apart from that, what about the hundreds of young men and women and priests sacrificed and buried around the tomb at Abydos?'

Oh gawd, here we go, Danny would think to himself. *Here comes the dreaded arm.* 'But if they knew about mummification at the time, then there'd no problems, eh? Is that what you're saying?' It was time to concentrate.

'I'm convinced the Arm of Djer is the earliest evidence of mummification and that it *was* royal. And, yes, you're right. If they were mummified in Memphis, then transporting them that distance wouldn't have been a problem. When Petrie partially unwrapped the bandages he found four fabulous bracelets of gold, amethyst, lapis lazuli and turquoise, bearing the cartouche of the pharaoh arranged on the forearm. It, the arm, must have belonged to King Djer himself,' Helen said fervently.

'Well, surely anyone examining the arm and the bandages would be able to tell? Wait on: if it was a royal tomb, what happened to the body? The pharaoh?'

'The tomb robbers got there long before Petrie. They'd broken up the body, knowing that they'd find a king's ransom among the bandages – jewellery and the like. Then they set fire to the burial chamber.'

'So how come this Petrie fellow found the arm?'

Helen shrugged. 'Who knows? Perhaps one of the robbers meant to come back for it later without his mates knowing.'

'So the arm is all that's left of the pharaoh?'

Helen sighed. 'I wish.'

'Hang on! You just said this bloke Petrie found it in a crevice.'

'He did, and then he photographed it and delivered it to the Boulaq Museum in Cairo, where the bracelets were removed for display.'

'Yeah, but there's still the arm?'

'No.'

'What? They threw it away?'

'Well it disappeared, but you're probably right.'

'Jesus!'

Helen laughed. 'I guess they figured they had dozens of mummified bodies. An extra arm here or there didn't much matter.'

'Well, with no arm, you're up shit creek without a paddle, aren't you?'

'You have such a charming turn of phrase, darling . . . but no. Have a look at this.' Helen turned to a green leather-bound tome that lay on her desk and opened it to show a black-and-white photograph of the arm with the bracelets hand-coloured occupying an entire page. 'See, if you look carefully, there's a stain on the inside layers of the wrappings.'

'Yeah, probably the result of damp, and being stuck in that crevice.'

'But what if it isn't? What if the stains are resin and other embalming agents?'

'Helen, how can you possibly tell from a photograph?'

'Don't be such a spoilsport, Danny Dunn. *Of course* I'm not basing my thesis on a single photograph. Flinders Petrie must have taken samples of linen from the Arm of Djer. They must still exist, somewhere.'

'Where? I mean, where do you think?'

'I don't know. Cairo, perhaps; the Kasr-el-Aini Medical School, where they unwrapped and studied the mummies? The Museum?'

'The selfsame that lost the royal bloody arm? Don't like your chances, babe.'

Helen sighed. 'I'd so love to prove them all wrong. Emery, in particular. He's a stubborn old coot. Besides, wearing culottes in that heat was ridiculous! He wouldn't touch the local food, and his poor wife, Molly, ran out of recipes for bully beef and rice . . . and tinned beetroot! He loved it, so we had it with every meal.'

'You mean you'd travel to Cairo in the hope of finding a piece of ancient bandage to examine for possible resin marks?' Something in his voice must have betrayed his incredulity, because Helen's tone changed.

'Now, listen to me, Mr Big-shot Lawyer! If you were prosecuting a murder and a crucial clue involved a potential wild goose chase to some faraway place, would you ignore it?' Helen didn't wait for an answer. 'Of course you wouldn't! And that's what an archaeologist does – follows clues hidden in history.' She tossed her handsome head. 'Anyway, it's clearly not possible.'

'What isn't possible?'

'Going to Cairo.'

'Oh, I dunno,' Danny replied.

'Danny, what do you mean?' Helen cried, clutching his arm. She was suddenly excited, her eyes shining.

The law partnership was prospering, and they were well past their early financial problems. 'We can manage it. I'll talk to Franz.' But Danny couldn't resist adding, 'I must say, it's a bloody long way to go to look for a stained bandage that could have been tossed in the rubbish bin sixty years ago.'

'Well then I won't go,' Helen said, her voice flat, as if the air had suddenly been squeezed out of her. Then, not wanting to show her disappointment, she said firmly, 'I probably need to be around. Sam seems a little distracted at present, and Gabrielle wants to start music lessons, or so she says.'

'Sam distracted – what's that mean?'

'Her teacher says she's not paying attention in class.'

Danny frowned. 'Have you spoken to her?'

'Of course.'

'What did she say?'

Helen chuckled. 'She said she was concentrating on the 1968 Olympics.'

Danny was forced to laugh. 'But that's years away!'

'I pointed that out to her, but she said Dawn Fraser had visited her school and told them you have to plan a long way ahead if you want to win gold.'

'Funny little thing. Sam has always been the more competitive of the two. When we're rowing I often have to slow her down. It's a bit of a worry really.'

'What is?'

'That she's outstripping Gabby already.'

'Gabby has other things on her mind,' Helen added, a trifle acerbically. 'She wants to play the violin, she tells me.'

'What – at this age she knows already?' Danny said, mimicking Franz mimicking his mother.

'Some kids from the Sydney Conservatorium came to the school to play for them. They demonstrated all the instruments, and Gabby apparently fell in love with the violin. Or perhaps it was with the violinist,' Helen said dryly. 'Anyway, she came home and said, "Mummy, can I have a violin for my birthday?" Then she added, "I've fallen in love and I'm going to play in the Sydney Symphony Orchestra . . . or maybe I'll be a soloist – I haven't made up my mind yet."' Helen paused. 'So, you see, it's an important stage in their development. Best I stay home and concentrate on the living.'

'Mum says she wants to spend less time in the pub,' Danny said suddenly.

'Yes, she told me.'

'Told you what?'

'She'd like more time with her grandchildren.'

'Yeah, she's had forty years in pubs, so you can't really blame her. And Dad can probably do the actual day-to-day running of the Hero. She'd still do the books, the orders, supervise the cleaners. Now she's driving, she can take the twins to school and pick them up, and I daresay she'd be happy to supervise their homework and give them their tea, either at the pub or here.'

'What are you trying to tell me, Danny?'

'That you're going to Egypt to find your stained bandage.' Danny laughed. 'After all, if you're right, it'll knock the socks off your supervisor.'

'Darling, I *know* I'm right; I just need the evidence – the proof,' Helen insisted, 'and if I'm right, it'll knock the socks off the entire world of archaeology.'

'Be careful, sweetheart. One of the partners at Stephen James & Stapleton had a favourite saying: "There's many a slip between mug and lip." Don't make a right fool of yourself in front of your university colleagues. As Pineapple Joe would say, "Keep *schtum* until maybe you got double proof."'

Helen was not to be outdone. 'Or, as Sammy says, "A certainty is a dog that usually comes last at Harold Park." You're right, of course. But there are two things I am absolutely certain of – my husband and my mother-in-law. Thank you, darling.' Helen rose from her desk, walked over to the small leather couch and perched on Danny's lap. Wrapping her arms around his neck she kissed him deeply, then drew back and said, 'Which reminds me, Daniel Corrib Dunn. You haven't done your French homework for four days. Your teacher is getting anxious!' She grinned, looking at him lovingly. 'I'll call Brenda in the morning and talk to her. How lucky am I, to have the mother I've always wanted in Brenda, and the man I've always wanted in you. You know, I really think I could have been a great publican's daughter. I like a good pub: the atmosphere, the noise, the camaraderie – it's pretty fundamental.'

'Whatever that means,' Danny replied, unimpressed. 'It's the pot where people come to get pissed, the pisspot. I guess that's pretty basic. Getting back to your trip, how would you like to fly to Egypt?'

'What? By aeroplane?' Helen asked, surprised.

'I know you're a positive angel, darling, but yes. I looked into it a while ago, when you first started talking about Cairo in that special tone of voice you have.' He smiled. 'I think, from memory, Qantas flies to Tehran, then Iranian Airways would take you to Cairo. It'll take you a day or two, but it's a damn sight better than two weeks by P&O and another two weeks home. It'll mean you'll spend less time away from us, yet still have more time for research.'

'Oh, how exciting! I've never been in an aeroplane.'

'You'll be the first in the family to take an overseas flight, not counting the twin-engine Dakota that took us from Bangkok to the hospital in Rangoon.' Danny laughed. 'Flying costs the same as a first-class berth on P&O. The posh people all prefer to fly these days, my dear.'

'In that event, I'll stick out like a sore thumb,' Helen grinned.

During her time away they received an airmail letter from Helen every week, the single sheet of blue paper crammed with her smallest writing, full of funny stories that made the twins giggle, featuring her adventures with four major characters in the Cairo museum, where she was attempting to establish the whereabouts of the samples of the bandage that once covered the long-ago discarded arm of King Djer.

There was Ben Bin Bandage, the mummy restorer, who went to great lengths to show Helen all the wrong bandages. 'But madam mustn't be so fussy pot. I can find you bandage nearly, exactly, almost identical, the same, only one thousand years the difference!' Dr Abdul 'My Goodness' No, who was responsible for unwinding mummies, whose first reaction to any of her requests was, 'My goodness no, madam! These bandages, they are for the unwinding of, not for the taking of and using of and finding old resins maybe on the inside of that which was never seen before and I think is the poppycock and nonsense of!" Fatima Frankincense, the mummy-stuffing herb expert: 'We are mixing secret spices for the pharaohs and also for madam's very delicious dinner tonight! Madam is having dreams after eating. She is beautiful Cleopatra on royal barge sailing with very, very important Roman soldier, Mark Antonia, friend of Julie Caesar, down the Nile and hiding sometimes in papyrus. And very nice things they are happening inside there indeed! And lastly, Mohammed the Mummy Minder: 'Madam, if you want I can find you whole arm with bandage complete, not shitty small piece. They are having plenty resin, very cheap, genuine pharaoh, every satisfaction guaranteed! Goodwill to all mens!'

But reading between the lines of Helen's letters it was apparent to Danny, Brenda and Half Dunn that all was not going well in the search for the elusive resin-stained bandage. Then a month after she arrived Danny received a cable from Cairo sent directly to his office.

NO LUCK BANDAGE CAIRO STOP
GOING TO LONDON FURTHER SEARCH STOP
SEND SEVENTY POUNDS C/O EGYPTOLOGY DEPARTMENT
UNIVERSITY COLLEGE LONDON STOP
LOVE HELEN

For three weeks Helen continued her search in the Petrie Museum at University College London without success. With her money rapidly running out she knew she would soon be forced to come home. Then she came across an entry in the register that simply read 'Linen, Abydos, Dynasty 1'. Within an hour she had located the ancient samples, which were stored together with a swatch of the finest modern Irish linen, put there by Flinders Petrie as a comparison. Included was a note in his handwriting comparing the quality of First Dynasty linen with the best modern cloth, exactly as she'd read in the green book. Within a day she examined the Egyptian linen under a microscope and identified what she thought were minute traces of resin. Not long after, a university archaeological chemist verified the resin content, as well as the presence of two additional agents required in the mummification process. Helen was jubilant! She now had the indisputable evidence to support a groundbreaking piece of original research. The snip of a girl from Australia would have to be taken seriously in the clubrooms of the Athenaeum in Piccadilly and the hallowed halls of international academe.

On Helen's return to Australia, Danny and the twins, Brenda and Half Dunn waited excitedly at Sydney Airport terminal for her to emerge from customs. The twins held a handmade placard that read: WELL DUNN, MUM! and Danny another that said, YOU HAVE EVERY RESIN TO BE PROUD!

Now, in January 1960, Helen handed Danny a bound copy of her dissertation. Twelve copies had been printed and bound by the University of Sydney Press. He opened it to the title page:

Royal Tomb or Cenotaph?
Reassessing the Evidence from
First Dynasty Saqqara and Umm el-Qa'ab, Abydos,
with
Special Reference to the Arm of King Djer
****

Thesis submitted in fulfilment of the requirements for the degree of
Doctor of Philosophy
by
Helen Brown, B. A. (Hons), M.A., University of Sydney
January 1960

It would take at least a year, maybe more, for Helen's dissertation to be read and marked, and in the meantime life marched on at a steady pace, much as usual. Danny was getting nowhere with the council or the police over the noise and overcrowded tenancies in Brokendown Street, as it had become known to one and all.

Tommy O'Hearn, the ex-soap-factory shop steward, Half Dunn's nemesis, he of the water-polo and scuffed patent-leather shoe incident, was now the state member for Balmain, his seat won uncontested in the recent election of the Cahill Labor government. Danny had watched as O'Hearn soap-boxed in all the pubs with a swagger and a smug smile that he was aching to wipe off his fat face. The bad back that had prevented O'Hearn joining up had miraculously come good after the war was over. Funny that.

Danny had discussed with Half Dunn the prospect of taking the council to court over the blatant violation of the *Landlord and Tenant Act* but his father was quick to put the kibosh on the idea.

'Danny, this isn't just a few councillors getting a backhander from a local developer – they're simply the small fry. Tommy O'Hearn's not a lot bigger. This goes all the way to the Premier's Department and the Police Commissioner. Too many windmills to tilt at, Don "Nifty" Quixote. Take my advice: bide your time, son. I haven't spent thirty years on a bar stool at the Hero without learning that every dog has his day; sooner or later these bastards will get what's coming to them. Something will happen, just you wait and see, mate.'

'Jesus, Dad, how long does a man have to wait? I used to think we were the salt of the earth here in Balmain – tough, strong, independent, working class and proud of it. I believed that there are only two kinds of people: those who come from Balmain and those who wish they did. But now I realise it's all bullshit. It's the place where the Labor Party was born, but what good has that ever done us?'

'Fair go, Danny —'

'The bloody coal depot, the power station belching smoke into the air so that most Balmain kids can be heard coughing half a block away! The soap factories, chemical factories and any form of dirty industry nobody else wanted were all welcome in Balmain, right along the harbour's edge. The Balmain part of the harbour has more effluent and crap poured into it each day than anywhere else in Sydney, Dad. I should know. Some mornings when the twins and I go out on the harbour it's like rowing in a cesspool.'

'You seem to forget people needed jobs, urgently. The factories, Mort Dock, coaling ships, the power station – they were jobs for the workers,' Half Dunn argued.

'Sure, that's why we have the lowest per capita income of any suburb in Sydney. They brought all the lowly paid shit jobs to Balmain. All the fucking misery! Child abuse and wife abuse are bloody endemic. If it wasn't for the "Shut up and put up, you're from Balmain" ethos, I'd have the battered wives and kids of Balmain queuing at the front door every Monday morning all the way to Rozelle.'

'C'mon, Danny. We run a pub. You know that kind of thing happens everywhere. Balmain doesn't have an exclusive on wife-bashing.'

'You're right, but low pay, unemployment and drink go hand in hand with abuse and violence. During the Great Depression and right up to the start of the war we had the highest rate of unemployment in metropolitan Sydney.'

'Don't I know it,' Half Dunn said. 'Your mother and I took over the Hero at the worst possible time. It's down to her hard work and brains that we survived.'

'Well, you'll be happy to know we're still bottom of the list. Yet we still vote Labor. As far as the Labor Party goes, we grant them permission to shit on their own doorstep! We're taken for granted and exploited and we cheer every time we get kicked in the teeth! Up the fucking toothless Tigers!'

Half Dunn grinned. 'Son, I wouldn't be calling them that in the main bar; the mighty Tigers are struggling a bit this season.'

But Danny would not be distracted. 'Now they're dumping the wretched of the earth in Brokendown Street and getting a kickback from a slum-landlord syndicate, and once again we're letting the bastards get away with it.'

'You sound like someone who's preparing to go into politics, Danny. You planning to take on the Tommy O'Hearns of this world, eh?'

'Nah, bullshit, Dad. I'm a criminal lawyer. But I tell you what, mate, I've defended some of the truly bad boys in the last few years, and yet the real crims are in state parliament in Macquarie Street and at police headquarters – the sycophantic bastards that follow the flash money from the so-called respectable families and city syndicates that have the real power in this city.'

'I don't disagree with you, son, but what would you do to change things? Finding fault is easy – we're all experts at pot and kettle calling.'

The days when Half Dunn, fuelled by eight or ten schooners, had a theory about everything that amounted to bugger all of nothing were long gone. His native intelligence had surfaced, once his brain wasn't addled with drink, and these days his opinions were usually worth careful consideration. His reformation had started with the war, when he began to listen to war news on the radio and traced its progress on a map of the world. He'd always read Danny's university essays, a habit he continued throughout Danny's law degree, acquiring an education of sorts.

Half Dunn, unlike Danny, loved to listen to Helen talk about Ancient Egypt and seemed never to get enough of her stories. He recycled them in his own pub yarns until half the drinkers in Balmain had a nodding acquaintance with at least one pharaoh. Half Dunn could draw a crowd in the pub when he talked about the dwarfs that were buried close to the pharaoh and the role they had played in life and in court. The sex lives of the Egyptian nobles was another favourite topic. Half Dunn had an excellent ear and he'd spent so many years propped at the bar that he'd become a bit of a chameleon, shaping his stories to his audience. When he told stories to the twins, who learned much more from him on the subject than they did from Helen, he spoke simply, in language small children could understand and enjoy, but when he regaled the drinkers in the pub, he used their idiom. Danny, dropping by the pub to visit his parents, once heard him tell an entire story in the voice of one of the regulars at the Hero. 'Lemme tell ya, those pharaohs didn't fuck around, mate. They shacked up with their sisters and daughters, even married them, the dirty bastards,' Half Dunn began.

'Yer jokin'. That for real?' Davo, one of the regulars, asked.

'Yeah, fair dinkum,' Half Dunn said, adding, 'They also had as many wives as they wanted in their harem, kids everywhere, wives and concubines, plottin', even killin' each other and havin' a go at the old man himself when they got half a chance. Tell yer what, it weren't no friendly atmosphere – it was on fer one an' all in them royal harems.'

'What's a concubine?' Bullnose asked.

'A whore, only exclusive! The palace was crawlin' with real good-lookin' sorts.'

'So what's the dirty bugger doin' screwin' his sister and his daughter, then?'

Half Dunn ignored this. 'Mind you, when the old bloke died, not that he was always that old – they had boy kings, too – but when they'd catch a bad cold or somethin' we wouldn't take no notice of, they'd cark it, 'cause they were ratshit from all the in-breedin' that come from their old man shaggin' his rellos.'

'Serves the buggers right,' said Simmo, another regular.

Half Dunn wasn't going to let his story turn into a discussion on Ancient Egyptian morality, so he pressed on. 'Anyway, once they died, they'd turn the bastards into mummies, wrapping bandages, layer after layer like you've seen 'em in pictures.' He stopped, pausing for effect, his look taking in each of them in turn. 'But what you ain't seen is what they done to his fuckin' brain.' The speaker paused again for the effect this would have on his audience.

'Yeah, what?' several of the group cried. It was obvious that Half Dunn now had his audience by the short and curlies. Most of the blokes standing around him hadn't taken a swig from their schooners for several minutes.

'Nuthin' trivial, I gotta tell yer.'

'What? They reckoned like . . . the brain was sacred?' Davo suggested.

'Nah, just the flamin' opposite, mate. They reckoned it weren't no use in the afterlife so they had to get rid of all that grey mush and shit in the pharaoh's skull.'

'Yeah, that'd be right,' Bluey volunteered. 'I mean, human brains look the same as sheep's brains. If yer didn't know what they were for, you wouldn't put much store by havin' 'em with you in heaven, would ya?'

'Not heaven, mate, the *afterlife!* They didn't have no Jesus,' Half Dunn said in a spectacular demonstration of the mindset of the group.

'So go on, tell us . . . what'd they do?' another one of the group asked impatiently.

'Do? What, to the brain?'

'Yeah.'

'They pulled it out through the poor bastard's nose.'

'Jesus, that'd hurt!' someone exclaimed, getting a cheap laugh.

'They got this dirty great metal pick sort of . . . well, not so big, I suppose, but evil lookin', and they broke the bone with it, then they jiggled it around in the cavity until the brains run out.'

'How'd they know when it was all out?' Simmo asked.

'Jesus, Simmo, how the fuck would I know!' Half Dunn exclaimed.

A voice from the back of the group said, 'They could'a weighed it; the male brain always weighs about the same.'

'Yer kiddin'? London to a brick my brain weighs more than Simmo's,' said Half Dunn with conviction.

'Y'd lose the bet, it's the same.'

'There yer go – they weighed the fucker. Easy,' Half Dunn said. Several of the group took the opportunity to take a swig of beer. 'But that weren't all,' he volunteered, then paused until he had the group's attention once again.

Danny, who'd taken up a cloth and was pretending to polish beer glasses, strained to hear every word so that he could retell it, blow by blow, to Helen in bed that night. He knew Half Dunn was good, but this was masterful.

'Bluey here was sayin' about sheep brains,' Half Dunn continued at last. 'Well, you ain't heard nothin' yet, mate. They sliced open the pharaoh's left side. Don't ask me why the left. Then they pulled out the liver, lungs, stomach and the intestines.'

'What about the heart?' Davo asked.

'Yeah, good point, glad you asked. The Ancient Egyptians believed the heart was the business end, the real McCoy. Where they got their intelligence, memory, reason, all the good stuff. They left it in so it could be used in the afterlife.'

'Yeah, stands to reason, don't it?' Flossy, who hadn't hitherto said a word, remarked.

'How's that then?' said the bloke who'd volunteered the information about the brain's weight.

'Yeah, what's yer point, Flossy?' Half Dunn added.

'Well, if yer didn't know that the grey mushy stuff was your brain and yer intelligence and reason, you'd reckon it was yer heart them things come from, wouldn't ya?' Flossy explained. 'I mean, stands to reason, don't it? Pumpin' blood every which way over yer body, it makes sense it could carry messages down all them arteries and little veins and stuff.'

'Shit, Flossy's right, yer know! I reckon we'd do the same if we didn't already know about the brain,' said Bluey.

Everyone nodded. Flossy's point was valid, but Danny saw that Half Dunn didn't want to be distracted. 'So, now they got the brains and the liver and lights out, they have to dry the bugger so he don't rot.' He chuckled. 'Bloody clever, them Gypos. They done the same as yer do with fish – they got this special salt from some lake and they packed the empty body in it for forty days exactly.'

'Why forty days?' a new voice asked. 'Fish don't need forty days.'

'How the fuck would I know why forty days, Neilo? Maybe that's how long it takes fer all the mummy juices t' run out, for the fucker to dry, because what they do next is rinse it in piss.'

This got a laugh all round and the mercurial Half Dunn, quick to correct himself, went on, 'No, mate, I don't mean piss-piss. I meant piss that you drink!' He pointed to his untouched middy.

'Beer? They rinse it in beer,' Bluey asked, clearly impressed.

'No, ya drongo, not beer. They've got this palm wine they use for rinsing the dried-out body and then they fill all the cavities with spices and bandages soaked in this resin stuff.'

'Cavities? Ya mean the arsehole and the gob?'

'Jesus, Froggy, what other cavities do yiz reckon we got? Except for yer personal flippin' brain box, of course!'

'What about where they took the brains outa the nose and the hole they made to get the liver and all that – them's cavities,' Froggy protested.

'Yeah, maybe,' Half Dunn said, wanting to press on. 'All them bandages and the other shit they pack into the cavities was so the body would look the right shape. Once they've got it lookin' fair dinkum again they'd anoint it with heated resin and this perfumed oil.'

'Frankincense,' said a voice from the back.

'Eh?' Several heads turned to look at him. 'What the fuck's frankenwhatchamacallit?' Simmo asked.

'Like in the Bible, where it says they anointed him in frankincense and myrrh. Didn't yer learn that in Sunday school, Simmo?'

'Mate, I'm Greek Orthodox.'

'Yeah, right,' Half Dunn said, trying not to laugh. 'Anyway, then they wrapped them in these special bandages like ya see at the movies,' he paused, 'but before that they put false eyes in and did the hair fancy like, sort of poofter style.'

'Eyes, there ya go, they's cavities,' Froggy protested again.

Half Dunn, the supreme actor, sighed. 'I just said they put false bloody eyes in 'em!' He gazed around at his audience, and paused before adding, 'So, there you go – Bob's yer uncle – the pharaoh's ready for resurrection and eternal bliss.' Half Dunn brought his long-neglected middy to his lips, hesitated, examined the glass then said, 'Fuckin' piss's gone flat. Whose shout?'

People no longer left the Hero shaking their heads, thinking Half Dunn was a bullshit merchant, all hot air and hype. Instead, these days they listened or asked questions and took his answers seriously, frequently asking his advice as well. He'd discovered he had a mind that could grasp a difficult concept and render it easy to understand. He'd cut his grog consumption to four middies a day and had taken to walking twice a day down Darling Street to the ferry terminal and back for exercise. It was as if the weight he'd lost had been composed of foolishness disguised as fat. Now, stripped down to thirteen stone, what intellectual flesh was left was well worth considering.

Danny, too, knew that Half Dunn had a point when he suggested that every dog had its day, and that Danny should perhaps wait before taking the council to court over breaches of the *Landlord and Tenant Act*. Now, intrigued, Half Dunn asked his son, 'Well, how do you see the future of Balmain? More of the same?'

Danny, put on the spot, decided to share some of the ideas he and Helen often talked about. 'This suburb is like a can of sardines: we're sealed off – with the fish packed in tight, all the same size and appearance. We look the same, think the same, behave the same, vote the same, with the result that very little that makes a difference to people generally happens to us. We're stuck in a time warp and led by the nose by corrupt politicians. Worst of all, we believe our own bullshit. It's a big year if the Tigers win the premiership because that confirms our superior status.

'If Dawnie wins gold again at the Rome Olympics this year, then we all win; she's the proof that we're especially talented and unique. But what about the suburbs that spawned John and Ilsa Konrads or Murray Rose, who'll all most likely win gold, Rose possibly more than once?

People in those suburbs don't carry on as if they're personally responsible for their athletes' success. Hoo-bloody-ray for our Dawnie! Poor bloody kid. It's not the weight of Australia she carries on her shoulders, but the expectations of bloody Balmain. A mongrel like Tommy O'Hearn couldn't get elected to run a fiddlestick competition in any other Sydney suburb – he's well on his way to becoming a lush, the twins have a canary with a higher IQ, but simply because he was born in Balmain we allow the Labor Party to use him as their glove puppet.'

'Okay, mate, so get on with it. What do you propose we do?' Half Dunn asked, a little impatiently.

'Rip the top off the sardine can and let in some fresh air. This is potentially one of the most beautiful suburbs in Sydney. If you imagine looking down on Balmain from the air, the peninsula has three fingers running out into the harbour: Louisa Road, Wharf Road and Darling Street. More people have harbour views here than just about any suburb in Sydney. We have more harbour-front land than Point Piper; the only difference is that we use it for factories that pollute the harbour and the really rich use Point Piper for palatial homes and yacht moorings.' Danny looked up at Half Dunn. 'Our real estate, unlike the Eastern Suburbs or the North Shore, is cheap as chips.' He paused. Half Dunn could see he was genuinely excited. 'Okay, so as Lachlan would say, here's the advertising pitch: cheap real estate; water views; potential harbour-front dwellings; a short ferry ride to the city; parks; schools; and the potential for restaurants and cafés and a complete cosmopolitan culture; young people coming in with talent, education, drive and different values.'

'And the people who have always been here, what about them? What if they don't want to leave?' Half Dunn asked.

'They will.'

'Now wait on, mate! Wait a cotton-pickin' minute! You're the one always defending the common people. Now you want them to sell their prime real estate to a bunch of wealthy wankers! Why is that?'

'Christ, Dad, we're selling harbour-front houses to slum landlords who are partitioning them into plywood cubicles to house an influx of the hopeless and the hapless, as Franz calls them, because nobody wants them. People who own their houses in Balmain are forced to stay because the semi-slum they live in is unsaleable!'

'Whoa, Danny. Most Balmain people maintain their homes well. It's their home – in most cases it has been for several generations. They may not want to up stakes and go any more than you do!'

Danny, taken aback somewhat, searched for a reply. 'Just because a house is cared for and the front lawn is clipped doesn't mean it isn't in a depressed area and therefore worthless as real estate.'

'Yeah, sure, but real estate isn't everything. I daresay there's unhappy people in Point Piper.'

'Not if you believe Franz.' Danny laughed, pleased to lighten the tone. 'Of course! It's a free country. People can stay if they wish – nothing to stop them. My point is that right now they can't sell the only asset they've got. Open Balmain up to young professionals and the houses people own will triple in value and still be a bargain for the new owners. It will allow the older people to get out and retire down the coast, or up north, to Queensland, allow the sardines to jump out of the can.'

'And you think this can be done?'

Danny nodded. 'Yes, as a matter of fact, I think it can. The world is changing. If John F. Kennedy is elected to the White House, even Australia is going to have to change. But not as long as state Labor uses Balmain as a dumping ground for unwanted industry and as housing for the underclass in return for feathering their nests. I doubt very much that they can be made to see the grand vision.'

Half Dunn laughed. 'Never mind the state – I'm having trouble seeing the grand vision, as you call it, myself. I admit, things could be a damn sight better, but why can't we make them better for the folk who live here, not for a bunch of whackers who commute to work in the city in suits and ties?'

Danny had to laugh despite himself. 'That, in a nutshell, describes me, Dad.'

'Yeah, well, you know what I mean,' Half Dunn growled. 'It would be nice to see the place prosper, but why do we have to tip out all the current inhabitants?'

'Because we need a new attitude, and this place is totally reactionary. We cop all the shit and think it's Shinola.'

'What's that mean?'

'What?'

'Shinola.'

'It's an American expression – "He can't tell shit from Shinola" – shit from boot polish. Dad, the point I'm making is that the status quo has existed for so long and we're so accustomed to copping it sweet that we don't know the difference. You don't need to be told it's very cosy for Macquarie Street and Sussex Street. Where else can you dump an unwanted industry with all the industrial facilities for a generous kickback? We need something big to happen that will shake the monkeys out of the trees, new people who start asking questions, who are not going to let Labor, or any other state government, get away with things.'

'And you wouldn't consider standing for the next state election?'

'What? As a Liberal and expect to win in Balmain? That'll be the frosty Friday!'

'No, mate, as an independent. Stand against Tommy O'Hearn.'

'What? Against the Labor political machine? C'mon, get real, Dad! Besides, with all the pro bono wife- and kid-battering cases I've taken on over the years, I've alienated half the men in Balmain and put the other half in the clink for a spell.' Danny grinned. 'I walked into the Tradesman's Arms the other day and the whole pub suddenly went quiet.'

'Mate, that's your whole strategy!'

'What is?'

'Women! All the women at Brenda's shandy soirees are always asking her if you'll stand – go into politics. You should know better than most – women are beginning to demand their rights.'

'Nah, not here in Balmain. When it comes to the crunch they'll still do as their old man tells them. Half the bastards I want to prosecute are let off because their wives beg me not to pursue it.'

'I don't agree. It's not like a trade union vote where you're publically shamed if you vote against a union motion. It's a secret ballot. Danny, the women *love* you! You've fought for them and their kids and you've won. You've got half the men in Balmain on the run.' Half Dunn laughed, suddenly recalling something. 'Black-eyed Susan, remember you took Ron, her old man, to court and he got six months in Long Bay? Well, according to Brenda, she jokingly complained at the soiree last Thursday that she had nothing to say because she hasn't had a bashing, or even her trademark black eye, for two months and she's missing the whingeing. Ron is permanently off the piss, shit-scared he might find himself back in the clink.'

Danny grinned, then said, 'Mate, no way! An independent in Balmain would be about as effective as a fart in a thunderstorm!'

Danny, like most of us, judged the progress of his life by the stuff he took seriously at the time. But often, when you look back, the serious stuff turns out to be unimportant, and a minor event you hardly noticed becomes a turning point that greatly affects the path you subsequently take in your life.

Sammy and Bullnose were over at Danny's place working in the garden, which, under Helen's direction, had been restored to its former splendour and was now one of the truly great gardens in Balmain or, for that matter, any of the surrounding suburbs. Helen tried to get the twins interested in gardening but had to admit they only helped because they loved the stories the two old men would tell them, although Sam begged to be allowed to operate the new Victa lawnmower. Helen suspected that when she wasn't around, Bullnose would let her. Both he and Sammy doted on the girls and the feeling appeared to be reciprocated. Gabrielle spent quite a lot of time in the rose garden, making an awful squawking sound on her new violin and claiming the roses loved it. 'Mummy, there's heaps more since I played for them. Ask Sammy and Bullnose if you don't believe me.'

Helen always responded modestly when people admired the garden. 'It always had great bones – lovely mature trees, azaleas, camellias – and the old-fashioned rose garden just needed pruning back and a bit of food. Roses take some killing off – tough as old witches – and the perfume is divine.' She would laugh as she summed up. 'Sammy and Bullnose do all the hard work three days a week, the twins ride in the wheelbarrow and I take all the credit for the result.'

Just a few days after Danny had had his heart-to-heart with Half Dunn over the state of Balmain, a terrace wall in the garden collapsed and needed to be reconstructed. Danny, while undergoing his weekly massage, asked Bullnose if he would rebuild it. Frankly, he hoped the old retired bricklayer would excuse himself on the grounds that what he used to call his 'arty-ritis' was too bad for him to take on the job. But he also knew they regarded the garden as their own and that bringing in a bricklayer from outside might upset them. 'Mate, you're not as young as you used to be. If the bricklaying is a bit much, I'll get someone in,' he said, then added hurriedly, 'You'd still be in charge. You know, supervise the job.'

As he suspected, both men wouldn't have a bar of it. 'Nah, Danny, Sammy'll do the barra, you hire a cement mixer and we'll mix the cement and I'll handle them bricks, no risk. Need a week, I reckon. Not as fast as I used t' be.'

Danny already paid them the going daily rate for gardeners, plus the mandatory six schooners in return for his weekly massage. He would have liked to pay them more but they wouldn't hear of it. 'Okay, bricklayer's rates then. I insist.'

Bullnose looked questioningly at Sammy, who said, 'Righto, thanks, Danny. The mongrels have put up the rent; be very useful.'

'Look, why don't I pick you up from your digs after we get back from rowing? Say eight o'clock?'

'Whaffor?' Bullnose protested. Sammy shot him a meaningful glance, but it was too late. 'We only live down the road,' Bullnose added.

Danny, ignoring Sammy's hands on his back, sat up on the new massage table he'd bought for the old masseur. 'Hang on. You told me you lived in Mrs Bursell's boarding house, bottom of Darling Street?'

'Yeah, she carked it a year ago and her daughter and the family got the house.' Sammy shrugged. 'Had to move, mate.'

'Into Brokendown Street – ferchrissake, why didn't you tell me?'

'Dunno,' Bullnose replied, glancing at Sammy for help.

'Except for this house, it's not an address a man would want to brag about,' Sammy said quietly.

'Yeah, before was different. Mrs Bursell's was good – she give us our tucker and all. This is a real shithouse place!' Bullnose said in his clumsy manner.

'Why don't you apply for public housing? You're both pensioners, always paid your taxes,' Danny said.

'Yeah, we done that,' Sammy said.

'We was told it was a ten-year waiting list,' Bullnose added.

'It's a scam, mate. It's who you know – we can't afford a bribe to jump the list. They're giving preference to the Poms, the migrants that come over here because they were bloody useless where they come from in the first place,' Sammy said bitterly.

Bullnose was quick to add, 'Mate, them whingin' Pommy bastards, bloody ten-pound tourists, they get all the government housing. Good Aussies like Sammy and me, we're history – not a flaming chance, mate. Snowball's hope in hell. If the Poms don't get them Housing Commission flats the fuckin' Reffos do, and if there's anythin' left over, the bloody Dagos with ten stealin', stinkin' snotty-nosed kids are packed in tighter than a can of IXL peaches.'

It was Sammy's turn again. 'It's no better if you try to get, y'know, like a private one-bedroom flat. They take one look at yiz, see yer no spring chicken, ask where y' work, and when you tell them you're a pensioner they slam the front door so hard it frightens the animals in the zoo across the bloody harbour.'

Danny knew that marginal people like Sammy and Bullnose would never get a private lease; rented properties were rare enough, but no landlord would consider them acceptable tenants. The same applied to single mothers, ageing widows or the mentally ill. The slum landlords of properties in places like Brokendown Street or of sub-standard boarding houses who took their pensions in return for a bed and one badly cooked meal a day were the only ones who would have them.

Danny suddenly made up his mind. 'Look, we've been mates a long time, in fact, since I was a nipper.' He turned to Sammy. 'Without you working on my back, Sammy, I'd probably be in a wheelchair, or at least I'd be using a stick.' He looked at both men in turn. 'Now listen, I've got an idea I've been thinking about but I was waiting for the right time, thinking you were cosy enough at Mrs Bursell's. Helen says the garden could use you another couple of days a week – well, that's Monday to Friday, full time. As you know, the basement isn't being used. It's got a separate entrance off the garden, it's dry, the water pipes go down there and they're in good nick, and so does the electricity. It wouldn't take a lot to turn it into a great little flat.' Danny grinned. 'That way I'd be able to keep an eye on you two old reprobates.'

The two old men stood silently looking down at their feet for so long that Danny thought they were trying – or at least Sammy was – to find a nice way to refuse his offer. Then Sammy, squinting up at him, said, 'Only if we work for no pay, Danny, just the schooners.'

Danny laughed. 'Sorry, mate. Helen would kick my arse all the way to Cairo. No way.'

'Okay. Well, if we get paid for doin' the garden, we'll give you our old-age pensions for rent. That's seven quid a week,' Bullnose said.

'So you want to turn me into a slum landlord, is that it?' Danny asked, shaking his head. 'Look at it this way. You do some of the hard yakka to convert it, to build the flat. It's obviously going to need a bit of brickwork, plumbing . . . we'll get an electrician in to do the wiring, and we'll have to put in a kitchen and a bathroom. What you can't do Half Dunn will take care of; he can find us a plumber or someone else who can do the job.'

'Mate, me old man was an electrician at Morts. I used to work with him during the school holidays. I can do all that shit with me eyes closed,' Sammy volunteered.

'Done a fair bit o' plumbin' meself in me time,' Bullnose added, not to be outdone.

Danny hesitated. 'This would have been a while back, Sammy. We'll see when the time comes, eh, Bullnose?' Changing the subject quickly away from the two do-it-yourself experts, he went on to say, 'There's the furniture left over from our flat that we had before we bought the house. We'll get a couple of single beds and mattresses. When it's all done you two will have a home and I'll have an asset, a nice little flat in the basement. Thanks anyway, Bullnose. It's a generous offer, but I don't need your pension. The asset I'll gain is sufficient payment. Do you reckon you can get by where you are for the next three or four months while we get the basement converted?'

It was obvious Danny wasn't going to take no for an answer. Both men, again staring at their boots, nodded. The two tough, proud old blokes were too overcome to reply. And so it was decided with a nod and handshake.

Danny now had a firsthand source of information about the houses and tenants in Brokendown Street and soon gained an insight into what was going on. Twenty-eight houses, all of them directly across the road from the factories lining the waterfront, and all once the substantial homes of factory managers, had been abandoned in the 1930s and allowed to fall into disrepair because of the effluvial stink and smoke from the factories. While now, thirty years on, the conditions were marginally better, the once respectable houses were virtually slum dwellings. It transpired that all of them had been purchased by the same syndicate for a song and converted into low-cost accommodation for the poor, all of whom were, generally speaking, on the bones of their arse, the people nobody wanted.

While this was blatant exploitation of the poor by the rich, Danny, who had studied the *Landlord and Tenant Act* carefully on the numerous occasions he'd taken his complaints to the council, saw that a paradox existed in the Act. In its amended form it was intended to grant the state control of rents, presumably to protect tenants and landlords. However, rents had generally been set too low and had not kept pace with the cost of living. Honest landlords, unable to make a fair return on their investment, left the rental market. This left only government housing and the rogue landlords and syndicates who simply ignored the legislation, bribed council health inspectors, bought up sub-standard properties cheaply and charged whatever rent the market would bear, aware that the poor and defenceless could never afford to seek redress in the courts. The Sammys and Bullnoses of this world were lambs to the slaughter, with nowhere to go except into the clutches of unscrupulous landlords.

Now, with the two old blokes on the inside, Danny was better able to understand the prevailing conditions in Brokendown Street. In fact, apart from repairing badly leaking roofs, totally defunct plumbing and electrical wiring where it no longer worked, the slum landlords did precious little, at the same time packing in a great many more tenants than these properties were meant to house. They partitioned even a modest bedroom into four cells with cheap plywood partitions, splitting the wiring at the ceiling rose and running taped flex to light bulbs hanging above each cubicle.

At most, two of these plywood cubicles might have a window; the other two would not, a single overhead light bulb being the only source of light. Windows were barred to prevent a moonlight flit, as was the back door. The only entrance and exit was the front door, kept under almost constant surveillance and locked at 9 p.m., except on Friday and Saturday nights.

Fifteen people would share the original bathroom and kitchen, with their unreliable power and water supply. Electrical circuits were overloaded and the wiring usually done by amateurs, because qualified electricians risked losing their licences if they followed the owner's instructions. This, in turn, created huge fire hazards. Fire extinguishers and hoses simply weren't supplied.

Premises converted in this way provided rental income that was usually ten times greater than that allowed under the Act. Brokendown Street, reduced to near-Dickensian conditions, was proving a veritable goldmine for its owners. Sammy and Bullnose explained the rules for living in one of these converted shit holes to Danny. Well, there was only one rule, really – the landlord's word was law. Any complaint resulted in the threat of eviction or a beating if a tenant couldn't fight back. It was known as CNO: 'Clout 'n' Out'. But in fact it was far worse: standover tactics were common, tenants who complained were often beaten severely and women were sexually assaulted. The 'managers' were thugs, and often enough drunken thugs. No receipts were issued for rent or bonds. Any work tenants did on a place to ensure their own safety or comfort was not credited. Councils, except for collecting the garbage, stayed well away, their councillors happy to receive a regular brown envelope.

Bullnose, with Sammy acting as cement-machine mixer and barrow boy, rebuilt the terrace wall and then enthusiastically set about constructing their new home in the cellar. They weren't fast but they were thorough and Danny was surprised at the skills they brought to the task. In fact Sammy did do the wiring and Bullnose the plumbing, and in their absence Half Dunn, at Danny's request, sent down a certified electrician and plumber who were regulars at the Hero to inspect the result. The electrician claimed the work was first rate and laughed when he saw the switchboard. 'Perfectly good, but I haven't seen it done like that since my dad's time,' he said. The plumber suggested one or two small changes to the configuration of the pipes to prevent the possibility of the kitchen sink clogging and an air block forming in the shower recess, and that was about the extent of it.

Danny visited J. B. Sharp, Fine Traditional and Modern Furnishings, and ordered two beds and mattresses. He was duly confronted by Mr Sid Sharp, the son of the founder, who wore a bowler hat all day and quite possibly all night, inside and outside. He'd never been seen without it and there were frequent but pointless bets laid over whether he was bald as a bandicoot, but nobody ever found out.

He was also famous for his driving and owned a big maroon 1939 Buick, all chrome and show-off, which he drove with an abandon that sent everyone running for cover. He'd get into the car, put it into low gear and slam his foot down hard on the accelerator so that the big V8 engine screamed for mercy. Then, releasing the handbrake, off he'd go, ignoring traffic lights and stop signs, with one hand permanently jammed on the horn to warn off anyone silly enough to approach. His driving knowledge never extended beyond what he considered to be the five essentials: handbrake, low gear, accelerator, horn and brakes. Though he'd had countless accidents miraculously he'd never killed anyone.

In desperation Sergeant McCusky, the local police sergeant, had finally revoked his driving licence and the big automobile now stood permanently parked outside the shop, all the dings removed, maroon duco polished to a mirror shine, its whitewall tyres pumped and perfect, the leather upholstery glossy, while on the driver's door, beautifully painted in a gold copperplate script, were the words:

Sergeant McCusky
Is a right mug lair!
The bastard went and busted me.
That's just not fair!

*

J. B. Sharp Esq.

'Danny, glad you came in, son,' Sid Sharp called in welcome. 'As a matter of fact I've got a bone to pick with you,' he said, stabbing Danny lightly in the chest with a pudgy finger.

'Oh? What is it, Mr Sharp?'

'Dining-room suite. You know the rules. When you get married, son —'

'Oh, yes, right. But I've . . . we've been married for years, Mr Sharp.'

Sid tapped his forehead. 'Elephants never forget, son.'

'But the flat we lived in was too small – there wasn't room for a table and chairs,' Danny protested.

'And now with that big house by the water surrounded by the stink of factories, that you and – Helen, isn't it – foolishly bought?'

Danny charitably ignored the remark. Sharpy was famous for his direct manner. 'Yeah, but when we bought it the original furniture was still there. We restored a beautiful old cedar table – French-polished it – and upholstered the twelve matching chairs.'

'Twelve! My word, that's a big table. Righto, son, you're forgiven for not getting one from J. B. Sharp.'

What the old man was alluding to was a Balmain wedding tradition. J. B. Sharp Pty Ltd had been established by his father in 1890, and Sid hadn't changed the name. Since the time of the coal mines the firm had allowed local engaged couples to select a dining-room suite – table, chairs and sideboard – from the shop and then permitted them to pay it off in their own time. When the suite was finally paid off, the old bloke would present the family with a locally made bentwood rocking chair. This was his private joke, as some couples were indeed grandparents before they made the final payment. Some few never did pay him. 'Not because they're dishonest,' the old man would explain. 'Life is short and the struggle is long.' Danny was reminded that Pineapple Joe had taken the idea of his pay-as-you-wear suits for Balmain lads from J. B. Sharp.

The contention over the dining-room suite resolved, Sid Sharp patted Danny on the shoulder and asked, 'What can I do for you, my boy?'

'I need two single beds with hard mattresses,' Danny answered.

'For the twins, eh? They must be growing up. Hard mattresses, that's good.'

Danny simply grunted. No point in telling him about the arrangement in the cellar. By tomorrow morning it would be known to one and all that he'd taken on a couple of boarders.

'I hear your twins are still rowing with you,' Sid chuckled. 'But now they're regular porpoises in the pool as well. Two new Dawnies in the making, eh?' He paused. 'You want to pay off the beds instead of a dining-room suite?'

Danny laughed, shaking his head. 'Nice of you, Mr Sharp, but it's okay. We can manage.'

'I always said you would have played for Australia if it wasn't for what the war did to you. Mind you, that's not a real bad second-hand face the Yanks gave you.'

Danny couldn't possibly take umbrage. Sid knew everything about everyone on the peninsula and his directness or lack of subtlety was more than compensated for by his kindness.

Danny, having selected the beds and mattresses, prepared to leave, the old man accompanying him from the shop to the pavement, where traditionally furniture was displayed. A small boy stood close by. 'Ah, I see you still use a dog whacker,' Danny laughed.

'Dogs don't change,' the old man said laconically. The dog whacker was a small boy who watched out for stray dogs that threatened to piss on the legs of the furniture on display.

Danny grinned. 'I remember doing dog whacking one school holiday soon after we'd arrived in Balmain from Wagga. I can't say it was the most fulfilling job I've ever had, but in the process I got to know every stray mutt in Balmain.' He turned to old Mr Sharp. 'Thank you for your help, Mr Sharp. Wouldn't be the same around here without you.'

'Don't worry, there'll always be a Sharp. My son Jack will take over from me, and then his son, baby John will. He's already got the gift of the gab. Wouldn't surprise me if he becomes a politician.' Sid laughed. He looked directly at Danny. 'I just want to say this before you go, son. It's good what you've done for the women around here. Too much nasty stuff been happening for too long.' He grinned. 'I hear they're calling it the Danny Dunn wing at Long Bay. You should be proud of yourself, my boy.'

The basement flat was all but complete except for laying the lino in the kitchen and bathroom. The original clay floor tiles that covered the basement were still in good condition, but what with Bullnose's arty-ritis and it being late April with a cold winter promised, Danny had ordered Feltex to be laid over the remaining area of the flat and had a Warmray slow-combustion heater installed.

It was all over bar the shouting and Sammy and Bullnose were justly pleased with themselves; they'd done a grand job and had only to wait for the lino and carpet to be laid before they could move in the beds and the rest of the furniture. In the twins' words, they'd be snug as a bug in a rug. Only one week to go to moving day.

At 2 a.m. on Saturday the 30th of April, Danny was jerked awake by the sirens of several fire engines approaching. He jumped out of bed, shaking Helen awake. 'Fire!' he yelled.

'Where?' Helen cried.

'Close! Smell the smoke?'

Danny ran out to the upstairs verandah in his pyjamas while Helen, who slept naked, hurriedly put on her dressing-gown against the autumn chill and followed him outside. A house in Brokendown Street had gone up in smoke, the flames already leaping high into the night sky. Danny counted along the houses. 'Oh shit! It's Sammy and Bullnose!' he cried. 'Jesus, no. No, no!'

Helen clutched his arm, 'Hurry, Danny! They may have got out – they could be safe!' she said, her eyes brimming with sudden tears.

CHAPTER TEN

DANNY FLUNG ON HIS rowing gear – a pair of gym shorts, an old Tigers football jumper and a scruffy pair of tennis shoes – and ran. As he approached the fire, a generator started up suddenly and the scene was bathed in light from three spotlights rigged up by the fire brigade. Danny found Bullnose on the pavement at the edge of the light, strapped to an ambulance stretcher well clear of the blazing boarding house. Only his head showed above the blanket, the skin on his face blackened but already peeling in places, showing a dozen or so bright-red patches of raw flesh the size of postage stamps. His eyes were closed, his eyebrows and hair burnt off. The old man was sobbing, calling out distractedly, 'Sammy! Sammy!' Danny dropped to his haunches beside him, panting.

'Bullnose, mate, it's Danny!' he gasped, sucking in air.

Bullnose managed to open one eye. 'Sammy! Sammy's in there! Lemme out! Lemme out! Sammy! Sammy!' he shouted, his body struggling against the straps, and then suddenly he was seized by a paroxysm of coughing.

'Steady, mate, take it easy,' Danny said. He looked up at the house. The back of it was ablaze, sheets of flame leaping into the sky. The firemen had only just managed to get their hoses going, but the looping jets of water emptied into the inferno seemed to have no noticeable effect, although clearly the firemen were trying to stop the flames spreading to the front of the old house.

Two ambulance men ran over. 'Sorry, sir, we've got to get this man to Emergency,' one of them shouted above the roar of the flames.

'He's got a mate – did they get him out?' Danny cried, still breathing heavily but trying to stay calm.

The wind gusted around and they were able to talk normally.

'He's all we've got out, sir,' the first and older of the two men replied.

'Meter board! Meter board!' Bullnose whimpered, then was once again overcome by an attack of coughing.

'Smoke inhalation, but he's not too bad,' the assistant volunteered.

'Is he going to be okay?' Danny asked fearfully.

'He's not burned too badly – face mostly. It's the shock.' He shrugged. 'But I'm not a doctor. Some people can die of shock,' he said quietly. 'Especially the old ones.'

'He's got a mate,' Danny repeated.

'Afraid there's no way of knowing who's still in there. If there's people in the back, they won't be needing us.' The first man shook his head. 'Back windows are barred and the back door too . . . they've got Buckley's. Those who come out the front are all there's goin' t'be comin' out.'

'It happens all the time with these slum boarding houses,' the assistant said.

They bent down simultaneously and lifted the semi-conscious Bullnose. The first attendant nodded down at him. 'This old bloke got lucky. He almost made it to the front door, so the firemen could get to him.'

'His mate would have been close by,' Danny said helplessly.

'Yeah, well, like I said, some of the people in the front of the house got out before it filled with smoke. No good going in there now – smoke'd kill yer sooner than the fire.'

'I'm sorry, sir, we have to be going,' the second attendant urged.

'Where are you taking him?' Danny asked.

'This time of the mornin' . . . St Vincent's.'

Danny walked beside the stretcher to the ambulance, where he touched Bullnose lightly on the shoulder, trying to hide his panic. 'See you tomorrow, mate.' He waited by the ambulance until its rear doors were closed. 'Thanks,' he called to the two attendants, then ran over to a group of a dozen or so people, survivors who had obviously come out of the house, one or two in pyjamas, most wrapped in blankets issued by the firemen. All were standing, except for one old woman who was huddled under a red and grey army blanket, her grey hair loose and completely obscuring her face. She was weeping hysterically. Danny knew Sammy wouldn't be among them. Obviously, if he'd been okay or able to move he would have been with Bullnose. Nobody took any notice of the hysterical old woman. Danny stepped over and shook her, but she continued to wail, so he slapped her across the face, hard enough to shock her but not hurt her, the way he'd done countless times in the prison camp when men, at the end of their tethers, suddenly lost control. The woman collapsed onto her side and the blanket fell open to reveal her emaciated body, but her wails changed to quiet sobbing.

A young lad, maybe seventeen or so, with the unfocused look usually worn by the mentally retarded, was sucking his thumb. 'She fell down,' he said, pointing. 'Look.'

'All right, Jimmy,' an old bloke said. 'Don't point at her. She'll be all right.'

Danny hurriedly covered the woman, then gently lifted her into a sitting position, brushing the hair from her face. 'You'll be okay, love,' he said, holding onto her for a moment, while checking the shocked faces around them, hoping, but also knowing it was in vain, that he would see Sammy's among them. He turned back to the old crone and placed his hands gently on her shoulders. 'You okay, love?' The old woman, unable to speak, looked at Danny, her eyes frightened, then she nodded and a tear ran down her cheek. 'Good girl. Help is coming,' Danny said to comfort her. Then, rising to his feet he looked at the group. 'Anybody see anyone else hurt . . . any other survivors?' he asked.

The old bloke gestured towards the flames. 'Few dead, I reckon.

Burning flesh, know it from the war. They been caught out the back. Windas barred, back door too. Mongrels done that,' he growled. He seemed the only one able to respond.

'Do you know Sammy Laidlaw?' Danny asked him.

'Yeah, but I ain't seen him,' the man replied, then, peering at Danny he said, 'You're Danny Dunn, the lawyer bloke, ain't ya?'

Danny nodded. 'Yeah. And you are?'

'Jack . . . Jack Medlow. Yeah, you sent me son-in-law to Long Bay for a spell, mate.' He paused momentarily, then added, 'Good onya, Mr Dunn. Drunken bastard beat me daughter and the kids regular.' Then he turned and spat to the side. 'Dirty mongrel, couldn't keep his filthy hands off me little granddaughter.'

Helen, fully dressed in slacks, jumper and the gumboots she used in the garden, suddenly appeared at Danny's side. Taking his arm she looked anxiously up into his face. 'What's happened, darling? Did you find Sammy and Bullnose?' she asked.

Danny excused himself, drew her aside and explained the situation to his increasingly tearful and protesting wife. Finally, brushing away her tears, Helen sniffed and nodded. 'Come, Danny, there's nothing we can do here. The twins may wake up and find themselves alone in the house. Let's go home. I have something I have to tell you.'

Danny turned and pointed to the old woman who was now lying in the foetal position. 'We have to take her – she's in a bad way. She can't stay out here all night. She has nothing on under that blanket.'

Helen hurried over to the old woman, bent and shook her gently, then lifted her arm and felt for a pulse. 'Danny!' she cried.

He strode over. 'What?'

'I can't find a pulse,' Helen said, concerned.

Danny dropped to his haunches beside the old woman and searched for a pulse, first on her wrist, then in the angle of her jaw. 'Nothing,' he announced. He opened the blanket, rolled her gently onto her back and put his ear to her chest, listening. Then suddenly he threw back the blanket altogether and began to press forcefully and rhythmically on her sternum. The survivors crowded around, mute. 'Helen, move 'em back,' Danny gasped, continuing to pump. But after several minutes there was no change. 'It's no use,' he said at last.

'Here, let me take over,' Helen cried.

There was the sound of police sirens in the distance and everyone looked up to see the cars' flashing lights exploding in bursts of blue against the night sky, and reflecting off the harbour water.

'About bloody time! Bastards don't like comin' down here,' Jack Medlow snorted. They all watched as a police car and a paddy wagon drew up beside the fire engines. 'Maybe they'll arrest Lenny Green,' he said hopefully. This drew a titter from the survivors, who'd shown little concern for the dying old woman, too numb or too used to misery to respond, but at the mention of Lenny Green they seemed to come to life. 'Manager,' Jack explained to Danny.

'Danny, I think it's hopeless,' Helen said, panting. Then, rising, she drew the blanket back over the motionless body.

It was almost 4 a.m. when Helen and Danny got back home. Danny had made a statement to the police sergeant and provided his office phone number. He knew all the local police, having gone to school or played football with most of them, but had been surprised to see that this lot were not from Balmain but from police headquarters in the city – no doubt the reason for their late arrival.

Helen made tea and they sat in the wicker chairs on the upstairs verandah, too exhausted and overcome to go back to bed. The twins had, thankfully, slept through the disaster. It seemed the firemen had finally gained control and had kept the fire from spreading to the front of the house, although much of the back half had been gutted. Two more police cars and a police bus arrived on the scene and, shortly after, a large black Bedford van appeared. Six men in white overalls jumped from the back carrying what looked like stretchers, though not the hospital kind. 'Morgue van,' Danny said quietly. 'They're moving the bodies quickly. No forensics – that's unusual.'

The morgue attendants carried out eight stretchers covered in what looked from a distance like green canvas sheets. 'Funny, they're not treating it as a potential crime scene,' Danny remarked, as he watched the police leave without cordoning off the house.

Helen made a fresh pot of tea, and toast with Vegemite for them to have as they watched the dawn opening up the new day. The fire was finally out and the smoke had cleared, except for a few innocent-looking grey spirals. All the survivors had been transported elsewhere in the police bus, and as the last of the stretchers was placed in the black van and the doors closed, Danny, suddenly overcome, let out a sob. 'Sammy!' he cried, as the tears began to flow.

Helen came over and knelt on the tiles beside the wicker chair. The dawn sky was just starting to colour as she silently took Danny in her arms and held him against her, allowing him to weep. After a while Danny sniffed and wiped at his eyes, then, accepting Helen's handkerchief absentmindedly, blew his nose. Realising what he'd done he shoved it into a pocket. 'I'm sorry about that, darling. I guess I lost it. You get used to people not dying around you,' he said quietly.

'Don't apologise. The fact that you can still cry for a mate makes me love you even more, if that's possible.' She kissed him tenderly. 'I think after you've had your tea we should go to bed, don't you?'

'The twins will be up soon,' Danny nodded in the direction of the harbour, 'expecting to go out.'

'I'll tell them,' Helen said.

Danny lifted his cup. 'You said you had something to tell me.'

'It can wait, darling. Beddy-byes now,' Helen replied, smiling.

'No, tell me,' Danny insisted. 'Please.' He was enjoying Helen's hand massaging the back of his neck.

She turned slightly, her hand still on his neck. 'Riley owns the house that burned down. As well as all the others in the street. He's a slum landlord . . . rather, he's head of the syndicate that —'

'Jesus!' Danny shot out of the chair, his teacup smashing on the tiled verandah. He spun around to face her. 'How long have you known this, Helen?'

'Don't be angry, darling. Not that long,' Helen said, alarmed by his reaction.

'Angry? Jesus Christ, I'm furious! Sammy's dead and Bullnose . . . who fucking knows!'

If Danny expected Helen to be contrite, he was in for a big surprise. Her voice was suddenly cool and measured. 'That's precisely why I didn't tell you; it's because of them, and because you're reacting exactly as I feared you would!'

'Eh? Come again? Because of *them*! One of *them* is dead, and the other may be dying in hospital as we speak!'

'I didn't start the fire, Danny!' Helen said sharply. 'I'm not responsible.'

'You knew that Riley was the slum landlord and you didn't tell me? Jesus, Helen!'

'And that would have made a difference? Stopped the fire? Prevented Sammy's death?' Helen cried.

Danny, fighting to gain control, dropped his voice. 'So when did you propose to tell me?'

'In precisely one week, after Sammy and Bullnose had moved into the flat. That way Riley wouldn't have been able to get his standover man to beat them up.'

Danny sighed, and flopped back into the chair. 'Helen, you'll have to explain that piece of exquisitely feminine logic. After all, I'm a mere male.'

'And acting like one, my dear,' Helen suggested coolly, his sarcasm no match for her own.

'So?'

'Well, if anyone tries to leave one of Riley's boarding houses, a goon pays them a visit and threatens them with a severe beating. If the intimidation isn't enough to change their minds, they usually meet with a nasty accident that lands them in hospital.' Helen paused for emphasis. 'Or worse, if they threaten to go to the Housing Commission and spill the beans, they're taken by motor boat a mile beyond the Heads and told to swim home. The following morning the body is washed up at Camp Cove, Bondi, Tamarama or Coogee beaches.' She shrugged and spread her hands. 'The suicide of a nameless, homeless person of no fixed address usually rates about two inches on the fourth page of the *Herald*.'

'Christ, how do you know all this?'

Helen ignored Danny's question and went on. 'The manager pins up the cutting so the other "boarders" see it, together with a sympathy note from the management and staff.'

'And you didn't trust me enough to tell me this? I ask again, how long have you known? Do . . . I mean, *did* Sammy and Bullnose know?'

'I've known for about a month. It's taken that long for me to gather all the information I needed. And no, apart from knowing, like every other boarder, not to talk to anyone if they intended leaving, I don't believe they know – knew – any of the details. But, yes, I did ask them not to say anything about leaving. I told them that arrangements had been made to get them safely out next Saturday morning.'

'And that's when you planned to tell me about Riley?'

'Yes. After we'd gone to fetch them and brought their stuff back in the car.'

'And may I ask how you found out about Riley?'

'The lawyer, the other bidder on the house. Remember he withdrew early. It only occurred to me about two months ago that he might have been bidding for the people who owned the other houses in Brokendown Street. I guess he expected to pick it up for a song, that he'd probably be the lone bidder. When we turned up he pulled out early. I got his name from the Birchgrove real estate agency; the guy who owns it is a friend of Dad's.'

'So?'

Helen hesitated. 'Danny, you don't want to know.'

'Oh, but I do!'

'I accidentally on purpose befriended one of his legal secretaries – I was curious, that's all. I found out her boss was representing a Double Bay syndicate buying up slum houses.' Helen shrugged. 'The rest cost me a couple of martinis after work. She got a little drunk – well, a lot, actually – and told me about the standover men and the motorboat out to sea. She claims she wasn't supposed to know, but the goons came into her boss's office to get paid and she heard them talking. It didn't take much to get it out of her; it had obviously been playing on her conscience.'

Danny shook his head, still much too angry to give Helen credit for her clever detective work. 'Helen, ferchrissake, I'm a criminal lawyer! I am *accustomed* to keeping evidence to myself until it's needed. What is this? Were you frightened I'd blab?'

'Yes.'

'Jesus! You didn't trust me, did you?'

'Darling, you're one of the most intelligent men I've ever met, but also one of the most emotional. I love you for your good mind but even more for your good heart. You genuinely care about people, little people. Every time some ingrate goes to jail for beating his wife and kids, I can barely contain my pride. But with Glossy Denmeade's death, it's different. My heart sinks each time I look down at your shiny boots. "One day he's going to catch up with Riley," I think to myself, and I know that's not going to be a great day in the life of our family.'

'What do you mean?' Danny demanded. 'You thought I'd be unable to contain myself and go and find Riley and personally harm him?' Danny suggested, aghast.

'Well?'

'Bullshit!'

Helen's eyebrow arched. 'Oh?'

'Well? . . . Oh? . . . Are you incapable of anything other than monosyllabic replies?' Danny said, frustrated and unable to find a ready response.

'For goodness sake, darling!' Helen cried. 'You've been trying to get to the bottom of these slum boarding houses for how long? And we're still nowhere. The council doesn't want to know. Tommy O'Hearn is protecting them, or, as you say, riding shotgun for them. The Labor

Party, the state government and the police are taking brown envelopes. You've become pretty obsessed with the whole thing and you've been obsessed with finding Riley since the end of the war. Now both obsessions merge into one and you're going to treat it as due process? Now that, my dear friend, is total *bullshit!*' Helen shouted. 'You couldn't get to Riley in a court of law if you tried. You have absolutely no proof of any wrongdoing. You're not going to get any of those poor devils into the witness box; they're all terrified of Riley's goons, and the tragedy is that they have nowhere else to go. Other than directly assaulting him, your hands are tied.'

'Sammy and Bullnose, they would have testified,' Danny said, taken aback by her vehemence.

'Perhaps. Once they were away from there. My original point, I believe,' Helen, calm again, sighed and shrugged. 'I was afraid you'd take the law into your own hands. Half Dunn is right. You have to wait for an opportunity. I was scared you wouldn't take his advice. If you'd attempted anything while Sammy and Bullnose were still in the boarding house, it wouldn't have taken long for Riley to see the connection and send in his standover men to take revenge on the two of them *and* on you. A boat trip beyond the Heads was not out of the question.' Helen paused. 'Danny, you'd never have forgiven yourself . . . *I'd* never forgive *myself.*'

Despite his anger, Danny was beginning to understand, if not agree with, Helen's concern. 'I don't think you're right. I've waited too long to blow the chance to get to the bastard.'

Helen smiled. 'Okay, here's a hypothetical situation: you're in Tokyo at a legal convention. You go to the toilets, a door opens and you're confronted by Colonel Mori. There's nobody around. What would you do?'

Danny thought for a moment. 'I don't know,' he sighed, shaking his head.

'Well, I think I do,' Helen said quietly. 'You once told me you were taught how to kill a man in ten seconds, silently.'

'You think I'd kill him?'

'Yes.'

'You *really* think so?'

Helen didn't answer for a moment. 'Okay, so Mori is your nemesis. He's also Japanese and the enemy. How much worse is Riley? Riley is one of us, he isn't the enemy, yet he still acted as he did over Glossy Denmeade's boots.' Helen tossed her pretty head.

'So, when Sammy and Bullnose were safely in the flat, when you eventually decided to tell me about Riley, you thought I'd what? Kill him?' Danny asked, most of the fight gone out of him.

Helen, playing for time, stooped to pick up a piece of broken saucer. Looking down at her feet she said softly, 'Darling, you know the war did things to your head. You're not always in total command of your emotions, or of your temper. Craig Woon believes that prisoners who went through what you endured are potentially loose cannons. I know you think about Riley every day of your life, every morning when you pull on your boots.' Helen looked directly at Danny. 'I don't know, I just don't know!' Her voice started to quaver. 'I didn't know what to do!' she wailed.

Danny rose from his chair. 'Helen, Helen, come here.' He took her in his arms, holding her tight against his chest. 'Not even Riley would make me do anything to harm you and the twins.' Holding his sobbing wife, Danny watched the sun rise over the harbour, wondering what the day would bring. Half Dunn was right: with Sammy's death and the deaths of the others in the fire, an opportunity had come at last.

'Daddy, when are we going rowing?' Sam asked, her voice coming from the doorway behind them.

'Why are you crying, Mummy?' Gabby said. 'Is it because you broke a cup?' she asked, seeing the mess on the verandah tiles.

Oh gawd, how are we going to tell them about Sammy? Danny thought suddenly.

Helen removed herself from his embrace and, calling the twins to her, gathered them into her arms. 'There's been a terrible fire, darlings,' she said, pointing at the burned-out house. 'Bullnose has been hurt and they've taken him to the hospital.'

'And Sammy, is he hurt too?' Sam asked, as they both ran to the edge of the verandah to look at the site of the blaze. They were in their pyjamas without dressing-gowns or slippers.

'No, darling.'

'Is he dead?' Gabby asked.

'Yes,' Helen said quietly, in her final monosyllabic answer for the night – or was it the day? So much had happened.

'Can I use the Victa lawnmower on my own now?' Sam asked at once.

Gabby was quiet for a time, thinking. Then she said earnestly, 'Can I play my violin at Uncle Sammy's funeral? I know he'd like that.' Then she said, 'And I'll pick a nice bunch of roses – pink ones and some yellow – for Uncle Bullnose to smell in the hospital. He always says, "Everything's coming up roses."'

'And I'll sing the Tigers' song for Uncle Sammy,' Sam announced, not to be outdone.

'That's very nice,' Helen said, struggling for control. 'I'm sure they'd like that. Now run along and play in your room until Grandma comes to take you to school. Daddy needs to go to sleep for a couple of hours, so no noise, you two, please,' she instructed.

'Is dead forever and ever?' Gabby asked seriously.

'Until heaven,' Sam replied.

'It is forever and ever, sweetheart,' Danny said, kneeling down and giving her a hug. 'We're all very sad.'

Danny grabbed a couple of hours' sleep, while Helen called St Vincent's to see if they could visit Bullnose. She had a lecture to give in the afternoon but would be free in the evening. It seemed that apart from the burns to his face and one hand, and a very sore chest, Bullnose was recovering. Still under heavy sedation for pain and shock, he was nevertheless able to see visitors for a short time between six and eight.

Still weary and heavy-hearted, Danny went into the office to review a court case he had the following morning. Franz came in to him mid-afternoon and slapped the *Daily Mirror* down on his desk. 'Your fire made the front page.'

Danny stared at the newspaper.

Eight Die in Boarding-house Inferno

He read the report quickly while Franz waited – it was the usual stuff, the what, when and where of the tragedy. Only two of the eight dead had been identified because the files containing their details had been severely damaged by water and smoke. Police, with the cooperation of the building's management, hoped to release details later in the day.

The report went on to say:

The bodies of six of the deceased are thought to be too badly burned to be identified. One victim found by firemen in the front section of the building is believed to have succumbed to smoke inhalation. Police identified the man as Samuel Herman Laidlaw, a World War I veteran and retired masseur at the Balmain Leagues Club, where he was a popular member. An elderly woman, identified as Sarah Jane Bassett, is believed to have died of a heart attack on the footpath after being rescued from the burning building. All attempts to resuscitate her failed.

The bodies of the deceased were transported to the city morgue, where it is hoped relatives may be able to identify personal possessions such as rings and other items worn by the fire victims.

Firemen rescued one boarding-house guest who had managed to reach the front hallway of the house before smoke overcame him. He was transported by ambulance to St Vincent's Emergency and is believed to be suffering from smoke inhalation and second-degree burns to his face. His name has not been released as police have yet to interview him.

Police are investigating the fact that the rear windows and rear door of the boarding house, possible escape routes, were permanently barred and locked. The manager of the boarding house, Mr Lenny Green, was not available for interview.

At this stage police inquiries indicate that there are no suspicious circumstances. The cause of the fire is believed to be a boarding-house guest smoking in bed, a common cause of fires in such establishments.

Danny looked up at Franz. 'Not a lot there to work with, except the barred windows and back door. I have a three o'clock appointment at the morgue to identify Sammy.'

'Take a camera.'

'What? Why? The morgue does that – it's part of the coroner's inquiry – 10 x 8 black-and-whites.'

Franz ignored his objection. 'Better still, I'll come with you. I don't trust you with my Leica,' he said.

'Sure,' Danny said, puzzled, 'but I still don't understand.'

'My old man phoned.' Franz pointed to the newspaper. 'He's read about the fire – I've talked to him about your neighbourhood troubles.' He smiled. 'When I told him about Bullnose and Sammy, he said it's essential to have pictures of the body that you've taken yourself, and also of the site of the fire.'

'Hey, c'mon, mate! This isn't Nazi Germany,' Danny protested.

'But it's nevertheless sensible advice. You didn't know my dad was a journalist in Austria, did you? One of the reasons we left was because the Nazis outlawed Jewish journalists. He was also part of the left-wing intelligentsia, not a good combination at the time. He's seen sufficient exploitation of the poor to last him a lifetime. What's happening in those boarding houses isn't unique or new. By the way, his area was crime investigation and, as he put it to me, "Already when you got a picture of the crime scene, it doesn't tell lies in the court like the advocate."'

Danny laughed. 'I don't think they go in for body tampering much at the Sydney City Morgue. But I agree about the site of the fire. Good point.'

'Leave it to me, but we'll have to hurry. If the police didn't cordon off the site last night, we'll be able to get a good look at the building before anyone gets in and removes any suspicious evidence.'

'We've got a qualified insurance assessor on the books, haven't we?'

'Not an assessor – no such animal – an insurance loss adjustor,' Franz corrected. 'Bob James. He's so naturally suspicious it wouldn't surprise me if he made his wife taste his dinner before he ate it. Works for all the big insurance companies. We used him on that big warehouse fire last year when we were representing the NSW Insurance Company.'

'Can you get this James bloke out in a hurry?'

'If he's not interstate. He gets his bratwurst from my mum. She always makes him a special batch – more caraway seeds, or something. It might be as well to accompany him.'

Danny gave him a sceptical look but said nothing.

'My dad's advice again, mate. But didn't you say Bullnose yelled out "meter board" when he was lying on the pavement? If the meter board hasn't been totally destroyed, we need a picture of it, the barred windows, the back door, the bedroom partitions, wiring details . . .'

Danny sighed then rubbed his eyes. 'And *I'm* supposed to be the criminal lawyer! I guess I'm not thinking straight; long night. You're dead right about the fire scene, and the pictures in the morgue can't hurt. Please thank your dad. Tell him we're grateful his instinctive distrust as a journo is still in fine working order.'

Franz laughed. 'He's given me the same advice – "take before-and-after pictures of a property; you'd be amazed at what goes missing between the auction and settlement". By the way, do you know anyone at the Balmain Police Station, in case we have any problems getting onto the site?'

'Sure do. I was a foundation member of the Balmain Police Boys Club as a nipper and I'm on the board of governors. Larry Miller is the sergeant in charge of the cop station as well as the club.' Danny picked up the phone. 'I'll give him a call. You call your insurance bloke, find out when we can go out. Have you got your camera here?'

'Not *we*, *I'll* go with Bob! If you're going to be representing Sammy at the inquest, it's not such a bad idea to keep *schtum* for the time being. Anyway, you were probably recognised last night, but that's easily explained, since you live up the street. On the other hand, you don't want to be seen snooping around, digging among the ashes with a camera.'

'What are you doing as a conveyancing solicitor? You'd have been a damn good criminal lawyer,' Danny grinned.

'If that's a compliment, thank you. I hope to justify my parents' faith in me and end up a rich man instead.'

Franz went to his office to contact the insurance bloke, and Danny dialled the morgue and then the Balmain police. He got through to Sergeant Miller, who assured him that the insurance loss adjustor and his assistant would be allowed to inspect the site of the fire. 'Oh, Larry, mate, do me a favour. Just log that a fire insurance adjustor called Bob James phoned and asked if he and his photographer could visit the site.'

'Sure, Danny, no problem. Glad you're onto it. Can o' worms, that whole street.'

Franz popped his head around the door. 'Okay, Bob James is free, so I'm off.'

'Mortuary, three o'clock. Will you be back in time?' Danny asked.

'I'll meet you there!' Franz replied.

Helen and Danny arrived at St Vincent's at precisely six that evening, after Danny had performed his last duty for poor Sammy Laidlaw – sadly identifying his old friend. They found Bullnose sufficiently recovered to be moved out of Emergency into a men's ward in the general part of the hospital. Had the duty nurse not led them to his bed they would have had no way of recognising him; his head was swathed in bandages with only a slit for his mouth and another for his eyes. 'I've seen Egyptian mummies with fewer bandages on their heads,' Helen laughed softly, bending down and gently kissing his swaddled forehead.

'Gidday, old fella!' Danny called, trying to sound cheerful. 'If you can't talk, just nod your head.'

'I can talk,' Bullnose said slowly, 'I musta had me hand over me mouth and nose to keep out the smoke when the meter board zapped Sammy and the flash got me face.' He withdrew his right hand from under the blanket to show the bandage. 'Yer gunna go after them mongrels, ain't ya, Danny?'

'Yeah,' Danny said quietly. 'Yeah, I'm going to do that, Bullnose.'

'Sammy . . . he wouldn't wanna die fer nuthin'.'

'I know, Bullnose. We can talk about it when you're a little better.'

'Gabrielle picked these roses for you and Samantha bought you a lollipop,' Helen said softly. 'She chose a raspberry flavour and assured me it was your favourite. When I asked her how she knew, she said, "Easy, because it's mine." Come to think of it, in your bandaged condition a lollipop on a stick is a very practical choice.' Helen placed the roses on the metal cabinet beside the bed. 'I'll see if I can find a vase.'

After she'd left, Danny took the chair beside the old man's bed. 'Have the police been to see you yet?' he asked.

'Nah, youse're the first. Nurse says they usually leave it a day unless you're about to cark it.'

'Okay, but understand that it won't be the Balmain mob – Larry Miller and the boys you know from football – so I want you to listen to me carefully, Bullnose. Tell the truth, but *only* answer their questions, understand? *Don't* volunteer any information.'

Bullnose nodded. 'But if they ask me exactly what happened, t'explain like?'

'Trust me, they won't. But now listen, mate, I want you to remember every question they ask, in the order they ask them. They may even try to verbal you. I don't think so, but they might. Everything they ask and say, even among themselves, as well as your answers. Do you think you can do that?'

Bullnose made a small disgusted sound in his throat. 'You know me, Danny. Memory like an elephant.'

'Remember, tell the truth, but *don't* volunteer anything on your own. If anything, play dumb, okay?'

'I am dumb, Danny,' Bullnose said quietly. 'Sammy were the smart one.' His eyes welled with sudden tears. 'We's bin mates sixty-three years, since I was six and he were seven. We done Gallipoli and then Flanders, Ypres, Passchendaele. It were a Frenchy sheila taught him t'massage first, then he done a course when we come back and worked as a masseur for a few years. He was gunna be a physiotherapist. He was that clever, he done one year, passed an' all, then the Depression come and he couldn't go on with it. I done bricklayin' and he done that.' Bullnose dabbed at his brimming eyes with a bandaged hand. 'I'm sorry, Danny . . . fuckin' meter board. I told him t'leave it be – we would'a got outta there safe.

Silly bugger wanted t'save them people screamin' out the back, and —'
He started to sob.

Helen returned holding a vase and saw immediately how upset he
was. Placing it carefully on the metal cabinet, she set about arranging the
roses, deliberately making small talk while the old man collected himself.
'Gabrielle came racing home from swimming training this afternoon,
terrified she wouldn't have time to pick these . . . Pink because she's a
girl and yellow because it's your favourite, she said . . . Samantha says
if you don't like the lollipop to give it back, but she knows you won't
because its raspberry . . . but if you don't, *really* don't like it, she'll ask
her grandma to give her one of those Anzac biscuits she knows you like.'

Bullnose had recovered sufficiently to give Helen a wan smile. 'You
tell 'em both thanks, Helen. Tell Gabby, thank you for the pink and
yella roses – they're bonza! Ask Sam how did she know that raspberry
is my favourite. Tell 'em I'll soon be back, but they gotta look after the
garden for me in the meantime and not forget to turn the compost heap.
They won't like that.' He laughed. 'Gabby says it's where the flowers go
to poo and Sam asked why do we let them poo in our backyard? That
little scallywag, Sam.' Bullnose chuckled. 'She told Sammy he could
have one of her gold medals to wear around his neck 'cos she won't be
able to wear them all after the 1968 Olympics, but *only* if he lets her use
the Victa lawnmower *now*.'

Danny shook his head and smiled indulgently. 'She's a worry all
right.'

The ward sister entered, white on white on white, all of it somehow
starched and angled; even her nose seemed sharp on her stern face.
Clearly nothing had changed in hospitals since the twins were born,
certainly not the bossy attitude of the nursing staff. 'I'm afraid you'll have
to go now. It's time to change the patient's dressings. Say goodnight to
your guests, please . . .' she checked the clipboard at the end of the bed,
adding, 'Mr Daintree.'

On the pavement outside the hospital, walking to where they'd
parked the car, Danny suddenly stopped and turned to Helen. 'Darling,

Primo's is only a few minutes' drive from here. What say we have dinner in town? Brenda won't mind putting the kids to bed, and we'll be home before ten.' He pointed. 'Look, there's a phone box, a sign that we should. We can call Mum now.'

'Darling, that would be lovely, but you must be exhausted after last night. Are you sure?'

'Hey, look who's talking. You've been up just as long as I have.'

'No, I cheated. I went to bed after you left for the office and then only had to go in for one lecture this afternoon, first-year students, simple stuff I can do in my sleep.'

'I can sleep tonight,' Danny said, 'and we won't be late. I want to make it up to you for being such a shit last night. Dinner at Primo's will, I hope, be a reasonable start to an apology. What say?'

'Oh, sweetheart, I'd love to. But I'm not really dressed for it and we don't have a booking.'

Danny grinned. 'I'll greet the maître d' with the "universal handshake", as Franz's dad calls it.'

'What if it doesn't work?'

'In that case, we'll be witnessing a genuine miracle. We meet all the requirements: we're sober, you're beautiful, I'm wearing a suit and tie, and we're both Caucasian.' Danny paused. 'Most importantly, a magic quid will have been transferred from one palm to another.'

'And I left my good lippy at home,' Helen moaned.

When the date of the inquest was announced, Danny immediately dictated a letter to Keri Light, the new legal secretary he shared with Franz, addressed to the coroner's office seeking leave to appear on behalf of Mr Bullmore Nosbert Daintree. Both these unfortunate Christian names had quickly been converted in the schoolyard to Bullnose, the moniker that had served him well for almost seventy years.

A week later Keri, sitting at the front desk while Amanda, the receptionist, was at lunch, called through to say, 'Mr Dunn, I don't know if this is a joke, but a Mr *Lawless*, who says he's from the attorney-general's office, is on the phone.'

'Yeah, that's right. Put him on.' He heard Keri giggle before she made the transfer. 'Good afternoon, Nick. This is a surprise. What can I do for you?'

Nick Lawless was an outspoken civil servant, regarded by some lawyers as a man who often abused his position. He'd served under five state Labor ministers and there were those among the legal profession who believed he regarded himself as the de facto attorney-general. Danny reasoned that, blessed or cursed with such a surname, he was more or less forced to prove himself, and they'd always had a cordial, if not chummy, relationship.

'Danny, what's this I see? You're listed as appearing for one of the victims in the Balmain boarding-house fire? I thought battered wives and kids were more your thing . . .'

Danny forced a small chuckle. 'Well, yeah, I suppose so, Nick. It's just that the man works . . . er, worked for me as a part-time gardener. I want to see that the poor old bugger is looked after, that's all.'

The civil servant's tone softened noticeably. 'Heart on your sleeve again, eh, Danny? When are you going to learn that the poor will always be among us? You can't have the Jew boy earning all the dough while you go in to bat for the little people.'

Danny winced. 'Is there something you're not telling me, Nick?' he asked, hoping he sounded sufficiently ingenuous.

'No, son. We were just a tad concerned when a lawyer of your reputation bobbed up on the inquest list, that's all.'

'Are you sure? I sense you're worried about something.' Danny didn't want to appear too naïve or Nick Lawless would smell a rat. He was arrogant but no fool.

'No, nothing, mate,' Lawless answered with a chuckle, far too old a hand to be wrong-footed. 'Heffron's under a bit of pressure, taking over so unexpectedly after Cahill died. He still feels he's on probation. The

Minister for Housing thinks he should have been the chosen one, so he wants a show of strength over this . . . er, boarding-house fire. When we saw Nifty Dunn on the list . . . well, there's one or two people got a little antsy. We don't want a shit fight just at the moment.' Another chuckle followed. 'Mate, what can I say? Usual big boys' games.' He paused. 'Righto then, if you're just looking after this old bloke, I guess that's okay.'

Danny realised it was all bullshit, but it was quality bullshit and he would have expected nothing less from the senior civil servant. 'Well, as a matter of fact I'm pretty busy at the moment, Nick. I thought it would be a fairly open-and-shut case, all over in a day or two. I'd just like to see that the old bloke gets a fair suck of the sav.'

'Thanks, Danny. Leave it to me; I'll pass that on. The coroner, old Harry Prout, is on the verge of retirement. I'm sure he doesn't want the newspapers all over this one. Nor does my boss, ha ha.'

'No, I don't suppose that ever serves a useful purpose,' Danny replied, thinking how useful a newspaper exposé might be in the case, and that perhaps he should give someone a discreet call. 'Nice to talk with you, Nick.'

Danny put down the phone. He remembered Half Dunn's 'every dog has his day' advice. *You'll keep, Lawless,* he thought.

Danny walked through to Franz's office. 'Just had Lawless from the attorney-general's office on the phone. Wanted to know why I was on the inquest list.'

'Got the wind up?'

'Hopefully I managed to reassure him it was simply good old Danny doing another pro bono.'

'Not the sort of guy you'd invite to your son's bar mitzvah,' Franz remarked.

'Oh, you've noticed?'

'Bastard doesn't do a whole lot to hide his anti-Semitism.'

'Franz, I suspect even if I can get the coroner to refer it to the attorney-general for trial, Riley will have his arse well and truly covered.

We need to know more about him: his social position, standing in the community, friends in high places, associates, family – that sort of thing. Our man from Vaucluse, Bryan Penman, just might be useful. Do you think you could approach him? It's not appropriate for me to do it.'

'Why? Because you got him off a murder rap? You think you'd be putting him in an awkward position?'

'Yeah, kind of. Puts him under an obligation.'

'Shouldn't be a problem. I'll talk to my mum and dad.'

'You can be sure if things get too hot, Riley will have someone lined up to take the rap. His sort always does. Besides, it's standard practice.'

Franz gave him a straight look. 'Danny, I know how badly you want Riley, how long you've waited to nail him, but don't be blinded by the need for revenge.'

'What do you mean by that?' Danny asked, a little defensively.

'Treat it like any other case. Remember Old Sharp's advice – there's many a slip between mug and lip, so don't be the mug.'

'Hey, mate, that's a bit close to the bone! You think I could be emotionally blinded? Jesus! First Helen, now you!'

'Two very sensible people making the same observation, it seems,' Franz said coolly. 'Treat it the same as any other case.'

'But it isn't the fucking same! Eight people are dead. Eight people have effectively been murdered!'

'See what I mean? You're on your white charger and tilting at windmills. You haven't proved that anyone has been murdered. I may only be a conveyancing solicitor, but as I understand it, this is an inquest into the cause of an accident, not a murder trial. Right now Nick Lawless is talking to somebody who's talking to somebody who'll talk to Riley's mob and tell them Nifty Dunn is representing Bullnose at the inquest. I don't for one second believe you allayed his suspicions.' Franz paused. 'No, that's not quite fair. You probably did. But Lawless is as cunning as a shithouse rat. Besides, you're a pretty high-profile lawyer. He'll pass the word around as a matter of routine, and by this afternoon Riley will have his lawyers briefing the best available barrister in town.'

Danny was silent, drumming his fingers on Franz's desk, thinking, then finally he said, 'Okay, maybe you're right. What are you suggesting?'

'I'm suggesting I don't contact Bryan Penman. Nobody gossips like the very rich. Initially Riley mustn't be seen to be your target. You first have to prove criminal neglect: that the fire was an accident waiting to happen, that the meter board and the wiring were faulty and that the owners were aware of this and neglected to do anything about it. Even if you're successful, that doesn't necessarily get you to Riley. They'll have a scapegoat – the manager probably.'

'Lenny Green, yeah, I'd anticipated that. My job will be to establish a direct and admissible link between the cause of the fire and Riley.'

'I don't like your chances, Danny,' Franz responded.

Danny ignored this. 'We need to get Green to testify that he informed Riley of the danger and that Riley ignored his advice.'

'If a conversation such as that ever took place,' Franz said, sceptical.

'It took place, or it will have,' Danny said, almost as a throwaway line. 'Green is definitely the key. They'll persuade him that the inquest will be a whitewash and the most he'll face is a rap on the knuckles.'

'And your job is to persuade him otherwise?'

'Well, not exactly *my* job, someone else's. I've called Bumper Barnett.'

'The hastily-retired-on-a-full-pension Kings Cross detective sergeant?'

'The same. He comes recommended by Perc Galea.'

'But if you can't talk to Bryan Penman, how can you approach Galea for help? He's one of your clients, too.'

'Galea is different. The criminal world runs on dishing dirt.'

'And high society doesn't?' Franz exclaimed, surprised. 'It'd be good if Lenny Green has a criminal background, would it not?'

'Probably better if he doesn't. We don't want the court automatically regarding him as a mendacious ex-crim. Bumper will, I hope, put the fear of God into him.' Danny reached over and lifted the gold Parker pen from its marble and bronze snout. Franz referred to the pen as the Bar Mitzvah Boy's Burden, claiming he'd received twenty-three identical pens on the day he turned thirteen. Danny tossed it from one hand to the other, then said carefully, 'Mate, I'd be really grateful if you acted as my sounding board in this. Perhaps even sit in court with me, act as my instructing solicitor. You and Helen might be right – I want him too much. Always dangerous with my . . . er, personality.'

'Sure. The debating team together again, eh?'

Two days later Bumper Barnett attended a briefing with Danny and Franz in the spare office they referred to as the boardroom. He reported what he'd managed to find out about Lenny Green, and then they settled down to discuss tactics.

Danny was a big man himself, over six foot, but next to Barnett he appeared merely average. The ex-policeman was close to six foot nine, and his shoulders seemed almost half that measure. He carried a beer gut that would have put Half Dunn to shame when was in his prime. This abdominal bulwark, rotund and rock hard, was the source of his nickname and served as a formidable weapon. His huge stomach took the place of a police truncheon or a pair of fists. He would literally 'bump' crims into submission, working them into the corner of a room where he'd repeatedly bump them until they confessed or collapsed. An added advantage was that they never had a mark on them to show the severe beating they'd received. *'I swear I never laid a hand on him, Your Honour.'*

In his day, Bumper Barnett couldn't be called an honest cop, but then he couldn't be called a corrupt one either. He'd acted as bagman in the Cross and Darlinghurst area, personally delivering the weekly take from the brothels, sly-grog operators, SP bookmakers and gambling joints to the safe in the premier's office, to which only he and the premier had the combination. In return he'd received a small stipend that the premier referred to as his weekly bonus. It was never going to make him a rich man.

He was respected by the major crims because he never used the information they gave him for any purpose other than the one he'd told them about. He kept his word and never doublecrossed them or accepted a personal bribe. He was fearless and respected no man above another; he did things his own way, accepted what he couldn't change and served the general community conscientiously, so that no honest citizen had any reason to fear him and most criminals had a great many reasons to do so if Bumper decided to come after them.

He came unstuck leaving a brothel late one Saturday night, where he'd gone to collect the bagman's share of the night's takings. A young hoon on the pavement was beating up one of the girls from the establishment. Bumper grabbed him by the shirtfront and gave him a bump that sent him careening into a parked car, breaking his shoulder and several ribs.

Unfortunately for Bumper the drunk turned out to be the assistant police commissioner's eighteen-year-old son, celebrating the end of his final-year school exams with his mates, so it proved to be a career-terminating bump. The pro, it seemed, had embraced the kid, pretending to persuade him to come inside with her, but had then neatly plucked his wallet from the inside pocket of his jacket and dropped it while trying to conceal it inside her bra.

Bumper Barnett was subsequently given the choice of serving out the remainder of his police career in Wilcannia, a three-pub town out west on the banks of the Darling River, or resigning quietly on a full police pension. He chose the latter and maintained the goodwill of the Kings Cross community as well as the respect of the criminal fraternity. In the process he earned twice as much as he had as a policeman, doing useful tasks such as the one Danny had now asked him to undertake.

Lenny Green, the boarding-house manager, turned out to be a recidivist, in and out of the clink since his teens. It was the usual story: Parramatta Boys Home, reform school for delinquency, mostly stealing cars, then breaking and entering, nothing big or well planned, just typical small-time criminal stuff that got a light sentence so that he was

in and out of jail like a yo-yo. He'd been clean for five years and prior
to taking over the boarding house had been for a short time a general
factotum at a strip club in Kings Cross. 'Like most of his kind he's not
very bright,' Bumper Barnett concluded. 'He'd probably 'fess up if he was
worked on a bit.'

'Spot on, Bumper,' Danny said. 'Convince him that the inquest is
going to take off like a rocket and he's going to be tied to the stick. Let
him understand there's a very real risk that he's going to jail for a very
long time.'

Bumper nodded. 'Mr Dunn, Lenny Green is about to discover that
the only way out is to tell the truth, that the truth will set him free. He'll
come to understand that committing perjury will have two disastrous
consequences: he'll end up getting the book thrown at him and he'll
have earned my disrespect.'

'Okay, we'll leave all that to you, Bumper. By the way, see what you
can find out about Riley, and the Double Bay Syndicate, as I believe
it's called. I don't want you knocking on doors or making any direct
inquiries, just ear-to-the-ground stuff. Find out if Riley's involved in
anything else that's got a nasty whiff to it.' He paused. 'Righto, let's try
to work out what the opposition may be planning to do at the inquest.'
He turned to his partner. 'Franz, what do you reckon?'

'Well, the locked back door and the barred windows that prevented
the eight people escaping are not going to go away. So, they'll have to
try to coerce, persuade, make it worthwhile for Lenny Green to take the
blame for criminal neglect. If the sentence he receives is a token rap
over the knuckles, a few months in jail with a big payout waiting in the
bank for him when he comes out, he may agree.'

'With respect, Mr Landsman, he *will* agree,' Bumper said. 'Two
consequences if he doesn't: Riley will have him badly beaten up and
he'll miss out on the equivalent of two years' pay. It doesn't make a lot of
sense to refuse.'

'So the manner of the inquest is established and the result is more or
less a foregone conclusion?' Franz suggested.

'It's not quite that clear-cut. The crowd at the morgue are pretty independent and will give the facts as they see them. The idea will be for the inquest to run on formal lines: no unpredictable questions and no suggestion that manslaughter is involved – only an unfortunate error of judgment and a consequent light penalty for Green,' Danny said.

'Fires in boarding houses, especially this kind, are not uncommon,' Bumper added. 'Drunks fall asleep with lighted cigarettes. Believe me, once a coir mattress starts to burn it's bloody hard to put out. Happens in the Cross all the time.'

'So we're concluding that the bars on the window and the locked back door, not the meter board, will become the focus of the inquiry.'

Danny nodded.

'But what about Sammy and the meter board? The on-site pictures I took with James – the insurance loss adjustor,' Franz explained to Bumper, 'and the picture of Sammy's arm taken at the morgue tell a very different story,' he said vehemently.

'Ah, that's where we hope to surprise them,' Danny said, smiling, then adding, 'Thank Christ for your dad's initiative and the pictures you had James take, Franz.'

Franz sighed. 'Mate, in my world Christ doesn't get the credit for very much. In our opinion he was nothing but a troublemaker.'

CHAPTER ELEVEN

NOBODY ON DANNY'S SIDE of the court proceedings was surprised at the approach taken by the lawyer and barrister representing the Double Bay Syndicate. As Bumper Barnett remarked, 'When you're not expecting difficult questions you won't go looking for clever answers.' When Danny left virtually all the questioning to the coroner and the barrister assisting him, Riley's mob relaxed. Nick Lawless had been correct; Nifty Dunn wasn't there to stir things up.

The Coroner's Court was far from full, due to the lack of relatives of either the deceased or the survivors, although Danny felt sure they would magically appear if there was even a whiff of compensation for the victims. He was also gratified to see Riley in court; he had thought it might be necessary to have him summonsed. Riley's presence indicated that they were confident the inquiry would go as planned. Danny was careful to keep his expression neutral when he happened to face the area where Riley sat, acting as if he had little or no interest in his presence, and that any animosity from the past had faded with time.

Danny nodded to the barrister assisting the coroner, Ray Onions, a reliable old stager who usually didn't set out to rock the boat. His Worship, Harry Prout, the coroner, while not the sharpest knife in the kitchen drawer, had achieved senior magistrate status by dint of his methodical and persistent approach to his work, and had been moved over to the coroner's office to see out the last two years before he was due to retire.

While Riley's mob would have thought themselves fortunate to have him in the chair, Danny had the same reaction but for a different reason. He'd known Prout as a magistrate and had a fair amount of respect for him. If he wasn't the blade used to carve the Sunday roast, he nevertheless possessed one characteristic that might be useful – like most people who secretly know they're not among the elite in their chosen field, he hated to think someone was trying to put something over him. On two occasions Danny had benefited from this trait in his court when it was apparent police had verballed two of his clients. Danny noted that Prout seemed particularly grumpy this morning and concluded that his arthritis must be playing up. In a court where everything needs to run smoothly, a cantankerous magistrate can do a fair amount of damage if the pot is sufficiently stirred. Persistent pain often leads to bad temper.

In addition, Riley's people, taking no chances with Nifty Dunn's appearance on behalf of one of the survivors, had taken the precaution of hiring a top gunslinger, a barrister by the name of Steel Hammer (you wonder sometimes what parents must be thinking when they name their child), who was known in the legal profession as 'The Hammer' because of his forceful and intimidating manner. Many imagined that he must have been the school bully in his day, assuming that Sydney Grammar had one such. The way the hearing was going, Hammer, like Danny, was proving somewhat overqualified.

The proceedings had started predictably enough with the police and fire-brigade experts reciting their evidence – tragic affair, cause of fire unknown, no suspicious circumstances, although the fire-brigade expert pointed out that permanently barred windows on a building used for accommodation, 'other than as a prison, a police station, or a mental institution, Your Honour,' was unusual.

'When you examined the premises, notwithstanding the barred windows and locked door, was the interior of the building in its original condition, apart from cosmetic work and repairs, or had it been substantially modified?' Danny asked during his cross-examination.

'Well, yes, it had been modified, in so much as it was altered to accommodate additional people,' the expert replied.

'What? More rooms added?'

'In a manner of speaking, yes.'

'Would you explain to the court how this was done?'

'The rooms had been divided into smaller rooms.'

'I see . . .'

'Objection! Your Worship, this is standard practice in the renovation of older premises for this purpose,' Hammer protested.

Danny affected surprise. 'Your Worship, I was not about to question the manner of the renovation.'

Harry Prout gave Hammer a look of irritation. 'Please go ahead, Mr Dunn.'

'My question is, were there any changes made to the electrical wiring?'

'Yes, each of the smaller areas required a light source of its own.'

'I see. And how would you describe these smaller areas?'

'They were cubicles.'

'How many of these cubicles would you say were contained within one average-sized room?'

'Four.'

And each had a completely independent source of light?'

'Yes.'

'These four independent sources of light led from the previous central rosette in the room, is that correct?'

'Yes.'

Hammer got to his feet. 'Objection, the witness has previously stated that the cause of the fire was unknown, but offered the unprompted opinion that it was most likely to have been caused by a tenant falling asleep with a lighted cigarette. No mention was made of the electrical wiring.'

'Objection overruled, Mr Hammer. No question has previously been asked concerning the wiring,' Harry Prout retorted. 'You may proceed, Mr Dunn.'

'No further questions, Your Worship,' Danny said, resuming his seat beside Franz.

A look of annoyance crossed the coroner's face. It was clear he had anticipated something more from Danny when he'd overruled Hammer's objection. Danny was pleased; he wanted the old magistrate to think they were all playing possum and to assume there was a cosy little agreement overseen by the attorney-general's office.

'Call Gareth Lachlan Riley!' the coroner's clerk announced. Ray Onions, the barrister assisting the coroner, proceeded to ask Riley a list of very routine questions and received equally routine and seemingly rehearsed answers. In fact, Franz was having trouble hiding his amusement. Riley's answers were almost precisely what had been anticipated in their pre-trial briefing: yes, he was the managing director and a shareholder in the Double Bay Syndicate; no, he wasn't aware of any pre-existing problems with the premises – as a matter of fact the Syndicate chose their managers with some care and gave them a degree of autonomy once they had established a set of criteria for the managers to follow. He believed these were accepted by boarding-house guests. No, he hadn't visited the specific building recently, in fact not for some time, but there were no complaints, and Mr Green, as previously stated, was a highly competent and popular manager. He chuckled, 'One thing you learn in our business is that people never hesitate to complain when they think they are not getting the service they believe is due to them. We have over eighty establishments on our books, in Balmain, Newtown, Paddington, Parramatta and Kings Cross; inevitably there are fires to put out and I attend to these first and foremost.'

'Perhaps not the most appropriate metaphor in this case,' Onions replied, causing a titter of mirth throughout the court. 'Thank you, Mr Riley,' he concluded.

'Do you have any questions for this witness, Mr Dunn?'

'Not at this time, Your Worship.'

The coroner, glaring meaningfully at Danny, said rather acerbically, 'Perhaps you could remind me why you are in attendance in court, Mr Dunn?'

'I am representing the interests of Mr Bullmore Nosbert Daintree, Your Worship.'

The coroner nodded and turned to Riley. 'You may step down, Mr Riley. However, as a witness in this inquest you are required to remain available,' he glanced at Danny, his right eyebrow slightly raised, 'for what appears to be the unlikely event that any questions arise from the evidence of subsequent witnesses.'

'Yes, certainly. Thank you, Your Worship.' Riley darted a tentative glance at Danny and then ventured a brittle, somewhat ambiguous smile, one that could have been taken as mere recognition or as a gesture of mollification – 'Let's let bygones be bygones.'

Hammer, Riley's barrister, asked for and was granted permission to speak.

Oozing sincerity and in a nicely modulated private-school accent, he began. 'My client has asked me to stress how very distressed he personally feels over this terrible disaster. He would like the court to know that his syndicate has found alternative accommodation, at its own expense, in a private hotel for the survivors of the fire until such time as they can make their own arrangements. He has also made a significant contribution to the funeral costs of the deceased, allowing them to be buried with dignity as private citizens and not at a cost to the state. Finally, he has made a donation to St Vincent's Hospital, after the rejection of his offer to pay the hospital costs for the boarder who sustained severe burns escaping the fire.' He shot a glance at Danny.

'Very commendable, I'm sure,' Harry Prout sniffed. He wasn't having a good day.

Danny had decided not to call Bullnose to the witness stand. The police had interviewed him in hospital and he had done as Danny had asked him and replayed every question, using the precise words of the police officers. It soon became apparent that the police were simply going through the motions of acquiring a record of interview and not much else. But they had asked Bullnose whether he had seen any others attempting to escape the blazing house.

'Yes,' Bullnose replied.

'Did you know this person?'

'Yes,' had been the reply again.

'Did you see what happened to him?'

'Yes.'

'Can you describe what you saw?'

'He tried to shut down the meter board, which was going apeshit,' Bullnose said.

'What do you mean by that?'

'It was an electrical fire, and sparks were shooting everywhere. He reckoned he could shut it down. People upstairs were screaming.'

The sergeant conducting the interview had said, 'Don't record that,' to the policeman taking notes. Then he'd turned back to Bullnose. 'Are you a qualified electrician?' he demanded.

'No.'

'Then this is only an opinion?'

'Yes.'

'But not an expert one?'

'No.'

'C'mon, the smoke in the front hallway was too dense for you to see anything.'

'It was dense but —'

'I suggest to you that you only imagined you could see,' the sergeant said, cutting him short. 'You don't want to get yourself into unnecessary trouble, Mr Daintree.'

'Trouble?'

'Yes, we don't want to have to take this further. Do you smoke?'

'Yes.'

'Did you have a drink on the night of the fire?'

'Yes, but —'

'Well then, I think we'll let the fire brigade tell the coroner what caused the fire. Do you understand, Mr Daintree?'

'Yes.'

'Put this down,' the sergeant said to the policeman taking notes of the interview. 'The interview terminated when the witness claimed that while attempting to leave the premises, due to the quantity of smoke in the front hallway, he was unable to see more than a few inches ahead.'

Danny had listened to this with great interest. He was after Riley, not the cops, and now he knew that everyone was working together.

Ray Onions called Lenny Green to the witness stand. Green was not a big man nor an imposing one. Knowing of his past, Danny thought he could see in him the results of a poor and loveless childhood. Green seemed to bear all the marks of emotional and physical neglect produced by a notorious boys' home and the Great Depression. He had received as little emotional and intellectual nurturing as he had good nutritious food, and the result was that he was a sad example of society's lack of care. If he'd been a plant, he'd have been a weed growing from a crack in an asphalt pavement, determined to cling to life, even though no one cared whether he did so or not. It was no wonder Bumper Barnett had pronounced him a pushover – one who didn't have to tell an untruth to implicate Riley but instead had merely to be persuaded to tell the truth.

It was Sammy who, six months earlier, had first alerted Green to the fact that the meter-board wiring couldn't carry the load placed on it and was an accident waiting to happen. Green, recognising that he would be blamed if anything happened, notified the syndicate by writing to Riley and sending the letter by mail, but without results. In addition he'd sent a copy of the same note to Riley via the rent collector, that is, the man from head office who picked up the rent that the managers had already collected from their tenants. Green had done this on two further occasions, each time mailing the original and sending one of three carbon copies via the rent collector. All three notes had been addressed to Riley. After the third, Riley had visited, but instead of examining the meter board or bringing someone with him who was capable of making an assessment, he'd brought a notorious standover man, known in the criminal world as Shocker Docker. Docker had made Green unlock the back door and led him out into the overgrown and weed-infested backyard where, in Riley's presence, he'd given him a savage beating, finally knocking him unconscious, then throwing him into a blackberry thicket.

'Why didn't he simply resign, get the hell out of there?' Franz had asked Bumper.

Bumper laughed. 'It's a different world, Mr Landsman. Green's a small-time crim with nowhere to hide and no personal protection. If he buggers off, next thing he's arrested on suspicion of rape or armed robbery, with the girl and witnesses standing by, or the shopkeeper identifying him in a police line-up. Worse still, he's invited on a trip out to sea. So, when there was a fire, Riley made a deal with him – he takes the rap, is guaranteed a light sentence, and there's a reward waiting for him when he gets out.'

'But how does he know Riley will pay up when he comes out?'

'It's a matter of honour among thieves, Mr Landsman. It's arranged through a third party who holds the money for a small percentage. Besides, Riley is not a criminal as such. He simply uses crims as the strong-arm part of his operation. He has to keep his word or they will lose respect. He, or his syndicate, are believed to own seventy or eighty of these cheap doss houses; they couldn't run their business without goons riding shotgun.'

'And you've managed to persuade him to go along with us and tell the truth?' Franz asked.

'Maybe,' Danny had laughed. 'It will depend on how we handle things at the inquiry. We're up against some formidable and determined opposition, and I keep reminding myself that this is only a coroner's inquiry, that I'm not trying to expose the whole corrupt system – police, councils and politicians. All I'm trying to do is to get Riley to commit perjury, and the whole mess will begin to unravel if the coroner believes there is sufficient evidence to go to trial. The one thing we've got going for us is the coroner, Harry Prout. He's his own man and I don't believe he can be bought.'

Franz turned to Danny with a grin, shaking his head. 'And to think all I have to worry about is the previous owner of a property nicking the Victa lawnmower and the garden tools in a private transaction. Last week I nearly had a transaction involving a 500-acre prime stud property in Bowral fall through because the previous owner's wife dug up all the daffodil bulbs in the garden. His lawyer somewhat bizarrely claimed that what was underground wasn't included in the contract.'

'Riley's not going to be easy to pin down, Mr Dunn,' Bumper Barnett said. 'I did what you asked and picked up what I could on him. Apart from what we already know there isn't a lot of dirt attached. Your man Riley is prominent in business and social circles, as I think you know. He's pretty well connected and sits on the boards of several government and charitable bodies. Not much old money left but he's from one of those Sydney families who have single-digit numberplates on their cars. He married well and his wife inherited a packet in mining stock, most of it BHP. She's on the Black and White Ball Committee and very hoity-toity. Here's the joke: one of his charities is the Parramatta Boys' Home!'

'You're right – he's got his arse well covered. That's the problem with social position and money: if you achieve the former it doesn't much matter how you make the latter.'

'Providing you don't get caught and you're not Jewish,' Franz added.

Bumper Barnett paused and rubbed his chin. 'You know, as a former cop, something worries me in all this business with Lenny Green.'

'Oh?' Danny asked curiously.

'Yeah. I asked myself, why would Riley bother to go out to visit Green after the third meter-board complaint? It would have been much more sensible to send a goon to beat the crap out of him, and leave it at that. He'd achieve the same result, only he, Riley, wouldn't be directly involved . . . implicated. It doesn't make sense.'

'You're right, it doesn't,' Danny agreed.

'So I dropped in to see Perc.'

'Galea – the crime boss?' Franz asked.

'Yeah, Mr Dunn's mate,' Bumper grinned, looking at Danny.

'Don't ever say that in public, Bumper. I represented him in court; we got lucky, that's all,' Danny said quickly.

'Mr Dunn, he thinks the sun shines out of your backside. He called a mate on the phone and they were yakking on a bit and then Perc puts down the phone. "It seems your man Riley is some kind of pervert, Bumper," he says to me. "He gets off on seeing people beaten up."

'"Yeah? I've known mongrel cops like that," I say.

'"No, no," he says, "not like a bad cop. He don't do the beating up himself – he's too much of a fucking coward."

'"Just watches?"

'"Yeah, sort of."

'"So? Why not go to Rushcutters Bay Stadium, Saturday-night fights, two guys knocking the living shit out of each other?" I suggest.

'"Nah, that don't work for him. It's blokes he's got power over. He needs the – how can I put it – the personal power, that's what turns him on."

'"You mean he's a sadist?"

'"That's a big word for me, mate. I'm a wog," Perc says. "The fact that he can personally cause some poor bastard to become mincemeat is his shtick."'

'That's Yiddish!' Franz exclaimed.

Bumper ignored the remark. Shtick was a common underworld expression. 'Galea says his mate swears Riley cracks a fat, panting and groaning, watching some poor bastard take a beating at his instigation. It happens somewhere to someone in one of his doss houses every week.' He paused for emphasis. 'Riley didn't visit Lenny Green to teach him a lesson for complaining about the meter board. Green was simply that week's opportunity to get his rocks off. That week's power play! Jesus!'

'Christ! Glossy Denmeade's boots!' Danny exclaimed. 'That's why he chose someone from my company and not his own. As an officer he had the power to humiliate Glossy, make him beg, but had he done the same in his own company his blokes would talk about it. Glossy's boots were famous in the entire battalion. He would have known we were being shipped out and as company sergeant major I couldn't get back at him. Maximum result, minimum fallout, the dirty bastard!'

Now, with Lenny Green in the witness box, Ray Onions began with the usual questions, after establishing that Green had been the manager of the premises in question for the past four years, and that Green couldn't imagine what might have started the fire.

'Mr Green, you were left pretty much alone to run the premises as you saw fit. Is that so?'

'Yes, sir, that is correct.'

A sense of torpor descended over the court as the barrister assisting the coroner reiterated the statements made by Green to the police and in turn received largely monosyllabic replies. Several of the court reporters got up and left – they would phone in later to get the predictable findings: death by misadventure, with a rap over the knuckles for Green, the manager, under the *Landlord and Tenant Act* because of the barred windows and locked door. There would be a light sentence to follow when the matter came to court. It was a half-column piece in the back half of the newspaper, less if it was a busy news night.

Ray Onions concluded his questioning. Steel Hammer was regretting that he'd bothered to read the brief he'd been sent; there had been no barking, no finger pointed accusingly at the witness demanding answers, no scope for pushing witnesses around, no bombast required, not a single caution from the coroner. He was practically falling asleep. It was apparent to him that the deal, whatever it was, had been well organised, and even Nifty Dunn, for whom he had a measure of respect, had been 'well briefed'. It was going to be an easy day at the office and Riley had promised to see what he could do about tickets to the Black and White Ball. He was going to return home to his wife tonight a hero.

Harry Prout, now in a thoroughly bad humour, glared at Danny, 'Any questions for this witness, Mr Dunn?'

'Yes, Your Worship.' Danny stood. 'Mr Green, I ask you now to listen carefully. Were the facts stated by you in the police record of interview an accurate account of your actions and those of others prior to and during the fire?'

Green hesitated. 'No, sir, they wasn't.'

Franz swallowed and tried to suppress a smile. Green was on side. A sudden excited murmur ran through the courtroom and there was a loud bang as the front legs of Hammer's chair hit the deck.

Harry Prout came alive and banged his gavel, calling for order. Then, with silence restored and the reporters poised over their shorthand pads, he said, 'Mr Green, I must caution you, making a false statement to the police is a very serious offence. Are you aware of the trouble you may be causing for yourself?'

'It ain't gunna be half as bad as what they threatened, what they did to old Charlie McFadden last year,' Green replied, his fear palpable.

'Oh? Can you tell the court what these threats were, Mr Green?' Danny asked.

'Like Charlie, if I didn't cooperate, keep me mouth shut, they was gunna dump me a mile out t'sea and tell me to swim home.'

'They? Who made this threat? Is that person in this court?'

Lenny Green pointed to Riley. 'Mr Riley, sir. He come round the mornin' after the fire.'

Steel Hammer jumped to his feet. 'Objection! Your Worship, I must protest. This witness, now a self-confessed liar, is making unsubstantiated and extremely serious allegations against my client, one of this city's most respected businessmen.'

'Please sit down, Mr Hammer! It is the business of my court to examine all the facts relating to this tragic matter and you may be assured I shall do just that.' Harry Prout shot Danny a barely concealed look of encouragement. 'Mr Dunn, you may continue with this witness.'

'Mr Green, as the coroner has pointed out, lying to the police is a serious offence. You must have believed Mr Riley was capable of carrying out his threats?'

'Objection, Your Worship. My learned friend is leading the witness.'

'Objection sustained. Counsel will refrain from leading the witness.'

'Let me put it to you this way, Mr Green. Did you have good cause, based on past experience, to believe that Mr Riley would carry out this alleged threat?'

'Yes, sir, he – Mr Riley – had Shocker Docker with him. When I complained the last time about the meter board, two months back, it was him who knocked the livin' sh— – sorry, sir – that beat me with a pickaxe handle in the backyard, with Mr Riley watchin' on.' Lenny Green sniffed then, looking directly at Riley, and wiped his nose on the back of his hand. 'They left me unconscious, lying in the blackberry bush.'

'Is that David Docker, the notorious standover man?'

'Yes, the same, sir. Him and Badman Burgess, they do the beatings for Riley. He, Burgess, give me a proper hidin' two years ago.'

'Objection, Your Worship,' Hammer cried. 'We have no substantiation for this alleged assault, no witnesses, and we are being asked to accept the word of a recidivist.'

'Objection overruled. Did I not hear your client earlier applaud Mr Green as a capable and reliable manager in whom he placed full trust? Would you like the clerk of the court to read his exact words from the record?'

'No, Your Worship. My client is now conscious of having totally misplaced his trust.'

The coroner turned to Danny. 'However, Mr Hammer's point is valid, Mr Dunn. Can your client substantiate his claim of the alleged beating?'

'Yes, Your Worship. I intend to produce a witness who is ready to testify under oath that he saw the beating take place.'

Danny resumed his examination of Lenny Green. 'Mr Green, you have testified that you alerted Mr Riley on three separate occasions to the potential risk of the meter board causing a fire. Are you an expert in such matters, an electrician, perhaps?'

'No, sir, it was Sammy Laidlaw told me.'

'The deceased? One of the victims in the fire?'

'Yes, sir.'

'And he was an electrician?'

'No, sir, he done massage.' This brought a gush of laughter from the gallery. 'But he said he knew about these old meter boards; he said he was apprenticed to his father, who was an electrician before the war, but after he come back he didn't take it up again.'

'But you had reason to believe he knew what he was talking about?'

'Yes, sir. He showed me where they'd put the copper wire across the two fuse boxes.'

Danny turned to the coroner. 'Your Worship, I intend to bring an expert witness to the stand to explain in simple terms this matter of the copper wire.' Turning back to Green, he said, 'And you communicated on three separate occasions with Mr Riley, warning him of the danger posed by the meter board?'

'Yes, sir.'

'And can you prove this?'

'Yes, sir. I told the rent collector, Garry Griffin, about the meter board, then I made an entry in the book we have to keep to record any trouble . . . er, complaints from the boarders, and then there are the letters.'

'Letters?'

'Yes, I wrote to Mr Riley. I took a carbon copy of the letter and posted it to meself and then I posted the original to his office in Double Bay. I done this all three times.' Lenny Green looked decidedly pleased with himself. 'So, Mr Riley got me letter. I posted the first carbon to meself and the second one I give to Gary to give to Riley.'

'Yes, thank you, Mr Green. I think the court understands. Mr Riley received two copies and you kept one.' Danny turned to Harry Prout. 'Your Worship, I submit to the court three unopened envelopes stamped and clearly dated, each approximately two months apart. Mr Green assures me they contain the appropriate carbon copies of the letters sent by him to Mr Riley. I invite the court to open them.'

Hammer jumped to his feet. 'Your Worship, I beg leave of this court to consult with my client.'

'Very well, Mr Hammer.' The coroner banged his gavel three times. 'This court will adjourn for luncheon. We will resume at 2 p.m. sharp. In the meantime I shall retire to my chambers and examine these letters.'

At the resumption of the hearing, with no further questions for Lenny Green, Hammer requested permission to put Riley on the witness stand and also to examine the three letters Green purported to have sent to his client.

'Mr Riley, would you please look at these three letters,' he began. Riley opened each in turn, read them briefly and replaced them in the envelopes. 'Now, sir, do you recall having received the originals of these carbon copies in the mail?'

'No, sir, I do not.'

'Do you recall any instance when Mr Garry Griffin, your rent collector, verbally informed you of Mr Green's concern for the safety of the meter board?'

'No, sir.'

Hammer turned to the coroner. 'Your Worship, I ask permission for Mr Garry Griffin to appear.'

'Permission granted.'

After Griffin was summoned and made his way to the witness stand, Hammer took him through the preliminaries, then said, 'Mr Griffin, if you had been required to pass on a message, an *important* message concerning the *safety* of the residents of a particular boarding house, would you have neglected to do so?'

'Of course not.'

'Will you point out Mr Green in this courtroom, please?'

Griffin pointed to Lenny Green. 'Yeah, him, there.'

'Did you ever receive a message, or three messages in all, each on a separate occasion, to pass on to Mr Riley, concerning the safety of the meter board?'

Griffin shook his head energetically. 'No, absolutely not.'

'Your Worship, I put it to this court that Mr Green, for reasons of his own, has devised an elaborate plot to implicate my client in this meter-board fiasco. I ask that you strike this evidence from the record.'

Harry Prout seemed surprised at the request, but apart from raising his eyebrows managed to restrain himself. 'However interesting such a theory may be, this inquiry does not accept the notion of a plot to implicate your client, unless you are prepared to offer a great deal more evidence of Mr Green's ulterior motives, Mr Hammer. This suggestion, notion, request is not accepted and will not appear on the record of this inquiry unless you wish to offer such proof. Do you wish to do so now?'

'Not at this time, Your Worship.'

The coroner turned to Danny. 'Do you wish to cross-examine the witness, Mr Dunn?'

Danny rose to his feet and in a paraphrase of Steel Hammer said, 'Your Worship, I put it to this court that my learned friend, for reasons of his own, has devised an elaborate plot in his lunch hour to implicate Mr Green in what he calls this meter-board fiasco!'

A roar of laughter travelled through the courtroom and was only silenced by a great deal of gavel banging from the coroner. 'You will withdraw your statement, Mr Dunn,' Harry Prout demanded.

'I withdraw the statement, Your Worship, and do not wish to cross-examine this witness. But I request permission to present a witness to substantiate Mr Green's assertion that Mr Riley visited the premises upon receiving the third notification of the faulty meter board, and that Mr Green did receive a beating instigated by Mr Riley on that occasion. May I call Mr Jack Steven Medlow, Your Worship?'

'Call Jack Steven Medlow!' the clerk of the court announced.

It was the old man Danny had met on the night of the fire, who had congratulated him on putting away the son-in-law who had been beating his daughter and her kids and sexually abusing his granddaughter. 'Mr Medlow, how long have you known Mr Lenny Green, the manager of the boarding house where you resided until it was recently burnt down?'

'Ever since I moved in three year ago, Mr Dunn.'

'Would you say he was a popular manager? Generally speaking, was he well liked?'

'No, sir, he's a mong—, not popular.'

'Is it true that you witnessed him being assaulted?'

'Me and the lad, we seen it happen, Mr Dunn.'

'The lad?'

'Young Jimmy Clark.'

'Can you explain the circumstances?'

'Circumstances?'

'Yes, where you were and what you saw?'

'I don't know why he was beaten up. It happened about a month before the fire. We was in the back of the house, upstairs. I was helping Jimmy to make a kite when he looked out the window. "Uncle Jack, look!" he shouts. I go to the window and there's Lenny Green and these two men in the backyard. One's looking and t'other – a real big bloke – is standing over him and Lenny is on his knees in front of the first bloke – who looks like a toff, good suit and all, and he's begging him not to hurt him, sobbing like, and clutching his shiny shoes. But the bloke just looks down at him with this sort of smile on his face. He's got his hands in his trouser pockets like he's jingling change, then he nods to the big bloke who starts walloping the bejesus out of Lenny. He's using a pick handle and I think he's gunna kill him. But then Lenny collapses like and I reckon he's unconscious, because the big bloke kicks him in the ribs maybe three times and he don't move. Then he grabs him by the collar and drags him through the paspalum and the weeds into a big clump of blackberries that grows against the back fence.'

'And the second man, can you tell me how he was reacting to Mr Green being beaten?' Danny asked.

'Well, he didn't shout out or nothing like that, if that's what you mean. He just watched,' Jack Medlow replied.

'Can you tell the court what happened next, Mr Medlow?'

'Nothin'. They left. We heard the car but we didn't see it – we were in the back of the house, like I said. The boy was very upset and he wanted to run down and help Lenny Green. But I told him we couldn't get involved. It weren't nothing to do with us. I told him Lenny probably had it coming to him. But you know how it is with them kids when they, yer know, 'aven't got all their marbles; they don't see the harm in anyone. So the lad don't take no notice of me and he runs downstairs and the back door is open and he goes out to help Lenny, who hasn't moved in the blackberries. So I go down and together we carry him into the house. He's bleeding something terrible and I reckon we're gunna have to call an ambulance. I send the lad to fetch the kitchen workers but they don't want nothing to do with it. Then Lenny comes to and we take him to his room out front next to the office and he says not to call nobody – he can take care of himself.'

'Mr Medlow, do you recognise anyone in this courtroom who may have been one of the men present in the backyard?'

'Yes, sir, Mr Dunn.' The old bloke turned and pointed at Riley. 'He were the one that stood and watched with his hands in his pockets.'

Danny turned to Harry Prout. 'Your Worship, I wish this court to record that the witness pointed to Mr Riley.' He turned back to Jack Medlow. 'Thank you for your cooperation, Mr Medlow. I have no more questions.'

The court had come alive as the coroner turned to Steel Hammer. 'Do you have any questions for this witness, Mr Hammer?'

Hammer rose, pushing out his gut and his chin, his right-hand thumb hooked into the waistband of his trousers. He stood silent for a moment and glared at Jack Medlow, then barked, 'Mr Medlow, you constantly referred to . . .' he glanced down at his notes, 'let me see, yes . . . the young lad, Jimmy Clark, Jimmy, the boy, and then someone who, I quote, "yer know, 'asn't got all their marbles". What did you mean by that?'

'Jimmy Clark has Down Syndrome, sir.'

'And how old is Jimmy Clark?'

'Fifteen.'

'And, as you put it, he hasn't got all his marbles. You mean he is mentally retarded, is that right?'

'Yes, but —'

'Thank you, Mr Medlow. I don't require any more explanation. What is your age, sir?'

'Seventy-nine.'

'Mr Medlow, how good is your eyesight?'

'It's real good now.'

'Oh, how so?'

'Well, sir, I had two cataracts removed and now I can see good as new.'

'Mr Medlow, how far do you estimate the distance was from the upstairs window to where these two men were alleged to be in the backyard?'

Jack Medlow seemed to be thinking for some time.

'Come now, Mr Medlow, did you not say it was the boy who was mentally retarded?' Hammer barked.

A murmur of protest rose from the gallery. 'Counsel will withdraw that inference,' the coroner said. 'It will be struck from the record.'

'Certainly, Your Worship. I withdraw the inference.'

'Forty feet for the bloke with the pick-axe handle, forty-one feet for Lenny.' He pointed at Riley. 'Forty-two feet for jingle balls!' Jack Medlow said. 'Yeah, I reckon that's it.'

The old man's certainty and irreverence brought another roar of laughter from the gallery and Harry Prout brought down his gavel repeatedly. 'This court will come to silence!' he demanded.

Hammer had met his match. 'Your Worship, both the testimony against and the identification of my client have come from a near-octogenarian who has had recent surgery to both his eyes and who claims to have acted in cooperation with a mentally retarded fifteen-year-old boy. I submit that his statement should not be admitted as evidence.'

Danny jumped to his feet. 'Objection, Your Worship. While Jimmy Clark is too young to appear as a witness,' he turned briefly to Franz, who handed him two sheets of paper, 'I submit for the court record a certificate from a leading psychiatric doctor that states that Jimmy Clark is perfectly capable of acting in a rational and responsible manner and has the mental age of an eleven-year-old. Furthermore, I have here the results of a recent eye test which indicates that Mr Medlow has excellent long-distance vision.' Danny handed the two certificates to the clerk of the court.

'Objection sustained. Thank you, Mr Dunn.' The coroner turned to Steel Hammer. 'I must remind you, Mr Hammer, that it is my responsibility to decide what evidence is acceptable to this court and what is not. There is no jury to influence here and, I assure you, I am not easily intimidated. You may continue.'

'I have no more questions at this point, Your Worship.'

Harry Prout, still bristling with annoyance, glared at Hammer. 'You do not make yourself clear, Mr Hammer. Do you wish the court to dismiss this witness or retain him for later questioning?'

'I have no more questions for this witness, Your Worship,' Hammer said, his features turning a deeper shade of crimson. It was clear his easy day at the office was beginning to turn decidedly sour.

Danny rose. 'I request permission to call Mr Robert James as an expert witness in relation to the true cause of the fire.'

'Permission granted, Mr Dunn.'

'Objection, Your Worship,' Hammer barked. 'We already have expert testimony from the New South Wales Fire Brigade as to the most likely cause of the fire.'

'No, Mr Hammer, your objection is overruled. Mr James has appeared before me on several occasions and I have consistently found his testimony to be cogent. I should remind you that eight people have died and it is my responsibility to investigate the cause of those deaths, and make recommendations to the attorney-general as to whether anyone should be charged with any relevant offences. You may proceed, Mr Dunn.'

'Mr James, as a freelance loss adjuster, have you appeared for several major insurance companies?'

'Yes, sir.'

'What, in your opinion, was the source of the fire and where did it start?'

'From the intensity of the damage in the kitchen area compared to the remainder of the back of the house, it almost certainly started in the kitchen. The ignition site was either the electric stove or the electric water heater. I believe a short circuit in one of these two appliances melted the insulation, isolating the 415-volt circuits leading to the kitchen.'

'Mr James, surely when a short circuit occurs, the fuse terminals contained in a normal domestic fuse box are designed to burn out, cutting the flow of current before a fire can occur?'

'Correct. But in this case, the fuse terminals in both fuse boxes – the 220 volt and 415 volt – had been bridged with heavy copper wire.'

'Ah, Mr Green's reference to copper wire,' Danny noted.

James continued. 'The current would not cut out, as would be normal in the event of a short circuit in the system, but would continue to flow, overheating and eventually burning the insulation material protecting the circuits and causing the area around the wires to burst into flames.'

'Can you explain to the court why the fuse boxes were not destroyed completely?' Danny asked.

'Yes, sir. The materials supporting the fuses are fire resistant and I was able to photograph the fuse box the following morning to show the partly melted copper-wire bridge in both fuse boxes.'

'Your Worship, I wish to submit these photographs supporting Mr James's evidence. We are most fortunate that the fire brigade arrived so promptly and that the front section and hallway weren't destroyed.'

Danny turned back to his witness. 'Mr James, I ask you, is such bridging of fuses normal or acceptable practice?'

'No, sir, it is not only dangerous but also illegal. It would render any insurance cover void.'

'Why, in your opinion, would anyone resort to such a criminally stupid act?'

James, his face serious, replied, 'The cost of wiring premises such as this, with all the modifications to the rooms and the redistribution of electrical current, would be very expensive, sir. By bridging the fuses with copper wire they would be attempting to avoid fuses blowing, which would otherwise have led to the need for expensive rewiring.'

'Mr James, did you see any evidence supporting the previous testimony that the fire was probably started by someone smoking in bed?'

James paused, an old hand in the witness box. 'In this instance I could find no evidence that the fire started in this manner or, for that matter, that it started in any of the cubicles . . . er, bedrooms. The original short almost certainly occurred in the kitchen area in one of two appliances requiring 415 volts.'

'Objection, Your Worship,' Hammer cried, jumping to his feet. 'The kitchen was entirely destroyed. How can the witness maintain with absolute certainty that a 415-volt short started the fire and not someone, as previous experts have attested, upstairs with a lighted cigarette left to burn after they fell asleep?'

'Your worship, before you rule on my learned friend's objection I believe we can offer further proof,' Danny said hurriedly.

'Very well, Mr Dunn.'

'How can you be certain the fire started from a 415-volt short in one of two kitchen appliances requiring such voltage, Mr James?' Danny asked.

'The victim discovered in the hallway proves this conclusively, Mr Dunn. Unfortunately the body – all the bodies were removed illegally before photographs of them could be taken on the site. But I have closely examined the photographs taken in the morgue, as well as those taken by your associate, Mr Landsman.'

'Your Worship, I now tender these photographs. All have been certified by the forensic pathologist examining the bodies and carry his signature.' Franz rose and handed the photographs to the clerk. Danny turned back to James. 'Please continue, Mr James.'

'Well, sir, as you would know, a 240-volt shock is nasty and in some circumstances can kill a person, but a 415-volt shock will cause devastating burns and is far more likely to cause death.

'The photograph shows that the right hand and arm of the deceased found in the hallway beside the meter board is charred to the bone, and remarkably the handle of the brass switch knife is still fused to the remains of the fingers of his right hand. It indicates that he was attempting to turn off the power by pulling the brass switch knife downwards, but with the insulation melted around the knife he was, in effect, grasping a bare, electrically alive piece of red-hot metal. I believe he would have died instantly.'

'Can you venture an opinion about why the deceased would have done such a thing?'

For once James looked surprised. 'Why, to cut the current, to prevent the fire, sir.'

Danny, anticipating an objection, cut in quickly. 'But you said the knife handle was red hot. Would he not have seen this?'

'The hallway would have been filled with smoke. It is entirely possible that, acting in an emergency, he would not have been aware of the condition of the knife switch.'

Danny expected an immediate objection from Hammer – it was a leading question and James had offered a personal opinion in reply – but to his surprise it didn't come. At that precise moment he knew he'd won.

'And, Mr James, could there be any other reason for attempting to throw the switch?' Danny asked.

'No, sir, the switch has only one reason to exist, and that's to shut down the power. It is reasonable to conclude that Mr Laidlaw was attempting to save the lives of the people trapped upstairs and died in the attempt.'

Danny glanced up into the gallery to see Helen with her arms around Bullnose, who was weeping for his old mate. He could also see the expression of intense pride on his wife's pretty face.

Harry Prout was regarded by his younger associates as an old-school magistrate, sliding unnoticed towards the end of his forty years on the bench. He was neither brilliant nor dull, notorious nor outstanding. He had done his job and, although wiser, was going to leave it as honest and straightforward as he had been on his first day on the bench. He had made mistakes, some poor judgments, but they were all his own doing. He had never succumbed to pressure or coercion, and his honesty was as plain and unambiguous as he was himself.

When Green's evidence damning Riley emerged, Prout immediately saw that he was dealing with more than simply a corrupt man with a predilection for perversions that were almost beyond his comprehension as a Presbyterian elder. He saw clearly that he was dealing with larger and systemic corruption that might exist within a municipal council aided and abetted by the police force, the housing commission and therefore the state government. But it was not his job to follow up on this, other than to recommend that the attorney-general's department pursue the issue. He had merely to decide whether Riley had knowingly neglected to ensure the safety of the people in the boarding house and consequently whether he faced the possibility of a charge of manslaughter or even murder.

Almost from the moment Harry Prout began his summing up, aided by a surprisingly animated Ray Onions, Danny knew it spelt disaster for Riley and his Double Bay Syndicate.

'I find the eight deceased victims perished because of an electrical fire resulting from wilfully neglectful conduct on the part of the owners of the premises. Their actions were carried out with a knowing and callous disregard for the consequences. I also recommend that the attorney-general investigate whether the owners of the property were aided and abetted by the failure of council staff, and other government bodies responsible for the safety of tenants, to carry out their duties. I would anticipate strong public interest in this matter, relating as it does to the safety of our citizens.

'I am, in particular, concerned with what appears to be a blatant attempt by Mr Gareth Lachlan Riley to coerce witnesses appearing at this inquest into giving false evidence to protect himself and others. Other parties who should be investigated include Leonard Arthur Green, Sergeant James Patrick White, Mr David Seamus Docker, Mr

Garry Wilfred Griffin, and the directors of the Double Bay Syndicate. All have played a part in these tragic events or in this inquiry, and the evidence they have tendered on behalf of the defendant has proved to be of doubtful veracity. I venture to say there may be others whose names have not appeared in this hearing, all of whom may have shown a contempt for the rules and regulations protecting the citizens of this state, who may have to answer to the attorney-general's department.

'I also wish to comment on the apparent lack of diligence on the part of the police responsible for investigating this tragic affair and their failure to carry out a full and proper investigation of the fire, in particular, their insistence, against all precedent, that the bodies of the deceased be removed before a proper on-site forensic examination.

'Finally, the conduct of Mr Daniel Corrib Dunn, representing one of the surviving victims, has been exemplary and I wish to thank him for the service he has rendered to this coronial inquest on behalf of his client. I wish him and his client and all the victims of this tragic event well in any subsequent actions they may take to pursue damages for the pain, loss and suffering they may have experienced.'

The reporters rushed for the exit. Here was a story they'd been waiting for, a real story that had legs, one they suspected could lead them up the rungs to the very top of the political ladder. Everyone knew that the government was on the nose and that all and sundry were taking bribes. The trick was to prove it. When business and government collude it is extremely difficult to obtain proof of such collusion. It took a case such as this one to wedge the door open a fraction. No government could ignore the findings of the chief coroner, and the attorney-general would have no way of preventing Riley from standing trial for, at the least, a manslaughter charge. Any attempt to do so would indicate clearly that the state government was up to its neck in corruption. Thanks to the separation of powers, once someone was within the court system the government was no longer in control. The justice system was flawed, but it wasn't corrupt and couldn't be manipulated. They had no choice – Riley had to be sacrificed.

While previous cases had achieved notoriety for Nifty Dunn, this one had all the trimmings required for a media bonanza. There were questions in the house and for once the opposition had a field day, in fact a week where, for the first time in years, they had Labor, if not on the canvas, certainly in a corner, covering up while trying to recover from wobbly knees. The coroner's inquiry was the preliminary bout, but everyone knew Riley's trial would be the big stoush.

Danny's 'heroic' role in the inquest was played up by the media for all it was worth. As a story it had all the elements of a pantomime: a proper villain who was exploiting the poor and the helpless, the strongest possible suggestion of a corrupt system that was aiding and abetting him, and a noble hero who was prepared to tilt at the tallest windmills and had elected to do so at no charge.

In fact, Danny was made in media heaven: he was a war hero who sported a rakish eye patch and whose face, showing clear marks of suffering at the hands of the Japanese, drew immediate sympathy. He dressed like a prince and yet he was clearly a man of the people, with a set of social convictions they could readily admire. The usual dirt-diggers found none. His wife was clever and pretty and plainly her own person, a one-time lieutenant colonel in Australian intelligence and soon to be one of only a small number of the country's female academics to have been awarded her doctorate. Somebody leaked the news that Bullnose Daintree, one of the victims of the fire, had been given permanent refuge in the Dunn home, which, despite Danny's attempts at clarification, only increased his heroic status.

The story of the twins out rowing with their father on the harbour four mornings a week also gave Danny the imprimatur of caring father and family man, and to Brenda's joy the *Women's Weekly* did an entire article praising the virtues of the high-profile lawyer and the academic who still managed to be ideal parents to their twin daughters.

Nor did the media neglect the twins in the scramble for more material. Gabrielle was portrayed as a violinist who showed early promise and Samantha was being spoken of as potentially the next Dawn Fraser, ready for the 1966 Commonwealth Games and then the 1968 Olympics, when she would be seventeen years old.

While basing any predictions on the pre-teen talents of either twin was drawing a pretty long bow, this didn't stop the newspapers and magazines from speculating, much to the increasing annoyance of their mother, particularly when she caught Sam cutting out articles from magazines and pasting them into her school scrapbook.

'Samantha, what are you doing?' Helen asked sharply.

'Fixing my scrapbook, Mummy,' Samantha replied, surprised at the tone of her mother's voice.

'Not with that scuttlebutt, darling,' Helen said, realising that Sam was unaware of what she was doing.

'What's scuttlebutt?' Sam asked.

'Gossip, tittle-tattle, rubbish, that sort of thing.'

'But why can't I paste it into my book?'

'Because what it says is simply not true about any of us. The journalists exaggerate to make a good story. For instance, comparing you to Dawn Fraser is nonsense, it's —'

'No it's not, Mummy. I'm going to win three gold medals just like her.'

'Darling, you don't know that.'

Sam looked at her mother, her expression shocked. 'Yes I do. I promised Sammy!' She pointed to the article already pasted into her scrapbook. 'They're only saying what's going to happen.'

'Samantha, it's very good to have ambition, but one thing we don't do is count our chickens before they hatch, and in this case you haven't even laid the eggs.'

'I have! I have so! My coach says I'm doing the same times as Dawn did when she was eleven, and I'm only nine! So that's fair!'

'Darling, Dawn didn't go around at ten or eleven telling everyone she was going to win three gold medals; she just went and did it.' Helen made a mental note to have a quiet word with the twins' swimming coach.

'Well, so shall I!'

'Samantha, I want you to take that article out of your scrapbook at once. You're getting much too big for your boots. In eight years' time, that's nearly as long again as you've been alive, you may get your chance to prove you're right, but until that time we need to be modest.'

Sam looked again at her mother. 'You just don't understand, Mummy! I'm simply not the modest type!'

Helen was hard put to maintain a straight face. 'Perhaps you should take a leaf out of Gabrielle's book. She doesn't boast about the violin, does she now?'

'Mummy, that's silly! There's nothing to boast about! The kids at school put their hands over their ears when she plays; doesn't matter how nice she sounds. They're calling her Catgut. As a matter of fact she's going through a very hard time and I'm helping her. I've told her not to worry, her time will come. And besides, I'm going to give her one of my gold medals!'

Danny might have expected a downturn in business in the period before the Riley trial. After all, he was being touted as the lawyer who had exposed government corruption, finally bringing into the open what everyone already knew. Those colluding with or benefiting from corruption were most often from the big end of town, and not necessarily even Labor supporters, but businessmen are, after all, pragmatists, and seize what opportunities they can. Supporting Danny might have been foolish but there was an election coming up and they might just have been hedging their bets. Whatever the reason, Danny and Franz were offered more work than they could possibly handle, and Danny's reputation amongst the criminal class had, paradoxically, grown.

As for Gareth Lachlan Riley, the coroner's findings began an inexorable process that would lead to his ultimate destruction. He and his wife were found to be the sole directors of the Double Bay Syndicate, the other members from the protestant social elite having proved much too savvy to agree to sit on the board. The business had been highly profitable and their original contributions had long since been returned with a substantial profit. As Franz put it, it was time to cut their losses and head for the Bellevue Hill(s), the exclusive suburb on the rise above Double Bay where most of them had residences.

Every door was suddenly closed to Riley. The brown-envelope mob big and small – municipal councillors, members of parliament, ministers and senior public servants – refused to accept his calls. His wife, Kathleen, resigned from the Black and White Ball Committee, as well as from numerous other high-profile charity organisations.

Riley had committed the ultimate offence of being found out. Fanned by the righteous flames of the new talkback radio, television and the newspapers, former recipients of Riley's largesse now looked blank when his name was mentioned, and silently and collectively decided he was to be abandoned to a fate none of them could alter even if they'd wanted to – the usual escape clause for those who routinely compromise their principles. A reinvigorated police investigation quickly provided a damning prosecution brief for the committal proceedings. Six months after the coroner's inquiry, Riley was arraigned to face committal proceedings in the Darlinghurst Magistrates Court. The senior magistrate decided that a prima facie case had been established on a raft of charges, the most serious of these being manslaughter.

Several days before the hearing was due to begin, Danny received a call from Steel Hammer, Riley's barrister.

'How are you, dear boy?'

Danny, slightly taken aback, recovered quickly. 'Well, I can't say this isn't a surprise, Steel. To what do I owe this honour?'

'Thought you might like to have lunch. The Australian, tomorrow?'

'I'm pretty busy, mate, and it's awfully short notice. Is it important?' Danny said, regaining the initiative.

Steel chuckled. 'Let me put it this way: my client wants to make a gesture – I think, an important one.'

'Riley?'

'Yes, we go to court in three days. I must say I'm relieved to see the court hasn't appointed you as prosecutor. Young bloke called Wilder, heard of him?'

'Can't say I have.'

'We're submitting a not guilty plea.'

'Hmm, no comment, except to say young doesn't necessarily mean dumb.'

Steel Hammer laughed. 'What are you saying – you don't like our chances?'

'I wouldn't want to venture an opinion; besides, I'm not a betting man. My business with Riley is over.'

'Well, no, actually. I think he has one final piece of business he wishes me to conduct with you on his behalf, hence the lunch.'

'Okay. The Australian? That the golf club at Rose Bay or the Australia club?'

'The golf club.'

Danny chuckled. 'I'm a tyke, mate. You sure it's kosher?' he said cleverly, bringing a Jewish reference in as well.

Hammer sighed theatrically. 'Oh well, I'm sure it will be perfectly fine. I guess there are one or two papists on the kitchen and dining-room staff.'

'Wouldn't be too sure, we're usually fairly particular where we work,' Danny replied.

Hammer laughed. 'One o'clock then, parking lot is at the back of the club house. Look forward to seeing you. Cheerio then, old son.'

Franz was away finalising a property deal in Orange so Danny had no one to talk to about the luncheon appointment at the dreaded Australian Golf Club. But at dinner that night he mentioned the upcoming trial to Helen.

'Lucky he didn't get charged with murder,' Helen said.

'No, unlucky. This magistrate's obviously after him.'

'What do you mean, darling? Isn't it the lesser charge?' Helen asked, curious.

'Juries are more likely to convict on a manslaughter charge than on murder and it carries a maximum sentence of life imprisonment. Besides, you have to prove intent for murder, which would not be possible in this case. Eight dead in a fire isn't going to get him off lightly. He'd be better off pleading guilty. Fighting this one would be foolish. One look at the photographs, particularly of Sammy after his attempt to save those poor people, and any sympathy vote is gone.'

'If you say it would be foolish to plead not guilty, why wouldn't his barrister advise him not to do so?'

'Can't say. Perhaps Riley chose to ignore the advice of Hammer, who, by the way, called me today.'

'What – Riley's barrister? I should have thought you'd be the last person he'd want to speak to.'

'Well, yes, I admit it came as a surprise. He's invited me to have lunch with him tomorrow. You'll never guess where.'

Helen laughed. 'Next time give me a hard question. The Australian Gold Club, of course!'

'You bugger!'

'I'm not just a pretty face, Daniel Corrib Dunn. Whatever for?'

'That's just it, I have absolutely no idea.'

At lunch the following day Steel Hammer seemed relaxed and his usual urbane self. He was surprised when Danny declined the offer of a good bottle of red, but went ahead and ordered it anyway. Danny ordered a soda, lime and bitters in a tall glass. Hammer clutched his wine and began. 'Before I say anything else, Danny, it would be remiss of me not to say what a fine demolition job you did on my client at the coroner's inquiry, speaking purely professionally, of course.'

'Of course . . . and thanks,' Danny replied. 'No hard feelings, then?'

'Good lord, no, dear boy. All a part of our profession. Sometimes the law is an ass and sometimes it makes an ass out of us. The thing is, my client was assured it would be all right on the day.'

'Lawless from the attorney-general's department?' Danny ventured.

'I see you're already a step ahead of me, old son.'

'Yeah, well, there are nicer human beings on the planet.'

'Quite. Since the inquiry, Riley has discovered the friends he thought he had in high places are no longer taking his calls. Once things blew up they didn't want a bar of him.'

'That's understandable. He's not exactly flavour of the month.' Danny paused. 'Steel, I'm afraid I don't give a toss. My history with Riley goes way back. If you're looking for sympathy you've come to the wrong man.'

'Oh dear no. You're quite wrong. In fact my client, in a sense anyway, wishes to show remorse.'

'Huh?' Danny was stunned. 'Are you joking? Riley and remorse – that's an impossible juxtaposition, an oxymoron.'

'Well, of course, the remorse does come with a sting in the tail, though I hasten to say not one intended for you.'

'Riley realises he can't undo the past, but he wants to get back at the people who happily took his money and then, as happily, left him in the shit to fend for himself.'

'Who? His fellow shareholders? He's got Buckley's. No, the brown-envelope mob. It extends all the way from the bottom rung to the top of the ladder,' replied Hammer.

'And you're not going to make this a part of your defence?'

Steel Hammer sipped at his wine. 'If the prosecutor – Wilder – has half a brain, you know he'll make it difficult to introduce this information as admissible evidence in the context of a manslaughter charge.'

'You're right. And the media, they'd lap it up?'

'Yes, we thought of that, but to what purpose? The media already have their villain. It's not going to help Riley if he's seen as dobbing in his corrupt mates.'

'Does he care?'

'Well, yes. While he wants the material used to the utmost effect, he genuinely wants to apologise, in as much as he can, for the business of Glossy Denmeade's boots.'

'How do you know about that? He told you?' Danny said, his surprise obvious.

'Yes.'

'I'm not sure we – that is, those of us who came back from the camps – would be prepared to accept an apology. I certainly wouldn't accept one from him.'

Steel Hammer sighed. 'Be that as it may, he wants me to give this to you.' He reached down beside his chair and then handed a large manila envelope to Danny. 'Open it,' he instructed.

Danny withdrew a half-inch-thick wad of foolscap sheets and began to read the top typewritten page. It was immediately apparent what it was, as well as the fifty or so pages that followed. 'Shit!' Each of the pages was headed with a name and address followed by dates and amounts but also, surprisingly, bank account numbers in a number of cases. Danny would later do his homework and discover that the fifty people receiving kickbacks extended across the spectrum – housing-commission personnel, police, right up to an assistant commissioner, and various members of the councils in which the eighty or so slum boarding houses were to be found. In addition, the list of politicians included all the local members, as well as the ministers for housing, health and social welfare.

'God, this is dynamite!'

'Riley said I should give it to you. Of course, at this stage it's only allegations, but he said it will stand up in court. On the last page is a list of witnesses over the eight years.'

Danny looked at Hammer, bemused. 'If there are any strings attached, forget it. Why me . . . why of all people give it to me?'

'Well, come to think of it, it's not a bad choice. You have a reputation for going after the bad guys. You may have brought him undone but that doesn't mean he doesn't admire your persistence. Maybe it's his way of saying he's sorry, and there are no strings attached. What he did say to me was, "Tell Dunn to use this in any way he likes and I'll back him up in court. I have a feeling the bastards are going to come after him. Having this list will help."' Riley's barrister paused. 'I agree, you've upset a lot of powerful politicos with this one, Danny.'

Danny leaned back. 'Well, whoever would have thought this possible? Tell him thanks.'

'Right then, I recommend the roast beef – they carve it at the table – and the Yorkshire pudding is special,' Steel Hammer said, unfolding his napkin and reaching over to refill his glass.

Helen, of course, was most anxious to hear what happened at the lunch and called Danny's office mid-afternoon, unable to wait any longer. 'Danny, how'd you go?' she asked when he came on the phone.

Danny pretended not to understand. 'Go with what? Unusual for you to call in the middle of the afternoon, darling,' he said, teasing her further.

'Bastard! At lunch?'

'Oh, that.'

'Danny, I could cheerfully kill you sometimes! Was it good or bad?'

'Frankly, I'm not sure, but it changes a lot of things . . . but then again, maybe not. Look, I'll be home early. I'll tell you then. It's a bit complicated over the phone. Do you think the twins could stay at Mum's tonight?'

'What about Samantha's swimming? Saturday is a big training day.'

'I'll pick her up at the Hero, 7 a.m. sharp,' Danny said. 'Perhaps we could go to dinner. Nothing over the top – Charity's in Darling Street? The pasta's great. It's Friday night, so we'd better book.'

At Charity's that night Danny handed the envelope to Helen. 'Take a squiz at this, darling.'

'Is this what Riley's barrister gave you?' Helen asked, accepting the envelope.

'Yeah, all the king's horses and all the king's men. Riley's pay-off sheets.'

Helen started to read. 'Heavens to Betsy! If I wasn't a lady I'd say, "Jesus!" Half the local council is in on it – Jack O'Shea, deputy mayor.' She flipped pages looking for more names she recognised. 'The housing minister and that ingrate O'Hearn, our odious local member; every time I see him he's got fatter and more oleaginous in his manner. Will you go to the police with this?'

Danny laughed. 'Not your best idea, my love. There are at least half a dozen senior officers' names on that list, including Don Barnes, one of the assistant commissioners.'

'What then?'

'There's an election coming up.'

'So?'

Danny was silent and Helen said suddenly, 'Danny, you're not?'

'Not what?'

'Going to stand?'

Danny gave Helen a wry grin. 'Darling, if I use this list now and Labor loses the election, who do you think they'll blame?'

'So, what are you saying – you'll use it to get elected? As blackmail?' Helen, deeply shocked, was as plain spoken as ever.

'No, of course not! *Jesus*, Helen!'

'Well, thank God for that!'

'If you were a Catholic, I'd make the priest order you to say three hundred Hail Marys and ask God to forgive you! The only way to fix something like this, as well as get Balmain out of the doldrums, is from the inside. I want your permission to stand for preselection, to put my name up against the fat oleaginous bastard, as you put it.'

'Danny, you're dreaming. They wouldn't stand for that for one moment! You're already on the nose from the inquiry.'

'Well, I don't suppose they could stop me nominating. What do you think?'

'I think you're out of your mind. They'll find a dozen ways of rejecting your nomination. Danny, for heaven's sake, you're anathema to the Labor Party at the moment.'

'But we're both still members.'

'Until they find a way of throwing us out on our necks.'

'Yeah, maybe, but there's no harm in trying.'

Helen pointed at the manila envelope. 'And what are you going to do about that?'

'Nothing for the moment. Let's just think of it as insurance and not confuse the issues.'

'Danny, are you sure about nominating for preselection? Walking into the lion's den with all those hungry resentful lions waiting?'

'If you'll be there with me, darling. At least it will bring everything to a head and we'll know what to do next.'

Helen smiled. 'I'm not sure it's a good idea for both of us to be eaten. Who will take care of the twins? Sometimes, Daniel Corrib Dunn, I wish you weren't so bloody obsessed.'

The following Monday Danny put in his nomination to the preselection committee and waited for the reaction. It wasn't long in coming. The phone rang on Wednesday morning and Keri put the call through to Danny. 'It's a Mr Jack O'Shea. The president. He didn't say what of.'

'Ah, put him through, Keri. He's president of the Balmain branch of the Labor Party; I've been expecting his call.' Danny waited until he heard the click. 'Hello, that you, Jack?'

'Danny, comrade, I'm ringing 'bout you nominatin' for the seat.'

'Oh, yeah.'

'Look, mate, fair go. The party is coppin' a fair bit of bad publicity – but then you'd know all about that.'

'Go on,' Danny urged.

'Well, we don't want a nasty preselection fight, do we?'

'Why does it have to be nasty, Jack? The branch members will decide; I'll accept that.'

'Comrade, there's an election coming. We got to present a united front – you know what I mean, mate.'

'Yeah, business as usual, let's not rock the boat, eh? Don't you think it might be time to represent the people of Balmain and not shonky mates and outside business interests? Isn't that what local branches are all about? Some people may think it's time to introduce a little fresh blood.'

O'Shea's tone of voice quickly changed. 'Danny, don't give me that shit! The only blood shed around Balmain will be yours. We was takin' care of old people 'til you came along! We lost four hundred old people when they closed them boarding houses down your street; shops lost their profits, pubs; old people thrown onto the street because of what you gone and done – everyone losing because of it. Wait 'til we're through with you, mate! You won't know your fucking arse from yer elbow! You don't have the fuckin' numbers and you ain't gunna turn this suburb into a place for fuckin' poofters and lawyers!'

The man was so far over the top that Danny found he wasn't even angry. O'Shea was the perfect example of everything that was wrong with Balmain, everything Danny was fighting to change. 'Well, we'll see, won't we, Jack? I'm not withdrawing. Last time I looked we were still living in a free country.'

The Labor apparatchiks went to work with a vengeance, and money flowed like water in the pubs as O'Hearn's mob spread lager goodwill to one and all. The rumour mill began to grind, and the wives of two shop stewards claimed that Danny had raped them when he was in his late teens – a time in his young life when he had had to beat back the girls with a stick. But the old business of calling a man a pig was once again successful, and, as Helen had feared, Danny lost the preselection by the narrowest of margins.

'Well, Don Quixote, what now?' Helen asked as she and Danny spent the evening together on the upstairs verandah, she with a glass of white wine and he with his evening pot of tea.

'Fuck 'em, darling. I'll stand as an Independent. I'm not going to let them get away with dishing the dirt like that. We came within a hair's breadth of winning; it's worth another go, if only to show the bastards we're not beaten.'

'Please, darling, don't. You won't stand a chance, and you know the rules – stand against a Labor candidate and you forfeit your membership of the party.'

'Do we really care? I mean, after what's happened?'

'Well, no, I don't.'

'Well? Don't forget Dr Evatt did it – stood as an Independent in 1927 and won!'

'Hmm, not quite the same though, is it? Please think about it carefully, Danny. I know you're feeling hurt, but it's a big step and you don't want to lose twice. Wouldn't it be far better to wait until the election after this one – let the air clear a little?'

Danny thought for a moment. 'No, bugger it! If I lose I'll have had the experience, or I'll know not to try next time.'

'Not *if* – you will lose, darling, but I'm with you every inch of the way. This isn't the first windmill you've toppled, to everyone's surprise.'

'Okay, but nothing changes. This is going to be your year, Helen. You worked hard for that doctorate and your career is not going to suffer for the sake of mine. This election is not to interfere. When you're busy, Brenda will be at my side and Half Dunn will be my campaign manager. Agreed?'

Helen rose from her wicker chair, sat on his lap and kissed him. 'Yes, my impetuous leader!'

Riley pleaded not guilty and received twelve years' jail on the manslaughter charge. 'Were it not for your war service,' the judge intoned, 'I would have considered a life sentence.' In addition, he received a further five years for attempting to pervert the course of justice. Riley had fallen far from the heights of Bellevue Hill.

His wife, Kathleen, pleading that she was a token director and knew nothing about the business, subsequently received a six-month sentence, which for her proved to be life, for every social aspiration she might ever have entertained was denied her forever.

Danny was still not through with Riley. *Four Corners*, the new serious-minded weekly news program on ABC-TV, had prepared an exposé on slum landlords. Danny didn't reveal to them the existence of the Riley list, nor did he give them any details of the story of Glossy Denmeade's boots; instead, he suggested that they visit the Reverend Ayliffe's widow and request permission to peruse his war diaries in which the Anglican parson had written a full account of the incident. After John Ayliffe's death, Danny had kept his diary, fountain pen and wristwatch and returned them to his wife when he got back to Australia. He told *Four Corners* that if, having read the account in the diary, they wished to know more, he would arrange a lunch at the George Street RSL for the director and cameraman to meet several ex-prisoners of war who had been with him on the Burma Railway. He regretted that he couldn't be present at the lunch, for reasons that would become obvious. This time Danny wasn't taking any chances; the Reverend Ayliffe was an officer, not an enlisted man, so the league of gentlemen soldiers would be unable to deny the story.

The program about Riley and Glossy Denmeade's boots caused a sensation and reignite the whole issue of corruption, and although the *Four Corners* team lacked the firm evidence needed to prove government corruption, it wasn't hard for viewers to make up their own minds. Danny received a great deal of publicity for standing as an Independent in Balmain. People began to speculate that he might even win.

But Labor won after scurrilous rumours were spread in the last week before the election. Danny lost, but only on a count-back, the margin just eleven votes. He had scared the living daylights out of the Labor Party, which had automatically expelled him, and had lived to fight another day. Danny, instead of being put well and truly in his place, remained, in local Labor terms, Public Enemy Number One.

Riley made the headlines one last time before hanging himself in his cell. Glossy's boots were put on display in the foyer of the George Street RSL, and for a week the lunchtime queue to view them stretched an entire city block.

But the Glossy Denmeade story had one more twist: Gwen Ayliffe gave her husband's war diaries to the Canberra War Memorial. As soon as they were read, it was discovered that the Reverend Ayliffe had dealt in some detail with Sergeant Major Dunn's leadership during the time he was responsible for the prisoners in the camp. There were descriptions of the numerous occasions when Danny had stood up to Colonel Mori on behalf of his men, at real peril to himself. On a number of occasions, Captain Ayliffe had recommended a citation for Sergeant Major Dunn. Belated proceedings were instigated by the director, and on Anzac Day 1962, in a ceremony at Government House in Sydney, the Governor-General awarded Daniel Corrib Dunn the Military Medal. Moments after it had been pinned to his chest, Helen whispered, 'Take back what you said about all officers, Sergeant Major Dunn.'

But 1962 was really Helen's year, when she was awarded her doctorate from University College London. She was certainly not the first Australian woman to earn a doctorate, but she was only the second to have earned it in Egyptology, a discipline dominated by men. Women were not generally willing or able to spend long periods away from their families at digs in Egypt, so Egyptology research was restricted to very committed single women, who had to fight for recognition and often faced extraordinary challenges in what was regarded as a 'man's world'.

Helen had already achieved the status of senior lecturer at Sydney University, and if you had asked a member of the faculty (almost all male) what she might expect in the years to come, even the most charitable would not have been encouraging: senior lecturer for ten to twenty years and then perhaps an associate professorship if she were too remarkable to overlook, but elevation beyond that would be, frankly, impossible. Australian academia provided safe jobs with reasonable retirement plans, and although there were a few stars, some of whom resided in the Ancient History department, none of them were women.

At first, Helen had pinned her hopes on one of the new universities that were being mooted by the federal government. One such was

Macquarie University, due to begin its first undergraduate year in 1967 and two years later to establish a Department of Ancient History. With a doctorate under her belt and seven years to impress (lobby might be a better word), she'd hoped to secure the position of senior lecturer at Macquarie and take it from there. One thing was certain: she would never be given a more senior position at Sydney.

But Helen soon learned that all positions at the new Macquarie University, from senior lecturer up, would be advertised internationally, and that the minimum experience required would be ten years post-doctoral practice. Further inquiry revealed that any university in the world with a vacancy in ancient history was always swamped with highly qualified applicants. The dean of the still-to-be-opened Macquarie University advised Helen that her lack of post-doctoral teaching experience would almost certainly eliminate her in the first round.

A tiny terror was beginning to make itself felt within her; she was essentially a woman who needed stimuli – what Danny would call action – and with her doctorate behind her and the predictable years of teaching stretching ahead, she was beginning to question her choice of vocation. In just a few years the twins would be teenagers and increasingly independent, Gabrielle occupied with music and Sam with swimming.

Helen had found that she couldn't ignore Danny's political campaign and discovered, to her surprise, that she was a very good strategist. Coming so close to winning against all the odds had made her realise how very much she missed the thrust and parry of life outside the university. Danny was almost certainly committed to fighting the next election. Far from being discouraged, he'd had a glimpse of victory and what it might mean. 'Darling, the only way things will change is if we are in a position to influence them, to call at least some of the shots.' Helen was beginning to realise that she might never be able to call any of the shots in her academic life.

Brenda was still enjoying being a grandmother and doted on the twins. She'd pick them up in the morning, and then take them from school to swimming training and then, as often as not, back to the Hero for a spoil afternoon tea before bringing them home. Helen and Brenda had always got on like a house on fire and Helen admired her enormously. The Hero was by now the biggest pub in Balmain, and Brenda, always careful with money, was, by local standards, now a wealthy woman. But more and more Brenda spoke of retiring. She'd been in pub life for forty-two of her sixty years, and with six o'clock closing no longer the law and pubs open until ten at night, she was feeling the strain. While Half Dunn had come good, so to speak, and ran the pub after six, he too wasn't getting any younger.

This had all come to a head when Rose, Brenda's ageing mother, visited the chickens early one afternoon and didn't return. Patrick went looking for her that evening, and found her sitting with her back against the laying boxes, dead from a heart attack or, as Brenda silently believed, a broken heart.

Brenda had driven down to Wagga for the funeral and afterwards stayed for a week to try to persuade Patrick to return with her to Sydney. He'd stubbornly refused. 'This is my bed of thorns and this is where I shall lay, girlie.' She'd secretly been grateful that he'd wanted to stay put – a cantankerous 83-year-old man was not what she needed in her life – but she was aware of her responsibilities as his oldest living child. Before she returned to Sydney, she'd elicited a promise, in return for a weekly stipend, that her twin sisters would take turns visiting the farm once a week to check on his welfare. The arrangement wasn't to last long; a month after Rose's death, Patrick left a short note on the kitchen table, held down with a jar of Rose's homemade marmalade. Brusque to the last it simply read:

Gone to join Rose.

He'd put the barrel of his single-gauge shotgun to his mouth and pulled the trigger.

Brenda returned from Wagga after she had given Patrick a funeral with all the trimmings, which was attended by the twins and their fifteen children, all of whom were dry-eyed throughout the ceremony. At the wake, held at her old pub, Brenda watched as her sisters, brothers-in-law and several nieces and nephews got motherless drunk, then summoned a taxi to take them all home in two separate trips.

She was devastated that her father, in comparatively good health for his age, would think to take his life, and she wept quietly at the realisation that he had loved her mother but had been too bitter with life to show her affection of any kind. And her mother, the soft enduring Rose, had finally given up and died of a broken heart. While Brenda and Half Dunn had grown closer over the years, she returned from Wagga determined to mend any matters between them and to give him the love he deserved in return for the loyalty he had shown her.

She'd been back only a few days when she drew Helen aside after delivering the twins home one afternoon and asked if she would come to dinner the next night.

'We'd love to. It's a Friday, so the twins can stay up later, and I'm sure Danny will be free.'

'No, me darlin' girl, this is just you and me. Mick has been told to make himself scarce and I was hoping Danny would be home to look after the twins.'

Helen often spent time alone with Brenda, and they regularly had lunch together at Charity's, where they knew the chef – Pamela, a pretty Queensland girl – and her husband Graham, who was chief bottle-washer and roustabout, as well as a gifted clarinet player. Italian pasta dishes dominated, and although the food was plain, it was excellent. The whole family ate their evening meal at the Hero once or twice a month, usually on a Saturday evening, so it was an unusual request but one to which Helen was quick to agree. She knew Brenda must have something on her mind.

Brenda had prepared a macaroni cheese and she served it with a salad almost immediately after Helen arrived. Then, over a cup of tea, she said, 'Helen, it's now sixteen years into your marriage and I feel I know a great deal about you, darlin', and all of it's good.'

Helen grinned, waiting. 'But?'

'I've never seen you sew.'

Helen breathed a sigh of relief. She hadn't known what to expect after being summoned, albeit nicely, by her mother-in-law to dinner at the Hero. Certainly, she could never have guessed it was to discuss sewing. 'I suppose that's because I don't. Until Mrs O'Shea left to stay with her son in Queensland, she did the mending and, I confess, while we did a little embroidery at school, it wasn't called the Presbyterian Ladies' College for nothing. Sewing was thought to be only slightly ahead of scrubbing floors in the skills required to prepare us for marriage. In fact, anything you couldn't do out of bed while wearing white gloves and a hat – apart from a little genteel cooking, perhaps – was deeply frowned upon.'

'Embroidery? Well, I suppose that's something,' Brenda said.

'If you don't mind my asking, it does seem a curious question. Is it important?' Helen asked, intrigued.

'Yes and no. I daresay you can learn, and embroidery isn't a bad place to start.'

'Brenda, what on earth are you talking about? By the way, I should confess that I wasn't all that interested in embroidery,' Helen added, laughing. 'My mum used to finish off most of the pieces I attempted – I remember once throwing a particularly nauseating piece out of the train window – but without her help I'd never have passed what was sneeringly known as domestic science.'

'Would you be after learning if I was to show you?' Brenda asked, still not explaining. 'You see, I don't want to pass it on to one of the twins' daughters – my twin sisters, I mean, not your twins – they're a poor and disappointing lot and really can't be entrusted with such an important family matter.'

Helen held up her hand. 'Brenda, you have to stop right there.' She took a quick breath. 'What are you talking about?'

'Why, the quilt, of course!'

'What quilt?'

'Well, I'll be darned, that boy really *can* keep his mouth shut,' Brenda said, pleased. 'Mick says he told Danny about it, but asked him to keep it confidential.'

'When? Danny doesn't keep much from me.'

'In 1945, after he got back from the war.'

'Maybe he did, that was a long time ago,' Helen said, feeling a little exasperated.

'You'd have remembered if he had, darlin',' Brenda assured her. 'Come along, I've laid it out in the dining room.' She rose and Helen followed her.

Laid out on the table, its sides almost reaching the floor, was a multi-coloured quilt that, at first glance, looked as if it was made up of different-sized patches of cloth, completely lacking the symmetry usually associated with an Irish quilt. Nevertheless, it was vibrant and eye-catching and might even have been described as spectacular, except for the traditional border. It seemed to be made up of isolated scenes peppered with Celtic crosses.

'Goodness!' Helen exclaimed, not sure how to react.

'It's the quilt of Sorrow and Travail with the Far Corner of Joy,' Brenda explained, as if such a name were natural enough. 'Come, let me take you through the generations – only five, I fear, because it was only then that my great-great grandmother Caoilainn learned the gentle art of quilting, when she was serving as a lady's maid at Kylemore Castle, County Connaught.' Brenda lifted part of the great quilt that hung over one end of the table. 'See, it is embroidered here in Gaelic. I'll translate it for you.'

'Brenda, you never said you spoke Gaelic!'

'No, no, darlin', that I don't. These words were taught to me by Rose.' Brenda first read them in Gaelic and then recited them in English.

This is the work of Caoilainn and it be
with the greatest humility dedicated to:
The most pious Saint Caoilainn who quickly

won the esteem and affection of her sister
nuns by her exactness to every duty, as
also by her sweet temper, gentle confiding
disposition and unaffected piety.

The more Helen looked at the quilt, the more fascinated she became with it. It wasn't a thing of great beauty, yet it was undoubtedly a magnificent repository of memory and, judging by the dates, it was a real expression of Ireland's history. Brenda explained that it dealt with seven generations, because Caoilainn, whose splendid name meant 'fair and slender', had started her quilt with the stories of her grandfather and then her father, so that the first incident concerning her family dated back to the middle of the eighteenth century. It was a two-hundred-year history of the major events in the lives of an Irish family, and it struck Helen like a bolt that she was now a part of it, part of the quilt, part of the trail of sorrow and travail with the far corner of joy.

'Let me take you through the history of one side of Danny's family, which, of course, is now one side of the twins' family, and then I'll explain why you are here tonight.'

Helen listened, fascinated, as Brenda took her through each incident she knew about, although there were many whose meaning had been lost in time that she couldn't explain. The scenes, montages and symbols, often very crudely done in appliqué and embroidery, were quite bewildering but also wonderful. Some had a short explanation stitched beside them in Gaelic and later in English, while a few had quite long explanations. Each quilt-maker decided for herself what she wished to represent without recourse to any other family members. The quilt was never on display, never explained, and the decision to record sorrow and travail, or to pay a rare visit to work in the far corner of joy, was absolutely the responsibility of the oldest woman in any particular generation.

But by looking at the dates, diligently embroidered beside often mystifying or quixotic scenes wrought with scraps of appliquéd cloth, Helen realised several of them involved even earlier events. The quilt, she estimated, covered a period of two hundred years, but it seemed fairly certain that the oldest images would have derived from oral history recorded by the first of the quilters. These seemed to start around 1740, then in 1798 came the Irish Rebellion. The 1829 emancipation of the Catholics was commemorated in the far corner of joy, but travail and sorrow followed in 1845 with the beginning of the potato famine, then again in 1867 with the abortive Fenian uprising.

Helen couldn't identify any of the events that followed, until the First World War, by which time Brenda's parents were already in Australia. Rose had added the deaths of her two sons, slaughtered in Britain's unholy war fighting against the Germans. It was curious, or perhaps poignantly sad, that the only item in the far corner of joy was the Catholic emancipation, until Rose's addition of the birth of her little son, the first of the family to be born on Australian soil. Brenda had added Danny's birth, and now it would be Helen's task to add the birth of the twins, a responsibility she would take very seriously. Brenda had earlier pointed out a small paragraph embroidered in Gaelic, which explained that the quilt had been blessed with holy water and a promise made that, come what may, whether travail or disaster, the quilt must remain forever within the family.

The back of the ancient quilt was also uniquely revealing for it carried the outline of a tree with hundreds of names and birth dates, each on a single green leaf. But at the base of the tree lay hundreds of leaves in autumnal colours, yellows, reds, purples, russet, pinks and browns, and on each leaf was embroidered the same name as appeared on a green leaf, and the date of that family member's death.

'Helen, you are the next in line as Keeper of the Quilt. Will you accept? And, in your turn, will you hand it over to one of the twins?' Brenda finally asked.

Helen wasn't in the least religious but nevertheless found 'the oath', as Brenda described it, and the responsibility for the quilt overwhelmingly meaningful. Close to tears, she gazed at her mother-in-law, a woman she had learned to love and respect far more than she did her own mother. 'Brenda, I would be enormously honoured, but I cannot sew or appliqué. Any idea you may have of my embroidery skills should be dismissed from your mind, and I draw like an intelligent five-year-old.'

Brenda laughed. 'That, darlin', is why I called you in now and not on my deathbed. Are you willing to learn?'

Helen gulped. Of all the unlikely skills she might have thought to acquire, quilting, sewing, appliqué and embroidery were not among them. 'Mother, I am overwhelmed with the honour, but most fearful of the result,' she found herself saying, in a formal manner that seemed to be required in the presence of the eccentric but venerable quilt. Helen, biting her bottom lip, thought hard. It was a decision from which there could be no turning back. Finally, she spoke again. 'Yes,' she said, 'yes, I am prepared to learn, but you in turn must be prepared to tell me if I don't succeed.'

Brenda laughed. 'The entire quilt has been made by ordinary women; some of them knew their craft, and others knew little of it but accepted it as a part of their family life. Thank you, Helen. Can you give me four hours a week, one hour each night?'

'For how long?'

'You will decide that yourself. The only measure you have, the only comparison, is against those who went before you.'

And so began the quilting lessons, the bloody and cramped fingers, the tiny invisible stitches always too visible, constantly unpicked and done over, often a dozen times. Helen was a strong woman who held herself in high regard, not from any conceit but because she approached most things in life with full confidence that she would be able to do well if she only tried her best.

The task was twofold: to maintain the quilt, and to add the information, written or pictorial, that symbolised her own generation. Restoration involved carefully mending the work of the past while trying to preserve it's integrity. For historical clarity the embroidered words were repaired precisely, the spelling errors maintained, and the colours matched, even though they were often badly faded. The task was to match the original work as closely as possible and to preserve the quilt in its original form. Brenda, while competent, could claim no special talent, although some of the long-dead quilters might well have been considered serious artists.

After three months, Helen had gained sufficient humility to realise that she was dealing with a serious art form, and while she would perhaps always be an amateur, her naturally competitive spirit meant that, at the very least, she hoped to become a serious amateur. The curious thing was why she cared so much. Her work would seldom if ever be seen, and she wasn't competing with anyone except the long dead. Then one day she realised that she was doing what the tomb decorators did in ancient Egypt – making beautiful decorations to be admired by the ghosts and phantoms who peopled the afterworld, and, curiously, this notion spurred her on. She wanted to excel for her own sake; she wanted to know that, in her own eyes, she had not let herself down nor those who came before her. It was a strangely gratifying feeling.

As an Egyptologist, her task had been to attempt to reveal the past through a scrap of linen bandage impregnated with traces of resin; now, as a quilter, she was attempting to understand the travails and sorrows of life in another time, as well as express what was most significant about the life of her own family, visiting, she hoped, the far corner of joy which suggested that, in the field of human endeavour, sorrow was in far more ready supply than joy. As Keeper of the Quilt, she was at once anthropologist, art historian, custodian, restorer and potential contributor. Helen accepted this task with a zeal that, if it had been manifest in Danny, she might have judged obsessive.

In the time that she worked on the quilt with Brenda as her taskmistress, Helen grew very close to the older woman. They had always enjoyed each other's company and the differences in their backgrounds and education seemed to count for little: both were professionals, lived busy lives, and much of their free time was spent with their families, so that the intimacy women are capable of feeling with each other had never had time or space to truly blossom. Now, as they unpicked and stitched, patched and replaced, they talked endlessly. Brenda told of her stoic parents and the tragic deaths of her brothers, and of how this had left her father a bitter and cruel man. Her mother, Brenda and her sisters had become the butt of his cruelty, disdain and indifference. He had lost his sons, who had been butchered in the First World War by Britain, the great mother of all whores, leaving him with only the burden of daughters, for whom he had, if anything, a harsh love but little understanding. He simply handed these responsibilities to his wife. His irascible nature and stubbornness meant that he lay on a bed of thorns that Brenda had come to think was largely of his own making.

Unlike Helen, Brenda had had a childhood of grinding labour and fear. The terrible beatings her father had inflicted on her were more a consequence of his inner rage than of anything she might have done. And where Helen had searched for and found her soul mate, Brenda described the lonely years when she'd used Half Dunn, the lump of lard, to change her life, forcing him to marry her. Both women were grateful for their healthy babies – Helen had waited years for her twins, and Brenda had miscarried, finally visiting the far corner of joy with the birth of Daniel Corrib Dunn. With it came the determination that she would dedicate her life to making him into 'a somebody'. This confession had brought tears to Helen's eyes. 'Mum, you were always "a somebody", only you didn't know it,' she said softly, hugging Brenda to her breast.

Now, with everything beginning to change, Brenda spoke of preparing to retire. Half Dunn had lost weight, and with it the lassitude that had oppressed him. Brenda had discovered another person, someone she had first grown to like and now confessed to love, so that she wanted to get to know him – truly know him – at last. 'Retirement will be wonderful,' Helen said. 'We'll have more of you both; how lovely.'

'Ah, yes, my darlin', but first I must be rid of the pub – clearly, Danny won't be taking it over – and a sad day that is going to be, but with all the changes coming, I'm too old and tired . . .' She sighed. 'We'll just have to wait and see what turns up, my dear.'

Helen, for her part, was able to talk of her recent fears that all the effort in the world wasn't going to allow her to achieve the career in Egyptology she knew she was capable of. She admitted to her mother-in-law that while she was reconciled to Danny attempting to win at the next election, the idea of being a politician's wife wasn't enough for her. His obsession to change the world wasn't something she could or would want to stop, but neither was it one she shared. The twins would soon be teenagers and her role as a mother was likely to decrease; her greatest fear was that she would inevitably end up as just another academic during the day and her politician husband's grinning handbag at night, as they attended endless boring but necessary functions.

Brenda pressed her for more. She had become very involved with Danny's stand as an Independent and Helen knew she would back him to the hilt in the next election. Brenda understood that Danny was attempting to do for Balmain what she had done for herself through sheer hard work and determination. Danny wanted to help the people who were locked into a life of poverty over which they had little or no control, those men who bought her beer for the small comfort it brought them and who, together with their wives, were being led by the nose by Tommy O'Hearn. The fat slug had skipped enlistment, pretending to have flat feet, while her precious Danny had gone to fight for them, had suffered for them and now was willing to fight for them again – had already fought for them in the courts. Brenda was inordinately proud of Danny being a lawyer, especially the fact that his defence of Balmain women and their children meant that he was virtually idolised by those who attended Brenda's soirées, in fact by most of the women in Balmain. On the other hand, Brenda was equally enthralled by the prospect of Danny following in Doc Evatt's footsteps. 'Do you think Danny will win next time?' she asked.

Helen shrugged. 'Who knows, but I can say this for him: I've never seen him lose. He may be a dreamer, but he's prepared to do the hard yards, do the planning. Changing an entire social structure, one that's existed for a hundred years, is a frightening idea. This is the biggest project he'll ever attempt and I live in terror that it won't work and we'll . . . well, I suppose we'll get by, but he won't! For Danny, this is the end game.'

Brenda said nothing. She was thinking about Helen's need for independence, which she understood very well. She too had enjoyed life on her own terms; she herself had escaped virtual servitude as a sixteen-year-old maid in a pub. So, one afternoon while quilting she asked, 'Helen, are you sure you want to leave the university? You know how proud we are of what you've achieved. I can never get over the thrill I get when I talk about you as Dr Helen Dunn.'

'Mother Brenda, I'll still be a doctor if I'm washing dishes for a living. I must say, going to work and facing a lecture room full of students who think of Egyptology as simply a unit to add to their quota for the year is becoming less and less interesting, and elevation, even at one of the new universities, is, frankly, less and less likely. I sometimes feel like a mummy myself, wrapped in an endless career bandage that is slowly covering anything useful I have to offer the world.'

'Well then, darlin', I'll come straight out with it. Why don't you take over the pub? We'll back you. Things are changing fast, too fast for us, and we'll be left behind if we don't change with the times. Pubs are becoming restaurants and entertainment centres and goodness knows what else in the future.'

Helen, usually circumspect, looked at Brenda and, surprising even herself, replied, 'Yes, please.'

Brenda didn't make a fuss; she simply replied calmly, 'Good. And so now you will both change your lives; that's a brave decision but, I think, a good one, certainly not one I would have dared contemplate once I had my arms locked around the security of owning a pub.'

And so began Helen's apprenticeship, on the day she completed the restoration of a scene on the quilt of an eighteenth-century cannon depicted at the moment of discharge, the mouth of the great black metal monster exploding with sharp-coloured flames of appliquéd material. Flying in the air in front of the cannon was a soldier in uniform, who had obviously received the full force of the blast, his hat and bayoneted musket flying through the air, together with an arm and a leg detached from the body, both high above his head and moving in different directions. Then, as if in a different part of the scene, a young redheaded girl, in a dress the same colour as the soldier's uniform, watched him as he struggled with only one arm and the stump of the other on crutches. Under it all were several verses in Gaelic that Helen had been careful to embroider exactly as they had been. The whole scene had been badly faded when she began, and her restoration was a triumph, the result of a great many hours of work. Her skills had progressed to the point where she enjoyed the task and seldom these days pricked a finger; in fact, she was rather proud of the calluses that had formed on her thumb and forefinger.

Brenda, looking at the completed work, clapped her hands and exclaimed, 'My darlin', your apprenticeship is over! Now we begin your training as a publican.'

Helen was gazing at the words of what looked like a poem, or perhaps a song with a chorus, stitched with silk thread onto the linen background. 'Oh, how I'd love to know what they say,' she exclaimed.

'You would?' Brenda asked, suddenly looking serious.

'Of course. They took me nearly a month to embroider, each word a beautiful mystery. I may be forced to learn Gaelic.'

'No need for that,' Brenda said. 'Here's what they mean in English,' and she began to sing in her light, sweet voice.

> Here I sit on Buttermilk Hill,
> With salty eyes I cry my fill,
> And ev'ry tear would turn a mill,
> Danny's gone for a soldier.

> Shule shule shule aroo,
> Shule shule shule aroo.

And every tear would turn a mill,
  Danny's gone for a soldier.

With pipes and drums he marched away,
  He would not heed the words I'd say,
  He'll not come back for many a day,
    Danny's gone for a soldier.

  Shule shule shule aroo,
    Shule shule shule aroo.
  He'll not come back for many a day,
    Danny's gone for a soldier.

  Me, oh my, I loved him so,
    It broke my heart to see him go,
  And time will never heal my woe,
    Danny's gone for a soldier.

  Shule shule shule aroo,
    Shule shule shule aroo.
  And time will never heal my woe,
    Danny's gone for a soldier.

  I'll take my needle, take my reel,
  And try my broken heart to heal,
  I'll sew my quilt and wish him weal,
    Danny's gone for a soldier.

  Shule shule shule aroo,
    Shule shule shule aroo.
  I'll sew my quilt and wish him weal,
    Danny's gone for a soldier.

I'll dye my dress, I'll dye it red,
The colour of the blood he's shed,
For the lad I knew has from me fled,
Danny's gone for a soldier.

Shule shule shule aroo,
Shule shule shule aroo.
For the lad I knew has from me fled,
Danny's gone for a soldier.

'Oh, Brenda, that was lovely!' Helen exclaimed, her eyes shining.

'It's an old Irish folk song, but when Danny came home from the war I went to the quilt and there it was – it had happened before to my family – and that's why I quilted Danny and the Japanese,' Brenda said, saddened by the memory.

Helen had, of course, seen the section Brenda referred to when she had first shown her the quilt. She subsequently couldn't bear to look at it and always turned it away from her when she was working on a restoration. Brenda was no artist with appliqué, and her work was graphic, crude and raw enough to be compellingly gruesome. The scene depicted a Japanese officer and six soldiers surrounding an Australian soldier, his torso naked. The officer was holding a rifle with the butt poised directly above the soldier's face, but instead of Danny's face, there was a ragged red patch with a pool of blood running from it, disappearing under the brim of a slouch hat that lay on the ground close by. Beneath the depiction Brenda had embroidered in her own handwriting:

It broke my heart to see him go

Brenda, having completed the lovely ballad, sat thinking, then said quietly, 'Did you know, dear, that the twenty-eight houses in Brokendown Street are for sale? They're empty and nobody wants them. I hear Riley's wife will soon be out of jail, but the syndicate hasn't held together. Anyway, they're on the market and I believe they could be snapped up for a song.'

Helen laughed. 'Franz says they've all run up the hill to hide – Bellevue Hill. Mention the name Riley and they look vague and ask, "Who?" You wonder who would possibly be interested in the houses, don't you,' Helen remarked.

'If you think Danny can win, we ought to start believing in this change he speaks about,' Brenda said. 'So, why don't I buy the houses?' she asked, po-faced.

Helen was taken aback, struggling to grasp what Brenda was suggesting. 'What?' was all she could think to say, then, 'But . . . but you were talking of retiring . . .'

Brenda appeared to be thinking and Helen waited for her to speak. 'Well, you take over the Hero, darling, and I'll help you renovate the houses. We'll make it a display street – show people what Balmain could be like – and they'll be there to prove Danny's point at the next election. What do you say?'

Helen was seldom profane. 'Jesus!' she exclaimed, completely stunned. 'Brenda, how long has this been going on in your mind? There are a few pretty big "if"s in there as well, I have to say.'

'Oh? And who was it said just recently that you've never known him to lose? If a mother, together with a talented and brilliant daughter-in-law, can't back her equally brilliant son, what sort of family are we? We must have faith in our own, Dr Dunn.'

'Brenda, it's frightening, but terribly exciting,' Helen cried.

Brenda looked at Helen and it was obvious she was happy. 'You'll be the fourth-generation publican. If I buy the houses, and if Danny's right and he gets his way, we'll have twenty-eight waterfront houses. If he's wrong, well, they're going for a song and it won't be a terrible financial disaster, and I daresay we'll recover. Whatever happens, it won't happen overnight, and the pub will generate enough income to slowly do the houses up. Are you willing to bet on your husband, girlie?'

For a moment she sounded remarkably like Patrick, her father.

CHAPTER TWELVE

BRENDA WAS THE ONLY bidder for the twenty-eight houses in Brokendown Street, and despite the fact that she picked them up for a lot less than the value of the land they stood on, there were howls of mirth in the pubs of Balmain over her absurd acquisition. After the inquiry, the Minister for Housing, covering his arse, had been quick to find all the boarding-house residents' Housing-Commission accommodation superior to the slum cubicles they'd formerly occupied. The lodgers left with a zeal that expressed the general opinion of the properties, and most people assumed that Brenda, hitherto respected as a businesswoman of some standing, had suffered some sort of brainstorm.

Brokendown Street was well named; even the factories on the foreshore had fallen into disrepair, judging from the rusted corrugated-iron roofs, sagging fences and abandoned machinery. In fact, there were very few parts of Balmain that could match its air of decrepitude. The accumulation of human detritus in the rundown boarding houses had added to the general sense of desolation, and yet their removal only made the street seem even more godforsaken. Brokendown Street was a real-estate nightmare, and even Danny and Helen's well-kept house and garden was referred to by the locals as The Big Dunny.

At dinner on the evening of the day Brenda bought Brokendown

Street, and before it became the latest joke around the peninsula, Helen explained to Danny the idea behind the purchase, but instead of being flattered by the faith his mother and wife demonstrated in his future political career, he was more than a little bemused and annoyed. 'If this is your first step into the business world, Helen, you're heading for disaster!'

'Oh? And why is that?' she asked.

'Ferchrissake, blind Freddy knows Brokendown Street is Balmain's biggest shitheap! This house aside, of course.'

'Well, yes, but if we can show that the shitheap, as you refer to it, can become a desirable residential area, doesn't that demonstrate the potential of the rest of the peninsula? Isn't that an example of the changes you're standing for?'

'There are too many "if"s in that for it to be worth consideration.'

'These "if"s, as you call them, what are they?'

'Well, the biggest if is if I'm elected; the second is if Labor is thrown out; the third is if you can get the bank to lend you the money to renovate; the fourth is if we can get rid of the waterfront industry; the fifth is if the local trade union will allow you to renovate; the sixth is if council will rezone the waterfront area from industrial to residential; and the last if is if you can overcome all these ifs, will people want to live in Brokendown Street. Oh, and finally not if but when Brenda is certified insane and sent to Callan Park for buying the houses in the first place, your newfound career is going to be on the rocks.'

Helen shook her head slowly. 'There's only one if that matters: it's if we believe we are doing this for all the right reasons.' She smiled. 'If we do, we simply can't fail. As for my new career, not if but when you are elected and you get the waterfront zoning changed to residential and we own the entire waterfront on this part of the harbour, it just might turn out to be one of the better business decisions we are ever likely to make, Daniel Corrib Dunn.'

'Isn't that being a bit simplistic?' Danny said, immediately softening. He had long sensed Helen's frustration with her academic career and had been delighted when she suggested learning the pub game and eventually taking over from Brenda. Seeing her enthusiastic and happy meant a great deal to him.

'Not in the least. Failure would be *if* we didn't try. You don't always have to succeed not to fail. Now, tell me, are you on side and are we a team – Brenda, Half Dunn, you and me? Oh, and Lachlan, of course, to —'

'Lachlan? Why Lachlan?'

'Because you need him if you're going to win.'

'But, darling, we've been there before. He's Tommy O'Hearn's bloody brother-in-law!'

'He's also an account director at George Patterson, the biggest advertising agency in Australia. He's known you since the first day you stepped ashore after the war and he openly gives you credit for changing his life; he loves you more than a brother, let alone a brother-in-law. He can mount a better campaign for you than can anyone else in the country.'

'But have you explained that it might be awkward for him?'

'I didn't need to. He was rather hurt that you hadn't asked him to help in the last election.'

'But didn't you tell him we discussed it and thought it might compromise his relationship with his brother-in-law? The sitting member, after all!'

'Yes, of course I did. His reply was, "Helen, you could have asked! You don't understand: he's my brother-in-law; Danny's my big brother!" He was almost in tears. And I got the impression that there isn't a lot of love lost between the sitting member and Lachlan, by the way. Later he hinted that O'Hearn is a nasty drunk with a wicked temper and a sudden and unpredictable backhand – he's far from the loving family man he purports to be. Lachlan's sister and her two kids are anything but happy little Vegemites. So I called him and he's over the moon.'

'You could have asked me. After all, I'm the candidate,' Danny said, ever so slightly miffed.

Helen looked at him sternly. 'We better sort this out right at the beginning: if you want to call the shots, that's fine; I understand there can only be one boss.'

'But you think it ought to be you?' Danny said.

'Yes, I do.'

Danny folded Helen into his chest. 'I give in, but, sweetheart, you'll have to run the whole show for me. I'll be too busy running a law practice and knocking on doors, and . . .' He kissed her on the top of the head. 'Whereas you, on the other hand, are as free as a bird. Nothing much happening in your life, is there? Learning to run a pub, renovating a street, running a political campaign and being a mother – shouldn't prove too difficult.' He laughed.

'I'll manage. I've got a good team, and others will help, I'm sure. The women from Brenda's soiree will distribute leaflets and start the word-of-mouth, and Pineapple Joe is also on board. Lachlan's come up with a campaign name and a slogan —'

'Already?'

'It's brilliant. Want to hear it?'

'Of course. Do I have a choice?'

'What do you mean, do you have to approve it?'

'Yeah! After all, I'm the candidate.'

'But I'm the boss, remember?' Helen giggled. 'I hope it doesn't come to that. Are you ready?'

'Yup.'

'Tiger 13!'

'What?'

'Tiger 13!'

'*Tiger 13?* What the hell is that supposed to mean?'

'I'll tell you, but let's go upstairs to the verandah first; then we can look out at the constituency whose hearts we have to win.'

Several minutes later, seated on wicker chairs, with a fresh pot of tea for Danny and a glass of wine for herself, Helen began to explain. 'You only missed out by eleven votes last time, so we only have to keep the votes we got and get another couple – thirteen – to win. Thirteen votes in Tiger country.'

'Ah, Tiger 13! I see. Very clever . . . but thirteen is an unlucky number. Why not Tiger Dozen or Tiger Fourteen?'

'Danny, I'm ashamed of you. There are thirteen players in a rugby league team. Now, let's talk tactics.'

'Yes, ma'am,' Danny said with a grin. 'Right away, ma'am.'

'Well, the sooner you announce you're a candidate the better. We can call a press conference to announce that you're standing as an Independent at the next election, while your name's still fresh in the public's mind.'

'But isn't it a bit . . . well, early?'

'No. Let Tommy O'Hearn and the rest of them have a go at us early on so we get some idea of what they're likely to do. We lost last time because of the scurrilous rumours they circulated about you in the last week of the election, when you didn't have time to refute them. They've got a big propaganda machine and we've only got us. If we wait until the last few weeks of an election, they'll swamp us. If we play them over a couple of years, Balmain has time to get its collective mind around voting for an Independent.'

'Good one,' Danny grinned. 'I see . . . and the slogan?'

'"All we need is you." It's aimed at every individual who wants to think their vote is one of the thirteen.'

'That's good thinking, but shouldn't it have some sort of promise? You know – "All we need is you and we can make the changes needed in Balmain", something like that.'

'No, Lachlan says if we start to campaign early, like now, by the time the election comes in two and a bit years, everyone on the peninsula will know what we stand for, and they'll take the slogan as a personal call to help. Labor has been promising things with pretentious and grand slogans for donkey's years and they've never once delivered. People don't believe political promises; it's time we treated the voter as an adult . . . well, the ones who voted for us last time and the thirteen extra we want, anyway.'

'Tiger 13 it is then. When do we start?'

'Tomorrow. And I have another surprise – Pineapple Joe is dressing the team.'

'What? We're all wearing suits? Bit pretentious in a working-class suburb, don't you think?'

'No, silly, those new T-shirts all the kids are wearing. He's bought the Australian rights to a special stretchable ink called Plastisol; it makes screen-printing T-shirts more practical: you can wash them, the printing doesn't run or fade, and it stretches with the fabric. He reckons suits will always be good business, but times are changing, and this is going to make him a motza. It'll be a black T-shirt with the word "Tiger" in orange, the "13" in white, and the slogan in white across the back. He's donating a thousand and we'll sell them for campaign funds. "Helen, we are makink a goot deal: you are getting propergoose and money for makink funds and already I am gettink advertisink for mein beautiful new product."'

Danny laughed. 'What do you imagine this propergoose is we're getting?'

Helen laughed too. 'It took me a while; he meant propaganda.'

They had a good chuckle, glad Pineapple Joe was on their side. Everyone liked him, and even though, by Balmain standards, he was a rich man, no one resented him . . . well, perhaps only Tommy O'Hearn.

'Darling, when we were talking about my running the show, you said you had the practice and knocking on doors, and I thought you were going to add something else. What was it?' Helen asked.

'Helen, I don't want you to feel under any pressure; whatever happens, remember I love you and am deeply proud of you.' Danny took a breath. 'But we've got just two and a bit years to go before the election and I'm going to need a hard six months at the end to fight it if I'm to have a chance of winning. That leaves me two years; the twins are eleven now, so that takes them up to thirteen. These two years are critical in their swimming training and I need to be there for them; after that I hope they'll be under Forbes Carlile at Ryde pool.'

'Oh dear,' Helen said softly.

Danny, excited, missed or ignored her tone of voice. 'Can't you see it all works out beautifully? You're busy with Brenda, I have the twins under my control, establishing a training regime, then I go into parliament and can do the right thing there, because Carlile has taken over their training, and hopefully you're well on your way to renovating Brokendown Street. It all fits perfectly, darling!' Danny looked over at Helen and saw that she was studying her hands, which were folded in her lap. 'What?' he asked, 'What's wrong?'

Helen looked up slowly. 'Gabrielle doesn't want to continue swimming,' she said quietly.

'Don't be ridiculous!' Danny shouted. 'Who said? Gabby? She's only eleven, ferchrissake!'

'Yes, but a very serious-minded eleven. She was invited to the Conservatorium after her last music exam to play for them in their early-talent-spotting program. They were sufficiently impressed to say that she might qualify for a place in the Conservatorium when she's fourteen.'

Danny was suddenly furious. 'Jesus, Helen, now you tell me! How long have you known about this? You, above all people, know I've had long-term plans for their swimming!'

Helen remained calm; she knew the signs all too well. 'If her heart is elsewhere, she won't make the Olympic squad anyway. They may be twins but you know how different they can be. Samantha is determined to win three gold medals. Now she says she promised Sammy she'd do it for him. Gabrielle has her head and her heart in music. Danny, can't you see? She's only swimming to please you.'

Danny shook his head. 'Christ, I dunno, a man does his best and —'

Helen became angry. 'Danny, stop that! You're not to become depressed, get into one of your sloughs! The twins have always responded to you. What other kids do you know who have been out on the harbour at dawn since they were tots, rowing like galley slaves? They never complained. Then swimming training every day after school . . . they accepted it all without ever whingeing. And why? Let me tell you why,

Danny Corrib Dunn. Because they love and adore you! Now one of them shows a different talent – you might even say a splendid talent, one that's beyond your experience, one you can't personally manage – and you throw in the towel. So, are you going to deny Gabrielle her moment in the sun?'

Danny, furious, bit down on his reply. His mind was racing. He could almost see what was to come if he persisted – Helen had enough steely resolve in her not only to resist him, but also to beat him. If he insisted on Gabby continuing her swimming training, he'd have Helen to contend with, and if Gabby didn't win a medal or even get selected at seventeen, she'd have missed her chance at the Conservatorium. *Shit, shit, shit! There go the glorious headlines!* This had been his dream since the twins were born – twin gold. He'd dreamed about it and would happily have waited seventeen years for his moment in the sun, and made whatever sacrifices were required so his girls could compete for Australia as he might have done.

'They weren't treated like galley slaves,' he said darkly, getting abruptly to his feet. If he stayed a moment longer he was going to find himself in a row – a big one! 'I'm going to bed. I've had enough bullshit for one night!' He stomped inside, thinking there had to be something wrong with her logic. Didn't she realise that he was potentially sacrificing his political career on her behalf? Bloody women – they wanted everything and they were still not satisfied, tearing your children out of your arms. So much for a decent, honest dream, a nice harmless ambition; two gold medals out the window, just like that. Christ, it wasn't a lot to ask, was it? Bloody violin, the same bloody scales played hour after hour. What was the point? Danny was thoroughly cheesed off. First Brenda, then Helen; he'd spent his whole fucking life with women who didn't know their place. No wonder Half Dunn had expanded like a Michelin balloon – he'd buried all his resentment in fat!

Feeling a bit better after his grumble, he cleaned his teeth and climbed into bed. Then he realised he hadn't kissed the sleeping twins. No, bugger it – he'd only kiss Sam; bloody Gabby didn't deserve a kiss. Where'd all this music crap come from, anyway? As far as he knew, nobody in the family could even play the comb and paper. And how much had the bloody violin cost! It wouldn't end there, no way; next thing she'd be demanding a bloody Stradivarius or whatever it was called. Then he told himself he'd take back what he thought about Gabby letting him down. Bloody Helen was right: Gabby wouldn't make the squad if she didn't give it everything. She was already a foot behind Sam in the pool. He jumped out of bed and went through to the twins' room. He kissed both of them lightly on the forehead and immediately felt much happier. Bloody hell, he'd apologise to Helen in another lifetime – or in two days minimum. That was the best he could manage. He flopped back into bed and fell asleep.

Danny's candidature was announced on a Monday, hit the media on Tuesday, and on the Wednesday Franz strolled into Danny's office after lunch and perched on a corner of his desk, shoving the clutter of manila folders and red-taped briefs to one side. 'How do you ever find what you're looking for in this bloody mess?' he asked.

'I don't,' Danny replied. 'The beautiful Keri does. If she ever left, my part of the firm would collapse in a mountain of brown manila and red tape.'

'Got a minute?' Franz queried.

'Sure, what's up?'

'Dad's in my office; he'd like a word with you.'

'Of course! Glad to see he wants some credible legal advice.' Danny rose, laughing.

'No, no, stay. Sit. I'll bring him in.'

'Anything I should know?'

'Nothing he won't tell you himself – he doesn't confide in me.'

Danny stood as Josef Landsman entered, and extended his hand. 'Nice to see you, sir.' He indicated one of the two chairs in front of his desk. 'Please, won't you take a seat?'

'Ja, thank you, Danny. You are well?'

'Thank you, yes.'

'Do you want me to stay, Dad?' Franz asked.

Josef Landsman turned slowly to look at his son. 'Of course.'

Franz seated himself beside his father.

'What can I do for you?' Danny asked, his voice warm.

Josef Landsman drew back with a look of mock surprise, his cheeks slightly puffed. 'For me, nussing; for you, maybe somesing, eh? Danny, everyone was watching what you did ze uzzer night to announce you going to stand Independent. Ja, das is goot.'

Danny grinned. 'Not much choice; I can't stand for the Labor Party.'

'Ja, this I understand. Myself, in Germany I was Social Democrat.'

'That was the equivalent of what? The Labor Party?'

'No, for that zen you must be communist. More like Liberal Party here, maybe also a little bit za right-wing Labor.'

'I never thought of you as a Liberal, Mr Landsman.'

'Ja, when we came to this country, maybe yes, Mr Scullin, zen Mr Curtin and Mr Chifley, for zem I can be Labor; but what we got now here in zis place – rubbish!'

'My dad has always said your loyalty is to yourself; you vote for outcomes, not for parties,' Franz explained.

'Ja, das is goot, Franz, for your conscience you must vote.' He turned back to Danny. 'I am a plain man – I don't beat about za trees. You have thought maybe change to Liberal?'

Danny was taken aback and looked quickly at his partner. Franz threw up his hands. 'Don't look at me, mate, I'm just as surprised as you.'

'Ja, such things, when you talk zey fly like za butterfly out the window. Franz, he doesn't know nussing.'

'Well . . . I must say it comes as a bit of a surprise. Franz must have told you, I'm a Labor man, born and bred.'

Josef shrugged, spreading his hands. 'Ja, of course, before, but now, after what happened, maybe not?'

'Well, you're right in one respect: I've burned my bridges with the Labor Party.' Danny grinned. 'They'd pre-select Genghis Khan before me, which is why I'm standing as an Independent – might even win, at a pinch – but there'd be a lynch mob after me if I stood for the Libs.'

'Acht, politics! What is the difference? Let me tell you, my boy, Hester and me, ja, now we are Liberal, but next time, who knows? Maybe we vote Labor. First principle politics, all parties when they come to power they revolutionary, they make changes, everything is good, so again we vote them, next time not so good, bit scandal, bit corruption, bit, how you say . . . ?'

'Complacent?' Franz offered.

'Ja, complacent. Maybe again we vote them. Now they forget why they there, forget the people. They become corrupt, they don't care, they become . . .'

'Reactionary?' Franz offered again.

'Ja, exactly, now it is past zat time when they must vamoose. Now is time for change, bring in revolutionary party. In zis country, right now, zis moment, ja, revolutionary is Liberal Party comink from Mr Bob Askin in za next election. If you want, you can change things; now it must be za Liberal Party.'

'Goodness, Liberals revolutionary? That's a turn-up for the books. I'm not at all sure Bob Menzies would be pleased to know he's a revolutionary.' Danny paused, thinking. 'Could be awkward, Mr Landsman. In Balmain, Liberal is a dirty word.'

'Ja, of course, this is why we are talkink now, when comes 1965 maybe they are thinkink little bit different in Balmain.'

'If they were, it would be the first time in a hundred years. It's not about thinking differently, it's about *thinking* in the first instance. It's a year since the Riley conviction, and at the time the media was all over us like a rash and couldn't get enough of the government corruption it revealed. But nothing has changed and they voted Labor back in for the seventh time! Balmain has voted Labor since the party was formed and the party has been throwing shit at it from the start – coal mines, power stations, chemical factories, soap factories, foundries, marine workshops – most local kids have chest infections and snotty noses, the air above Balmain is perpetually foul and the water lapping its shores is the most polluted in the entire harbour. Franz here calls it a cesspool and he's not far wrong. And *still* they voted Labor.'

'But only by eleven votes,' Franz reminded him.

Josef Landsman nodded. 'Ja, peoples. What are they sayink? The more I see peoples, zen the more I am lovink mein dog.'

Danny, wanting to change tack, now said, 'I had no idea you were actively involved in state politics, Mr Josef.'

Josef Landsman drew back in horror. 'No, no, after Germany, never!'

Danny looked at Franz, bemused. 'Then why this invitation to join the Libs?'

'Ja, mein goot friend, also yours, Mr Bryan Penman, he comes to me and says, "Josef, Bob Askin, he would like to meet Mr Dunn. Maybe you could arrange? Maybe also dinner some place where nobody is seeink? Mr Penman house maybe, yes?"'

Danny thought for a moment, wishing Helen were with him to act as a sounding board, then decided to have a bet each way. 'Mr Josef, this comes as something of a surprise. I'd like to think about it, then hear what Mr Askin has to say. I'm sure Helen and I would be delighted to invite Mr Penman, Mr Askin and his wife – and yourself and Hester, of course – to dinner, preferably this coming Friday night.'

'Thank you, Danny, I will tell.' He balanced a brown paper carry bag precariously on a pile of files. 'Some nice cheeses, also bratwurst, compliments Hester. *Guter appetit*.'

Bob Askin was impressive for his ordinariness. He'd slowly risen up the ladder of Liberal politics by starting as president of the Rural Bank Association. Danny and Helen found his approach clear, honest and direct. He didn't make excuses for losing the last election: 'The politics of governing are learned through practice; we've simply been in the doldrums too long. Institutions and business are accustomed to Labor and they've made their arrangements; they know what to expect. But sooner or later smugness and apathy, the inevitable result of being in power too long, begin to affect them, corruption becomes apparent, and business and institutions see themselves as being tarred with the same brush. The public finally begins to take notice.'

'I always thought it was the other way around – the public grew weary of the government and threw them out,' Danny said. 'Are you saying it's the big end of town that decides?'

Askin was careful with his answer. 'Government, any government, has to work with business, the people who run the other side of things. If the two work together, the state is usually in good shape; if they're at odds, things start to fall apart and that affects jobs, housing and ultimately the utilities – roads, hospitals, transport . . . that's when people power comes into its own.'

'What are you saying – the people are a last resort?' Helen asked.

'No, of course not, but it might be true to say that people find out last. Half the effort of any government that has overstayed its term goes into closing down information, in effect, keeping the media barons on side. If they turn against you and go to the people, then the rest, as they say, is ancient history,' Askin replied.

'Well, in this state there's just a handful of media organisations, but I should think only two that truly matter: Fairfax and Packer,' Franz said.

Askin leaned back in his chair, hands spread wide. 'That's about it. If you don't have at least one of the big two, it makes it damn near impossible to win.'

'And the next election?' Helen asked.

'Ah, that's entirely different – jobs for the boys, corruption, incompetence, backstabbing, faction fights and plain old lassitude, the business of taking things for granted after more than two decades in office – that's when we'll be able to count on the support of the media . . . well, at least one of the big two, anyway.'

'What about policy, something people can hold on to?' Danny asked.

'To be truthful, this is really the first opportunity my party will have to use the media to publicise our policies,' Askin said.

'And the Liberals now have such media backing?' Bryan Penman, who had been quiet all evening, now spoke.

'Yes, Sir Frank Packer of Consolidated Press; that means Channel Nine and the *Telegraph* are on side for the 1965 elections.'

'Danny, I'll be perfectly honest with you, you're a media dream. You've been a lone drummer beating a march against corruption without ever appearing to be a crackpot. Our investigations show that you have gone to court pro bono on countless occasions for battered housewives and children; you exposed the slum landlords and the corruption of the council and Labor politicians; the people in the street love you; you didn't put a foot wrong in a tough media confrontation; your war record is exemplary; your time in a prison camp shows you know how to work with people, take charge, take the lead and take responsibility; you're a team player and your belated decoration is proof of your valour. Finally, the Labor Party has reason to hate you. It's everything we could hope for in a Liberal candidate.' Askin paused, and looked at Helen. 'And Dr Dunn, your wife, is also greatly to be admired for her work in the field of academia. The two of you make a formidable and, we believe, winning combination.'

Helen winced as she realised that her role in these grand plans would be as Danny's handbag. If this were the case, she intended being a crocodile-skin grip with a sharp snap, at the very least.

Askin paused and looked around, a boyish grin on his face. 'There, I can't remember ever having pissed that deeply into anyone's pocket. Well, not since my last meeting with Sir Frank, anyway.'

The dinner table erupted in laughter and this last admission probably did more for Bob Askin's credibility than the somewhat overblown praise that had preceded it.

'Bob, Helen and I live here and have no intention of moving, but to stand for the Liberal Party would be tantamount to suicide in Balmain.'

'Oh, of course! We understand. The idea would be to find you a safe seat somewhere else. Just agree to come on side and leave those details to me.'

Danny glanced over at Helen, hoping to get some unspoken reaction. In a barely noticeable gesture she lowered her eyes and shook her head. They were in agreement, so there would be no argument later over the decision he was about to make. 'Bob, while I am extremely flattered by your invitation to join and your offer of a safe seat, I am a Balmain boy and I am to be judged by the promises I make to my own people. I sink or swim by what they decide.'

Askin was silent, his chin on his chest. 'That is disappointing, truly disappointing, Danny. If you change your mind, will you let me know?'

'Of course, and thank you, Bob. Thank you also for your candid and open briefing, especially your willingness to accept Helen and me into your party. I regret I can't accept and I assure you what has been said here tonight won't go beyond this room.'

Askin was doing a fairly good job of hiding his annoyance. 'Danny, you must understand any power you will have as an Independent will be minuscule; you will simply be a spare part in the engine room of politics.'

'Then we must hope that the engine might have occasion to break down once in a while,' Danny replied.

Askin paused. 'Pity. You would have been good – all the makings of a minister, in which case the things you want to achieve become a lot easier.'

After the last of the guests had departed, Helen made Danny a mug of Milo, their usual bedtime drink. 'Darling, I couldn't have said it better, but I'm not sure we made a friend of Mr Askin. Do you think that part about being a minister with the power to change things was shorthand for "don't expect any help from us"?'

Danny laughed. 'You know what I kept thinking when he made the offer?'

'What?'

'That if I accepted a safe seat I'd be corrupted even before I got into parliament.'

'Looks like a rocky road down Brokendown Street, mate.' Helen sighed. 'Do you think we've done the right thing?'

Danny grinned. 'Growing up in Balmain, you start negotiating with the big boys in the playground in primary school, just to be allowed to eat your own sandwiches. The trick is to get elected; after that, I'll have to learn how to negotiate eating my own sandwiches with the people who run the show.'

'You've positively made up your mind, haven't you?' Helen asked one last time.

'Not to be a politician, but to be someone who brings about change.'

Helen knew that look. Danny's next obsession was building faster and faster. He had always been his own man – in a sense, always an independent – he would make it work; he always did.

Two days after the Askin dinner, Danny walked into Franz's office and flopped down in the old leather club chair that his partner had found at a Point Piper garage sale and of which he was inordinately proud – 'Touch of gravitas, mate, scruff marks and all. Where could you buy one like that outside an Englishman's club?'

'You mean they have garage sales in Point Piper?' Danny had quipped back.

'Yes, when they have to throw out the worn Persian carpets,' Franz had laughed.

Danny had to admit it was comfortable; perfect for an afternoon nap. 'Got a moment?' he said.

'Not really, but in your case I'll make an exception.' Franz grinned.

'Haven't seen you since the dinner at my place. What did you think?'

'What about? Askin? My mum's cooking? Which reminds me, she phoned to say she'd left a saucepan behind. Will you bring it in?'

'Yeah, sure. No, I mean, what did you think generally?'

'Generally speaking I'd say you turned down a bloody good offer. Christ, Danny, he almost guaranteed you a minister's portfolio.'

'Yeah, to sleep with the devil.'

'And with Labor you're on the side of the angels?'

'Well, no, but I'm standing as an Independent. My vote goes with whatever is the right thing to do.'

'C'mon, Danny, you're not naïve; your vote is meaningless if the party in power has a clear majority.'

'Yeah, I know, but —'

'But what?'

'Mate, I have to go in on my own terms. I might get lucky and it will be a close election and then I'll be able to make my presence felt.'

'It's a lot to hope for. What if it's a landslide?'

Danny shrugged. 'I'm only doing it for one reason and that's what I wanted to talk to you about.'

Franz glanced at his watch. 'How long will it take? If it's changing Balmain, we've talked it out before and I have nothing more to add —'

'To your cesspool argument . . . yeah, I know, but there's been a new development.'

'Mate, I'm meeting a property developer for lunch.'

'This is about the same thing – can you cancel?'

'No, I bloody can't! Jesus, Danny, we're just starting to make real money and you're talking of abandoning ship. Someone's got to stay at the helm. You can't practise while you're in politics, which leaves me and the two students we've got from law school. It effectively halves our income.'

'But I won't be taking any money out, we'll live on my parliamentary salary. Helen's also bringing a bit more home from the pub, although it doesn't yet match her uni salary. But it will, and soon. That's what I want to talk to you about.'

Franz sighed. 'I can't miss this lunch – the project is potentially huge!'

'Yeah, okay, but the one I'm going to talk about could be bigger.'

'Bullshit, Danny! Stick to wives and children, and leave the conveyancing to me, will ya?'

'You going to listen?' Danny demanded, not in the least put out by Franz's protests.

'You've got exactly half an hour.'

'Righto, now don't interrupt, no wisecracks, just listen – okay?'

'Yes, *mein Herr*!'

Danny began by telling Franz that Brenda had bought the twenty-eight houses in Brokendown Street, but got no further.

'So it's genetic, is it?' Franz said with a laugh. 'Errors of judgment or plain stupidity – which is it?'

'Franz! You promised. No smart-arse remarks!' Danny said. 'And wipe that superior Hebrew smile off your face.' He then outlined the political campaign to come, explaining that renovating the houses – or some of them, anyway – would demonstrate what could be done.

'Look, Danny, I'll give it to you straight: it all sounds pretty flaky to me. You can't just go around and change the social demographic of an entire suburb!'

'Why not? I thought you approved of my going into politics?'

Franz drew back. 'Mate, don't confuse me with Josef and Hester. My mum and dad didn't even mention it to me before Dad saw you here. It wasn't my idea — Jesus! I gotta go!'

Franz grabbed his briefcase and crossed the office.

'When will you be back?' Danny called.

Franz propped and turned to face him. 'When you're over your nervous breakdown!'

'My office, four o'clock!' Danny said.

'Yeah, okay.'

Franz returned around three-thirty. It may have been the half-bottle of wine he'd had at lunch, but he seemed in a better mood as he entered Danny's office and assumed his usual perch on the desk.

'Good lunch? Did we win?' Danny asked.

'Does a bird fly?' Franz said flippantly, the alcohol showing. He was usually pretty circumspect about his clients, his well-known discretion winning him more than a few contracts from the big end of town, where the development business wasn't always strictly above board. Franz, for instance, knew more about the getting things done between pollies and private individuals than did Danny. An appropriate contribution to election funds was the semi-honest way of getting a minister's ear, while the euphemistically named 'brown envelope' – a more personal contribution in return for influence – was so common with the incumbent Labor government as to be almost routine.

'So, are you too pissed to resume our talk?' Danny asked.

'You know, you never give up, do you, Danny? Balmain has been chugging along for well over a century. It was designed to be a city dump – somewhere to put all the utilities and mess-makers in one inner-city industrial location and service them with the poor, who are not entitled to clean air, or to notice stink and abomination, as long as they're given a sufficient serve of bread and circuses to keep them thinking they're happy. Up the fucking Tigers!'

'Yeah, I told you all that, but it can be changed. Look, I've got a proposition to put to you, one that could make us all rich, though that's not why I'm doing it.'

'While your contributions to this firm can be said to be important, making us all rich hasn't been one of them to date.'

'I guess you're right – it's not something I think about a lot.'

'Well, if every battered wife and abused child pro bono had been fee paying, we would be. But pro bono-ing the entire peninsula is going a bit bloody far.'

'Franz, it's not me you have to back, it's Helen and Brenda.'

'Yeah, well, that's another thing. Helen has just given up a secure job with a guaranteed pension to run a pub, something she knows bugger all about. Your mother wants to retire, your dad isn't exactly a ball of energy, you're standing as an Independent with no power to change anything in the next election, and you're asking me to become involved?'

'Mate, I know it doesn't look good on paper —'

'Good? Shit, Danny, there's not a single thing about it that's sound business or even basic commonsense!' Franz, who usually drank very sparingly, suddenly lost his temper. 'You're supposed to be bright, but this is the dumbest bunch of decisions I've seen in years! And just when things are looking up for the firm. We've got a more than enviable reputation for disputation and criminal law, and you're prepared to throw the whole lot away to save a recalcitrant fucking suburb from itself! This time, Don Quixote, there are too many windmills at the top of the hill, your lance is blunt and you're riding a donkey that's exhausted! If ever there was a well-named project it's Brokendown Street!' Franz snapped. 'What you need to do, mate, is go and see Craig Woon, now that he's a fully qualified psychiatrist, and get yourself certified!'

Danny looked calmly at Franz. 'Balmain is in better shape than the prison camp.'

'What's that supposed to mean, for God's sake?'

'It means this is not the hardest thing I've ever had to do.'

Franz gave Danny a look of bewilderment. 'You *really* believe you can pull this off, don't you?'

'Yes, but we need your help.'

'Mate, I'm getting close to being rich. For a Jew that's just another word for "safe". It hasn't been easy, but nowhere near as hard as it's been for my parents, who educated me and have a right to see me meet their expectations. Now, along comes some dumb Irishman with a proposition that is guaranteed to make me poor again!' Franz spread his arms. 'What do you expect me to say?'

'You'll never know unless you give it a go. If it looked easy, then everyone would be doing it. You have to see it differently. See the harbour not as a cesspool but as potentially one of the prettiest stretches of water in Sydney – quiet, tranquil and a stone's throw from the centre of the city. Under the crud lies a paradise. Things are looking up; we've finally recovered from the Depression and the war; there is a new upwardly mobile young generation emerging; this new contraceptive pill is going to change things for women; even Pineapple Joe is changing from men's suits to T-shirts. Can't you see we're paddling like mad but there's a good wave behind us, a big one, and if we catch it, it will take us all the way into shore?'

Franz sighed. 'Danny, what do you expect me to say?'

'Not say, do.'

'Okay, do?'

'Franz, you don't have to invest in it, though I think you'd be a fool if you didn't, but I want you to sit on the board, be the chairman. We need your know-how.'

'And someone to cop the shit when you go bankrupt?'

'Ah, come on, mate. Every night the twins and I sing a song, have done since they were three years old, and the last lines go, *And can you possibly tell me why . . . You dream of ice-cream and apple pie?* You're the schemer and I'm the dreamer – that's why we're such a terrific combination.'

Franz smiled. 'Maybe, but I've had a bit too much to drink. I'd like to discuss it with my parents. I'll talk to you tomorrow. But just so I know, who would be on such a board?'

'Just the family – Helen, Brenda and Half Dunn.'

'And you?'

'No, mate; hopefully I'll be in parliament. Can't be seen to have a vested interest.'

'I don't know, a vested interest in failure goes well with being an Independent, doesn't it?'

'You'll keep, son,' Danny replied, smiling. But at least Franz was paying him the courtesy of getting a serious second opinion. Josef and Hester had worked hard and prospered. They were shrewd, practical people who, Danny knew, had put their money into various developments – what the Americans called shopping malls – that were just beginning to appear in Australia.

Danny was accustomed to getting his way, except occasionally with Helen, but he felt fairly certain Franz wasn't going to deliver tidings of great joy and future opportunity to Josef and Hester. And that wasn't the end of Danny's disappointing day. The phone rang and shortly after the ever-astute Keri called out, 'Danny, I have a Mr O'Hearn on the phone.

He has an unpleasant tone, no "please" or "thank you", just your name as if it were a demand: "Danny Dunn!"'

'Yeah, that figures, put him through.'

Danny waited for the click. 'Hello, Danny Dunn?' he said in a neutral tone.

'Tommy here, Tommy O'Hearn.'

'That's what my secretary said. What ill omen presages this call?'

'Eh?'

'To what do I owe the pleasure, or is it business?'

'Jack O'Shea and me want to see you, mate. Termorra!'

'I'm booked out for tomorrow. How about Friday in my office . . . let me see, eleven o'clock okay? By the way, can you give me any indication of the reason for the call?'

'Yeah, mate, righto, eleven o'clock.' The phone went dead.

Bloody charming. Presage was obviously the right word, Danny sighed to himself.

When he got home, Danny unburdened himself to Helen about Franz's response, but she reacted calmly enough. 'Well, what can you expect? I seem to recall you were not without reservations yourself, darling. Of course we'd love to have him as our chairman, but only as a true believer.' She sighed then added, 'We'll muddle through on our own, I daresay. It's hard to see Josef and Hester giving it the thumbs up. But what do you think the odious Tommy O'Hearn wants?'

'No doubt he's on a message from his masters in Macquarie Street, although the fact that he's bringing Jack O'Shea with him is interesting, given that he's the mayor elect of Balmain. Whatever it is, you may be sure it isn't good news and has something to do with my standing as an Independent.'

Franz rang Keri just after nine o'clock the following morning to say he wouldn't be in until lunchtime and couldn't be contacted, but that he'd see Danny after lunch. Danny had a brief appearance to make in court, but, as usual, instead of an hour it took three, two of them waiting to be called. He got back to the office just before one to be told that

Franz and his parents were waiting for him in the boardroom and that Hester had brought a packed lunch.

Danny had a quick pee, washed his hands and then went straight to the boardroom. 'Mr Josef, Mrs Landsman, how nice.' He glanced quickly at Franz for some sort of reaction but got none.

'Chicken soup, Keri is makink warm, zen sandwiches – roast beef, cheese, tomato, Australian, togezzer on black bread, German,' Hester announced.

'I thought it only fair to bring Mum and Dad,' Franz said, 'that way you'll hear it from them.'

'Oh dear,' Danny said sitting down. 'Well, you were hardly ambivalent yesterday.'

To Danny's surprise it was Hester who spoke first. 'Helen, she is liking this Brokinkdown Street, Danny?'

'Yes, very much.'

'Very goot, and she is working to make zose houses nice?'

'Well, yes, that's the general idea, Mrs Landsman – to show people the potential, I mean, if the area is cleaned up.'

'Danny, why you are turnink Mr Askin's offer away?'

'Mr Josef, me being a Liberal politician would be like you turning into a gentile. I couldn't do it.'

Josef sniffed. 'Lots of Jew they are becomink gentiles when comes the war, also before zat, the Spanish Inquisition . . . sometimes we got to do, life is precious.'

'Yeah, well, I don't know what I'd do if it meant the lives of my family, but that's not the case here.'

'Ja, your answer is goot.'

Josef looked at Hester and they nodded slightly. 'We are goink this morning with Franz to see zat Brokinkdown Street. We would like very much to buy in this project, Danny, but only when I can be chairman,' Hester said.

Danny could hardly believe his ears. 'Buy in?' he asked, caught off guard, his surprise clearly showing.

'My mother makes all the financial decisions; she learned to do so when my dad was in the internment camp.' Franz smiled. 'Her track record is pretty impressive.'

Danny was lost for words but eventually said, 'Of course. But didn't Franz explain?'

'Mate, I gave them the full cesspool theory, the whole bloody disaster!' Franz said. 'But my mum loved it, she says it's the perfect investment.'

'Huh? She said that?'

Franz turned to his mother. 'Ask her.'

'Danny, for Brokinkdown Street, ven you look, everysing is bad, terrible, terrible! But zen you look again, only one change and everything is goot now. When zose factories by the harbour is taken away and no more bad things zey are putting in zat water, zen everysing is goot.' She clapped her hands. 'Twenty-eight properties, harbour-front, oi vey! Mein goodness!' Her laughter almost sounded like a mischievous giggle. 'Maybe I talk to Helen and Brenda, three womens togezzer.'

Danny glanced quickly at Franz, who shrugged. 'I'm not a woman, mate, what would I know?'

'Well, will you be part of it?' Danny asked.

'No way, José! In business with my mum, are you crazy?'

Danny turned to Hester Landsman. 'This comes as quite a surprise, Mrs Landsman, and, of course, it's not my decision. Can I arrange a meeting with Helen and Brenda?' He looked at Josef. 'Will you be included, Mr Josef?'

Josef put his hand up in a gesture of surrender. 'Hester only, one is enough. Two Landsmans, zat is too much,' he chuckled.

And so, to cut a long story short, Brokendown Street Property Investment Pty Ltd was formed, with Helen as managing director, and Brenda and Hester as the other two directors, taking turns month about at being chairman. The Landsmans, through their investment company, owned forty-nine per cent, Brenda forty-nine per cent, and Helen, for political reasons, owned only two per cent, though carried the deciding vote in any disagreement. They all shared equally in any profits. All that was needed now was for Danny to be elected, and somehow get the zoning for the Balmain foreshore changed to residential. Two very big *ifs*.

The visit from Tommy O'Hearn and Jack O'Shea, or, as it became known, the visit from the two Os, duly began on the dot of eleven o'clock on the day following the Landsman family meeting. Tommy O'Hearn, fat as a pig from feeding at the political trough, and Jack O'Shea, president of the local Labor branch, would-be mayor, and beanstalk slim, were announced by the switch and ushered into the boardroom by Keri, who took their order for, in both cases, tea with three sugars. Danny entered and both men remained seated, neither offering to shake his hand. 'I see,' Danny said, smiling, 'you've come on business.'

'Too right, mate,' Tommy O'Hearn said, tapping the fingers of his right hand on the boardroom table.

O'Hearn was wearing a cheap, badly fitted, grey Terylene suit, with the collar button of his white shirt undone behind a red tie (Labor colours), pulled down an inch or so to give him room to breathe. O'Shea, equally in uniform, but in his case, working-class dressed up, sported a short back and sides with a quiff that was heavily Brylcreemed (a little dab will do ya), brown slacks, brown shoes and a yellow shirt with the collar turned over a brown sports jacket. Pineapple Joe, Danny silently observed, was going to be called upon to do a severe makeover if Jack O'Shea were to pass muster as the new mayor.

This reminded Danny of a story Lachlan had told him. Tommy O'Hearn had ordered a new suit from Pineapple Joe and when it was ready he'd asked him to send it around and not to bother with the bill; it was to be Joe's contribution to the local Labor party. Tommy added that he required two more contributions to the party every year. Joe had delivered the suit in one of his famous Pineapple Joe suit packs with a pineapple stencil on the outside. When O'Hearn unzipped it, he discovered that the suit was held together with pins. Pineapple Joe had added a note that read, *You are tryink to stitching me up! Try now stitching up your own suit, big fat Nobody Smarty Pants!* Not only was Joe's English improving, but he was probably the only person on the peninsula who was totally bulletproof. He didn't owe anyone anything and, until Tommy O'Hearn came along, he had no enemies.

Keri entered the boardroom with tea and a tin of Arnott's Assorted, offering it to them. Jack O'Shea picked carefully, like a kid not accustomed to treats, finally selecting four, all with some sort of filling. Tommy O'Hearn simply took two handfuls without looking and deposited them on the table beside his teacup. Neither bothered to register Keri's expression as she departed.

Danny sat on the opposite side of the two Labor officials. 'Well, obviously you're not here looking for a good lawyer. What can I do for you, gentlemen?' he asked.

'Danny, you done the wrong thing by the party,' O'Hearn began.

'A matter of loyalty,' O'Shea added.

'Oh, and why is that?'

'You know why, mate!' O'Hearn spat.

O'Shea, a biscuit filled with bright pink cream halfway to his mouth, paused. 'Brokendown Street, them boarding houses, getting all them poor people evicted,' he accused.

'Oh, I see, exploiting the poor, is that it?'

'Yeah, you got it in one, mate. Poor buggers had nowhere to go. We was trying to make sure they was took care of.'

'Correct me if I'm wrong, but I think the court proved fairly conclusively that there were several others who were taken care of, and it wasn't the old and the poor.'

Tommy O'Hearn, mouth crammed full of biscuit, simply shook his head, while Jack O'Shea looked at him as if to say, 'Shall I tell him or will you?' O'Hearn nodded to his partner in crime.

'We seen where your mother bought them houses – them boarding houses. I always took her for a smart woman.'

'We all make mistakes,' Danny grunted.

O'Hearn dipped a biscuit into his tea. 'Yeah, well, never can tell what stupid things people will do, can ya?'

'Meaning what?'

'It could be that the council is thinking of condemning the lot, eyesore on the beautiful harbour,' Jack O'Shea ventured.

Danny paused, then started to clap. 'Now you're talking! Good on ya, Jack, bloody excellent move. Get rid of the factories and warehouses, buy my mum out – I'm sure she'd be happy to accommodate the council for a small profit – and that'll give you a mile of harbour-front to turn into a park and plant trees; kids can play, sail boats, fly kites, race billycarts.' He turned and leaned over the table towards O'Shea. 'Jack, mate, you'll be the most popular mayor ever and you'll have my own and everyone else's support!'

'Whoa! Steady on! Factories mean workers' jobs,' O'Hearn said, spitting biscuit crumbs, totally taken aback at Danny's unexpected reaction. 'Not in the party's interest, mate. Can't condemn a perfectly good factory, now, can we?'

Danny put on a disappointed face. 'Jesus, for a moment there I thought you were fair dinkum, that things were going to happen at last. I should have known better,' he said, playing it for all it was worth.

'We're not into stealin' the bread out of the workers' mouths, mate; we leave that to the fuckin' lawyers. But them houses, that's different. Court said they was slum dwellings. They're empty – only two things can happen to them: pull 'em down or renovate. Like Jack said, they's an eyesore.' He looked at O'Shea. 'Can't have that now, can we, Mr Mayor?'

Jack O'Shea shook his head. 'They're rubbish, mate. Can't have rubbish on the foreshore. Gotta clean it up. Be me first job as the new mayor, I reckon.'

'What, pull them down and build new ones – new houses?' Danny asked.

'Nah, shouldn'ta been there in the first place. Prime industrial site that,' Tommy O'Hearn said, adding, 'Close to the city, deep waterfront – need a bit of dredging for the big ships to come in, that's all – lotsa new jobs for the workers.'

'What if my mother decides to renovate? Using union labour, of course,' Danny added quickly.

'Of course, don't want no troubles with the union, mate,' Tommy O'Hearn said complacently.

'But then the unions wouldn't be able to find anyone prepared to work on the project. Council fines for non-compliance would follow.' Danny paused. 'That it?'

'You know you always did catch on pretty quick, Danny,' O'Hearn said, enjoying himself.

'And what do I have to do to avoid this, Tommy?'

'Simple, comrade,' O'Hearn said smiling. 'You don't stand as an Independent.'

'And everyone backs off?'

O'Shea spread his hands and smiled. 'Simple, ain't it, mate?'

'And if I do stand?'

'Well, Jack here is on the council and he's gunna be the next mayor. The land on the foreshore is both residential and industrial; they done that way back in the 1890s when the workers lived next to the factories. It's high time it were changed, only it's harbourside property, so it's both state and council. We reckon it should be classified industrial – jobs for the workers. Me being the member for Balmain, and Jack here the next mayor, shouldn't be too hard to get that legislation through parliament and council. We'll give 25-year leases for the factory owners already there, the same for newcomers. Won't be any houses left standing, mate. Maybe your mother could build warehouses after she's pulled down what's there, that's if she can get any union labour to work for her, and as you know we don't let no scab labour into Balmain. Looks like a rock and a hard place, Danny, don'tcha reckon?'

'What? You scared I'm going to kick your arse at the next election, Tommy?' Danny said.

'Nah, mate. Balmain's always been Labor, always will be, but why make trouble for yourself if it ain't necessary?' O'Hearn shrugged.

'Yeah, you're scared all right, Tommy.' Danny smiled. 'Oh, yes, and Jack, with an Independent in, it might give people the idea that the council could benefit from a change as well. What do you say?'

'Bullshit!' O'Shea said. 'That'll be the fuckin' day!'

Danny reached over and picked up the boardroom phone. 'Keri, can you bring in the lists on my desk, the copy we made? Thanks. Oh, Keri, bring in a toilet roll as well, will you?'

Tommy O'Hearn looked at Jack O'Shea and couldn't resist: 'What, you've shit yer pants, have yer, mate?'

Keri brought in a roll of toilet paper and a copy of Riley's list on which were underlined all the names of everyone on the council, and on the Labor councils where the boarding houses had been, as well as public servants, police and politicians, right up to the Minister for Housing. Among them, of course, were the names of Tommy O'Hearn and Jack O'Shea, together with the date and amount of every payment, going back five or more years. The names of the witnesses were not included.

'Perhaps you'd like to find your name and verify the amount you received as a bribe,' Danny said. 'I have a list of twenty-two witnesses who are prepared to testify in court.'

He handed the sheets over to the two men and watched as O'Shea's hands began to shake, and O'Hearn's face darkened two shades of apoplectic scarlet and a bright trickle of sweat ran down the side of his face into where his neck would once have been.

'Now, please, gentlemen, I am a criminal lawyer, and one not without some reputation. I know how to use this information if I have to. But then, of course, you'd know that. I'm not asking you to do anything, because if I did, it would be the same as the blackmail you have just attempted to use on me. Whatever decision my mother makes about the Brokendown Street houses must be processed in the normal manner through council; whatever workmen she hires to help her must be allowed to work and we will use union labour whenever there is a union man qualified to do the job. If the foreshore is reclassified as an exclusively industrial zone, I will act immediately. I intend standing as an Independent and I expect a clean fight, so please don't disappoint me. Of course, if in the meantime anything should happen to me, or to anyone close to me, there are instructions left on how to act and where to send this information. Now, I think you should leave.'

Both men rose, then O'Hearn said, 'How do we know you won't use this list anyway?'

'You don't, mate. You don't,' Danny said quietly. 'Oh, Jack, I wonder if you'd do me a small favour?'

'What?' O'Shea demanded, not happy.

'In your next council meeting, could you please gazette the name of the street where my mother has the houses, changing it from Gull Street to Brokendown Street? That's what most people have come to call it.' O'Shea nodded, and headed for the door. As they reached it Danny called out, 'Hey, Tommy, you forgot the shit paper!'

After dinner that evening, while the twins did their homework in their room, Danny and Helen retired to the upstairs verandah with a glass of wine and a pot of tea, and he told her the details of the meeting with the Two Os, omitting the toilet-roll incident. It was a very Balmain boys thing to do, but he knew she wouldn't see the joke – only the cheap shot it so obviously was. Helen then told him about the meeting she and Brenda had had with Hester Landsman.

'Do you reckon you and Brenda can work with her?' Danny asked. 'You've got all the bases covered in one sense – Catholic, Jew and Protestant.'

Helen rolled her eyes. 'Well, Brenda liked her and I've always liked her. She isn't aggressive, but she certainly knows her onions. The only really serious question she asked was, did we think you'd win the election? I told her I'd never seen you give up on anything you'd made up your mind to do. "Ja, Franz says also the same," she said, and that seemed to satisfy her.'

'She didn't have any hints on how I might change the zoning if I did manage to get in as an Independent, did she?'

'No, not exactly, but when I told her about your determination, she

THE STORY OF DANNY DUNN   469

said, "Ja, such a man will win, zen from the inside comes za changes." I guess she meant you can't make changes standing outside looking in. By the way, she couldn't believe what Brenda had paid for the entire street.' Helen laughed. 'She wanted to write a cheque out for her share on the spot, in case we changed our minds.'

'Well, the sooner Franz puts the deal together the better,' Danny advised. 'It would be very wise to start renovating at least your first house as soon as possible – show the Two Os you mean business and put their integrity to the test.'

'Their survival instinct, don't you mean? Neither of them would know the meaning of the word integrity.'

And so the first year of renovations got underway, and Tommy O'Hearn, with Labor back in power, made no move against them. Union labour was plentiful. Leichhardt Council, now under Mayor Jack O'Shea, did nothing, beyond the usual bureaucratic trials, to obstruct progress, and Helen, largely in charge day to day, was not only learning a great deal from the trusted workmen Half Dunn was sending from the pub, but loving it. Much to the disgust of the twins, she'd traded in her Mini Minor for a Holden ute and sometimes even wore blue King Gee overalls and workmen's boots.

Danny and Brenda shared responsibility for the twins' care, and Helen somehow managed, with Brenda riding shotgun, to run the pub during the day and also be on site when she was needed. Fortunately, Brokendown Street was only five minutes away from the Hero, and Half Dunn took over the pub in the evening, allowing Helen time with her girls.

Late one night, when Danny and Helen were about to go to bed, the phone rang.

Helen answered, slightly alarmed by a call at that hour. 'Hello?'

'Hi-ya, Helen. It's Billy calling ya'all from N'awlins. How yer doin', honey?'

'Billy! How lovely!'

'By mah reckoning it's eight o'clock your time. Not too late for you folks, I hope?'

'Billy, it's eight o'clock in Perth, ten o'clock here in Sydney, but it wouldn't matter what time it is – it's lovely to hear from you.'

'Why thank you, honey, but business first, in case this line cuts out on us. I'm coming to Australia November 5, on Pan Am flight 62. Can you book me a hotel close to where you folks live and meet me at the airport?'

'Billy, delighted, but of course you *must* stay with us.'

'That'll be nice, Helen.' He chuckled. 'I'm gonna need me a good lawyer and I do declare I know just the right one.'

'Hang on, I'll call him, but in case the line cuts out I'll say goodbye. I'm so excited you're coming.' Helen laughed. 'We speak so often of our time with you that the twins think you're a character out of a storybook!'

Billy chuckled. 'Bye now, honey, see y'all soon.'

'Danny, it's Billy – Billy du Bois calling from New Orleans,' Helen cried.

CHAPTER THIRTEEN

HELEN WATCHED THE ONCE-A-DAY Pan Am flight coming in to land. It had been sixteen years since they'd seen Billy du Bois and she was naturally a little nervous, not least because Danny was unable to be with her – he was in court all day – and the car had been booked in for a service. She'd been obliged to bring her Holden ute, the front mudguard of which had taken a knock from a forklift truck on the building site. She found herself worrying that it wasn't the sort of vehicle Billy would be accustomed to, and worse still, that he might think she was a stereotypical female driver. *Come on, girl, you've got a doctorate and you're thinking like a high-school student with 'L' plates*, she castigated herself.

The 707 jet taxied into a landing bay and Helen made her way to the reception area outside the customs hall. She was certain she'd recognise Billy – after all, there couldn't be too many passengers who were six feet four inches tall, with the build to match, coming through the door wheeling a baggage cart – and, of course, she was correct. He emerged, a hulk of a man immaculately dressed in a grey custom-made suit, cream silk shirt and russet tie, and wearing a cream panama hat which showed sufficient hair for Helen to see that it was streaked with grey. He wasn't fat but he was deep-chested and just beginning to thicken around the waist. He'd always had presence because of his size, but now he was imposing; he was a man who couldn't possibly be ignored. He didn't see her because he was talking to a slim, fair man wearing jeans tucked into cowboy boots, a white marine-style T-shirt, a leather bomber jacket and a cream Stetson with James Dean sunglasses perched on the brim. Most of the other men coming through customs wore suits so that the bloke Billy was talking to appeared somewhat incongruous among the formally dressed passengers now being swept up by chattering families wearing their Sunday best. The second man must have been at least six feet tall but he looked small and slight beside Billy's bulk. Helen was reminded what a truly good-looking man Billy was.

'Billy! Billy du Bois! Over here!' she shouted, waving.

At the sound of his name Billy looked up, saw Helen and waved, turning his baggage trolley towards her. To Helen's surprise the second man followed him. 'Helen, honey, howdy!' Billy swept her into a huge bear hug, so that the people standing nearby laughed and the blond man smiled as his eyes met Helen's. 'You're just as beautiful as ever, baby doll!' he boomed.

'Welcome to Australia, Billy! It's so lovely to see you!'

'Helen, this is Dallas.'

'Dallas?'

'Yeah, he's from Texas, but not from Dallas,' Billy chuckled. 'That's his real name – Dallas Honeywell, my partner. Dallas, this is Helen Dunn – Dr Helen Dunn.'

'Howdy, Dr Dunn, nice to know you.' Dallas offered his hand.

Helen took it and smiled. 'Welcome, Dallas. Please, it's Helen, and don't take too much notice of the doctor.' She released his hand. 'We don't stand on ceremony in Australia, and besides, right at this moment I'm a bartender and building-site manager.'

'Helen, I apologise for the change of plans, but Dallas only got back to N'awlins from Vegas the day before yesterday and told me he was free to come along. We tried to call, but the time difference was against us, so we took a chance, but we'll stay in a hotel —'

'You'll do no such thing; we have seven bedrooms and plenty of linen. You'll both be very welcome.'

'We don't need a bedroom each, honey,' Billy chuckled. 'In fact, we don't need separate beds. Dallas here is more than jest mah business partner.'

'Oh!' Helen said, momentarily taken aback, not at the realisation that Billy was homosexual but that it had never occurred to her. In all the letters they'd exchanged over the years, she'd never thought to ask him about his love life or lack of a wife. A six foot four inch master sergeant on a Harley-Davidson motorcycle who single-handedly liberated a Japanese prisoner-of-war camp didn't fit the stereotype. Billy was handsome, generous, intelligent and charming, a man most women would drool over, and every inch a man's man. She knew he spent a lot of time in Las Vegas, the centre of the world for firm young female flesh, and had assumed he liked to play the field. Helen smiled, attempting to hide her surprise, and said warmly, 'Billy, we love you, and I'm sure we will love Dallas, too.'

Dallas smiled. 'Much appreciated, ma'am . . . er, Helen. Folk in the small Baptist-belt town in Texas where I hail from don't take too kindly to the notion.'

'I'm afraid we're not a lot better here, Dallas. Homosexuality is still a crime in Australia, and quite recently Danny defended one of our major writers, proving conclusively that the police had attempted to blackmail him in order to extort money. While Danny won the case, the police were let off with a rap on the knuckles, and Danny said the only reason he won was because his client came from an old, moneyed and very influential family and was revered by the literati.'

They had left the concourse and were on the way to the parking lot. 'Ain't any different back home, Helen,' Billy grinned, reassured. 'But we ain't here to look for action; we're a couple and we don't play around. Now, answer this question, please: "Are there no flies in Australia?"'

'Of course, probably enough to cover the state of Texas,' Helen laughed.

'Bugs?' Billy asked again.

'You mean insects? Sure, Sydney is the cockroach capital of the world. But why do you ask? We've got mosquito netting on every window.'

'Well, as soon as they opened the doors of the plane this guy in white overalls and a face mask steps in, an aerosol can in each hand, and he walks down the centre of the plane and sprays us all with some kinda insecticide that don't smell so good. I said to Dallas, "What do you suppose? They're trying to kill American bugs?"'

Helen laughed. 'You're right about the bugs, Billy.' She then explained the concept of 'island Australia'.

They had reached the car park before Helen remembered she had brought the ute. Slim-hipped or not, there was no way the two men would fit in the cabin of her Holden ute unless Dallas sat on Billy's lap, and even then it might be tricky with the height of the roof. Also, given the conversation of just a few moments before, it would not be a good look. 'Oh dear, I'd forgotten about the ute!' she cried. 'You won't fit in, we'll have to get a taxi!'

Dallas chuckled. 'Hell, ma'am, I grew up sittin' in the back of a pick-up: six brothers and mah big sis, Kate – she sat in the front with mah folk, Heck and Billy-Jo.' He loaded their bags into the back of the ute then vaulted in after them, settling himself comfortably. 'Okay, let's go!' he called, banging on the roof.

On the way in, Billy asked about Danny and his looming political career, and Helen explained about Balmain and her leaving the university to run the pub and supervise the renovation of Brokendown Street. 'It's a strange time for us,' she confessed, 'and I'm still getting over the change from Dr Dunn, senior lecturer in Egyptology, to site forewoman and publican. Most of the older workmen call me "girlie" and the young ones "boss", while the patrons in the pub just call me "Doc Gyppo".'

Helen then outlined how Brenda had taken over much of the care of the twins and Danny helped with their swimming training. 'Samantha, in particular, but Gabrielle as well until she sits for the entry exam to the Conservatorium. Danny believes, and so does their coach, that Sam could make the Commonwealth Games in Jamaica in 1966.'

'But I seem to remember Danny saying something about rowing . . .' Billy said.

'Yes, you're right. For a long time Danny wasn't sure whether he wanted the girls to be champion swimmers or champion rowers,' Helen smiled, 'but swimming seems to have won out over rowing. They still go out sometimes, but mainly for fun now.'

'Hey, that's really something! And Gabrielle, she's a musician? That's one hell of a family. What instrument does she play?'

'The violin. She's talented but there's so much competition with the violin. She may switch to the viola or even the cello, but she loves her violin.'

'Honey, you tell her if she passes her exams, her Uncle Billy is going to get her the best brand-new violin or viola or cello money can buy, and Dallas and me are going to be cheering Samantha in Jamaica if she makes . . . what did you say they were?'

'The British Empire and Commonwealth Games – thirty-four nations competing.'

'Jamaica, that's almost next door. We'll be there,' Billy assured her.

'That would be nice. We'll all meet up if she makes the team,' Helen said. 'You can tell them yourself. The twins are very excited about meeting you.'

'Dallas went out and bought them both a Stetson; he just hopes he's got the size right. He wanted to get them a pair of cowgirl boots but I told him better hold off till next time, when we can be sure of the size.'

The twins loved their Stetsons – even though they were rather too big for them, with paper stuffed inside the headbands the girls thought they were the bee's knees – and they both took to the two Americans immediately, too. It turned out Dallas played the harmonica and knew hundreds of folk tunes. Before long he and Gabby were engrossed in learning 'House of the Rising Sun'. 'It's a traditional song, but there's this new singer called Bob Dylan who's just released a recording. Plays one mean harmonica, Gabby.' Gabby immediately fell in love with Dallas, Dylan and folk music.

Sitting on the upstairs verandah after dinner, watching the lights on the harbour, Danny said, 'Billy, tell us a bit more about these poker machines. No offence, but I find it hard to take them seriously. But you reckon they're the way of the future, eh?'

'I sure do. My family has made a lot of money out of the poker-machine business, and as a hotel-owning family, you should be interested too.'

'Don't mind him,' said Helen with a laugh. 'He thinks anything other than the law or sport is frivolous. I'm interested. Please, go on.'

'Well, honey, William "Billy" du Bois Incorporated has about fifteen per cent of the slot-machine market in Nevada, where they're legal, and twenty per cent of the unofficial . . . well, hell, the illegal machines in the rest of the country. We had a big share of the market in Havana, Cuba – maybe thirty per cent – but that commie Castro closed down the casinos. But since Kennedy got the better of him last month, and we can all breathe easy again, we're hopeful that business may be back to normal before too long.'

Danny shook his head and said, 'Cuba? They brought us to the brink of nuclear war! If —'

'Hold your horses, darling,' Helen interrupted. 'I really do want to hear what Billy has to say about these machines.'

'Well, I was just about to say that maybe it's time we looked elsewhere. We'd like to take a look-see at Australia. We ain't the first American company in your market but we reckon we are the best, and by most standards the game here is almost honest. You have over a thousand clubs in this great state with over ten thousand machines in operation. That is just about a big enough market for us to enter with the Willy Billy duB slot machine. We don't do penny-ante, but your market is going to grow. Once your state government sees the amount of tax revenue they can harvest for doing nothing, they'll soon be addicted. The next three years will see the number of machines double and, yessir, we aim to be here. And as sure as night follows day, the other states will open their markets.'

Danny looked doubtful. 'This is a country that gambles on horses and dogs, Billy. I know the pokies are going great guns, but wait till the wowsers start yelling . . .'

'Wowsers?' Dallas said, puzzled. 'That's a word I ain't heard before, but the way it comes to mah ears it don't sound good.'

'The church groups, temperance groups – they're a fairly formidable lobby.'

'But horses and dogs are okay?'

'Yeah, but like your country, off-course betting isn't allowed, in theory.'

Billy laughed. 'So how is it done, who owns the scam? You ain't got a strong mafia . . .'

'We refer to it as SP bookmaking. Almost every pub has an operator, except the Hero – Mum's always been dead against it. It's illegal, but big business all the same, and I can't see that changing.'

'Okay, so here's mah next question: what is the ratio of men to women amongst punters on the horses and dogs?'

'I can't answer that except to say that men would be the overwhelming majority.'

'Ah ha, and what if I told you that slot machines, one-arm bandits, are mostly played by women?'

'Good lord! Are you sure? That simply wouldn't have occurred to me.' Danny turned to Helen. 'Next time we're at the Tigers' let's check that out.'

'Brenda likes to have a flutter,' Helen remarked, adding, 'didn't you know that?'

'Mum?' said Danny. It was a new insight into a mother who, as far as he knew, had worked hard for every penny she'd ever made.

Dallas, who had largely been silent, now said, 'The grind, that's where the dough is: small time, many times – it all adds up. In this business we think small and often. In the horse races you can make how many bets? Maybe ten in an afternoon of racing. A lotta folk study the form and only lay one or two bets, but on the bandits they can have one every twenny seconds.'

'But . . . but, surely, the state can only sustain so many clubs and the clubs can only own so many machines; soon enough the market is going to be saturated. Where's the new business for your company going to come from?' Helen asked. 'I mean, you can't keep supplying machines to a limited number of outlets, can you?'

'Ah, that's where you're wrong,' Billy said. 'Gamblers are addicted to challenge and to change. They love new models. Every year we bring out new features, like more reels, multi-line payouts, bigger payouts – it goes on forever.'

'Hey, wait on, surely if you increase the size of the payouts, you kill the goose that lays the golden egg!' Danny cried.

'Goddamnit, Danny, you ain't thinking like a businessman. If a quarter can make you a jackpot of a thousand dollars instead of fifty, that's very exciting news, but, of course, the jackpot comes along a lot less often.'

Helen laughed. 'I guess tapping into human weakness has always been the perfect business.'

'Well, Helen, honey, you're an anthropologist, you can answer that better than I can,' Billy ventured.

'Ah ha, yes, gambling was a feature of ancient Egypt; it's been around for some time,' Helen said.

'Ancient Egypt, hey? I'd surely like to hear about that. But you're right, gambling is ingrained in the human psyche.'

Helen nodded. 'I'm sure you're correct, but why would a club buy your machines when they're used to other brands?'

'Good question, Helen,' Dallas said. 'Now we're into my area, ma'am. You see, the whole business is full of crooks. The problem ain't the club committee – they don't work in the club, and they're usually a bunch of good citizens who ain't around at one o'clock in the morning when the machines are serviced and the money accounted for. It's the management and staff who run the club or the casino who often cain't resist temptation.'

'The point is, you don't miss what you've never had,' Billy cut in.

'Which reminds me,' Helen said suddenly, glancing at Danny. 'Brenda told me of a scam she uncovered yesterday, which I haven't had time to tell you about. I missed it completely. She's fired Ray Hankin over it.'

'Ray Hankin! But he's been there ten years running the bar. That can't be true – I'd trust him with my life; he was in my battalion in Singapore, salt of the earth.'

'Well, it seems he's been salting it away, all right. Brenda discovered it purely by chance.' Helen turned to Billy and Dallas. 'Would you mind if I quickly explained this to Danny?' she asked.

'You want us to leave, honey?'

'No, no, of course not! But it means interrupting you and we're anxious to hear more. It's just that the bar manager may call Danny at work tomorrow pleading innocence, and he needs to know what's going on, but with all the excitement of your arrival, I forgot to tell him.'

'Go right ahead, Helen. We've got all night. We'll be too jet-lagged to sleep much,' Dallas said.

Helen smiled briefly, then began. 'It seems Ray buys a couple of bottles of Johnnie Walker for thirty-five shillings and brings them to the bar when he comes to work. When the legitimate Hero bottle is empty he replaces it with one of his own. As you know, the mark-up on spirits is one hundred per cent, so he sells his own bottle for three pounds ten shillings in nips, making a hundred per cent profit. Brenda didn't catch on because the bottle stock isn't short and the till is perfectly reconciled. She told me you all used to joke about him replacing his Holden every two years, and how his stock answer was that he preferred cars to wine, women and song. Judging by his new Holdens, he's been running this scam for ten years. He's cheated her out of thousands!'

'Christ, that's sad. I persuaded her to give him the job in the first place because he was having the usual post-war problems. Brenda kept his job open even though he'd sometimes be away for days on end when the things in his head got too much for him. How did Mum find out?'

'Purely by chance. She moved his bag to get something and heard the bottles clink, and she thought he might have helped himself from the storeroom, but when she checked, everything was there. It didn't take her long to work out what was happening, so she put a mark on the labels of all the Scotch in stock and kept an eye on the bar bottle. Sure enough, an unmarked bottle turned up on the rack. She let Ray do it three times before she confronted him, then fired him on the spot.'

Danny turned to Billy and Dallas. 'I guess that's pretty much what you were talking about with the pokies.'

Billy shook his head and sighed. 'Greed and temptation; humans can't resist either. But, thank the good Lord, as long as they exist, the gambling business will be profitable.'

'The ancient Egyptians had a game called *senet*, a kind of combination of backgammon, draughts and chess, on which they often wagered their fortunes – houses, slaves, concubines, the lot. They believed it was given to them in a book of magic written by the god Thoth, and so, literally, was a gift from a god.'

'Well, we have much to thank the good god Thoth for. Shall I continue?' Dallas asked.

'Of course. Sorry about the interruption,' Helen said.

'No, ma'am. I reckoned I knew every scam in the book, but I ain't heard that one before. So, at the end of a busy grind every machine becomes a cash cow ready for milking. The secret is to get the money out of the milk pail before it can be counted.

'The scam is usually in place from the beginning. The slot-machine agency, generally owned by a crime syndicate, sells the machines to the committee and then "interviews" the manager – it's called "familiarising" him with their machines. That's when the scam is first set up. It's the club management's reward for keeping a particular agent's machines and "updating" them from time to time.

'If the club committee has never seen accurate figures for a machine, then they don't miss the fifteen or twenty per cent taken off the top each night. As Billy says, you don't miss what you never had, and your barman was the same with his Scotch bottle. He sees to it the till reconciles. And with slot machines, the till is like a car's odometer, only the manager is shown how to wind the day's tally back to the amount left after the percentage has been skimmed off.' Dallas laughed.

'Nice work if you can get it,' Danny said. 'Is there nothing to prevent this happening?'

'Absolutely!' Billy said. 'Our new Willy Billy duB machine can accurately meter every take from every linked machine. One reading tells you the individual take and the combined take for the day's grind.'

'And it can't be tampered with?'

'Ain't nothing cain't be tampered with, but doing so is well beyond the knowledge of the average club manager and requires roughly two hours' work by a slot-machine mechanic. That makes a Willy Billy duB slot machine very popular with club owners and committees, and very *unpopular* with managers and staff.' Billy chuckled, then went on. 'Our sales pitch is simple enough. We guarantee to increase takings for the club by ten per cent, while giving the player exactly the same percentage payout. It's an irresistible offer, especially as we give a fortnight's trial. The result is always above the guaranteed ten per cent. Suddenly they see the light – the club is doing real well – and now the committee or the owner *does* know what he's been missing. This usually results in a new manager and new casino or club staff, the removal of all the rival machines, and a clean club making good money.'

Danny laughed. 'And a poker-machine supplier named *William "Billy" du Bois Incorporated* with a whole new bunch of enemies.'

'You got it,' Billy grinned. 'It's a tough game, but not if you know how to handle things.' He looked over at his partner. 'That's where Dallas comes in.'

'Is this what happens in America? Las Vegas?' Danny asked.

'Of course,' Dallas replied.

'Well, if you're using Australia as a test market for the new Willy

Billy duB machines, aren't you going to run into trouble when you put them in back home?'

'No, Danny, when everything is corrupt it's much easier to handle. You see, the casinos are owned by the mob – the mafia. If they catch a card dealer cheating or a staff slot-machine scam, they take the culprit for a ride into the desert and he or she is buried in a shallow grave with a hand sticking up above the sand holding a blackjack card or a silver dollar in their cold dead fingers. The point is that the mob do the skimming themselves before the government man takes his share as tax, so stealing from the mafia ain't wise.'

'And where do we come in?' Danny asked.

'You can be our agent or simply our lawyer, or both. What we do in our company is completely honest and above board, and we would expect the same from our agent in Australia. But our business has been in this game now for forty years and I just want you to know the parameters. If you take on our agency, you're gonna make, if you'll excuse the French, a shitload of dough, but in order to keep the hoods away you're going to need to include a security operation as part of the operating costs. You'll get our machines on consignment so your starting costs will be minimal. Dallas will show you how to keep the bad guys away. If you're not happy to come in,' Billy spread his hands and smiled, 'Danny, I love you like a brother and you'll still have our legal work. We're not going to have any trouble appointing an agent; we know the Packer organisation is interested, as are several other parties.'

Danny looked at Helen. 'Billy, you don't understand, this is not my decision. I'm no businessman – just ask my partner, Franz!' He smiled at his wife. 'If Helen's interested, she will make the decision, not me. This would be her operation, that is, Helen and her partners.'

Helen smiled. 'Billy, of course we want to be your agent, but you'll have to meet my two partners first – Brenda Dunn and Hester Landsman.'

The first opportunity Danny had to talk to Helen about Billy being queer was in their bedroom that night. He wandered out of the bathroom, still cleaning his teeth, the toothbrush working and the paste frothing.

'Can'tgetoverBilly,' he said.

'Can't understand a word, darling.'

'Okay. Justamo.' Danny turned towards the bathroom and reappeared in the bedroom a couple of minutes later.

'Now, what was all that about?' Helen asked, climbing into bed.

'Billy! Who'd ever have thought?'

'Does it really matter?' Helen replied, right eyebrow arched.

Danny didn't answer, thinking, then said, 'When he appeared at the gates of the prison camp on his Harley with the sidecar loaded with smokes, he was the toughest son of a bitch I'd ever seen. He looked like a giant . . . in fact he was a giant! This huge monolith suddenly appearing in front of several hundred starving, spindly-legged, sallow-cheeked, hollow-chested human wrecks. He decked the two Jap guards at the gate as if he were swatting a couple of flies. When he told us he'd come to liberate us on his own, there wasn't a man present who didn't believe he was capable of doing so. This bloke was Jesus Christ in an army uniform garlanded with ammo belts.' Danny paused. 'I just don't believe it – Billy a shirt lifter, a pillow biter, a pansy. Christ, no way!'

Helen suddenly sat bolt upright in bed and glared at him. 'Oh, how charming, Daniel Corrib Dunn. Are you telling me you're a poofter basher?'

'Nah, just a very fucking surprised lawyer.'

'And what? You're disappointed? It changes things?'

'Helen, I've been carrying this image of Billy in my head for how long? Seventeen or so years. You know, great mate, good bloke, tough guy, the quintessential male, and now . . .'

'So what's changed, Danny? Come on, I know you better than that. He's still all those things, as well as generous and smart and kind. He's handing us an opportunity the richest family in Australia would grab if given half a chance, and offering, in effect, to finance us into the business. As far as I'm concerned he's still all the things you said he was and more – much, much more.'

'You mean you weren't surprised when he told you? C'mon, Helen, be honest.'

'Of course I was, momentarily. But then it all made sense, his not taking a wife – as good a man as a woman might find and still single. In retrospect, I should have worked it out years ago, but, of course, I was stuck with the same macho image of him as you were. I've never had a thing about homosexuality – there were heaps of homosexual men in intelligence during the war – but I guess I was thinking in stereotypes all the same, even though I've occasionally fantasised about women.'

Danny crawled into bed beside her. 'Well, at least it's not another man,' he grunted, then started to laugh. 'I guess I'll get over it. I still love the bastard, he's still my mate, but, Jesus, I'm still gobsmacked.'

'Speaking of gobsmacked, darling,' Helen said, running her hand down his chest. 'How about getting that gob smacking? It's high time I tested your French. If you don't use a language, you lose it.'

'Sure you don't want to call in one of your girlfriends?' Danny said, kissing her softly on the mouth.

'Certainly not,' she said sleepily. 'We'll start tonight with lesson number sixty-nine, darling.'

The meeting with Billy, Dallas, Brenda, Hester and Helen went well, and they agreed unanimously to set up the HBH agency – the first initials of the three directors – for the Willy Billy duB machines. The new agency was to be a subsidiary of Brokendown Street Property Investment Pty Ltd.

When Dallas warned them that things could get a bit rough and that they were going to need a security team, they took it in their stride. 'Gangsters from Germany I know already,' Hester said; Brenda had witnessed more pub fights than she'd had hot breakfasts; and Helen had

had military training. These were not three women who would be easily intimidated.

'Danny used an ex-police detective sergeant, Bumper Barnett, when he was investigating Riley. Perhaps you should interview him, Dallas? He knows the crime scene in Sydney well and he's got a fearsome reputation,' Helen said.

Hester was quick to agree. 'Ja, Franz also, he is saying so.'

'What – a bent cop?' Dallas said, alarmed. 'Helen, ma'am, they're a breed not to be trusted.'

'No, he's straight – no convictions – but he's somewhat in disgrace. To use a Billy word, he "misconceived" what was happening outside a brothel in Kings Cross and beat up the eighteen-year-old son of one of our assistant police commissioners. It was a matter of being sent to the bush or resigning from the force. Now he acts as a freelancer and commands a lot of respect on both sides of the legal fence.'

'Will he come on board? I mean, as permanent staff? This ain't no freelance job.'

'I don't know – we'll have to ask him.' Helen turned to Hester. 'Can you ask Franz to give you his phone number? I'd prefer to keep Danny completely out of this. You never know who's watching, with him standing for parliament. We've learned that misconstruction is one of the sharpest knives in the political armoury. Danny calls it, "Calling a man a pig".'

Dallas laughed. 'That's from Texas, ma'am, Vice-President Johnson. He's the expert at hog-calling.'

Billy said, 'You know, ladies, we've never had an all-female Willy Billy duB agency; in fact, we've never had a woman executive. Dallas and I are greatly looking forward to our association with the HBH Agency.'

It was agreed that Brenda would work with Dallas on the security arrangements, but that Half Dunn would run the sales operation and be the troubleshooter, dealing with the club committees if anything went wrong. He would return to the States with Billy and Dallas and be placed on the Willy Billy duB sales team for three months to familiarise him with sales and slot-machine training. As Danny said later, while this was the first job his father had ever had outside the pub, he'd been, in a sense, training for it all his life. Half Dunn could hardly stop beaming; he was being taken seriously at last, and, what's more, in a business for which he could dress in his Runyonesque style.

Dallas and Brenda interviewed Bumper Barnett the day after the meeting. The interview took place upstairs at the Hero, and it was a no-fuss affair conducted around the kitchen table. While Bumper was surprised that Danny wasn't present, Brenda was well enough known in her own right as a Balmain publican, and he paid her due respect as she explained the business. She finished by saying, 'We want someone exclusively, Mr Barnett. You will not be free to work for anyone else. This is a legitimate business and we plan to keep it that way, and so we want you to respond in the same way as you did when you were in the force. Before Dallas briefs you, I have to ask, do you want the job?'

'Well, Mrs Dunn, I've never worked for a woman and —'

'Three women, Mr Barnett,' Brenda cut in.

'Ah, yes, but who will I answer to?'

'Me,' Brenda said, 'and in my absence, my husband, Mick. Are you interested?'

'Definitely, madam.'

'It's Brenda or Mrs Dunn; I don't run a brothel,' Brenda said, in one stroke asserting her authority. 'I don't want you to make up your mind until Mr Honeywell has outlined your duties. After that we'll settle on a suitable salary. I expect you to haggle, but don't expect to win.'

Bumper laughed. 'My mum was Irish and I never won an argument with her. I'll tell you what I hope to take home every week and you can decide, Brenda.'

Dallas was impressed. 'Detective Sergeant Barnett,' he began, paying homage to Bumper's former police rank, 'y'all would know security ain't about physical presence; it's all about perceptions – what's goin' on in the would-be perpetrator's head.'

Bumper Barnett beamed. 'You're right, mate,' he said. 'The silent threat; it's how good law-keeping works.'

'Exactly, that's why Vegas is the most law-abiding town in America; the small-time hoods know if they gonna make trouble, they gonna end up disappeared without leavin' a farewell note for their family. You need the bad guys to know that if they try anything they're gonna get hammered.'

'Yeah, right. But I have to be honest with you both, Sydney isn't that kind of city, and if I tried anything like that, the cops would have my guts for garters. Besides, a one-man law enforcement agency is not gunna work.'

'Right on, buddy. What you've just said gives me confidence you know the game. But we don't want a bunch of ragtag hoods with brain damage looking after our slot machines. We need people the punks know they cain't take no liberties with, with reputations but not crime records, who can back you up when needed. This is your town – have you got any ideas?'

Bumper thought for a moment. 'Lennie McPherson, he's a local Balmain boy . . . Abe Saffron . . .' He thought again, then shook his head. 'Nah, not right them two . . . Oh Jesus, yes! Er, excuse my French, Mrs D. Of course, Perc Galea. Bloody perfect! He's a colourful racing identity, he has no form, he loves Danny Dunn, and he's got the right reputation and organisation to back him up. But . . .'

'But what?'

'He don't strike me as the kind of bloke that's going to work for a salary.'

Dallas looked over at Brenda. 'I'm sure we can find a way to interest him. Can y'all organise a meeting?' he asked.

'Sure, when?'

'Tomorrow?'

'I'll try, mate.'

'Day after if you have to, no later,' Dallas said. 'Time's gettin' real short. Don't pay to be away too long.'

Bumper Barnett wasn't present when Brenda and Dallas met Perc Galea, upstairs at the Hero. Galea listened as they outlined the business. 'I'm horses and dogs,' he said when they finished, 'but I don't suppose the pokies are all that different. Probably knock into a mate or two.' He sighed, shaking his head slowly. 'Afraid I can't do it for five per cent, Mrs Dunn, Mr Honeywell – ten per cent of the business and I just might be interested.'

To Dallas's surprise, Brenda laughed. 'If we offered five per cent to any big businessman in this town he'd snap it up and pay good money for the privilege. It's a more than decent offer for the use of your reputation, Mr Galea. If Mr Honeywell is right and it's all about perceptions, there'll be very little work involved. We've given you a set of sales projections, and I should add they're very conservative.' Brenda looked directly into his eyes. 'Now, I'm going to make you one more offer, Mr Galea. We'll give you seven per cent if you agree right here on the spot. If you want to go home and crunch the numbers and come back to us tomorrow, then it will revert to a five per cent share. If that's not acceptable, I quite understand, no hard feelings; we'll simply make other arrangements.' She continued to stare down the colourful racing identity. 'This is not a one-horse race, but Danny trusts you implicitly and wanted me to give you right of first refusal.' Brenda held her gaze as she waited for Galea's reply.

Perhaps there was something in his Italian background that made him respect older women, or perhaps it was his respect for Brenda's son. 'You're a tough lady, Mrs Dunn. Maybe you should come work for me, hey?'

Brenda, still unflinching, sniffed. 'The only time I ever worked for anyone else I was sixteen and found myself on my hands and knees scrubbing floors.'

'Okay, you got a deal, Mrs Dunn; we'll shake hands on seven per cent. Now, maybe Mr Honeywell here can tell me what to expect.'

The American's respect for Brenda was growing by the minute. 'If'n y'all don't mind, I'd be obliged, now we're in business together, if you'd call me Dallas. Can I call you Perc?'

Galea grinned. 'Yeah, so long as you don't call me Percy.'

'Thanks, Perc, welcome to the Willy Billy duB family. I guess it ain't gonna be much different to Stateside. What we'll require is for the heavy hitters to know you are in business with Willy Billy duB slot machines.'

'I see – what you want is a bit of respect. But if it ain't shown it can be followed up with a bit of biff. Is that right, mate?'

'That's right, Perc. Bumper Barnett will tell you when the biff is needed,' Brenda replied.

'Ah, a good man,' Galea said. 'A very good biff man himself. Matter of fact, I got a lotta respect for him; as a cop he didn't take no apples.'

Billy, Dallas and Half Dunn left for New Orleans a week later, with their new agency established and the promise of the first shipment of machines arriving in the warehouse shortly after Half Dunn's return. Christmas came and went and it would take a good six months of the following year to get the Willy Billy duB agency up and running.

By March the next year Helen had finished renovating three of the houses in Brokendown Street (now its official designation). They were painted white, and neat as a new pin. Bullnose had seen to the landscaping and planted jacaranda trees outside each of them. 'It'll take a few years for 'em to grow, but it'll look bonza with them purple flowers and the white houses.'

Lachlan's new wife, Erin Walsh, who had somewhat outrageously kept her maiden name, persuaded Lachlan to buy one of the houses as their first home. She was a young fashion designer who sensed the start of a new age; fashion for young women was coming out of America and London that she described as 'Beat and Peer'. She had read Jack Kerouac's On the Road and embraced the Beat generation, the precursor to the hippy explosion. She was designing dresses, pants, T-shirts, shorts and shirts in outrageous colours, florals and geometric patterns that ignored all the fashion dictates from France and Italy, and were intended for young people rather than the privileged rich. She was designing clothes that said it was okay to look for personal freedom, and that whispered about sex, drugs and jazz.

She named her fashion label Brokendown, after the street she and Lachlan now lived in, and opened a shop (she refused to call it a boutique) in Darling Street, in partnership with Pineapple Joe. Balmain housewives out doing their grocery shopping visited it for a laugh, and the staff at Freda's Frocks called it an eyesore, a disgrace and an insult to womanhood. 'Entirely appropriate name for that label,' they would sniff, 'entirely lacking in any sense of style or decorum.'

However, younger people loved it and on Saturday mornings shoppers sometimes had to queue to get into the shop. It soon became apparent that the young women Lachlan termed the 'early adopters' were coming from all over Sydney to shop at Brokendown. Pineapple Joe's foray into T-shirts had been mad enough, the locals thought, but this new venture was really over the top. That crazy young woman wore beads and bangles and colours that clashed hideously, and she obviously didn't wear a step-in under those sacks that passed for dresses; why, the way her body moved was nothing short of obscene.

When she introduced miniskirts and vinyl boots that were inspired by the London fashion designer Mary Quant, they reckoned she had finally gone too far. They loved Joe, but the gossips now suggested there might be a streak of dirty old man in him that nobody had been aware of before. Otherwise, why would he partner in business with a young woman who was obviously not quite right in the head, who wore skirts up to her crotch that ought to have her arrested for indecent exposure.

But Erin Walsh had started something that wasn't going to go away. The next two renovated houses in Brokendown Street were snapped up by two young couples in advertising, friends of Lachlan. Helen soon had deposits from young married couples on six more homes which were yet to be renovated. While the first three renovations were financed by Brenda and Hester, Harry Farmer from the Bank of New South Wales was happy to finance the next six once he'd seen the deposits. When they were eventually sold, Brenda would have recovered the money she'd paid for all twenty-eight houses.

Some of the Balmain folk were beginning to sense some sort of change was in the air, and Danny's door-knocking and his Tiger 13 message were beginning to become more meaningful. While, of course, Danny wanted everyone's vote, Lachlan had established that women were Danny's true believers. They were the ones most trapped in the eternal cycle of poverty, who had always mindlessly voted the way their husbands had told them to. Danny, without making it obvious, targeted the female vote. It was from them he'd earned a silent gratitude for his stand against domestic violence, and, as Lachlan pointed out, voting Tiger 13 was a way they could repay his caring for them over the years.

Tommy O'Hearn and Labor's advertising agency, McCann Erickson – under the tsar of political advertising, the irascible and redoubtable Sim Rubensohn – soon realised that, for the first time, Balmain was a potentially vulnerable seat, and targeted the male vote. The local Labor slogan, printed in black on white T-shirts and distributed free, appealed directly to local pride and the unique 'Balmain Boy' image. As was usual with Sim Rubensohn, the approach was right on the money, direct and designed to appeal to the working-class male mind.

Balmain
Jobs for workers
Not homes for wankers
Vote Labor

The battle of the sexes was on, and Danny and his team always ended a visit to a household or group with the words, 'Remember your ballot is secret and how you vote is a private matter for your conscience and nobody else's.' This mantra was repeated so many times that voting for Danny was simply referred to as 'The Conscience Vote'. With two years to go it was a long haul, but pleasingly more and more women, and some of the men, were beginning to sport Tiger 13 T-shirts.

Danny gave every appearance of accepting Gabby's choice of music over swimming, but he was nevertheless bitterly disappointed. By nature a dreamer, but also a believer, he often followed his dreams to the point of absurdity, but he was never left wondering what might have been.

This wasn't always easy on Helen, who had to live with a man rigidly determined to pursue a course once he had made up his mind. She had to take the good with the bad. For instance, Danny may have dealt with Riley, but he still had a reckoning to come with Colonel Mori, the Japanese commander of the prison camp; conversely, he was determined that Spike Jones, the little medical orderly who had risked his life to hide the flag, should get the recognition he deserved.

In his speech when he received the Military Medal from the governor-general, Danny had spoken about Jones and the system that denied brave men recognition because an officer hadn't witnessed their acts. 'It discounts the word of the ordinary soldier who is prepared to give his life for his country. In return his country thinks so little of him that his word cannot be trusted. It is not the beribboned generals who preserve freedom and democracy, it is men like the little Welshman Paul Jones who keep the flag of freedom flying,' he ended.

Afterwards at the reception, the Governor-General, Viscount De L'Isle, approached Danny and said, 'Mr Dunn, would you kindly send me the details of Private Jones? I am not only Australia's governor-general, and I will attempt to use what influence I have at home to see that he receives the recognition he undoubtedly deserves.'

'Thank you, sir,' Danny answered, realising that he'd broken his promise to himself and called an officer 'sir'.

Six months later in a ceremony held at the British War Museum, where the Union Jack that had flown over the camp on the morning of the Japanese surrender was on display, Private Paul 'Spike' Jones was awarded the DSO by the Duke of Edinburgh for distinguished service while a prisoner of war under the Japanese.

Danny had flown over as a guest of the British Government to see Spike's bravery recognised. Immediately after the little medic had received his medal, a choir from his hometown of Pontypridd sang the anthem, 'Land of our Fathers', the first verse and chorus in English and two more in Welsh.

> *The land of my fathers is dear unto me*
> *The land of the poets, the land of the free*
> *Her patriots and heroes her warriors so brave*
> *For freedom their life's blood they gave.*

> **Chorus:**
> *Wales! Wales!*
> *Pledged am I to Wales*
> *Whilst seas surround*
> *This land so proud*
> *Oh, long may our tongue remain.*

Danny had forgotten that Spike Jones hadn't seen his new face. When they finally met up after the ceremony, the little Welshman took one look at him and exclaimed, 'No, it can't be, can it? My goodness, it is!'

The two men embraced. 'Congratulations, Spike. Only eighteen years overdue, mate!' said Danny.

The two old men o' war spent a week together in Pontypridd, where the mayor had given them both a civic reception and where Danny, much to Spike's embarrassment, told them the story of Paul Jones in the prisoner-of-war camp. It appeared the following day on the front page of the *South Wales Argus* and the day after that in most of the other Welsh newspapers. At long last, the man of peace who'd held his head high in a time of war, Private Paul Jones, Royal Army Medical Corps, became a national hero. Sergeant Major Danny Dunn had finally kept his promise.

Danny flew back to Australia in a Qantas 707. As he settled into his first-class seat, compliments of the British Government, he said softly to himself, *One down, one to go. Mori, you Japanese son of a bitch. You're next, you bastard.*

But in the meantime he had more than enough on his plate, keeping up with a thriving law practice; knocking on doors in the evenings and at weekends, explaining his hopes for Balmain; and getting involved with Sam's swimming.

The law was his work, campaigning as an Independent was about making change happen, but training Sam was his passion. Gabby had passed her music exams with flying colours, and at twelve years of age was accepted into the Conservatorium High School, effectively ending her swimming career. Danny struggled to find any enthusiasm for Gabby's music, but while he didn't say so, her choice left him free to concentrate completely on Sam.

At twelve, Sam was showing a determination to win that made her pit herself against girls of fifteen and sixteen, whom she as often as not beat in the fifty- and hundred-metres freestyle, although she wasn't yet strong enough to be a consistent winner in the two-hundred metres. But Danny believed if he could work with her and Harry Gallagher for the next two years, she would be ready for the British Empire and Commonwealth Games, and while it wasn't the toughest competition in the world, it would be an indication of her potential, and great preparation for the next Olympic Games.

Danny had read Forbes Carlile's book as soon as it had come out. *Forbes Carlile on Swimming* was the first modern book on the subject, and Danny became determined that Carlile become Sam's coach after the games in Jamaica. Sam's times were already indicating that if she progressed as expected, at fourteen she'd have a very good chance of representing Australia in the West Indies.

In the interim he developed a program with her coach for Sam to match other up-and-coming swimmers. The Balmain pool – 73.3 yards long – proved inappropriate for this type of serious training. It was tidal and salt water rather than chlorinated, at low tide the walls were seen to be covered in barnacles, and it wasn't unusual for the pool to be invaded by jelly blubbers and other stingers. The stormwater drains flowed into it after rain, causing the pool to be closed because of pollution. So Sam was moved to Drummoyne pool, known to all as 'Crummy Drummy', and while Danny continued to coach her, she was still under the watchful eye of Harry Gallagher, who coached Dawn Fraser. Because of Harry's association with Balmain, he had always given Danny the benefit of his knowledge.

Sam would need to swim twice a day and throughout the winter, so Danny decided to train her in the channel that sent warm water from the Balmain Power Station into the harbour, where she could swim against the current. He had a pair of foot-hugging rubber slippers fashioned for her so she wouldn't cut her feet on the oyster shells that grew on the channel walls. The prevailing theory was that sheer endurance, using what was known as two-beat kicking, was the key to a swimmer's success, and that future champions were built on distances swum each day under the slogan 'miles make champions'.

Sam was swimming twice a day, six days a week, with each session a total of two and a half miles of what was known as interval training: one-, two- and four-hundred metres at ninety per cent effort broken by a minute between each of slow recovery swimming. This was supplemented by weights training – nothing too strenuous – followed by calisthenics for flexibility and mobility. In all of this Harry Gallagher was working on perfecting her stroke technique. It was tough going and required a great deal of pluck and character from a young girl who was about to go through puberty, but Sam never complained. On the top of every page in the logbook recording her distances she wrote, *Three gold for Sammy*.

While the twins were tall and naturally athletic, the physical differences between them began to show as Sam's training continued: her broad shoulders, tight stomach and muscular legs made Gabby look slender and almost fragile (which she wasn't) by comparison. With Gabby away at the Conservatorium High School, the twins were parted for the first time in their lives, and surprisingly it was Sam who seemed to miss her twin most. Whether it was her twin's absence or the pressure of her training program, Sam missed out on a scholarship to Sydney Girls High and moved up into first year at Balmain High School.

The twins had always been together and as a combination they were never challenged in the school playground, but with Gabby gone and Sam in perpetual training, she no longer had time to spend with her friends and found herself increasingly isolated at school. The twins had always been popular, with Sam the leader and mischief-maker, and Gabby the one who made the peace when things went too far. But now, with Sam seeming to lose interest in playground shenanigans, a group of girls from Rozelle, a neighbouring suburb, took control of the playground and began to pick on her. Sam was a pretty confident kid and it didn't worry her too much – she had lots of backup from the kids she'd grown up with in Balmain. For the most part she took the teasing in her stride, until one day one of the Rozelle kids, a large, lumpish bully named Rosie Bilson, who led the group that tormented the playground, stole her training logbook from her schoolbag. Surrounded by her mates, Rosie circled Sam, holding up the logbook and sneering, 'Three Gold for Sammy! Three gold for Sammy!' The group took up the chant, expecting Sam to laugh it off or hopefully beg for her precious logbook, but Sam said not a word, and simply whacked Rosie Bilson hard on the side of the head with her closed fist, then jumped her, knocking her to the ground. Sam then grabbed Rosie by the hair and smashed her head into the ground three times; then, leaping to her feet, she turned to face the startled gang of girls. 'Who's next?' she hissed.

The screaming Rozelle mob rushed her and Sam was beaten to the ground. Balmain girls ran from all directions to come to her aid, and the skirmish was soon over, but Sam had received a kick to the face and her left eye was rapidly closing. The Rozelle gang backed away, two of them lifting a sobbing Rosie Bilson to her feet and leading her off. Sam, dry-eyed, picked up the logbook and stalked off without another word. The Balmain girls were triumphant, cheering – Sam had recovered the contested playground in the best Balmain tradition. When later in class her history teacher noted her closed and rapidly purpling eye and demanded an explanation, Sam explained with a smirk and a suitably foolhardy look that she'd whacked her eye on a branch when she'd been fielding a ball at rounders, perpetuating the legend that Balmain girls don't cry and neither do they blab. That night two hundred or so Balmain schoolkids proudly recounted the story to their mothers and Danny was a couple of hundred votes closer to being elected the Independent member for Balmain.

But, of course, Helen, having accepted the story of the rounders ball and the mishap with the branch, soon learned the truth at the afternoon soiree. That evening after the twins were asleep, she confronted a tired Danny, first telling him the story, then adding, 'For God's sake, Danny, it all happened over a silly logbook! Children tease each other all the time – she shouldn't have reacted violently like that. Besides, she lied to us. Sam never lies. The child is under too much pressure – it's got to stop!'

'Silly logbook!' Danny, suddenly and unreasonably furious, shouted. 'Did you say silly logbook? There's nothing silly about it! That's Sam's whole life you're talking about!'

But Helen wasn't going to back off. 'What life? Samantha doesn't have a life! She has swimming. The child is exhausted and she's become obsessed. Whenever I talk to her about doing something else she looks at me and says, "I'm fine, Mum. I'm learning to win." Well, she isn't fine, you hear! Her school marks are down and she's perpetually tired. It may not have occurred to you, but she's growing up. The child is going through puberty and all she can think of is gold medals to please her father!' Helen burst into tears.

'Bullshit! She can stop any time she likes. What about Gabby, hey? Did I stop her from giving up, throwing in the towel?'

'Giving up?' Helen shouted through her tears. 'She did no such thing! She happens to be a talented musician!'

'Well, yeah, she's probably going to end up in some orchestra full of long-haired gits and poofters, but if that's what *you* want . . . *she* wants, who am I to argue? But don't you go trying to mess up Sam's head, okay?'

'It's already messed up! Can't you see, she's obsessed, like you! Three gold for Sammy! She says it in her sleep!'

But Danny wasn't listening. 'I won't have it, Helen. As a matter of fact I'm bloody proud of her for whaling on that kid for stealing her logbook. It shows she's got the guts it's going to take to get her to Jamaica in '66 and then Mexico in '68. You keep your hands off *my* twin, Helen!'

'*Your* twin!' Helen screamed. 'She's not *yours*, she's *ours*! How can you say something so cruel?'

Danny, realising he'd gone too far, forced himself to calm down, but he couldn't stop himself from having a final dig. 'Yeah, well, its true. You had your way with Gabby and now you want Sam!'

'That's just not fair!' Helen cried.

'Helen, you're the one who's under stress. You're working too hard – the pub, the houses, the pokies. You're a big-time success, but what about your family? Business is booming, but you need a rest!'

'I'll take one after the fucking election!'

'Helen, *ferchrissake*, we're well on our way to becoming rich. You've proved you can succeed outside the university; you're the one who's becoming obsessed!'

Helen sniffed, knuckling back her tears. 'Don't change the subject. We're talking about Sam. Danny, can't you see – Sam's becoming *you*! You're a damaged person. You admit the war did that to you, and that's understandable, but you're turning swimming into Sam's war! It isn't fair; she's too young to have her life ruined.'

'Ruined? Don't be bloody ridiculous! Sam loves what she's doing! She's the one who wakes me up in the morning to go to training.' Danny paused, then said, grim-faced, 'If you try to undermine me with Sam, I warn you, there's going to be trouble!' He rose from his chair. 'And now I'm going to bed. I have to be up at five-thirty for swimming training. To go to war!' he added, then stomped towards the door, where he turned and shouted, 'And stop that goddamned bawling, will ya!'

'I'm not bawling!' Helen cried, then, on a sudden furious impulse, she grabbed the wine bottle and hurled it at him with all her might. 'You bastard!' she screamed.

Red wine traced a bright arc through the air, then the bottle smashed in a great scarlet splash against the wall to the left of the lounge-room door.

'Go to bed, Helen, you're drunk!' Danny said coldly, closing the door behind him. He turned to see the twins in their pyjamas, standing in the hallway clutching each other, terrified looks on their faces. Sam's left eye was still swollen and purple, but her right was wide and staring. 'Go to your mother, Gabby . . . Sam, you go to bed,' her father commanded.

'No!' Sam cried. 'My mother needs me!'

CHAPTER FOURTEEN

NEW YEAR'S EVE 1964, and Danny and Helen sat on the upstairs verandah alone and happily so. They enjoyed being together when the weary old year petered out and the new arrived with sweet promise. The twins, now thirteen, were at a party at the home of one of Gabby's Conservatorium High School friends in Double Bay and had been given permission to see in the new year. Brenda would pick them up after attending the midnight service at St Mary's Cathedral.

Danny and Helen always shared a bottle of French champagne on New Year's Eve, one of the few times Danny allowed himself to drink. They had toasted every momentous occasion in their lives with it, from the unforgettable, joyously disastrous exploding jeroboam when Danny graduated and became 'a somebody'; to Helen's announcement that she was pregnant; the birth of the twins; the night they'd left for America; the day Danny was awarded his belated medal; and, of course, every New Year's Eve since.

They referred to the occasion as the 'Calling of the Year', both of them sitting quietly and reviewing what had happened in their lives since the last calling. Helen and Danny loved these talks. They served to clear the air of any misunderstandings between them or hurts, and were often illuminating and surprising when they considered the repercussions of apparently innocent or unimportant actions. It was both reassuring and exciting, because they were reminded that the coming year might well hold unforeseen adventures.

While Danny's life had settled into a repetitious and sometimes tedious round of seeding his message of change in the hope that it would blossom during the state election in 1965, Helen's had been packed with challenges that tested her intellect, ingenuity, diplomacy and stamina, and moreover she'd thrived.

She was running the pub during the day, backed up by Half Dunn, who took over at night. The houses in Brokendown Street were selling like hotcakes, some even before they were renovated, and others almost immediately after they were completed and put up for sale. The formula for renovating the houses had been well established by now and their team of workmen knew the processes by heart, so, beyond her daily inspection, Helen had less and less occasion to supervise progress.

The pub was continuing to show a healthy profit and she had plans to incorporate a restaurant into the popular summer beer garden. The success of Billy and Dallas's poker machines had surpassed their expectations, and combined with the steady sale of the renovated houses, Helen was making money hand over fist. The HBH Agency and Brokendown Street Property Investment Pty Ltd had paid off the bank loans they'd needed to finance the purchase and renovation of the Brokendown Street houses and the poker-machine business. The time would soon arrive when they would have to look around for a new investment. Helen was starting to think about opening two or three boutique hotels in the CBD, with good luncheon restaurants and superior accommodation for overseas business executives who wanted a quiet and relaxing stay.

Brenda, now finally free of the responsibility of running the pub, blossomed into an increasingly devoted grandmother, looking after the busy routines of the twins, who at thirteen were becoming more and more independent. Where once their lives had been almost as identical as their faces, now their activities diverged more and more, and often the girls' only chance to enjoy their old intimacy came in their shared bedroom each night.

With time on her hands, Brenda became responsible for the Willy Billy duB machines, which she referred to as her 'naughty job'. She'd spend the mornings and early afternoons touring the clubs that ran HBH machines, talking to the managers or 'troubleshooting', as she called it. She'd always put a couple of pounds through the pokies she so dearly loved, then do a bit of shopping as she went from one to another of the five or six clubs she'd visit most weekdays. She would then race to pick Sam up from school, drive her to the Drummoyne pool for training, and get back home moments before Gabby arrived by ferry from the Con. Danny would pick up Sam, or she'd get a lift or take the tram home. Life free of the polished bar and the smell of hops was sweet for Brenda. She'd also discovered while troubleshooting in the pubs that she was an excellent saleswoman; club committees and managers loved the tough little Irish redhead who understood their concerns, having been in the hospitality business all her life.

Eighteen of the twenty-eight houses in Brokendown Street had been renovated, and Danny now indicated them with a sweep of his champagne glass. 'Sweetheart, it's been your year. Really, you've got your side of the street looking wonderful. Let's hope next year I'll win, and I can start clearing up the dirt and pollution at the water's edge so that the children who will inevitably live in your houses will be able to play in clean harbour water.'

'Darling, perhaps it's time. I can't help feeling things are beginning to change. Maybe it's because I'm mixing with a broader range of people than I was —'

'Publican, builder, sales agent for poker machines . . . it doesn't get much broader,' said Danny.

Helen smiled and continued. 'I'm starting to see things differently. You can . . . well, feel it in the air. Things are changing.'

'What – in Balmain or the whole country?'

Helen thought for a moment. 'I don't suppose I can speak for the whole country. But don't you agree that things feel different? It's as though people's thinking has shifted up a gear. I'm not sure I can put my finger on it, but . . . well, as I said, it's in the air.'

'Yeah, perhaps. Things don't change a lot in the law – same villains, same transactions for Franz – and Sam's morning training sessions don't differ much. Weekdays I'm in a bit of a rut.' Danny laughed. 'I've been that busy knocking on doors every weekend, spreading the message of change, I probably haven't had time to notice any of it happening. That's the trouble with life – you get so caught up with the detail you miss the big picture.'

'I guess you're right, but I'm still at heart an anthropologist and the young people I see around . . . well, they seem to me to be jumping out of their skins, expecting a different world from the one we live in now,' Helen reflected.

'Hmm, maybe . . . I'm not so sure. Humans don't change fundamentally, do they? Isn't that your field? Civilisations die because they can't adapt?'

'Probably because the elders of the tribe took no heed of what the young were saying,' Helen said. 'When you look at the big picture, you realise that the past two years have been different, not only for me, but I think for Australia, even the world. Maybe it's television; there are no more dark corners to hide in.'

'Television is going to change the way we live,' Danny said.

But Helen hadn't finished. 'Even the small things . . . when I started taking over the soirees from Brenda just on two years ago, it was still a shandy-and-gossip session, while the women did their knitting, or shelled peas or peeled potatoes. Most opinions about anything beyond what happened in the kitchen or with the kids were introduced by the words, "My husband says . . .". Now that's seldom the case; they talk about change, their hopes, the future, more or less on their own terms.'

'Gawd, that's going a bit far – Balmain housewives thinking for themselves!' Danny exclaimed.

'Don't be rude, Danny Dunn! If you're going to be elected, they're going to be the ones to do it,' Helen chided.

'You're right, darling, I take that back. I'll wash my mouth out with soap later. In truth, the women have always been the backbone of Balmain, keeping it together. Left to the blokes, gawd knows what would have happened.'

Helen laughed. 'In the case of Balmain I think you're wrong. They did leave it to the men, and look at the mess they've made!'

'If you're talking about politics, you're probably right. Few women were politically involved. They never questioned their loyalty to Labor. Balmain *is* Labor, always has been, always will be. But I have to say, I'm getting a slightly better reception when I door-knock these days. We still get the odd bloke in blue singlet and thongs, with a dent in his lower lip where the roll-yer-own sits permanently, telling us to bugger off, but it's less often. Did I tell you Lachlan's got the agency – or rather, their young research bloke, Hugh Mackay – to do a 'How will you vote?' questionnaire for us? The Tiger 13 team are taking it around as soon as the men go back to work mid-January.'

'What – you're writing off the men completely?'

'Not completely, but I think women will respond more honestly without the old man standing behind them scratching his crotch. We'll see the men when they're on the job.'

'But isn't that risky? What about peer-group pressure? And they work locally in the docks and workshops, so it's harder for them to see how cleaning up Balmain will benefit them,' Helen said.

'Yeah, but it's better than going into the pubs. I think we have to accept that we've lost the majority of the male vote. "Jobs for Workers" is a slogan they imbibed with mother's milk. Smoke stacks, noise and soap factories pouring shit into the harbour are what put bread on the table – they can't see beyond that. Some of the younger guys may see it differently and vote Tiger 13, but the rest of the Balmain boys won't change.'

'Well, if the soiree girls are any indication, you've got the women's vote sewn up. One of them asked me the other day how many "free cases" you've done, standing up for beaten wives and children. When I said I didn't know exactly but it was well over two hundred, she said, "Never mind him talking about changes to the harbour and getting rid of the stink; far as I'm concerned he's okay. I haven't been beat up in two years. Danny sent Norm Cross, our neighbour, to Long Bay for beating his wife, Elsie, and the kids, and that scared the livin' shit outta Bill, me husband. That'll do me. Danny's got me vote." Then one of the others piped up and said that when a husband on the peninsula comes home aggro from the pub and wants to take it out on her and the kids, the standard line is "You touch us and you're *done*, mate, Danny *Dunn!*"'

'That's nice,' Danny said, laughing. 'But it probably won't help with the male vote. As Billy du Bois would say, Tommy O'Hearn is going to kick arse this election, pull in all the favours he reckons he's owed. I'm told he was out among the Christmas shoppers in Darling Street, wearing a Santa cap and giving away Labor's new T-shirts.'

Helen laughed too. 'That reminds me, the twins saw him. Samantha put it rather well. She said, "Mum, it was disgusting! He's repulsive. He walks like Godzilla and he's so fat he looks like he's about to give birth to triplets!" She said he was sweating like a pig so the white T-shirt was soaked and clung to his stomach and chest, and all his black stomach and chest hairs were showing through. And the words on the front of the T-shirt said, "100% Genuine Balmain Boy, Vote Labor." "Yuck!" as Sam said. Then Gabby said, "It was truly revolting, Mum. Is Dad going to beat Tommy O'Hearn in the election?"'

'It's curious that they've changed the original T-shirt message; I thought it was spot on for the local voter,' Danny observed.

'You mean "Jobs for workers, not homes for wankers"?'

'Yeah.'

'Then you would have thought wrong,' Helen remarked.

'Oh? And why's that?' Danny asked, surprised.

'The reason is staring you in the face, Daniel Corrib Dunn; it's Brokendown Street!'

'Eh? I'm still not with you.'

'When that slogan first came out it probably *was* spot on,' Helen explained. 'Brenda was the laughing stock of the peninsula, but now nobody's laughing. Now one side of the street is neat and fresh with the beginnings of nice gardens, and eighteen crisp new bungalows that were snapped up by, if you like, the "wankers" on the Labor T-shirts. Of the ten homes remaining I've got deposits on five. Harry Farmer is begging us to borrow money. He's hit the jackpot – he got a performance bonus last year and is hoping for one again this year. And everyone in Balmain is starting to wonder what their place is worth.'

'I suppose so, although it's pretty hard to fathom. The dirt and the pollution remain for all to see across the street, so why on earth is everyone going crazy for them? It isn't logical.'

'It's perfectly logical. Young couples buying in are convinced it's only a matter of time. We tell them we honestly don't know when, if ever, the front will be cleaned up and they nod and say, "It will happen, just you watch. Nifty Dunn will get in." The confidence is there and, like I said, the young are on the move.'

'Jeez, I hope it's justified.'

'It will be,' Helen said confidently. 'Change is in the air.'

'Yeah, I'm yet to be convinced,' Danny growled. 'You know, even if I'm elected, it won't be easy for me to get the harbour front and the other industrial areas rezoned. If Labor gets back, I've got Buckley's, and if Askin wins with a big majority, it might be just as hard.'

Helen smiled lovingly at Danny. 'It won't be as hard as persuading Colonel Mori not to kill one of your men in the camp. Like Bob Dylan says, "The times they are a-changin'", and the Labor Party isn't stupid to be changing their slogan. They realise you've got a damn good chance of winning.' She thought for a moment. 'Although, I actually think they're making just as big a mistake with their "100% Genuine Balmain Boy, Vote Labor" slogan; it's playing right into our hands.'

'How's that?' Danny asked. 'The Balmain Boy thing has always worked before. It's a cliché but it's effective.'

Helen grinned. 'It didn't even occur to them to do a T-shirt that says, "100% Genuine Balmain Girl, Vote Labor"! And, by the way, that's not me making an astute observation; it comes straight from last week's soiree – the ladies shelling peas and peeling potatoes got the message loud and clear that their votes were simply taken for granted.'

'Shit! I never thought of that.'

'That's because you're a man,' Helen said, adding, 'You probably haven't noticed that women are beginning to see themselves in a different light. There's a long way to go, but at least it's started.'

'What's started?'

'Women thinking for themselves – not letting their husbands decide what's good for them.'

'So, tell me, why did I have to end up with the original trailblazer?' Danny laughed.

'Ha ha. But, Danny, you must have noticed. The signs are there for all to see, and it's not just women and girls. Look at Erin's shop! Saturday mornings are a near riot, with kids swarming in from everywhere, and Billy has offered to finance her expansion into Las Vegas. Pineapple Joe's happy as a sand boy with his investment.'

'Yeah, Joe's bought the whole change package, I have to admit. I saw him the other day while I was getting petrol. Now, instead of wearing a suit, he's wearing one of his exclusive Pineapple-brand T-shirts . . . not a pretty sight, I might add. The T-shirt was covered with Campbell's soup cans. "Gone into the soup business, Joe?" I said. "What you talkink about, Danny?" he replied, stabbing at a soup can on his chest. "This soups can's genuine Andy Wall Hole, American pops artist!" Then he gave me the drill. "Suits, finish, finito! Now I am sellink four suits, maybe, in vun month! Danny, lissen to me. Mister Bobs Dylan, he is sayink everythink that was before now is blowink in za wind and zat za times zey are a-changin – you heard zat song maybe on ze radio? Last week I'm sellink tree hundred T-shirt, bit a cotton, some paint, one pound five shilling, thank you, very much oblige, sir." He stuck his forefinger in the air. "One T-shirt I am makink on silk screen in mine special paint, no crack, can stretch, wash like a baby bottom, ten minutes!" Then he tapped me on the chest. "One suit five pounds ten shilling, tree days I am workink finger to bones, and wool material for makink cost two pounds already. You know what is costing me T-shirt raw materials?"' Danny chuckled, wagging his finger in imitation of his old friend. '"Let me tell you, sonny boy . . . five shilling, paint include."'

Helen laughed. 'You do know he financed Erin Walsh and owns half of her Brokendown label, don't you? Remember, he's donating a thousand Tiger 13 T-shirts to your election team to wear and give away during election week.' She smiled ruefully. 'I think it's conscience money. He said not to tell you until closer to the election because, "I got to see a mans about a dogs, because I can make new Labor T-shirt more cheaps and colourfast zen za schmuck they got makink now, who is robbink and cheatink zem mitout sight." I think he meant robbing them blind, but, anyway, he's supplying the enemy, the old scoundrel.'

'Maybe you're right about change,' Danny mused. 'But who was it said the more things change, the more they stay the same?'

'Oh, Danny, even the twins are aware of it,' Helen said. 'Gabby and Sam are mad about the Beatles – they were so excited about the tour. And Gabby's been a Bob Dylan fan since Dallas taught her that song of his. And his latest album's called *The Times They Are a-Changin*'!'

'Hmph,' Danny grunted. 'I agree, it's certainly not Frank Sinatra and Duke Ellington. But nothing's changed in sport, although I can't see why they awarded the bloody Japs the Olympics —'

'You were saying?' Helen prompted gently.

'Well, Dawnie won the 100-metres – Sam nearly burst, she was so excited – and Betty Cuthbert won the 400-metres; Emerson won Wimbledon and we won the Ashes, which only goes to prove the things that really matter haven't changed much in Australia. Elsewhere? Hard to say. Kennedy's assassination is bound to bring change, and Bob Menzies reintroducing national service looks ominous. You can be sure it won't just be military advisers he sends off to Vietnam next year. You mark my words, darling, that silly bastard's going to involve us in this stoush, along with America. It's all very well for him to say national service is character-building, good for the youth of the nation, that sort of thing, but what does he know about war? I don't remember too many men coming out of the Burma Railway better men than they went in. Character-building, my arse. More like shitting yourself in the jungle wondering how the hell someone got you into this mess in the first place! We've been fighting the communists in Malaya for how long? Ever since World War Two ended. Now we're fighting them in Borneo, even if it's on the quiet against that lunatic Sukarno. Next thing, Sir Robert Fucking Gordon Menzies will want us to start some character-building against Ho Chi Minh!'

'Good thing you didn't take Askin's offer and stand as a Liberal, darling,' Helen said. 'Mr Menzies would call you a communist for talking like that!'

'How'd we get onto all this, anyway?' Danny asked, irritated. 'Aren't we supposed to be remembering our year, the highs and lows?'

Helen pointed to his glass. 'You've hardly touched your champagne, darling. It'll go flat.' She held out her empty one. 'I think I need another, please, for a toast to the new year. We're about to enter 1965, the Year of the Independent!' She rose, set her champagne glass down, then sat on Danny's lap and put her arms around him. 'I love you, Daniel Corrib Dunn!'

'I love you, too, darling,' Danny replied softly. 'We've been married nearly twenty years, and you're still as gorgeous as the first day I set eyes on you.'

'I know how we can welcome in the new year,' she giggled mischievously, standing up and wriggling out of her panties.

'Let me guess – the twins are out for another half hour at least – Scrabble?'

Helen kissed him. 'No, darling,' she said, working away at his belt and zipper, their kiss deepening as she pulled his trousers down over the spontaneous erection struggling to be free of his underpants.

'I thought you said women were only *beginning* to be assertive?' he gasped. 'So it looks like Scrabble's out, then?'

"Fraid so,' Helen said, straddling him and lowering herself slowly, enticingly, as she kissed him again.

'Next time we're calling the year, we'll remember this as the moonlit New Year's Eve we spent out on the tiles!'

'Mmm,' she murmured, lifting herself away from him. 'How's your back, darling?'

'Never better,' Danny whispered, gripping her to him as the car horns and fireworks marked the start of a new year.

'Happy New Year, darling,' Helen said, gazing into his eyes.

'Very happy,' said Danny.

Brenda dropped the twins off half an hour later, and they tumbled out onto the verandah full of stories of the fireworks they'd seen, and the great food, and the boy who told Gabby he liked her, then kissed Sam at twelve o'clock. Danny and Helen listened, their hands linked, then, as the stories faltered, and first Sam and then Gabby began to rub their eyes, Helen sent them off to bed.

'No training tomorrow, Sam,' Danny called after them. 'I'll give you the day off.'

Helen and Danny allowed the twins few privileges, and although they were comfortably off, in many ways they lived a similar life to most of the working-class kids at their school and in the neighbourhood. The rules were simple: mind your manners, do as you're told and don't argue, eat what's put in front of you, get out of the house and go and play on the street or in the park, be home by sunset, and never ever get into a car with a stranger. Saturday afternoons were spent at the movies, if you could wheedle a sixpence out of your dad or mum or your brother who did a paper run, and everyone went to Sunday school, then the lucky ones came home to a roast-lamb lunch, with mint sauce, roast potatoes and pumpkin, followed by apple pie or red jelly and ice-cream. Wise mothers never tamper with perfection. Despite the Sunday-school attendance,

Balmain wasn't, generally speaking, big on religion, and while respectful to priests, parsons, rabbis and preachers, the church figured in their lives for the most part only in christenings, confirmations, weddings and funerals. In summer most kids were to be found at the Balmain pool, and in winter at the football, if the Tigers were playing at home.

Boys got into fights, belonged to gangs and made billycarts in which they constantly risked their lives, breaking bones, grazing knees and splitting their heads open. Girls belonged to groups and imagined themselves different and special, with secret words and hand signs and the flower of the day concealed in their knickers. They swore serious oaths to eat only a certain colour ice-cream until they met a handsome prince, who would scoop them up and ride off with them on a white horse. While there was a certain amount of snootiness in their groups, and regular quarrels, the word 'superior' wasn't an adjective they understood. Nobody had any money, and a new and unusual ribbon in a girl's hair provided a serious, if temporary, elevation in her status among her classmates. As with their friends, most of what the twins did went largely unsupervised, apart from Sam's rigorous training sessions.

Sam and Gabby had always attended the movie matinee, and had spent most of the Monday lunchbreak retelling the story to those kids who hadn't been able to go because their parents were skint. Gabby was the master storyteller, and sometimes girls who'd seen the movie sat in just to hear her version, complete with theme music sung in her sweet true voice. Sam, if she felt like it, would do the sound effects – horses galloping, dogs barking, birds in the garden, cows, goats and donkeys in the countryside, creaking doors, frightened gasps or hysterical screams, deathly groans, ghostly moans or ghoulish laughter. If a male villain featured, she'd sometimes agree to do his part, but only if he was particularly nasty.

A Monday performance by the twins, complete with background music and sound effects, had drawn a sizeable crowd, and many who'd attended the original movie had declared the twins' version decidedly the better of the two, particularly on those occasions when Gabby organised audience participation. But, popular as these movie re-creations were, the other girls their age still exhibited a certain wariness towards Sam and Gabby. It was to do with them being identical twins and therefore freaks of nature – mixed in the same milkshake blender, two brains that worked as one; naturally they were therefore thought to possess mysterious powers. Oddly enough, the movie re-creations were taken to be further evidence of this. How else could Sam possibly anticipate the sound effects, expressions and even actions that were required when Gabby didn't look at her or give any signals to cue her? At first, both went to some trouble to deny this bizarre synchronicity, but it only seemed to confirm the fact of their special power in the minds of the other kids. Any doubts were immediately erased if either twin was attacked verbally or physically. The two girls suddenly became ferocious – a single being that fought back with venom and tenacity – so that on several occasions, two, three or even four assailants were no match for Sam and Gabby in a spat or a fight.

Sam and Gabby had almost unconsciously learned to exploit their status as twins. It was irresistible – even the teachers were somewhat in awe of them. They invariably came first and second in every subject, swapping positions regularly, one never consistently brighter than the other. Even after the girls had been separated and were attending different schools, they were both put up a grade partway through their first year of secondary school, despite Sam's obsession with training and apparent indifference to her schoolwork. It was as if there were an invisible cord connecting the two of them, no matter how great the distance between them.

Curiously, they hadn't fraternised or belonged to the same groups at primary school. These all-girl tribes had secrets, rules and sworn oaths to protect their customs, and Sam and Gabby ably demonstrated that they could each be trusted to keep the dark secrets of their separate groups. These were matters involving such deeply important things as ice-cream colours and flavours, code words, future husbands, copying homework, sandwich swaps and initiation rites, the most daring of which was going an entire school day without wearing underpants.

While they were fiercely loyal to their friends, this wasn't always reciprocated. Suspicion about the power of identical twins persisted, and Sam and Gabby never felt entirely accepted. Then there was the added burden of having a father who was responsible for sending several of their classmates' fathers to Long Bay jail. While this was often perceived as just and fair, with mother and kids grateful for the respite from regular beatings, there was also great hardship as the family struggled to make do without a dad's salary. This seemed yet another manifestation of the latent power the twins exerted. The fact that they were also thought to be beautiful only compounded things.

There was yet another factor that divided Sam and Gabby from their schoolmates. By virtue of their parents' economic circumstances and education, the girls were permitted to dream larger and more exotic dreams, to have bigger plans, to live in anticipation of grander futures. While there was the example of Balmain's own Dawnie, the daughter of a working-class family, who had brought fame and glory to the suburb as well as to her country, very few girls sought to follow her example; it just seemed too far out of reach. Dawn Fraser was yet another kind of freak. For the most part the other girls lacked any sense of choice over their future. This torpor, this lack of excitement, the almost total absence of ambition or goals was already evident in primary school, so that when girls eventually reached high school, they were effectively conditioned to the prospect of leading the compliant life of a Balmain housewife. At best they'd leave school after the Intermediate Certificate, and have a go at nursing or hairdressing, but more often than not, this spark of ambition was extinguished when they found themselves with a bun in the oven from a back-seat dalliance in a hoon's souped-up Holden. Of course there were exceptions, but very few, and those girls who showed unusual ability invariably obtained a scholarship to Sydney Girls High.

When Sam started swimming seriously, a fissure opened between the twins as Gabby's interest in music grew and Sam's determination to win three gold for Sammy fuelled her punishing training regime. But there was another wedge driven between them, by a Latvian girl named

Katerina, who arrived at Balmain High School one term. She was the most exotic creature Sam had ever seen, and before long she'd developed a full-blown crush on the new girl. A passing glance from this tall, dark-eyed, raven-haired, sombre creature would cause Sam's knees to tremble. Katerina seemed to have nothing in common with the rest of the girls and stood aloof: mature, condescending and superior. What's more, she was bloody tough, and when Sam had asked if they could be friends, Katerina had thought about it for ages before declaring, 'Okay, but we take no shit from nobody, right? That's the rule!' This single statement had brought Sam almost to the point of collapse and she immediately promised total obedience. She couldn't wait to tell Gabby about her new friend, and that night she acted out the whole thing, hands on hips, eyes downcast in the condescending manner of the Latvian girl, as she delivered the immortal line, 'Okay, but we take no shit from nobody, right?'

Gabby, once she'd met the fabled Katerina, dismissed the whole thing with a toss of her head and an impatient sigh, declaring, 'She has a cruel smile and she's got a haircut like a boy. I can't stand her.' In one slash of the tongue, the ties were severed, and the Dunn twins began, unknowingly, to separate, albeit very slowly and not in all things. Being a twin had always been like having an animated and sentient shadow, with whom you could share a mischievous look, a secret smirk or burst of giggles at something incomprehensible to others. Gabby and Sam had spoken the private unspoken language of twins and inhabited a secret world that others could never penetrate, but as their different personalities began to emerge, their close affinity began to dissipate. Gabby bonded with Helen, sensing that Danny disapproved of her decision to choose music and had neither sympathy for nor understanding of it, whereas Sam, always Daddy's favourite girl, became even more so, but while she loved Danny deeply, she was ever fearful of her father's mood swings and sudden outbursts of blazing temper.

Danny was, for the most part, a loving and caring father, but when the demons struck he could be cruel and unforgiving with his twin daughters, who far too often bore the brunt of his anger. A length of the pool not completed within a second of the required time would send him into a towering rage; an item of swimming gear forgotten and the twin involved would find herself trembling at the thought of yet another angry outburst. While he never laid a hand on them, his tongue was his razor, honed on the strop of his court appearances, and often it cut deeply. Sam coped much better than Gabby, taking Danny's rebukes in silence and still adoring her father in spite of his rages, while Gabby increasingly sought refuge in the comparative calm and comfort of her mother's presence.

It wasn't surprising that Sam bonded with the tough, uncompromising Katerina and that Gabby avoided her. Katerina's family spoke little English. Her father was a peasant in every sense of the word, and a vicious and cruel drunk. She'd frequently appear at school with a black eye or covered in nasty bruises and welts. When Sam sympathised, Katerina would look her in the eye and say, with what Gabby described as her cruel smile, 'It's okay, kid. When I'm seventeen, I'm gonna kill the fucking bastard!' She seemed so powerful, so resolute, that Sam had not the slightest doubt she would carry out her threat, and the thought of it would send shivers down her back. The closest Sam ever got to having a similar sentiment was when Danny was directing a spurt of unwarranted fury at her. A sentence would form in her head and she would silently pronounce her own version of Katerina's coarse pledge: *It's okay. When I'm seventeen, I'm gonna win three Olympic gold medals and I'm gonna stick them up your arse, Daddy!* This served greatly to ameliorate the effect of Danny's sudden and violent rages. The difference between Sam and Katerina was that Sam knew without a shred of doubt that her father adored her and would have happily given his life if it meant hers could be saved.

The unlikely friendship between Katerina and Sam continued, and Sam soon learned that she had more than one protector prepared to look out for her, no matter what the cost. One day a group of boys cornered Sam in the playground, teasing her, laughing at the time she spent swimming, holding their noses and saying she stank like a fish. The leader and main tormentor was a boy of thirteen named Denis Haze, nicknamed, appropriately, Dense Haze. Sam was giving almost as good as she got, and quite enjoying the boys' attention, despite their childish insults, when Katerina stormed onto the scene like a virago and let fly with a vicious punch, socking Dense Haze in the eye. He collapsed, clutching at his wounded face, and the others backed off, eyeing the two girls warily. 'Fuck off, shithead!' Katerina yelled, then, glaring at his mates, said challengingly, 'Come on, who's next?' To Sam's surprise they slunk away with their tails between their legs, Katerina muttering, 'Fucking dogs,' as she checked that Sam was unhurt, before giving the hapless mob a send-off with a flourishing two-finger salute.

If Katerina taught Sam the art of the surprise attack, she also taught her a new use for the two fingers she'd used in her contemptuous salute, introducing Sam to the surprising and secret pleasure of masturbation. The timing was good; the twins had only just stopped sharing a double bed and moved into beds of their own, and while they could easily have had rooms of their own, it had never occurred to them. Sam's new knowledge of another use for a body part she'd never really thought about was immediately conveyed to her twin one night as they were preparing for bed.

'You're not supposed to touch down there!' Gabby admonished Sam.

'Why not?' Sam replied.

'Because it's dirty and you'll get wee on your fingers, silly,' Gabby replied, lost for another explanation.

'No you don't. You just get a nice feeling, like you're blissing out,' Sam replied.

'If we were allowed, Mum would have told us,' Gabby said.

'They didn't tell us about weeing and we discovered that,' Sam countered.

'You don't *discover* weeing! It just happens – you can't help it. Why don't you ask Mum?'

'No!' Sam cried, instinctively uneasy.

'And why not?' Gabby said in her annoyingly self-righteous voice.

'Because Katerina said it's a special kids' secret and that parents don't have to know about it,' Sam fabricated wildly.

'See! I told you it wouldn't be allowed,' Gabby said triumphantly. 'That Katerina is evil.'

'She's not! She just knows things you don't need to share with parents like a big baby. Grow up, kid!' Sam said, using a Katerina expression.

'Yes, like swearing and saying the "f" word and the "s" word.'

'Those boys *were* fucking shitheads,' Sam said, savouring both words almost as much as Gabby's disapproval.

'You're just showing off, Sam! You ought to be ashamed of yourself,' Gabby replied, hopping into bed.

'Well, I'm going to do it, anyway,' Sam concluded defiantly. 'You don't know what you're missing out on.'

'Go ahead, be disgusting!' Gabby said, turning over huffily to present her back to her twin.

They never discussed the subject again, but Sam knew Gabby too well, and was positive that she wouldn't be able to resist the temptation. However, neither twin had any idea that this secret pleasure had a name or that it was connected with the big no-no word – sex. Not long after Katerina introduced Sam to 'the joy that lies below', her family moved to Adelaide, where Katerina's father had taken a job as a painter with Kelvinator, spraying fridges. Katerina's last words to Sam were, 'In four years you'll see me on the TV because I'm still gonna kill the bastard! Promise you'll come and see me in prison and bring me cigarettes.' Sam unhesitatingly agreed.

That Katerina's gift of self-knowledge had a sexual connection only became apparent as Sam matured and discovered that the need to pleasure herself was somehow heightened when she read certain passages in her father's books. Danny, like his father, was addicted to cheap paperbacks – Zane Grey, Nevil Shute, Mickey Spillane, Damon Runyon, Harold Robbins, Hammond Innes, Alistair MacLean. They were by no means pornographic, but they contained enough prurient passages not only to satisfy their mostly male readership, but Sam's innocent erotic life under the blankets, too.

She finally woke up to the fact that what she was doing was sexual while reading a Mickey Spillane novel. She came across a sentence that read: *Her thighs were as smooth as whipped cream on a silk bedspread.* In a thrice Sam knew she was the heart and soul of the femme fatale in Mickey's story, and had to hurry into her bedroom in the middle of a quiet Sunday afternoon to play out the scene between the gangster and his girl under the blankets. While it didn't strike her like a bolt of lightning out of the blue, she became conscious that the innocence of her childhood was over and that she desperately wanted to be kissed by a boy.

A year or so before, the twins had attended an evening for girls aged twelve to sixteen run by the Anglican Church that was held in the Balmain Town Hall, and billed improbably as 'The Birds, the Bees, You and God'. Most of their school friends were in attendance, and the lecture was given by a large, stern-faced matron wearing heavy, horn-rimmed glasses, with a pouter-pigeon breast and steel-grey hair swept up and tied in a neat bun at the back of her head. She introduced herself as Mrs Polkinghorne, which her audience of giggling teenage girls instantly translated to Mrs Pokinghorn. She was said to be a leading child psychologist, a profession most of her young female audience had never heard of, with the possible exception of the two Dunn girls.

What followed was a lot of information about menstruation – how to wear 'sanitary napkins', and how to keep oneself clean and 'fresh'. There was no mention of emotions or urges of any kind, although Mrs Polkinghorne 'touched on' masturbation, which she referred to as 'severe self-abuse'. She cautioned that it was dangerous to the wellbeing of young girls, spoiled them for marriage, and was responsible for unspecified, but nonetheless dire, health problems. It was a nasty habit that should be avoided at all costs. Sexual relations were a gift from God and could only be sanctioned within the bonds of 'Holy Matrimony'. An intact hymen was a gift whose value was 'beyond rubies'. Tampering with God's laws could lead to dire consequences. She advised that a good way to cope with any unusual feelings 'down there' was to take a cold bath. Neither twin had the faintest idea that she was referring to the pleasure each of them gave themselves in bed after the light was switched out.

Many complicated and incomprehensible diagrams followed, one of which included bisected testicles and a penis that seemed to be inside something they were told was a vagina – words new to the vocabulary of the majority of the girls present. This was referred to as 'penetration', an act that was under no circumstances to be performed before marriage, according to Mrs Polkinghorne, who referred to the ceremony as 'Holy Matrimony', no doubt because she was on the National Women's Council of the Anglican Church. She talked about the dire consequences of teenage pregnancy and of ways to spot it, which included puffy ankles and missing a period. As a great many of the girls had never even kissed a boy and had yet to experience a period, they were unsure whether to worry or not, and almost all immediately glanced down to check their ankles.

Mrs Polkinghorne relaxed a little when she spoke of the happy events that could arise *after* Holy Matrimony. The blood that had been little more than a hygiene issue in the earlier part of her talk was now 'food for the foetus during the gestation period'. This piece of information was not well received; babies, suddenly known as foetuses, drinking their mother's blood was beyond the comprehension of the audience, many of whom afterwards confessed they felt like throwing up.

Finally, she paused and asked her stunned and puzzled audience if there were any questions. There were none. She handed out little purple books to each thoroughly bewildered girl. They contained pictures of happy families with the father as often as not holding a Bible, and groups of smiling American girls who obviously didn't touch themselves in secret places and wore two-tone shoes and white socks, which everyone knew from the movies were called bobbysocks. On almost every page the girls were told that making babies was God's glorious gift to humanity but *only* within the sanctity of marriage. Having babies before marriage was referred to as the devil's work.

The entire process left the young audience thoroughly confused, and Sam and Gabby both secretly feared they'd destroyed any chance they might have had to enjoy a happy marriage and produce healthy babies. Neither of them went to church regularly, and had not had any idea of what they were supposed to avoid.

Helen observed the twins' long faces when they got home and she asked them how the lecture had gone.

Sam hesitated for a moment and then said, 'I can't have a baby.'

'Oh? Why is that?'

'You can't have one unless you've got puffy ankles and you miss a period, but the blood from your period feeds the baby, so it's a bit confusing,' Gabby explained.

Sam held up the purple book. 'It's all in here, Mum.'

'What nonsense have they been telling you? Let me see that,' Helen cried, reaching for the booklet. 'Perhaps I should have followed my instincts and talked to you about the birds and bees myself, but I thought this might be a better option.'

'And that's another thing,' Gabby said, 'she didn't mention birds or bees even once.'

'Who didn't?' Helen asked.

'Mrs Pokinghorn,' Sam said, and the twins started to giggle uncontrollably.

'She wasn't called that!' Helen exclaimed, incredulous.

'She was, Mum, she *really* was,' the twins answered simultaneously, giggling and clutching each other, relieved at having passed the burden of the sanctity of marriage, and all that it involved, to their mother.

Helen flicked through the booklet quickly. 'This is absolute rubbish!' she told them. 'Come and sit next to me and we'll begin all over again.'

Two months after Helen had given the twins a comprehensive, or at least sufficient, knowledge of their pubescent bodies, Sam woke at dawn one morning to go to swimming training, and as usual made her way to the bathroom in the dark so as not to wake Gabby. Switching on the bathroom light, she pulled down her pyjama pants to have a wee, and to her horror saw blood on the inside of her thigh and was immediately aware of where it had come from. Despite Helen having told them to expect this, she was panic-stricken. She'd pleasured herself to sleep the night before, and all she could think about was that she'd gone too far and broken her body and done herself an irreparable injury. Terrified, she could see at once that she'd have to go to the doctor and have an operation . . . he'd have to sew her up, and everyone would know!

There was a knock on the bathroom door, then her father's voice. 'Hurry up, Sam, gotta get going, sweetheart.'

'Daddy, I can't, not today!' Sam cried.

'Eh? What's the matter?' Danny asked.

'I'm sick,' Sam said, unable to explain.

There was a pause. 'Sick? You were okay last night. How sick?'

Sam burst into tears. 'I don't know!'

'Can I come in?'

'No!' Sam shrilled in panic.

Helen had told Danny about Mrs Polkinghorne's lecture and they'd had a good laugh about the twins mishearing her surname. Then she'd informed him that she'd given them their first sex talk, beginning with an explanation of periods. While he knew he should have expected this inevitable occurrence, he remembered feeling somewhat shocked at the prospect of his little girls turning into women.

'Surely not for a while yet?' he'd remarked.

'Well, mine came two days after my thirteenth birthday,' Helen had replied. 'Both their little bodies are beginning to change. You mean you haven't noticed Sam in her bathers?'

'No, of course not!' he'd replied, indignant at the question.

Helen had sighed. 'Men!'

Remembering this, Danny suddenly cottoned on to what might have happened to Sam. 'I'll get your mother,' he called softly.

He heard Sam sniff, then her tearful reply. 'Yes, thanks, Dad.'

Danny was aware that he was trying to keep his own voice normal, and he had an immediate sense that things had changed between himself and his daughter.

Gabby's first period followed almost six months later, although hers arrived with plenty of warning. For almost four months she experienced excruciating pain from cramps that kept her away from the Con High School, sometimes for a couple of days, and when her periods came they were often preceded by terrible headaches. The sudden cramps, often arriving without warning in the middle of a lesson, made playing the violin almost impossible. She wanted to double over and clutch her stomach. Fortunately, her tutor, Miss Rabbinowitz, immediately understood. To make matters worse, Gabby's periods were heavy and left her feeling weak for several days.

Sam soon enough adjusted to having her periods and, in fact, it made her feel rather grown up. While she continued to enjoy the pleasure her fingers brought her, her fantasies changed and she now saw herself as closer to Marilyn Monroe than Dawn Fraser, her previous idol.

Also, for the first time in her life, she realised that she was actually very pretty. Gabby, although identical to her twin, never felt the same pleasure about her looks. By the time they'd reached the age of sixteen, Sam had begun to dress prettily, and Erin Walsh began to use her as a model in her Saturday morning fashion parades, where she was starting to attract the attention of the young photographers who came along. Sam's tanned body and long legs revealed by a mini-skirt were being seen in the magazines, where editorials would often mention that she was a gold-medal hope in the coming Mexico Olympics. Sam loved the attention and the way young blokes looked at her.

Gabby, on the other hand, had a quite different take on how she wanted to appear. She wore no make-up and dressed in the dowdy styles of the hippy movement, thinking this a more appropriate image for a talented young musician. While the violin was her serious classical instrument, she took happily and easily to the guitar and the music of the time, never forgetting her early introduction to Dylan and his harmonica with Dallas. She did make a single concession to her physical appearance – she loved beads and bangles, often wearing as many as a dozen bright strands around her neck and lots of cheap brightly coloured plastic bangles on each wrist, unless she was playing her violin, of course. Despite her attempts to dress down and look plain, her brilliant titian hair, always worn with a freshly picked bloom from the garden, and the gift of her father's violet-blue eyes outshone her attempts at self-effacement and she remained extraordinarily and effortlessly pretty.

The 1965 state elections were to be held in May, and Danny and his Tiger 13 team campaigned almost ceaselessly in the months leading up to it. The questionnaire Hugh Mackay had prepared showed that Danny could expect around forty per cent of the women's vote but no more than ten per cent of the men's. Calculations revealed that this wasn't quite enough to win the seat, especially with Labor throwing everything but the kitchen sink behind Tommy O'Hearn. It was said that he was doing so much back-slapping in the thirty-odd pubs – not including the Hero – on the peninsula that his right hand had grown calluses. The slap on the back usually included a free middy followed by the words, 'Hope we can count on you, mate!' And Danny knew that for the most part Tommy could. If there was any ambivalence under the slapped back, a beer usually sealed the issue for Labor. Those were the unspoken local rules, and while Tommy was fat, he wasn't a fool.

Danny listed thirteen changes as his campaign pledge, using a train analogy that had first come from Helen, one night when they were sitting on the verandah after dinner and she had referred to Danny as an engine of change.

'So I'm a train driver now, am I?'

'Perhaps,' Helen had said, suddenly serious. 'If you think of change as a train, then each manifestation of change is like a separate wagon. The renovation of Brokendown Street is just one of the wagons. The new fashion industry started by Erin Walsh and her friends is another; darling Pineapple Joe with his T-shirt factory yet another. Two real-estate companies who usually stick to the posh suburbs have hung up their shingle in Darling Street – that's another wagon. Even Harry Farmer lending money for a house that isn't tied to a thirty-five-year mortgage is a wagon.' Helen hesitated. 'Now, if you can just get into parliament as an Independent and pressure them to change the zoning laws, that's when we'll get the train out of the goods yard and onto the track, heading somewhere that matters.'

'I like the analogy of the train,' Danny had said. 'I'll use that.' And he had. Most of the wagons appealed to women: clean air over Balmain was one such wagon, another was a park for kids to play where the soap factories currently stood. It became known as the Tiger Train, and in the last months of the campaign, many of Pineapple Joe's donated T-shirts featured a train with thirteen trucks forming a band around the midriff, each truck announcing a separate change. Labor voters named it 'The Dunny Train' because they thought it disappeared up its own arsehole, and his campaign workers were referred to as the 'Truckers and Shunts', the play on two similar-sounding words never failing to produce a grin among male Labor voters.

For the first time since Doc Evatt had stood as an Independent thirty-eight years earlier, the election became a rowdy, contentious, quarrelsome affair. Fights ensued outside the pubs and women openly defied their husbands by wearing Tiger 13 T-shirts. Wife bashings increased and the incidence of the Saturday-night drunken 'naughty' decreased decidedly as the household vote was split down the centre. Three of Danny's young male campaign workers were beaten up when each had unwisely entered a pub just before ten-o'clock closing, while most of his female volunteers were regularly verbally abused, referred to as 'Dunny sluts'. All of them eventually took it in their stride; it was, they realised, all part of the dirty game of politics.

Polling day finally arrived and by seven o'clock that night, an hour after the polling booths closed, the ABC-TV announcer in the tally room counted the safe seats for Labor, blithely including Balmain as a traditional Labor seat. But not long after, he announced the first big surprise of the election: the Independent, Daniel Dunn, running in the seat of Balmain, seemed to be winning, but it would be a close finish. 'Nifty Dunn has once again caught us all napping,' he announced cheerfully.

The celebration party was held in the gardens of Helen and Danny's home, at the far end of the partially restored Brokendown Street. Pineapple Joe, wearing a T-shirt with a picture of a house made out of a pineapple above the words 'Pineapple Real Estate', announced that he was going into the local real-estate business. 'Houses we are soon sellink to more of za wankers!' he announced, slapping Danny on the back.

Danny thanked him for his support, and Joe had the good grace to look somewhat sheepish. He was aware that the member for Balmain knew about him winning the contract to produce Labor T-shirts for the election, not only for Balmain, but for all the seats in the state Legislative Assembly, in the process making himself a small fortune. 'Danny, business is business, but for mein friend, anythink you are wantink – you understan'.' He then tapped the side of his head with his forefinger. 'But also I must be using always mein intellects.' Whereupon he pulled a T-shirt from his trouser pocket and laughingly declared, 'Maybe, God forbid, today you are losink already, Danny.' He then held up the T-shirt that read:

Wankers go home!

A month before state parliament was due to reconvene, Danny had moved into his small backbencher's office in the old parliament building in Macquarie Street. It had taken two weeks before the overall results were finally confirmed. Labor had lost the popular vote but the Liberals would need the help of the two Independents to govern, as the major parties in the Legislative Assembly were tied.

Danny had only been ensconced in Parliament House two days when Bob Askin rang to congratulate him and ask if he could drop around to see him. Danny was surprised that he didn't suggest his own office for the meeting, but he'd been expecting the call.

'Yes, of course, Bob, drop around anytime, but you'd be best to come alone; my office can only accommodate one visitor's chair.' It was, of course, his way of saying he wanted a private talk with the tough-minded Liberal leader.

'I'll be around in ten minutes,' Askin replied.

Danny grinned to himself – Nifty's luck had held. Nobody had expected the election to be this close. Most pundits had predicted an easy win for the Liberals, who themselves had been caught with their pants down, reasonably expecting that after Labor had been in government for twenty-four years and were known to be corrupt, the election would be a cakewalk. If it had been, then Danny was under no illusions – he'd have been about as welcome in the Liberal ranks as a loud fart in a crowded lift. But things had gone well, very well, and he knew he was in the box seat.

Askin arrived promptly and Danny moved his chair to face the guest chair without the desk separating them. It was a small gesture and probably one that would go unnoticed, but then you never knew.

'Welcome, and congratulations. It looks like you'll be the first non-Labor Premier in twenty-four years,' Danny began after they'd seated themselves.

Bob Askin grinned. 'Not hard to tell why I'm here, is it? The last time we met I pissed in your pocket, to no avail, and it seems your gamble to stand as an Independent has paid off. Now I'm prepared to do so again,' and he gave a distinctly braying politician's laugh.

'I shouldn't think that's necessary, Bob. The Labor Party happily accepted my resignation and I can't say they've taken their defeat in Balmain with good grace.' He shrugged. 'So I guess you've got the inside running.'

'The offer to join us still stands, Danny. But, of course, it isn't immediately a useful move for you. Nevertheless, you should think about your long-term future in politics.'

'Hmm, perhaps you're right. I'll have to think about it,' Danny said.

'I guess that means you won't,' Askin grinned, correctly reading the unstated refusal in Danny's answer.

'Bob, I'm not a politician and probably never will be; I simply wouldn't be comfortable changing horses after my electorate had just voted me in as an Independent. Voting Labor out for the first time since Doc Evatt doesn't by any means indicate that my electorate is prepared to endorse the Libs.'

'What do you mean?' Askin looked slightly alarmed. 'You're not on our side?'

'No, I didn't say that. I'm an Independent and I intend to stay that way. However, my vote comes with a specific agenda.'

Askin gave a sigh of relief. 'Naturally, we'd expect that. But there are other enticements – overseas trade missions, a seat on useful committees, inclusion in important inquiries, a few other small lurks and perks. Such a pity you won't join us – you'd make an excellent minister.'

'Thank you, Bob, but I'm not really a good committee man.'

'You're a lawyer, a damn good one, Danny, accustomed to convincing a jury . . . We don't want ministers who look for consensus, but ones with a clear point of view they intend to have accepted.'

'Well, there you go then, I'll always try to make my case persuasively.' Danny gave a cheeky laugh. 'In the meantime, you have my permission to move into the Premier's office.'

'Tell me so that I can prepare my team, what is it you specifically want to achieve in your first term?' Askin asked.

Danny looked him in the eye. 'I want Balmain and the other industrialised suburbs on the harbour turned into decent places to live. We're two-thirds of the way through the twentieth century and the government is still using these suburbs as if we were in the nineteenth! When Charles Dickens visited Sydney last century he described the foulness of Sydney Harbour and it hasn't changed, for crying out loud!

This is choice waterfrontage, and people deserve to live and bring up their families in healthy attractive surroundings, and not have to tolerate foul air, polluted water and possibly the highest incidence of asthma and bronchial problems in the country.'

'How do you suggest we do that? I imagine there are one or two industrial heavy hitters who might kick up a fuss.'

'Of course, the two soap factories for a start. The key is rezoning. If you change the zoning and at the same time give the old polluting industries the right incentive to move to the industrial estates starting on the fringes of the metropolitan area, they may be interested. Our survey shows that ninety-five per cent of existing industry located along the edges of the harbour does not depend on water transport.'

'So we give them a bribe to relocate – is that what you're suggesting?'

'Yes, but a real incentive, a generous one. Western Sydney is where the population is increasingly shifting and they need the employment the industries will provide. The increased land prices the harbour factory sites will fetch once the area is zoned residential or even light industrial will be a further temptation.' Danny shrugged. 'It's not that difficult and it's good government.'

Askin shook his head. 'I see the carrot clearly, but we'll need a stick. There are jobs involved, the local people won't like it.'

'I don't know about that. Balmain just voted for it.'

'Danny, this is a lousy media story – people having to travel vast distances to get to jobs that were formerly on their doorstep; some may even be forced to uproot and relocate. The serious TV docos will have a bonanza, and so will radio and the print media.'

'Then give the media an even bigger story, one with real legs, one that all of Sydney can embrace.'

'For instance?'

'The decline in Sydney's environment. *All* of Sydney's environment! The water and air pollution that's affecting us all, from Vaucluse to Pymble. Our harbour has been used as a sewer for over a century and a half, and we've been pumping shit into the air for almost as long. Take a team of scientists and a TV crew out to Balmain and have them analyse the stuff the soap factories, foundries and marine workshops are pouring into the harbour. That's your stick. You simply say your government has decided to make Sydney the cleanest harbour city in the southern hemisphere. We're building the world's most spectacular Opera House and we're not going to allow it to be swimming in a cesspool! It's a long-term platform that just might get you elected with a working majority next time around.'

Askin looked hard at Danny. 'This wouldn't have something to do with the twenty-eight houses you own on the Balmain harbourfront, would it?'

Danny nodded his head, laughing. 'Yes, of course it has. When my mother bought them she was the laughing stock of Balmain; the people simply couldn't believe anyone could be that stupid. But we went ahead nevertheless, and young couples came to take a look at the nice, neat, renovated little houses and started to buy them. Nothing had changed, except that people started to take notice; they began to see that change was possible. We've sold all but five houses, and they'll be sold the moment they're renovated and long before any rezoning might take place. My mother and wife and others who own them have already reaped the benefits. This is not about being greedy or about making money, it's about instilling hope. We haven't bought any more properties and, if it gives you any comfort, we won't be doing so – well, not in Balmain, anyway.'

Bob Askin rose. 'I can't see why not. I'm happy you've benefitted. It's going to be interesting having you more or less on our side, Danny. It will be some weeks before we're properly underway and can formulate and pass legislation. In the meantime there's a trade delegation going to Japan in a week – away for ten days – would you like to be included?'

At the mention of Japan, Danny started, but immediately collected himself. 'Japan, eh? Hmm, can't say I'm overly fond of the Japanese,' he said dryly.

'There are no strings attached. Both major parties are included in the group and the addition of an Independent is always sound politics. You'll be back before parliament opens. If I'm not mistaken, Tommy O'Hearn was on the original Labor list of people to go. You'll enjoy it, and of course you're welcome to take your wife.'

'May I think about it for twenty-four hours, please?'

Bob Askin had reached the door. 'Of course!' he said, then paused with one hand on the doorframe. 'By the way, thank you for my office,' he grinned.

'You're welcome. Oh, and, Bob, this rezoning legislation needs to happen in the first twelve months of your government, with the regulations to back it firmly in place. I don't wish to be left like a shag on a rock if a couple of by-elections make you complacent and you have a majority in your own right.'

Bob Askin straightened and gave Danny a mock salute. 'As one sergeant to another, I promise. But you must understand that legislation doesn't happen overnight.'

Danny nodded. 'Why don't you get your mate, Frank Packer, on side? That will bring in Channel Nine, the *Daily Telegraph* and the *Women's Weekly*. Not such a bad start, eh?'

Askin nodded. 'I now realise they don't call you "Nifty Dunn" for nothing. By the way, talking of offices, this one is ridiculous. I'll allocate you a better one.'

Danny shrugged. 'This one will do.'

'No, no, allow me the pleasure of turfing out some old Labor parrot from his nice comfy perch. Some of them haven't said a word in the house for fifteen years beyond squawking "aye" or "nay" when nudged awake for a vote.'

Danny and Helen travelled first class to Japan, the politicians not being averse to squandering taxpayers' money. They were ten minutes out from Tokyo's Haneda Airport, with the seatbelt sign already on, just as the sun, a great red orb against an almost pewter sky, was setting. It was the original of the image on the Japanese flag and immediately made Danny feel uneasy. He nudged Helen. 'Take a look at the sunset, it's giving me the creeps.'

Helen glanced through the plane window. 'Darling, it's only a sunset. I've seen similar ones from our top verandah.'

'Yeah, but at home it's the sun setting, here it's the dreaded fried egg.'

'Danny, we went through all this when you decided to come. It's over twenty years ago. You know the Japanese fighting in the Pacific, Malaya and Singapore suffered terribly. The people who are likely to be our hosts were ten-year-old kids when the war ended.'

'I'll bet that bastard Mori isn't dead,' Danny growled.

Helen touched him on the arm. 'You promised me you wouldn't dwell on him, darling. If you do, I'm taking the first plane home in the morning,' she warned. 'We both need a holiday – you're exhausted after the election and . . . well, I'm just plain exhausted. This is a trade junket. A couple of dreary tours through a motorcycle factory and a shipyard to see the ships they're building for our iron ore, three receptions and a fair bit of bowing and laughing at jokes we don't get, and then we're supposed to enjoy ourselves.' Helen looked at him appealingly. 'Don't spoil it.'

'Okay, okay, I'm sorry. Bloody silly, I know, but for a moment that sun brought everything back.' Danny smiled. 'Don't worry, I'll be all right, you'll see – the life of the flaming party. These are blokes I have to get to know.'

The delegation was met at the airport and escorted in four black limos to the Imperial Hotel, where, to their surprise, they were shown to a suite. Danny turned to Helen, who was just about to inspect the bathroom, and laughed. 'Bob doesn't miss a trick, but this is very nice. Did I tell you he moved me from a hole in the wall to a big office with my own secretary – leather couches, oil painting of the First Fleet on the wall, the works.'

Helen called from the bathroom. 'We'll have to have a bath – there's no shower – and the bath will fit all but about two feet of you. It's very posh. Take what you can get from Askin, darling. I can't help feeling that the moment they have a majority you'll be last week's bread.'

They spent the day looking around and came to realise that Tokyo made Sydney look like a backward village. That evening they attended a reception near the Imperial Palace as guests of the Australian embassy. The embassy, a magnificent traditional Japanese building, closer to a small palace than to a large residence, had been seized from the Japanese as war reparations, according to Tony Blackmore, a military attaché who introduced himself to Danny. 'Even after twenty years, Japanese businessmen tell us it's time to give it back – when they've had too much to drink, of course, which is quite often.'

Danny laughed politely.

Tony – a captain, Danny noticed – went on with a grin, 'They've got Buckley's. We like this rather grand pad. Even the Brits and the Yanks envy us.'

Danny warmed to him, despite his officer status. He had no pretentions and was just the sort of young bloke you'd like to think represented your country abroad.

A little later in the evening, when Helen had repaired to the powder room with several of the other wives, Danny approached the attaché. 'Do we, you know, keep a list of the . . . the bad guys who got back . . . I mean, the Japs?'

It was an awkwardly phrased question but Tony seemed to understand immediately. 'Mr Dunn, as a matter of diplomatic procedure we prepare a file on all the important visitors who come to Japan. I know you're a decorated ex-POW from the Burma Railway.' He grinned. 'We're briefed to avoid questions like that one.'

Danny laughed at his forthright manner. 'First, please call me Danny. And, second, if you know anything about state politics, you'll know that independent members, unless they're needed to achieve a majority, have about the same importance in parliament as the tea lady, probably less. But I've often wondered if it's all been swept under the carpet and everyone conveniently forgets the war ever happened.'

Tony Blackmore looked serious for a moment. 'No, not quite. We keep files on all the old Class A war criminals.' Then, changing the subject, he asked, 'How does it feel to be in Japan?'

As a lawyer, Danny knew how to persist with a line of questioning. He told the attaché about the sunset, adding, 'I wouldn't mind ten minutes with Colonel Mori, the Japanese commandant who ran our camp. The Yanks repatriated him without a trial to run the family industrial complex – business before justice, expediency before accountability.' Danny sighed. 'Water under the bridge, I guess. I must be getting old and bitter.' He paused, then shook his head. 'No, that's a lie. I've dreamed for years of catching up with the bastard.'

'You wouldn't be the first to say that. We even have a precedent, though it was long before my posting to Japan – a Qantas pilot, a former RAAF pilot, captured at the fall of Singapore and, like yourself, a prisoner of war under the Japanese on the Burma Railway. By some extraordinary coincidence he was in a bar in the Shinjuku district and recognised the barman as one of the Japanese officers from his camp in Thailand. He completely lost it and pulled him over the bar and very nearly beat him to death. He got away before the police arrived and came straight to the embassy and reported the incident.'

'What happened then?'

'Well, I believe the ambassador, himself ex-RAAF, got him on a flight back home using a diplomatic passport and a fair degree of bluff.'

'And then?'

'I honestly don't know any more than that. Canberra kept it very hush-hush and it never made the papers back home. The diplomatic blokes aren't too keen on military intelligence stirring things up; it upsets the business cocktail circuit.'

'You sound like you don't agree with a policy of amelioration.'

'Know thy enemy – that's our motto in intelligence. The only thing the Japs are sorry about is that they lost the war.'

'You mean you could find Colonel Mori if you wanted to?'

'Hmm . . . I must say, it doesn't sound too difficult. If he is a big noise in industry, then that would make it even simpler. I'll have a quiet look for you.'

'You will?' Danny asked, surprised. 'I'm obliged to you.'

'I'll call you at your hotel if I find anything. But you have to promise me, no violence.' Tony Blackmore looked sternly at Danny. 'You're not carrying a handgun in your luggage, are you?'

'Good Lord, no!' he exclaimed.

'Dangerous weapon, knife, garrotte?'

'I'd have to kill him with a ballpoint pen,' Danny grinned.

'It's been know to happen. I'm sorry, but I had to ask, and I apologise for doing so, sir. It's just that possession of a handgun by a foreigner in Japan means a life sentence.'

'Why are you offering to do this for me, Tony?' Danny asked, looking directly at the young army officer. 'You said yourself you're briefed otherwise.'

'You're a member of parliament, so I take it you're not a nutcase willing to create a huge diplomatic incident between our country and the local mob. But, as a matter of fact, I do have a reason, sir. My brother Jack survived the Burma Railway and got back to his family. I've witnessed what the demons can do to a man, the effect they had on his family. Unable to deal with them – the demons, that is – he finally committed suicide three years ago.' Then he added quietly, 'He always said, "I just want to tell the bastards, see them face to face, show them what they've done!"'

'Jesus, I'm sorry,' Danny said, taken aback.

'Would it honestly help to confront this Colonel Mori?' Tony asked.

'I don't know,' Danny replied. 'I honestly don't know. But I do know I have no wish to kill him.'

'Would it help if I came along?'

Before Danny could reply he looked up to see Helen approaching. 'My wife's coming, mate. She wouldn't be too keen to hear any of this,' Danny said, sotto voce.

'I quite understand, sir. I'll call you tomorrow.'

The following afternoon they returned from a visit to a motorcycle factory outside Tokyo. They'd been told that Japan was set to dominate the world motorcycle market. This, it was explained, had not been the case ten years previously when British and European manufacturers owned the market.

'They may have lost the war, but they seem to be winning the peace,' Danny remarked, as they reached their hotel.

Helen nodded. 'Nobody could ever accuse the Japanese of laziness.'

Danny went over to reception to get the key to their suite and the desk clerk gave him a meaningful look as he handed him a note and said in halting English, 'We not put . . . unner door, sir, by special instruction . . . that come telephone.'

Danny glanced at it briefly. It was a message from Tony Blackmore, asking him to call before five. He pocketed the note and walked over to Helen, who was standing at the lift, and handed her the key. 'You go ahead, darling, I want to see if I can find an English newspaper.'

He got through to the embassy from a guest phone in the foyer and was put through to Captain Blackmore. 'Tony, Danny Dunn.'

'Thanks for calling back, Danny. How was the bike factory?'

'Pretty good, although I think my wife would have happily given it a miss. To her they're just things on two wheels that make a lot of noise and are usually ridden by hoons.'

'Your Colonel Mori . . . interesting story,' the attaché began.

'Oh, you found him?'

'Yes, it wasn't difficult. He's retired.'

'Retired? He wasn't that old.'

'That's the interesting bit. As you know, the Americans brought him back to run a family engineering company – huge business – a significant part of rebuilding the Japanese economy. He assumed control for six years and in 1951 suddenly announced he was retiring.'

'What, for health reasons?' Danny asked.

'No, not at all. His announcement caused a bit of a fuss with the

Japanese Government, and the Americans weren't all that chuffed either. They'd absolved him from standing trial for war crimes and now he was opting out of the rebuilding of the local economy.'

'Don't tell me, mate! Lesser war criminals got the death penalty. I still get pretty worked up thinking about it.'

'That's the whole point. He announced at the time that his purpose for retiring was to atone for his actions during the war!'

'C'mon, you're bullshitting me,' Danny exclaimed, clearly astonished.

'He's become a monk at a Buddhist temple in Kyoto.'

'Fair dinkum. And he's still there? Still a monk?'

'Yes, the Chion-in temple in Kyoto. It's a major centre for Amida Buddhism here.'

'Amida? Is that significant?'

'Apparently they believe even the worst disciple can attain enlightenment by meditation and devotion to Buddha. Prostitutes, war criminals . . .' Tony laughed. 'Politicians . . .'

'Surely not politicians,' Danny replied. 'May I ask, can I visit this temple?'

'Sure,' came the reply.

CHAPTER FIFTEEN

JAPAN, GENERALLY SPEAKING, IS no longer a pretty place. Too many people work in ugly functional buildings and go home to equally soulless high-rise apartments. Beauty is to be found in the foreground, in small exquisite details; the broader landscape seems to have been sacrificed to progress, with very little thought given to rewarding the eye with unsullied countryside or rustic villages. Shinto, not exactly a religion, involves worship of the spirits that live in nature, and yet the Japanese have been prepared to sacrifice the countryside and nature itself for the dubious trappings of progress. The unavoidable outcome of an industrialised nation grown too big for the landmass it occupies is that Japan's architectural soul has been gobbled up, and many of its lovely quiet places have been lost. Kyoto, Japan's former capital, is the marvellous exception.

It is a small city that has maintained its heritage and still allows people a glimpse of the old Japan, with its temples, ancient monuments, tea houses, gardens, monks and geisha in cobbled alleys; a place wonderfully redolent of the past. Kyoto allows a people who have embraced Western modernity to remember where they came from and for a day or so to enjoy the richness of their remarkable heritage. Every year, millions of Japanese make the pilgrimage to Kyoto to renew their sense of who they are, and foreign visitors eager to discover a Japan that essentially no longer exists flock to this small city to catch a glimpse of pre-industrial Japan. And so the parliamentary delegation from New South Wales was inevitably taken to the place where, together with Mount Fuji, seven out of every ten Japanese picture postcards originate.

If anyone thought it odd that Captain Tony Blackmore, the Australian military intelligence attaché, accompanied the group on this particular day, they said nothing. He and Danny had hatched a conspiracy, planning to slip away for an hour to visit the Chion-in temple where Mori lived as a monk.

On the train going to Kyoto the attaché, as arranged, approached Helen and Danny. 'It occurred to me, Danny, that you might be interested in several aspects of Japanese military history in one of the museums in Kyoto not usually on the tourist list.' He looked at Helen. 'Of course, you'd be welcome to come, Mrs Dunn. It's just that, if the idea appeals, we might skip lunch so that you don't miss any of the other sights – the Golden Temple, in particular.'

Danny pretended to think, then said, 'Hmm . . . yes. Sounds interesting. Can't say I'm too taken with Japanese tucker, anyway.' He turned to Helen. 'You wanted to attend the cooking demonstration at lunch, didn't you, darling? Would you mind if Tony and I gave it a miss?'

Helen smiled. 'No, of course not. Thank you, Captain Blackmore. I'm far more interested in sushi and tempura than I am in machine-guns and ordnance. My military life is long past.'

'Helen was a lieutenant colonel in military intelligence during the war,' Danny explained.

Blackmore grinned. 'Yes, I picked it up in your file, Mrs Dunn. You were the highest ranking female officer in Australian army intelligence at the time. I very nearly saluted you when you approached at the embassy reception.'

'Goodness, you *have* done your homework, Captain Blackmore,' Helen exclaimed, amused, although Danny could see she was pleased. 'It's probably because I was the only one in the unit with a masters degree that included decoding Egyptian hieroglyphics.' She turned to Danny. 'Darling, you don't think this museum might upset you, do you? Bring back unfortunate memories, like the tour yesterday?'

Tony Blackmore jumped in. 'Oh, I shouldn't think so. This is traditional stuff, ancient weaponry, personal armour – nothing to do with the last big Pacific stoush.'

Danny didn't like deceiving Helen and promised himself he'd tell her all about it later, unless, of course, it all went horribly wrong with Mori, but at least the deception had been simple.

The incident on the previous day Helen referred to had occurred when the delegation had visited the Yakusuni Shrine in Tokyo – the national resting place of the spirits of Japan's war dead. Helen had suggested they give it a miss, for obvious reasons, but Danny had insisted they go. 'I fought the buggers; the more Japs I see safely dead the better.' The tour had been uneventful, even interesting, and hadn't aroused any particular emotion in him other than what might be expected from someone who had fought an enemy they had grown to hate.

They had almost completed the tour when they entered a hall that contained a large number of Japanese tourists, including several young children, who were being photographed standing in front of a locomotive by their parents. Danny's heart skipped a beat when he realised it was engine No. 31 of the Mitsubishi C56–44 class, which had been used on the Burma Railway, then sent back to Japan to be perfectly restored. He called over to their interpreter and guide to read and translate the large notice explaining the exhibit. The interpreter translated it for him, and Danny soon realised that there was no mention of the atrocities committed or the lives lost building the railway. Instead, it extolled it as a remarkable engineering feat and a demonstration of the superiority of Japanese technology, pointing out that 'the enemy' had claimed that such a railway was impossible to build. The translator, having completed his translation, added in a proud voice, 'Where other nations fail, the Japanese see a challenge and conquer it.' He bowed, thanking them for the honour of allowing him to translate.

Danny was thunderstuck at what he took to be the real arrogance under the feigned humility of most Japanese people. He had become accustomed to Japanese functionaries merely expressing 'regret' for their atrocities during the war, but small children being photographed beside the engine with a sign boasting about a project that had cost over 90 000 men's lives and ruined the futures of countless others was breathtakingly arrogant and unfeeling.

While the other delegates went in to lunch and a demonstration of Japanese food preparation, Danny and Tony Blackmore left in a taxi for the Chion-in temple. In the taxi, Danny took the opportunity to question the military attaché about his background. He didn't appear all that much younger than Danny, and if his brother had been a prisoner on the Burma Railway, he too must have had a war history. However, as it turned out, Tony Blackmore was the youngest of five children and had missed the Pacific War, but had joined army intelligence in time for the war in Korea. He already spoke Chinese and Russian, and when he'd been initially stationed in Japan, he'd learned Japanese, 'the language,' as he put it, 'of our Ally, now that Russian and Chinese are the languages of our enemies. I need to be fairly fluent in all three, as our Allies can often cause more trouble than our enemies.' This was his second tour of Japan since the conclusion of the Korean War.

Danny realised that the advantage of having Tony Blackmore with him was that they wouldn't need an interpreter. He was certain his Japanese would be too rusty to deliver effectively what he intended to tell the cruel ex-camp commandant turned Buddhist monk.

Lying in bed the previous night, Danny had rehearsed his confrontation with Mori a dozen or more times in his rusty Japanese, while flicking through his phrasebook, which proved frustratingly inadequate. Now he decided to ask Tony for the words he was unsure about. He still wasn't entirely sure he could articulate what he wanted to say, even in English. It is much easier to describe a man as a bastard than to confront him as one.

Danny knew very little about Buddhism and had always supposed that Shinto was the more common belief in Japan. 'Isn't it unusual to have someone like Mori become a monk in a Buddhist temple?' Danny asked, after their language session had come to an end and he had noted down the words he'd been unable to remember. 'I would have expected him to be Shinto.'

'No, not at all unusual,' Tony replied. 'Japan doesn't have a state religion, but you're right – Shinto has perhaps more adherents. Although it's hard to say, because the Japanese are fairly catholic in their religious beliefs. Shinto ritual, for instance, is usually employed for births, whereas Buddhist ritual is preferred for deaths. Most Japanese follow both and visit both Shinto shrines and Buddhist temples. It would be logical for Mori to seek his redemption as a Mahayana Buddhist monk, following the path to enlightenment through a monastic life of meditation and withdrawal. They believe that attempting to get others to reach a state of enlightenment is nearly impossible when you can barely help yourself. The idea is to confine yourself to the temple and work on your own enlightenment.'

'Bloody convenient, if you ask me,' Danny sniffed. 'You can be an utter bastard all your life, then, when you're old, you can buy an insurance policy from God or Buddha or whoever you've chosen to back.'

'Dunn, that's an Irish name, isn't it?' Tony Blackmore smiled, adding, 'Catholic?'

'I guess,' Danny replied.

'Well, as your local Father Murphy will tell you, it's never too late to return to the true faith, the true God. We do it all the time in Christianity. The Japanese are no different. Old people seeing the light after a lifetime of dark deeds is common in most faiths, I'd guess.'

The taxi dropped them outside the high stone wall surrounding the temple, and they walked unchallenged through an open wooden gate and into the large compound.

'Looks old,' Danny said, unconsciously lowering his voice.

'It is old, bloody old,' Tony replied.

Beyond the walls stood a series of tiered wooden buildings. Solid-looking and weathered, they gave the impression of having been there for a very long time. On many, the roof tiles were covered in moss and lichen. Dotted among the structures were great old trees, and the entire complex was surrounded by a beautifully manicured lawn. The chanting of monks punctuated by the tintinnabulation of small bells intruded into what might have been described as a serene silence. In a very real way, the sounds enhanced the sense of quietude.

'Christ!' Danny said under his breath. 'Who'd have thought?'

'Wrong God,' Tony shot back. 'This is the house of the fat guy with the smile.'

'I can see what you mean about trying to catch up with your inner self,' Danny remarked. 'Difficult to be a bastard in these surroundings.'

They'd reached the main temple and removed their shoes at the entrance, at the same time trying to adjust to the shadowy interior. The great hall was dimly lit by clusters of flickering candles that gleamed on an expanse of polished wooden floor stretching ahead of them to a large gold statue of Buddha, where a group of monks sat in a circle chanting with their heads bowed, intermittently ringing tiny bells.

A young monk, perhaps a novice, approached them, his every footstep making the floor sing as if it were specially sprung. 'It's called a nightingale floor,' Tony Blackmore explained quietly. 'It sings as you move over it to warn of an enemy approaching. Probably built around three centuries ago.'

The novice, smiling, bade them enter, then inquired if they were tourists and wished to be shown around. 'No,' Tony replied, 'We have come to visit the monk Mori-*san*.'

The young monk looked surprised. 'But you cannot be family?'

'No, old acquaintances. We are from his distant past, far away,' Tony explained.

'And you have come to see him before he attains the next step to enlightenment?'

'Yes,' Danny said, not sure what the young bloke meant. Then he added, 'We wish to pay our respects.'

'I will ask. Wait, please.' He turned and set off across the singing floorboards towards the circle of chanting monks, returning after he had consulted with one of them. 'He is still aware. You may come with me,' he said.

The floor sang or, Danny thought, made a wobbling sound as they crossed towards the chanting circle, and it wasn't until they reached it that he realised a monk lay at its centre. 'Christ, it's him – Mori!' he said in a shocked whisper. 'He's carking it. The bastard's dying!'

The monks continued to chant, ignoring their presence. Tony Blackmore touched Danny on the shoulder. 'Looks like we've arrived too late. Better leave, hey?' he whispered.

But Danny seemed not to hear. The Japanese words came to him clearly. He'd heard them a dozen times or more from Japanese guards as they'd beaten a prisoner to death for some trifling transgression. He stepped forward and gently placed his hands on the shoulders of two monks, forcing them to part sufficiently for him to step into the circle. Inside he dropped to his haunches beside Mori, who appeared to be still conscious. Looking directly into the dying man's eyes, he said, 'This is Sergeant Major Dunn, Colonel Mori.' A fleeting look of recognition appeared in Mori's eyes and a faint nod of his head signalled that he'd heard him, but there was no fear, and no remorse. Danny stared at that hated face, then leaned down and placed his mouth close to the dying monk's ear. In his rough Japanese he whispered, 'Die, you mongrel, you worthless piece of dog shit!' The chanting continued unabated, as he hissed, 'We are bound together for all time, Mori. May my spirit, and the spirits of those you harmed, haunt you for eternity!'

The monks droned on. As Danny rose, the two monks swayed to the left and right to allow him to leave the circle. Danny almost ran from the building, the floor bouncing and wobbling under his panic-stricken feet. Without waiting to put on his shoes, he reached the fresh air and barely made it to an ancient Sugi tree, a Japanese cedar, where he began to dry-retch. It was as if he were vomiting emotional bile, purging himself of the memories of the prison camp and the men who had died needlessly. Finally, his stomach turned and he threw up its contents.

Tony Blackmore stood, unmoving, a short distance away, holding Danny's shoes, and when Danny eventually approached him, he handed them over without a word. For the most part they were silent as they returned to the group, but just before they arrived, Danny turned and offered the military attaché his hand. 'Thanks, mate, I truly appreciate what you've done for me,' he said quietly.

'For my family too, Danny; for my brother Jack,' Tony replied.

It was not until New Year's Eve, when Helen and Danny once again sat on the upstairs verandah cracking the traditional bottle of Bollinger, that he told Helen the story of the final hours of the life of the one-time Colonel Mori. He couldn't bring himself to tell her the first part of what he'd said to the dying monk – they were words from the camp, and later he'd regretted using them. He simply told her that he had whispered to the dying man, 'We are bound together for all time, Mori. May my spirit, and the spirits of those you harmed, haunt you for eternity!' But in retrospect, even this gave him no sense of triumph or of a mission accomplished.

Nevertheless, Helen was appalled and said so. 'Danny, I don't know whether I believe in God, least of all a forgiving and merciful one, but I do believe in the human spirit, and you have sullied yours by saying what you said to Mori, and you immediately became a lesser man for it.' It was the closest he'd ever heard Helen come to making a moral judgment that left no room for appeal.

'Yes,' Danny said quietly. 'Yes, I know.'

1966 was the year of the British Empire and Commonwealth Games in Kingston, Jamaica. While Dawn Fraser, still at the height of her swimming career, would have been expected to return from Jamaica with four gold medals, a sanctimonious Amateur Swimming Union of Australia, flexing its muscles about the flag incident at the Tokyo Olympics, had banned her from competitive swimming for ten years, effectively terminating her career.

All of Balmain and most of sporting Australia were immediately up in arms, and Danny, as both a lawyer and the Independent member for the area, went in to bat for her reinstatement. He was to learn a salutary lesson: that dealing with fanatical amateurs who hold to what they believe is the moral high ground is not the same thing as working with professional and fair-minded people looking for a just and equitable solution to a problem.

As a lawyer, he could present a case that, if strong enough, could be expected to earn a not-guilty verdict or be dismissed. Similarly, in parliament, both sides were able to question and debate issues, and although deals were made from time to time, if they were clandestine or overtly unfair, the deal-makers risked exposure by the Opposition or the media.

His efforts to have the Balmain harbour-front rezoned as residential land was a case in point. Well argued on the floor of the house as beneficial not only to the immediate community but also to the city of Sydney and to the state, it met with the approval of all who had no special agenda. Most saw it as long overdue, a correction to blatant Labor Government corruption and inertia. However, none of these rules or traditions applied to the Amateur Swimming Union or the bodies controlling Australia's entrants in the Commonwealth Games or the Olympics.

Danny was more than a little surprised to discover a bias within the Swimming Union against so-called lower- or working-class swimmers, not dissimilar to the nonsense spouted by Hitler about racial purity that was supposedly supported by the 'science' of eugenics. Hitler had hoped to demonstrate the superiority of the German people at the 1936 Berlin Olympic Games, but despite Jesse Owens proving him disastrously wrong, he and the Nazis went on to murder six million Jews, Gypsies and other people they considered inferior.

The Swimming Union, using a high-minded and fanatically policed code of amateurism, tried to restrict the number of working-class Australian swimmers representing their country. In fairness, this concept originated from the International Olympic Committee, whose chief, Avery Brundage, was a notorious bully and Nazi sympathiser. Here in Australia, money was the weapon employed by the ranks of swimming officialdom to keep the sport socially pure and effectively only available to those with parents who could afford to sponsor their children's training and travel expenses. As the state or federal government made no contribution to the development of Australian athletes, this effectively kept the hoi polloi out of contention.

Danny's sense of fair play was immediately aroused. Dawn had been involved in the flag-stealing incident with a number of other Australian Olympians and hadn't instigated the prank herself, but despite that, she was the only participant to be punished with a career-ending sentence. This was especially galling because Dawn Fraser, the kid from the wrong side of the tracks, had the potential to become the greatest swimmer and possibly the greatest athlete in Australian history.

There had always been only one way for an impecunious swimmer to compete, and this was by accepting a life of severe financial hardship and hard work. Dawn had been permitted to compete in the first place because she had undergone this test and proved the depth of her character and her determination to compete, but now she had been deemed fundamentally unsound and disqualified from international competition. The sentiment in coaching circles was that the only one ever to beat Dawn Fraser was the Amateur Swimming Union of Australia.

Danny had tried everything in his power to have this decision reversed, including applying pressure from the state government and finally the media, but the Swimming Union proved to be a law unto themselves. This despotic and recalcitrant attitude of the swimming body, taking its cue from the all-powerful Avery Brundage, became known in swimming circles as 'Brundage's Bondage' and proved too strong for anyone to undo.

The word 'amateur' meant 'self-supporting', but without any sponsorship at all. As an example, if a local hairdressing salon gave a swimmer from a poor working-class family the money for a rail ticket to compete at a swimming meet, the swimmer was disqualified from ever competing for Australia. Money was seen as tarnishing the noble image of Olympic sport, and, it seemed, the image of the British Empire and Commonwealth Games.

Despite being warned at the outset that he would be punished for interfering, Danny had gone ahead on behalf of Balmain's beloved Dawnie. He could see little difference between this and the case of Paul Jones, the little Welshman who had been denied a military medal because there had been no officer present to attest to his quiet heroism. Danny had fought his entire life for a just system and he wasn't going to be easily scared off.

When the swimmers were selected to compete in Jamaica, Sam's name was not included on the list. In fairness, her times were not as good as they had been, but she was still consistently recording the fastest 100- and 200-metre times among Australian female swimmers.

This drop in her performance was a mystery to her coach but was put down to several bouts of bursitis and other injuries collectively known as 'swimmer's shoulder', and blamed on overtraining.

Sam, despite the occasional nagging injuries, the distances swum and the long hours, loved the training routine and the camaraderie of the other swimmers. She happily sacrificed the social life that Gabby was just beginning to lead – going out several times a week to perform at folk clubs with her guitar, or in the youth orchestra with her beloved violin. Having been put up a grade, both girls mixed with friends at least a year older than they were, and, like their classmates, they were now preparing for their Higher School Certificate the following year – a new final-year exam that would be introduced in 1967. It was a big load for both girls, neither of whom had yet turned fifteen, but they seemed to relish it.

Gabby had appeared several times on Brian Henderson's *Bandstand* on Channel Nine, singing folk songs from America, Britain, and occasionally Australia, and was frequently recognised and stopped by young people in the street. On one occasion on a Saturday morning she had been almost mobbed by the eager young crowd outside Erin Walsh's Brokendown shop. Photojournalists, present for a fashion show and prepared to capture Sam modelling the latest miniskirts, jostled to snap pictures of the popular young folk-singer twin, who was also a serious student at the Sydney Conservatorium. Gabby's talent for working the crowd, first demonstrated at primary school when she recounted the Saturday matinee movie, was standing her in good stead. She was very pretty, and modelled herself on American folk singers such as Joan Baez, whose music Dallas sent her regularly. Sam, hitherto the centre of attention, was not in the least concerned that she was being overshadowed by her musical twin. In fact, she shared in and enjoyed Gabby's success, knowing her own ambitions lay elsewhere.

Sam had lots of boy swimmers to amuse her, and she'd been grabbed and kissed and asked out by boys so often that she knew herself to be an object of desire and by far the prettiest swimmer in New South Wales. In fact, Sam was so attractive that both Danny and Helen had warned her about unwanted attention from men. Massages were routine after a training session, but in Sam's case they were always performed by Ursula Carlile out in the open. She was warned never to accept a massage from a male coach, an assistant or any other man. If she was away at a country or interstate swimming meet and Mrs Carlile couldn't be present, Sam was only to accept a massage in the open with other adults present. Sam knew from the other girls that sometimes a massage had nothing to do with curing sore muscles, and that some of them had been touched in inappropriate places by local coaches, assistants or helpers.

Sam's world consisted of pace clocks, goggles, the sharp slap of a rubber swimming cap over her ears, the constant smell of chlorine, bouts of ringworm, ear infections, sore eyes, rashes, dry skin and chlorine-induced asthma. Occasionally there would be a whack in the face or a split lip from a wooden paddle caused by a careless turn as one of the male swimmers in the next lane worked on his strength training. But through it all there was the constant urging and repeated reprimands of a fanatical father.

Rising at 4.30 a.m., Sam and Danny would head out in the dark for the Drummoyne pool, where she would swim four and a half miles in two hours. Australia had shifted to decimal currency in February, and metrification would follow in a few years, but for now Sam and Danny still used inches, feet, yards and miles. The distances were set at 200, 400 and 800 yards. In the afternoons Sam swam for another two hours, covering about three miles, mainly short distance stuff, such as fifty or a hundred yards.

Ever since Danny's entry into state parliament, she had been coached by Forbes and Ursula Carlile, as well as by assistant coach Tom Green when the Carliles were in Europe coaching the Dutch team. Karen Moras, three years younger than Sam and a working-class girl like Dawn Fraser, was another of the Carliles' 'Golden Fish', the term used for swimmers who had the potential, in the eyes of their coaches, to achieve gold either in the British Empire and Commonwealth Games or the Olympic Games. Sam was an obvious choice for selection to go to Jamaica.

The media put two and two together and started to cry foul at Sam not being chosen. The Swimming Union denied any wrongdoing, giving Sam's slower times as the reason she was passed over. The media retaliated by saying that no swimmer in Britain or the Commonwealth had achieved her performance times in the pool in the past year, but the swimming officials simply stonewalled, refusing to discuss their decision.

Sam was devastated. The week before the team was announced she'd reached parity with her previous times in the trials for selection for Jamaica, and an ebullient Forbes Carlile said he believed she was at the point of moving beyond them. In an interview before the team was announced, Carlile claimed his 'Golden Fish' was ready to take on the swimmers from Britain and the Commonwealth, and considered the Jamaica Games as the unofficial Australian trials for the Olympics in Mexico City in 1968.

But it was all to no avail: Danny was being punished for daring to challenge their decision to ban Dawnie, the working-class girl who threatened to be the greatest of all Australian swimmers. Poor Sam was caught between a rock and a hard place. Her loyalty to her father and the devastation she felt at the decision kept her in a constant state of turmoil. While, of course, she'd always denied it, she had been secretly confident that she would go to Jamaica – her times justified it and her consistent performances showed that, aside from unforeseen circumstances, she was a certainty for a gold in the 100- and 200-metres as well as a medal, if not a gold, as a member of the women's 4 × 100-metres medley. Sam wasn't vain or puffed up; she simply knew she was the best in her category and therefore expected to succeed. But there wasn't a swimmer or a coach in Australia who was under any illusions about why Danny's daughter was overlooked by the selectors – his attempts to have Dawn Fraser reinstated had been all over the media.

If Sam hadn't already known why she had been singled out for punishment, she soon did once she heard people refer to her as the 'second Balmain victim'. She couldn't bear to be seen at training or in public, where her fellow swimmers would pity her or people would expostulate or sympathise with her over her victimisation. For the first week she refused to go to training, and going to school was agony. Danny had promised her that he would not rest until the Swimming Union members changed their minds, but when Sam woke one morning to find that Danny had left for work so early that she'd missed him, she knew at once why.

Helen hugged Sam for a long time and simply allowed her to cry and to drown in her own misery. Finally, she held her daughter at arm's length, and looked directly into her eyes. 'Samantha, I'm going to tell you something about your father that we decided years ago – in fact before you and Gabrielle were born – never to tell you.'

Sam, despite herself, was curious. 'What?' she sniffed.

'Before the war, everyone knew that your dad would represent Australia in rugby league. In fact, if the war hadn't intervened, he was certain to have been selected for the next Kangaroo tour of Great Britain. So, you see, he too had to face disappointment and forego the honour of playing for his country. Like you and Dawn, he was the great hope of Balmain, and people loved him. Danny Dunn was the local hero and kids followed him as he walked down Darling Street.'

Sam nodded. 'Must have been tough, really tough.'

Helen then told the story of how Danny, captured by the Japanese, had gone to the rescue of a mate, because it was his duty to defend one of the men for whom he was responsible. She described how Danny had been savagely beaten. 'The attack was so vicious it fractured his back and all but ruined his face,' Helen said, now fighting back her own tears. 'Samantha, your father did that for a mate and because it was his duty. As a result of his fractured back he would never play for Australia or play any sport again, other than swimming and rowing his beloved skiff to keep fit.' Helen paused. 'When he tried to help Dawnie, he saw this as his duty as the member for Balmain. What you need to know is that he is your closest mate and would gladly give his life for you. He is desperately disappointed for you, and last night he cried in bed because he knows this is his fault and there's nothing he can do to fix it.'

'Oh, Mum, that's awful!' Sam whispered, awestruck at the thought of her father crying.

'No, listen to me, Samantha. You *must* understand. Given similar circumstances he'd do the same again. Your dad can't bear unfairness, and he'll always fight for the underdog against mindless, or even mindful, authority. He simply couldn't make an exception because you are his daughter.'

'I . . . I understand, I really do,' Sam said, 'but it's still so unfair!'

'Look, Dad and I talked last night, and we agreed that at nearly fifteen you are old enough to make your own decisions. So, if you *really* believe you can't continue with swimming, then we would understand if you decided to give up trying for the Mexico Olympics. You can change schools if you want to and concentrate on your HSC, then decide what you want to do with your life. What do you say, darling?'

Sam barely waited for Helen to finish. 'But, Mum, Dad has always wanted . . . he's always expected me to swim for Australia. I know how disappointed he was when Gabby stopped swimming! Remember, you had a terrible row and you threw that wine bottle at him. Gabby and I were scared stiff! Dad was furious!'

'Yes, I won't deny that, but first and foremost he wants you both to be happy. You've already got a drawer full of gold medals, Sam —'

'But I promised!' Sam interjected, clearly distressed.

'Darling, it's a big wide world. Whatever you do in life, the swimming you've done all these years has taught you character, determination and the will to succeed; none of it is wasted. Dad knows and accepts that.'

'No!' Sam cried, clearly alarmed at the suggestion. 'Three gold for Sammy! I promised!'

Helen looked sternly at her daughter. 'Are you sure, Samantha?'

Sam kissed her mother. 'Thanks, Mum, but I've made up my mind. I won't let Dad down.'

'I know, darling. So let's show him just what his daughter is made of, shall we? The Mexico Olympics are in two years' time. Let's make that your aim. But remember, if you miss out on selection, or a medal, we'll . . . he'll love you just as much. He just wants you to try your hardest.'

Sam sniffed and wiped away her tears with the backs of both hands. 'I'll do it,' she said, jutting out her chin.

Helen smiled, then, cupping Sam's face in her hands, she looked into her daughter's startling blue eyes, and kissed her gently on the cheek.

Sam rose to her feet. 'Where are you going?' Helen inquired.

'To find Gabby and apologise; she came in to comfort me and I told her to bugger off!'

'You didn't use the "f" word, I hope, Samantha?' Helen said sternly, though there was a twinkle in her eye.

Sam nodded. 'Sometimes it's the only word that's right, Mum! But she'll forgive me – I'm her twin.'

Danny, devastated, had talked with Helen long into the previous night, raging and swearing until he had vented most of his anger, then weeping helplessly with frustration and grief. On Helen's advice, he had agreed to talk to Sam, but after a sleepless night, he left early for work, putting off the confrontation until that evening.

He didn't beat around the bush. 'Sam, we all know why this happened. It's my fault, not yours, and I'm sorry, terribly sorry. Life sometimes doesn't deliver those things we feel entitled to. Events get in the way; unfair decisions, like this one, get made. We have to learn to bear these burdens or they crush us.'

'But, Dad, it's so unfair.' Sam's composure crumpled in the face of her father's distress. 'All you did was try to help Dawnie, and now they're punishing us! And what if I never get another chance, like Dawnie?' she lamented.

'Life always gives us another chance, darling,' Danny said, not entirely believing his own words. 'We just have to pick ourselves up, brush ourselves off and have another go. Let me tell you a true story. It's sad, but I think you're strong enough to hear it.' Danny then told Sam the story of a prisoner of war called George Watford who had been with him in Thailand. 'George rescued a starving mongrel dog and shared his food ration with her . . . she was an ugly little bitch, with lots of character. George grew to love her, I think more than his life, because by halving his food ration he was starving himself to death faster than any of us.' Sam, knuckling the tears from her eyes, listened intently. 'One day a Japanese soldier beat the dog to death with a pick handle, in front of George —'

'Oh, no! The poor little dog!' Sam burst into fresh tears.

Danny, noticing Sam's horrified expression for the first time, decided against telling her the fate of the dog. The soldier had taken an axe and chopped the scrawny pup into four pieces, then made the broken-hearted George cook and eat it.

Danny patted Sam on the shoulder, then continued. 'George Watford survived the camp, mostly due to getting his full rations back, and when he returned to Australia he studied to become a vet. He told me that he very nearly took his own life over the incident and I believed him. But he decided to live, and today he runs Australia's biggest animal shelter for the RSPCA. So, you see, darling, some things make us stronger, more determined and better, even though at the time we believe we lack the strength to survive.'

Sam nodded grimly, then attempted to smile. 'But, Dad, I need those gold medals to stick up your arse,' she wailed. Danny left his daughter's side, believing that, whatever happened, she was going to recover.

Danny resigned from parliament before the 1968 state elections. It had become clear to him that the Askin government had the potential to become as corrupt as the previous government – possibly even more corrupt – and that it was only the presence of the two Independents that kept them honest. The polls were indicating a big swing towards the Liberals, so Danny decided to resign as the member for Balmain, having achieved his purpose. The legislation to clean up Balmain and the other industrial waterfront areas around the harbour had finally gone through. Surprisingly, in the end, Labor made no attempt to block it in the Upper House.

Askin, true to his word, had offered the offending industries generous terms and financial help to relocate to the west. While the Waterside Workers Federation organised a protest march under the usual banner – 'Jobs for Waterside Workers!' – the local people quickly saw the benefits and only the diehard communists continued to thump the bar and demand their legal rights to air and water pollution.

Bob Askin visited Danny when it became clear that he was not going to stand for another term and offered him a safe Liberal seat. 'Danny, all the polls indicate a landslide for us. It looks very good and I could almost certainly offer you a ministry. One of the reasons for our predicted success is the harbour-front clean-up. We'd like to do the same in Newcastle and Wollongong, and you would make an excellent minister for state planning. What say?'

'Bob, I got lucky. I was here when you scraped into government on the bones of your arse; I'm under no illusions. With the greatest respect, you're Frank Packer's man and a big-money politician, whereas I'm, at heart, a poor man's politician. If you scratch me, you'll discover a blue singlet – wouldn't suit the crisp-white-shirt style of your blokes. Thank you, but it's time I went back to the law and put a few more wife beaters away.'

'Don't worry, Danny, there'll be plenty of work for you from my government.'

Danny laughed. 'As long as it isn't defending the indefensible.' He paused. 'Bob, I have to thank you for keeping your word and passing that legislation. It was my reason for going into politics in the first place.'

'No, Danny, it was the legislation the city and the state needed. Anything I can do for you in the future, just come and see me.'

Danny grinned. 'You wouldn't have any ideas about how to discredit the Amateur Swimming Union of Australia, would you?'

'Ah, you've proved to be a very good politician, Danny, astute and insightful, but with them, well, you were much too naïve. Too much Brundage's Bondage there for such as you and me.' The premier grinned. 'Frank Packer might have been able to help. If the silvertails who run the Swimming Union ran the country, we'd all be using a straight-arm salute. Still, I'll bring it up at the Premiers Conference in Canberra next year. I don't hold out much hope that the federal mob will listen, but it will be a nice relief from fighting for more hospital beds.'

Sam, somewhat to the surprise of everyone in Balmain, was selected for the Mexico Olympics, and the media began to refer to the three Golden Fish most likely to bring back gold – Sam, Karen Moras and Lynette McClements. On the new ABC-TV show *This Day Tonight*, swimming coach Forbes Carlile appeared as Bill Peach's guest to comment on the Olympic female swimmers.

'Do you think this is the beginning of another golden age in women's swimming and that we may discover another Dawn Fraser at these games?' Peach asked him.

Carlile was careful with his reply. 'A Dawn Fraser is a very rare fish – a natural swimmer who improves a little with training and technique but arrives virtually the perfect package. Having said that, our present female swimmers can compete and win against the rest of the world – Karen Moras, Lynette McClements and Samantha Dunn, to name only three, are among our Golden Fish for Mexico, and I expect them to do well.'

'No young Dawn doing laps in a side lane, then?' Peach asked.

'Well, as matter of fact, I have a young swimmer from Queensland starting to train with me. She's only twelve, but I haven't seen a talent such as hers since Dawn was a nipper.'

'And her name?'

'Shane Gould.'

Bill Peach turned to camera. 'Shane Gould, sounds like gold; remember, you heard it here first.' He turned back to Forbes Carlile. 'Do you think if Dawn Fraser were permitted to compete in Mexico, she'd have a good chance of taking the five gold medals people are saying she's capable of? Become the greatest swimmer in Australian history?'

Forbes laughed. 'I'm a swimming coach, not Nostradamus. One thing we all know in swimming is that there's many a slip between the starter's gun and the final touch. Even the best swimmers can have a bad day.' He paused. 'But having said that, in my opinion, Dawn Fraser *is* the greatest swimmer in Australian history.'

'The Olympic swimmers are in Townsville for training. Does it worry you that you and the other professional coaches – Harry Gallagher, for instance – are not permitted to accompany and train your own swimmers? Are you concerned that the Amateur Swimming Union of Australia has selected one chief coach, Don Talbot, to oversee the training for all the swimmers?'

'That's two questions,' Forbes replied. 'I'll answer the second one first. Don Talbot is an excellent coach and a good appointment, but having said that, we are asking a great deal of one coach and his helpers. Naturally, when you've worked with a swimmer, sometimes for years, you know every aspect of their character and training capacity, and when they are placed for a few weeks under a different coach it is likely to be difficult for them.' He looked directly at Bill Peach. 'Yes, frankly, it would be very nice to be able to be with your own swimmer, be the last person they talk to before mounting the starting block in Mexico.'

'So, you think this policy is the wrong one?'

'I didn't say that.'

Bill Peach changed tack. 'Your own swimmer, Samantha Dunn, some said at the time a certain gold medal winner at the Commonwealth Games in Jamaica two years ago, was omitted from the selection. Do you have anything to say about that?'

'Only that she was bitterly disappointed but hopes to justify her inclusion in the Olympic team,' Forbes parried.

'Do you have any qualms about the altitude affecting performances?' Bill Peach turned to camera again and explained. 'Mexico City is more than 7000 feet above sea level.'

'Of course, but I guess it's the same for all the competitors.'

'Not quite.'

'Oh?'

'The Mexican swimmers, for a start . . .'

Forbes Carlile laughed. 'Mexico isn't known for its swimmers.'

'You mean, they need all the help they can get?'

'I didn't say that.'

Bill Peach turned to the camera once more. 'Well, there you have it: no Dawn Fraser for Mexico City; the same coaching arrangements as the Commonwealth Games; rarefied altitude, pollution and rumours of possible social unrest; but at least we have Samantha Dunn back where she belongs.' The camera cut to a shot of Sam on the winner's podium winning gold at the national championships. Then, to Forbes Carlile as an off-camera Bill Peach thanked him for coming onto the program.

The camera cut back to Peach. 'Tomorrow night we have Percy Cerutty, the controversial coach of Herb Elliott, who will talk about our athletics team's chances against the Americans and West Indians. I leave you with this Cerutty quote: "Most coaches want to see how fast you run; I want to see how much guts you have." Goodnight.'

'Phew! Forbes only just got away with that,' Danny said, watching at home with Gabby. 'I wonder how poor Sam is going. She'll miss Forbes and Ursula.'

'It's not fair, Dad. She isn't even allowed to call us!'

'We'll see her in Mexico City, darling.'

'If they allow us to!' Gabby cried.

'Well, perhaps after she's swum her races and is free,' Danny said, silently agreeing with Gabby that everything was being done to discourage outside interference. He knew Sam would miss the support and reassurance of the people she knew, trusted and loved.

Sam was nearly seventeen, and this was the first time she had been parted from her family for more than a couple of nights for an interstate or country district swimming meet. Moral hygiene through sport – Olympic Chief Avery Brundage's philosophy – was eagerly adopted by the Amateur Swimming Union of Australia, even though it was as likely to hinder or upset young Australian athletes as it was to create a steely winning culture. Sam was a gregarious, outgoing young person and not accustomed to such isolation. Self-discipline was the last thing the swimmers lacked, having spent years rising at 4.30 a.m. and swimming three or four miles a day, while completing difficult and painful exercises, as well as coping with the normal exigencies of school and home life. Testosterone is not only present in males, and is enhanced by confidence, not denial.

However, Danny realised that not all swimming parents had the means to be present, and was therefore forced to conclude that Sam, like the others, would simply have to learn to manage on her own, though this should not have been necessary in the case of the coaches, who were prepared to raise the money to be with their swimmers. But all requests were denied by the Brundage cronies in the Amateur Swimming Union of Australia and the Olympic Swimming Association.

'Gab, don't forget we'll have her with us when we visit Billy and Dallas in New Orleans. And remember to take your Stetson! Did Sam take hers?'

'Mine looks pretty bad, but Sam's is worse,' Gabby laughed. 'She wears it everywhere, even once on the Brokendown catwalk. It got her on the cover of *Girl*!'

'Billy or Dallas will probably buy you each a new one, and if they don't, then I will,' Danny offered.

'You will not!' Gabby cried. 'I'll never part with mine. I've even worn it on *Bandstand*. I told Mr Henderson that I wouldn't perform without it.'

'You didn't!' Danny said, impressed. 'What happened then?'

'Well, he said that was the end of me appearing on *Bandstand*, so I started to walk off, but he called me back because the kids were all screaming at him and booing.'

'Gabby, you didn't tell me this. Does your mother know?'

'It wasn't a big deal, Dad. I'm a violinist, not a folk singer. *Bandstand* is only for fun.'

'So what happened next?'

'He said he was only kidding and to come back on, and then the kids booed him again for being such an idiot.'

'This all happened on live TV?'

'No, Dad, it's pre-recorded in the studio. They do three episodes at the same time.'

'And no repercussions afterwards?'

'Johnny O'Keefe came over and said, "Good on ya, kid."'

'And you've been invited back?'

'Yes, last week, but I told them I was going to the Olympics. Anyway, I wouldn't go onto *Bandstand* again unless I wore my Stetson.'

Danny grinned. 'Cheeky bugger! But you'd only worn it the once, and you've been on that show a fair bit – three or four times – haven't you?'

'Yes, but there was a principle involved!'

Danny laughed. 'Good one. You might start a trend.'

Gabby giggled. 'I already have. It's become a kids' thing, only they're using their dads' Akubras.'

'And what do you wear for concerts, now you're in the Conservatorium proper?'

'Oh, a black cloak and a fedora with the brim pulled down on one side!' Gabby grinned.

'With a flower?' Danny asked.

'Oh yes, a yellow rose from our garden, in memory of Sammy Laidlaw.'

'Bullnose would appreciate that. He said to me the other day, "Me arty-ritis is givin' me a bit a' stick, Danny. Yer'll have ter throw me in the compost heap when I can't prune them roses no more! Gabby'll go crook on me if she can't 'ave no yellow roses!"'

'I'd never go crook at Bullnose,' Gabby said with a smile.

'I'm not sure Sammy was much of a classical-music fan,' Danny went on, 'but I've been led to believe by your grandmother that it's the only kind of music they play in heaven, so he's probably got used to it by now. He's probably watching your progress and smiling, in between growing yellow roses in his heavenly garden.'

'Grandma loves the violin – or the fiddle, as she calls it. She says, "It's the sound of wild bush honey poured onto warm black rocks. That is, if *that* could be a sound, me darlin'." I've written a song I've called "Wild Bush Honey/ Warm Black Rocks". Wanna hear it?'

'Yeah, but maybe not right now, eh?' Danny said, turning his attention back to the television.

After arriving in Los Angeles, Danny and Gabby took a Continental Airlines flight to Mexico City. Helen had pleaded pressure of work by way of excuse for not joining them, something Danny and Gabby had puzzled over many times on the long flight. Danny, as usual, had done his homework and had grave doubts about the wisdom of bringing Gabby to one of the most dangerous cities in the world. But Sam was Gabby's twin and her anxiety to be close to her at her moment of triumph in the pool, an outcome Gabby never for one moment doubted, could not be dismissed. At the time of the Olympics, or perhaps because of the Olympics, Mexico City was like a human Krakatau, a volcano plugged by a sclerotic ruling class with the pressure of ten million, mostly poor, Indians, descendants of the Aztecs, building to an almighty eruption.

The people were kept under control by a combination of the army and the police, both organisations venal and corrupt in the extreme. Only the poor were fined or punished; the rich simply paid bribes. There was a saying in Mexico: 'It is easier to find a lone flea on an elephant than a rich man in jail.'

The poor inhabitants – you couldn't call them citizens because they had no rights – lived in shantytowns of flattened kerosene tins, canvas, plywood, corrugated iron, mud bricks and cardboard, without water or sanitation, while the rich, with their fortunes built on vast petroleum and oil resources, lived in unimaginable luxury, oblivious or uncaring. This was a city of private affluence and abject public squalor, where official buildings and private palaces stood in dirty streets and plazas crowded with beggars, the poor and the desperate.

With the world's eyes on Mexico, there was a chance to publicise the misery of most of the ten million inhabitants of the city. But the haves reacted to the riots as they'd always done and sent in the army and the police, who killed hundreds of students and rioters while the world and the Olympic organisers looked on and did nothing other than to have Brundage appear on the world's TV screens to assure everyone that the Mexican authorities had everything under control and that the glory of the Olympic tradition would continue.

Gabby and Danny arrived in the early evening, and by the time they had reached their hotel, Gabby was in tears at the poverty she had witnessed through the taxi window. They were welcomed by what seemed like a legion of spotlessly uniformed hotel staff, each more unctuous and fawning than the last, no doubt conscious of the privilege of holding down a regular job.

Danny had booked a small suite in the Hotel Majestic, an old and comfortable hotel with every amenity, close to the Zócalo, the plaza in the centre of the city. After the poverty they had witnessed coming in from the airport, it seemed an obscene extravagance.

The suite, despite being described as small, was spacious and deliciously old-fashioned, with high, dark wooden ceilings and several ornate silver-framed mirrors. The bathroom was large enough to throw an echo and contained an enormous four-legged bath and gleaming brass fixtures redolent of an advertisement in a Victorian almanac. But the water was steaming and plentiful, the beds commodious and well sprung, and the air-conditioning, while somewhat noisy, worked.

The Olympic Village, set in almost one hundred acres of lawns and wooded parkland in Pedregal de San Angel on the southern edge of the city, was just five minutes by car from the main stadia. It was designed as a new suburb with every amenity, so that the 7000 athletes and 800 officials had no reason, other than curiosity, to leave the village and enter the perilous city. To ensure that the athletes understood this, the entire area was surrounded by a high wire perimeter fence, patrolled by armed guards at the various entry points.

Sam lay on her bed in the small bedroom she shared with Judith Playfair. 'My legs feel heavy. Are yours okay?' she asked Judith.

'It's probably jet lag,' Judith said. 'Mine are fine.'

'Jet lag? We've already been here a week. Shouldn't it be over by now?' Sam asked.

'Perhaps it's the altitude, the two things combined. Maybe try a massage. I had one today; it was good,' Judith said.

'Me too, but I miss Ursula. It wasn't the same.'

'You're spoilt, Sam,' Judith said with a laugh.

'I know, but I miss my coach, don't you? I don't like what Don Talbot's assistant is making me do. It's different, the routines are different.' Sam turned on her elbow to face her fellow competitor. 'Judy, I'm scared.'

'Don't worry, we all are. We got accustomed to the change in coaches in Jamaica. There's not much you can do about it,' Judith advised. 'We all miss our coaches, Sam, but we don't have any say – you know that!'

'But everyone knows you guys didn't live up to your potential in Jamaica! Don't they realise that?'

'Grow up, Sam. It's not about us, it's about power! The little Hitlers. You have to tell yourself to forget what's giving you the shits and go for it – this may be your only Olympics.'

'Yeah, I suppose, but I'm not making it up about my legs.'

Six days later an excited Danny and Gabby sat in the swimming complex to watch Sam swim in her first heat for the 100-metres freestyle. Sam managed to spot them in the crowd and waved, while Gabby blew kisses down at her twin and Danny held both thumbs in the air.

'I'm so nervous, Dad, I think I'm going to be sick,' Gabby said.

'I'm carrying the other half of the butterfly colony, darling. She's done the work, now we can only hope it's enough.'

To their joy, Sam won her heat, but was well behind her best time. Hers was the fourth heat and the slowest up to that time, with three more to swim. Danny and Gabby waited anxiously to see if her time qualified her for the finals. 'Dad, she's four seconds behind her best time. Will it be enough?' Gabby cried, close to tears.

'If it is, then she's being very smart, sweetheart. Sam is saving herself for the finals.' But he knew his girl – Sam swam every race as if her life depended on it. Hers was an all-or-nothing personality; she put it on the line every time. He knew there was something wrong.

Danny was right, Sam had given it her best shot, but she'd woken up the day before the heats for the 100-metres with a stomach upset she'd at first put down to nerves. But on the morning of the heats, she'd started to cramp badly and had gone to the toilet several times. The coach made her top up her blood sugar with glucose, but she'd felt far from fit when the starter's gun went off. She was hugely relieved that she'd nevertheless made the finals. She'd be in the last lane, having only just scraped in, but she told herself the finals were two days away and the time recorded by the winner of the fastest heat was .07 of a second slower than Sam's best.

The night before the finals she started to vomit, and at nine o'clock Judith Playfair called the team doctor, Doctor Conning, who was unable to give her anything to stop the cramps and vomiting, because these were the first games where mandatory drug testing had been introduced. All he could do was try to maintain her fluids so that she didn't become dehydrated. He mixed her a cocktail of substances to increase her blood-sugar, but she seemed to throw them up almost as fast as she got them down. In the morning he gave Sam a final examination and called Don Talbot, advising him that he ought to pull her out of the race.

Don approached the miserable girl. 'Sam, the doctor says you're not good. He's advised us to pull you.'

Sam looked at him, unable to believe her ears. 'Mr Talbot, please, I have to race. I qualified – you can't pull me!' she cried.

'Sam, I'm responsible for your wellbeing. If I report this to Mr Patching, he'll accept the doctor's advice.'

'Please, please, Mr Talbot! I missed the Commonwealth Games. This may be the only chance I have to swim for Australia. You can't, please, you can't pull me!'

'Sam, you're entered in the 200-metres and the women's 4 × 100 medley; they're two days and a week away. You may recover by then.'

'And if I haven't? Please, sir . . . Mr Talbot, I've qualified for the final. Just let me swim; let me swim for my country!' Sam begged.

'I'll have another chat to the doctor, Sam. But understand, I'm your coach and your health comes first. I can't make any promises.'

Sam nodded, barely managing to hold back her tears. 'Thank you,' she said and waited until he'd left the room before she began to cry.

Don Talbot returned an hour later. 'Subject to the doctor's examination an hour before the race, so that the next fastest qualifier can be notified, you have my permission to compete.' He looked at her sternly. 'Sam, the doctor has the final word, okay?'

Sam nodded. 'Yes, thank you, sir.'

Dr Conning, the team doctor, was a nice enough bloke, who had been a competitor in the long jump at the Berlin Games. He examined her, questioning her closely. 'Samantha, you may get through the race, but you've got some sort of bug and I can't treat you or give you anything until afterwards. The only reason I'm going to allow you to swim is that the drugs you need to get rid of this bug will automatically disqualify you from the 200-metres freestyle and the medley. You're strong and you're fit and you may well recover on your own, so that you can swim in one or both of those races. Here are your options. You might as well understand that if you swim in an hour's time, you're unlikely to be in contention for a medal – you've lost too much fluid. If the race were any more than 100 metres, I wouldn't think of letting you compete. So, there you have it. Hope you recover without drugs and live to compete and win a possible medal another day, or be an also-ran in today's event – you decide.'

Sam was frightened and weak and wanted both her father and her twin to be with her. She felt sure that Danny would give her the strength she needed to compete, or to decide what she should do. But she was forbidden to call him. 'Now? I have to make up my mind now, doctor?' she asked almost in a whisper.

'Yes, you do, Samantha,' the doctor said gently. 'Tough decision.'

Sam tried to think what Danny would say, but all she could hear in her head was static. Then suddenly, quite clearly, she heard Katerina's voice: *Okay, but we take no shit from nobody, right? That's the rule!* 'I want to swim the 100-metres,' Sam said, looking the doctor straight in the eye.

Danny and Gabby sat in the stands waiting for the finals of the 100-metres women's freestyle. They were clutching Australian flags and wearing bright-yellow T-shirts with the words 'Go Sam!' on the front in dark-green lettering, compliments of Pineapple Joe.

The swimmers came out of the dressing-rooms and stood beside their respective blocks, waiting for the starter to ask them to mount. Danny was aware of Gabby trembling beside him and he put his arm around her to comfort her, but she suddenly burst into tears. 'There's something terribly wrong with Sam, Dad. I've been feeling it for days,' she sobbed.

'You're just nervous, sweetheart. It'll soon be over, darling.'

'No, it won't! She's ill – very, very ill. I know it!' Gabby gasped.

'Pull yourself together, Gabby. They're mounting the blocks,' Danny said, his own heart starting to pound. All those years, all those early mornings, all the lost tempers, all the tears, all the injuries, all for this one moment. There was a lump in his throat and he only just managed to say, 'Now, Gabby, watch.'

The starter's gun went off and the eight swimmers were away, Sam with a good start in the far lane. She touched in fifth place at the 50-metre mark, a good half metre behind the fourth swimmer. Danny wasn't aware that he was screaming as they raced towards the finish line. He knew Sam couldn't possibly win but she was overhauling the swimmer in fourth place, passed her with ten metres to go and then came up level with the American lying third. In a tremendous finish they touched at exactly the same time, seemingly a dead heat for bronze. Gabby was bawling her eyes out and Danny reached for his handkerchief, his eyes brimming.

This was the first time the Olympic Games used electronic as well as hand timing, announcing both results after every event. The microphone crackled and the chief swimming judge announced that the American swimmers had taken first and second places, and that the four judges using hand timing indicated Australia and America had finished in a dead heat for third. The crowd waited. 'The electronic timer gives it to America by one two-hundredth of a second. America takes the third placing,' the chief judge announced.

Danny suddenly realised that Gabby was screaming, 'Help her! Help her! Please, help Sam!' With the announcement over, all the other swimmers had started to leave the pool, but Sam lacked the strength. It was clear she could no longer even hold onto the edge of the pool or the lane rope, and she faltered and began to sink. The swimmer beside her, halfway out, turned and grabbed Sam's arm, supporting her while two officials ran over and pulled the unconscious girl from the water.

'That's my girl!' Danny sobbed.

CHAPTER SIXTEEN

AN UNCONSCIOUS SAM WAS placed on a gurney at the poolside and taken into the dressing-room, where she was given an intravenous electrolyte drip to rehydrate her exhausted body. Dr Conning, the team doctor, then accompanied her in the ambulance to the Olympic Village. She had regained consciousness and was fully aware of her surroundings by the time they approached the village. 'What happened?' she asked Dr Conning, who was seated beside her in the back.

'Well, my girl, what happened was possibly the most courageous 100-metre swim I've ever witnessed. You didn't get a medal, missed by two-hundredths of a second, but by God you deserved one!'

'No I didn't,' Sam answered flatly. 'I didn't win.'

The doctor shook his head. 'Sam, you couldn't win – nobody in your state of health could have. That you came so close to getting a place was a truly remarkable performance. I expected you to finish because I know how determined you are, but in last place and well behind. More importantly, I don't think you've done yourself any permanent damage. Luckily, the swimmer in the next lane got to you before you inhaled any water.'

'Will I be able to swim in the 200-metres freestyle heats tomorrow morning?' Sam asked.

'After seeing your performance this afternoon, nothing would surprise me. But in my opinion the answer is no, my dear; your Olympics is over. Until next time that is.'

'There won't be a next time,' Sam said softly. 'Please, Dr Conning, let me swim in tomorrow's heats. Please?' she begged.

'Now, Samantha, it's Don Talbot's decision, not mine, but he'll ask me what I think and I have to be truthful. I will be against it. It's not that we can't fix you – it's a simple enough matter of hydration and stopping your diarrhoea, and giving you a dextrose drip – it's just that we can't do it in time for tomorrow's heats. The 200-metres is in the morning and the women's 4 × 100-metres medley is in the afternoon. Despite your considerable courage, there's not a snowball's hope in hell of getting you going in time, my girl. You'll be right as rain in two or three days, but what you did today is going to take its toll, believe you me. You're going to be pretty whacked for the next twenty-four hours. By gosh, you were splendid, though,' he added admiringly.

They'd passed through the gates of the village and reached the Medical Centre, and soon Sam was sitting up comfortably in bed with a drip in her arm. 'I'm going to give you something to allow you to sleep for at least twelve hours,' Dr Conning said.

'But can I call my dad and my twin sister first, Dr Conning? They'll want to know what happened to me.'

'Yes, of course. In an hour you'll be strong enough to walk to the phone. I'll give you a sedative after that.'

Sam looked the doctor straight in the eyes, appealing to him one last time. 'Doctor, please don't say no to Don Talbot,' she pleaded. 'Just the 200-metres heats, that's all. I beg you! The medley, yes, I agree, I'd spoil the team's chances of getting into the finals.'

'Okay, Sam,' he sighed. 'I'll leave it until tomorrow. Your diarrhoea hasn't recurred since this morning, and that's a good sign, but I don't honestly hold out much hope that you'll be in good enough shape to swim.'

'Thank you, doctor,' Sam said, relieved, suddenly too tired to think.

But just then an orderly appeared and waited until Dr Conning noticed him.

'*Perdóneme*, doctor, *los padres de la chica estan esperando a la seguridad en la entrada del hospital*,' he announced in rapid Mexican Spanish.

'*No hablo* Spanish,' the doctor replied [I don't speak Spanish]. It was one of the more essential phrases the members of the Australian team had learned.

The orderly hesitated a moment, then, smiling, replied, 'Senor Doctore . . . excuse me. The papa and the senorita,' he pointed at Sam, 'of ze senorita is waiting at zi guardian telephono control entrada. *Por favor*, pleaze, zey can see ze senorita? Is okay, *por favor*?' He paused, then asked again, 'Is okay?'

'Speak of the devil,' Dr Conning laughed. 'They may spend an hour with you, Samantha, then you're going to have to sleep.' He nodded at the orderly. 'Is okay.' He turned again to Sam. 'You understand I will have to talk to your father.'

Sam nodded.

When Danny talked to her he was adamant. Sam was not going to take any further part in the Games. 'You've swum your race, sweetheart, and we're going home as soon as you're out of here. Gabby knew there was something very wrong with you and, of course, she was right.'

'But, Dad,' Sam cried, 'the doctor says we can wait until the morning to decide if I can swim!' She burst into fresh tears, completely overwrought. 'I've let you down, it's all been for nothing!' she wailed.

Gabby had flung herself at her sister, sobbing, and buried her face in Sam's lap. Now she shook her head as Danny said, 'Nothing is for nothing, darling, and you've never let me down – not for one moment. We are terribly, terribly proud of you, Sam!' Danny felt the tears coursing down his own cheeks.

In the taxi speeding to the village after the race, holding a distraught and sobbing Gabby in his arms, Danny had undergone an epiphany. His life suddenly seemed to be little more than a series of pathetic obsessions – Glossy's boots, Riley, Sammy Laidlaw, the medal for Spike

Jones, retribution on Colonel Mori's deathbed, O'Hearn and the polluted Balmain harbour-front; even his pro bono cases, though he'd helped numerous women and children, were all part of his anger at the world. It was, all of it, personal: his overreaction to and rejection of authority, his overweening sense of fair play – all seemed suddenly, pathetically, self-indulgent. Worst of all, he saw for an instant that he had been guilty at times of outright psychological bullying, and especially of his beloved and precious daughter Sam. Moreover, by differentiating between the twins, he'd done the same to Gabby. He also saw for the first time that an event that could be decided by two-hundredths of a second in a swimming lane, and yet potentially have consequences for the remainder of his daughter's existence, had no place in her life. It was all a terrible indictment of him. For a brief moment he saw that his inner demons and obsessions bordered on insanity. On that seemingly endless journey, he wondered how he was going to live with this awful realisation.

All Danny could think to do was to get Sam away from Mexico and try to make some restitution. He decided that when they got back to Sydney he'd call Craig Woon, now an eminent psychiatrist, and ask his advice. For the first time, Danny realised he needed more help than his beloved Helen could provide. He now understood why she had refused to come to Mexico, pleading pressure of work. It was so he could bask in the glory of what he'd achieved with his daughter, *his* twin, alone. Gabby had only been allowed to go because her presence was essential to Sam's wellbeing. Danny loathed himself for having thought this was apposite, for putting up only token resistance to his wife's decision. Her words came back to him clearly: 'Among several other urgent matters, there's a court appearance – quite annoying, really – the Builders Labourers Union. I'm a reluctant, but it seems essential, witness.' He was a lawyer. He knew how to get around that kind of situation! But he hadn't. Danny cringed inwardly. *What a pathetic fuckwit you are, Danny Dunn*, he silently acknowledged.

THE STORY OF DANNY DUNN 571

After Danny and Gabby departed, Sam slept for a good twelve hours, and when they returned the following morning at around 10 a.m., she'd been awake for ages and claimed she felt absolutely recovered, kissing them both happily. 'They took my drip out at six o'clock this morning,' Sam explained. 'I feel perfectly fine, t'riffic! I even went for a wee on my own.'

'Has the doctor seen you?' Danny asked, doubtful.

Sam's bottom lip dropped. 'Yes, he came with Don Talbot at seven o'clock.'

'Oh, Sam!' Gabby exclaimed, grabbing Sam's hand and holding it to her cheek.

'They made me walk down the corridor, so I ran instead.'

'And then?' Danny asked.

'They made me – I mean, Mr Talbot – made me do push-ups.'

'How many?'

'Fifty.'

'Pfft!' Danny flicked his hand dismissively. 'Nothing.'

'I collapsed on forty-two,' Sam admitted. 'Then Mr Talbot said, "C'mon, Sam, normally you'd be able to do two hundred on your ear, wouldn't you? The 200-metres freestyle heats are later today. Sorry, kid, no way."' Sam looked at her father, dry-eyed. 'Dad, it's all over.'

'Yeah, I guess it is,' he said with a rueful shrug. 'Glad to see you're taking it so well, darling.' To his surprise, Gabby was grinning. 'What's the grin for, Gabs?'

'Nothing,' Gabby said quickly.

'I'll see if you're well enough to leave and we'll go home, eh? Skip New Orleans . . .' Danny said.

'Dad, I'd like to stay for the closing ceremony,' Sam said firmly. 'I won't have another Olympics.'

Gabby turned her head away so her father couldn't see her expression.

Danny, lacking Gabby's instinctive understanding, was oblivious to Sam's reason for wanting to stay for the closing ceremony. He heard only one thing – that Sam had decided this would be her last Olympics. He could feel his anger rising suddenly – she was giving up! She would only be twenty-one next Olympics. It could all still happen – this wasn't the end. *Take it easy, mate,* a voice within him urged. He gulped, recovering. 'Yeah, fine. Want to say goodbye to all your mates, eh? Good idea.'

'I'd like to go to New Orleans after that, though,' Sam added, smiling.

Danny, now calm again, could hardly believe that his daughter, so totally mortified on the previous day, could be so calm today, apparently already reconciled to what must surely be the biggest disappointment of her young life, even bigger than missing out on Jamaica. He felt deeply gratified that she was demonstrating such maturity and sterling character traits. He allowed that she might be in shock and had perhaps slipped into a state of denial, and that it would all come out later. Still, he was grateful, for she seemed bright enough and even cheerful. 'When will they let you out of here?' he asked.

'Tomorrow, then I have to stay in the village all day. After that I can watch the rest of the swimming finals with you.'

In the cab going back to the hotel, Danny turned to Gabby. 'Back at the hospital, what were you grinning about? I even saw you turning away, trying to hide your amusement. What was all that about?'

'Dad, Sam's in love!' Gabby laughed, clapping her hands.

'What? How? What are you talking about, Gabby? She didn't say anything about —'

'Well she is!' Gabby said, her voice quite definite.

'In love?'

'Yes.'

'With whom, may I ask?'

Gabby shrugged. 'I don't know.'

'C'mon, Gabby, has she told you? I was there all the time . . . Sam said nothing to either of us.'

'She didn't have to, Dad. I'm her twin,' Gabby said, turning to look out of the taxi window so Danny wouldn't see her wide grin. She did wonder, though . . . the medical orderly was young and quite good-looking, but his hair was a bit greasy. Her instinct told her he wasn't the one. She knew Sam was on the pill. She'd been taking it to manage the timing of her periods.

The possibility of love at first sight may perhaps be genetically encoded into certain female brains, along with the belief that it is a euphoric condition that transports the newly smitten into a state of bliss transcending all else. Everything that happened before cupid's arrow struck, fixing its point in the centre of the heart, seems suddenly lacking in significance. Disappointment is a comparatively mild emotion when compared with the all-embracing feeling of new and true first love.

Although Sam had imagined countless trysts each night before going to sleep, and discovered new lovers within every book she read, her actual sexual experience amounted only to the odd grope and kiss at a barbecue or party after a swimming carnival. The few parties she'd attended were mostly with Gabby's Conservatorium High School friends. They were simple, alcohol-free affairs, organised along traditional Australian lines – the boys, mostly young musicians or brothers of the girls, separating themselves from the opposite sex and returning only to dance.

Both girls had passed their HSC the previous year. Gabby had gone on to the Conservatorium to study violin and become a full-on flowerchild, and in her spare time she continued to emerge as a rather winsome guitar-playing folk singer, thanks to several appearances on *Bandstand*.

Sam, on the other hand, had taken a year off before university in order to concentrate on her swimming and the coming October Olympics. She'd taken a part-time job at Brokendown as a sales assistant and regular model, but, as had always been the case, she was usually in bed by eight o'clock and up at four-thirty each morning for training, which left very little time in her life for romantic dalliance.

But now love came striding into Sam's life and into the Village Medical Centre ward, wearing a pair of striped pyjamas, in the form of a six-foot-two, blond, crew-cut, hazel-eyed American pentathlon athlete with a confident grin by the name of Gregory Beauregard Montgomery from the state of Louisiana. He'd collapsed in the 3000-metres under similar circumstances to Sam's.

'Hi there. Call me Greg, or Monty – take your pick,' he said, extending a bearlike paw. Before Sam could answer, he continued, still holding her hand, 'I know this is perhaps a little presumptuous, but we have no mutual friend to introduce us, so I am obliged to act in an unmannerly fashion, or I might never have the privilege and opportunity of meeting the prettiest mademoiselle I declare I have evah seen,' the American athlete said, smiling boyishly.

'Hello,' Sam replied, releasing her hand. 'That sounds to me like a well-rehearsed introduction, Monty.'

'Hell no, ma'am, cross mah heart, I don't meet too many pretty girls like you when I'm in mah pyjamas.'

'If I'm not mistaken, that's right out of Mickey Spillane's novel *Kiss Me Deadly*.' Sam giggled. 'You're a phony, Monty!'

Monty grinned. 'Now ain't that mah bad luck? She ain't jes purty, she's got brains. That makes her more deadly than a rattlesnake with a broken rattle.'

'Zane Grey, *Riders of the Purple Sage*,' Sam replied. 'You're a double phony, Monty. I think I'll call you "D.P.".'

'Call me anything you like but please tell me your name, mademoiselle,' the American boy pleaded, persisting with the French title commonly used in Louisiana.

'Hmm, let me see, sounds familiar,' Sam teased, pretending to be thinking. 'No, could be genuine,' she finally concluded. Smiling her most brilliant smile, she stretched out her hand. 'Gidday, D.P. My name is Sam, from Oz.' She deliberately used the Australian greeting common at the Games.

D.P. left Sam's bedside two hours later. He expected to stay one more night in the Medical Centre but couldn't be sure. 'They may let me out today. If they do, hey, I'll see you at the closing ceremony, okay?' He'd left only moments before Danny and Gabby arrived, by which time Sam was already well on the way to falling in love.

Whoever had designed the Village Medical Centre had not considered the consequences of having two wards in close proximity, each accommodating six testosterone-charged, extremely fit, young male and female athletes. Either that or they had mistakenly assumed that the reason the athletes found themselves in the Medical Centre would be sufficient to render them sexually sedated.

The Medical Centre wasn't designed for serious ailments. While there hadn't been any large outbreaks of Montezuma's Revenge or any other bug, there had inevitably been several serious injuries and some illness, but those affected had been transferred to a city hospital ward. Apart from the daily patch-ups of sprains, muscle tears, breaks and falls, with analgesics, salves and bandages, Sam and Greg were the sole two nocturnal inhabitants, separated by a single wall and not more than half a dozen paces between the entrance to either ward. It was a romantic accident waiting to happen.

Well after midnight, with the night orderly snoring in his tiny room at the end of the corridor, Sam and D.P. made love – Sam, for the first time, but the thousandth or more in her imagination. The boy from Louisiana was sufficiently unselfish to make it a lovely and loving experience.

To Danny's total mystification, Gabby had been right, and he met Gregory Beauregard Montgomery the Third at the Olympic stadium two days later. Sam had marched, or rather joined the American team in the casual parade that marked the closing ceremony, and Gabby, wearing one of Sam's two identical tracksuits, had slipped in with the Australians to enjoy the occasion. Both were having an absolute ball, and not a single person noticed that one swimmer had become two. Don Talbot came up to Gabby and pressed her shoulder. 'That was a great race, kid. I won't forget your courage in a hurry,' he shouted amidst the musical din of cheering athletes and applauding crowd.

'Thank you, Mr Talbot,' Gabby shouted, straight-faced.

'I think it's time you called me Don,' Talbot suggested, adding, 'Will you try for the next Olympics, Sam?'

'I think I'd like to learn to play the violin,' Gabby replied, but Talbot seemed not to register what she'd said.

'You'd only be twenty-one, and you've got the guts and the talent to succeed,' Talbot shouted, moving on.

'What, with the violin?' Gabby shouted back, grinning.

Talbot laughed. 'No, Samantha, but maybe the 400-metres?' he called back as he joined another bunch of Australian athletes in the happy crowd.

While D.P. didn't come from New Orleans, he'd graduated from Louisiana State University. He came from an old family and while he could well have qualified for track-and-field scholarships, it hadn't been necessary. He often stayed with an aunt in New Orleans, in a nice house not far from Billy and Dallas, who now lived in the beautiful old home in the French Quarter that Billy's parents and grandparents had occupied. Danny had instantly liked the young man and so had Gabby, so they had no qualms about him spending time with Sam. D.P. and Sam often took Gabby with them when they explored New Orleans.

Danny had previously called Helen and told her about Sam's disastrous Olympics, emphasising her courage, and then telling Helen about D.P., which was how they all referred to Sam's new boyfriend. 'Put Gabby on, darling. I must talk to her,' she'd said.

'Mum, Sam was incredibly brave!' Gabby shouted down the phone.

'Gabby, listen, make sure she's taking the pill,' Helen said urgently.

'Mum! You know Sam. She's not going to suddenly stop taking it.' Gabby laughed.

'Do you think it's been necessary?' Helen asked.

'Not sure, but I wouldn't be surprised,' Gabby replied.

'Oh my goodness!' Helen cried. 'You've both grown up so fast. Put Dad on again, darling.'

Sitting in a cocktail bar in New Orleans, Sam tasted her first martini, while D.P. told her he'd completed officer training just before going to the Olympics and would soon be heading for Vietnam.

'Vietnam!' Sam said, suddenly horror-struck.

'Honey, there ain't no other war Uncle Sam's losing,' D.P. replied, lifting his beer to his mouth and leaving a white foam moustache behind.

Sam grabbed a paper napkin and dabbed tenderly at his top lip. 'D.P., you can't go!' she cried. 'Why don't you become a draft dodger? You could go to Canada!'

'Mademoiselle Sam, mah family on mah mama's side has been in every war since the American Revolution. If I did that, mah family would see it as a betrayal of everything they stand for. Mah papa's family feel the same, even though they originally hail from France. We bin saluting the star-spangled banner for a hundred years.'

'But you might get killed,' Sam protested.

D.P. laughed. 'Now don't you worry none, Mademoiselle Sam. No gook is gonna get the ass of Second Lootenant Gregory Beauregard Montgomery the Third. Things are winding down, anyway. Even President Johnson's had enough. I'll do mah twelve months cowering behind a tank. It's speculated there won't be any more big battles.'

The twins left New Orleans with Sam in tears and promising to write to D.P. every week he was in Vietnam. Dallas had presented the twins with brand new Stetsons, which they'd graciously accepted, both thinking they'd never wear them. After the ugly sprawl, poverty and chaos of Mexico City and the hustle and thump of New Orleans, Sydney seemed like a calm, even backward, oasis. Sam enrolled at Sydney University to study law and Gabby entered her second year at the Con. That year, 1969, three years after the introduction of decimal currency, Helen told Danny that HBH had made a million dollars' profit, which they would use to buy two small hotels in the CBD.

Danny and Franz were also prospering, and Danny was flooded

with work from the Liberal government. It was slowly becoming apparent to him that the Askin government was developing all the bad habits of the former Labor government, and that he'd have to choose carefully and take on only those cases he felt good about. Danny's pro bono work continued. Despite the changes in Balmain and elsewhere, and the new prosperity, it seemed that Australia was still turning out approximately the same number of bastards, drunks, deadshits and wife beaters.

Once she was back home, Sam had conscientiously written to D.P. in New Orleans, and then, five months later, when he'd left for Vietnam, she wrote every week for the next three months. But, apart from a letter he'd sent several days after his arrival, she hadn't received a reply and became disappointed, then concerned and finally resentful. Danny had contacted the United States embassy and they'd eventually told him that D.P. was still in Vietnam, but they couldn't reveal his unit or his whereabouts.

Love cannot sustain itself on such a meagre diet of hopes and wishes and nothing in the mail. Eventually Sam had given up, although she still followed the fortunes of the American and Australian troops in Vietnam each night on the news. A report of a young Adelaide woman, a member of a Latvian migrant family, who'd murdered her father made Sam shriek for Gabby. Katerina was two years behind her deadline. Sam begged Danny to defend her, but he pointed out that his licence didn't allow him to practise in South Australia. Nevertheless, she persisted and he eventually organised and paid for a top Adelaide barrister to defend Katerina, with the result that the murder charge was downgraded to manslaughter. She'd finally received a five-year prison sentence, with the possibility of parole for good behaviour in three years.

That just about wrapped up the year, except that one early summer evening the phone rang and Gabby answered it. 'Hiya there, Gabby. This is D.P. here. Is Mademoiselle Sam home, please?' he asked politely, as if nothing had happened.

'D.P.! Where are you? Are you calling from Vietnam?' Gabby shrieked into the phone.

'No, honey, it's a place called Kings Cross. I'm on R&R.'

Sam had been pretty cross with him over the phone when he'd called. 'You bastard, D.P., you might have replied to my letters.'

D.P. pleaded with her, trying to explain. 'Sam, the news was never good. All I'd have had to say they'd have censored, except that I love you.' His soft, irresistible, deep southern drawl had done the rest and Sam had agreed to see him.

They'd started with a drink in the Macleay Street cocktail bar at the Chevron-Hilton, where D.P. was staying; Sam had a Bloody Mary and D.P. ordered a neat Kentucky bourbon.

'Not drinking beer any more?' Sam asked.

'Yeah, sometimes, in Nam, when it's hot.' He'd grinned. 'It's always hot, even when it's raining, and that seems to be most times. Even in hell it would be considered the number one shithole!'

'Is it really that bad?' Sam said, knowing that it was, but needing the small talk to become reacquainted, to feel comfortable in his presence after a year of not seeing him.

'It's worse than you can imagine. Most of the guys don't want to be there.'

'You mean some do?' Sam asked, surprised.

'The lifers, the regular army, they see it as the only war they've got. The rest of us, we jes want to get the hell outta there. And now this My Lai massacre has come out, we're not even sure we want to go Stateside. Folk back home are callin' us baby killers and spitting on us when we appear in uniform.'

'I wasn't going to bring that up. We were pretty shocked ourselves,' Sam said. 'It was sickening . . .'

D.P. was silent for a time, then abruptly changed the subject. 'All the guys reckon Sydney is the best place to go for R&R. No gooks, and most folk make you feel welcome. Ain't no one's spat on me yet.'

Sam smiled. 'Don't be too confident. You'd better not meet me at university.'

Sam and D.P. left the bar and found a disco not far from the Chevron, where they continued drinking and dancing until the early hours. Both of them were drunk – Sam, not for the first time, although never quite like this. She'd got pissed with uni friends on a Saturday night on three or four occasions, but had always left while she could still order a taxi without slurring her words. Now, standing in the hotel foyer, she told herself that if her mind was clear enough to be concerned that the bloke in the fancy uniform standing at the lift wouldn't allow her to go to D.P.'s room, then she was still in control. No more drinking, and a bit of a snuggle and a lie down, and she'd be right as rain. She was conscious that she'd broken Danny's curfew of one o'clock but, too pissed to care, promised herself she'd be home well before dawn.

D.P., grinning and swaying slightly, said, 'Guy at the counter asked me, "How come you blokes get all the good sorts?" Whadda fuck that mean?' he slurred. Sam realised that she had never heard him use the 'f' word before.

'I'll tell you when you're sober,' she grinned, following D.P. into the lift.

Upstairs in his room, he asked, 'You wanna . . . take a shower, Mademoi . . . selle Sam? Shit, I'm drunk.'

Sam, tired and sweaty, and her clothes smelling of stale cigarette smoke from the disco, agreed that a shower would be nice. 'I need to sober up. A shower might help,' she said. In fact, she was in much better shape than D.P., who had been drinking straight bourbon all night, while she'd skipped several rounds. She wasn't a regular drinker and now felt somewhat woozy, nicely relaxed, uninhibited and ready for a bit of reckless fun – the state of mind every male hopes to bring about in his partner when on a serious date.

Sam removed her clothes, leaving them lying on the bedroom

carpet, and when she was down to her panties she allowed them to drop to her ankles, stepped out of the left leg and kicked them at D.P., who caught the pretty black lacy nothing, laughing and bringing it to his lips. 'C'mon, soldier boy, get your exciting parts out of Uncle Sam's fancy dress – Raymond Chandler, *Farewell My Lovely*,' Sam giggled, now completely nude.

'Jesus, Sam, you're beautiful!' D.P. exclaimed, starting to undo his shirt buttons.

Sam knew she was gorgeous. She was still fit and swam a mile every day – or 1.6 kilometres, as they'd soon be calling it once the change to metric measurements was complete – and she worked out in the university gym.

They showered together, soaping each other, laughing and kissing and spurting water at one another. Then Sam, her skin flushed from the hot water, towelled D.P. down and, giggling, dried his erection. Kneeling, she took him gently in her mouth, something she'd never done before but had read about in Anaïs Nin's *The Four-Chambered Heart*, which had excited her enormously and led to countless nocturnal rubbings. 'Oh, Jesus, fuck! Wait on, honey!' D.P. moaned.

Sam grabbed an extra towel and followed him back to the bedroom, towelling her own body and head, then wrapping the fresh towel turban-style around her damp hair. She'd read about brewer's droop but happily D.P. seemed not to suffer from the condition; maybe bourbon was different and had the reverse effect. She felt much better – quite sober, really, although she knew she wasn't. She'd never before showered with a boy or taken his thingy (a childhood twinny word) in her mouth, but she had enjoyed both, and Sam knew she wanted more. Her imagined trysts were never in the back of a Holden or in somebody's spare bedroom at a party, like the couplings of some of her university friends. In fact, the three times she'd made love to D.P. hadn't exactly been romantic either – first the narrow Village Medical Centre cot, and twice, half-dressed in case his aunt returned from shopping, on the chaise longue in New Orleans. But she'd been in love, so it didn't matter. Now the double bed with crisp white sheets in Sydney's newest hotel seemed by contrast to be very posh and romantic. Besides, she was drunk and happy and horny as hell.

D.P. sat on the bed holding a bent teaspoon above the bedside table, heating it with a cheap plastic cigarette lighter.

'What are you doing?' Sam asked, a bit taken aback.

'Cooking up a little horse.' D.P. grinned.

'Horse . . . you mean heroin?' Sam asked, her knowledge of the drug only from books and movies.

'Uh huh,' D.P. said casually.

'Oh, God!' Sam cried in alarm.

'Now, Mademoiselle Sam, don't get excited, honey. I just use a little to take the edge off.'

'The edge?'

'Nam – it's how we cope.'

'But . . . but it's dangerous, D.P.!'

'Naw,' D.P. replied. 'Not if you jes taste, honey. A little taste, that's all.' He reached for the syringe on the small bedside table and used it to draw up the liquid in the teaspoon. 'You'll love it, the rush. We'll make love, and you'll fly! It's a high you'll never forget. You'll come like a choir of angels.'

Sam looked doubtful and D.P. laughed. 'I most sincerely promise, Mademoiselle Sam. And, honey, you can't get hooked on a little taste.'

'You sure?' Sam asked, still seeking reassurance.

D.P. gave her his boyish grin, the same look he'd worn when he'd walked into the Village Medical Centre ward in his pyjamas. Now he sat on the edge of the bed naked, the athlete's muscular body still clean and sharp, and Sam knew she wanted him badly. 'Honest Injun, trust me,' he said in his deep southern drawl.

'Okay, just once then,' Sam said, her heart beating furiously.

They made love and D.P. was right – the feeling transcended Sam's wildest nocturnal fantasies. The rush had started in her head and moved down throughout her entire body. It stayed with her while they made passionate love. When Sam finally reached orgasm, it was more marvellous than anything she'd experienced in the entire eighteen years of her life. It was also the first big thing, she knew, that she could never share with her twin. Sam now felt completely euphoric and sober.

Afterwards, propped up in bed against the big white pillows, she lay in D.P.'s arms with her head on his chest. 'How long have you been . . . ah, tasting?' Sam asked.

'That's easy,' D.P. replied. 'Ever since the Battle of Hamburger Hill.'

Sam grinned. 'The Americans do that so well!'

'Do what? Battles?'

'No, name them: The Battle of Wounded Knee, General Custer's Last Stand – and now the Battle at Hamburger Hill.'

'*Of* Hamburger Hill,' D.P. corrected.

'Will you tell me about it, or would you rather not?' Sam asked.

'Sure. Now we've had a little horse, I guess I can,' D.P. said.

'No, then don't,' Sam said gently. 'I don't want to bring back bad memories.'

'No, Mademoiselle Sam, I'd like to . . . yer know, get it off my chest. I haven't talked about it before.'

Sam noted that D.P. seemed almost sober and wasn't slurring his words.

'When did it happen? Recently?'

'No. I'd only just arrived in Vietnam – a greenhorn through and through. It was my first experience of the enemy – tenth to twentieth of May this year. You're supposed to be excited about your first battle, about leading a platoon – the usual bullshit, no guts no glory – but instead I was pooping my fatigues. The gooks were dug in on an outcrop 937 metres high; we called it Hill 937 before it got its other name.'

'Why Hamburger, though?' Sam asked.

'That comes later, honey. We got our ass whupped bad. Steep slopes covered in bamboo thickets and dense jungle, everything you don't want to find yourself fighting in. The hill, on the Laotian border, rose out of the A Shau Valley, and our job was to clear the valley. The motherfuckers – er, excuse my language, the NVA – were sitting upstairs picking us off, easy as you like. The valley was booby-trapped with landmines, bamboo pits, pillboxes that cost us dear to take out, seemingly manned by gooks positively happy to die. We were green, me and mah platoon; we were unfamiliar with the ways and means and the jungle. I had some experienced men, but mostly grunts – southern boys like me, jes outa high school. They were drafted, then after basic training, sent straight to Nam. Their mamas were still washing their socks, ironing their shirts, kissing them goodnight before bed . . . We didn't know our ass from our elbow, and with the other infantry we were tasked with destroying, that is, storming uphill through dense jungle and destroying three NVA battalions dug in real good. The enemy were good, seasoned fighters and they held the high ground. They also had a valley full of nasty surprises waiting for us below. Mademoiselle Sam, I was truly outta mah depth, I admit it, shaking like a leaf, expecting to die any moment. I was no brave officer, that's for sure. Mah sergeant, James P. Corn – they called him Jimmy Popcorn – a Negro from New Orleans, he took me aside and said, "Lootenant, yoh ain't gonna make it lessen I fix yoh some," and there in the valley, beside a stand of high bamboo creaking and groaning, he cooked me up some horse and injected me a taste. "Not too much," he said. "Jes a taste, mah good man, den you gonna fly up dat fuckin' hill, man!"'

'And it got you through the battle?' Sam asked.

'Honey, in Nam there ain't no *through*; there ain't no victory. We called it Hamburger Hill because they, the NVA, made mincemeat outta us – prime hamburger mince. Sure, we took the hill – seventy-two US dead and 372 wounded, over 600 NVA dead – that's way beyond acceptable, considering they had rifles, a few rockets and machine guns, and we'd thrown the whole of World War Two at them and then some.'

'NVA? You keep using the term.'

'North Vietnamese Army; they're gooks, but they're regular soldiers. Not civilians by day and Vietcong at night – men in uniform,' D.P.

explained. 'Yeah, we kinda won the Battle of Hamburger Hill, but I had three men left in my platoon, twelve dead, fifteen wounded.'

'Jimmy Popcorn?'

'Dead. When we got back, the colonel called me in to HQ. "Lootenant Montgomery, why are you not dead, son?" he asked. "You're a fuckin' disgrace – the worst platoon fatalities on Hill 937. Next time you come back dead and bring me more live men, and that's an order, you son of a bitch!" He picked up mah papers. "I see you were at the Olympics," he said.

'"Yessir!" I replied.

'"Pentathlon?"

'"Yessir," I said again.

'"Collapsed in the 3000-metres?"

'"Stomach cramps . . . severe diarrhoea, sir!"

'"Fucking coward, you mean. No guts. You let down America, son! You're doing it again! A fucking disgrace! A second lootenant is *supposed* to die! You are expendable, *not* your sergeant! Get the hell outta my sight, son!"'

'D.P., how awful! You poor, poor darling,' Sam said, kissing him.

'That ain't all, Mademoiselle Sam. Two weeks later we just up and abandoned Hamburger Hill. Gave it and the A Shau Valley right back to the gooks. "There you go, we've decided we don't want it after all; we've eaten all the hamburger we need."'

'But why?' Sam cried.

D.P. shrugged. 'Don't ask me, honey. There was no official explanation. We were just left to wonder why all our buddies had to die.' He turned and looked directly at Sam. 'There, that's another damn good reason for tasting horse.'

Sam got home just as dawn was breaking over the harbour. She'd been drunk, sobered up, tasted once again and then tasted D.P. again. Then, she'd been secretly shocked out of her socks when he'd said, after the second teaspoon boil-up, 'Mademoiselle Sam, I wanna lick you real bad.' But she was high as a kite and this wasn't a night to be prudish.

Besides, her inhibitions had long since deserted her. Later, she'd been delighted by the orgasm that followed, and more so when D.P. said, 'Ah, I've dreamed about having you, going down on you, babe. I jes knew you'd taste real good, the finest pussy, honey.'

Sam didn't know why, but D.P. saying that put her in mind of Gabby's hit song, 'Wild Bush Honey', now number five on the hit parade. She had added two more 'actuals' to what had hitherto been purely bedtime fantasies, but she couldn't remember being quite so bone weary since collapsing after the Olympic 100-metres final. Following the second heroin rush she seemed to be floating, a balloon slowly coming down to earth, not sure if she was going to hit something sharp and pop when she landed, but by the time she arrived home she was experiencing a raw, edgy, unfamiliar feeling she didn't like.

Danny was waiting for her. Sam knew that look on his face. He'd never beaten her, but she knew the fury about to explode within him would be far worse. Sam was spent, her usual inner resources gone. The years of learning to deal with his anger, cop it sweet, allow it to do the minimum damage, had dwindled to nothing. She waited, trembling, feeling close to collapse, as though she wanted him to beat her so she could crawl into a corner and die. 'Get your swimmers on and meet me at the skiff in five minutes,' Danny snapped. 'Go!'

Sam took the centre oars. She was cold in the spring dawn but soon warmed up as they rowed for an hour and a half until they reached South Head, at the entrance to Sydney Harbour. Apart from a few grunts, Danny hadn't spoken a word. Now he simply pointed to the water. 'Jump in. Swim home,' he commanded. It was 6.30 a.m.

Sam almost gave up on several occasions, too exhausted to continue. 'Swim, you little whore!' Danny demanded each time. At one stage when she tried to regain the side of the boat, he pushed her away with the end of an oar. Somehow Sam managed to get home. She tried to stand on the shelving pebbled beach next to the boathouse, but collapsed face down in the shallow water. Danny jumped from the skiff and grabbed her arm, pulling her roughly onto the beach, and left her there. Gabby came running from the house towards her unconscious twin, yelling. Danny stopped dragging the skiff up the ramp and pointed back at the house. 'Git!' he barked, with a flick of his head. 'Leave the trollop alone!'

Moments later, as Gabby hesitated, her hands to her face in shock and confusion, Helen raced across the front lawn, her face contorted with rage. She fell to her knees on the beach beside Sam. 'You bastard!' she screamed at Danny. 'You sick fucking bastard!' she howled, pulling Sam's head onto her lap.

Sam wasn't allowed to see D.P. again. She'd written him a letter explaining that she wasn't permitted to leave home, not even to attend university. Gabby had delivered it to the Chevron-Hilton. Sam was committed into Brenda's care, accompanying her as she visited clubs and checked the Willy duB pokies, Danny insisting that she was not to be left alone for a moment. During the course of the week, Brenda quietly asked Sam when her boyfriend was returning to Vietnam. Then, on the last day of his R&R, she indicated the telephone. 'I'll be in the garden for half an hour, darling,' she said.

Sam managed to get through to D.P. just before he was due to take the MACV (Military Assistance Command Vietnam) flight back to his base in Vietnam, what he called 'in country', because he was not permitted to reveal the landing field. They talked until the last minute. His final words to her were, 'Mademoiselle Sam, I love you. I'm coming to fetch you when I get back home, you hear, honey? Only two months to go, then my tour of Nam is over. Will you wait for me, lovely Sam?'

Sobbing, Sam agreed.

Six weeks later, when her last two letters had received no reply, she received a notification from the American Embassy in Canberra saying that Second Lieutenant Gregory Beauregard Montgomery of the Third Louisiana Light Infantry Unit had been killed in action in Vietnam. He had died in an enemy ambush of small-arms fire while on patrol in Thua Thien Province. He had left a request that she was to be notified in the event of his death.

Gabby, while still a serious student of the violin, was also still a rising folk star. Her hit song, known as 'Wild Bush Honey' rather than by its full title, had risen to the top of the local charts, and her pretty face, topped by a battered Stetson with a yellow rose in the hatband, was familiar to a generation, even though folk had a smaller following than rock. Johnny O'Keefe towered above the rest of the rock singers, and Little Pattie, beloved of the Australian forces in Vietnam, was a much bigger star, but Gabby had a growing following that she made no effort to cultivate. She thought of herself as a serious musician and a reluctant folk star, and refused the approaches of the big agents, leaving the contracts and recording deals to Half Dunn and Helen. It wasn't such a silly idea either – Half Dunn had long ago proved that he was an excellent negotiator, perhaps from all those years spent sitting at the main bar of the Hero, and since Brenda's retirement and during Helen's reign, he had really come into his own. Together they were a formidable combination: the old man who could talk up a deal better than almost anyone, and Helen, his brilliant, formidable and analytical partner, who could close a deal to their advantage faster than you could say 'Snap!', and spot a shonky one at a hundred yards.

Sam, on the other hand, had hit the wall. She'd scraped through her first year at Sydney University, but the old ebullient Sam was gone. Danny put it down to the inevitable disappointment of the Olympics, because, although she had a drawer full of medals from state and national titles, no Olympic gold snuggled among the gold-plated local ones.

Sam's personality allowed no compromise. From infancy she'd seen herself as a winner; Danny had told her she was a winner, and she'd suffered his demonic temper, obsessive personality and dictatorial manner because she believed him. He was her sun and her moon; he couldn't possibly be wrong and she must never let him down. If he screamed at her, his tongue cutting into her like a barber's razor, then it was her fault. It meant she wasn't trying hard enough. Sam had never swum for herself. Her mantra, *Three gold for Sammy*, was just another way of saying, 'Three gold for Danny'. Hester Landsman had once said to Helen in Sam's hearing, 'Darling, there is for us Jews a saying: *"Pray that you may never have to endure all that you can learn to bear"*.' Sam had learned to endure what she had to bear, and now that she had nothing to show for the years of sacrifice, she was beginning to unravel. She had few friends save those she had made through swimming – casual relationships based on their mutual interests. Where Gabby had amassed friends at the Con, Sam had no such emotional reservoir. Her school life at Balmain High had been about lessons; she'd never had the time for parties and the like.

She began to realise that her notoriety as a young swimmer, one Balmain folk saw as possibly their next Dawn Fraser, had replaced the need for friends to help her define herself and create her own identity. She was public property, the next Balmain Girl, national heroine, stepping into the large shoes once occupied by her father and left empty since the war. When she'd disappointed them, they wanted nothing further to do with her, and the older people muttered about her being the second Dunn to let them down. Even her modelling for Brokendown created less of an impression on fashion-conscious kids, who now simply remarked on the astonishing resemblance to her twin. When she appeared wearing her Stetson, people would ask, 'Hey, what happened to the yellow rose?'

Then, after silently trying to become reconciled to her new life as a law student and a nobody, D.P. had arrived back in her life – only for one night, but one that had changed everything. He had shown her how to lose herself, how to bear the pain. Then, as if that particular night was meant to be her metamorphosis, came that killing swim Danny had forced on her.

Helen had put her to bed and called the doctor, who'd given her a sedative. Danny had gone to work and when he returned that evening, Helen met him at the door, grim-faced. He'd attempted to kiss her, but she'd pulled away. 'Not this time. No way, Danny. We need to talk.' She'd turned and walked upstairs onto the verandah where she pointed to a wicker chair. 'Sit down, please,' she commanded coldly.

'Okay, so I was angry,' Danny said, sitting. 'The little whore was out all night.'

'The little whore! The little whore! Are you talking about my daughter?' Helen shouted.

'What else do you think they were doing? They were fucking!' Danny said, feeling his temper rising.

'And you know that?'

'What else? She spent the night in D.P.'s hotel room.'

'You hypocrite!' Even as she spoke, Helen knew there was no purpose in continuing. Besides, it wasn't why she wanted to confront him. 'What you did this morning was unforgiveable, it was pure insanity. You could have killed her!'

'She had to be taught a lesson. Her curfew was 1 a.m.! She disobeyed me. I simply won't have it!'

'Listen to me carefully, Danny. Since they were seven years old you've treated the twins as if they are your personal property.'

'Well, they are. Yours and mine.'

Helen shook her head vehemently. 'They are our *children*, *not* our slaves. Can't you see they're terrified of you? I managed to rescue Gabrielle, but you've destroyed Samantha. When she didn't achieve what *you* wanted, her life, as she saw it, was effectively over. She's been trying to pick up the pieces this year, trying to make some sense out of her life – out of the destruction your obsession has brought down on her head.'

'She's been okay, until D.P. called her – until last night,' Danny said.

'And you haven't noticed?'

'Noticed what?'

'That she is suffering from a loss of identity. You, of all people!'

'And what's that supposed to mean?'

'Danny Dunn – the beautiful young man, sporting hero, worshipped by the locals, certain to play rugby league for his country – goes off to war, returns broken, his former career expectations shattered, his mind not the same, filled with demons. It may not seem quite as dramatic, but a lot of that stuff is happening to Samantha. And last night, you, my friend, were Colonel Mori.'

'Jesus, that's not fair, Helen!' Danny shouted.

'Not fair! What you did last night can *never* be forgiven. I, for one, won't ever forgive you. You are damaged, but I always knew that, accepted that. God knows, it's not been easy standing by watching the demons within you destroying my child. When she didn't win gold at the Olympics, you know what? I was secretly glad. I thought that at last she'd be free of your influence. That she was still young enough to recover. I've watched her trying to cope, trying to heal. But last night was the end for me. It was sheer bastardry! You wanted your little slave back! It was – it is – sick! I want you to see Craig Woon. You've got to get help. If you don't you'll lose us all. We don't need you when you're like this!' Helen leaned forward until her face was inches from Danny's. 'Do you understand, Danny? Do you understand what I am saying? *We don't need you!*'

Danny rose from his chair and went downstairs, still in his business suit and Glossy Denmeade boots. He brought the skiff out of the boatshed and, jumping in, started to row into the darkened harbour.

In the early hours of the morning, Helen heard him coming up the stairs – she'd been awake all night – and switched on the bedside light. Danny entered the bedroom looking thoroughly dishevelled: he'd lost his eye patch, discarded his jacket and tie, and had a cut along the side of his face and a patch of blood on his white shirt.

'You up?' he said, stating the obvious. Helen remained silent. 'I'll see Craig Woon,' he growled.

Helen pulled the bedclothes away and rose. 'I'll make you a cup of tea,' she said.

Sam had grown silent. She hadn't said a word to Danny since the night with D.P. and the skiff. Danny had tried to apologise but to no avail. As far as she was concerned, he no longer existed. The willpower and the obsession he'd inculcated in his daughter she now exercised on him, proving her will was stronger than his. Helen, Brenda, Half Dunn – nobody could get through to her. Gabby, in an attempt to draw her out of herself, introduced Sam to some of her music friends. It was a mistake. Sam knew she must stay away from heroin, but that didn't include all the other painkillers available in the music scene. She began to hang around musicians, playing identical twin, merging her personality with Gabby's, first, the folk-rock musicians Gabby favoured, then, increasingly, the hard-rock musicians. Inevitably she discovered marijuana, and much more besides.

But sitting around listening to rock music – Col Joye and the Joy Boys, The Bee Gees, Normie Rowe, or the overseas heavy hitters Pink Floyd, The Doors, The Stones, The Beatles, Creedence Clearwater Revival, and the one and only Elvis – stoned and giggling, wasn't enough for Sam. She started to skip university, staying out late, then remaining in bed most of the day, and nothing anyone could say made any difference. She got kicked out of uni and took to hanging out at the Coogee Hotel at night with rock musicians euphemistically 'resting' but with no real work. She started to drink, mostly Scotch, but sometimes, pathetically, Kentucky bourbon. She'd come home drunk, sleep all day nursing a hangover, and go out again all night.

Helen tried to reason with her and Sam would appear to listen, but in the end she'd simply say to her mother, 'It's my life, Mum. If you don't like it, I'll move out.' She simply told Gabby to mind her own business. Helen persuaded her to see Craig Woon. She went once, then refused to return. Something inside Sam's head or heart had broken.

Helen had called Dr Woon. 'Craig, we're desperate. What can we do?'

'When I saw her, I felt she was suffering from depression, but I can't be sure. Helen, I need to see her several times more. If she'll agree to go into a clinic, perhaps we can find out. She's certainly suffering from a nervous breakdown – that's the old-fashioned word. It covers a multitude of sins and tells us nothing. The drugs aren't helping, either, and putting her on anti-depressants won't be sufficient, I fear.'

'She won't talk to Danny. It all started with the episode I'm sure he's told you about.'

'Sure, but it's too easy to say that. One unfortunate episode – a miscalculation on his part, harsh as it was – isn't going to cause her to change her entire character.'

'Then what?' Helen asked. 'We're at our wits' end. I feel we're going to lose her.'

'Helen, these things start way back. Something like the harbour swim can be the final straw, but that's all it was.'

'You mean it's something genetic?'

'Impossible to say, although there's some interesting stuff coming out about genetic predispositions. From observing Samantha's swimming career, I believe she is a "Type A" personality with highly addictive characteristics. They're the successful types, the high achievers, the high fliers, but when they crash, they do so as determinedly and in as spectacular a manner as when they succeed. They're the all-or-nothing types.'

'But isn't she too young for that sort of thing?' Helen asked. 'For goodness sake, she's about to turn eighteen. She hasn't had a life yet. She hasn't been such a high flier . . .'

'Oh, but that's where you're wrong, Helen. To achieve what she has achieved so far, Samantha has been under more pressure than most adults will have to endure in a lifetime, and after all that, she came crashing down – at least, that's probably how she would see it. She's hit the wall at full speed.'

'You mean not winning, not swimming all her races at the Olympics?'

'Yes, of course.'

'Craig, I know you have to maintain the confidentiality of your dealings with your patients, but you've been seeing Danny for quite a while now. Please, you've known him almost as long as I have. Is he the cause of Samantha's problems?'

'Helen, you're putting me in an awkward spot. Danny's my patient, so ethically —'

But Helen had had enough. 'He's also my husband! For God's sake, Craig, give me something to work with. My family is being destroyed and I don't know what to do. How do I get my daughter back? Is what's happened to her my husband's fault?'

'The answer is probably yes. But, having said that, not entirely.'

'Oh?'

'He wasn't able to have the same influence over Gabrielle, which tells me something.'

'What?'

'That at one level Samantha wanted it to happen; she needed to succeed, and she made up her mind to be a clone of her father.'

'What can we do about it?'

'This may seem a strange thing to say, but right now, without her father to depend on and without the structure of training, Samantha is suffering from low self-esteem. She doesn't know what to do, where to turn for directions.'

'Direction or directions?' Helen, ever analytical, asked.

'Both. Tell me about this boy from Vietnam,' Craig said.

'There's not much I can say. They spent the night together, then her father punished her, and shortly after that she got the news that he'd been killed.'

'Did she bond with him?'

'I shouldn't think so, not in one night. Surely that's not possible,' Helen said.

'That's not necessarily true. She knew him before; they were together in New Orleans. Did she tell you if they'd slept together?'

'No.'

'Did you ask her?'

'No, I simply made sure she was using the pill.'

'And this time, the night she spent with him here in Sydney?'

'She'd been through that trauma with her father. I wasn't going to exacerbate the situation by asking her.'

'Did Gabrielle ask?'

'No, but Gabrielle says she knows Sam slept with him.'

'How?'

'I don't know, Craig, it's a twin thing. They just seem to know.'

'There's every chance that Sam has associated her punishment for spending the night with her soldier boyfriend with her father demanding her back.'

'What, as his slave?'

'That's a tough word, but old lion, young lion. Danny was emotionally almost totally involved with his daughter.'

'What? In an indecent way?'

'No, of course not! But in a dependent way. Samantha is – was – what kept his demons at bay, kept him on a steady course. Perhaps he saw her as another version of his young self. Then, by choosing her boyfriend, she had, in his subconscious mind, chosen another guiding hand.'

'I see. But is it a two-way street? Would she blame her father for the boy's death?'

'Helen, we have to stop there. I'm venturing an opinion, and not necessarily an informed one. It's possible, but that's all I'm prepared to say. In confidence, Danny admits he's taken the Olympics thing badly, despite struggling against it.'

'Well, I have to tell you he's back on Mogadon, or sleeping tablets of some sort. He's been off them for years now.'

'Yes, I know. He asked me for a prescription. There are better things than Mogadon these days.'

'Is there something, anything, we can do for Sam?'

'Just love her, make her feel safe. We can give her something to help her if she'll submit herself for treatment.'

'Will she grow out of it?'

'Perhaps. She's young, fit, intelligent and attractive, and has a loving home and a future – all the components needed; it's certainly not impossible.'

At the Coogee Hotel, though, Sam discovered barbiturates, speed, and LSD, known as tabs. Barbiturates were easy to get – the doctors around Kings Cross and Darlinghurst would write a prescription if you simply looked forlorn, and pleaded that you were coming off heroin and looking for a soft landing.

Then one day Sam simply didn't come home. A day turned into a week. Gabby searched everywhere for her, but nobody had seen her at the Coogee Hotel or any of the other popular after-midnight watering holes frequented by rock musicians.

Danny put Bumper Barnett onto finding her. He had hundreds of copies of her photograph circulated; there wasn't a criminal or a prostitute or a shopkeeper in the Kings Cross area who wouldn't have recognised her. Bob Askin put the New South Wales Police onto it and cautioned them to keep it out of the media.

Another week passed. Several people called in to say they'd seen her, but it had been Gabby they'd seen. Gabby hadn't gone to the Con for two weeks and spent every day combing the Cross and Darlinghurst, and the nights with Danny, visiting every musician's haunt and likely bar in Sydney.

Sam wasn't in Sydney. She'd met a drummer at the Black Cat in the Cross. He belonged to a hard-rock band called Wild Dogs & Gentlemen, who were about to embark on a tour of several states.

The night they met, Sam had been sitting alone, miserable and silent. She'd scored some speed but it wasn't doing anything for her, barely taking the edge off her misery. The drummer had just finished a set – the last for the Wild Dogs & Gentlemen for the night – it was close to two in the morning, and the Black Cat was closing down. He walked up to Sam's table and said casually, 'Want a drink, beautiful?'

'Where?' Sam asked.

'There's a party in Newtown. Why don't you come? Plenty of acid – anything you like – dope . . .'

'And, surprise, surprise, I get to sleep with you,' Sam said. 'No thanks, I'm not a groupie.'

The drummer laughed, offering his hand. 'John.'

Sam took it, only just accepting it before letting it go. 'Sam.'

'Well, there you go, Sam. I only sleep with groupies and if you're not a groupie, then you're safe. But the music will be good, the gear even better, and you're too pretty to spend the night on your own.'

'Thanks, but no thanks,' Sam said.

John started to walk away, then stopped and turned back. 'We leave for Melbourne in the morning. Why don't you come?'

'What? Melbourne or Newtown?'

'We've got a two-week gig at the Rainbow Hotel in Fitzroy. You choose.'

'Give me one good reason, John.'

'Well, I'll let you decide, babe. But if you want something to help you make up your mind, my Kombi is parked a block away. I've got something in it that requires a needle and a teaspoon.' He reached into his jeans, tossed a blue plastic cigarette lighter into the air and caught it. 'And a bit of a flame. Oh yes, and a piece of rubber tubing. I reckon I've got enough to last the trip south.'

Sam got up and followed him out.

Two weeks later, the landlady of a cheap hotel in St Kilda Road that catered mostly for musicians called the Victorian Police. It wasn't the first victim she'd found dead from a heroin overdose, but it was certainly the most beautiful.

Sam's funeral was very simple: Franz, Jacob and Hester Landsman; Helen's parents, Barbara and Reg Brown; Bullnose; Lachlan and Erin; Pineapple Joe; Forbes and Ursula Carlile; Harry Gallagher; Brenda and Half Dunn; Gabby, Helen and Danny; and Father Patrick, the local Catholic priest. All the usual words and prayers were said, all the tears shed, clods thumped against the coffin, which carried a single yellow rose and Sam's battered Stetson. Somewhere a bird called, then another answered. High clouds drifted on a summer day, and the drone of a distant light plane could be heard if you concentrated.

Gabby broke from the small group, lifted her violin and started to play the opening notes of her song 'Wild Bush Honey'. After she'd played the haunting melody through once, she lowered the violin and began to sing, unaccompanied, the lyrics she'd rewritten for her twin.

> The sun doth shine today, my love,
> There's not a sign of rain;
> The bees are in the blossoms,
> And all our world is pain.

> Oh, wild bush honey's not as sweet as you,
> And warm black rocks won't last as long,
> As my heart's love so true, so true,
> As my heart's love for you.

> You've left us in the flower of youth,
> You've left us here to grieve,
> Oh, Sam, if you'd but known the truth,
> You'd ne'er have thought to leave.

> Oh, wild bush honey's not as sweet as you,
> And warm black rocks won't last as long,
> As my heart's love so true, so true,
> As our hearts' love for you.

EPILOGUE

HELEN WENT DOWN TO the cellar – the small, warm, dry room that housed the hot-water system where she kept the battered old trunk. She opened it and removed the quilt and the bag of cloth scraps. She took both upstairs to her study, the quilt now almost too heavy to carry. She spread it out carefully on the carpet and emptied the scraps of cloth beside it: pieces of the twins' christening gowns, a patch showing an embroidered teddy bear on the bib of a toddler's overalls, squares cut from their first school uniforms, several pieces from favourite teenage dresses, patches of silk from their first sets of 'sexy' knickers and bras, scraps of denim from their first pairs of teenage jeans – all scraps of the joy, angst and laughter of growing up.

Now to five generations of memory and tears she prepared to add a sixth. She had sketched the body of a young woman wearing green Speedo swimmers, her flaming red hair tumbling to her shoulders from beneath a battered Stetson. In an arc above her head were three gold medallions, above which she would embroider the words *Three Gold for Sammy*, and below, at the young woman's feet, the words:

Pray that you may never have to endure
all that you can learn to bear.
Samantha Dunn
1951–1970
R.I.P.

Helen began to weep. Her next task would be to introduce Gabby to the quilt she prayed she would never have to work on again.

A month later Helen had completed the quilt. It was late, but she'd wanted to finish it and return it to the trunk, to put Sam safely away, asleep with her ancestors. As she'd done for the past month, she'd locked her study door when she worked on the quilt. Around ten o'clock Danny tapped on the door. 'Come to say goodnight,' he called.

'Hang on, darling,' Helen called back, 'won't be a moment.' She hurriedly wrapped the quilt in a blanket she'd brought for the purpose and then unlocked the door. 'Sorry, busy,' she smiled, not explaining further. Danny could see the wicker needlework basket on her desk that he remembered from childhood. It had been Brenda's and was now Helen's and he knew its purpose, but he'd never seen the quilt.

'Women's business?' he said now, but not flippantly.

'Yes,' Helen said, making no attempt to explain.

'Well, I'm off to bed. Got to be up at sparrow fart. Going for a row in the skiff, so I need two kisses – one for now and one for the morning. Sleep late, darling, you're tired. I'll call you from the office.'

Helen kissed Danny twice, warmly. They'd both struggled since Sam's funeral. Danny had been very quiet and withdrawn, and Helen, lost in her own grief, hadn't made any effort to cheer him up; everything she had to spare went to her desolate surviving daughter. Danny hadn't been out in the skiff since the night of Sam's punishment, and she took it as a good sign that he was resuming his early-morning rowing. 'Don't go out for too long, darling – you haven't been rowing for months. You'll be stiff and sore tomorrow. And be careful of your back.'

Danny turned to go. He paused at the half-open door, his hand on

the knob. 'Helen, I love you. You have been my life . . . my everything.'
He hesitated. 'You know that, don't you?'

Helen smiled. 'Yes. Sleep tight, darling. Make sure the fleas don't
bite.'

Danny closed the door behind him and walked upstairs. On the way
to their bedroom he noticed a light under the twins' – Gabby's – bedroom
door and tapped lightly.

'Come in,' Gabby called, and as Danny entered she looked up from
her book in surprise. 'Oh, hello, Dad. I thought it might be Mum.' She
was sitting up in bed, propped up with pillows against the headboard,
a book resting open on her knees.

'Just passing, saw your light was still on,' Danny said, crossing the
room to the bed. He stood uncertainly, not stooping to kiss Gabby on
the cheek as she had expected. Instead he pointed to the edge of the
bed. 'May I?'

'Sure.' Gabby closed the book and shifted over to make room for
him to sit.

'I'm going out in the skiff tomorrow. Thought I'd just say goodnight.
Probably won't see you in the morning . . . be gone early.'

'I'm glad, it's been ages . . . ' Gabby, unconsciously paraphrasing
Helen, chided gently, 'Don't go too far or you're going to ache for days.'

Danny grinned. 'Your mother just said that.' He paused momentarily.
'Darling, I was just thinking . . . er, well . . . silly, I know . . . but do you
think we could sing the "Fish Tummy Song"?'

Gabby laughed, then smiled, and then her eyes welled, all in a matter
of moments. She nodded, unable to speak, shutting her eyes tightly
to squeeze back the sudden tears. Danny could feel his heart beating
rapidly as Gabby's voice came clear and clean, a beautiful contralto. The
bedtime song, the last words his darling daughters had heard every night
of their childhood, rose in his chest to join her.

Sam and Gabby, I heard someone say,
You haven't been terribly good today,

You've given the next-door neighbour's cat
A nasty whack with a ping-pong bat.
And can you possibly tell me why . . .
You pulled the wings off a butterfly?

May you eat boiled cabbage and pumpkin mash
And row inside the tummy of a great big fish
In a hollowed-out calabash!

Now, my girls, it's not very nice
When you torture poor little baby mice,
And squash the bug on the Persian rug,
With the brand-new rubber bathroom plug.
And can you possibly tell me why . . .
You made the butcher's parrot cry?

May you eat boiled cabbage and pumpkin mash
And row inside the tummy of a great big fish
In a hollowed-out calabash!

It's not very kind to creep up behind,
And frighten a lady who's almost blind,
And make a poor little slimy slug
Dance a waltz and a jitterbug.
And can you possibly tell me why . . .
You told a fat little pig he could fly?

May you eat boiled cabbage and pumpkin mash
And row inside the tummy of a great big fish
In a hollowed-out calabash!

Now it's really not good that you watched the dog
Eat up the frog on the log in the bog,

Or captured some tadpoles to put in the water
You gave to your favourite teacher's daughter.
And can you possibly tell me why . . .
The canary was dipped in bright blue dye?

May you eat boiled cabbage and pumpkin mash
And row inside the tummy of a great big fish
In a hollowed-out calabash!

But now is the time to go to sleep,
Snuggle right down and don't make a peep.
Grab your teddy and close your eyes,
Off you go to sleepy-byes.
And can you possibly tell me why . . .
You dream of ice-cream and apple pie?

May you eat boiled cabbage and pumpkin mash
And row inside the tummy of a great big fish
In a holloooooowed-ooout caaaalaabassssh!

Danny leaned over and kissed the now-sobbing Gabby lightly on the cheek. 'Thank you, sweetheart; know that I truly love you, my darling.' He rose, turned and walked towards the door, a big man with his dark hair speckled with grey and his girth starting to thicken, though his stomach remained flat. At the age of fifty he walked with a slight limp because of his bad back. He stooped slightly as he passed through the door, even though the lintel was still a good three inches above his head. Without turning he closed the door quietly behind him.

Helen didn't wake when Danny rose at four-thirty the next morning. Later, the crew from an Italian fishing boat returning through the

Heads would report that they'd seen a lone rower in a skiff in the choppy waves just beyond Sydney Heads at about six. They'd called out the name of the skiff, 'Calabash!' Then, 'You okay, mate?' The rower had raised his hand, indicating that he was in control, so they'd moved on.

Danny simply kept rowing.

Two days later the upturned *Calabash*, his beloved skiff, was washed onto Tamarama beach.

A week later, Helen, Gabby and Billy duBois stood on the point of South Head looking out to sea. Brenda and Half Dunn, suddenly old and bowed beneath the double blow of tragedy, stood nearby. Billy had flown from New Orleans for the memorial service and had attended the wake at the Hero, where it seemed most of Balmain had turned up uninvited.

The following day Billy had asked if he could visit the Heads that afternoon to say a final farewell to his buddy. It was a glorious summer afternoon, with a light nor'easter blowing in from the open ocean as they stood silently looking out to sea. Billy turned to Helen. 'He told me this happened to him when he sailed back home from the war, so I arranged it for the three women in his life. I hope you don't mind.'

A lone piper standing on a rock shelf to their right began to play, and the strains of the bagpipes drifted out across the water.

> Oh, Danny boy, the pipes, the pipes are calling,
> From glen to glen and down the mountain side;
> The summer's gone, and all the flowers are falling;
> 'Tis ye, 'tis ye, must go and I must bide.
>
> But come ye back when summer's in the meadow,
> Or when the valley's hushed and white with snow;

'Tis I'll be here in sunshine or in shadow;
Oh, Danny boy, oh, Danny boy, I love you so.

And if ye come when all the flowers are dying,
If I am dead, as dead I well may be,
Ye'll come and find the place where I am lying,
And kneel and say an 'Ave' there for me.

And I shall hear, though soft ye tread above me,
And o'er my grave, shall warmer, sweeter be,
Then if ye bend and tell me that ye love me,
Then I shall sleep in peace until ye come to me.

Danny Dunn
1920–1970
Rest in peace

ACKNOWLEDGEMENTS

This is my nineteenth book in twenty-one years, and while people are often kind about my work, I hasten to point out that without the generous support I receive and the knowledge of others freely given, none of those books would have been completed. It has become fashionable not to include acknowledgements in works of fiction, or to keep them to the minimum. And, as someone once told me, it is not necessary to thank the cat and the dog. But the role of the storyteller is made possible through the borrowing of experience and information from those who have done the actual spadework, and those who are invariably wiser and smarter than I am, and I am grateful to them. Every book is therefore a cleverly disguised list of generosity, kindness, support and the giving of wisdom hard-earned by others.

As only one of many such examples, I needed to know what it was like, really like, to be an amateur Olympic swimmer in the 1970s. My researchers and I conscientiously read the books and the tedious official histories. But it wasn't until Shane Gould MBE spent many hours, despite her own very busy schedule, detailing the information I needed that I was able to write several authentic narrative sequences – although any contentious conclusions I reached in the book, I should add, are my own. Thank you, Shane.

This book is the result of a great many such generous gestures. While your name and little more might appear below, what each of you did for me has made my storytelling possible.

Being a novelist's partner is a rotten job and one I wouldn't even consider undertaking from the non-tap-tap side. Christine Gee, to whom I dedicate this book, has been my constant and loving companion throughout. She is a person gifted with intelligence, understanding, patience, good humour, beauty and a natural vitality I cherish. In addition, she takes care of the endless miscellany of running a home, and also acts as my in-house researcher, reader and listener. Along with my longstanding and devoted personal assistant, Christine Lenton, Christine also manages the business aspects of our partnership. I thank her every day of our shared life together. I also want to pay tribute to her passion and commitment to the charities we jointly support, where Christine does the work and I accept the credit. These, not including the 150 or so charities to which she has sent signed copies of my books for raffles, auctions and door prizes, are: the Australian Himalayan Foundation, for which she is a proud Board member; the Thin Green Line Foundation, of which we are Ambassadors; Voiceless; the Taronga Conservation Society Australia; and Cure the Future – Cell and Gene Trust.

Secondly, I acknowledge my full-time professional researcher from Melbourne, Bruce Gee, who has partnered me for seven books and knows exactly what I want and how to reduce a tome to a couple of pages of relevance, or suggest a scenario that can prove extremely helpful. He is available at any hour of any day, and I consider myself very fortunate to be able to access his intellectual capacity, research skills and judgement. Then, in Sydney, for specific location and other tasks, I engaged Keri Light as a filmmaker, who worked to capture atmosphere and interviews on camera. My grateful thanks go to both of you.

I now need to thank the long list of friends and strangers who have contributed to this book: John Adamson, Yasuko Ando, John Atkin, Carole Baird, Malcolm Bruce, Peter Caine, Forbes Carlile MBE, Russell Coburn, Adam Courtenay, Barry Crocker, Tony Crosby, Lydia Davic, Owen Denmeade, Tony Freeman, Margaret Gee, Harry Gordon, Alex Hamill, Denis Hamill, Pat Hamilton, Sam and Alida Haskins, Ludwig Haskins, Oren Haskins, Jodie Iliani, Alan Jacobs, Jana Jones, Christine Lenton, Irwin Light, Margaret Mackenzie, Tex Moran, Penny Piccione, Susie Palfreyman, Roger Rigby, John Sharp, George Stone, Duncan Thomas, Debbie Tobin and Ken Wilder.

The institutes and organisations who helped, and the people within them to whom I am indebted, are: Amie Zar and Bruce Carter from the Local History Unit of Leichhardt Library; Kathleen Hamey et al at the Balmain Association; the University of Sydney Archives; the University of Sydney Law Library; the Mitchell Library; the NSW Conservatorium of Music; the Department of Ancient History at Macquarie University; and, lastly, Andrew Guerin of Rowing Australia.

While the writer and his publisher are essentially contractual partners, I have invariably received kindness, encouragement and accommodation from Penguin well beyond any contract I've signed – and this book has been no exception.

Firstly, my editor Nan McNab has been patient, understanding and mostly annoyingly right when we've argued. In all other matters she is equally difficult to fault. She edits each chapter as it comes to her at the end of the week without quite knowing what's in my mind, a task that would be a nightmare to most editors. Nan has responded with good humour, a great many late nights, tight deadlines and leaps of faith where her every footfall (largely in the dark) has proved securely placed. She is a very nice person and a delight to work with, and I thank her unequivocally for her contribution. Finally, she helped me scan the 'Fish Tummy Song' until the rhythm worked.

Rachel Scully, my inhouse editor, who rode shotgun with Nan all the way, was unrelenting, determined, considerate, passionate and disciplined about the outcome. I trust she got the book she hoped for – certainly I couldn't have hoped for a better and more involved editor, and I am truly grateful for her encouragement and help. Publishing professionals such as Rachel put their job on the line with almost every big book, and Penguin is blessed with her inclusion on their editorial staff.

Then there are those at Penguin without whom no book ever reaches a reader: Gabrielle Coyne, CEO; Robert Sessions, my publisher and Publishing Director of Penguin, who keeps his guiding hand on the tiller throughout; Julie Gibbs, who, though less directly involved, is always available to me for counsel; and Anne Rogan, Managing Editor, who is the nuts and bolts of everything from weekly chapter delivery to final proofs.

If the above are the principle decision-makers, those that follow are responsible for giving my book both polish and finish: proofreaders Sarina Rowell and Julia Carlomagno; typesetters Lisa and Ron Eady; Senior

Production Controller Nicole Brown; Art Director Deborah Brash; and senior designers Debra Billson, Tony Palmer and Cathy Larsen.

The marketing and selling of a book these days is a critical component to its success. Much as every author hopes his book will prove a runaway word-of-mouth success, releasing it to the reading world is fraught with danger. The marketing and sales staff are responsible for guiding a book through these turbulent waters and I am especially grateful to a team that has been with me a long time and performs this service very well indeed: Daniel Ruffino, Marketing and Publicity Director; Sally Bateman, General Manager, Marketing and Publicity; Anyez Lindop, Publicity Manager; Sharlene Vinall, Marketing Manger; Abigail Hockey, Advertising and Marketing Design Manager; Gordon McKenzie, Web Services and Multimedia Manager; and Vicky Axiotis, Publicity Assistant.

Every book needs to be sold and nobody does it better in my view than Peter Blake, Sales Director, and Louise Ryan, General Sales Manager, and, of course, every one of the Penguin sales reps. I thank you all for your efforts on my behalf.

Finally, every morning as I start to work, Cardamon and Mushka, two of our four cats (three of them rescued from a dastardly end) take up their editing positions in their baskets on my desk, while Timmy our mutt flops at my feet. With the exception of a walk for Tim, or cat-necessary business, they stay with me all day and, if necessary, all evening. The kitten Ophelia and the male tabby, Pirate, I regret to say are illiterate, but would nevertheless be upset if they were not included here. I thank them for their undoubted contribution to my daily wellbeing.

Thank you, all.

ALSO BY
BRYCE COURTENAY

THE POWER OF ONE

Born in a South Africa divided by racism and hatred, young Peekay will come to lead all the tribes of Africa. Through enduring friendships, he gains the strength he needs to win out. And in a final conflict with his childhood enemy, Peekay will fight to the death for justice . . .

Bryce Courtenay's classic bestseller is a story of triumph of the human spirit – a spellbinding tale for all ages.

TANDIA

Tandia is a child of all Africa: half Indian, half African, beautiful and intelligent, she is only sixteen when she is first brutalised by the police. Her fear of the white man leads her to join the black resistance movement, where she trains as a terrorist.

With her in the fight for justice is the one white man Tandia can trust, the welterweight champion of the world, Peekay. Now he must fight their common enemy in order to save both their lives.

APRIL FOOL'S DAY

In the end, love is more important than everything and it will conquer and overcome anything. Or that's how Damon saw it, anyway. Damon wanted a book that talked a lot about love.

Damon Courtenay died on the morning of April Fool's Day. In this tribute to his son, Bryce Courtenay lays bare the suffering behind this young man's life. Damon's story is one of lifelong struggle, his love for Celeste, the compassion of a family, and a fight to the end for integrity.

A testimony to the power of love, *April Fool's Day* is also about understanding: how when we confront our worst, we can become our best.

A powerful account of life and death from one of Australia's best authors.

THE AUSTRALIAN TRILOGY

THE POTATO FACTORY

Ikey Solomon and his partner in crime, Mary Abacus, make the harsh journey from thriving nineteenth-century London to the convict settlement of Van Diemen's Land. In the back-streets and dives of Hobart Town, Mary builds The Potato Factory, where she plans a new future. But her ambitions are threatened by Ikey's wife, Hannah, her old enemy. As each woman sets out to destroy the other, the families are brought to the edge of disaster.

TOMMO & HAWK

Brutally kidnapped and separated in childhood, Tommo and Hawk are reunited in Hobart Town. Together they escape their troubled pasts and set off on a journey into manhood. From whale hunting in the Pacific to the Maori wars in New Zealand, from the Rocks in Sydney to the miners' riots at the goldfields, Tommo and Hawk must learn each other's strengths and weaknesses in order to survive.

SOLOMON'S SONG

When Mary Abacus dies, she leaves her business empire in the hands of the warring Solomon family. Hawk Solomon is determined to bring together both sides of the tribe – but it is the new generation who must fight to change the future. Solomons are pitted against Solomons as the families are locked in a bitter struggle that crosses battlefields and continents to reach a powerful conclusion.

JESSICA

Jessica is based on the inspiring true story of a young girl's fight for justice against tremendous odds. A tomboy, Jessica is the pride of her father, as they work together on the struggling family farm. One quiet day, the peace of the bush is devastated by a terrible murder. Only Jessica is able to save the killer from the lynch mob – but will justice prevail in the courts?

Nine months later, a baby is born . . . with Jessica determined to guard the secret of the father's identity. The rivalry of Jessica and her beautiful sister for the love of the same man will echo throughout their lives – until finally the truth must be told.

Set in a harsh Australian bush against the outbreak of World War I, this novel is heartbreaking in its innocence, and shattering in its brutality.

WHITETHORN

From Bryce Courtenay comes *Whitethorn*, a novel of Africa. The time is 1939: White South Africa is a deeply divided nation with many of the Afrikaner people fanatically opposed to the English.

The world is on the brink of war and South Africa elects to fight for the Allied cause against Germany. Six-year-old Tom Fitzsaxby finds himself in The Boys Farm, an orphanage in a small remote town in the high mountains, where the Afrikaners side fanatically with Hitler's Germany.

Tom's English name alone proves sufficient for him to be racially ostracised. And so begin some of life's tougher lessons for the small, lonely boy.

Like the whitethorn, one of Africa's most enduring plants, Tom learns how to survive in the harsh climate of racial hatred. Then a terrible event sets him on a journey to ensure that justice is done. On the way, his most unexpected discovery is love.

THE PERSIMMON TREE

In the heartwood of the sacred persimmon tree is ebony,
the hardest, most beautiful of all woods. This is a
symbol of life, a heartwood that will outlast everything
man can make, a core within that, come what may,
cannot be broken and represents our inner strength and
divine spirit.

It is 1942 in the Dutch East Indies, and Nick Duncan
is a young Australian butterfly collector in search of a
single exotic butterfly. With invading Japanese forces
coming closer by the day, Nick falls in love with the
beguiling Anna Van Heerden.

Yet their time together is brief, as both are forced
into separate, dangerous escapes. They plan to reunite
and marry in Australia but it is several years before their
paths cross again, scarred forever by the dark events of
a long, cruel war.

Set against the dramatic backdrop of the Pacific
during the Second World War, Bryce Courtenay gives us
a story of love and friendship.

FISHING FOR STARS

Nick Duncan is a semi-retired, wealthy shipping magnate who lives in idyllic Beautiful Bay, Vanuatu, where he is known as the old patriarch of the islands. He is grieving the loss of his beguiling Eurasian true love, Anna, and is suffering for the first time from disturbing flashbacks to the Second World War.

So he puts pen to paper and tells the compelling tale of the life he has lived since his war-hero days. It's an adventurous life that has had at its heart the love of two passionate and unforgettable – but very different – women.

The seductive Anna Til and the beguiling Marg Hamilton have spent a lifetime in contest for Nick's devotion. Nick remains torn between them, and struggles between their two opposing worlds of economic exploitation and environmental crusade – until he is called upon to referee.